# ALSO FROM JOE BOOKS

Disney Frozen Cinestory Comic
Disney Cinderella Cinestory Comic
Disney 101 Dalmatians Cinestory Comic
Disney Princess Comics Treasury
Disney•Pixar Comics Treasury
Disney Darkwing Duck: The Definitively Dangerous Edition
Disney Frozen: The Story of the Movie in Comics
Disney Big Hero 6 Cinestory Comic
Disney•Pixar Inside Out Cinestory Comic
Disney•Pixar Inside Out Fun Book
Disney Gravity Falls Cinestory Comic Volume One
Disney•Pixar The Good Dinosaur Cinestory Comic
Disney•Pixar The Good Dinosaur Fun Book
Disney Zootopia Cinestory Comic
Disney Winnie the Pooh Cinestory Comic
Disney Descendants Wicked World Cinestory Comic Volume One
Disney Alice in Wonderland Cinestory Comic
Disney•Pixar Finding Nemo Cinestory Comic
Disney Star vs the Forces of Evil Cinestory Comic
Disney•Pixar Cars Cinestory Comic
Marvel Thor: Dueling with Giants

Don't miss our monthly comics…
Disney Princess
Disney Darkwing Duck
Disney•Pixar Finding Dory

And Disney Frozen, launching in July!

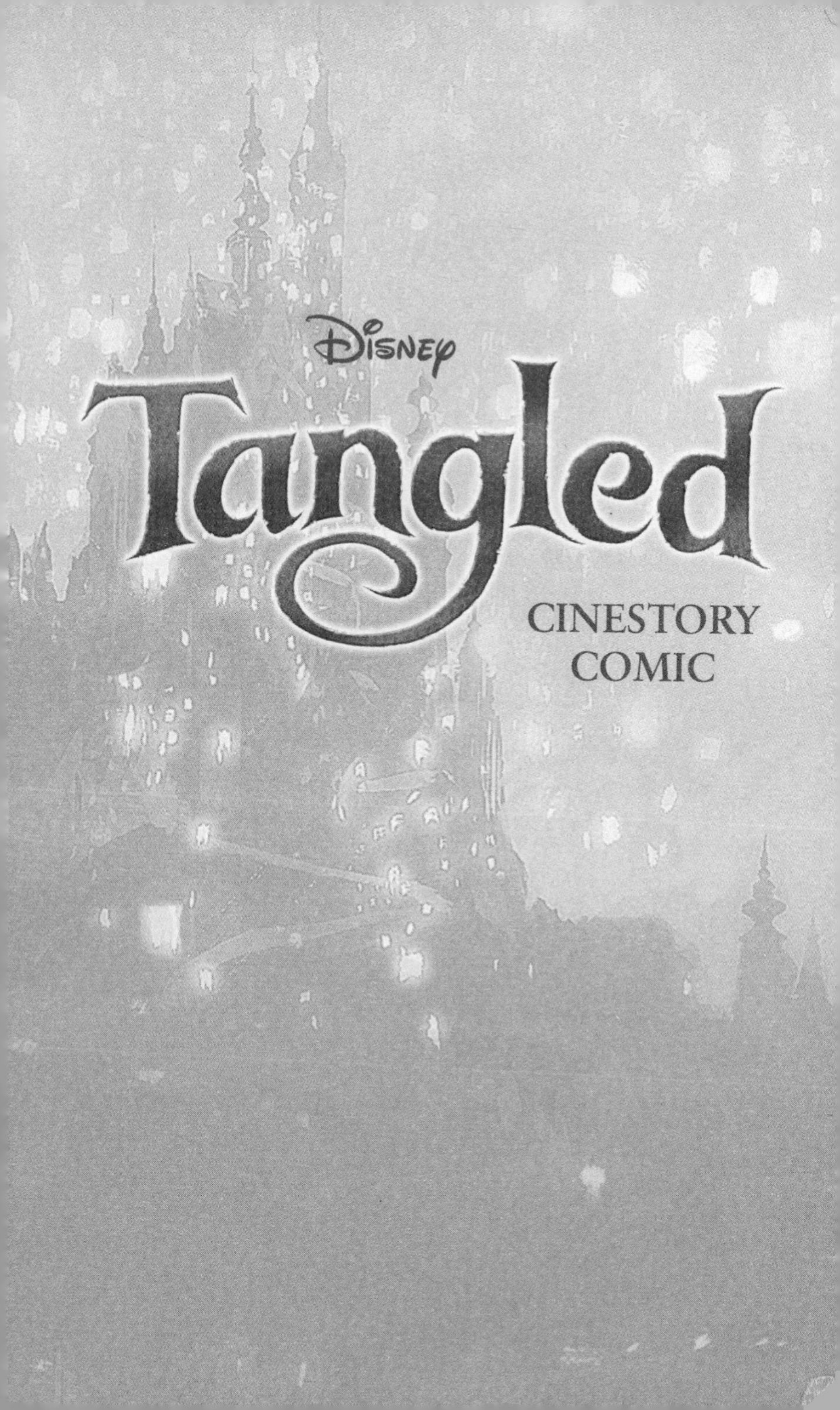

Disney

# Tangled

CINESTORY COMIC

JOE BOOKS LTD



Published simultaneously in the United States and Canada by Joe Books Ltd, 489 College Street, Suite 203, Toronto, Ontario, M6G 1A5

www.joebooks.com



First Joe Books Edition: September 2016

ISBN: 9781926516707
ISBN: 9781772753530 (ebook)



Library and Archives Canada Cataloguing in Publication information is available upon request

3 5 7 9 10 8 6 4 2 1

# Disney

# Tangled

## CINESTORY COMIC

ADAPTATION, DESIGN, LETTERING, LAYOUT AND EDITING
For Readhead Books: Jeremy Barlow, Ester Salguero, Eduardo
Alpuente, Alberto Garrido, Heidi Roux, Aaron Sparrow, Stephanie
Alouche, Heather Penner and Carolynn Prior.

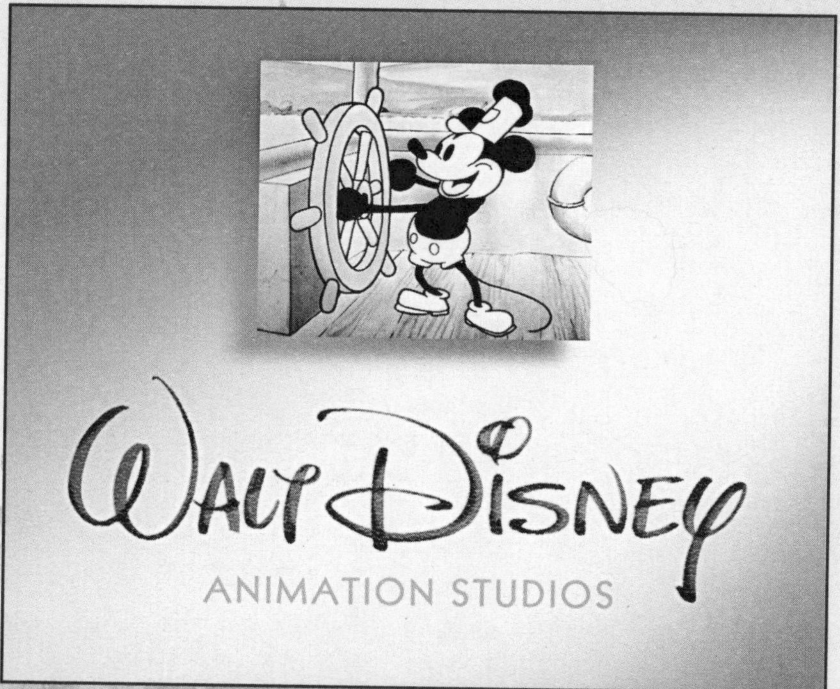
WALT DISNEY
ANIMATION STUDIOS

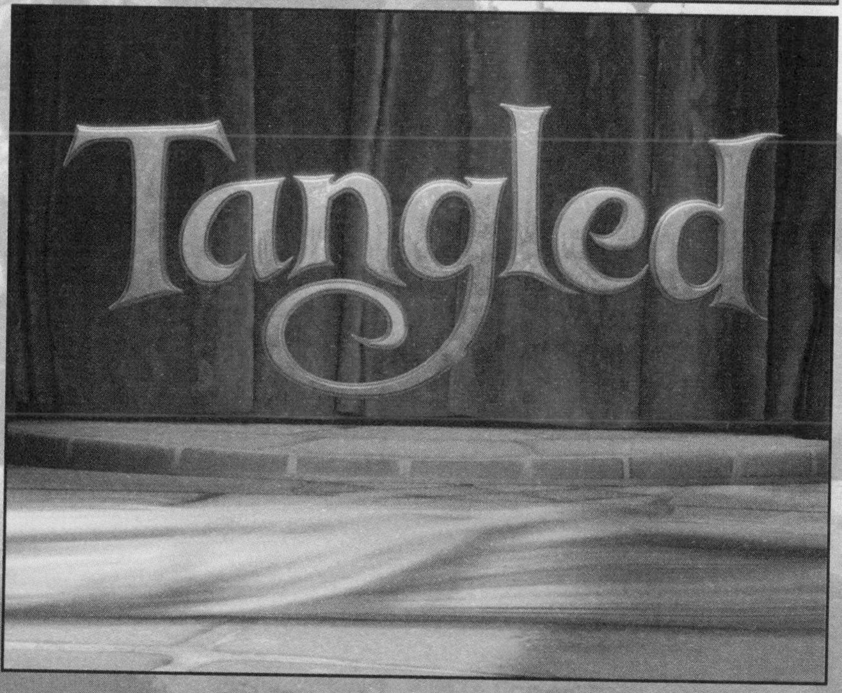
Tangled

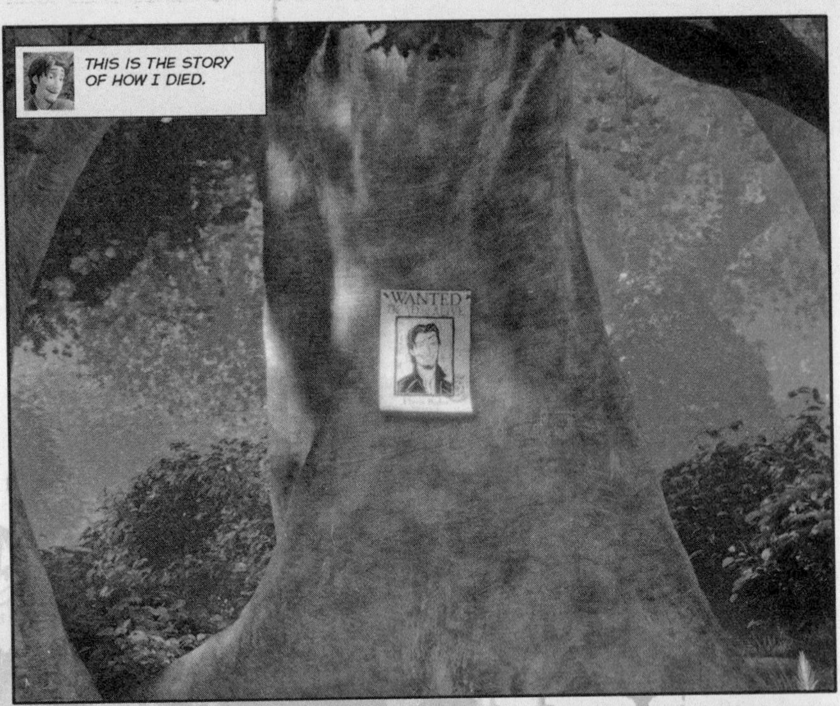
THIS IS THE STORY OF HOW I DIED.
WANTED

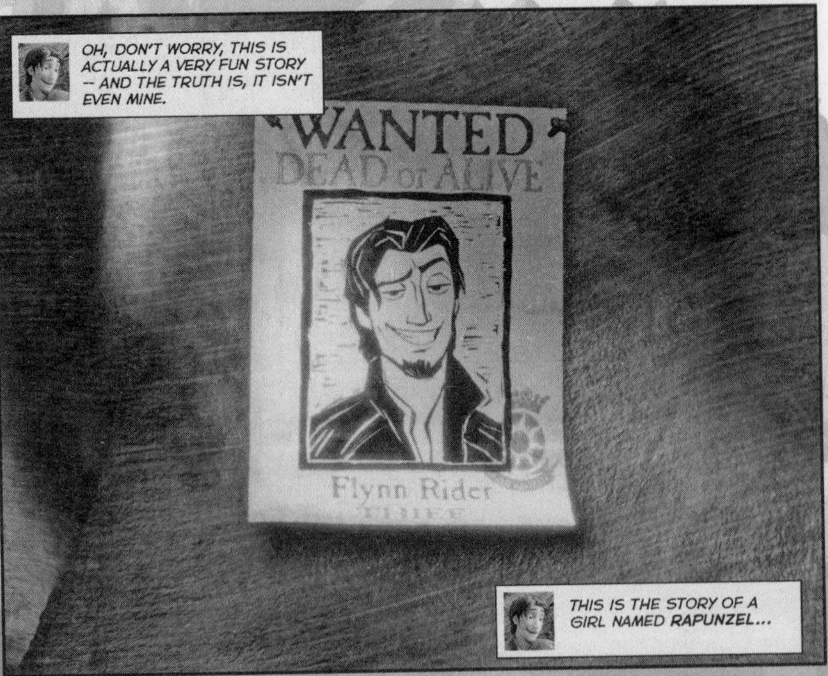
OH, DON'T WORRY, THIS IS ACTUALLY A VERY FUN STORY -- AND THE TRUTH IS, IT ISN'T EVEN MINE.
WANTED
DEAD or ALIVE
Flynn Rider
THIEF
THIS IS THE STORY OF A GIRL NAMED RAPUNZEL...

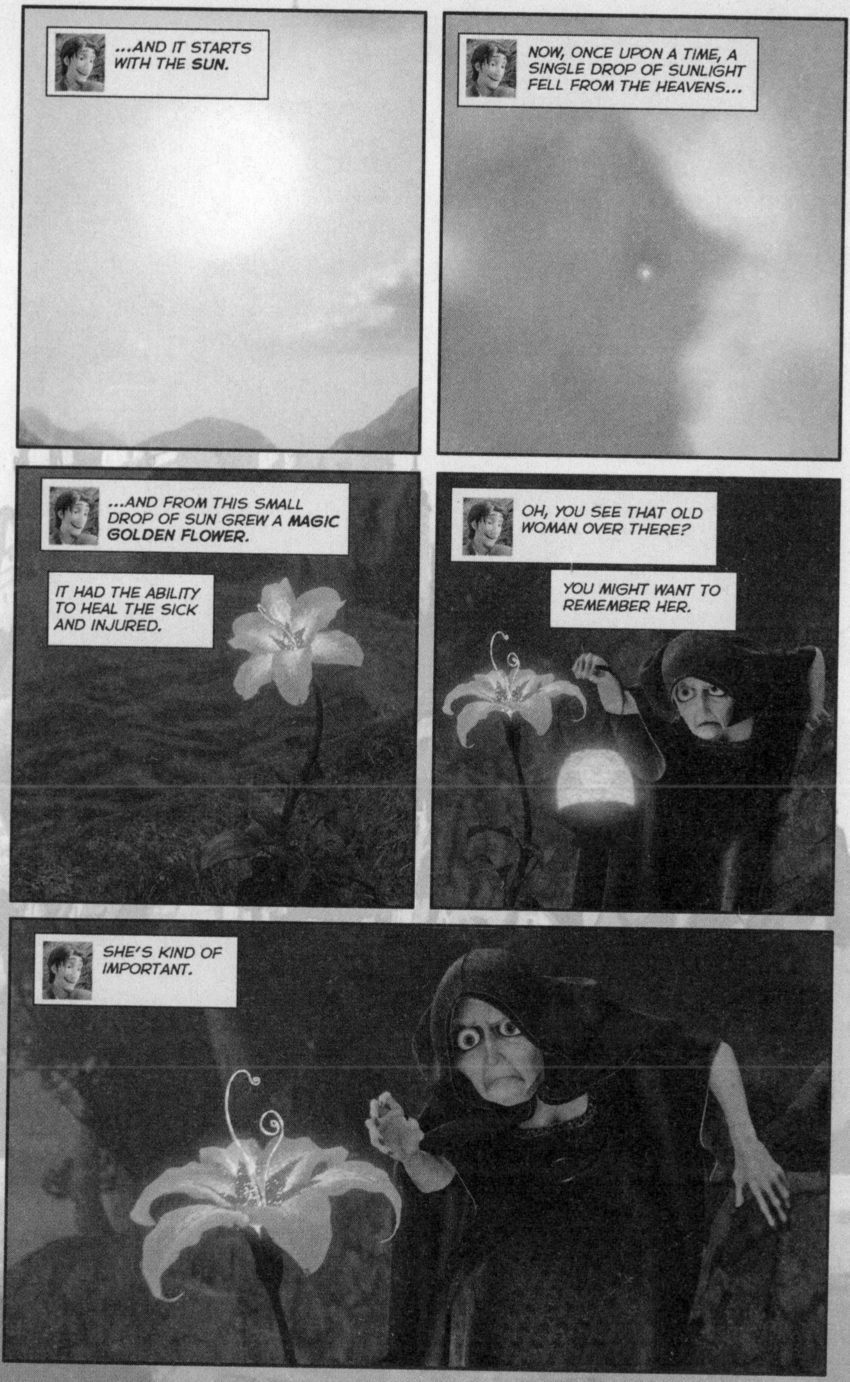
...AND IT STARTS WITH THE SUN.
NOW, ONCE UPON A TIME, A SINGLE DROP OF SUNLIGHT FELL FROM THE HEAVENS...
...AND FROM THIS SMALL DROP OF SUN GREW A MAGIC GOLDEN FLOWER.
IT HAD THE ABILITY TO HEAL THE SICK AND INJURED.
OH, YOU SEE THAT OLD WOMAN OVER THERE?
YOU MIGHT WANT TO REMEMBER HER.
SHE'S KIND OF IMPORTANT.

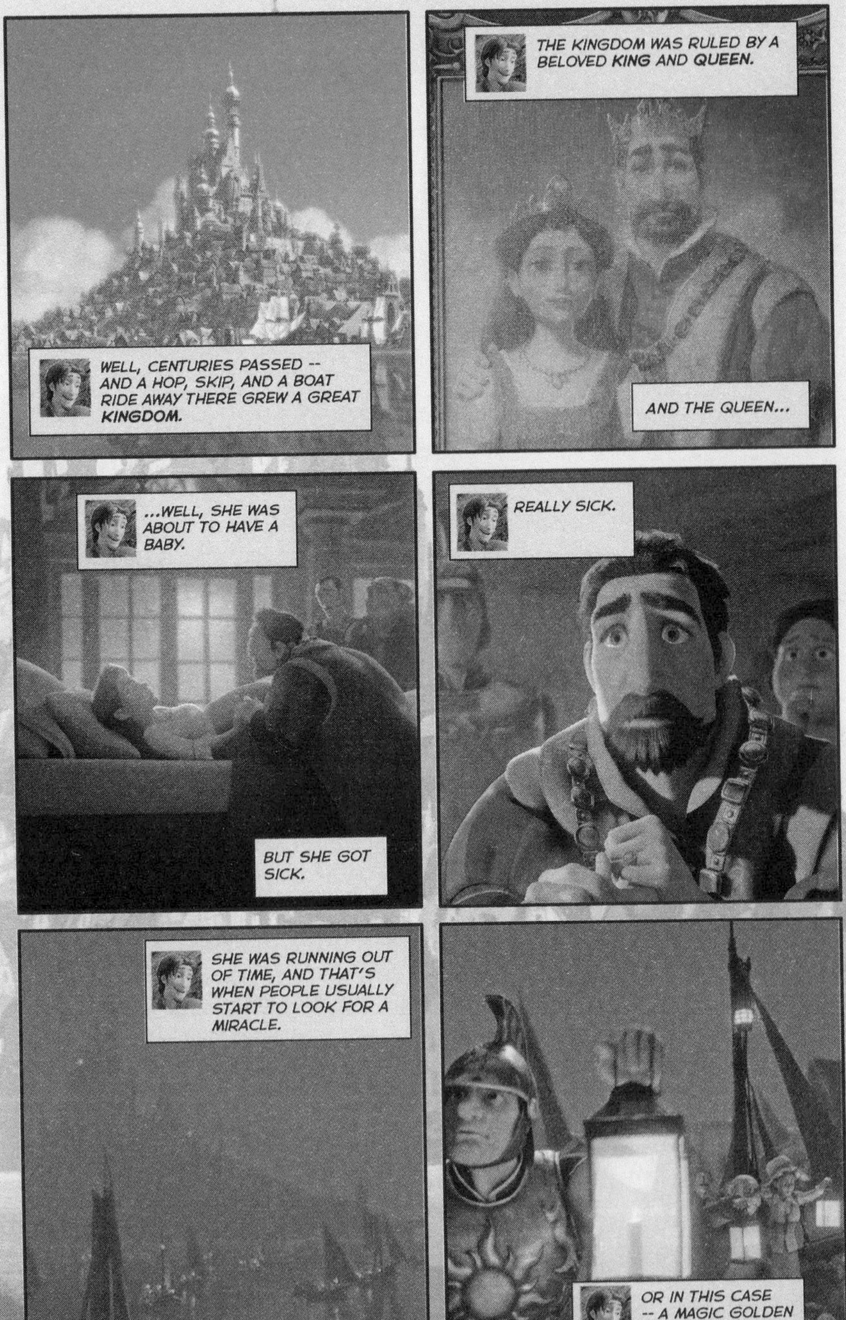
WELL, CENTURIES PASSED -- AND A HOP, SKIP, AND A BOAT RIDE AWAY THERE GREW A GREAT KINGDOM.
THE KINGDOM WAS RULED BY A BELOVED KING AND QUEEN.
AND THE QUEEN...
...WELL, SHE WAS ABOUT TO HAVE A BABY.
BUT SHE GOT SICK.
REALLY SICK.
SHE WAS RUNNING OUT OF TIME, AND THAT'S WHEN PEOPLE USUALLY START TO LOOK FOR A MIRACLE.
OR IN THIS CASE -- A MAGIC GOLDEN FLOWER.

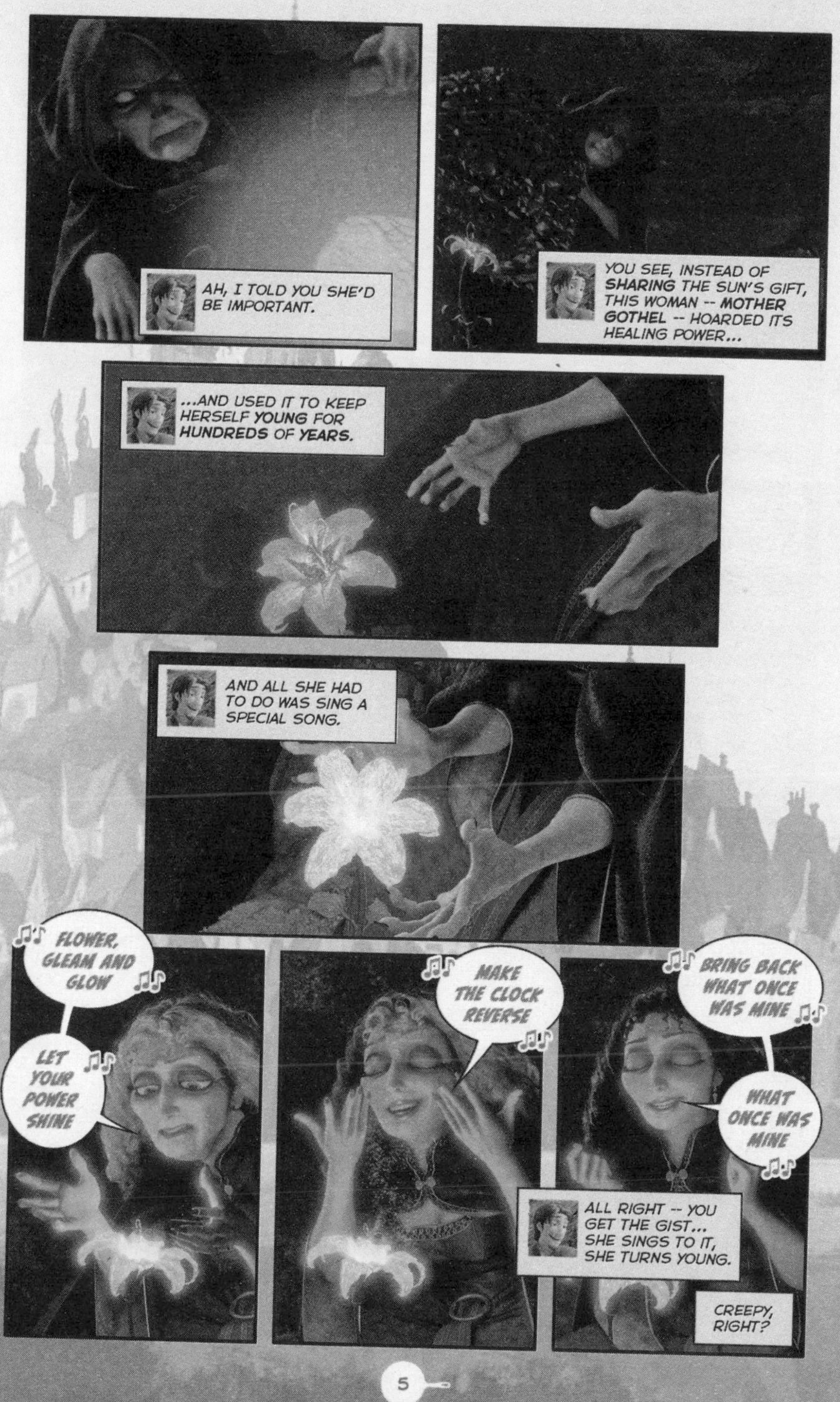
AH, I TOLD YOU SHE'D BE IMPORTANT.
YOU SEE, INSTEAD OF SHARING THE SUN'S GIFT, THIS WOMAN -- MOTHER GOTHEL -- HOARDED ITS HEALING POWER...
...AND USED IT TO KEEP HERSELF YOUNG FOR HUNDREDS OF YEARS.
AND ALL SHE HAD TO DO WAS SING A SPECIAL SONG.
FLOWER, GLEAM AND GLOW
LET YOUR POWER SHINE
MAKE THE CLOCK REVERSE
BRING BACK WHAT ONCE WAS MINE
WHAT ONCE WAS MINE
ALL RIGHT -- YOU GET THE GIST... SHE SINGS TO IT, SHE TURNS YOUNG.
CREEPY, RIGHT?

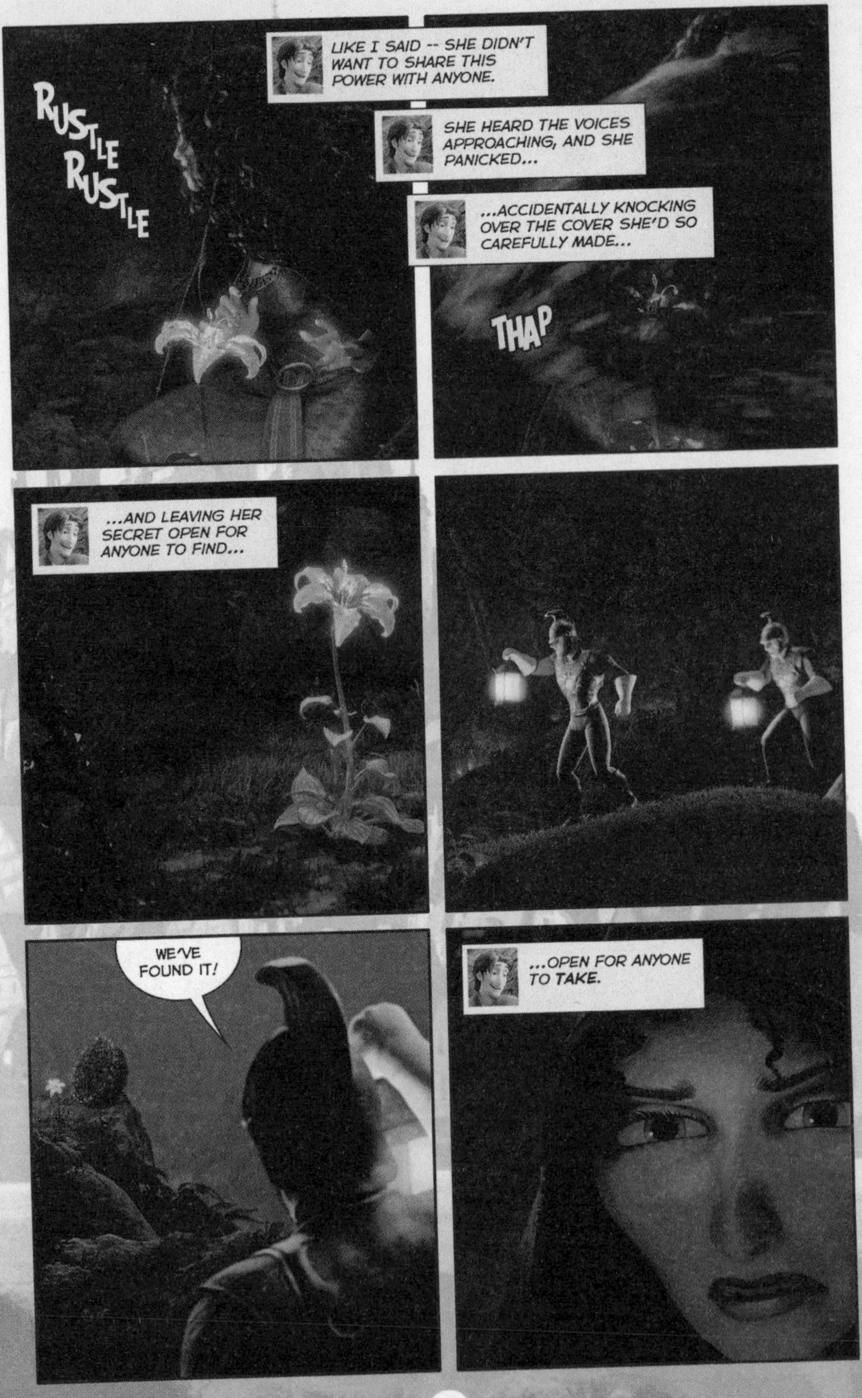

RUSTLE RUSTLE
LIKE I SAID -- SHE DIDN'T WANT TO SHARE THIS POWER WITH ANYONE.
SHE HEARD THE VOICES APPROACHING, AND SHE PANICKED...
...ACCIDENTALLY KNOCKING OVER THE COVER SHE'D SO CAREFULLY MADE...
THAP
...AND LEAVING HER SECRET OPEN FOR ANYONE TO FIND...
WE'VE FOUND IT!
...OPEN FOR ANYONE TO TAKE.

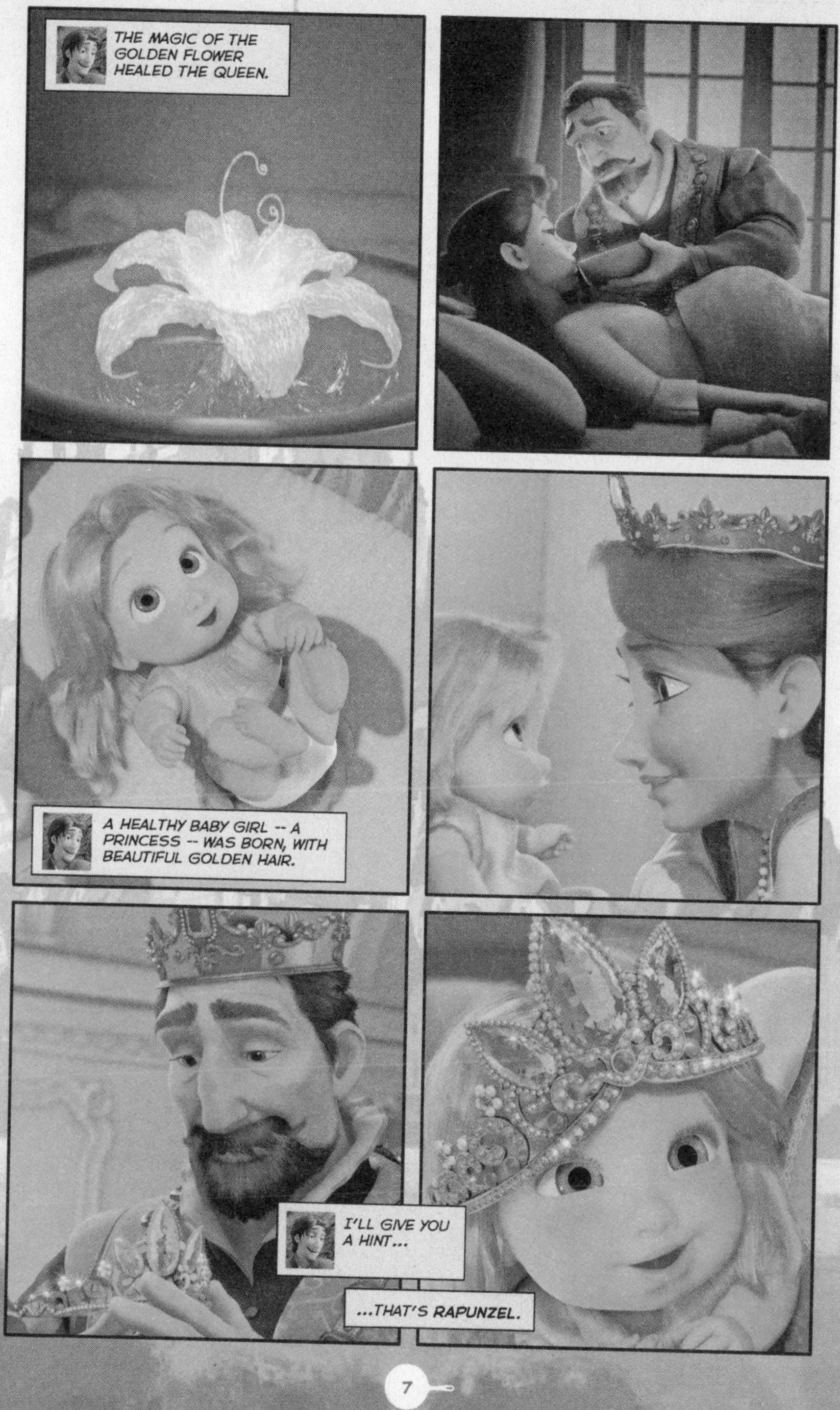
THE MAGIC OF THE GOLDEN FLOWER HEALED THE QUEEN.
A HEALTHY BABY GIRL -- A PRINCESS -- WAS BORN, WITH BEAUTIFUL GOLDEN HAIR.
I'LL GIVE YOU A HINT...
...THAT'S RAPUNZEL.

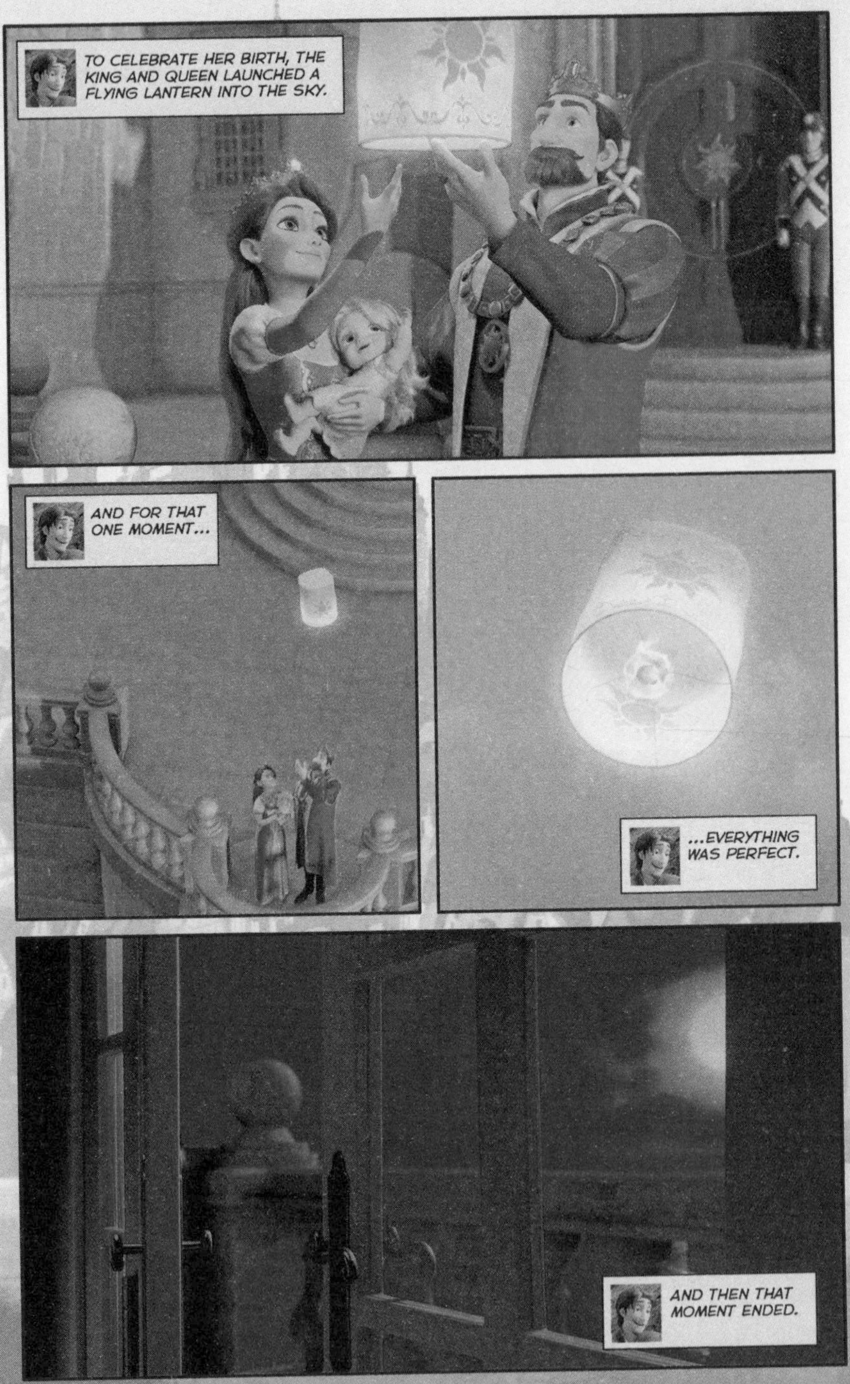
TO CELEBRATE HER BIRTH, THE KING AND QUEEN LAUNCHED A FLYING LANTERN INTO THE SKY.
AND FOR THAT ONE MOMENT...
...EVERYTHING WAS PERFECT.
AND THEN THAT MOMENT ENDED.

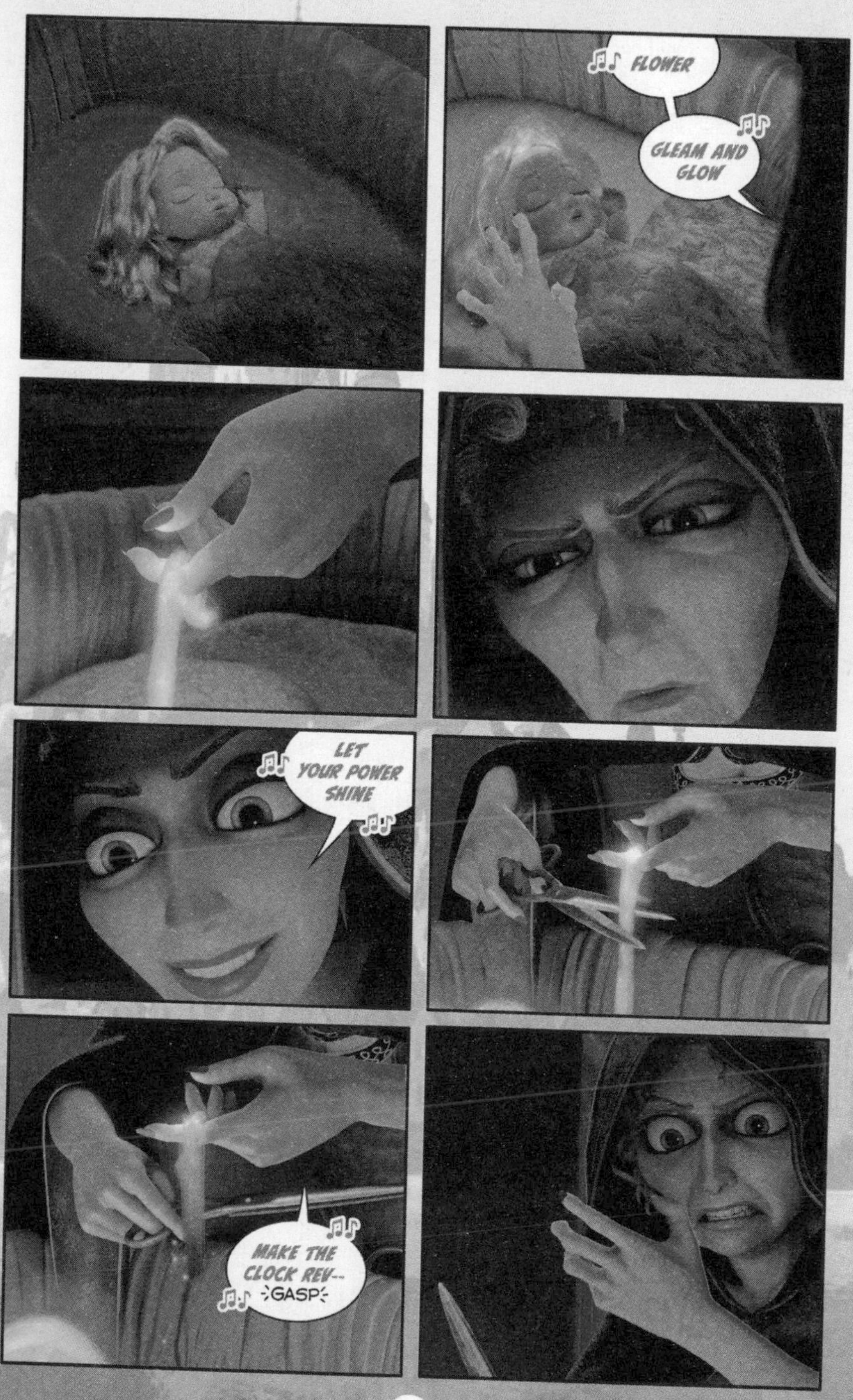
FLOWER
GLEAM AND GLOW
LET YOUR POWER SHINE
MAKE THE CLOCK REV-- GASP

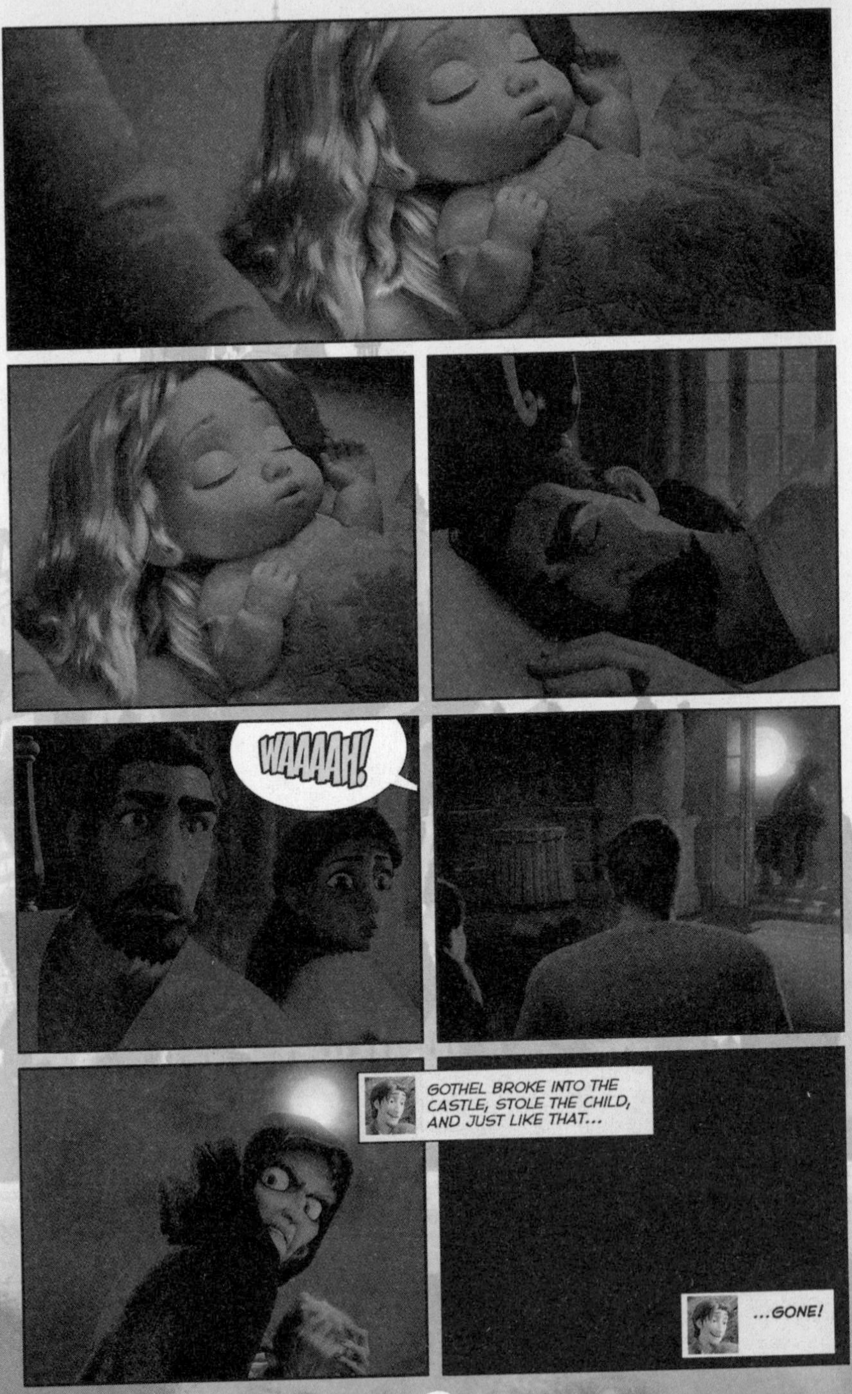
WAAAAH!
GOTHEL BROKE INTO THE CASTLE, STOLE THE CHILD, AND JUST LIKE THAT...
...GONE!

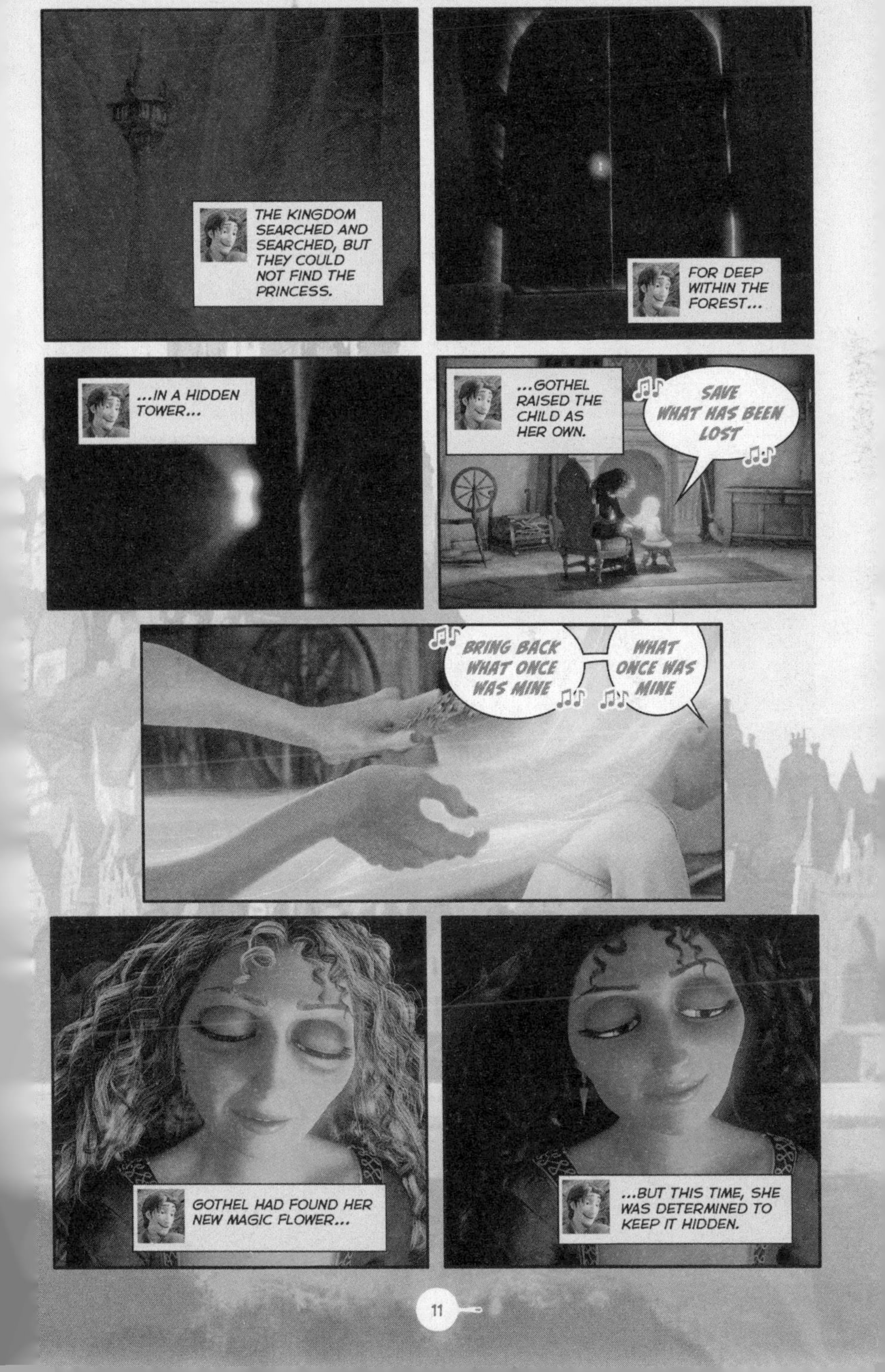
THE KINGDOM SEARCHED AND SEARCHED, BUT THEY COULD NOT FIND THE PRINCESS.
FOR DEEP WITHIN THE FOREST...
...IN A HIDDEN TOWER...
...GOTHEL RAISED THE CHILD AS HER OWN.
SAVE WHAT HAS BEEN LOST
BRING BACK WHAT ONCE WAS MINE
WHAT ONCE WAS MINE
GOTHEL HAD FOUND HER NEW MAGIC FLOWER...
...BUT THIS TIME, SHE WAS DETERMINED TO KEEP IT HIDDEN.

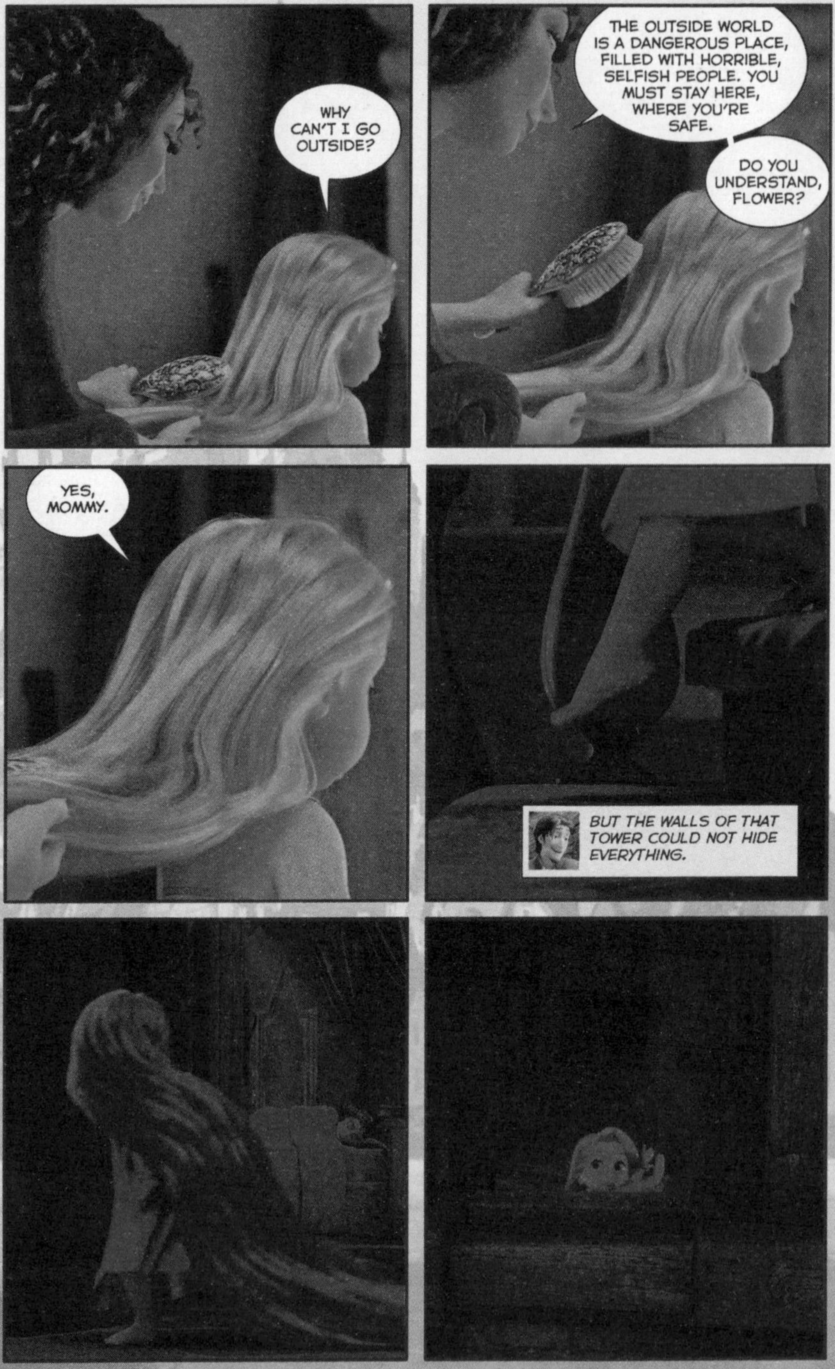
WHY CAN'T I GO OUTSIDE?
THE OUTSIDE WORLD IS A DANGEROUS PLACE, FILLED WITH HORRIBLE, SELFISH PEOPLE. YOU MUST STAY HERE, WHERE YOU'RE SAFE.
DO YOU UNDERSTAND, FLOWER?
YES, MOMMY.
BUT THE WALLS OF THAT TOWER COULD NOT HIDE EVERYTHING.

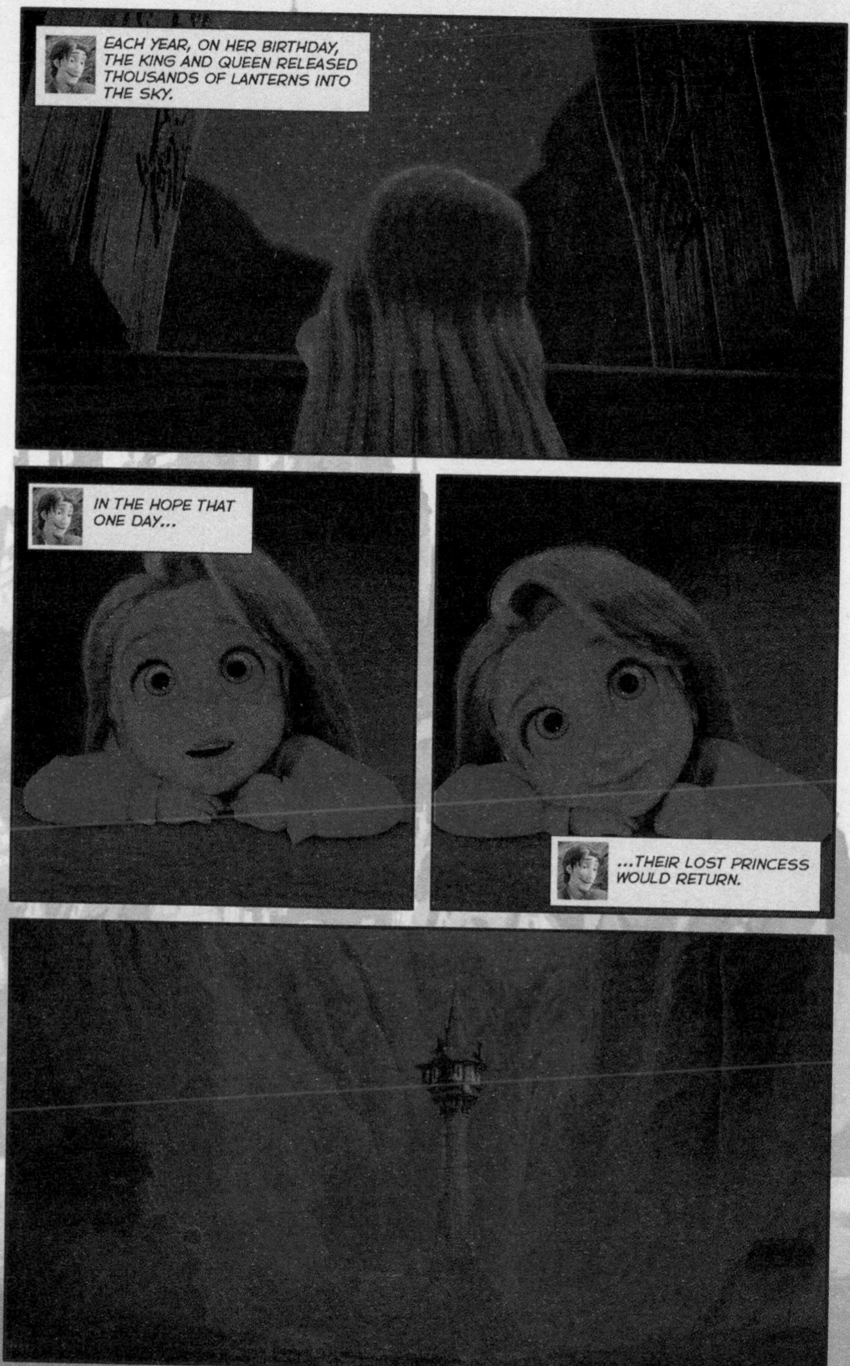
EACH YEAR, ON HER BIRTHDAY, THE KING AND QUEEN RELEASED THOUSANDS OF LANTERNS INTO THE SKY.
IN THE HOPE THAT ONE DAY...
...THEIR LOST PRINCESS WOULD RETURN.

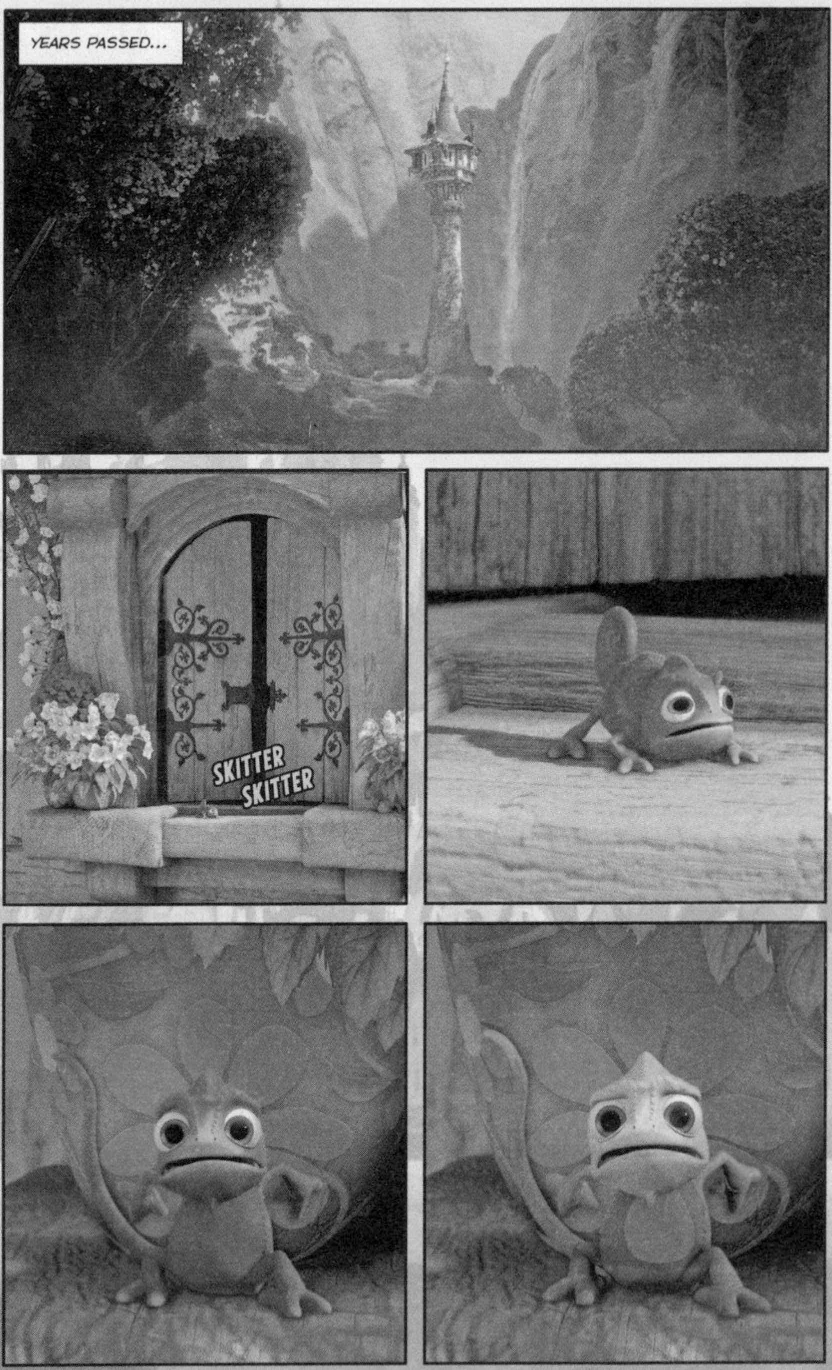
YEARS PASSED...
SKITTER
SKITTER

HA!

HMM. WELL, I GUESS PASCAL'S NOT HIDING OUT HERE.

HEE HEE HEE!

FWAP

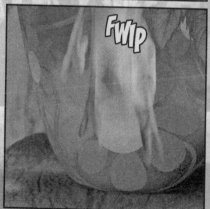

FWIP

GOTCHA!

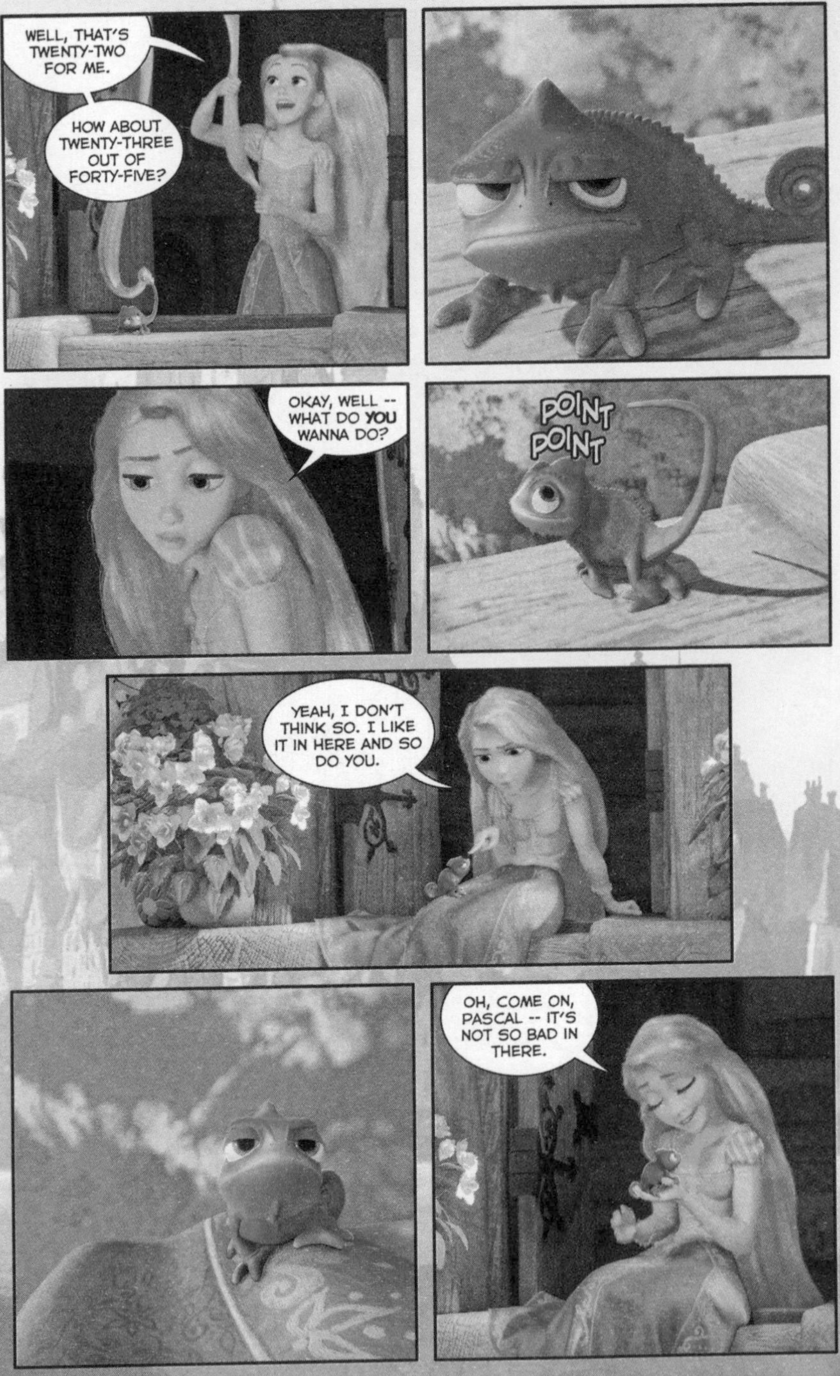
WELL, THAT'S TWENTY-TWO FOR ME.
HOW ABOUT TWENTY-THREE OUT OF FORTY-FIVE?
OKAY, WELL -- WHAT DO **YOU** WANNA DO?
POINT POINT
YEAH, I DON'T THINK SO. I LIKE IT IN HERE AND SO DO YOU.
OH, COME ON, PASCAL -- IT'S NOT SO BAD IN THERE.

SWOOSH

CHUNK

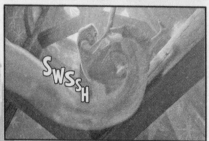

SWSSH

♫♪ SEVEN A.M., THE USUAL MORNING LINE-UP ♫♪

♫♪ START ON THE CHORES, AND SWEEP 'TIL THE FLOOR'S ALL CLEAN ♫♪

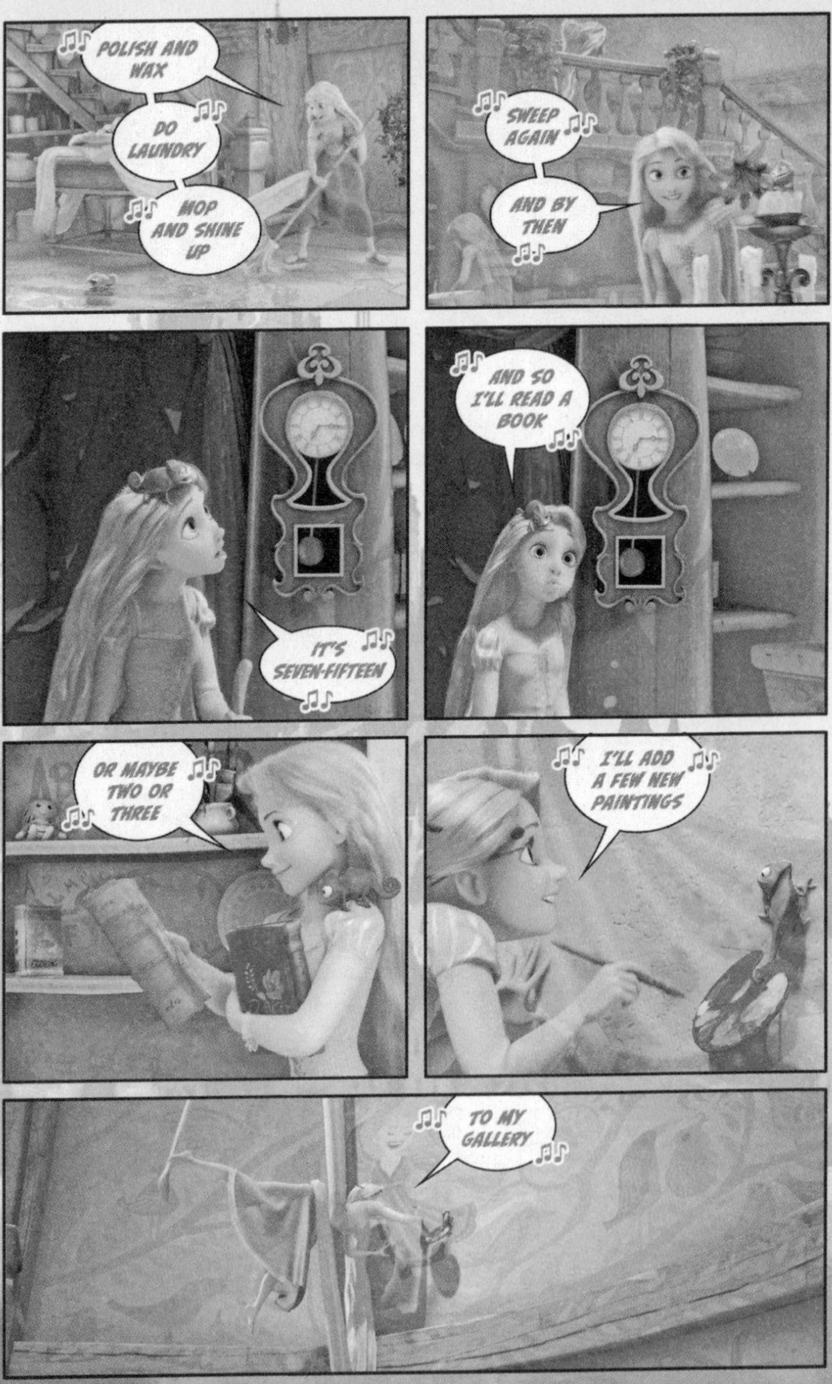
POLISH AND WAX
DO LAUNDRY
MOP AND SHINE UP
SWEEP AGAIN
AND BY THEN
IT'S SEVEN-FIFTEEN
AND SO I'LL READ A BOOK
OR MAYBE TWO OR THREE
I'LL ADD A FEW NEW PAINTINGS
TO MY GALLERY

I'LL PLAY GUITAR
AND KNIT
AND COOK, AND BASICALLY
WONDER "WHEN WILL MY LIFE BEGIN?"

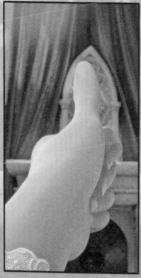

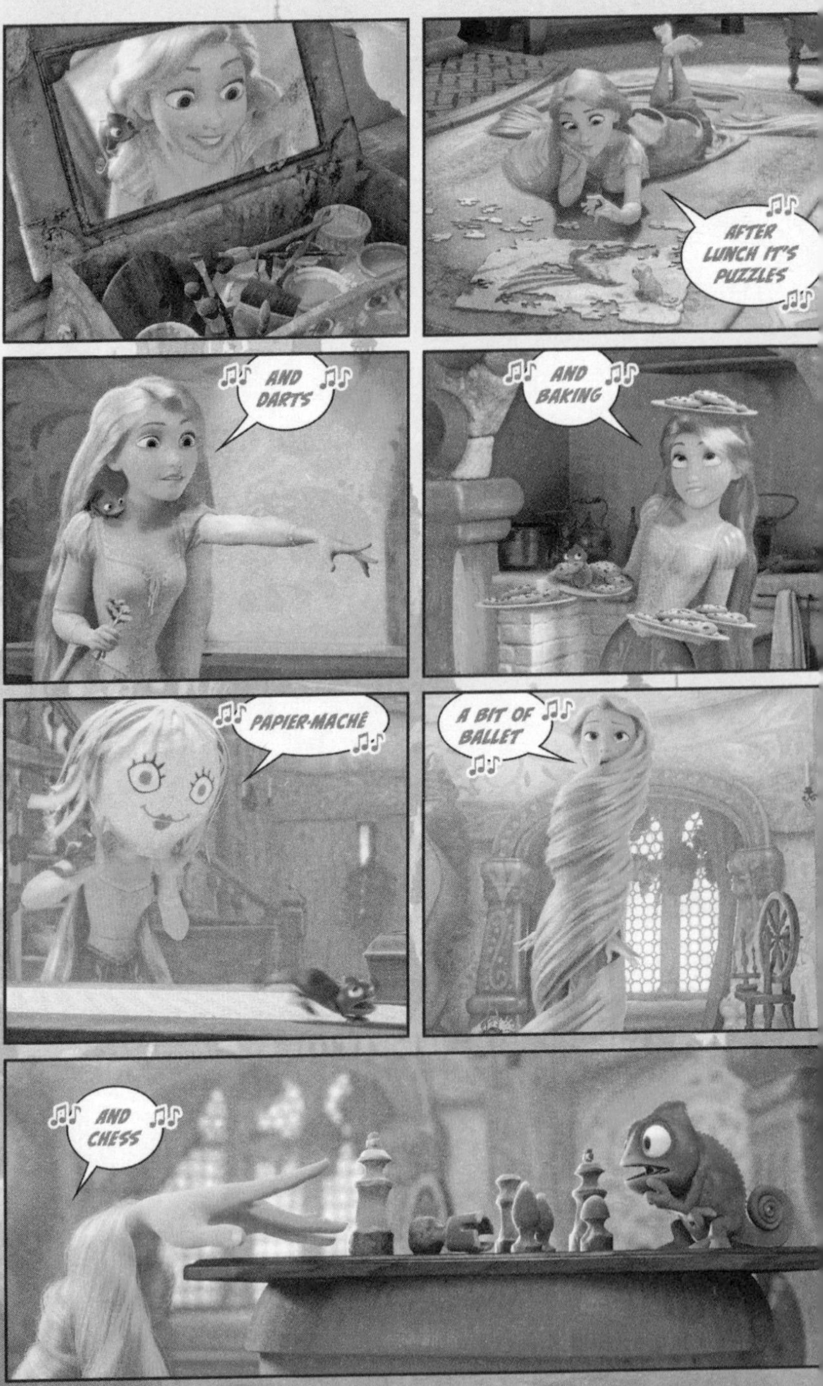
AFTER LUNCH IT'S PUZZLES
AND DARTS
AND BAKING
PAPIER-MACHÉ
A BIT OF BALLET
AND CHESS

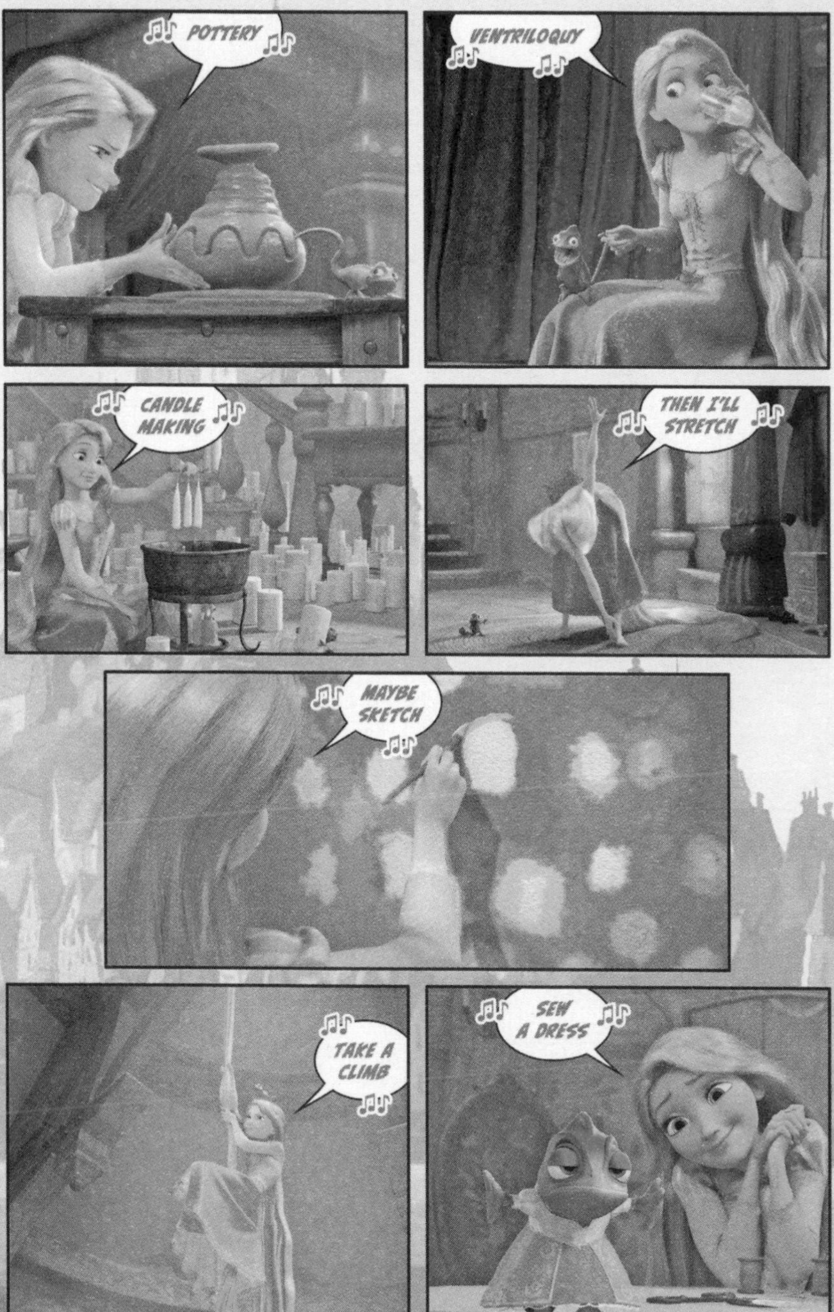
POTTERY
VENTRILOQUY
CANDLE MAKING
THEN I'LL STRETCH
MAYBE SKETCH
TAKE A CLIMB
SEW A DRESS

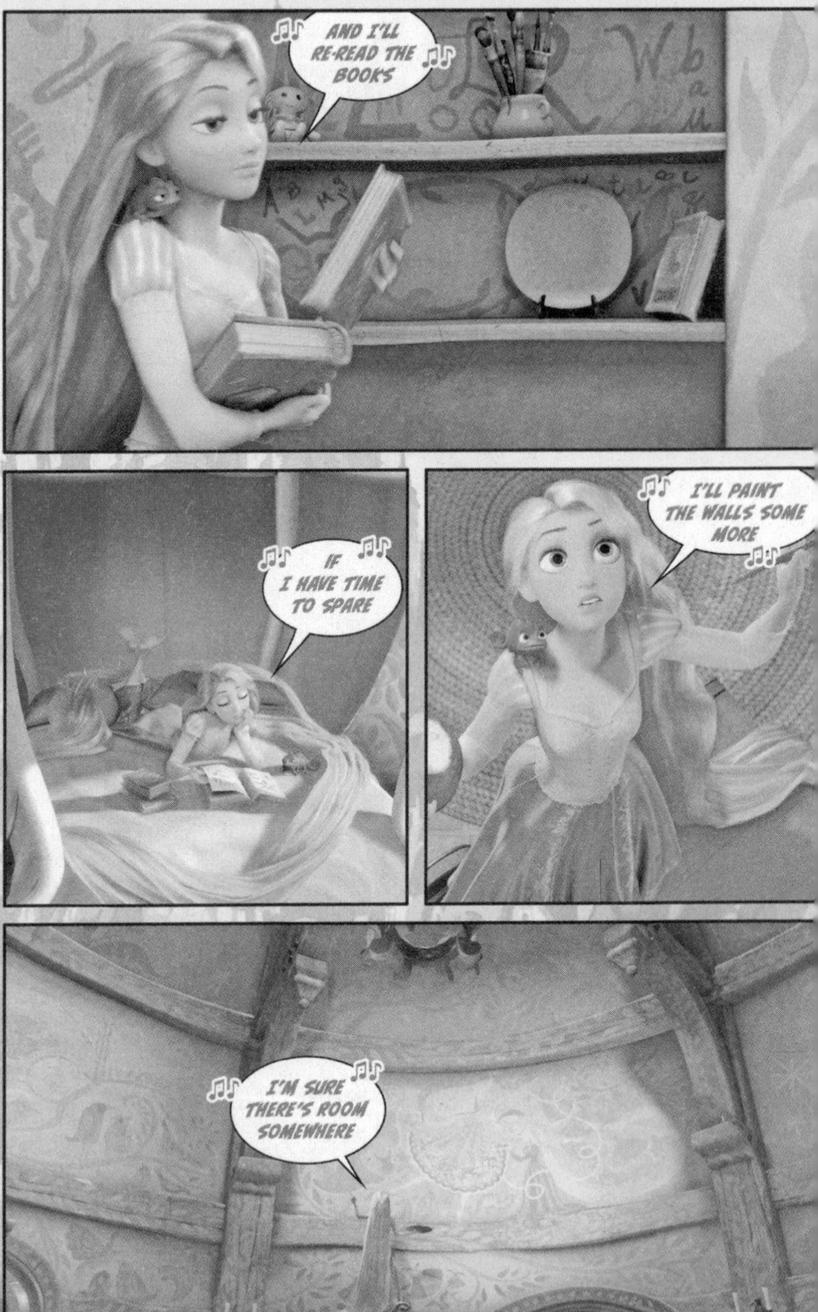
AND I'LL RE-READ THE BOOKS
IF I HAVE TIME TO SPARE
I'LL PAINT THE WALLS SOME MORE
I'M SURE THERE'S ROOM SOMEWHERE

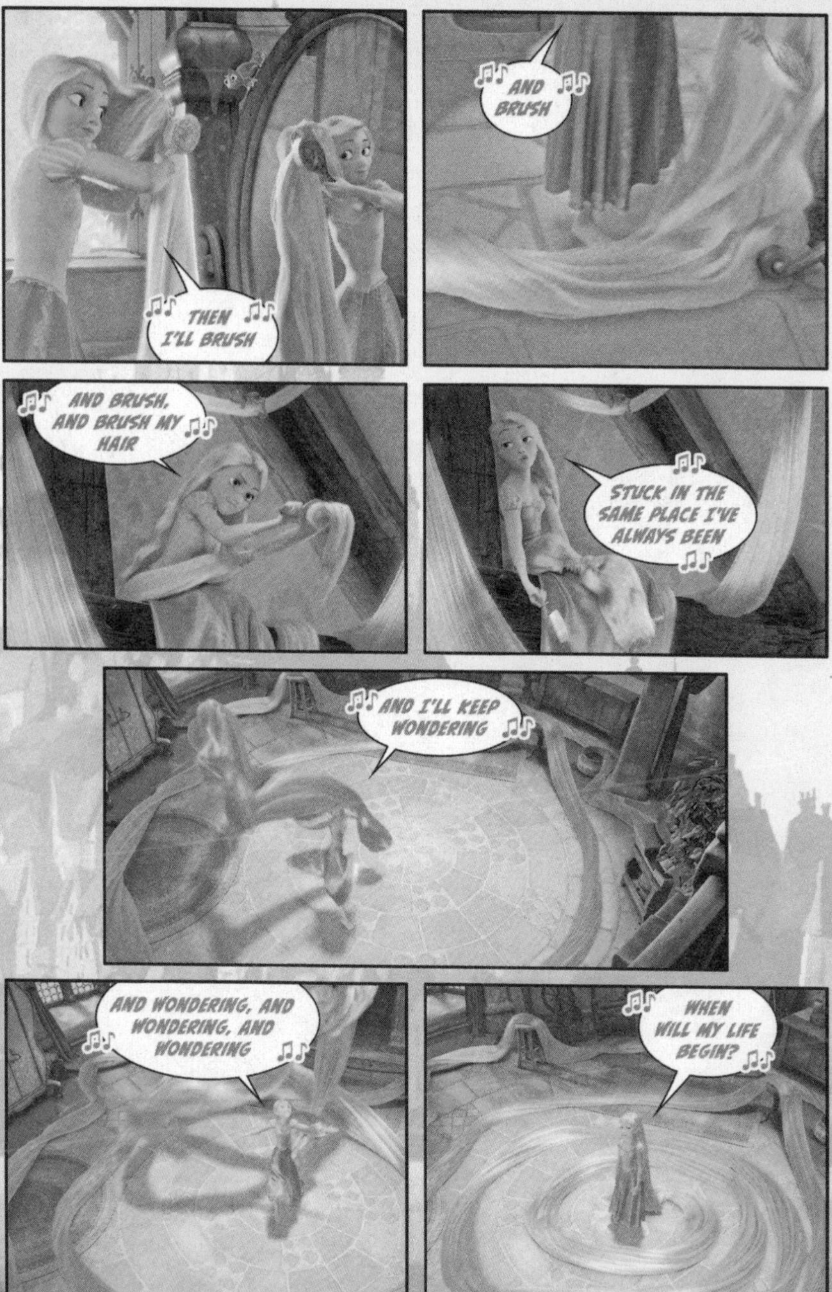
THEN I'LL BRUSH
AND BRUSH
AND BRUSH, AND BRUSH MY HAIR
STUCK IN THE SAME PLACE I'VE ALWAYS BEEN
AND I'LL KEEP WONDERING
AND WONDERING, AND WONDERING, AND WONDERING
WHEN WILL MY LIFE BEGIN?

♫♪ TOMORROW NIGHT ♫♪

♫♪ THE LIGHTS WILL APPEAR ♫♪

♫♪ JUST LIKE THEY DO ♫♪

♫♪ ON MY BIRTHDAY EACH YEAR ♫♪

♫♪ WHAT IS IT LIKE, OUT THERE WHERE THEY GLOW? ♫♪

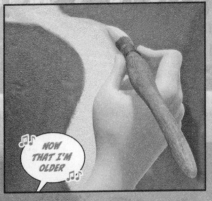

♫♪ NOW THAT I'M OLDER ♫♪

♫♪ MOTHER MIGHT JUST LET ME GO ♫♪

24

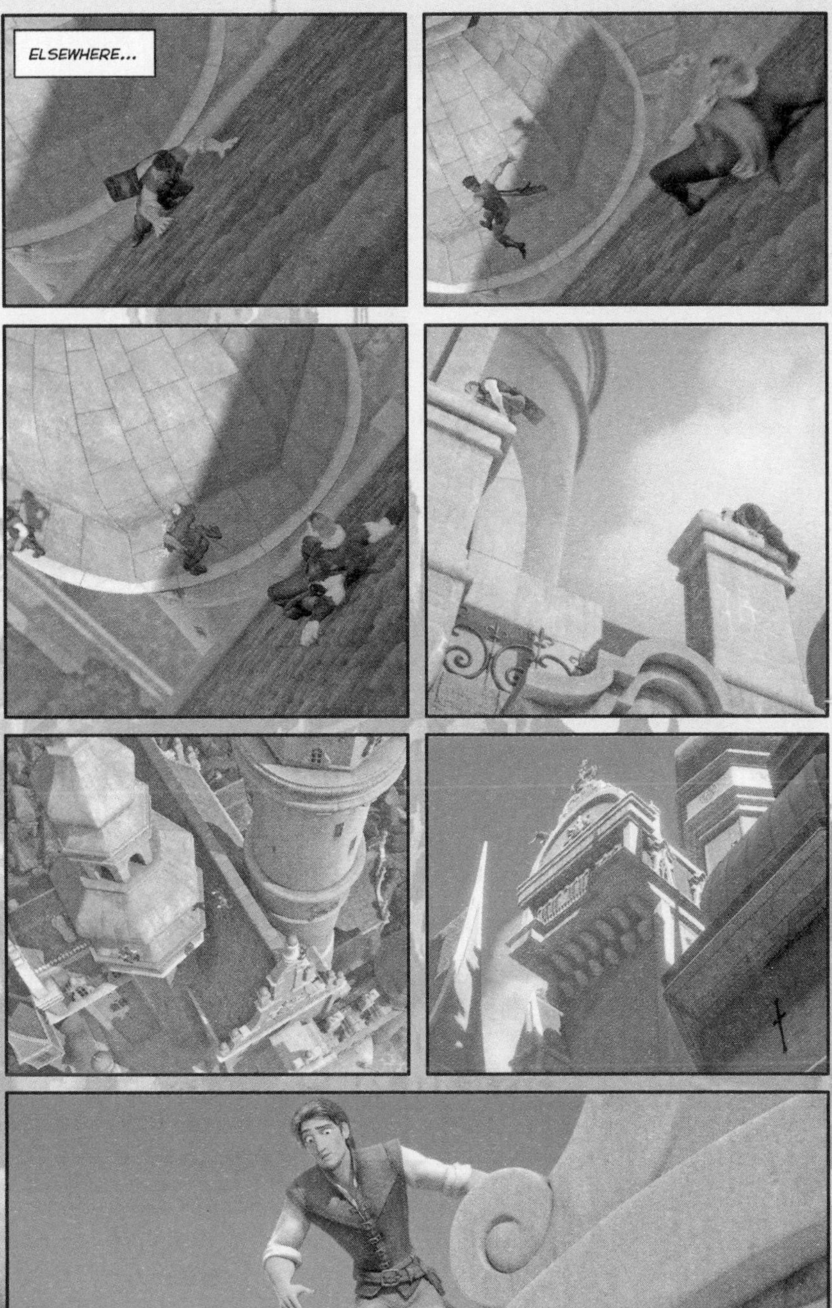
ELSEWHERE...

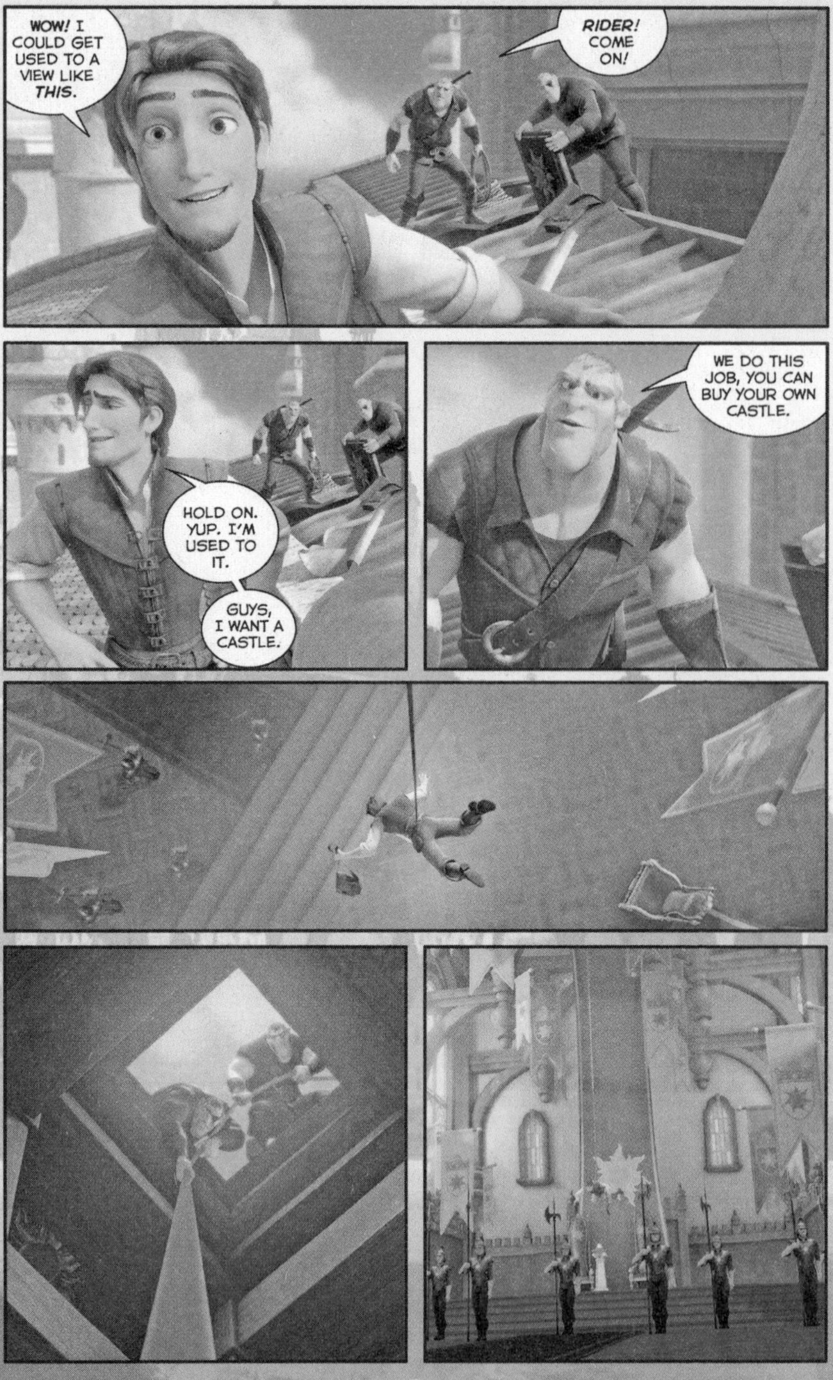
WOW! I COULD GET USED TO A VIEW LIKE THIS.
RIDER! COME ON!
HOLD ON. YUP. I'M USED TO IT.
GUYS, I WANT A CASTLE.
WE DO THIS JOB, YOU CAN BUY YOUR OWN CASTLE.

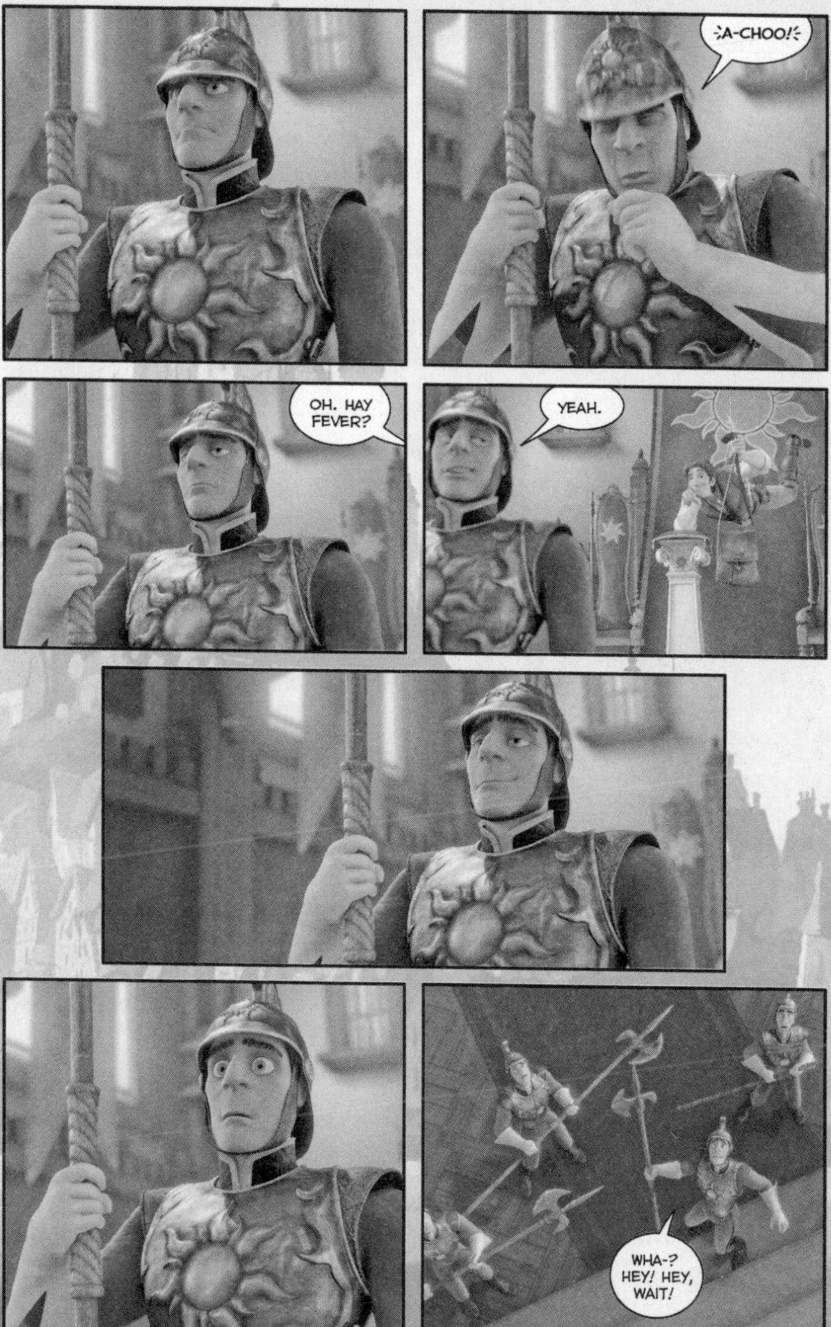
A-CHOO!
OH. HAY FEVER?
YEAH.
WHA-? HEY! HEY, WAIT!

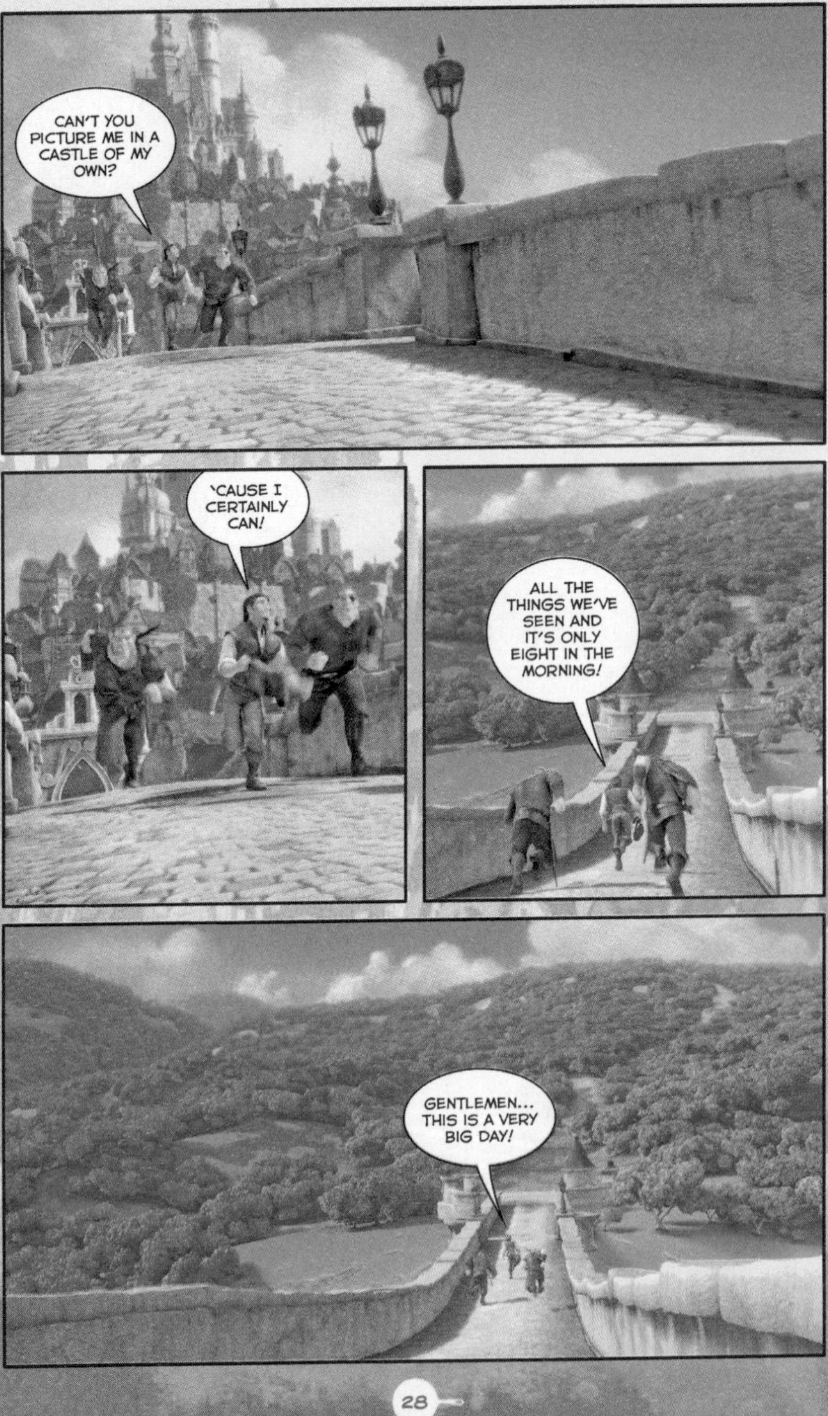
CAN'T YOU PICTURE ME IN A CASTLE OF MY OWN?
'CAUSE I CERTAINLY CAN!
ALL THE THINGS WE'VE SEEN AND IT'S ONLY EIGHT IN THE MORNING!
GENTLEMEN... THIS IS A VERY BIG DAY!

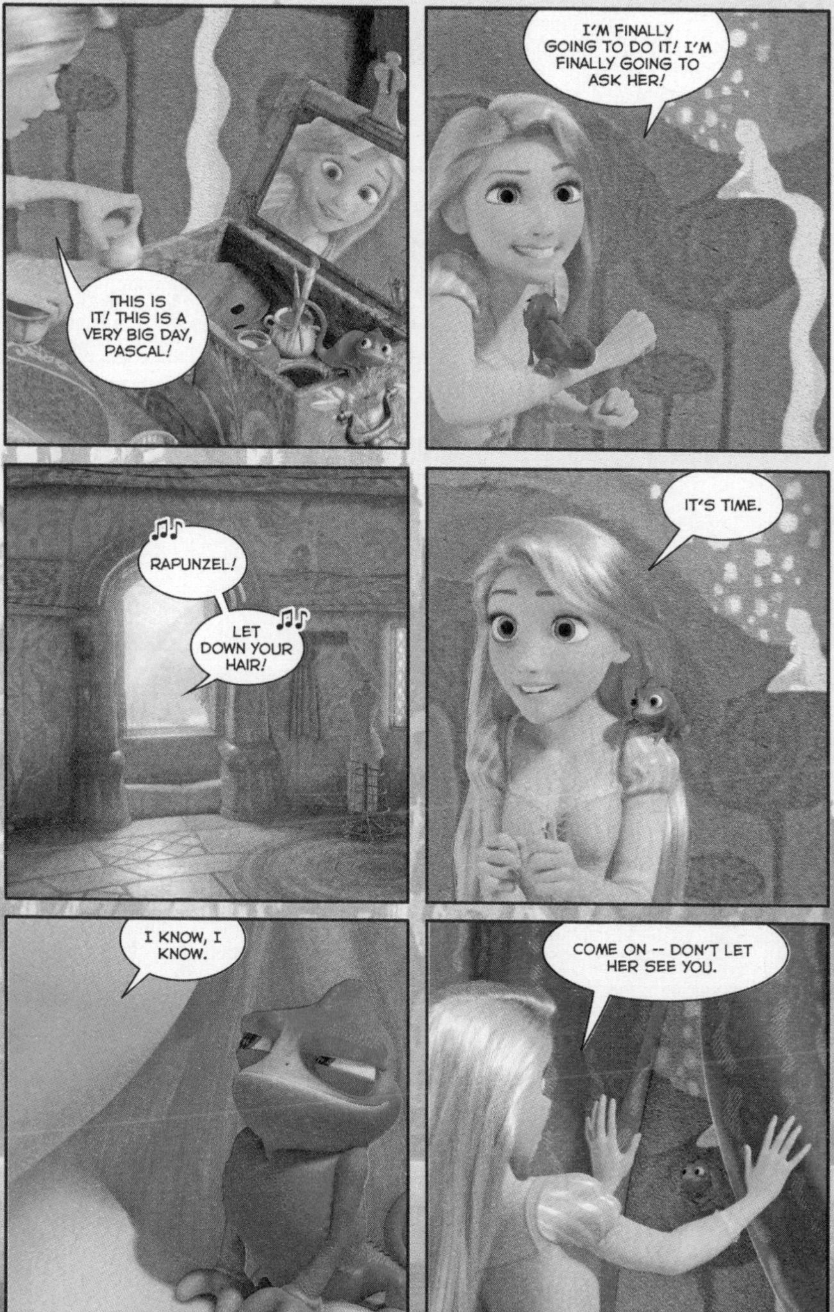
THIS IS IT! THIS IS A VERY BIG DAY, PASCAL!
I'M FINALLY GOING TO DO IT! I'M FINALLY GOING TO ASK HER!
RAPUNZEL!
LET DOWN YOUR HAIR!
IT'S TIME.
I KNOW, I KNOW.
COME ON -- DON'T LET HER SEE YOU.

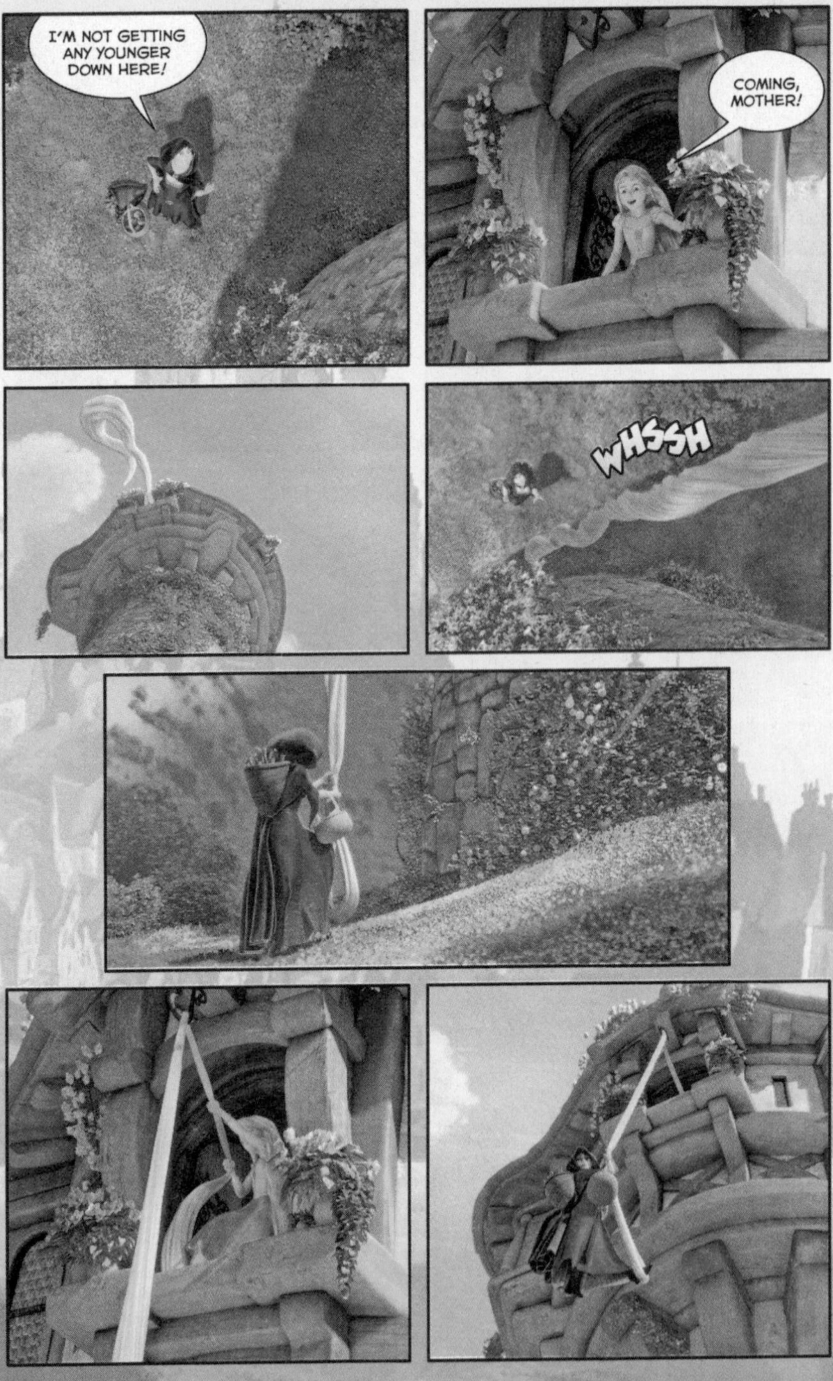
I'M NOT GETTING ANY YOUNGER DOWN HERE!
COMING, MOTHER!
WHSSH

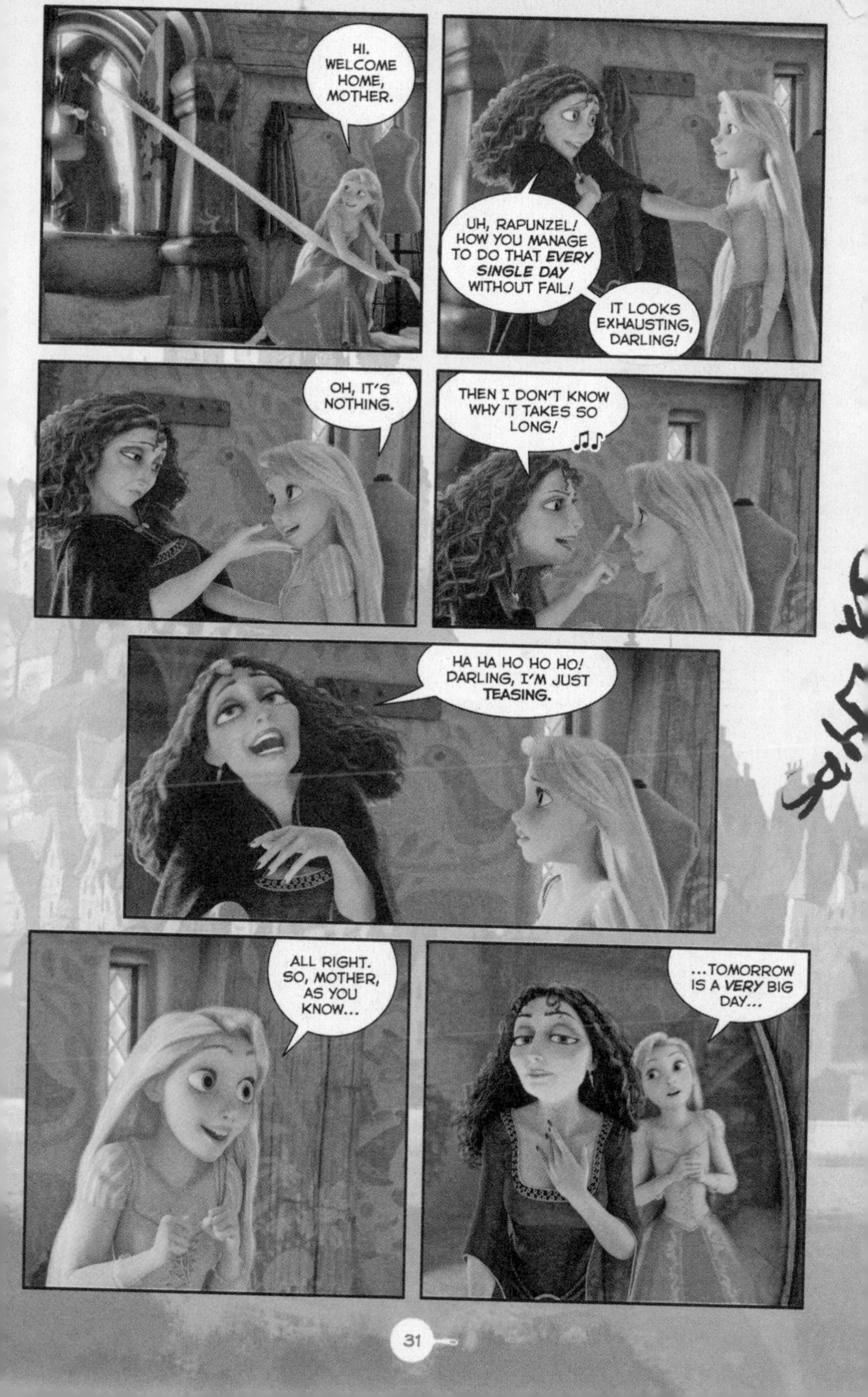
HI. WELCOME HOME, MOTHER.
UH, RAPUNZEL! HOW YOU MANAGE TO DO THAT *EVERY SINGLE DAY* WITHOUT FAIL!
IT LOOKS EXHAUSTING, DARLING!
OH, IT'S NOTHING.
THEN I DON'T KNOW WHY IT TAKES SO LONG!
HA HA HO HO HO! DARLING, I'M JUST **TEASING.**
ALL RIGHT. SO, MOTHER, AS YOU KNOW...
...TOMORROW IS A *VERY* BIG DAY...

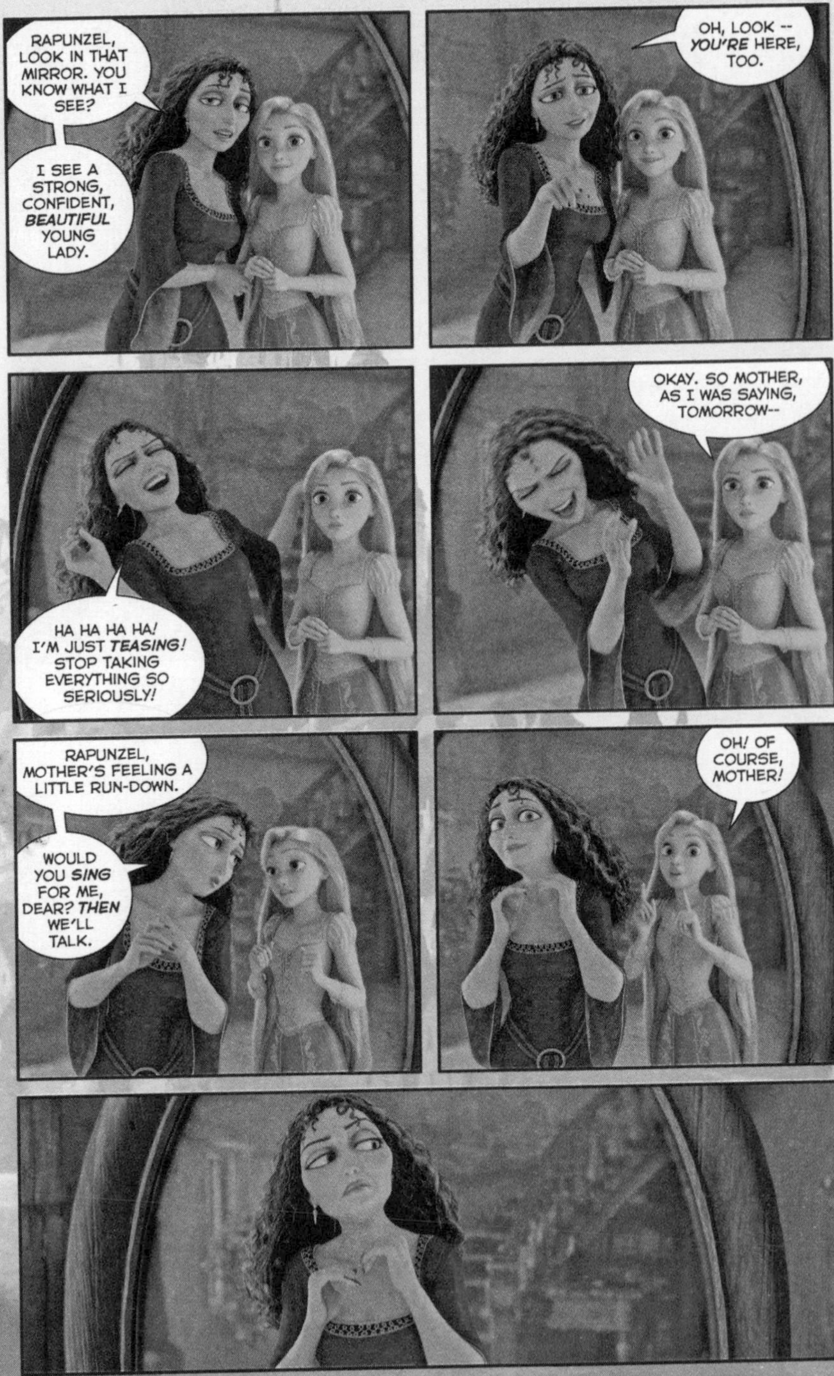
RAPUNZEL, LOOK IN THAT MIRROR. YOU KNOW WHAT I SEE?
I SEE A STRONG, CONFIDENT, BEAUTIFUL YOUNG LADY.
OH, LOOK -- YOU'RE HERE, TOO.
HA HA HA HA! I'M JUST TEASING! STOP TAKING EVERYTHING SO SERIOUSLY!
OKAY. SO MOTHER, AS I WAS SAYING, TOMORROW--
RAPUNZEL, MOTHER'S FEELING A LITTLE RUN-DOWN.
WOULD YOU SING FOR ME, DEAR? THEN WE'LL TALK.
OH! OF COURSE, MOTHER!

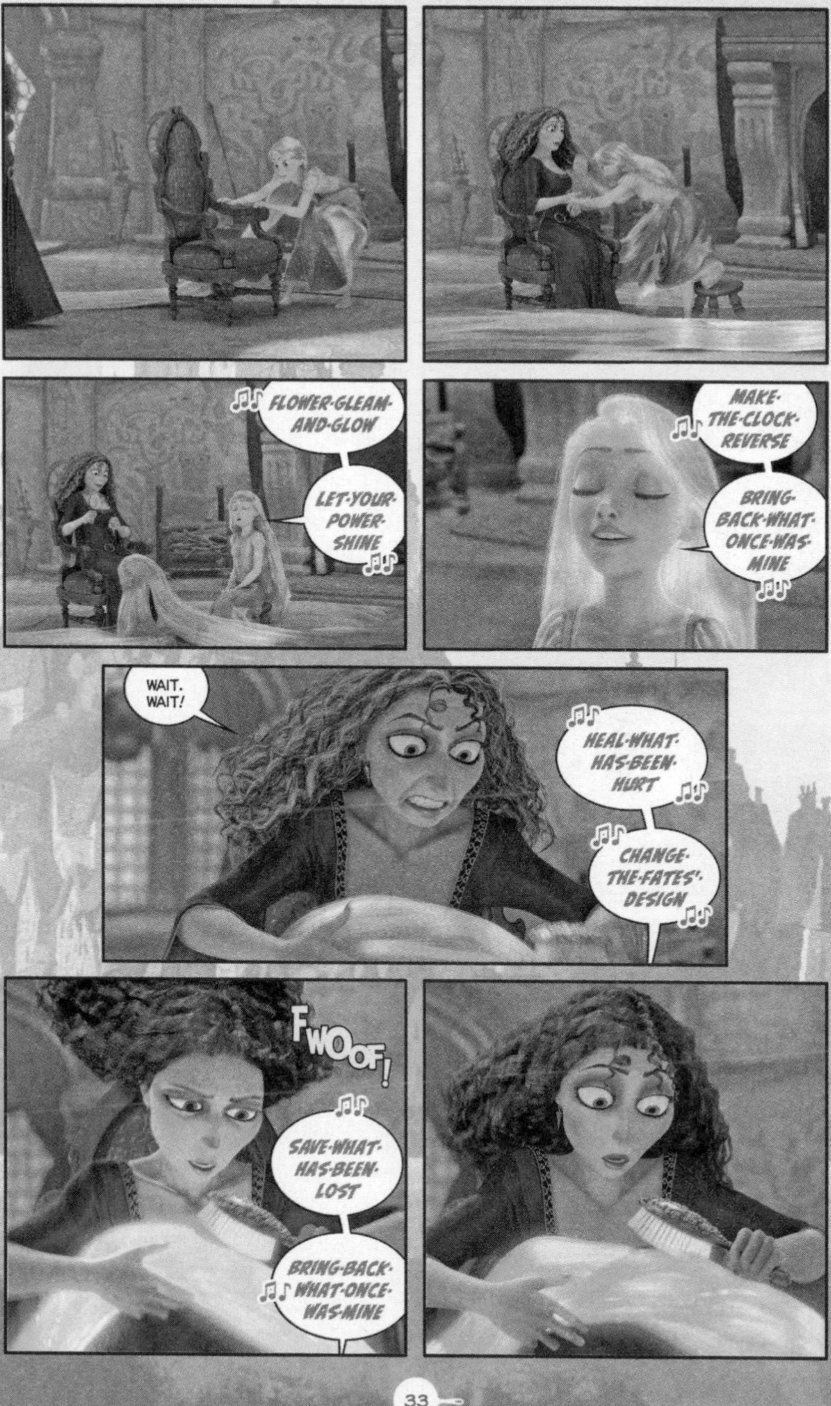
FLOWER-GLEAM-AND-GLOW
LET-YOUR-POWER-SHINE
MAKE-THE-CLOCK-REVERSE
BRING-BACK-WHAT-ONCE-WAS-MINE
WAIT. WAIT!
HEAL-WHAT-HAS-BEEN-HURT
CHANGE-THE-FATES'-DESIGN
FWOOF!
SAVE-WHAT-HAS-BEEN-LOST
BRING-BACK-WHAT-ONCE-WAS-MINE

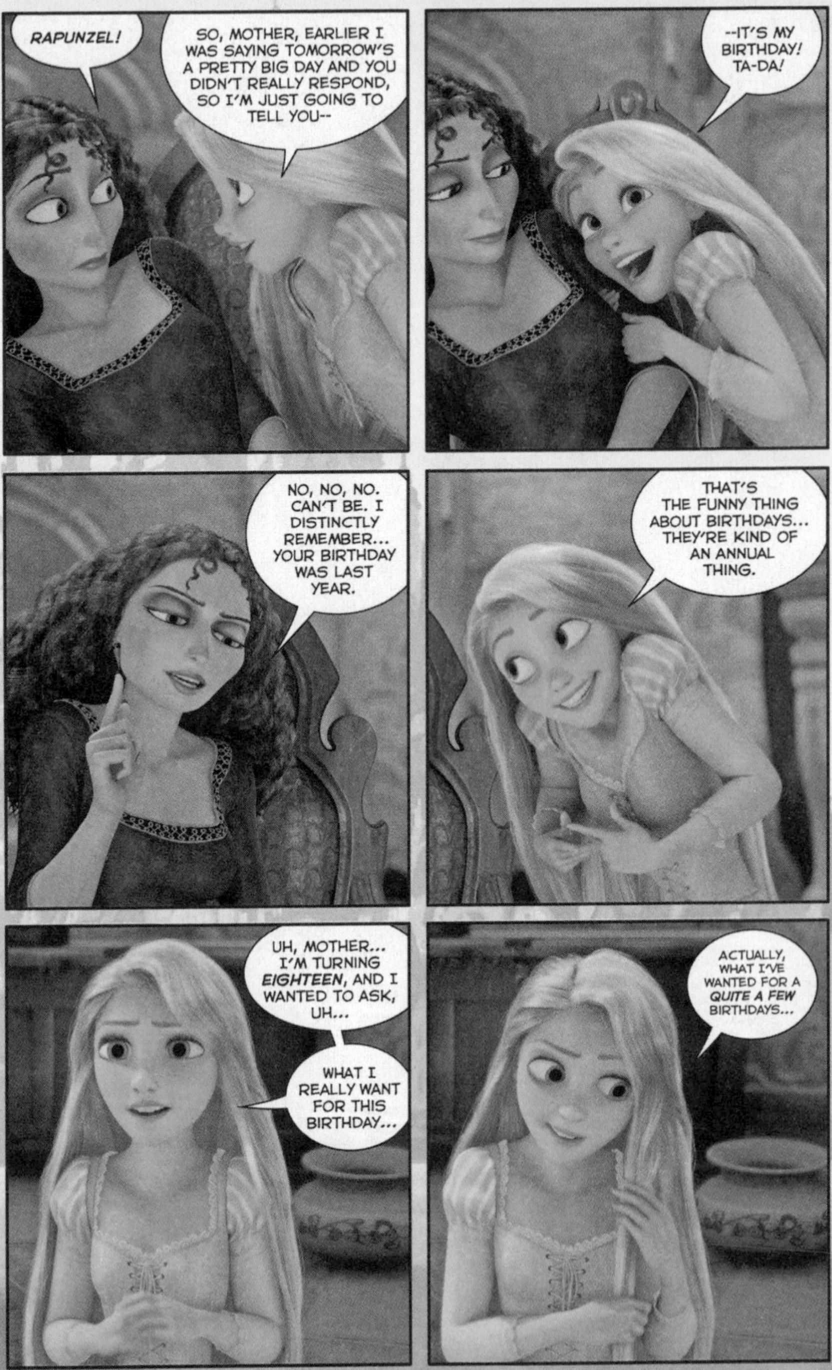
RAPUNZEL!
SO, MOTHER, EARLIER I WAS SAYING TOMORROW'S A PRETTY BIG DAY AND YOU DIDN'T REALLY RESPOND, SO I'M JUST GOING TO TELL YOU--
--IT'S MY BIRTHDAY! TA-DA!
NO, NO, NO. CAN'T BE. I DISTINCTLY REMEMBER... YOUR BIRTHDAY WAS LAST YEAR.
THAT'S THE FUNNY THING ABOUT BIRTHDAYS... THEY'RE KIND OF AN ANNUAL THING.
UH, MOTHER... I'M TURNING *EIGHTEEN*, AND I WANTED TO ASK, UH...
WHAT I REALLY WANT FOR THIS BIRTHDAY...
ACTUALLY, WHAT I'VE WANTED FOR A *QUITE A FEW* BIRTHDAYS...

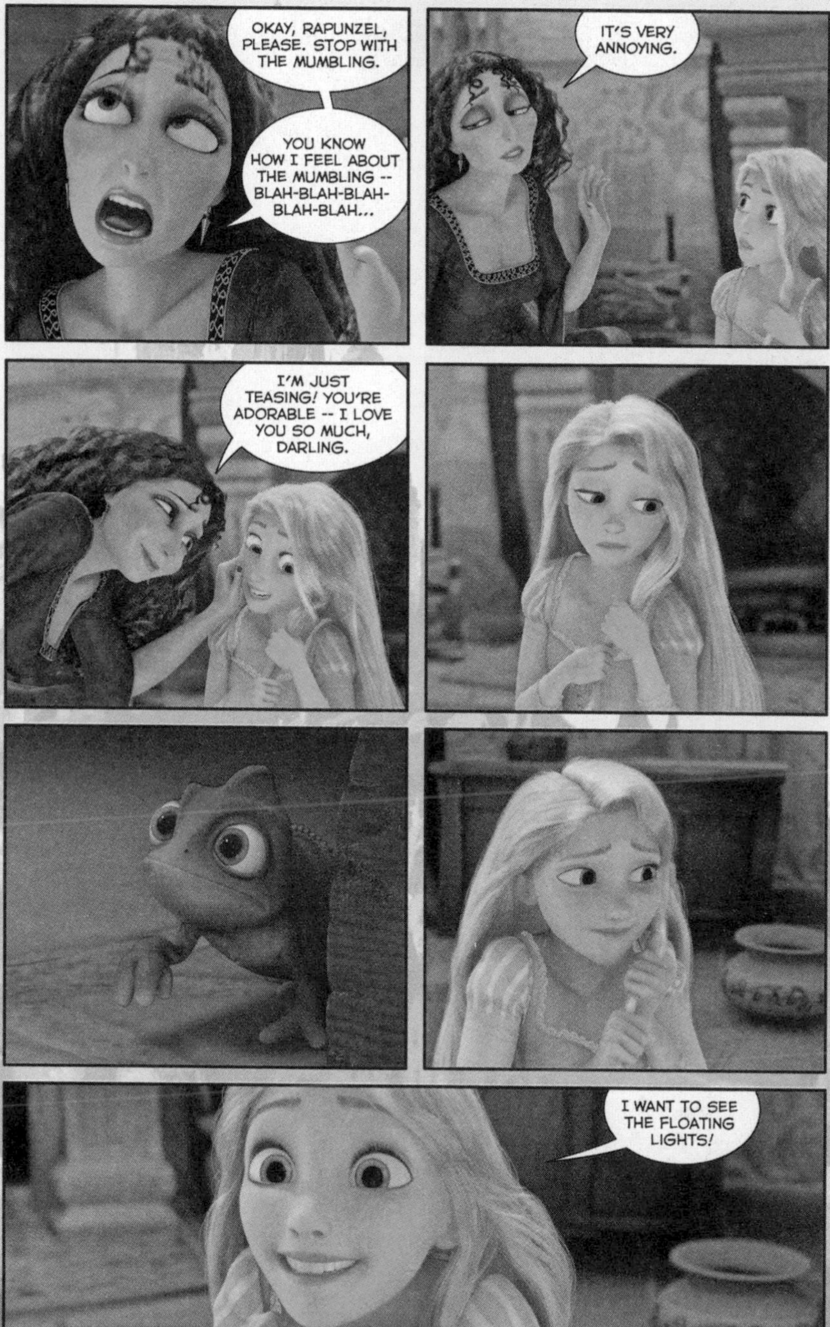
OKAY, RAPUNZEL, PLEASE. STOP WITH THE MUMBLING.
YOU KNOW HOW I FEEL ABOUT THE MUMBLING -- BLAH-BLAH-BLAH-BLAH-BLAH...
IT'S VERY ANNOYING.
I'M JUST TEASING! YOU'RE ADORABLE -- I LOVE YOU SO MUCH, DARLING.
I WANT TO SEE THE FLOATING LIGHTS!

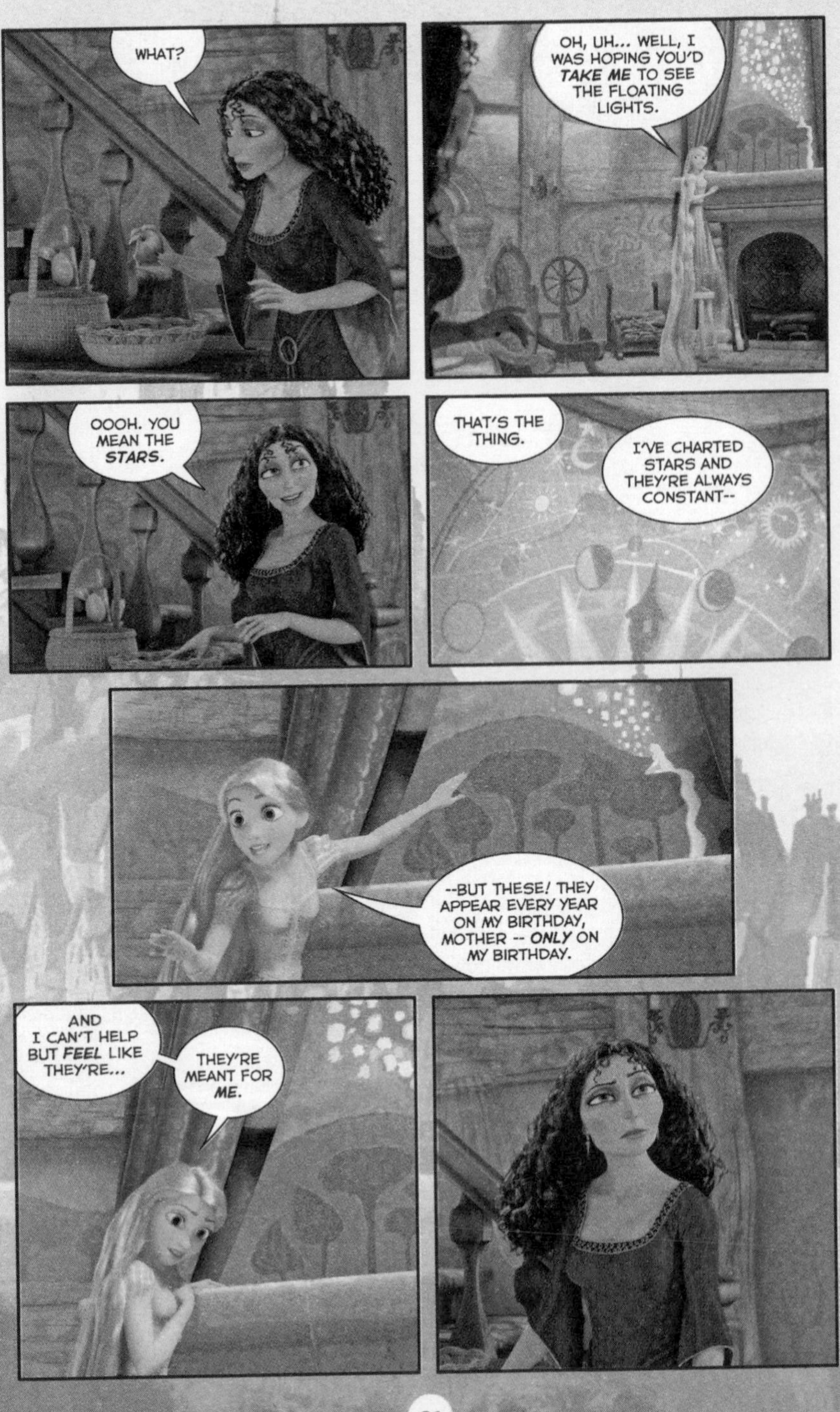
WHAT?
OH, UH... WELL, I WAS HOPING YOU'D TAKE ME TO SEE THE FLOATING LIGHTS.
OOOH. YOU MEAN THE STARS.
THAT'S THE THING.
I'VE CHARTED STARS AND THEY'RE ALWAYS CONSTANT--
--BUT THESE! THEY APPEAR EVERY YEAR ON MY BIRTHDAY, MOTHER -- ONLY ON MY BIRTHDAY.
AND I CAN'T HELP BUT FEEL LIKE THEY'RE...
THEY'RE MEANT FOR ME.

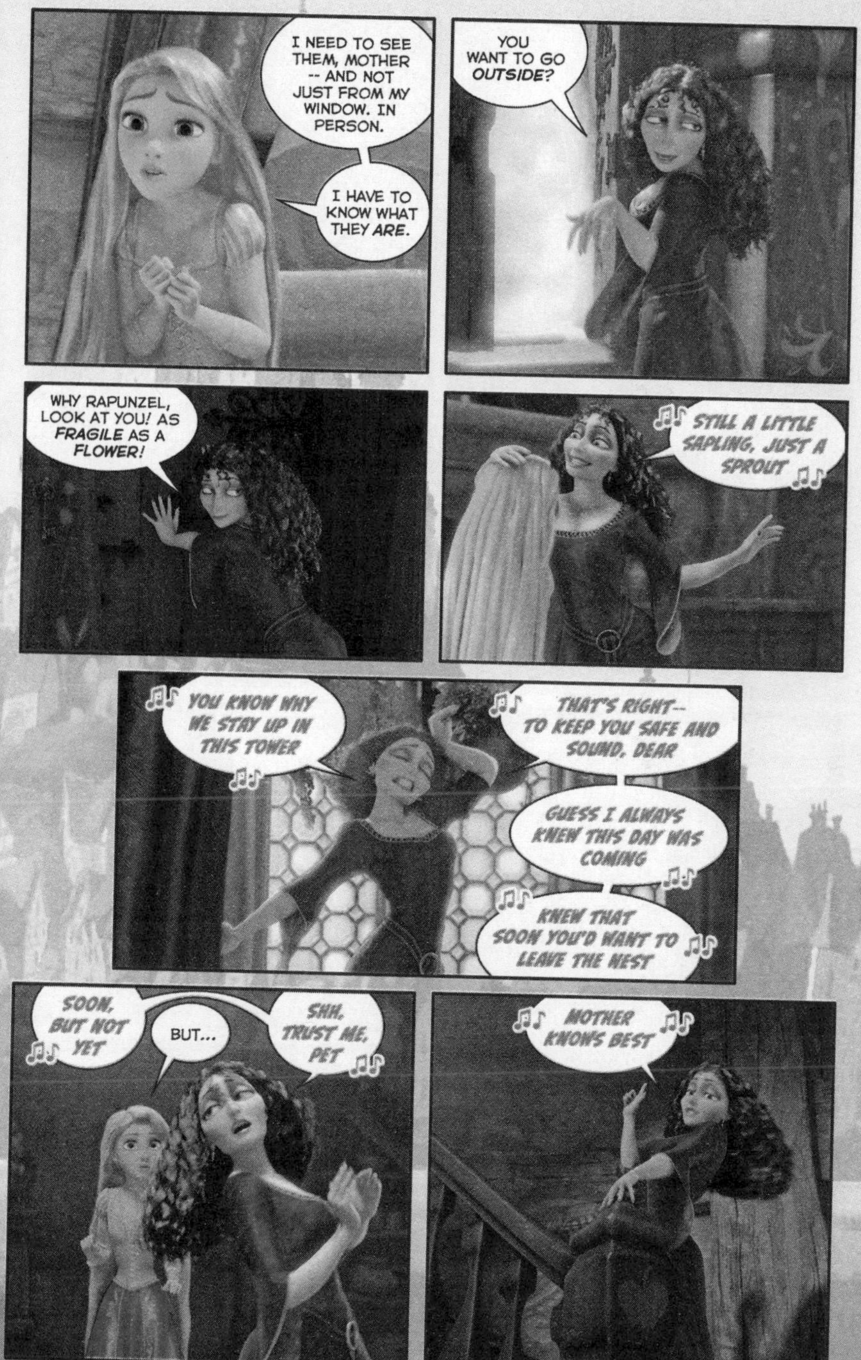

I NEED TO SEE THEM, MOTHER -- AND NOT JUST FROM MY WINDOW. IN PERSON.
I HAVE TO KNOW WHAT THEY ARE.
YOU WANT TO GO OUTSIDE?
WHY RAPUNZEL, LOOK AT YOU! AS FRAGILE AS A FLOWER!
STILL A LITTLE SAPLING, JUST A SPROUT
YOU KNOW WHY WE STAY UP IN THIS TOWER
THAT'S RIGHT-- TO KEEP YOU SAFE AND SOUND, DEAR
GUESS I ALWAYS KNEW THIS DAY WAS COMING
KNEW THAT SOON YOU'D WANT TO LEAVE THE NEST
SOON, BUT NOT YET
BUT...
SHH, TRUST ME, PET
MOTHER KNOWS BEST

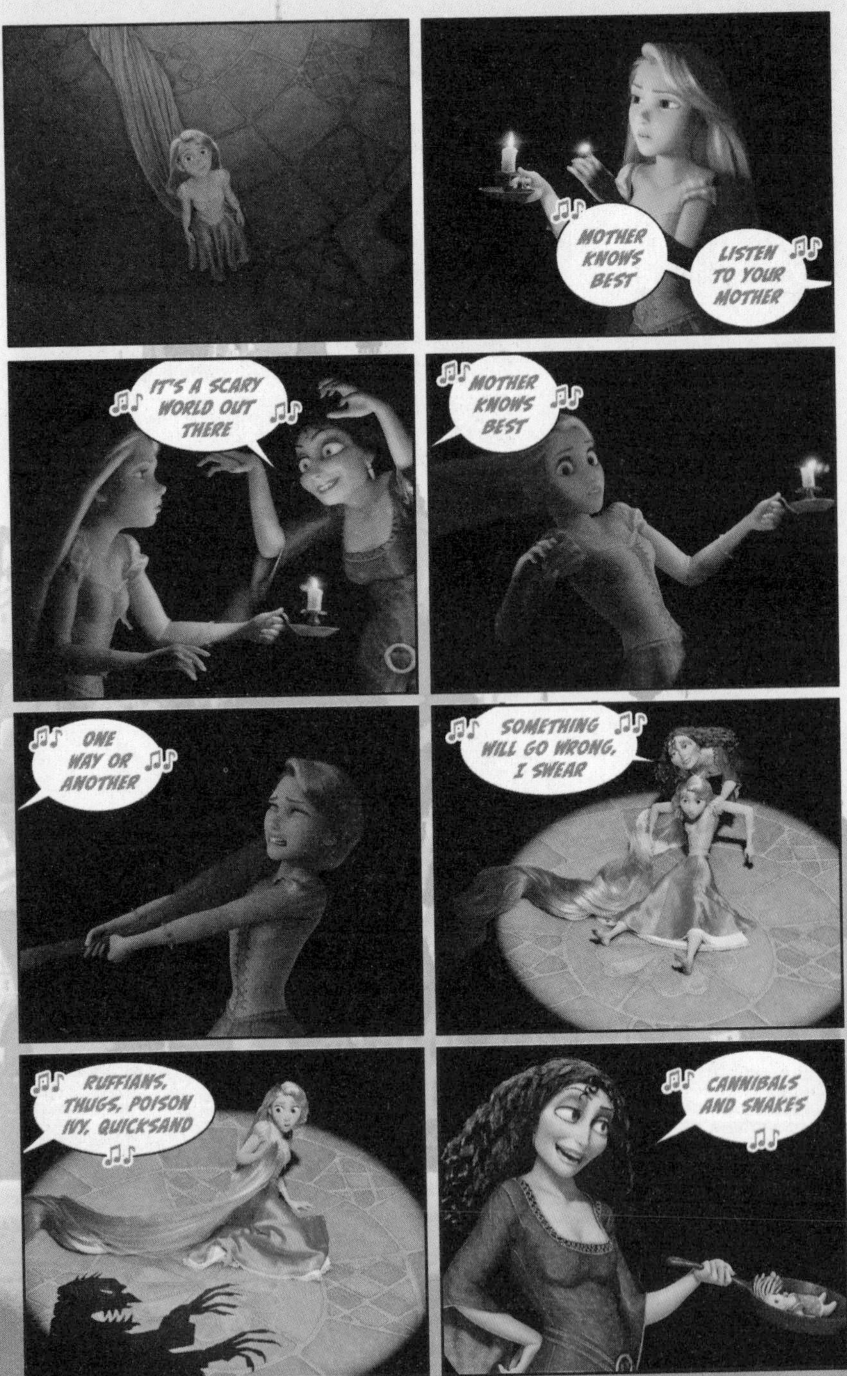
MOTHER KNOWS BEST
LISTEN TO YOUR MOTHER
IT'S A SCARY WORLD OUT THERE
MOTHER KNOWS BEST
ONE WAY OR ANOTHER
SOMETHING WILL GO WRONG, I SWEAR
RUFFIANS, THUGS, POISON IVY, QUICKSAND
CANNIBALS AND SNAKES

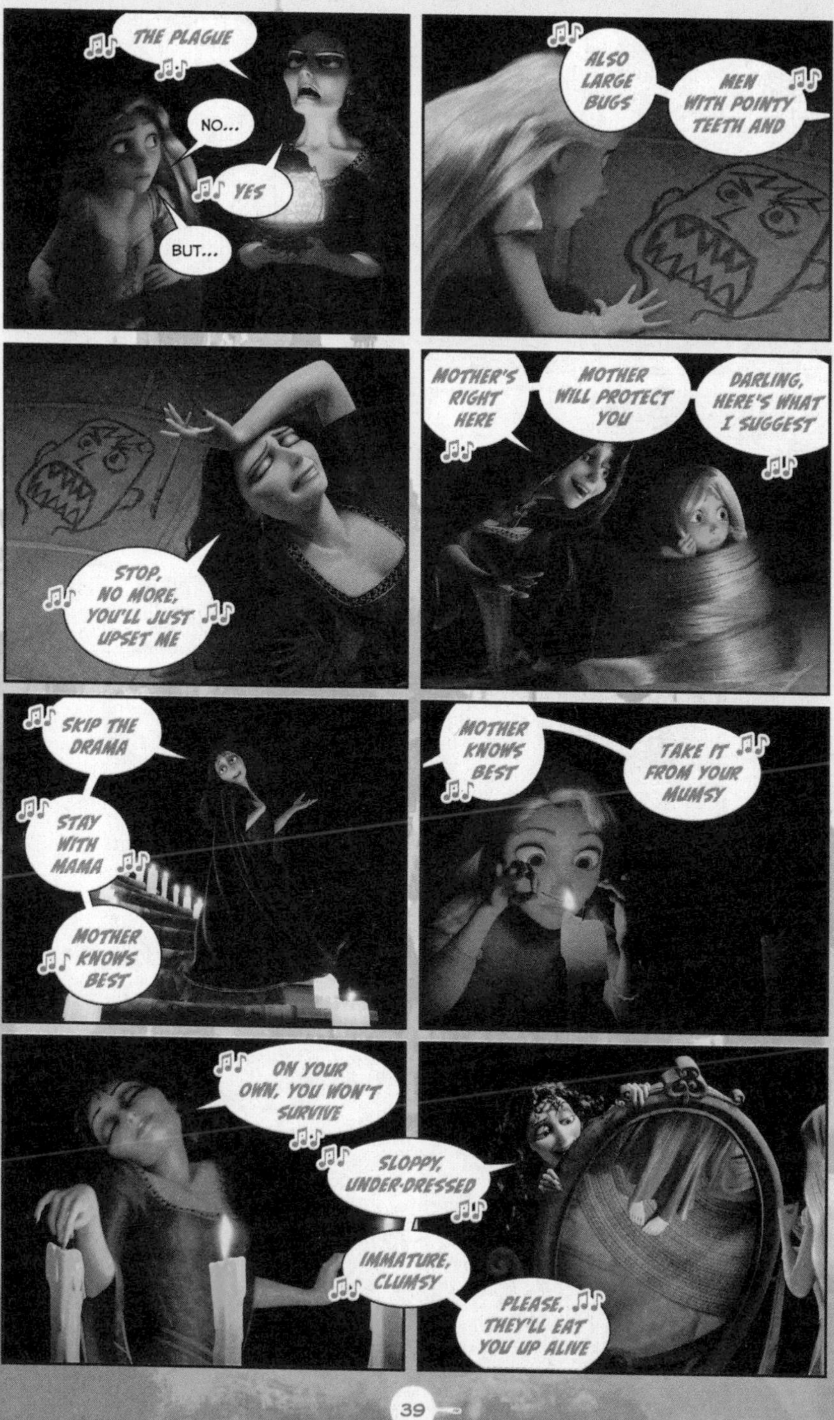
THE PLAGUE
NO...
YES
BUT...
ALSO LARGE BUGS
MEN WITH POINTY TEETH AND
STOP, NO MORE, YOU'LL JUST UPSET ME
MOTHER'S RIGHT HERE
MOTHER WILL PROTECT YOU
DARLING, HERE'S WHAT I SUGGEST
SKIP THE DRAMA
STAY WITH MAMA
MOTHER KNOWS BEST
MOTHER KNOWS BEST
TAKE IT FROM YOUR MUMSY
ON YOUR OWN, YOU WON'T SURVIVE
SLOPPY, UNDER-DRESSED
IMMATURE, CLUMSY
PLEASE, THEY'LL EAT YOU UP ALIVE

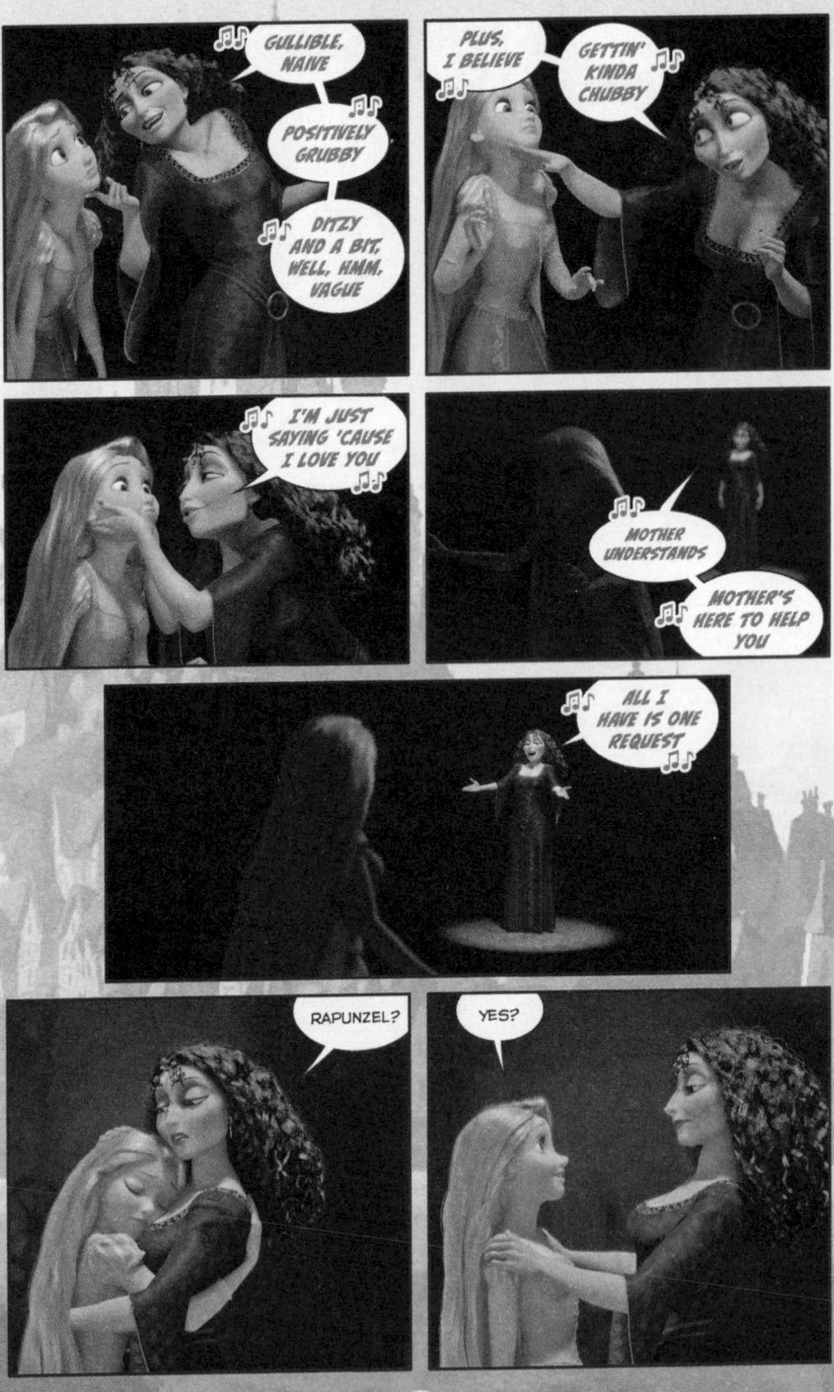
GULLIBLE, NAIVE
POSITIVELY GRUBBY
DITZY AND A BIT, WELL, HMM, VAGUE
PLUS, I BELIEVE
GETTIN' KINDA CHUBBY
I'M JUST SAYING 'CAUSE I LOVE YOU
MOTHER UNDERSTANDS
MOTHER'S HERE TO HELP YOU
ALL I HAVE IS ONE REQUEST
RAPUNZEL?
YES?

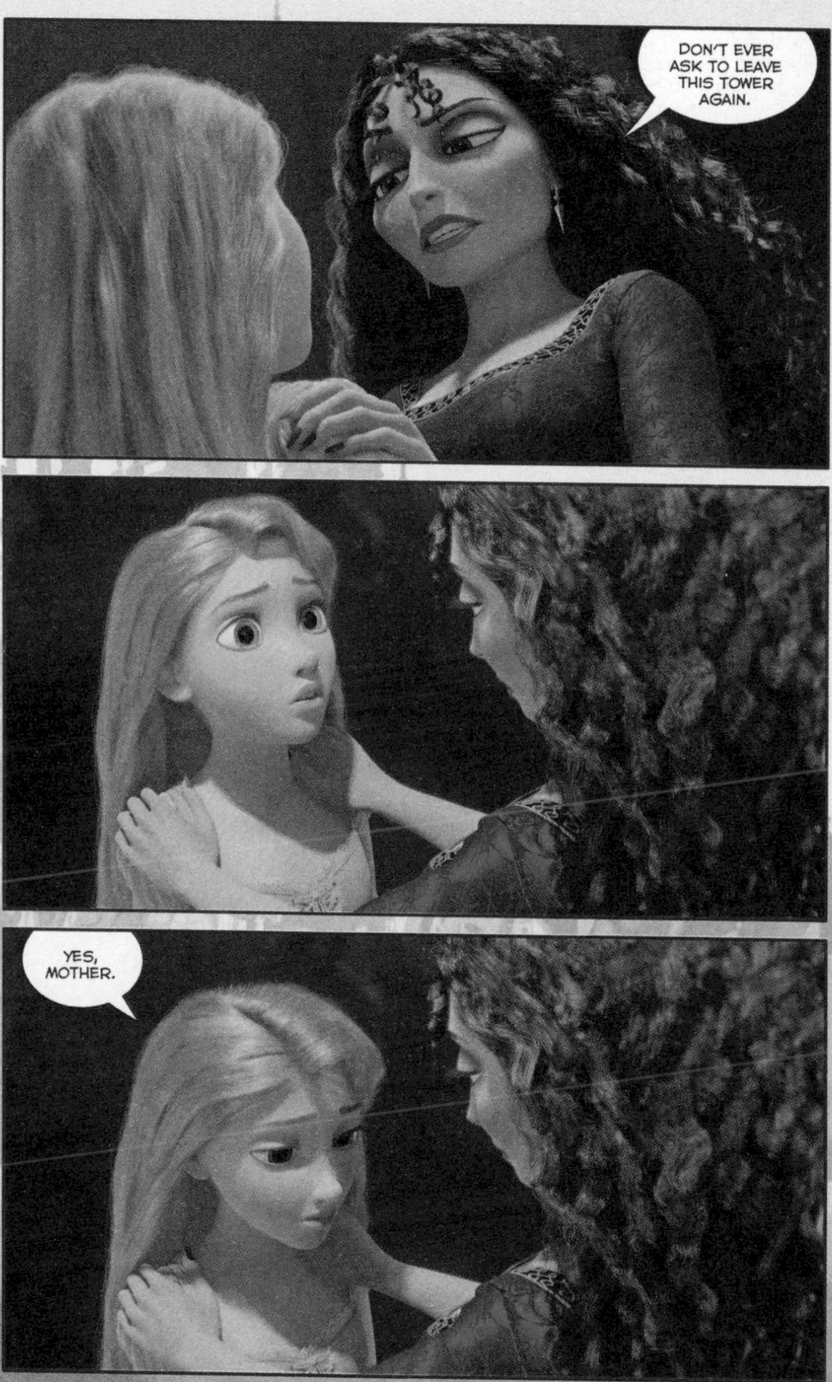
DON'T EVER ASK TO LEAVE THIS TOWER AGAIN.
YES, MOTHER.

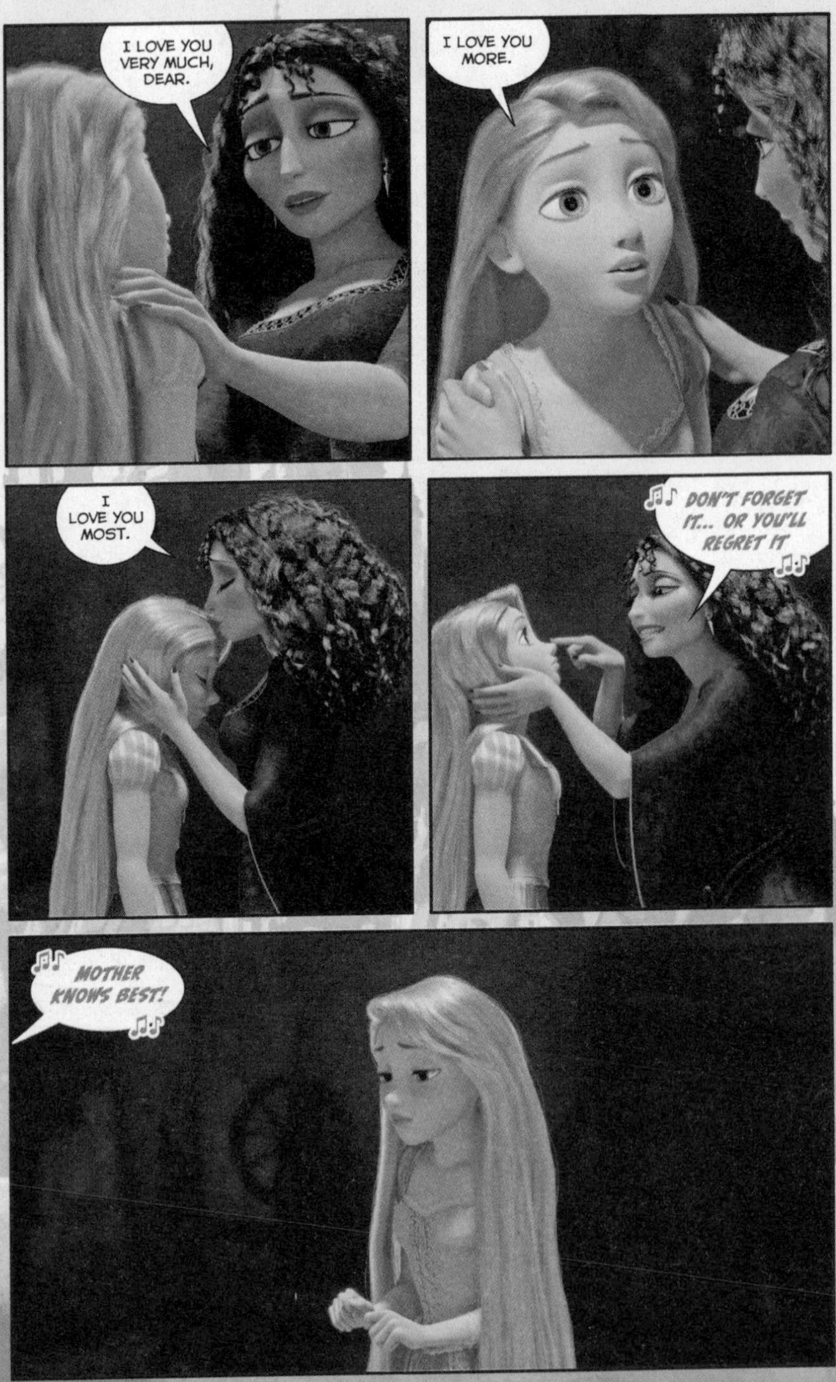
I LOVE YOU VERY MUCH, DEAR.
I LOVE YOU MORE.
I LOVE YOU MOST.
DON'T FORGET IT... OR YOU'LL REGRET IT
MOTHER KNOWS BEST!

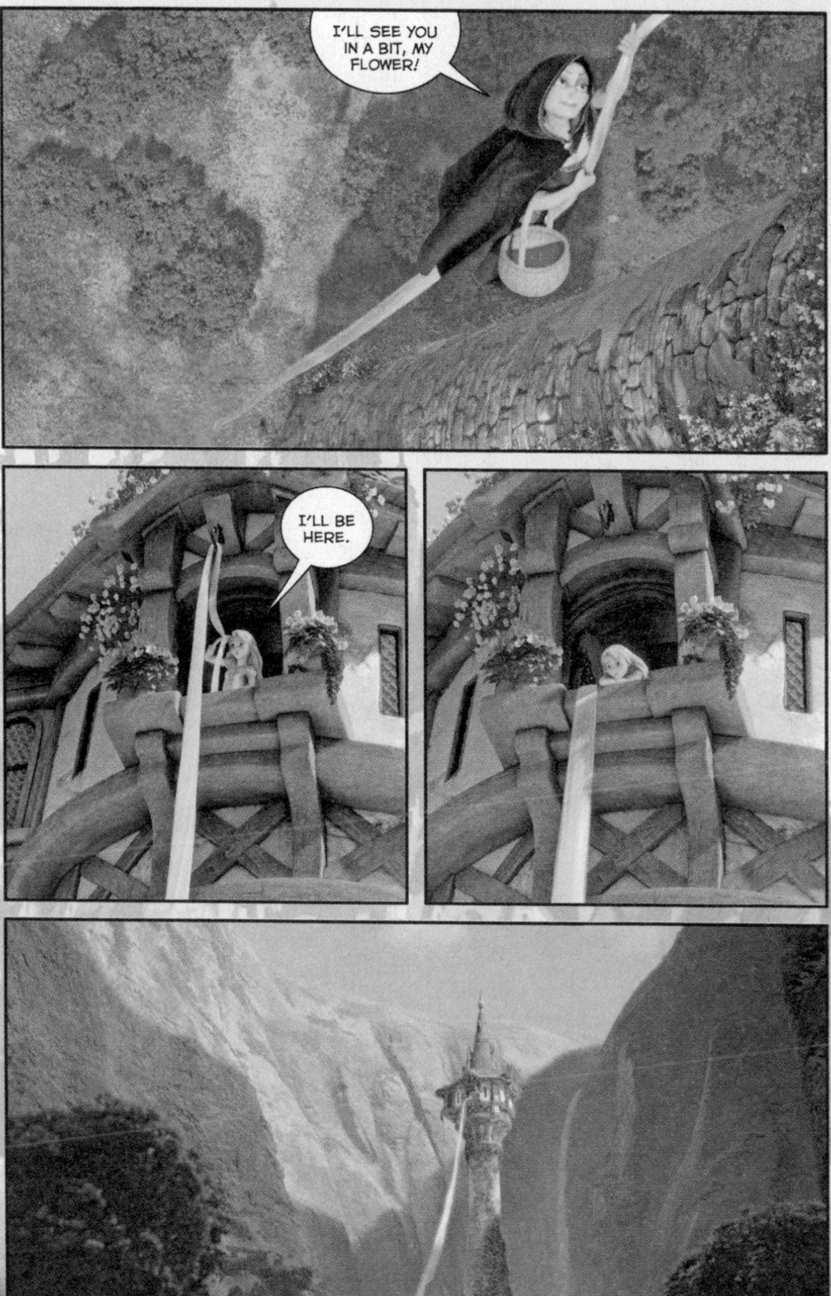
I'LL SEE YOU IN A BIT, MY FLOWER!
I'LL BE HERE.

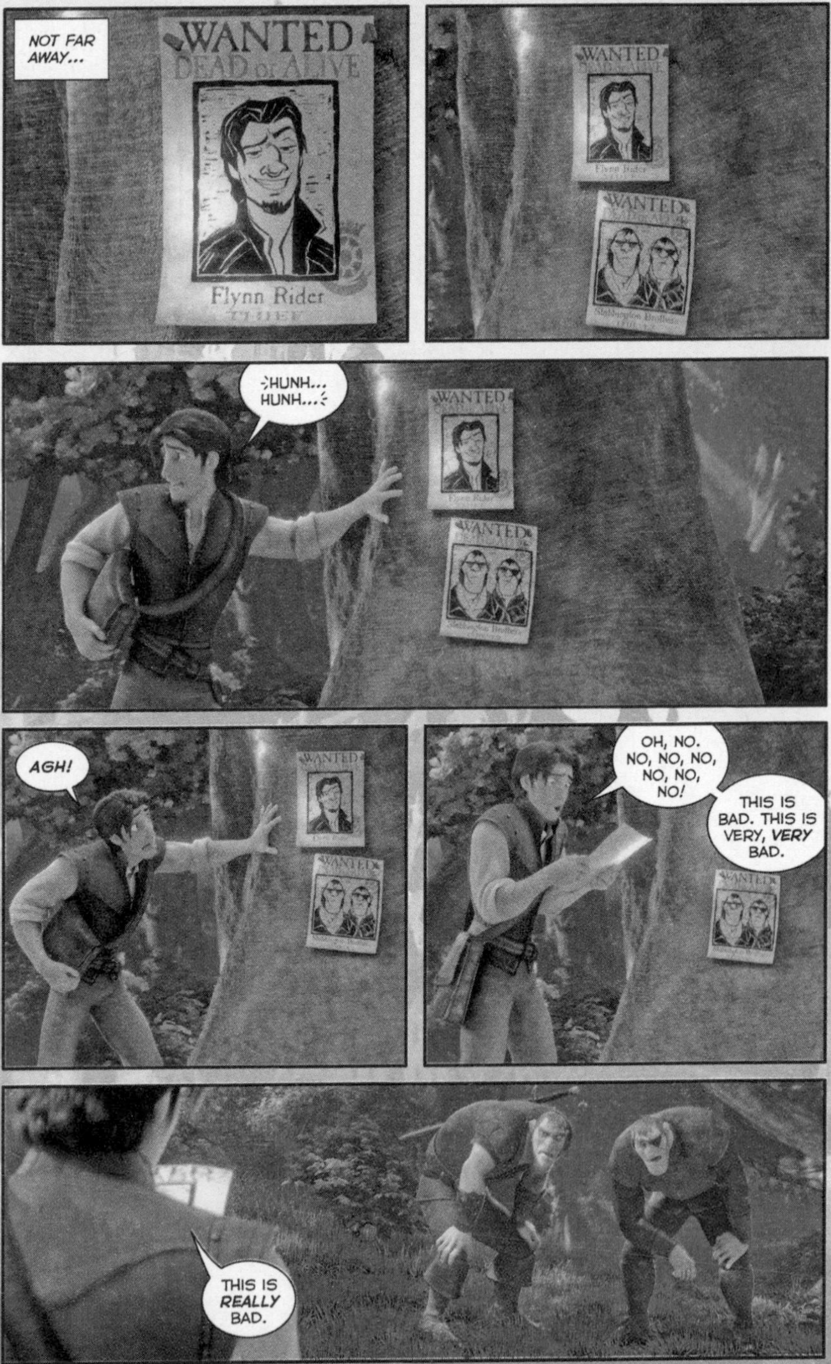
NOT FAR AWAY...
WANTED
DEAD or ALIVE
Flynn Rider
HUNH... HUNH...
AGH!
OH, NO. NO, NO, NO, NO, NO, NO!
THIS IS BAD. THIS IS VERY, VERY BAD.
THIS IS REALLY BAD.

THEY JUST CAN'T GET MY *NOSE* RIGHT!

WANTED DEAD OR ALIVE
Flynn Rider

WHO CARES?

WANTED DEAD OR ALIVE
Stabbington Brothers
THIEVES

THAT'S EASY TO SAY -- YOU GUYS LOOK *AMAZING!*

-WHINNY-

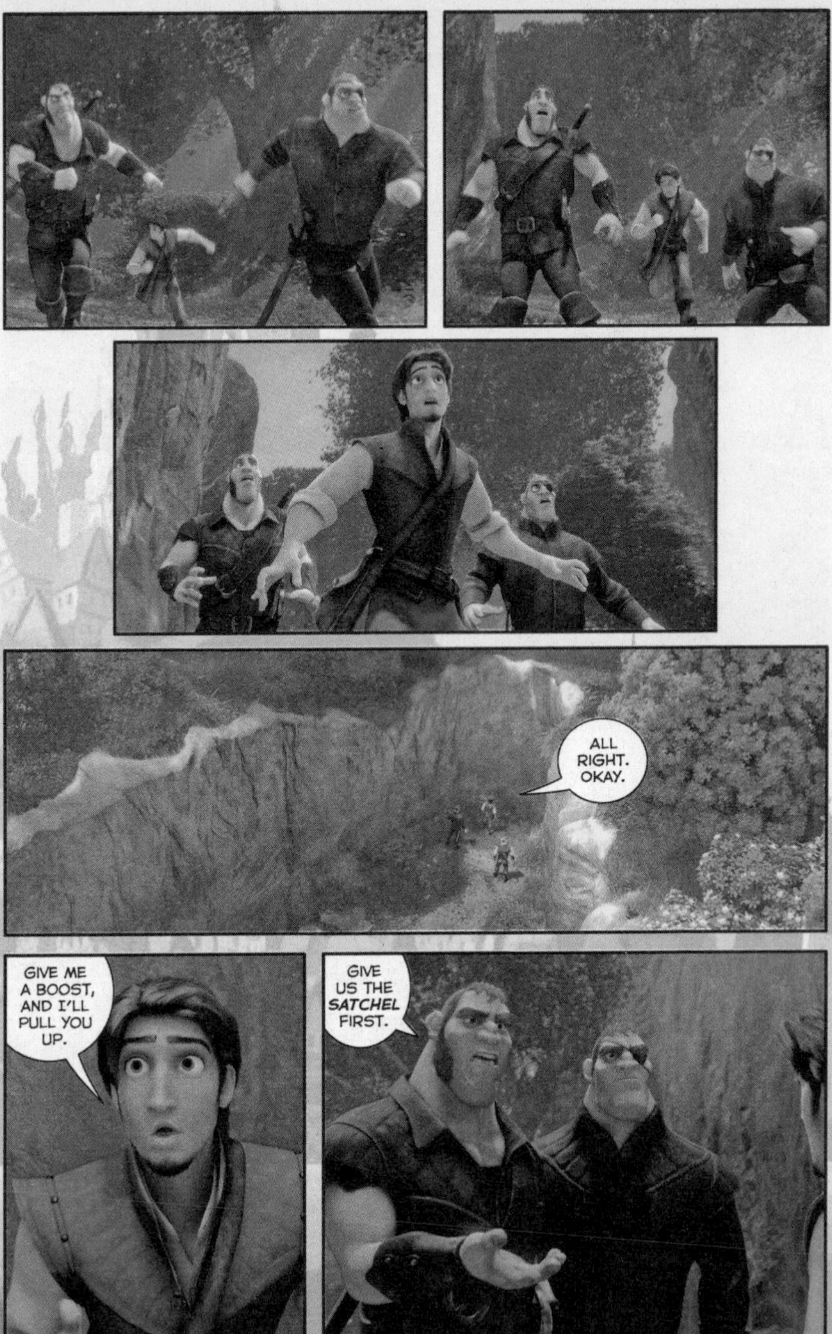
ALL RIGHT. OKAY.
GIVE ME A BOOST, AND I'LL PULL YOU UP.
GIVE US THE SATCHEL FIRST.

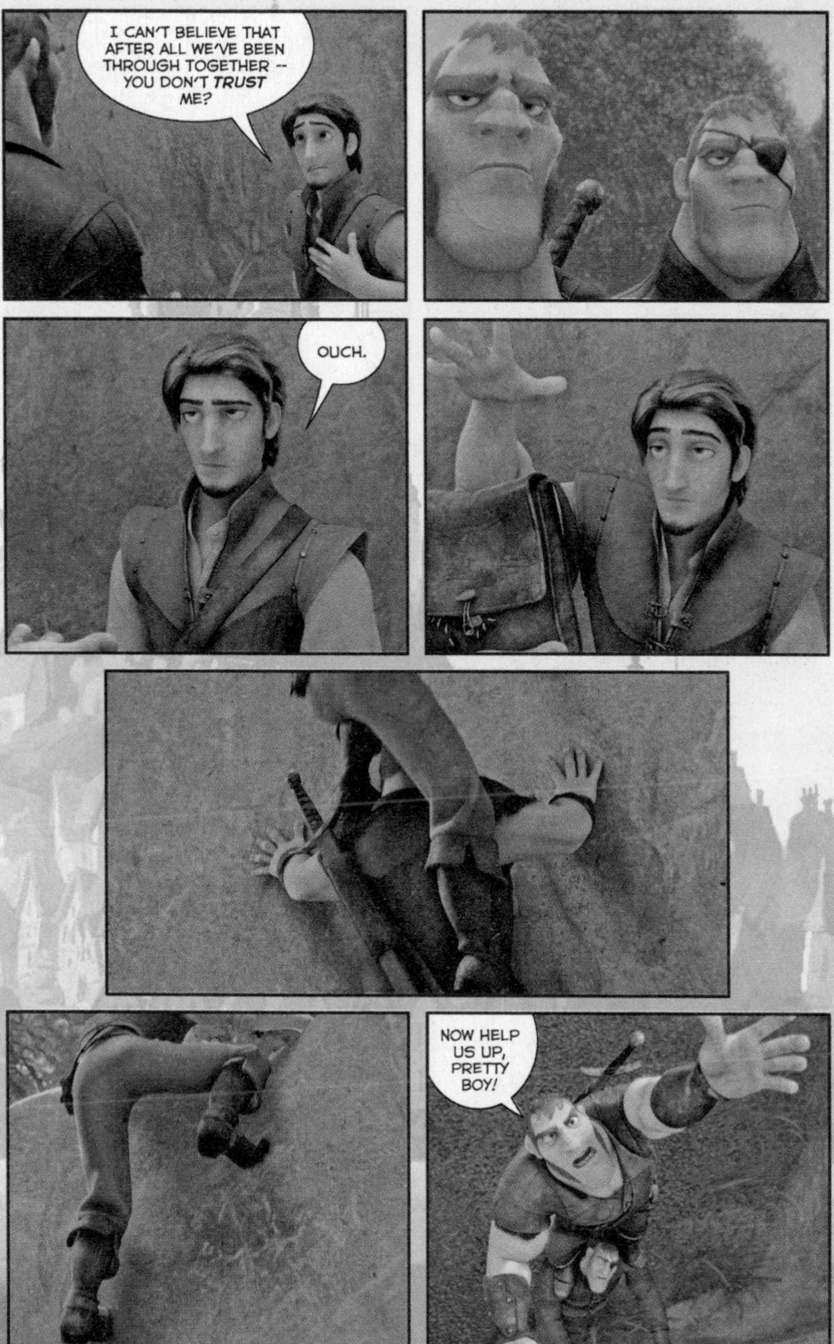
I CAN'T BELIEVE THAT AFTER ALL WE'VE BEEN THROUGH TOGETHER -- YOU DON'T *TRUST* ME?
OUCH.
NOW HELP US UP, PRETTY BOY!

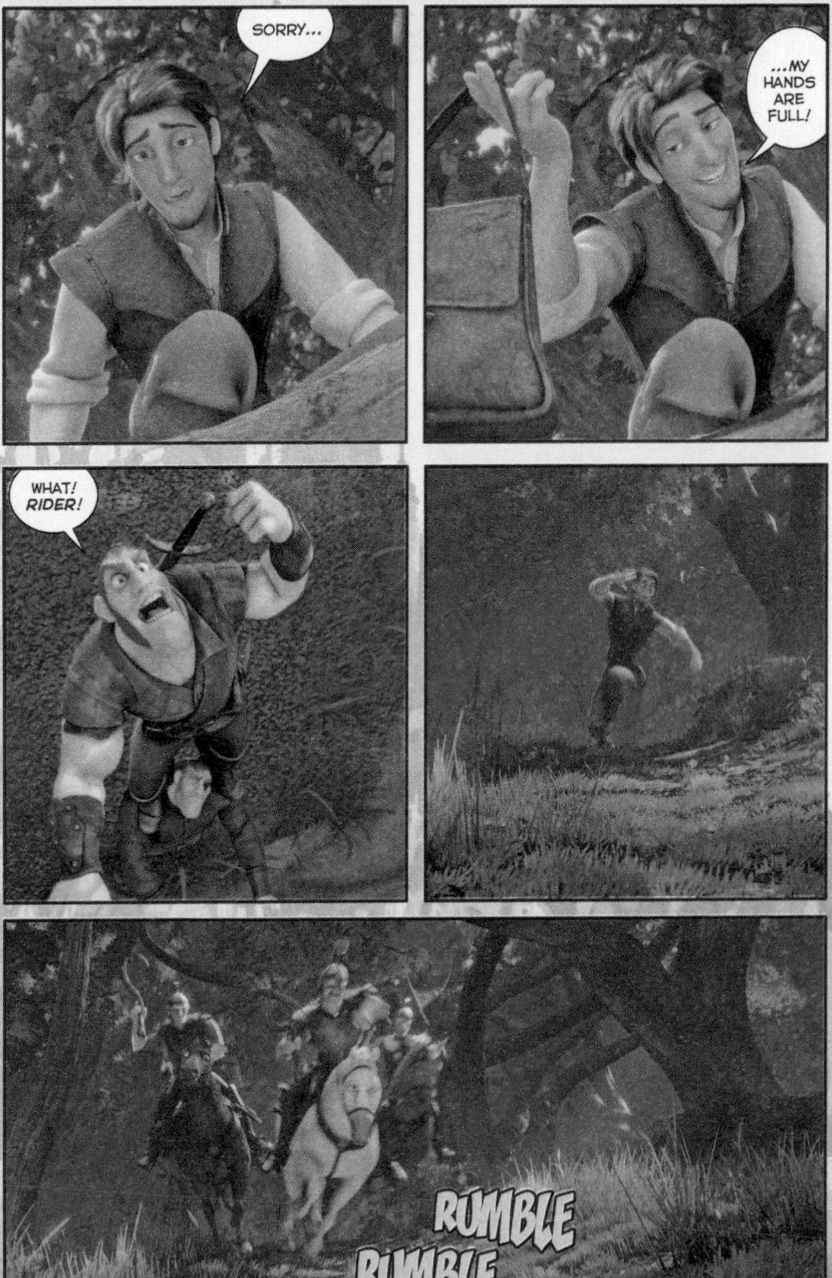

SORRY...
...MY HANDS ARE FULL!
WHAT! RIDER!
RUMBLE
RUMBLE

RETRIEVE THAT SATCHEL AT *ANY* COST!

YES, SIR!

NEEIIGH!!!

NEEIIGH!!!

NEEIIGH!!!

49

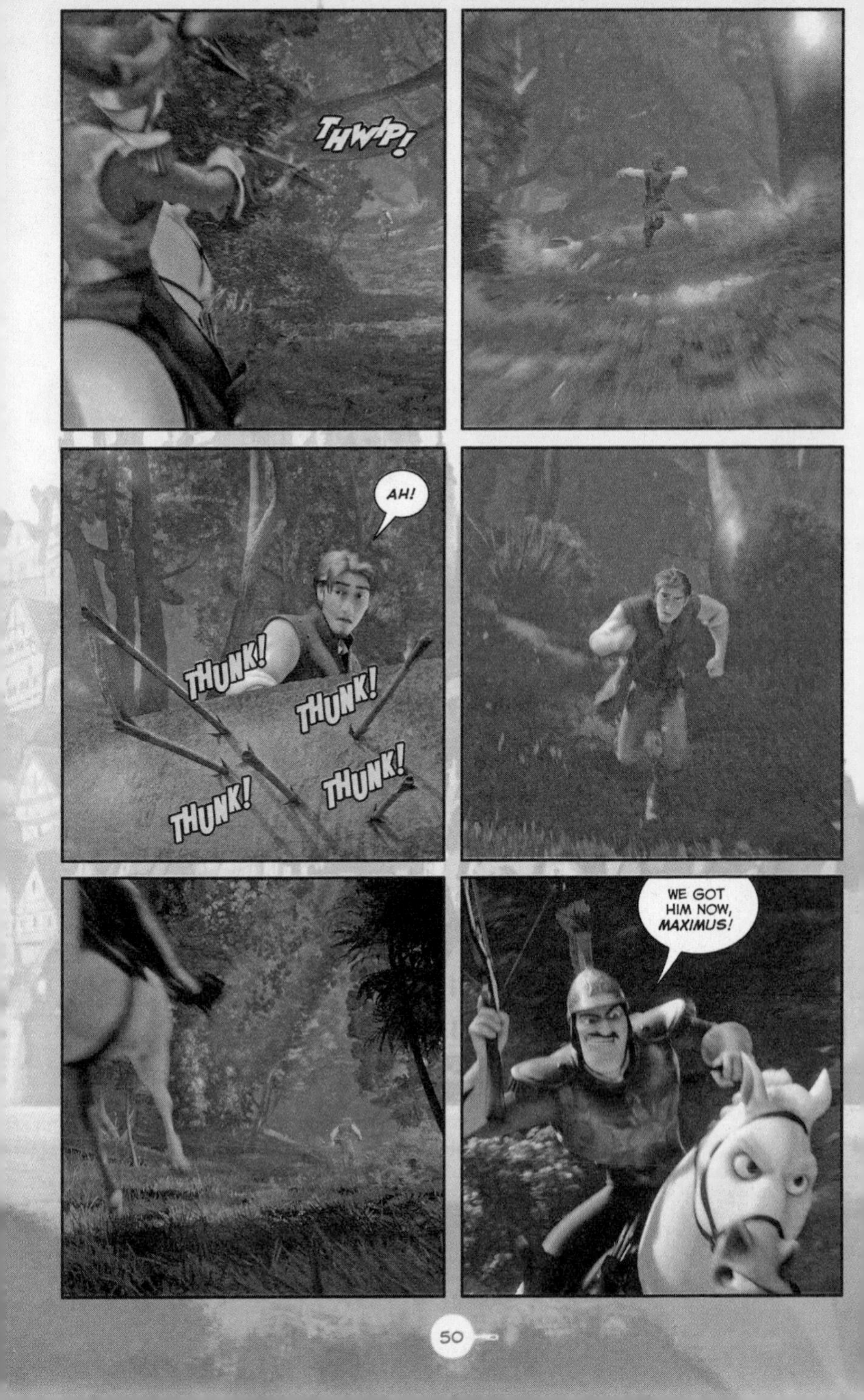
THWIP!
AH!
THUNK!
THUNK!
THUNK!
THUNK!
WE GOT HIM NOW, MAXIMUS!

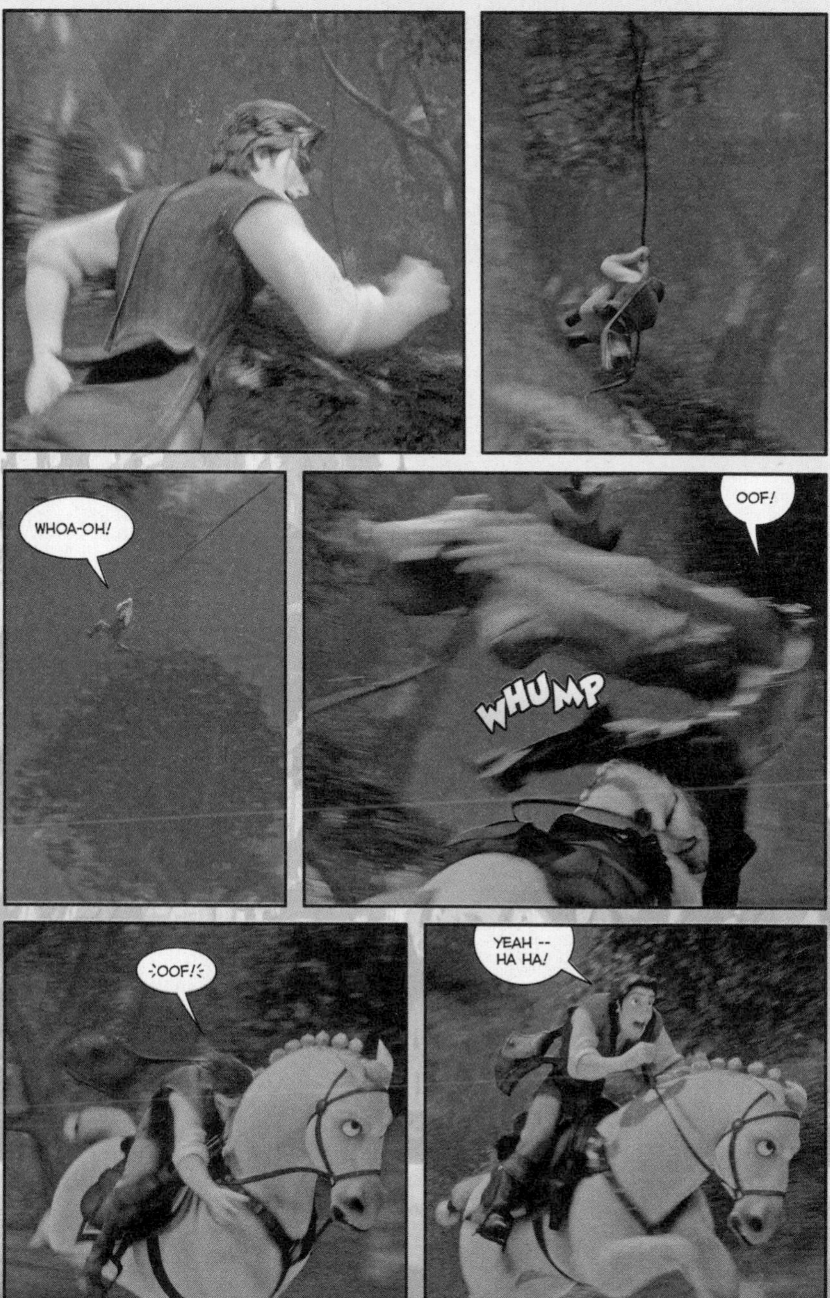
WHOA-OH!
OOF!
WHUMP
OOF!
YEAH -- HA HA!

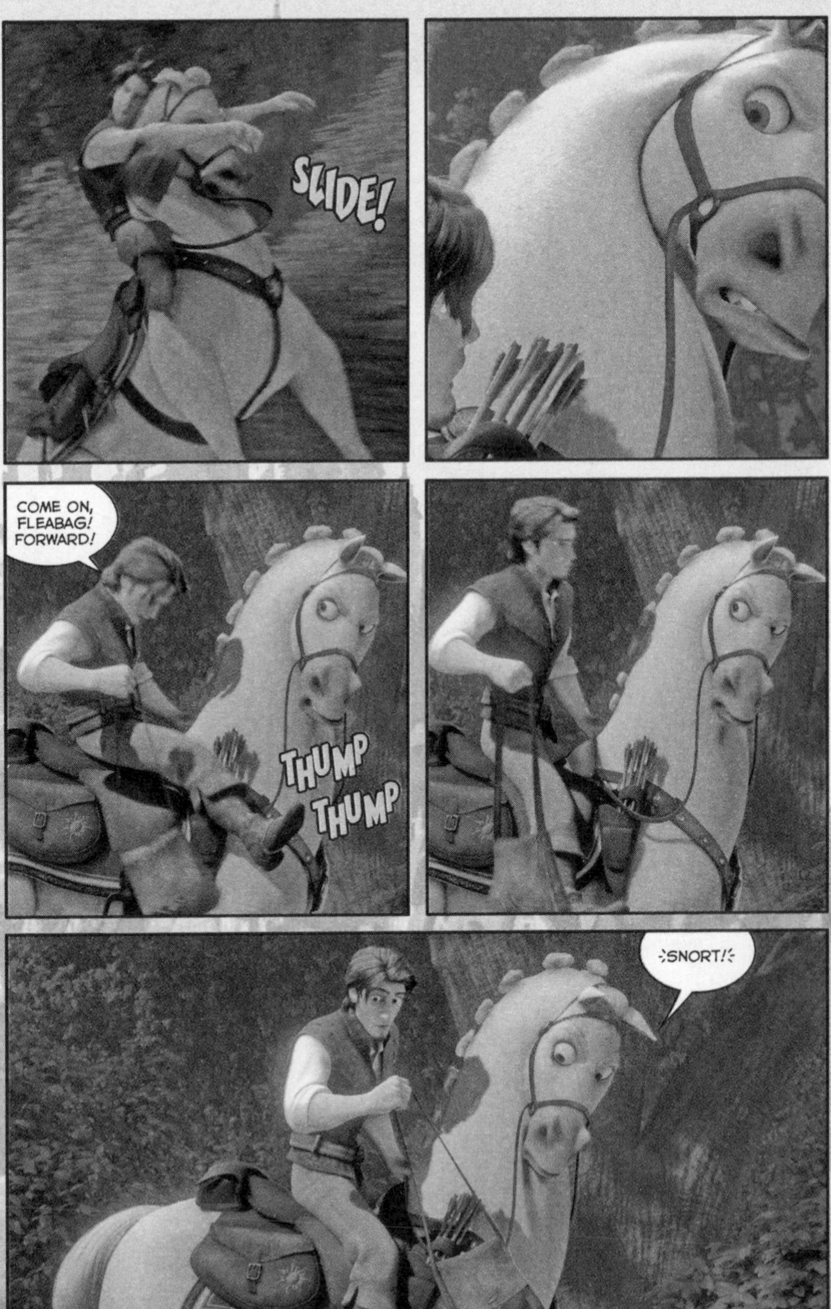
SLIDE!
COME ON, FLEABAG! FORWARD!
THUMP THUMP
SNORT!

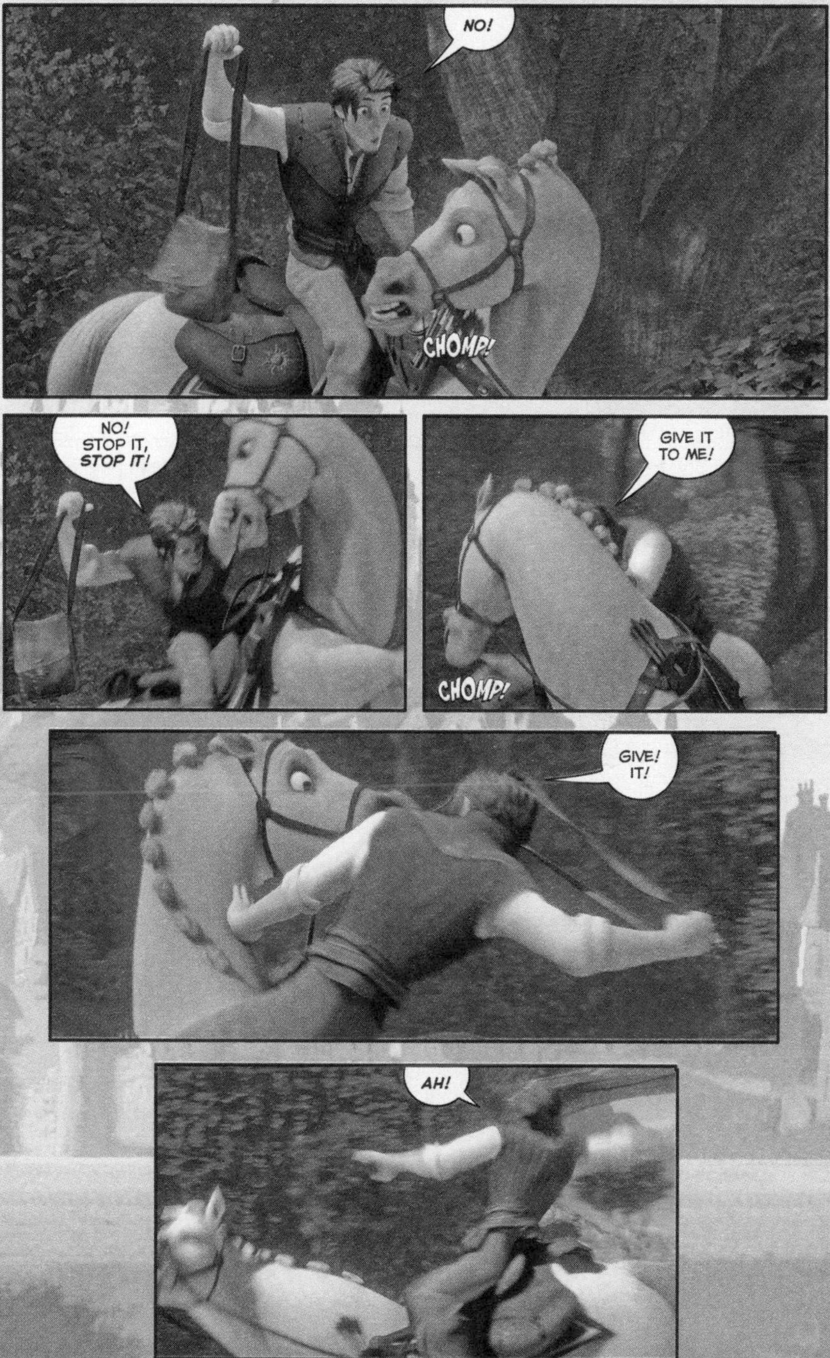
NO!
CHOMP!
NO! STOP IT, STOP IT!
GIVE IT TO ME!
CHOMP!
GIVE! IT!
AH!

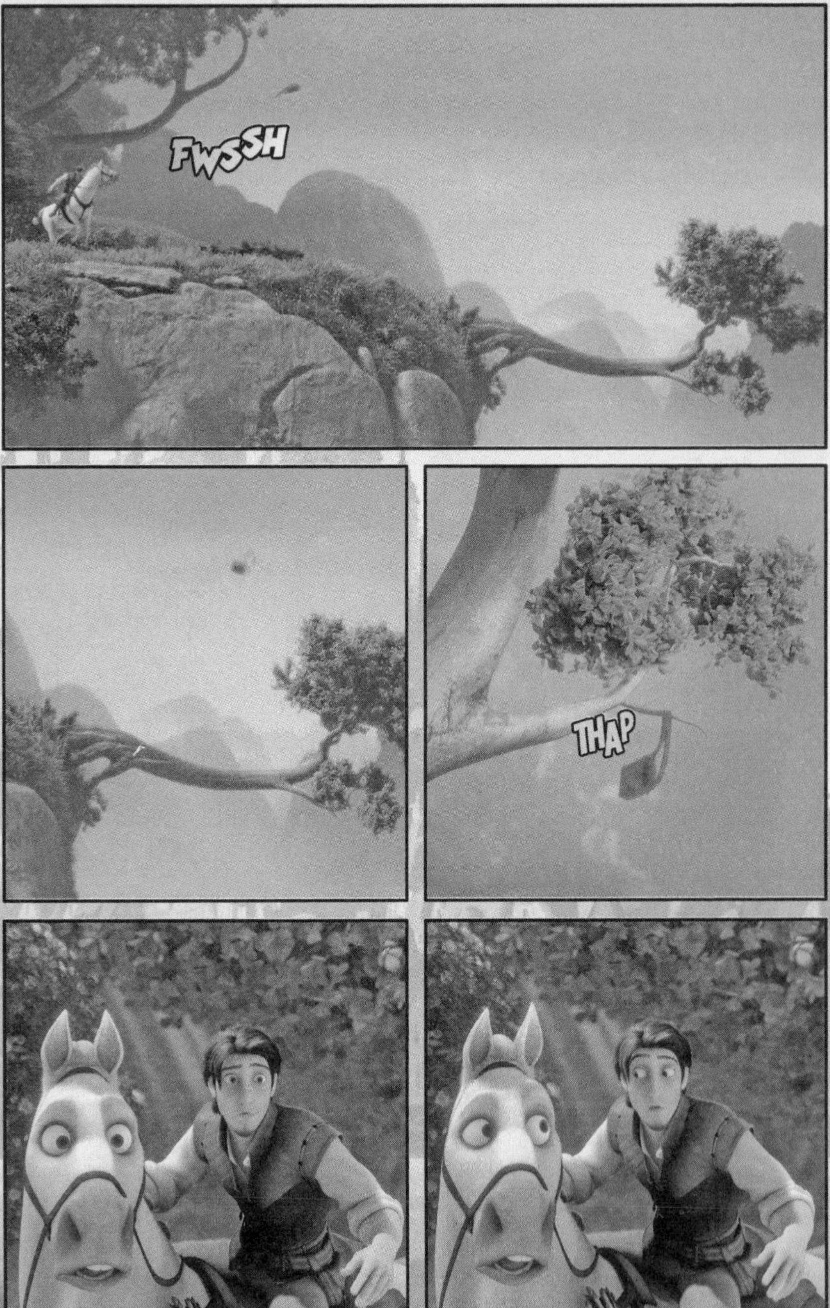
FWSSH
THAP

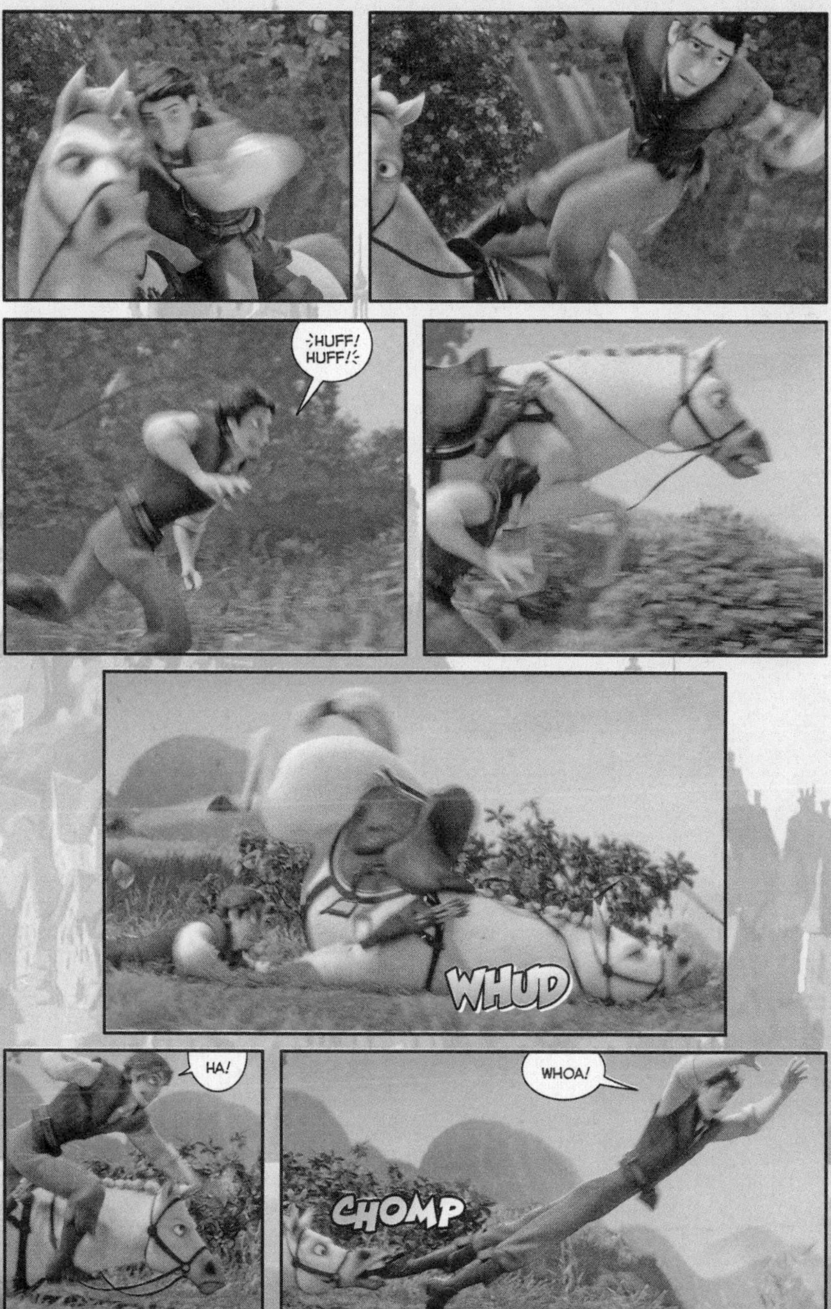
HUFF! HUFF!
WHUD
HA!
WHOA!
CHOMP

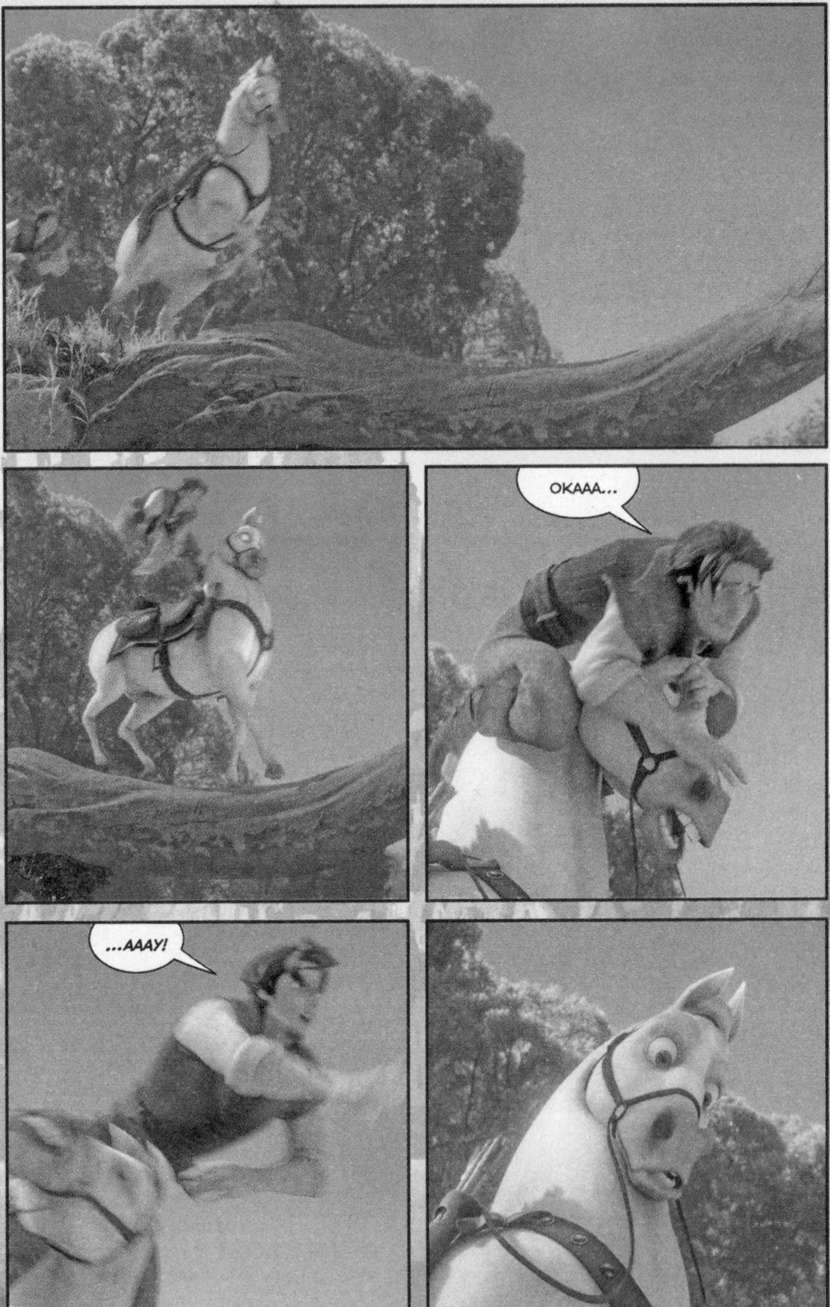
OKAAA...
...AAAY!

UH...

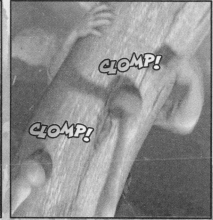

CLOMP!

CLOMP!

CLOMP!

CLOMP!

CLOMP!

CLOMP!

CLOMP!

CLOMP!

CLOMP!

CLOMP!

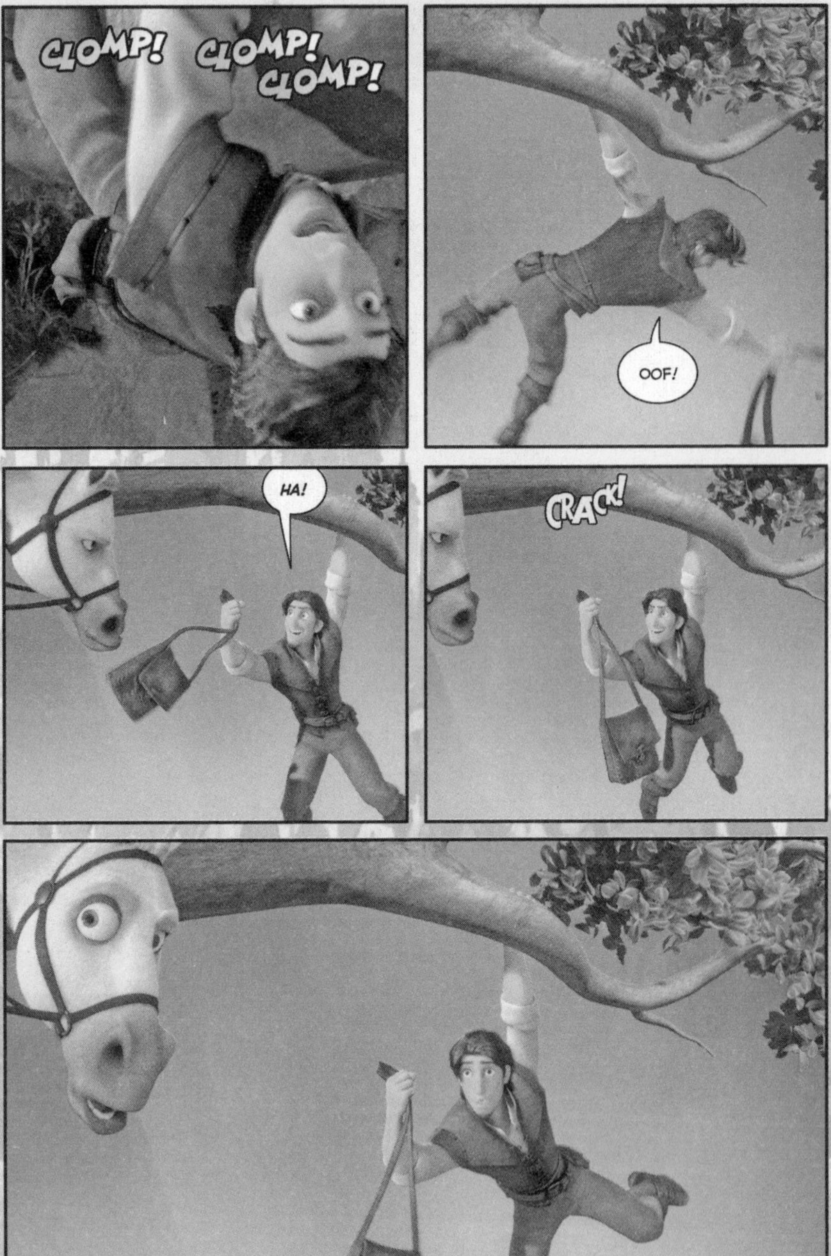
CLOMP! CLOMP! CLOMP!
OOF!
HA!
CRACK!

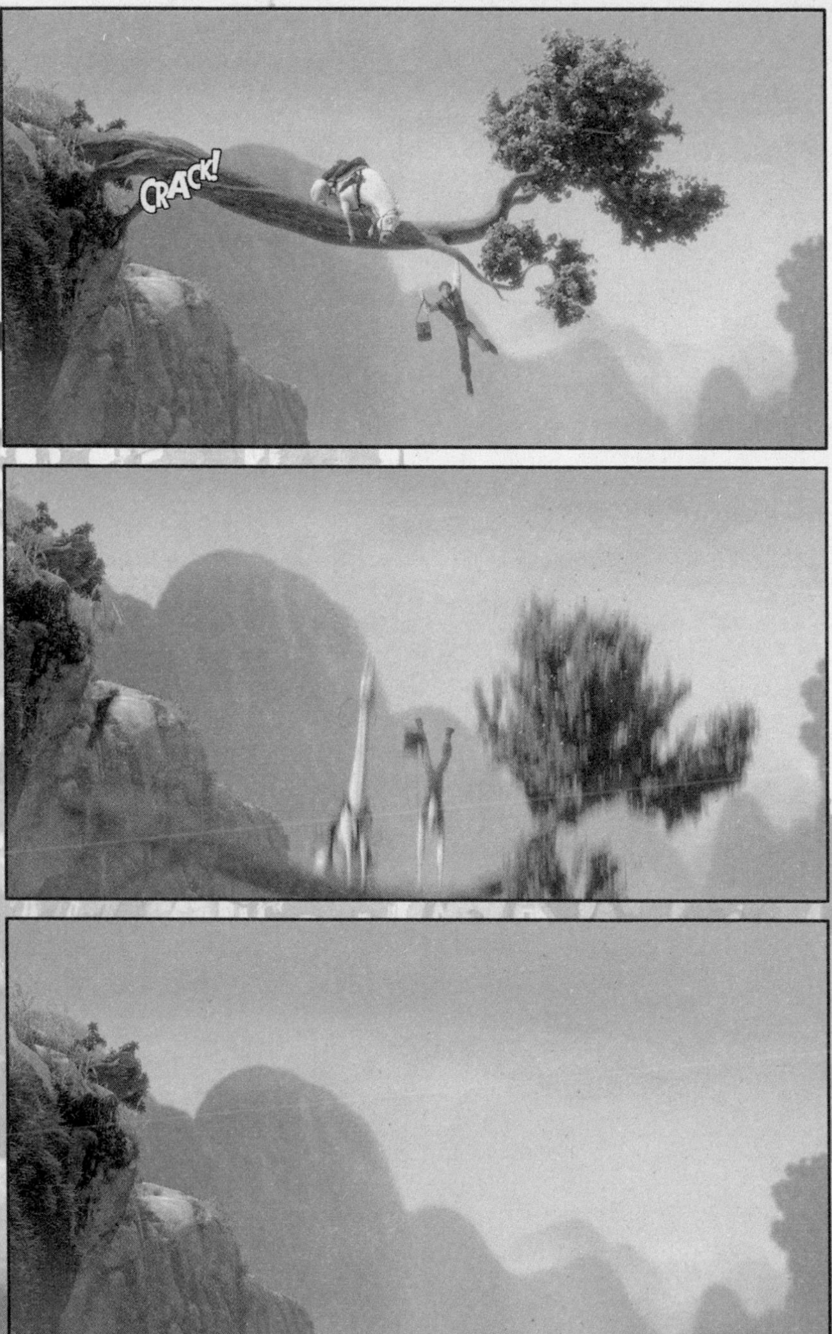
CRACK!

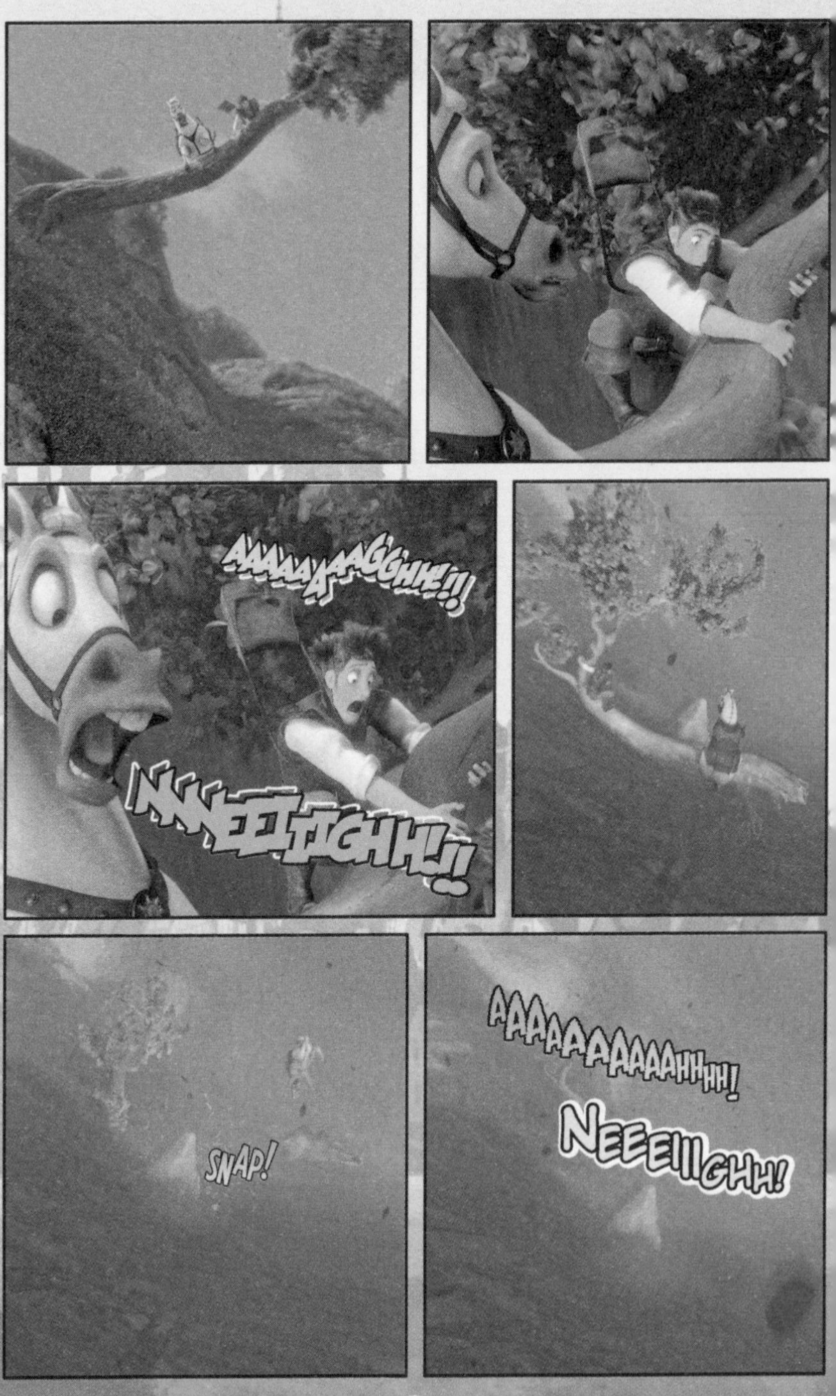
AAAAAAAAGGHH!!!
NNNEEIIIGHH!!!
SNAP!
AAAAAAAAAAAHHHH!
NEEEIIIGHH!

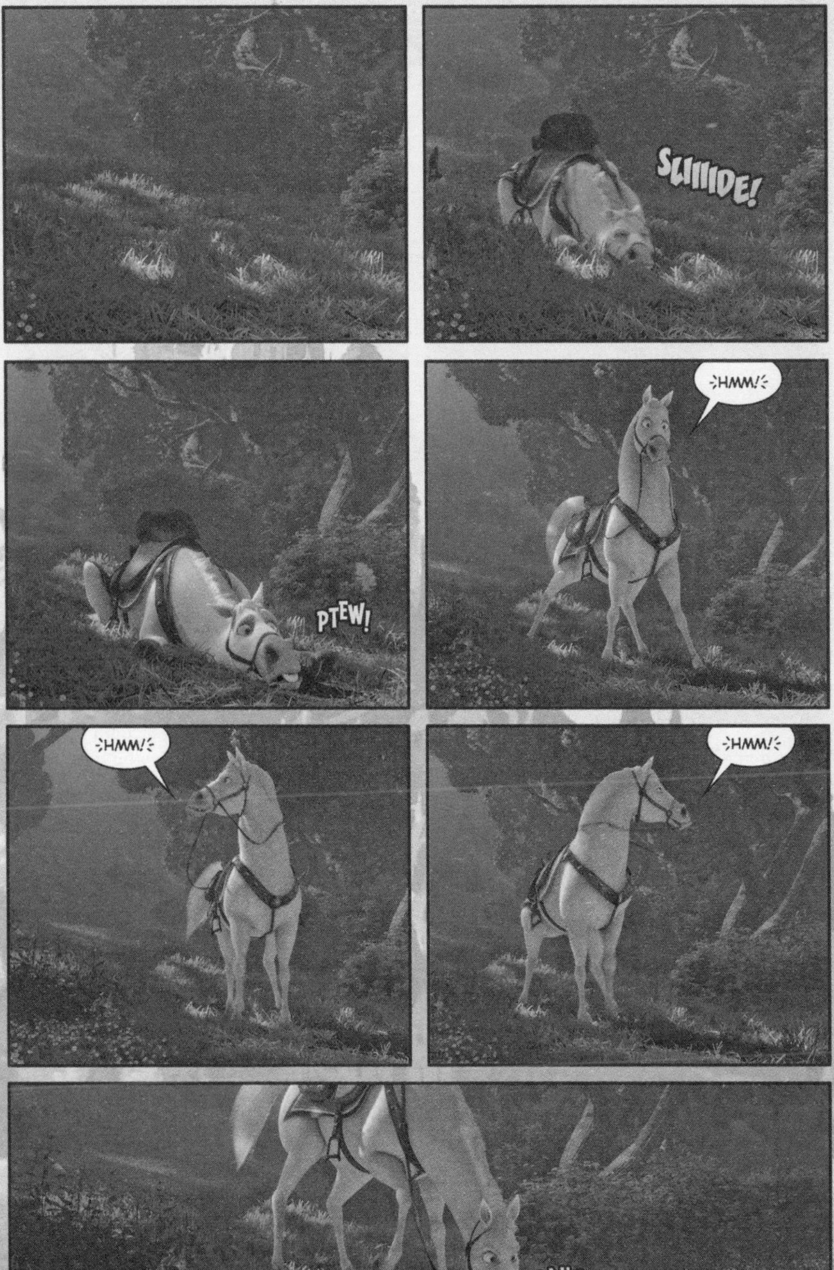
SLIIIIDE!
PTEW!
HMM!
HMM!
HMM!
SNIFF
SNIFF
SNIFF

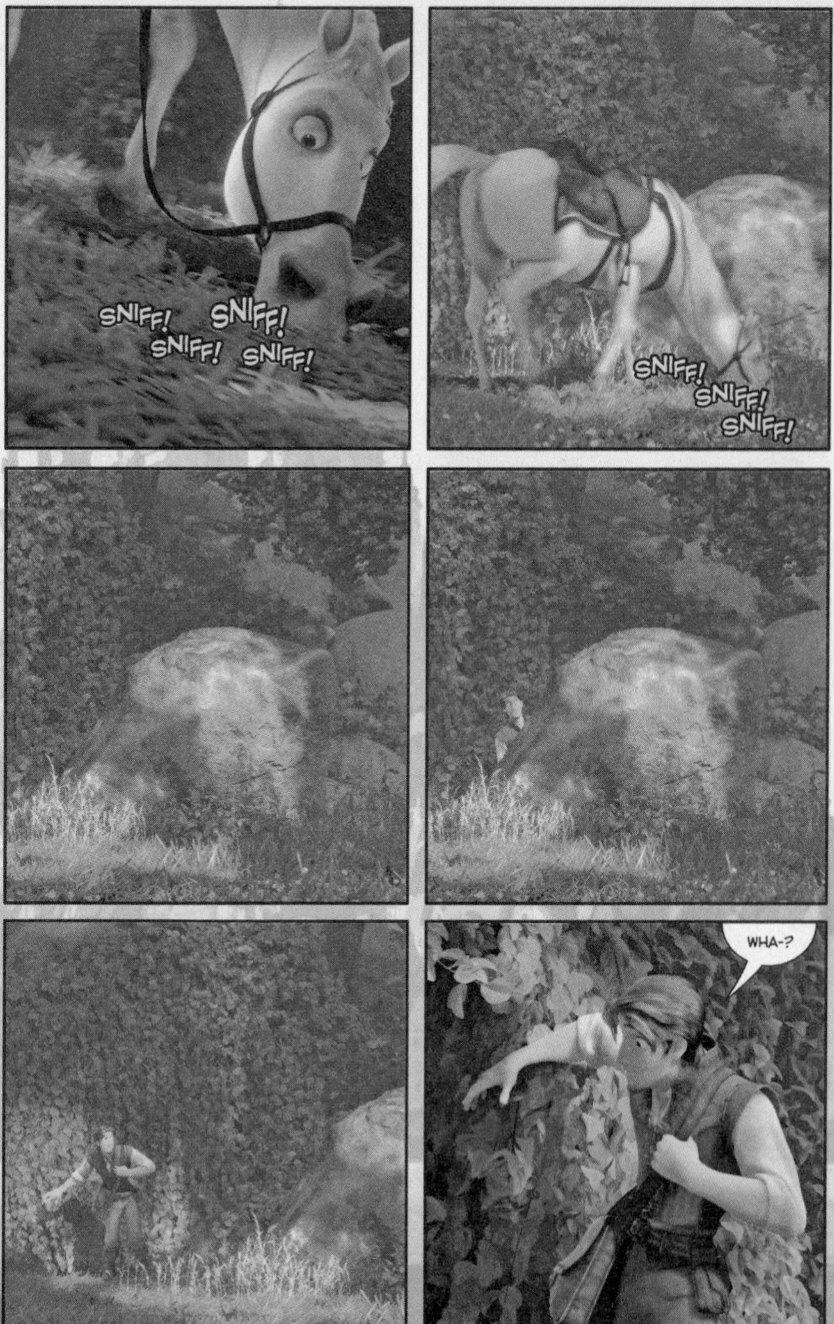
SNIFF!
SNIFF!
SNIFF!
SNIFF!
SNIFF!
SNIFF!
SNIFF!
WHA-?

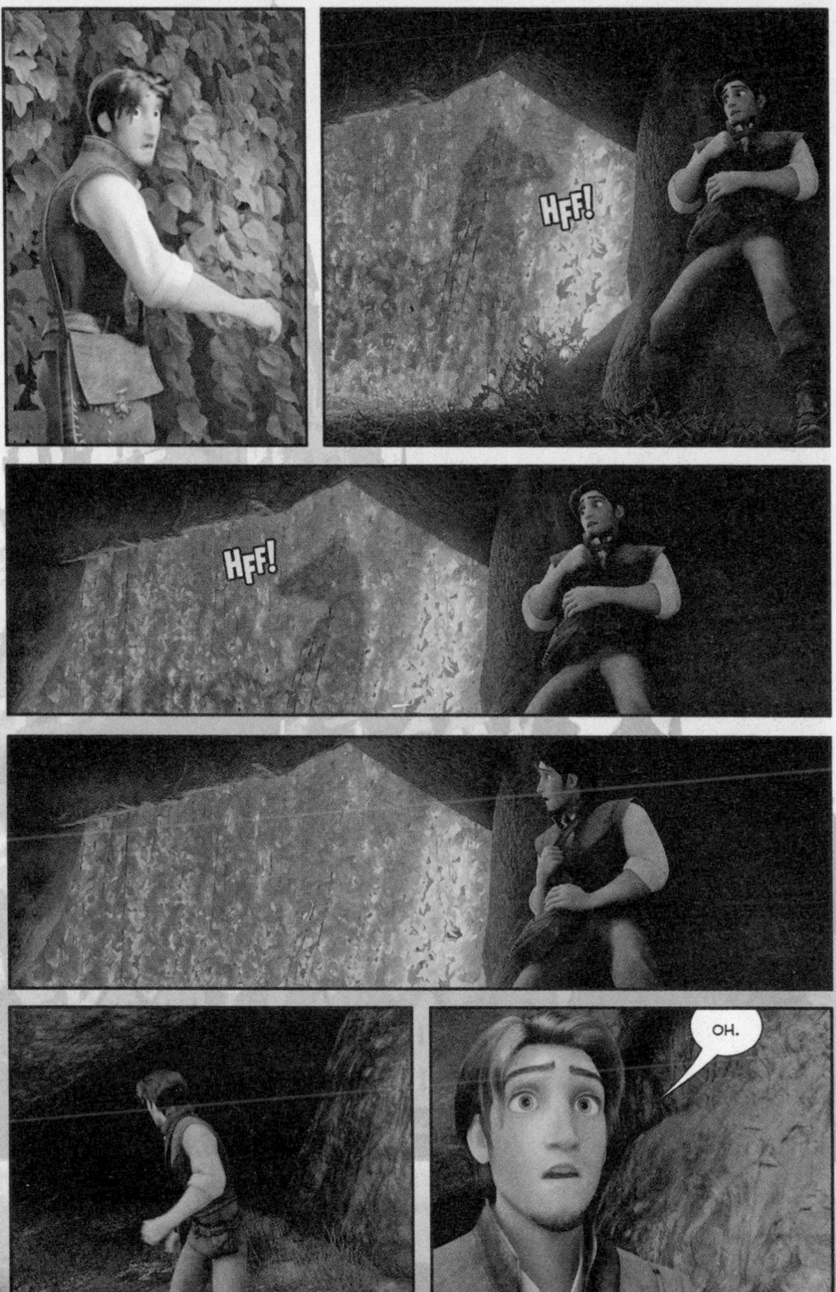
HFF!
HFF!
OH.

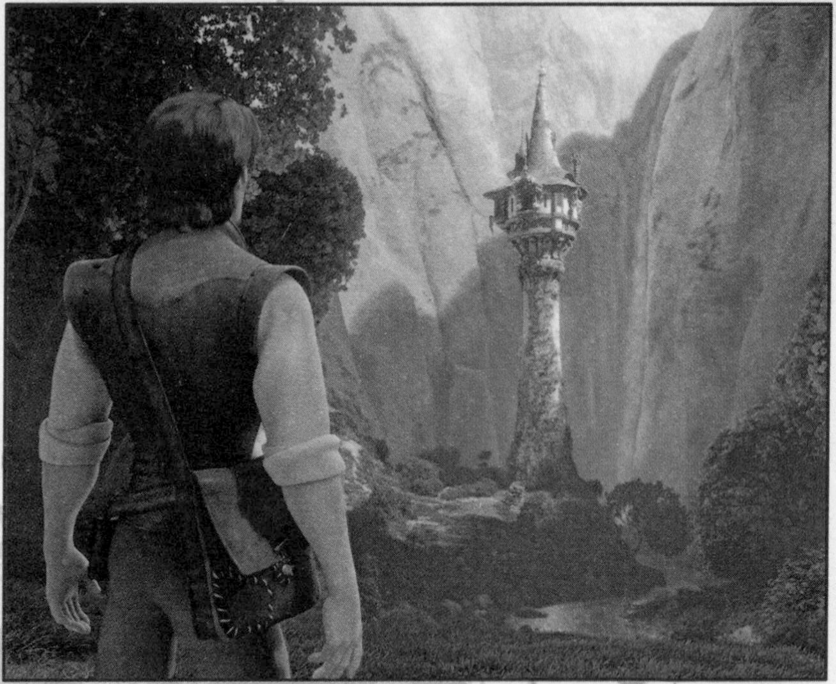

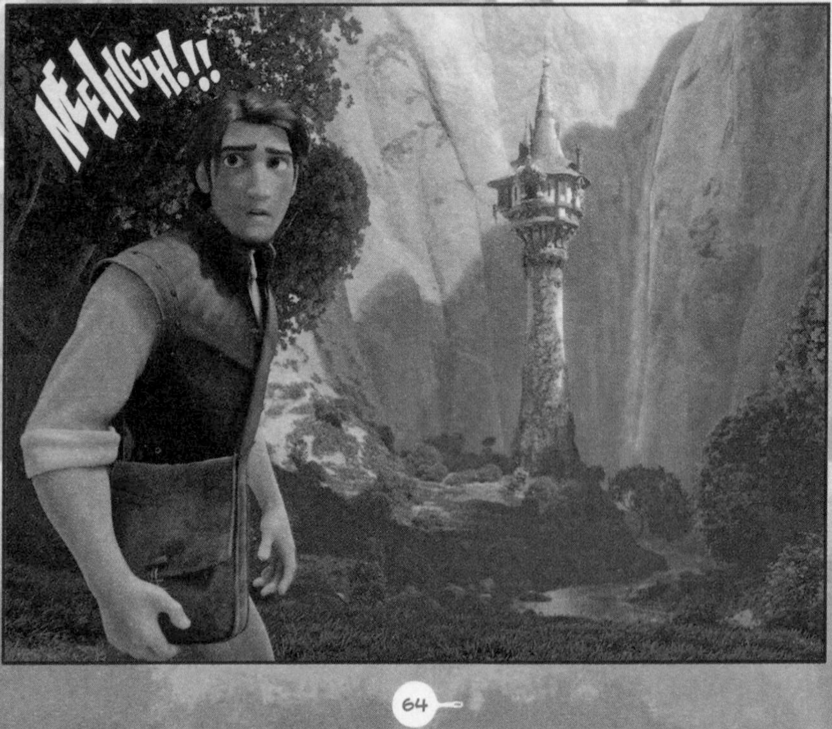
NEEIGH!!!

CHAK!

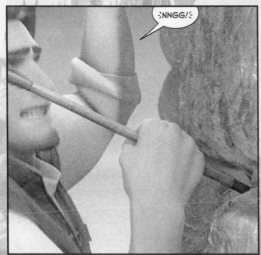

:NNGG!:

:NNGG!:

AH.

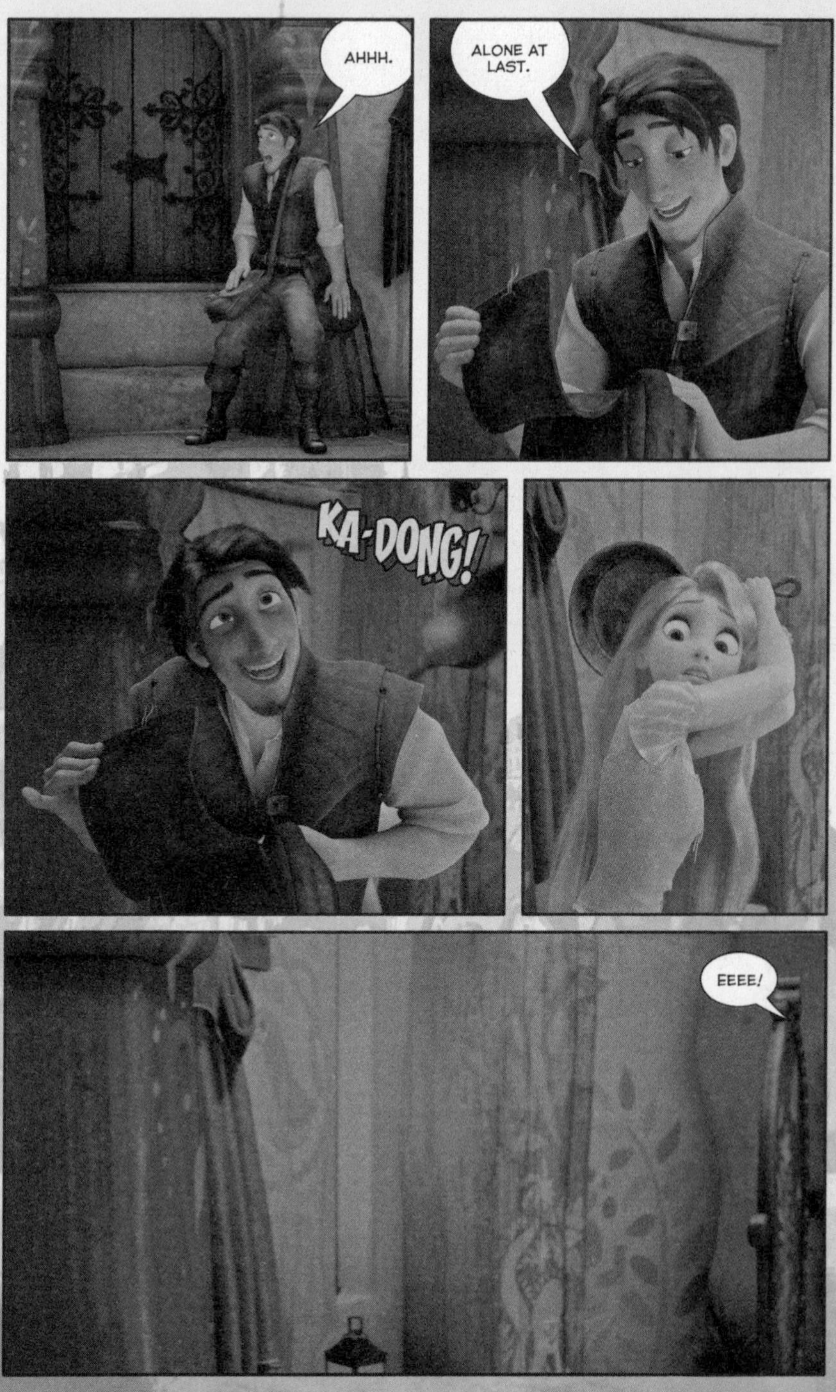
AHHH.
ALONE AT LAST.
KA-DONG!
EEEE!

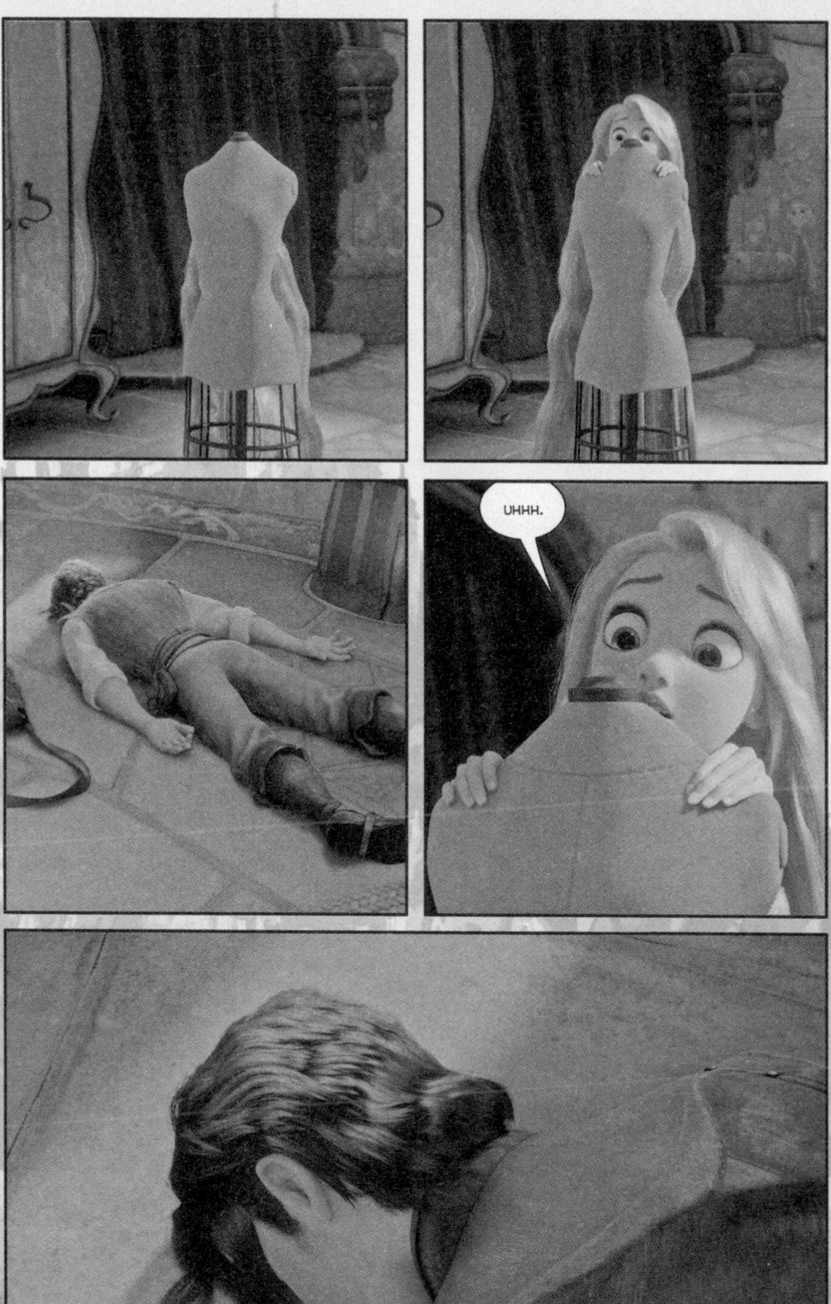
UHHH.

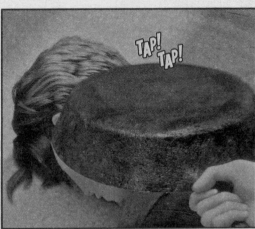

TAP! TAP!

PASCAL, WHAT DO WE DO?

SHRUG

GRRRR!

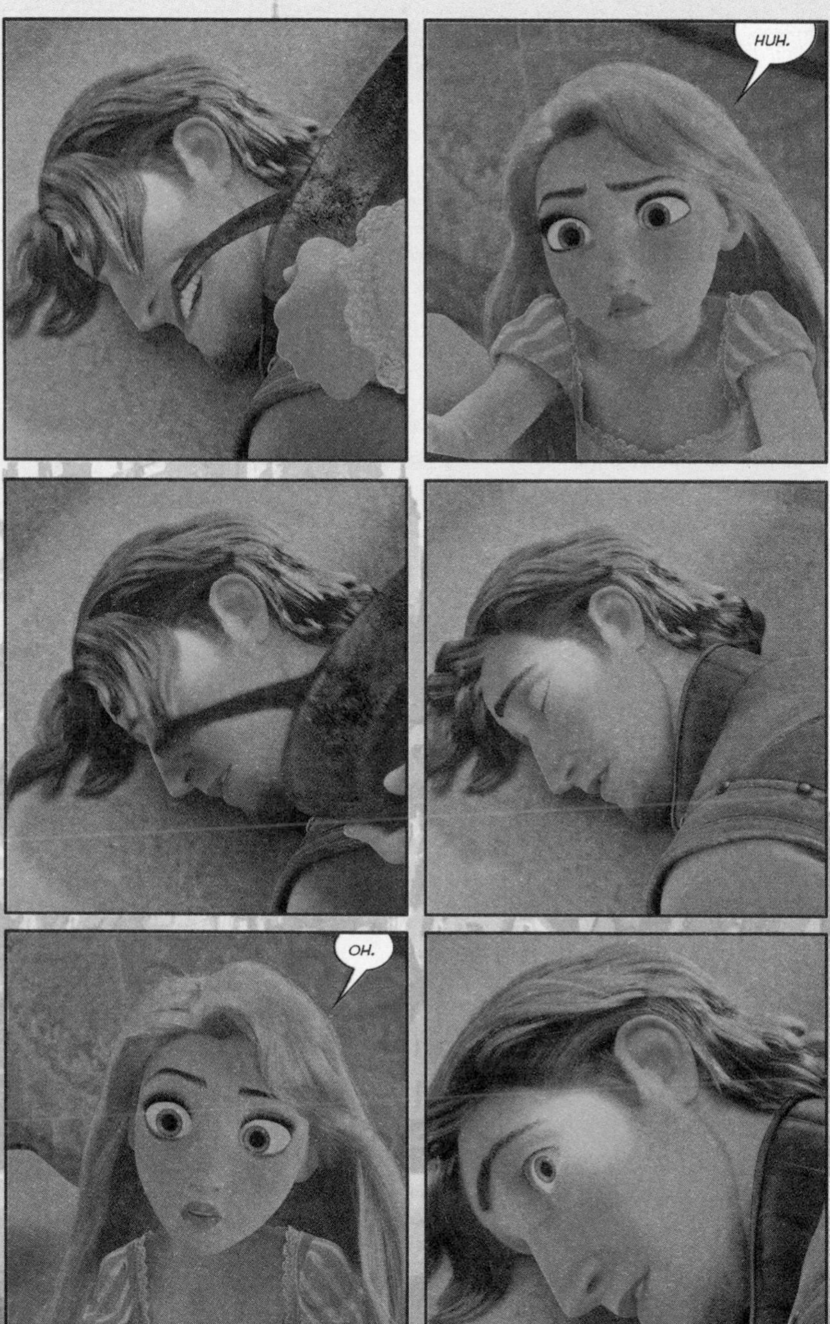
HUH.
OH.

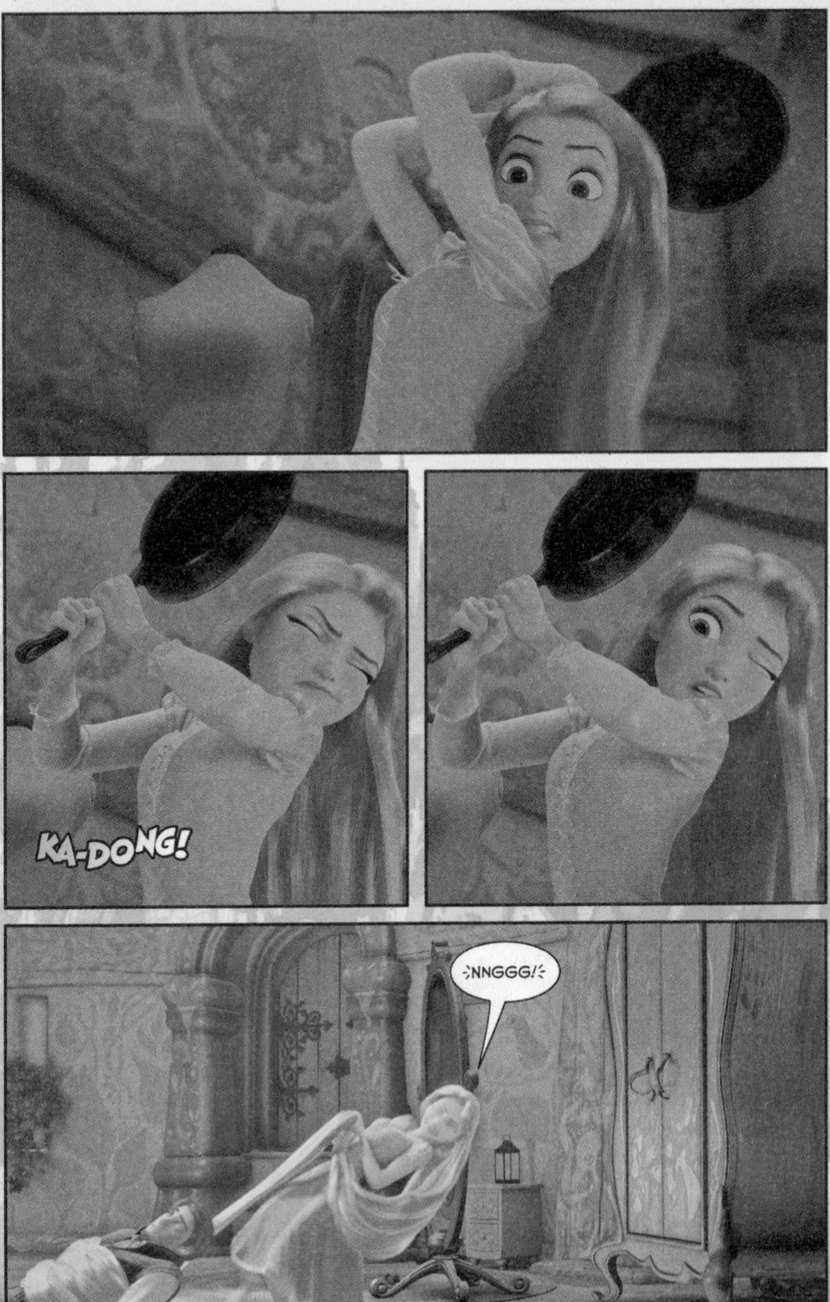
KA-DONG!
NNGGG!

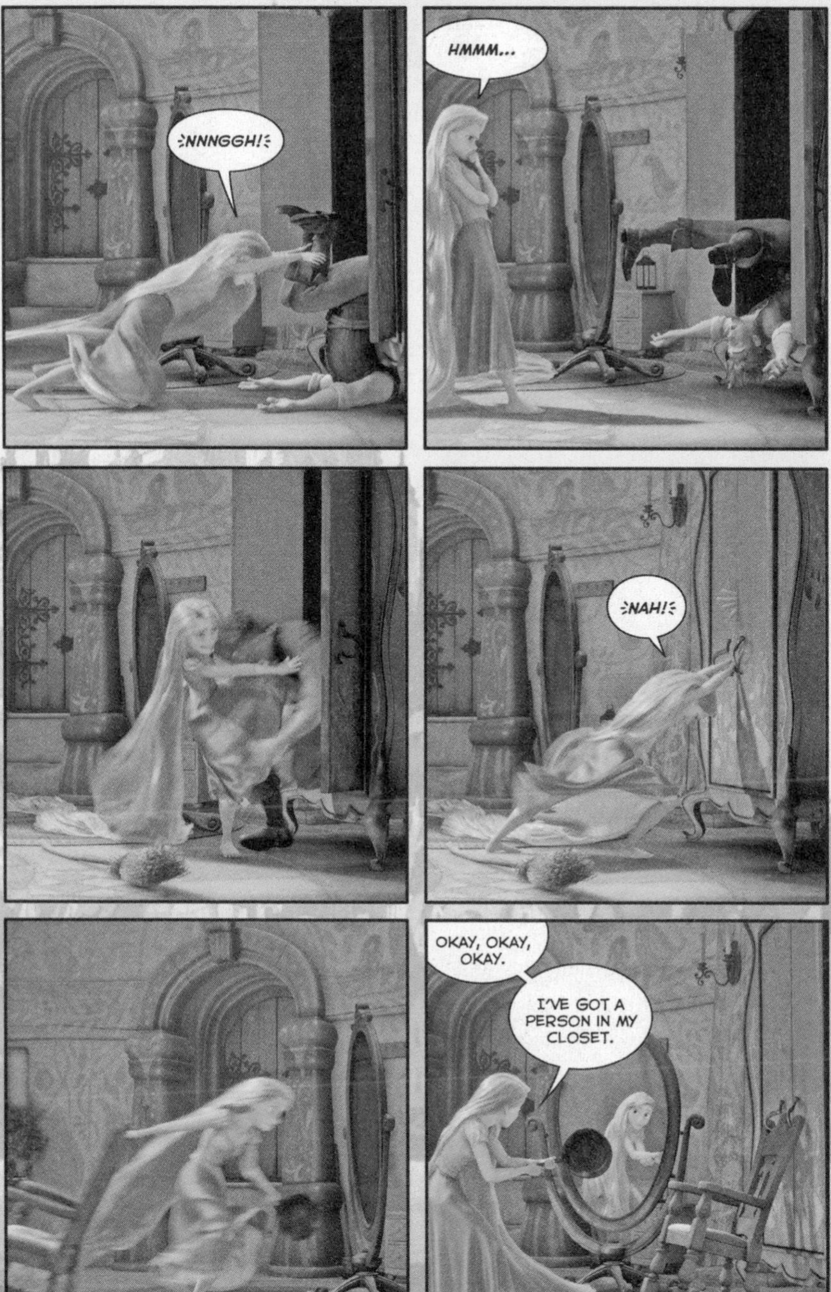
NNNGGH!
HMMM...
NAH!
OKAY, OKAY, OKAY.
I'VE GOT A PERSON IN MY CLOSET.

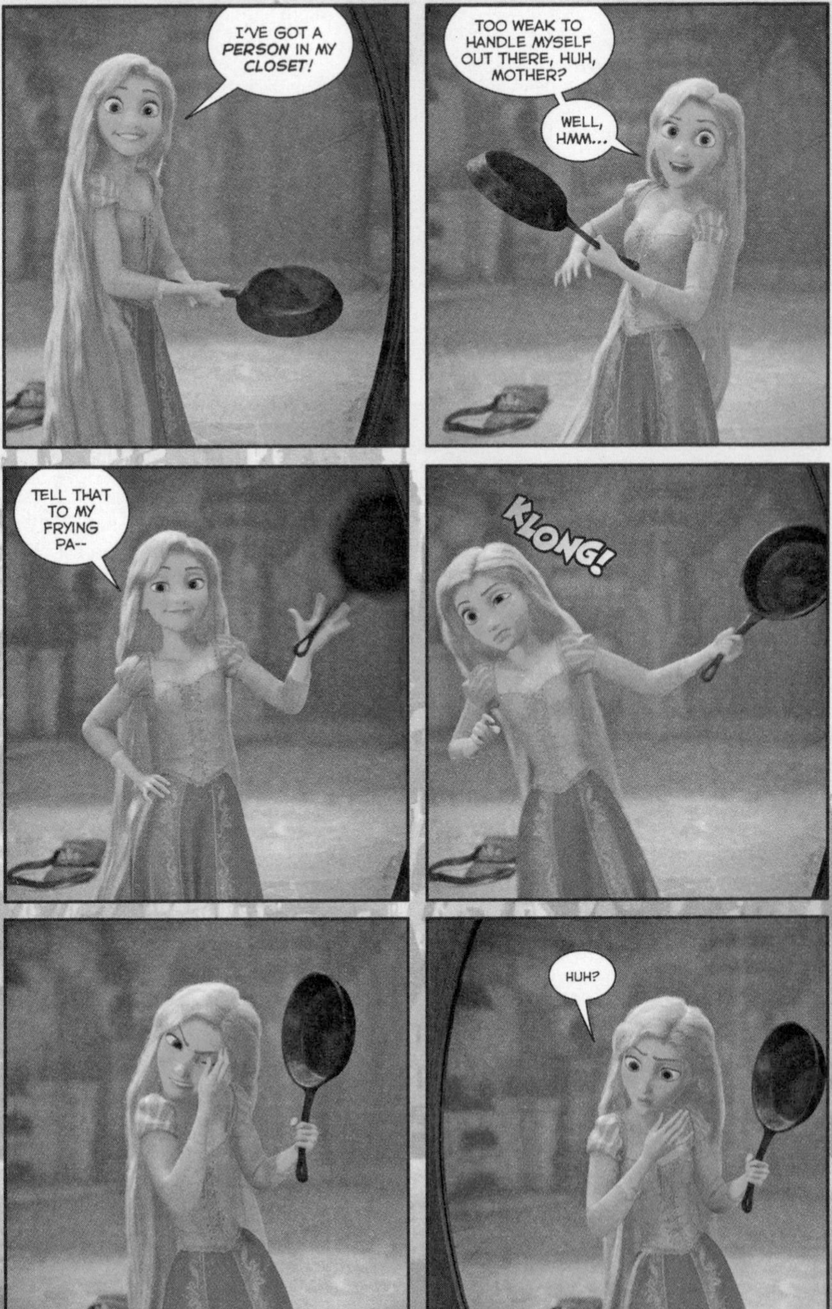
I'VE GOT A PERSON IN MY CLOSET!
TOO WEAK TO HANDLE MYSELF OUT THERE, HUH, MOTHER?
WELL, HMM...
TELL THAT TO MY FRYING PA--
KLONG!
HUH?

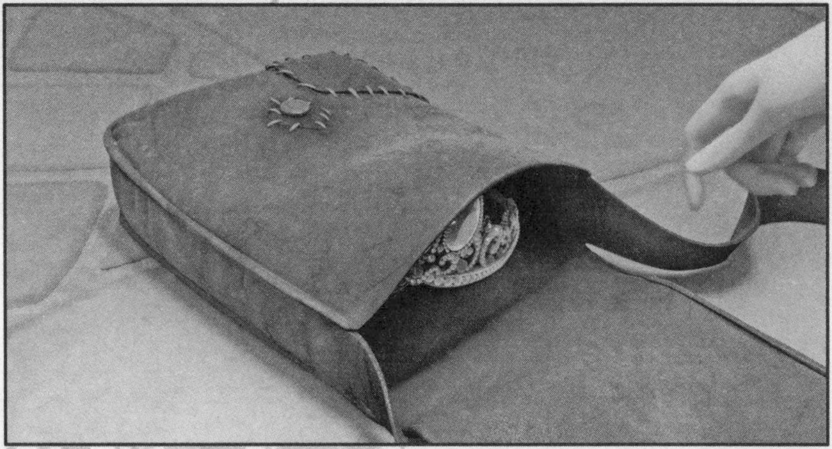

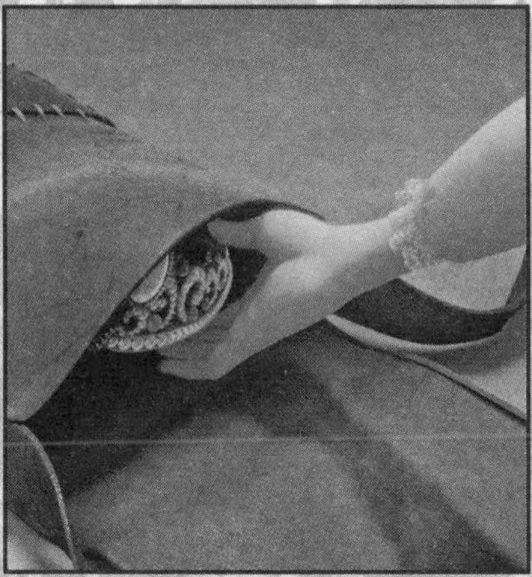

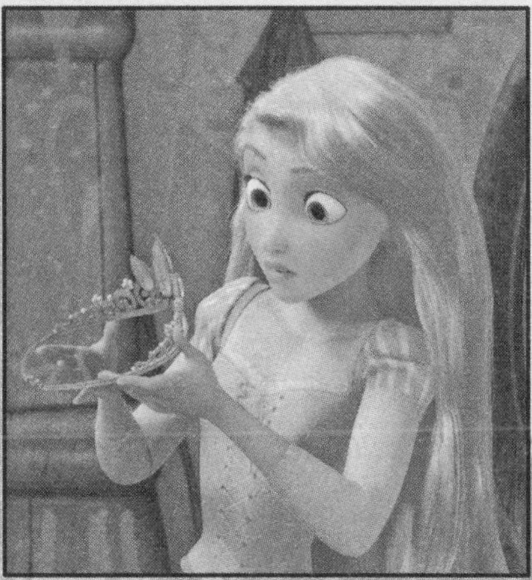

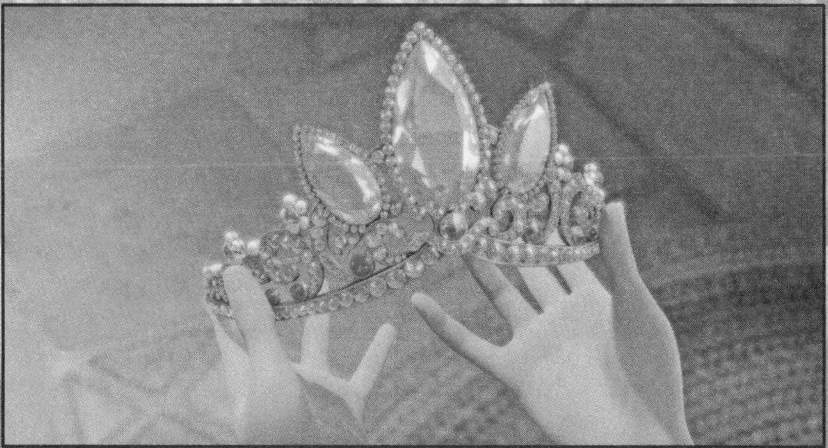

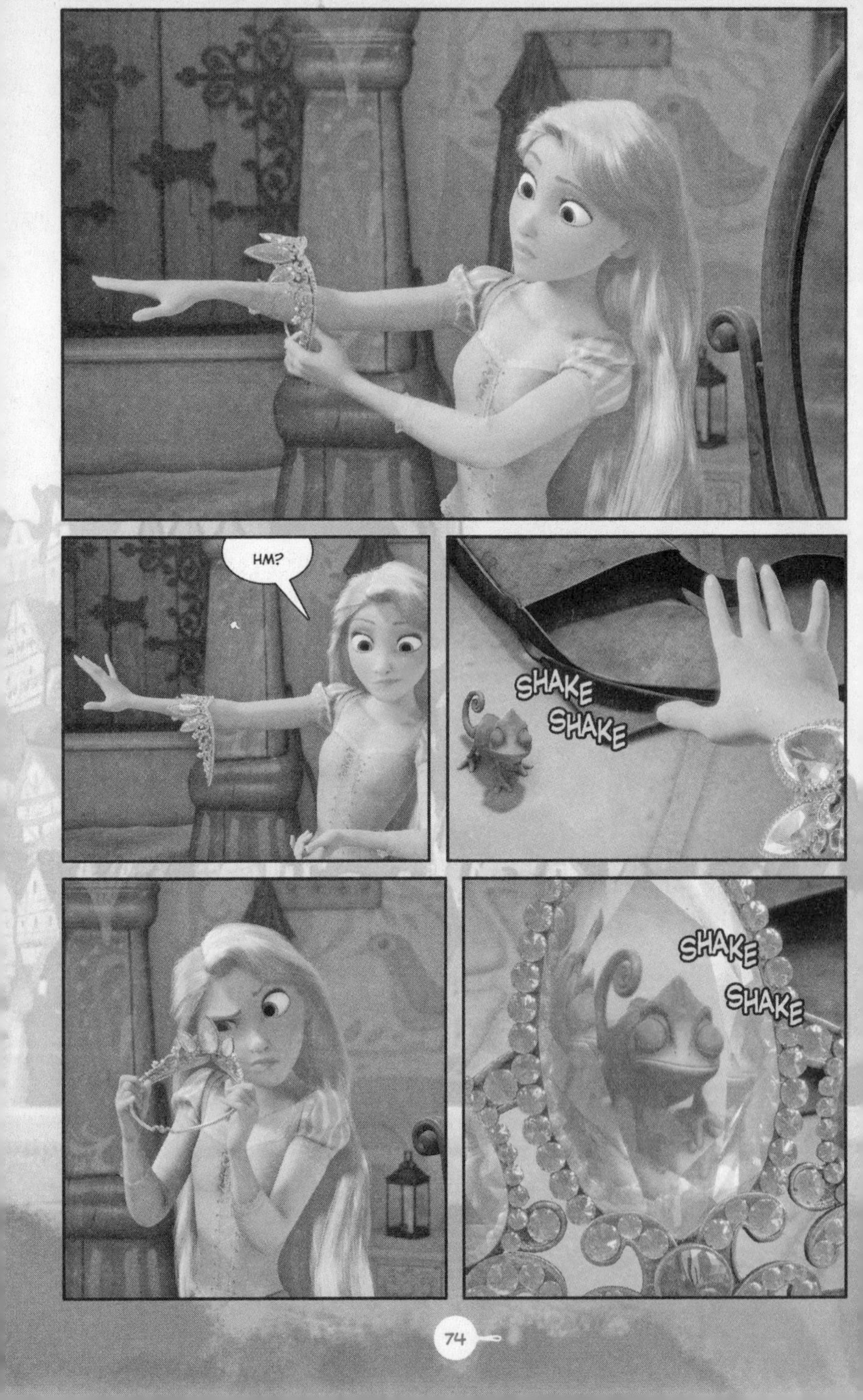
HM?
SHAKE
SHAKE
SHAKE
SHAKE

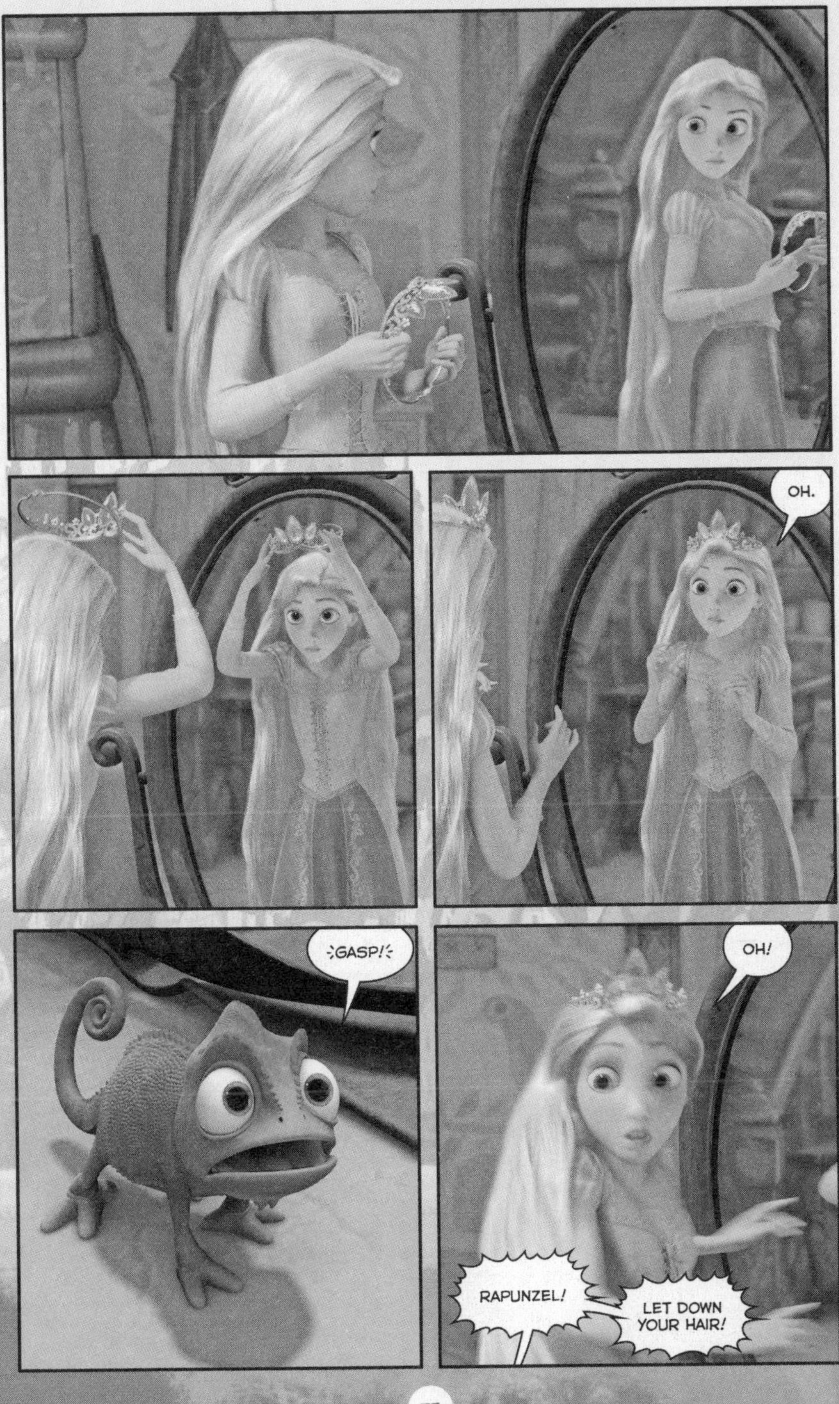
OH.
GASP!
OH!
RAPUNZEL!
LET DOWN YOUR HAIR!

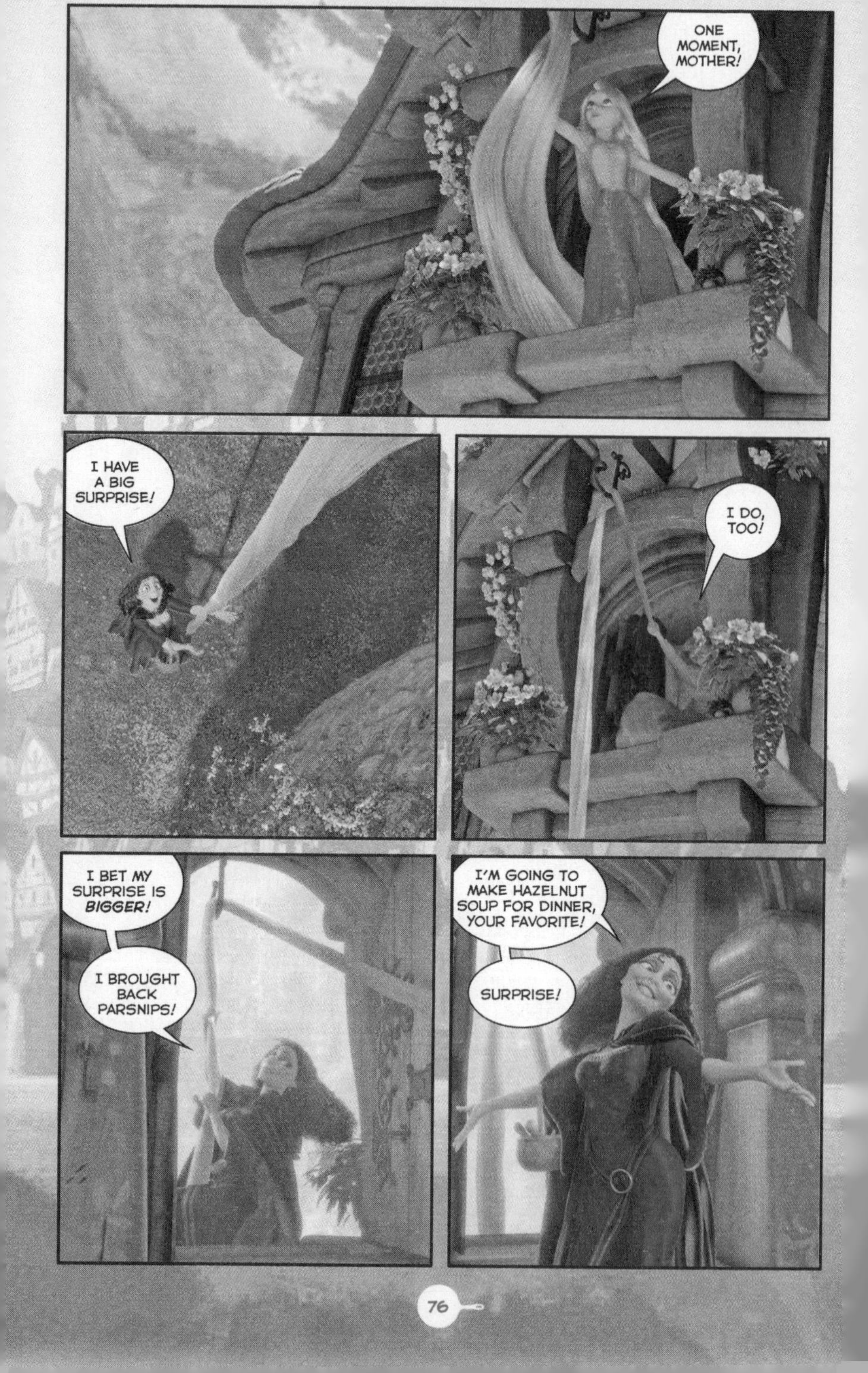
ONE MOMENT, MOTHER!
I HAVE A BIG SURPRISE!
I DO, TOO!
I BET MY SURPRISE IS *BIGGER*!
I BROUGHT BACK PARSNIPS!
I'M GOING TO MAKE HAZELNUT SOUP FOR DINNER, YOUR FAVORITE!
SURPRISE!

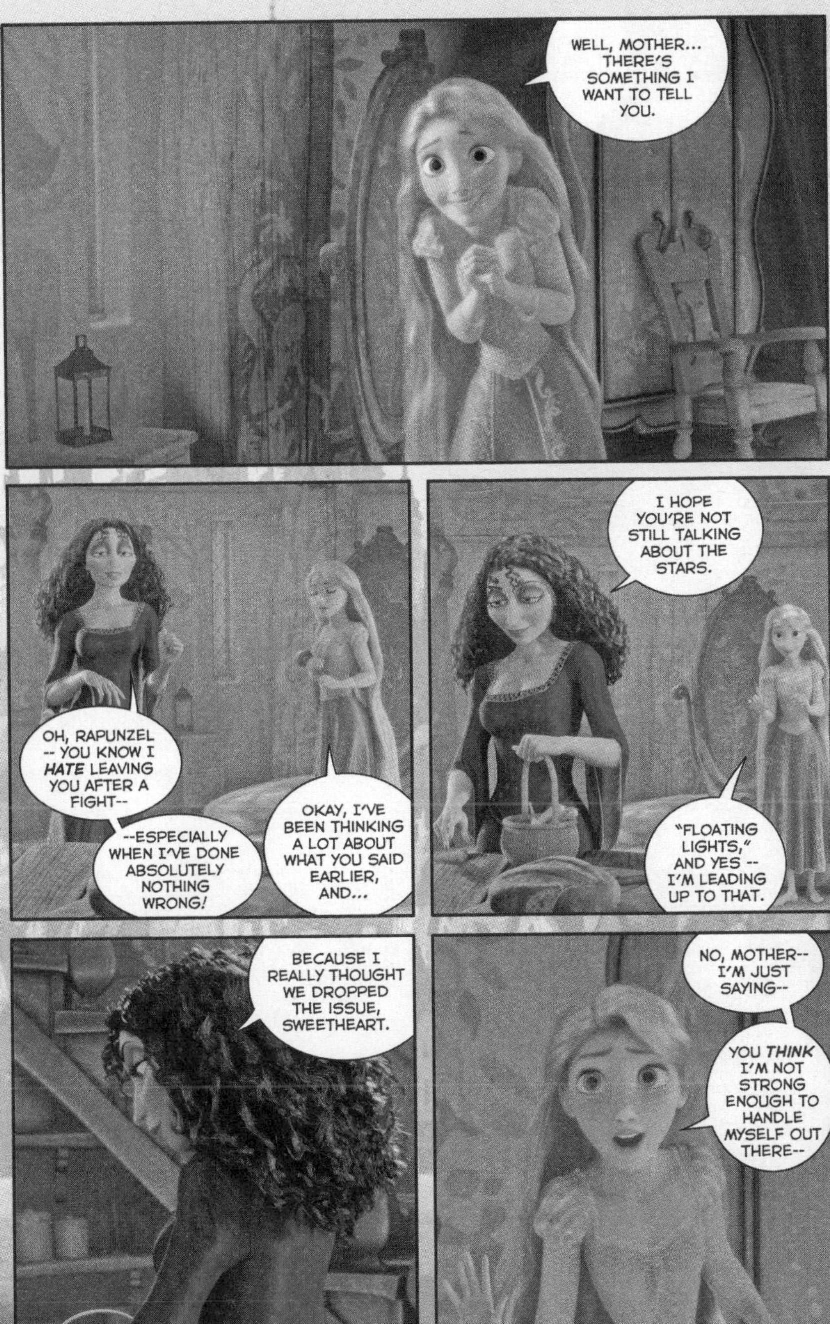

WELL, MOTHER... THERE'S SOMETHING I WANT TO TELL YOU.
OH, RAPUNZEL -- YOU KNOW I *HATE* LEAVING YOU AFTER A FIGHT--
--ESPECIALLY WHEN I'VE DONE ABSOLUTELY NOTHING WRONG!
OKAY, I'VE BEEN THINKING A LOT ABOUT WHAT YOU SAID EARLIER, AND...
I HOPE YOU'RE NOT STILL TALKING ABOUT THE STARS.
"FLOATING LIGHTS," AND YES -- I'M LEADING UP TO THAT.
BECAUSE I REALLY THOUGHT WE DROPPED THE ISSUE, SWEETHEART.
NO, MOTHER-- I'M JUST SAYING--
YOU *THINK* I'M NOT STRONG ENOUGH TO HANDLE MYSELF OUT THERE--

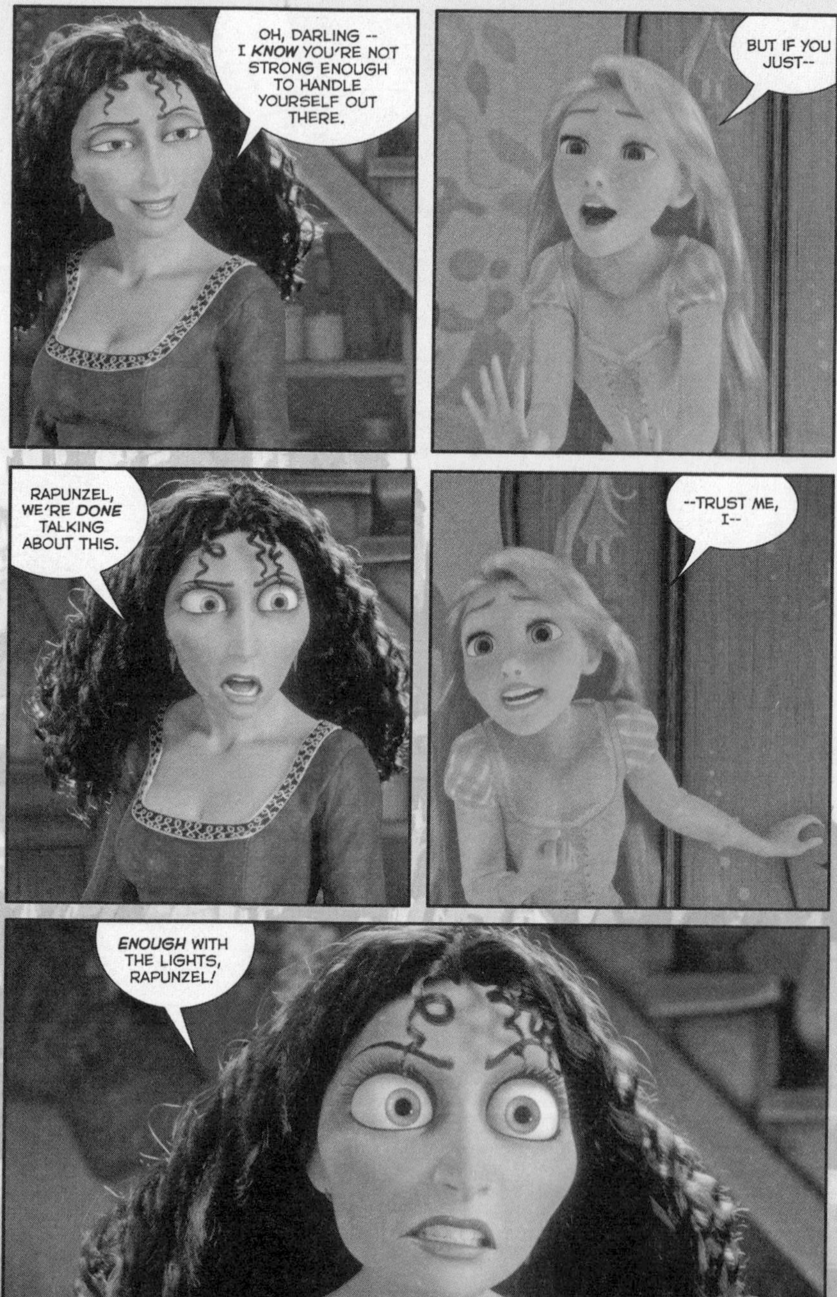
OH, DARLING -- I *KNOW* YOU'RE NOT STRONG ENOUGH TO HANDLE YOURSELF OUT THERE.
BUT IF YOU JUST--
RAPUNZEL, WE'RE *DONE* TALKING ABOUT THIS.
--TRUST ME, I--
*ENOUGH* WITH THE LIGHTS, RAPUNZEL!

YOU ARE NOT LEAVING THIS TOWER! EVER!

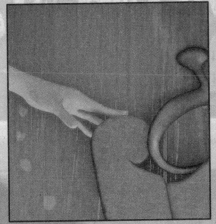

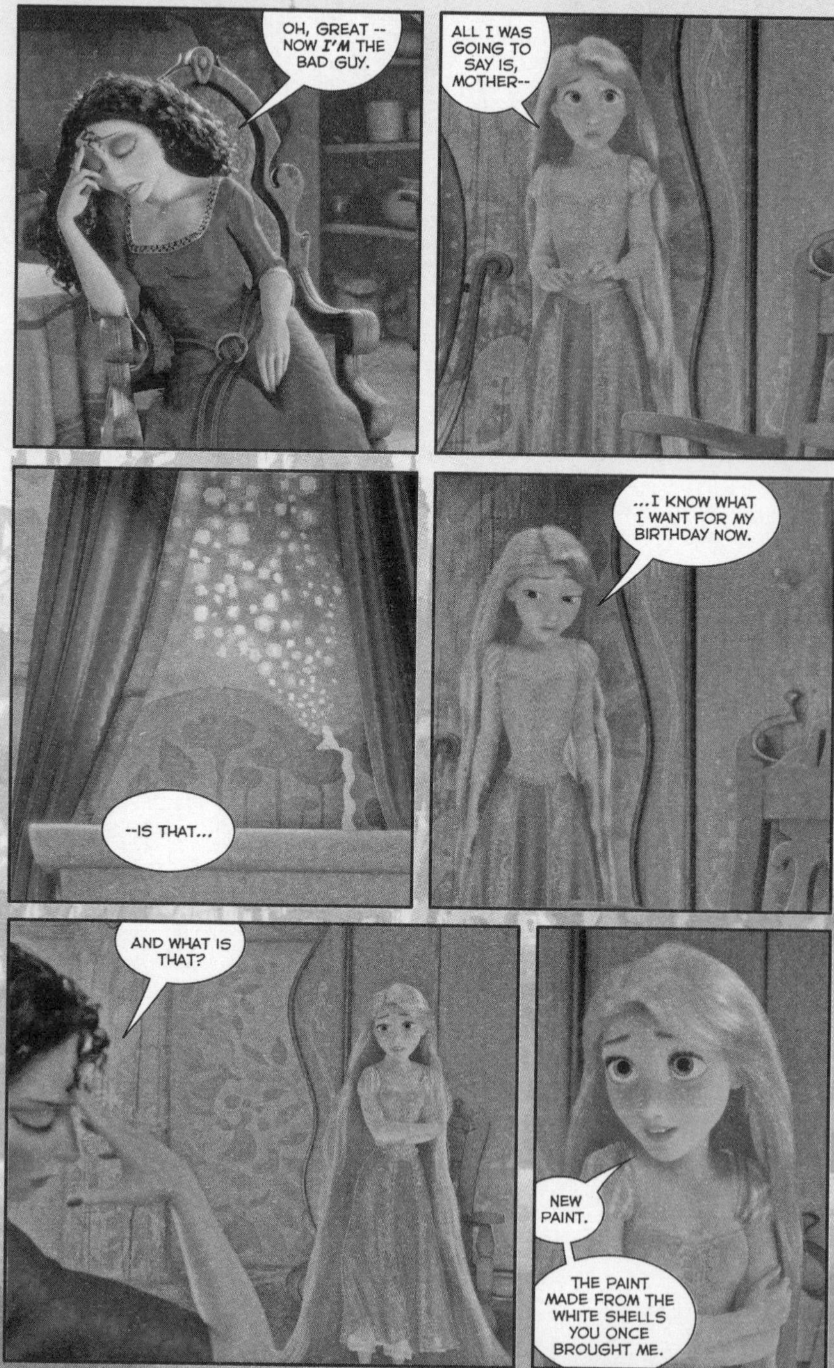
OH, GREAT -- NOW *I'M* THE BAD GUY.
ALL I WAS GOING TO SAY IS, MOTHER--
--IS THAT...
...I KNOW WHAT I WANT FOR MY BIRTHDAY NOW.
AND WHAT IS THAT?
NEW PAINT.
THE PAINT MADE FROM THE WHITE SHELLS YOU ONCE BROUGHT ME.

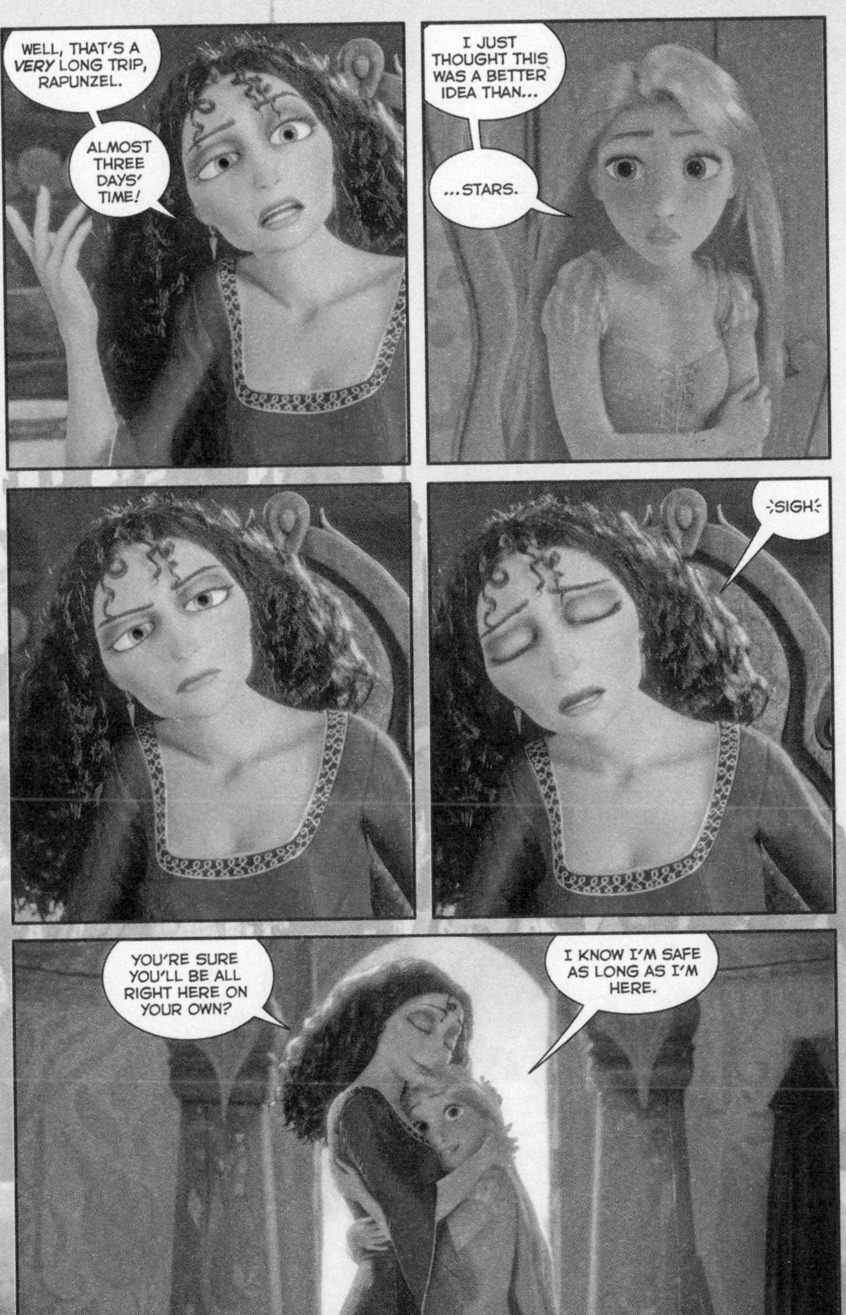
WELL, THAT'S A *VERY* LONG TRIP, RAPUNZEL.
ALMOST THREE DAYS' TIME!
I JUST THOUGHT THIS WAS A BETTER IDEA THAN...
...STARS.
SIGH
YOU'RE SURE YOU'LL BE ALL RIGHT HERE ON YOUR OWN?
I KNOW I'M SAFE AS LONG AS I'M HERE.

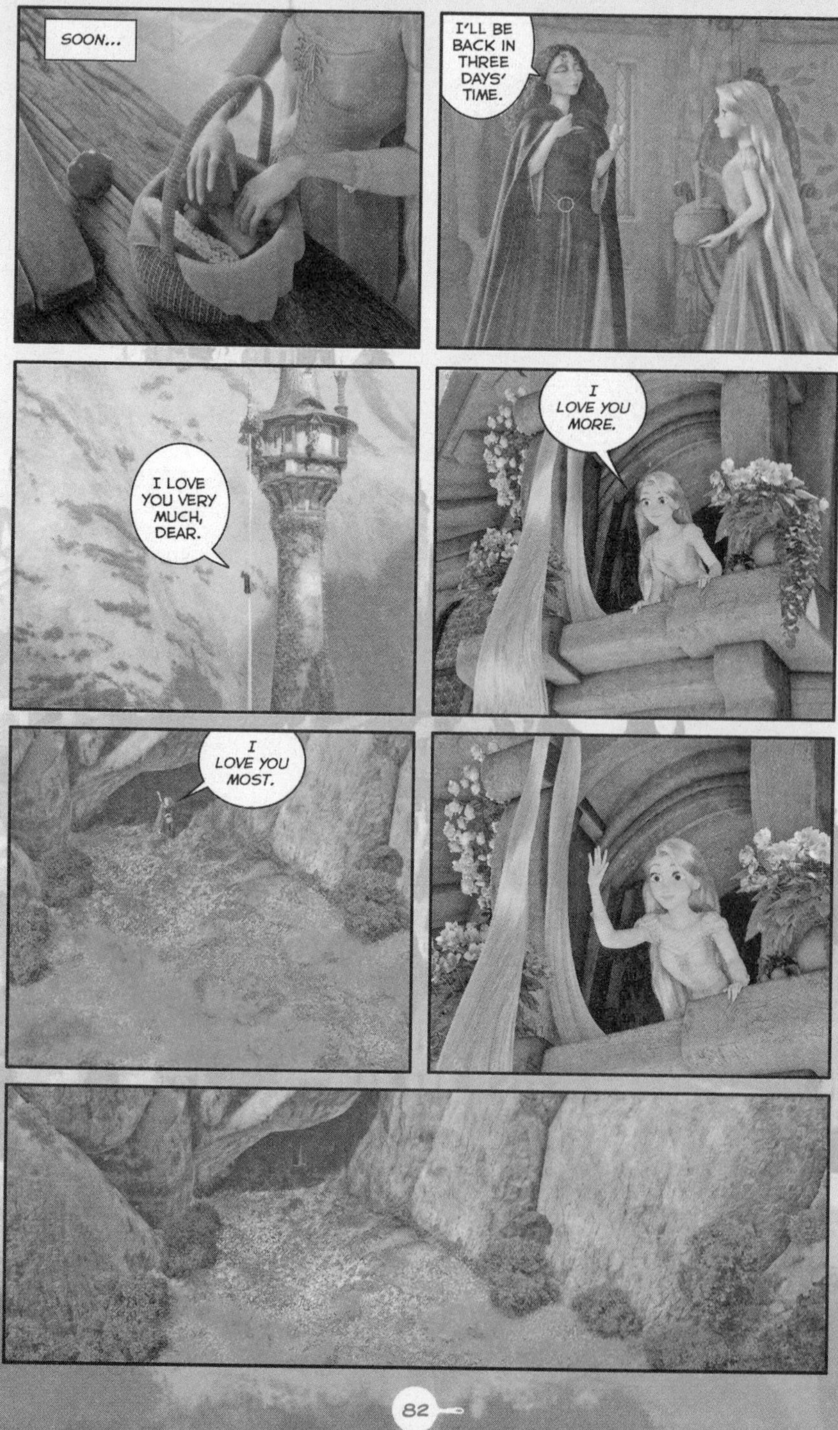
SOON...
I'LL BE BACK IN THREE DAYS' TIME.
I LOVE YOU VERY MUCH, DEAR.
I LOVE YOU MORE.
I LOVE YOU MOST.

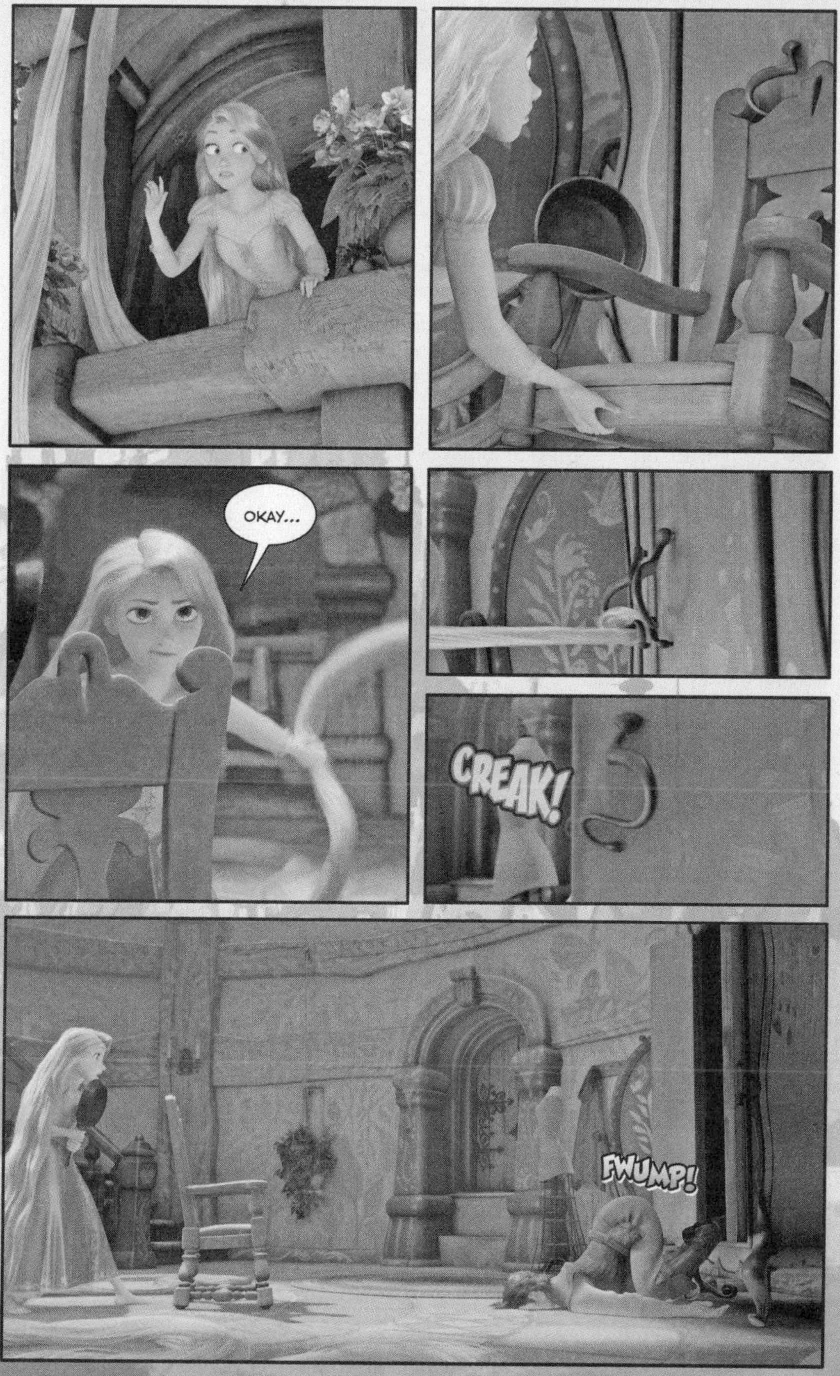
OKAY...
CREAK!
FWUMP!

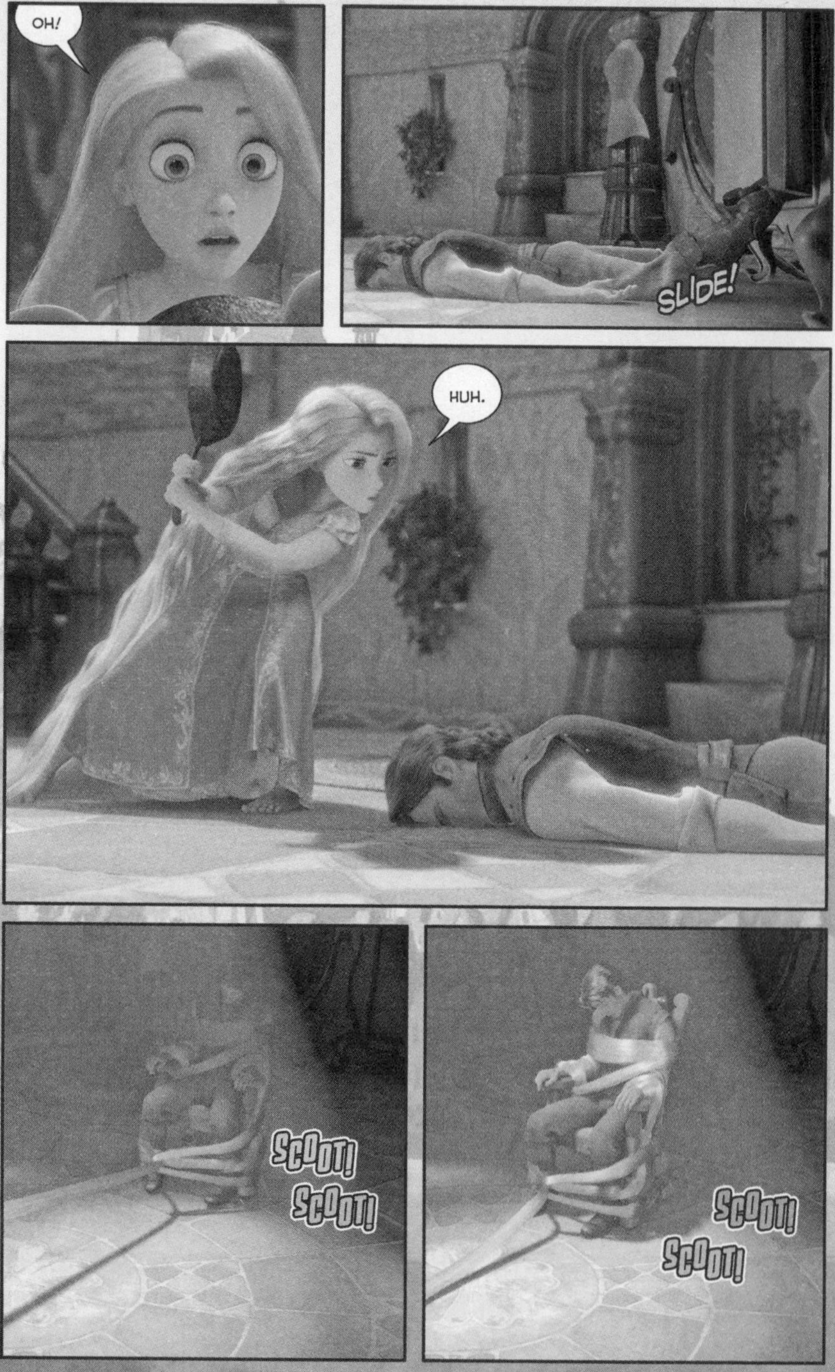
OH!
SLIDE!
HUH.
SCOOT!
SCOOT!
SCOOT!
SCOOT!

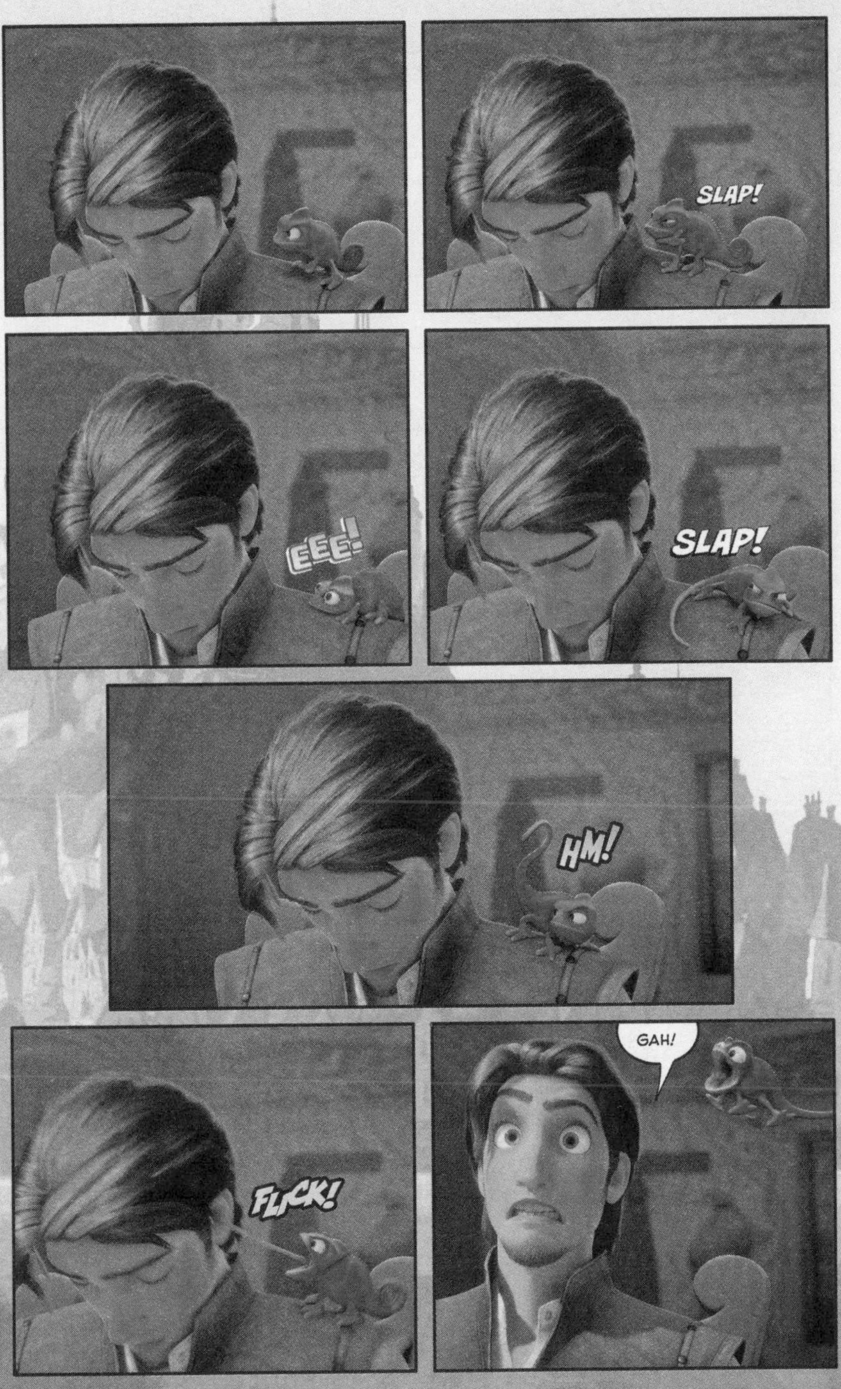
SLAP!
EEE!
SLAP!
HM!
FLICK!
GAH!

HUH? WHAT?

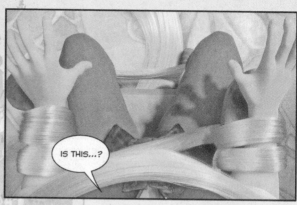

IS THIS...?

IS THIS... *HAIR?*

STRUGGLING ... STRUGGLING IS POINTLESS!

HUH?

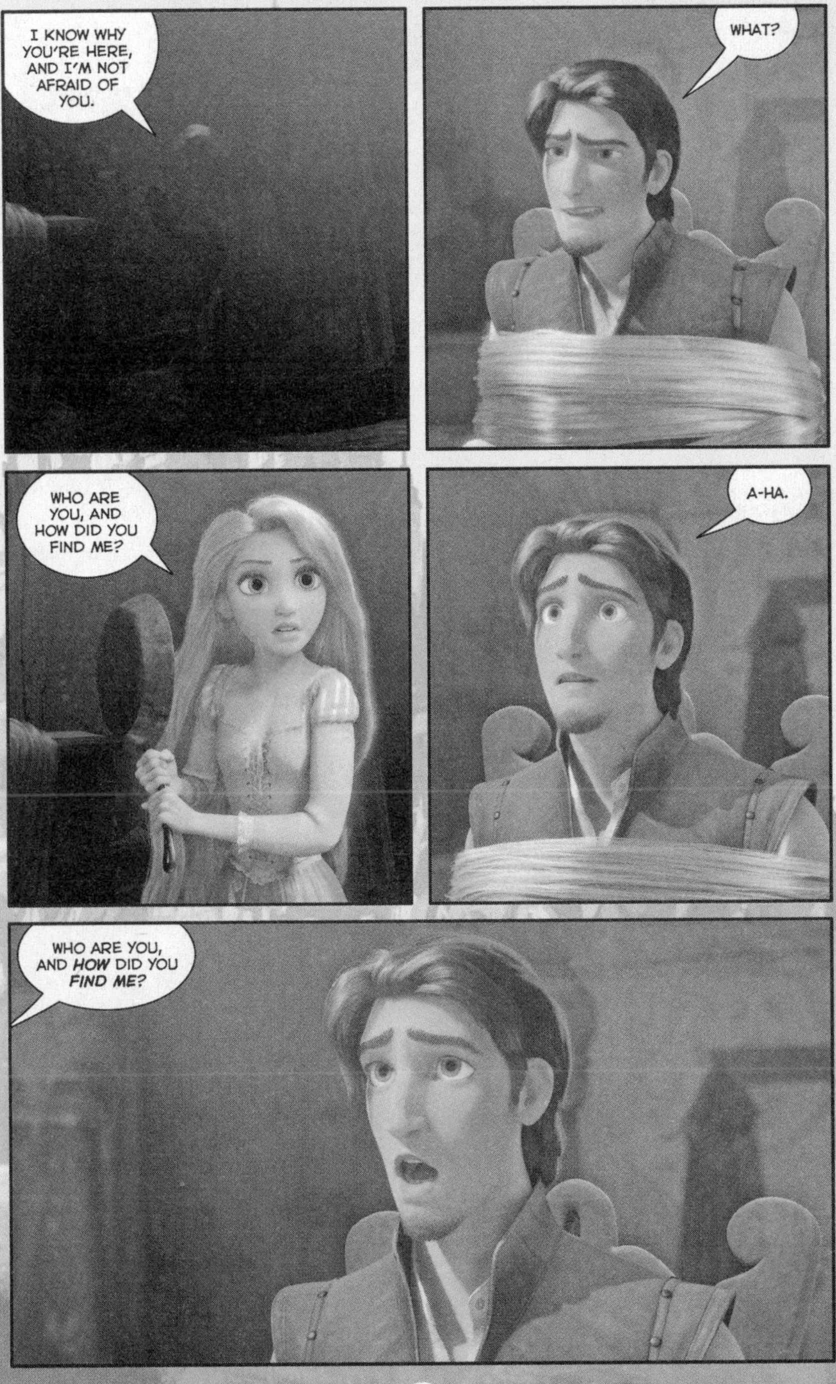
I KNOW WHY YOU'RE HERE, AND I'M NOT AFRAID OF YOU.
WHAT?
WHO ARE YOU, AND HOW DID YOU FIND ME?
A-HA.
WHO ARE YOU, AND *HOW* DID YOU *FIND ME?*

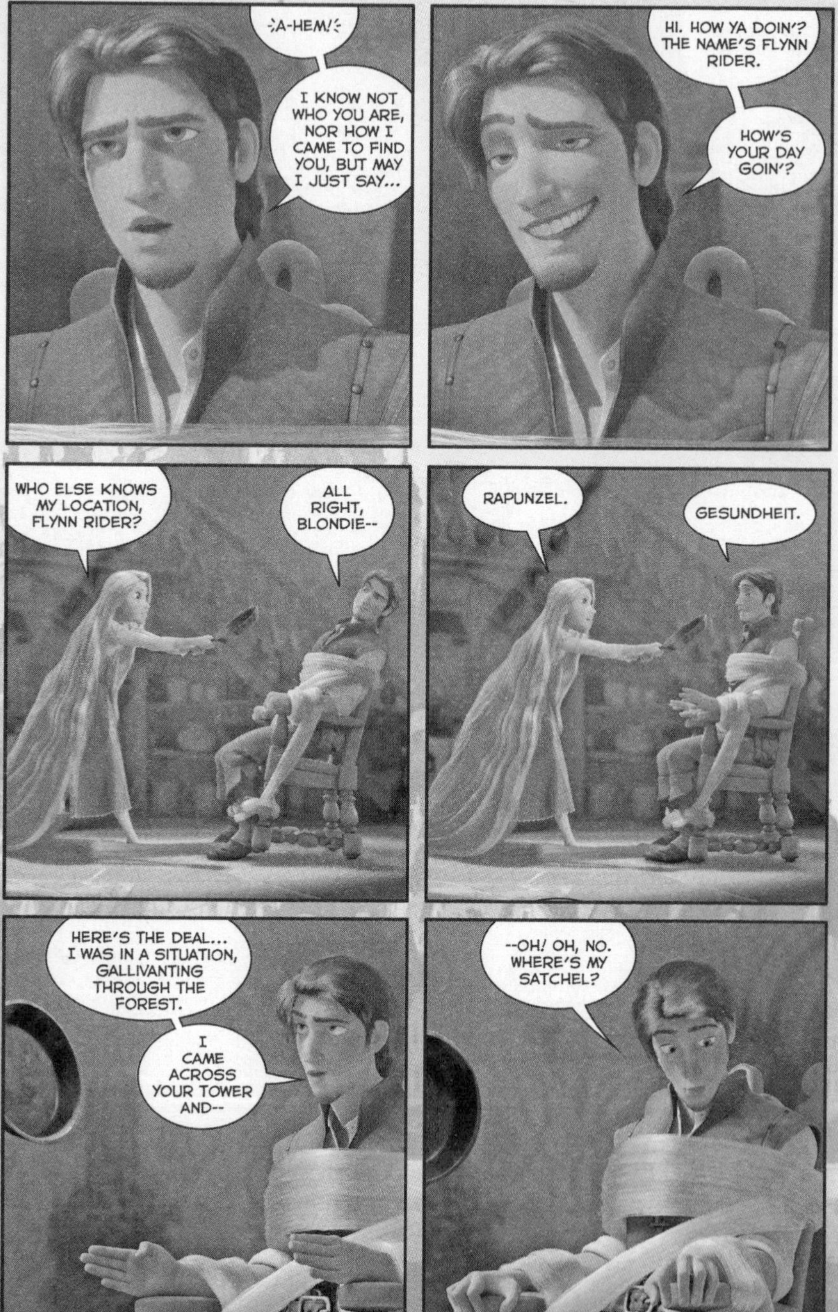

A-HEM!
I KNOW NOT WHO YOU ARE, NOR HOW I CAME TO FIND YOU, BUT MAY I JUST SAY...
HI. HOW YA DOIN'? THE NAME'S FLYNN RIDER.
HOW'S YOUR DAY GOIN'?
WHO ELSE KNOWS MY LOCATION, FLYNN RIDER?
ALL RIGHT, BLONDIE--
RAPUNZEL.
GESUNDHEIT.
HERE'S THE DEAL... I WAS IN A SITUATION, GALLIVANTING THROUGH THE FOREST.
I CAME ACROSS YOUR TOWER AND--
--OH! OH, NO. WHERE'S MY SATCHEL?

I'VE HIDDEN IT. SOMEWHERE YOU WILL NEVER FIND IT.

IT'S IN THAT POT, ISN'T IT?

KA-DONG!

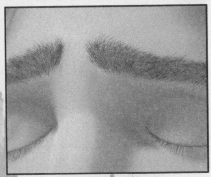

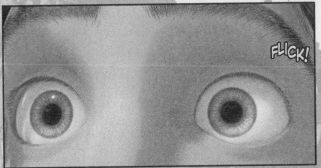

FLICK!

YIKES! WOULD YOU STOP THAT?!

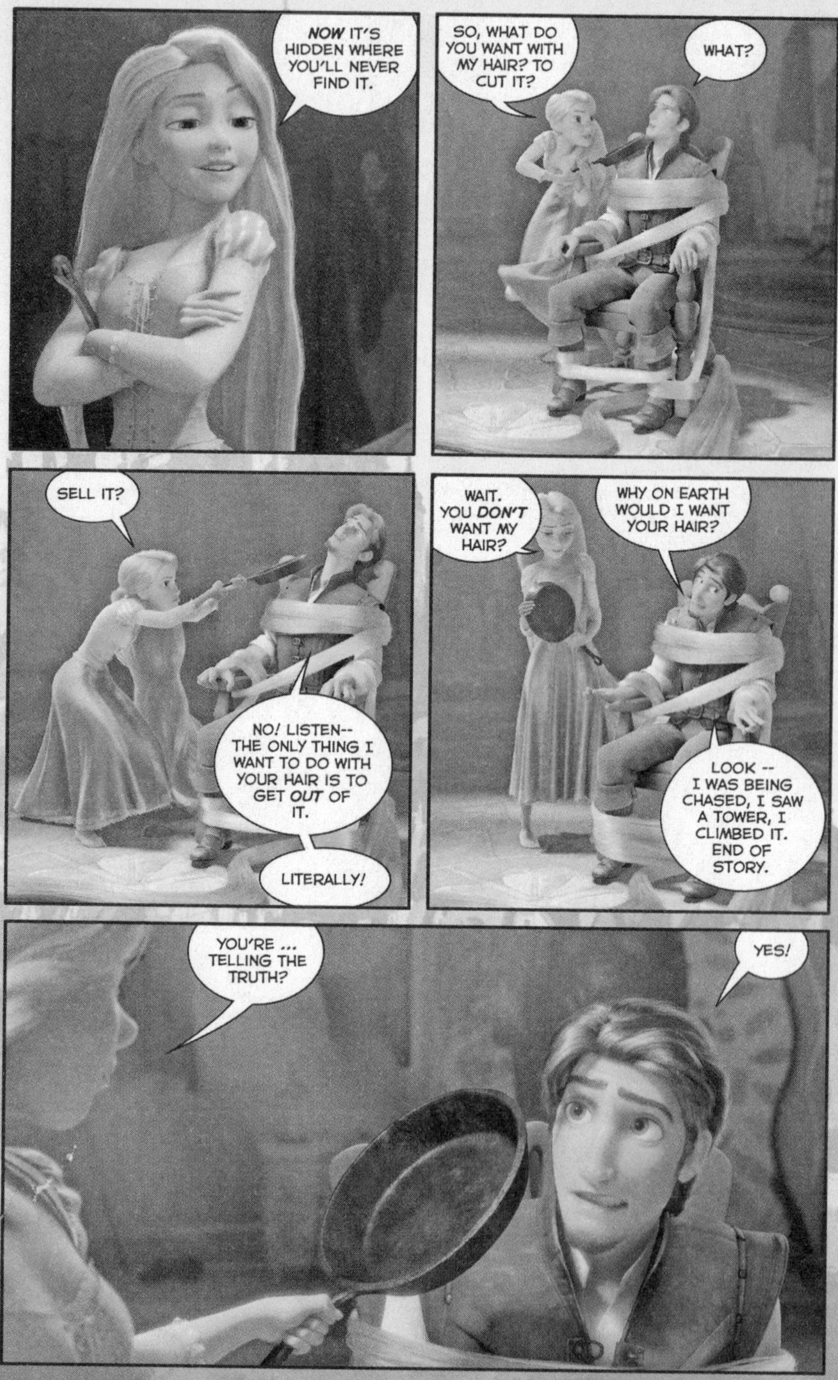
NOW IT'S HIDDEN WHERE YOU'LL NEVER FIND IT.
SO, WHAT DO YOU WANT WITH MY HAIR? TO CUT IT?
WHAT?
SELL IT?
NO! LISTEN-- THE ONLY THING I WANT TO DO WITH YOUR HAIR IS TO GET OUT OF IT.
LITERALLY!
WAIT. YOU DON'T WANT MY HAIR?
WHY ON EARTH WOULD I WANT YOUR HAIR?
LOOK -- I WAS BEING CHASED, I SAW A TOWER, I CLIMBED IT. END OF STORY.
YOU'RE ... TELLING THE TRUTH?
YES!

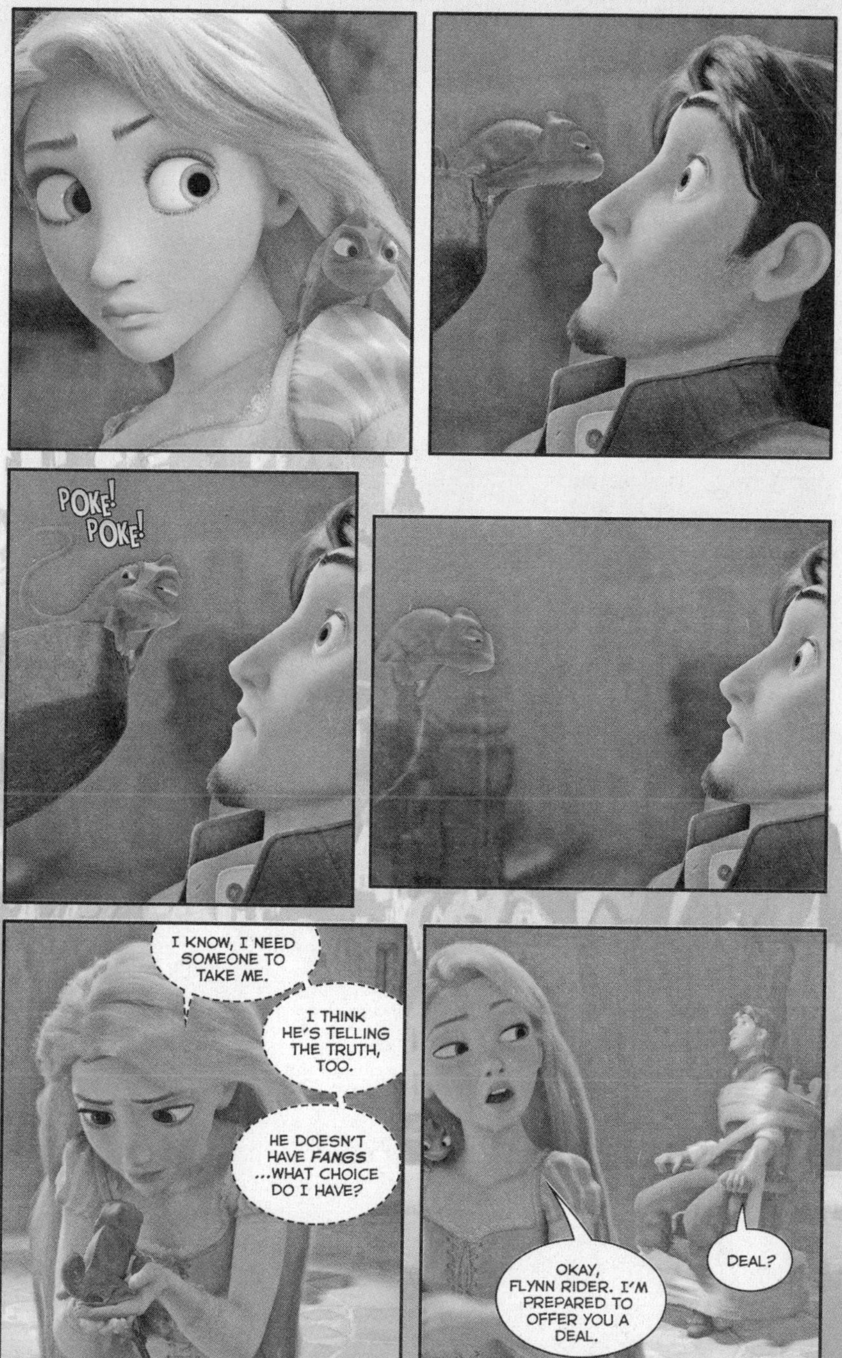
POKE! POKE!
I KNOW, I NEED SOMEONE TO TAKE ME.
I THINK HE'S TELLING THE TRUTH, TOO.
HE DOESN'T HAVE FANGS ...WHAT CHOICE DO I HAVE?
OKAY, FLYNN RIDER. I'M PREPARED TO OFFER YOU A DEAL.
DEAL?

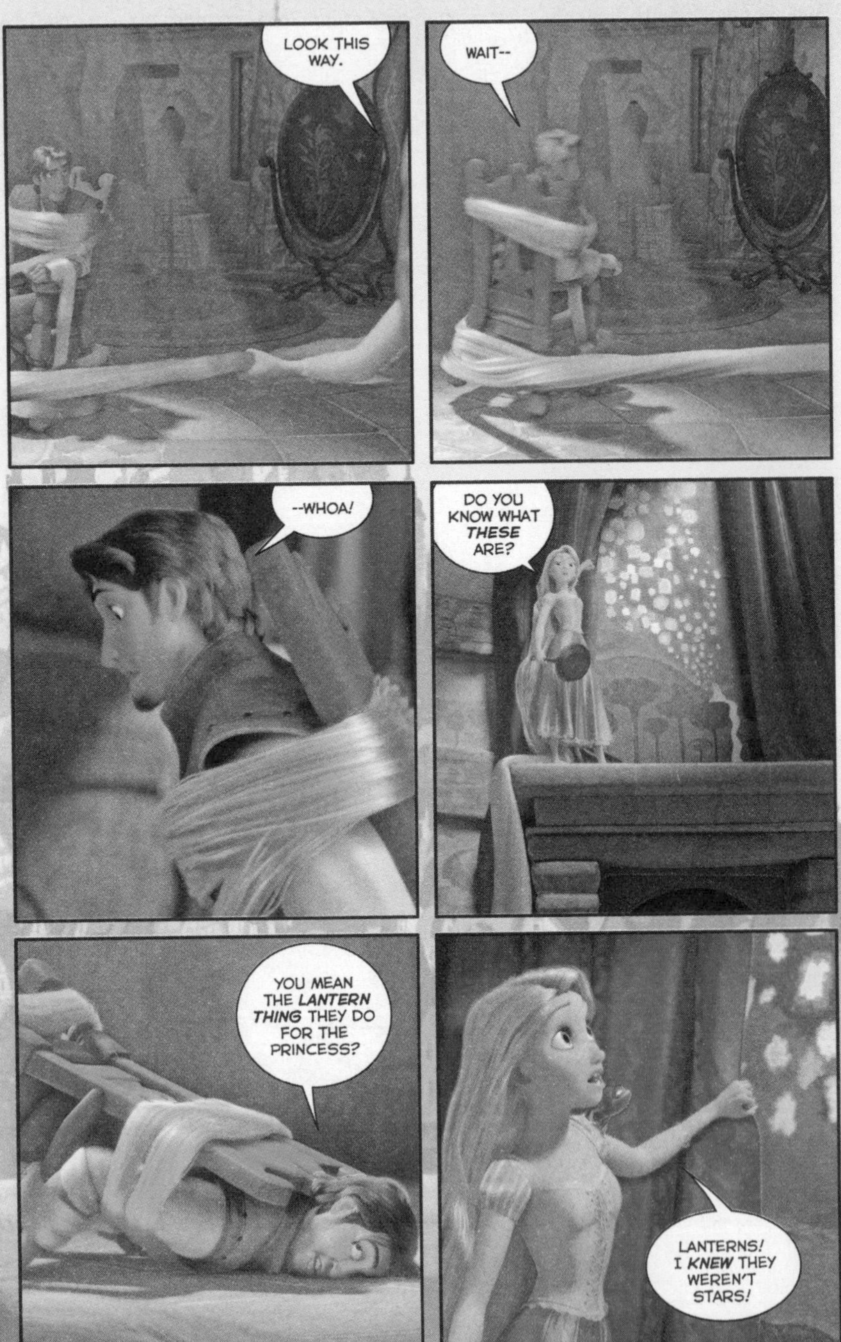
LOOK THIS WAY.
WAIT--
--WHOA!
DO YOU KNOW WHAT *THESE* ARE?
YOU MEAN THE *LANTERN THING* THEY DO FOR THE PRINCESS?
LANTERNS! I *KNEW* THEY WEREN'T STARS!

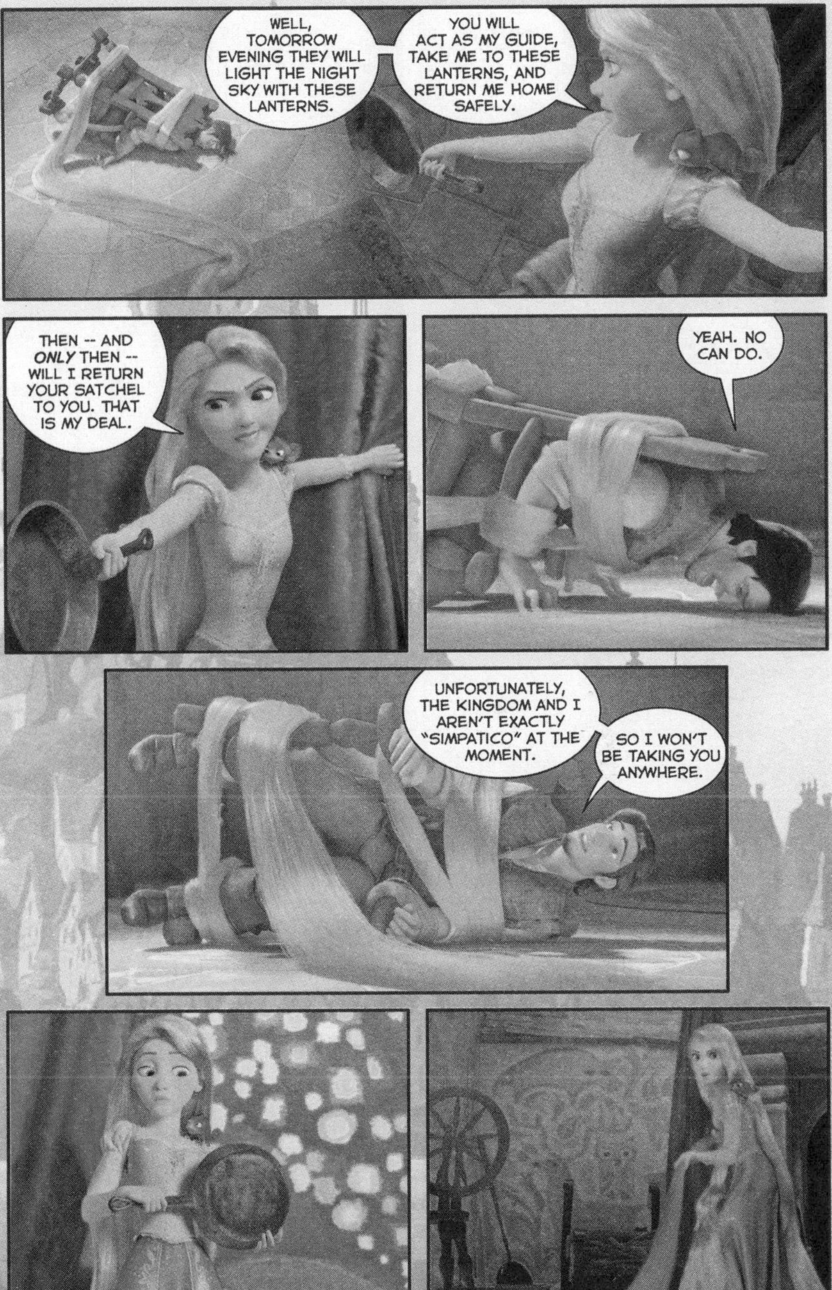
WELL, TOMORROW EVENING THEY WILL LIGHT THE NIGHT SKY WITH THESE LANTERNS.
YOU WILL ACT AS MY GUIDE, TAKE ME TO THESE LANTERNS, AND RETURN ME HOME SAFELY.
THEN -- AND *ONLY* THEN -- WILL I RETURN YOUR SATCHEL TO YOU. THAT IS MY DEAL.
YEAH. NO CAN DO.
UNFORTUNATELY, THE KINGDOM AND I AREN'T EXACTLY "SIMPATICO" AT THE MOMENT.
SO I WON'T BE TAKING YOU ANYWHERE.

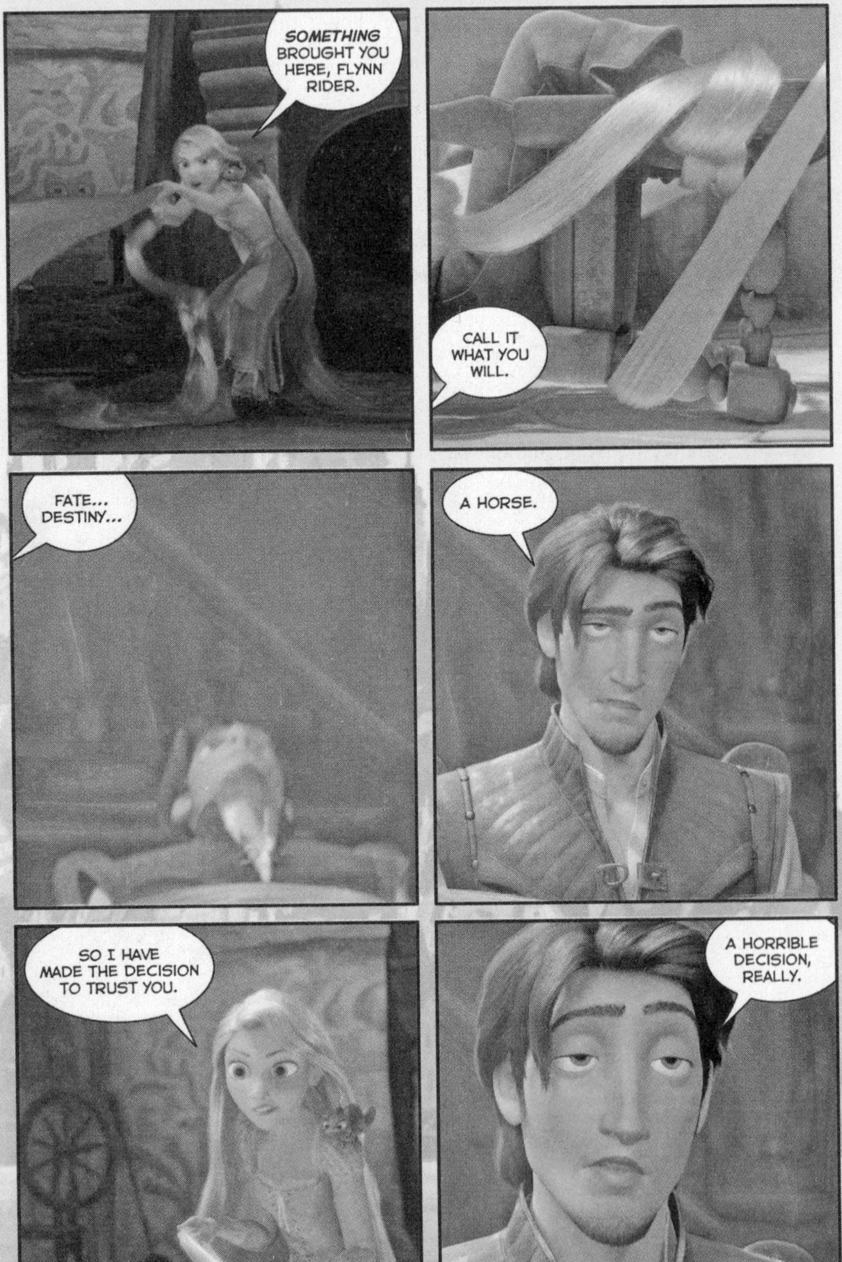
SOMETHING BROUGHT YOU HERE, FLYNN RIDER.
CALL IT WHAT YOU WILL.
FATE... DESTINY...
A HORSE.
SO I HAVE MADE THE DECISION TO TRUST YOU.
A HORRIBLE DECISION, REALLY.

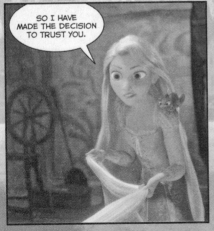

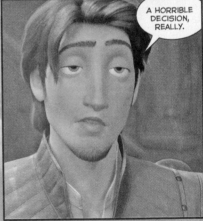

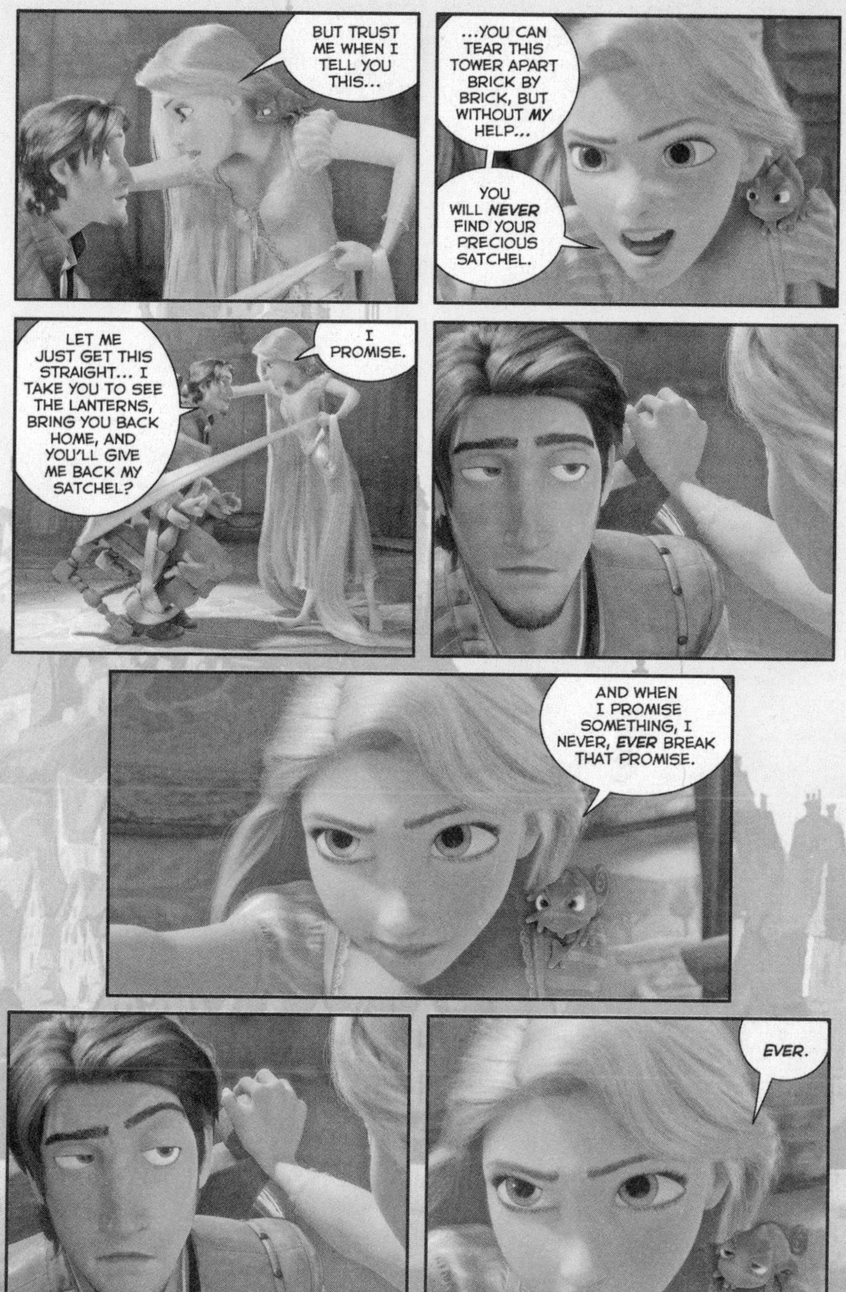
BUT TRUST ME WHEN I TELL YOU THIS...
...YOU CAN TEAR THIS TOWER APART BRICK BY BRICK, BUT WITHOUT *MY* HELP...
YOU WILL ***NEVER*** FIND YOUR PRECIOUS SATCHEL.
LET ME JUST GET THIS STRAIGHT... I TAKE YOU TO SEE THE LANTERNS, BRING YOU BACK HOME, AND YOU'LL GIVE ME BACK MY SATCHEL?
I PROMISE.
AND WHEN I PROMISE SOMETHING, I NEVER, ***EVER*** BREAK THAT PROMISE.
*EVER*.

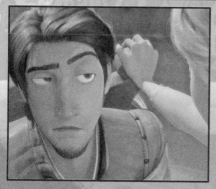

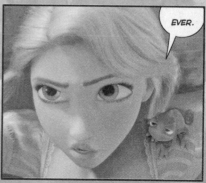

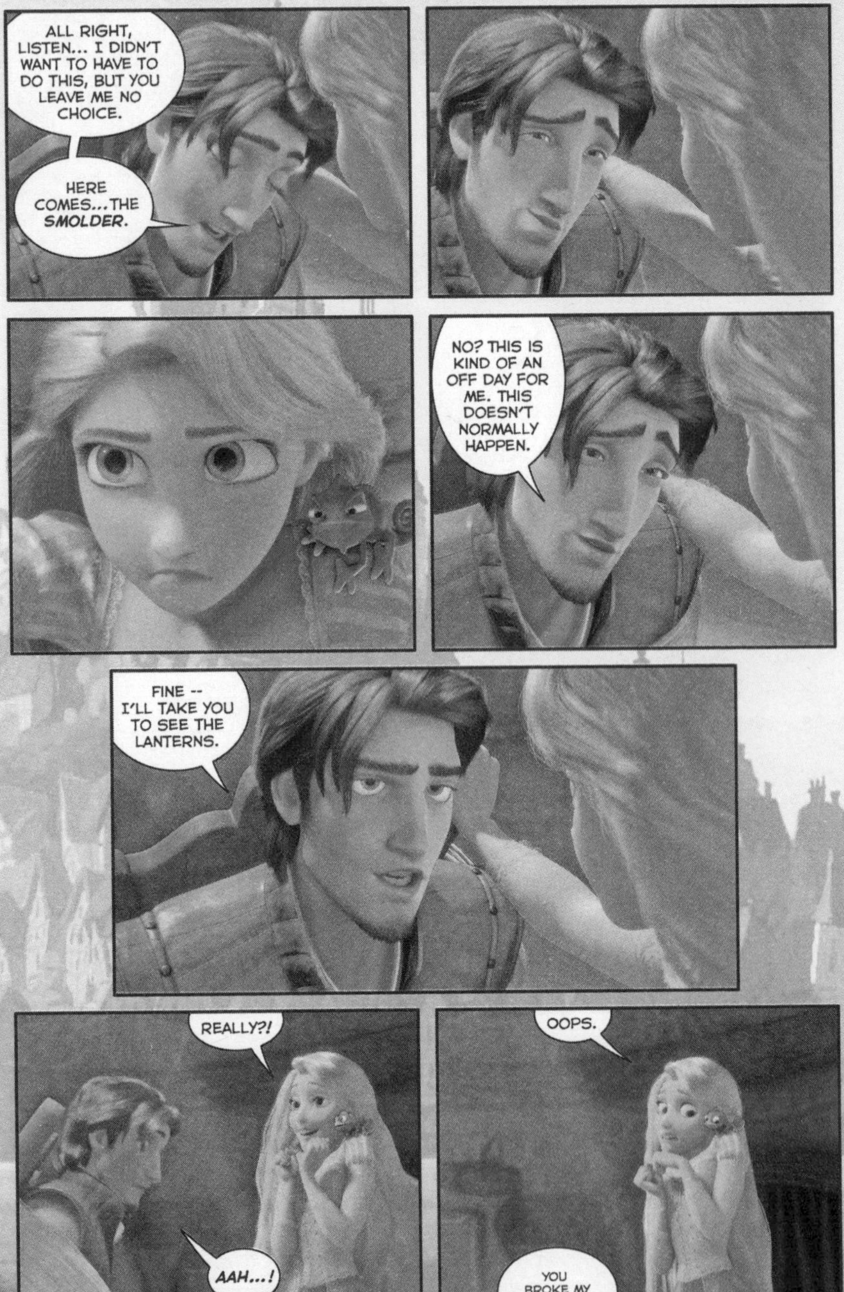
ALL RIGHT, LISTEN... I DIDN'T WANT TO HAVE TO DO THIS, BUT YOU LEAVE ME NO CHOICE.
HERE COMES...THE SMOLDER.
NO? THIS IS KIND OF AN OFF DAY FOR ME. THIS DOESN'T NORMALLY HAPPEN.
FINE -- I'LL TAKE YOU TO SEE THE LANTERNS.
REALLY?!
AAH...!
OOPS.
YOU BROKE MY SMOLDER.

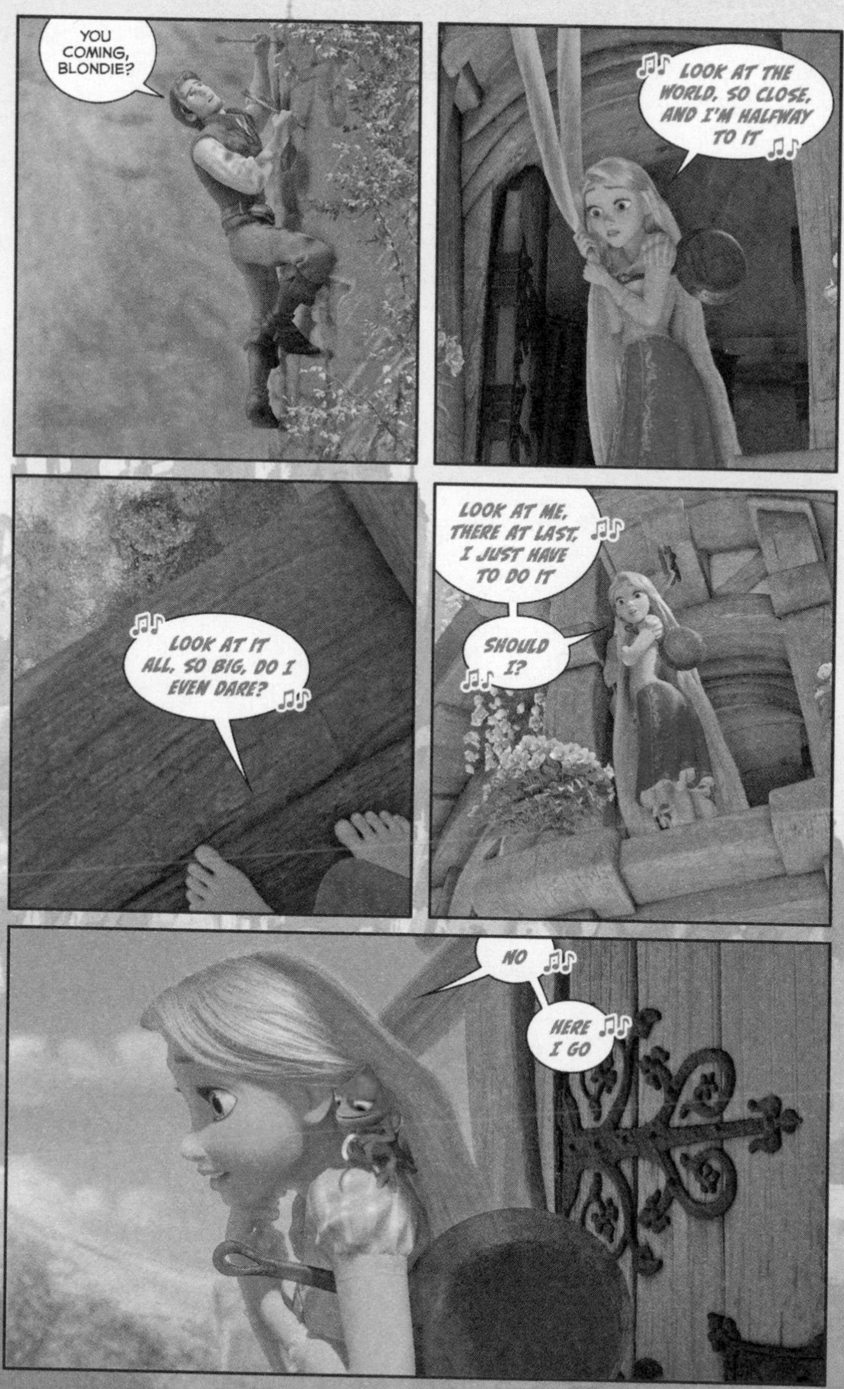
YOU COMING, BLONDIE?
LOOK AT THE WORLD, SO CLOSE, AND I'M HALFWAY TO IT
LOOK AT IT ALL, SO BIG, DO I EVEN DARE?
LOOK AT ME, THERE AT LAST, I JUST HAVE TO DO IT
SHOULD I?
NO
HERE I GO

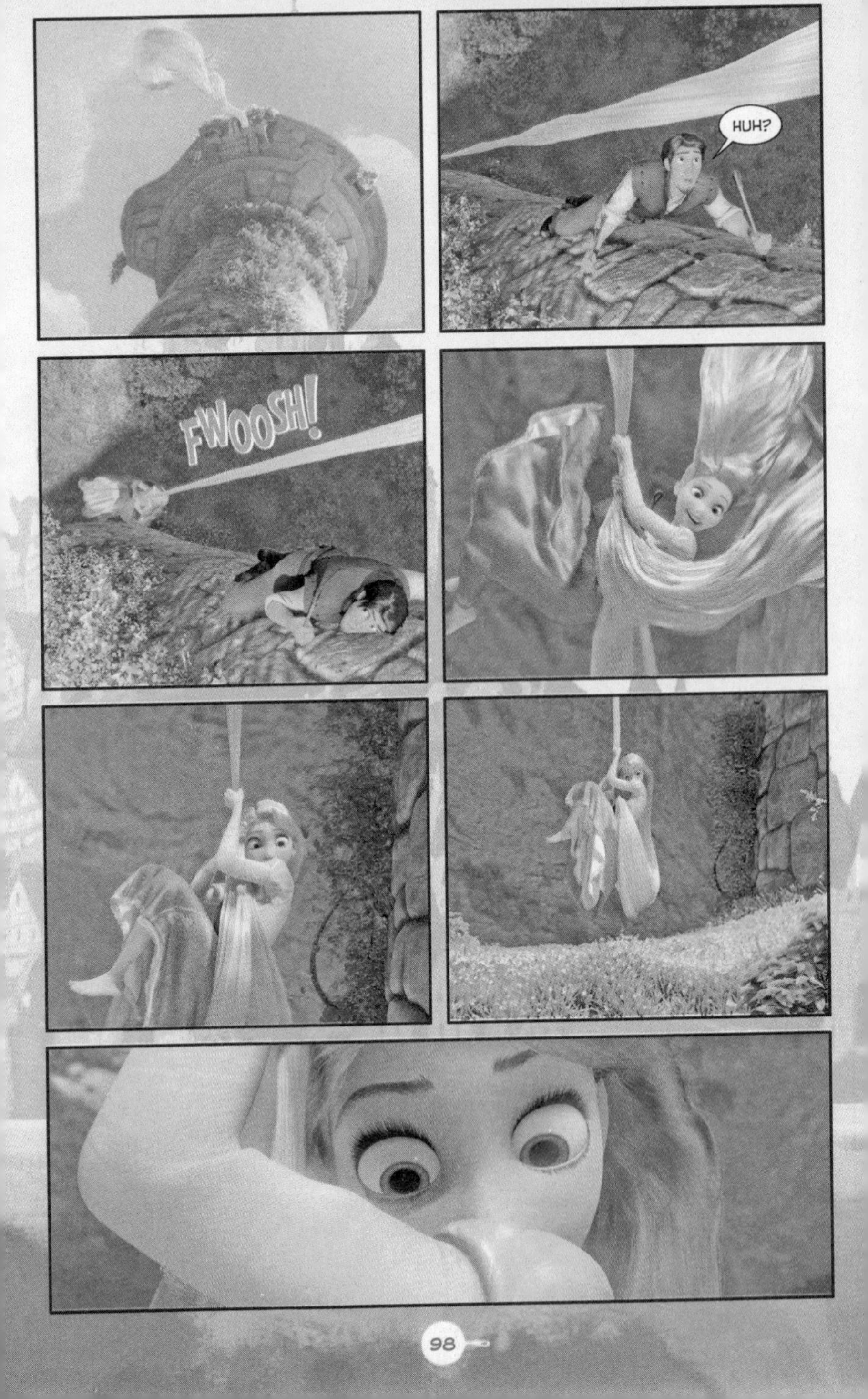
HUH?
FWOOSH!

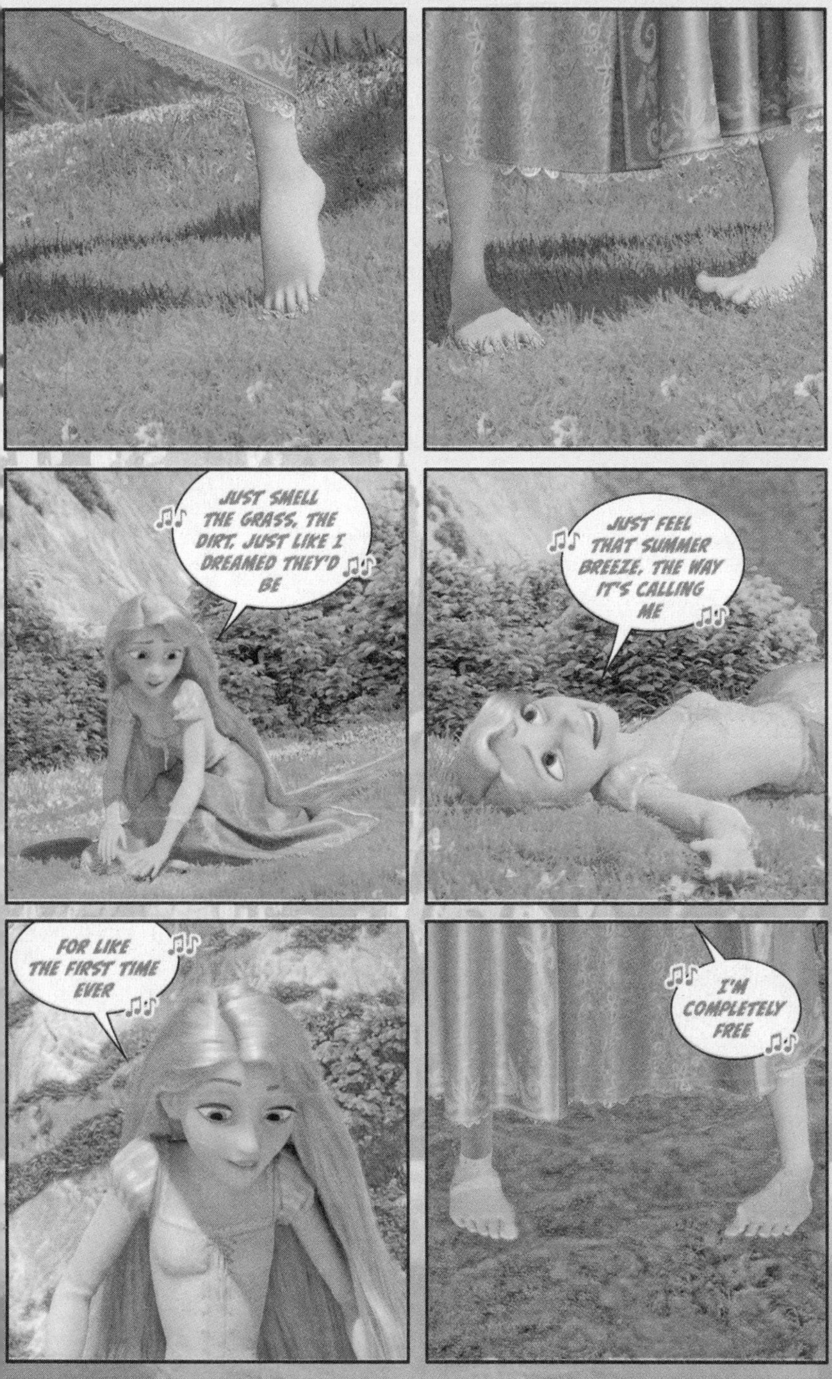
JUST SMELL THE GRASS, THE DIRT, JUST LIKE I DREAMED THEY'D BE
JUST FEEL THAT SUMMER BREEZE, THE WAY IT'S CALLING ME
FOR LIKE THE FIRST TIME EVER
I'M COMPLETELY FREE

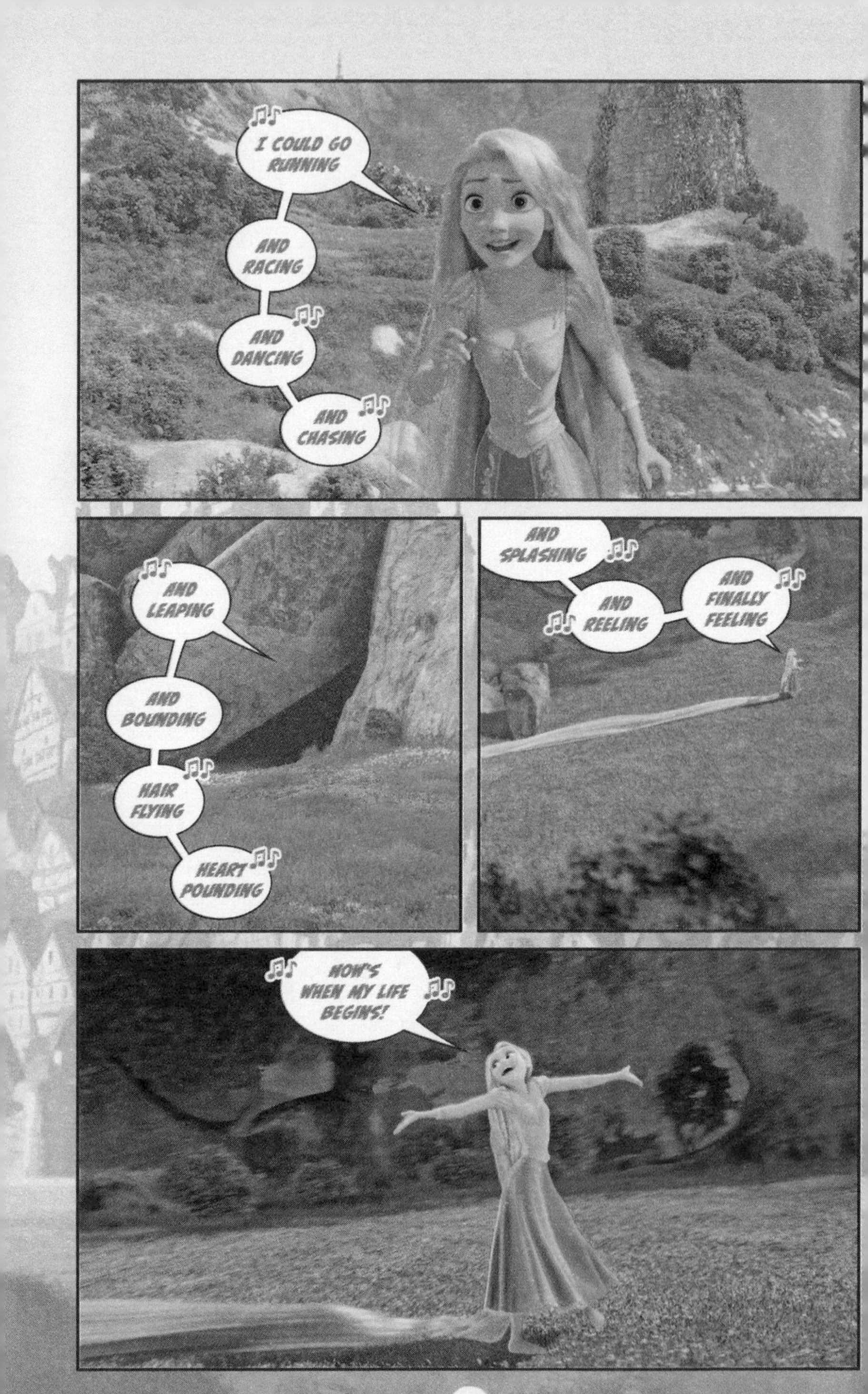
I COULD GO RUNNING
AND RACING
AND DANCING
AND CHASING
AND LEAPING
AND BOUNDING
HAIR FLYING
HEART POUNDING
AND SPLASHING
AND REELING
AND FINALLY FEELING
NOW'S WHEN MY LIFE BEGINS!

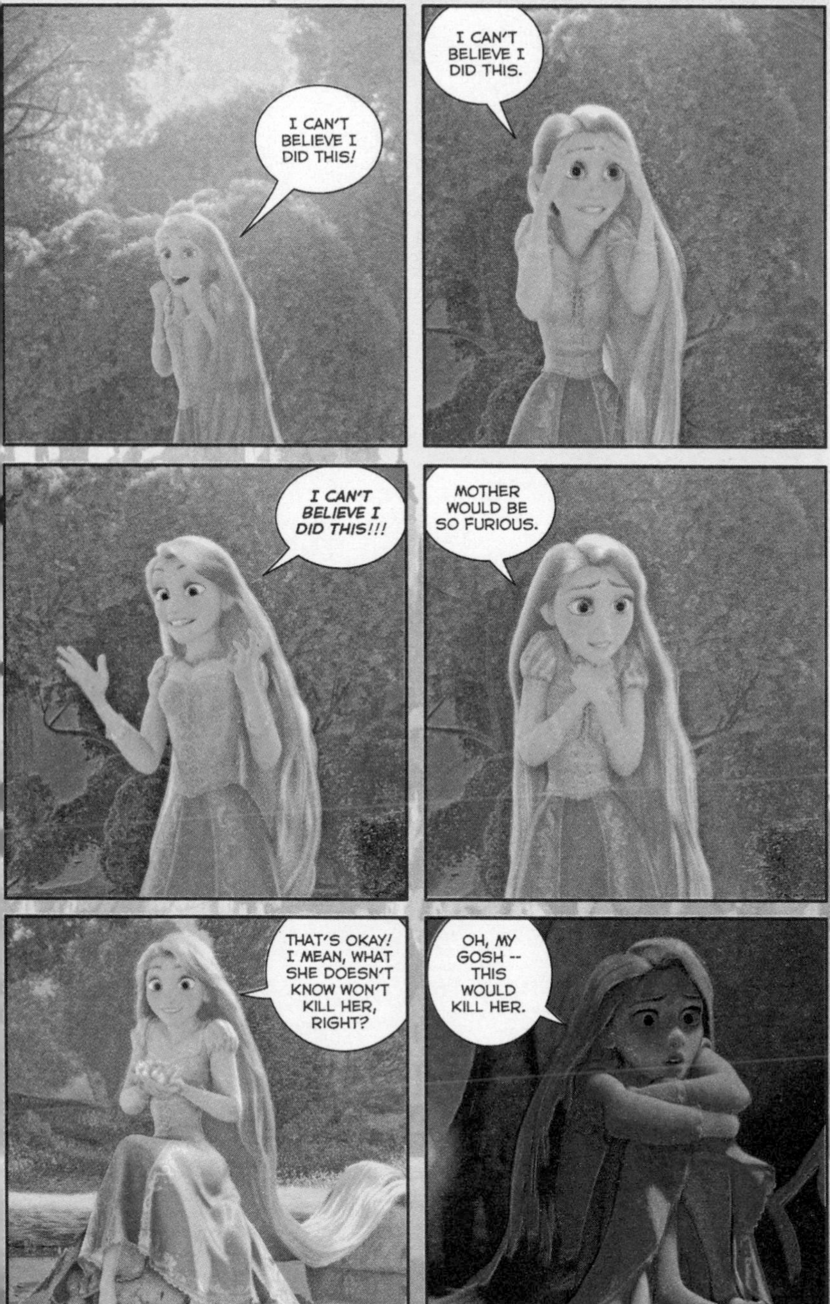
I CAN'T BELIEVE I DID THIS!
I CAN'T BELIEVE I DID THIS.
*I CAN'T BELIEVE I DID THIS!!!*
MOTHER WOULD BE SO FURIOUS.
THAT'S OKAY! I MEAN, WHAT SHE DOESN'T KNOW WON'T KILL HER, RIGHT?
OH, MY GOSH -- THIS WOULD KILL HER.

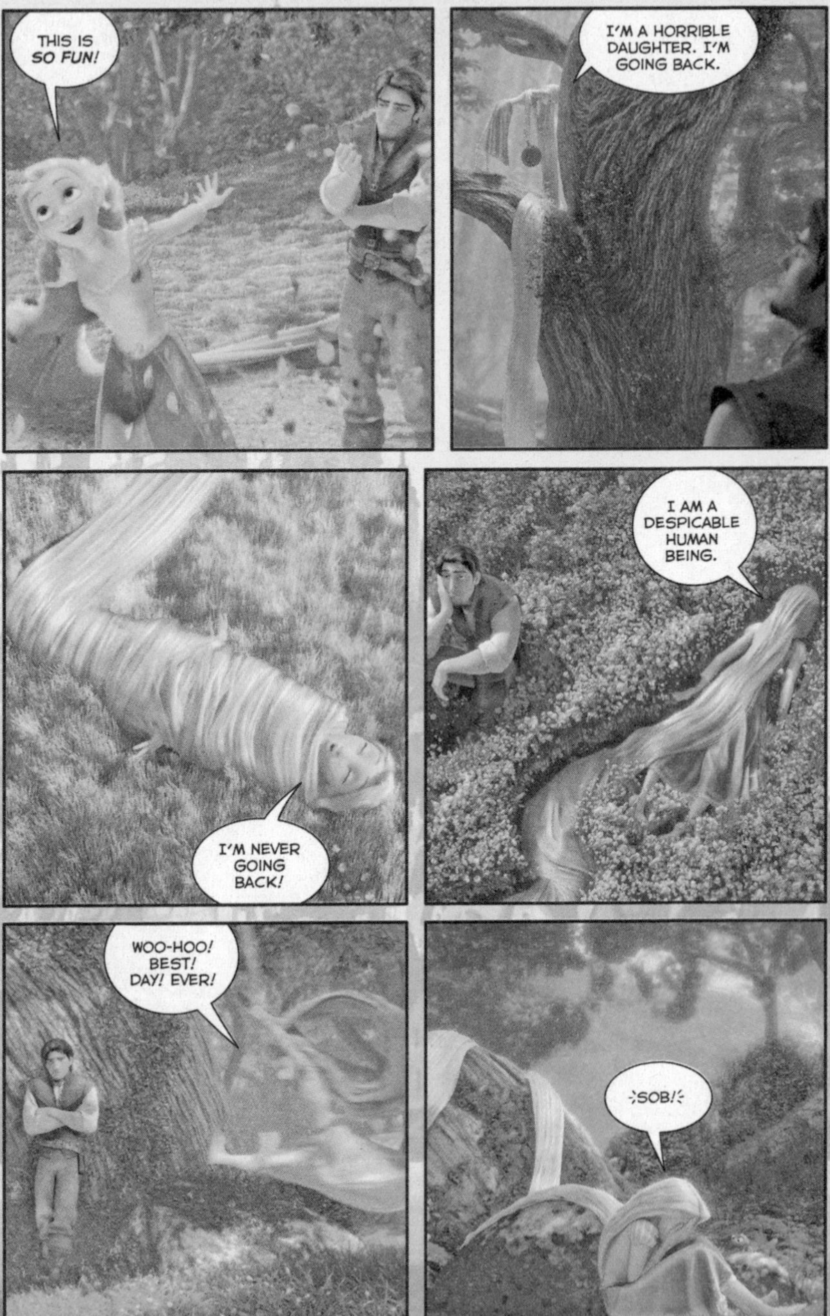
THIS IS SO FUN!
I'M A HORRIBLE DAUGHTER. I'M GOING BACK.
I'M NEVER GOING BACK!
I AM A DESPICABLE HUMAN BEING.
WOO-HOO! BEST! DAY! EVER!
SOB!

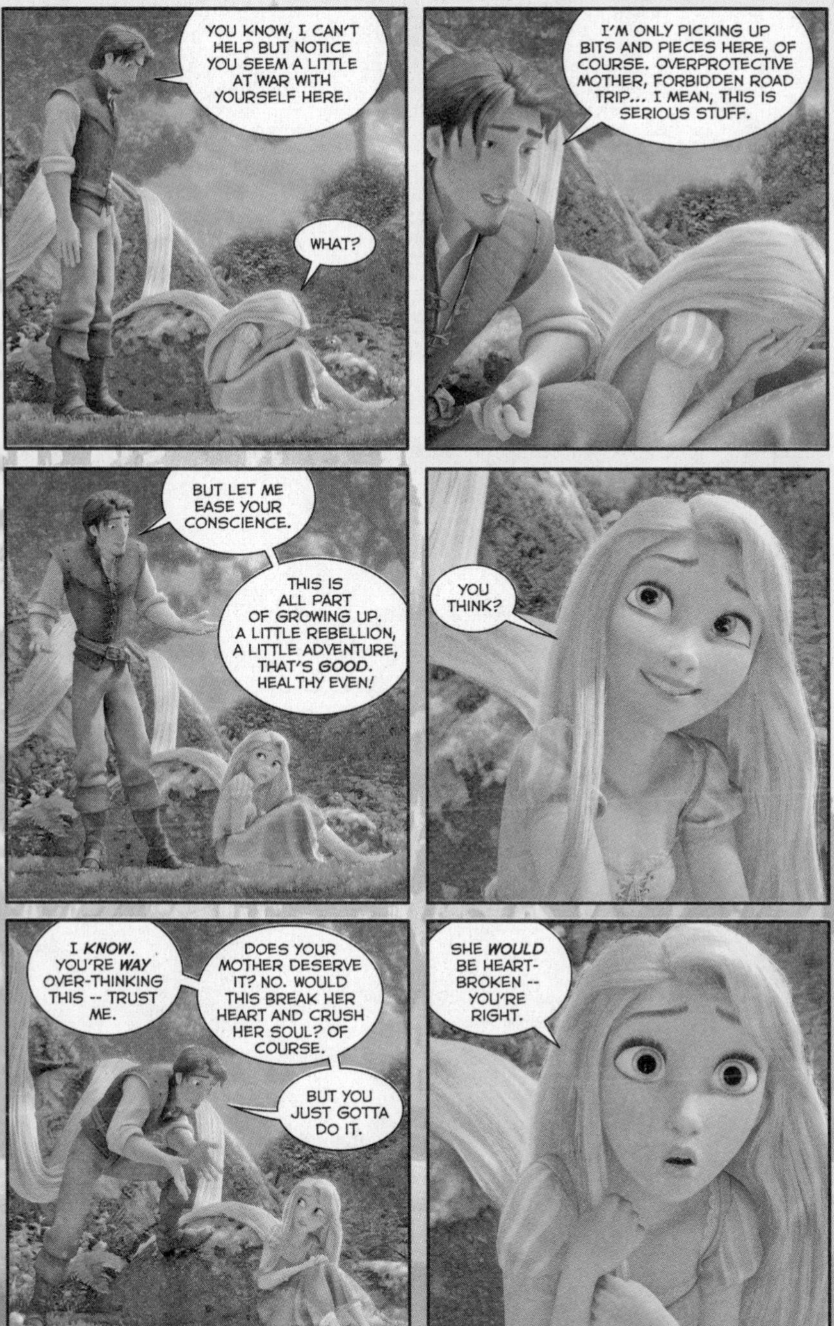

YOU KNOW, I CAN'T HELP BUT NOTICE YOU SEEM A LITTLE AT WAR WITH YOURSELF HERE.
WHAT?
I'M ONLY PICKING UP BITS AND PIECES HERE, OF COURSE. OVERPROTECTIVE MOTHER, FORBIDDEN ROAD TRIP... I MEAN, THIS IS SERIOUS STUFF.
BUT LET ME EASE YOUR CONSCIENCE.
THIS IS ALL PART OF GROWING UP. A LITTLE REBELLION, A LITTLE ADVENTURE, THAT'S *GOOD*. HEALTHY EVEN!
YOU THINK?
I *KNOW*. YOU'RE *WAY* OVER-THINKING THIS -- TRUST ME.
DOES YOUR MOTHER DESERVE IT? NO. WOULD THIS BREAK HER HEART AND CRUSH HER SOUL? OF COURSE.
BUT YOU JUST GOTTA DO IT.
SHE *WOULD* BE HEART-BROKEN -- YOU'RE RIGHT.

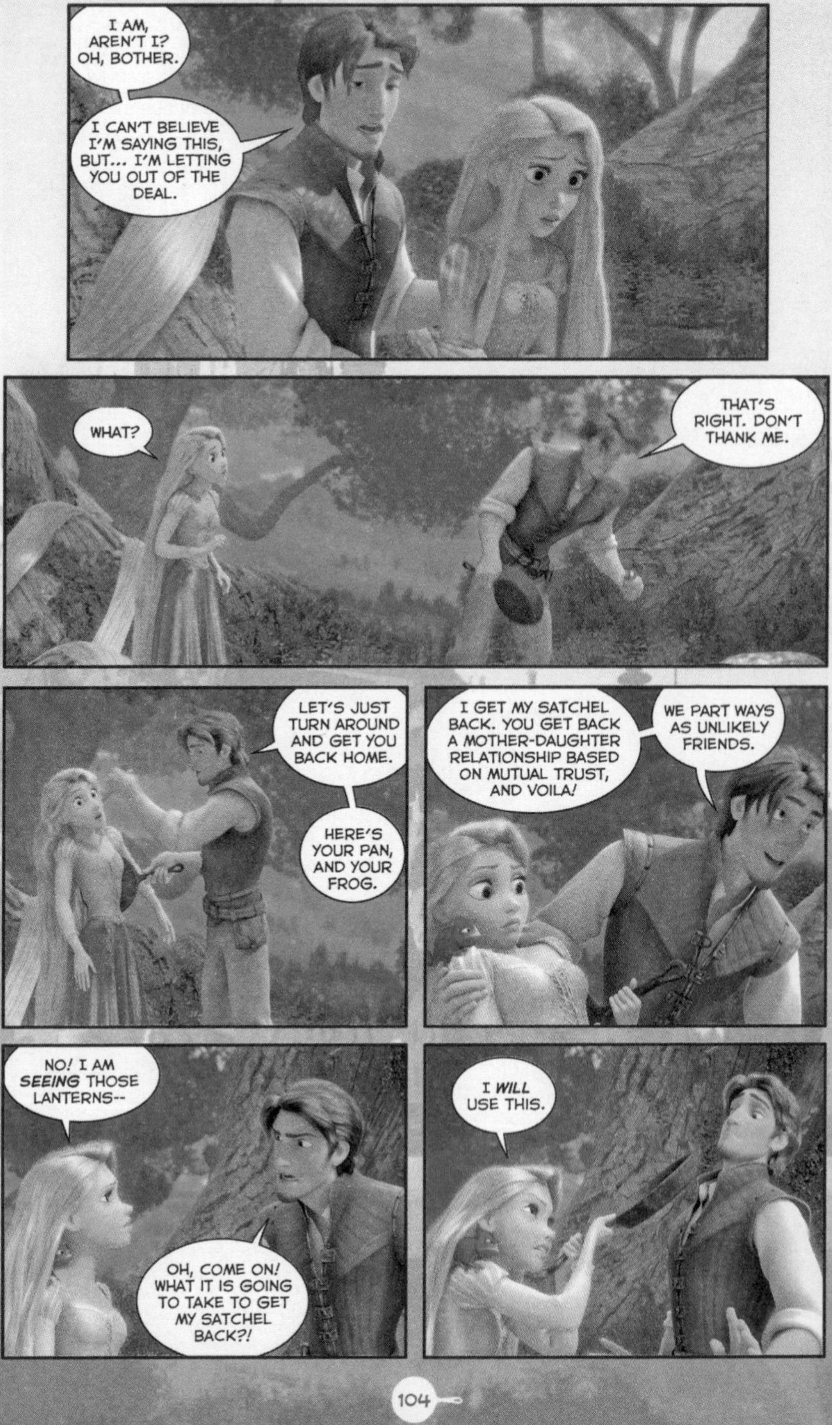
I AM, AREN'T I? OH, BOTHER.
I CAN'T BELIEVE I'M SAYING THIS, BUT... I'M LETTING YOU OUT OF THE DEAL.
WHAT?
THAT'S RIGHT. DON'T THANK ME.
LET'S JUST TURN AROUND AND GET YOU BACK HOME.
HERE'S YOUR PAN, AND YOUR FROG.
I GET MY SATCHEL BACK. YOU GET BACK A MOTHER-DAUGHTER RELATIONSHIP BASED ON MUTUAL TRUST, AND VOILA!
WE PART WAYS AS UNLIKELY FRIENDS.
NO! I AM *SEEING* THOSE LANTERNS--
OH, COME ON! WHAT IT IS GOING TO TAKE TO GET MY SATCHEL BACK?!
I *WILL* USE THIS.

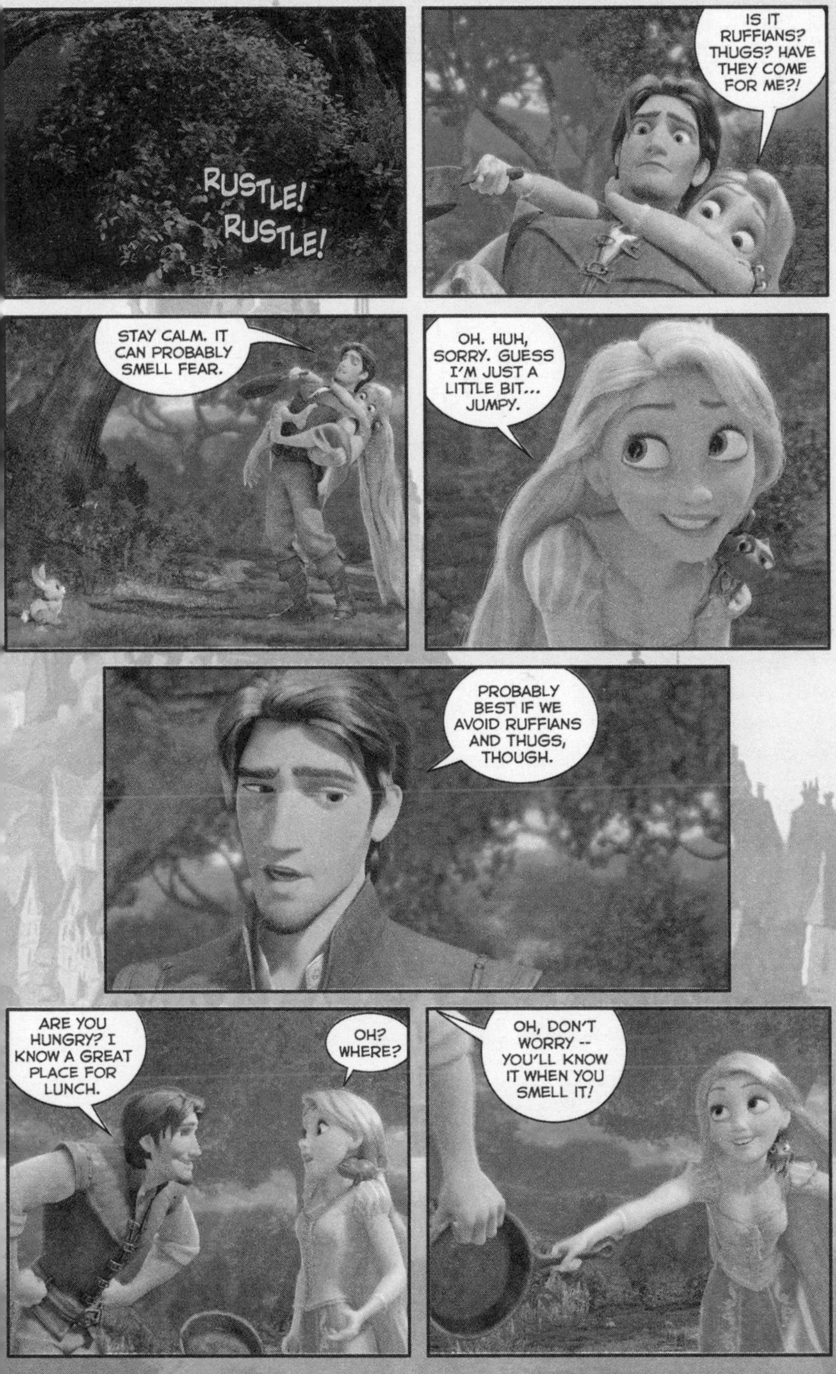

RUSTLE! RUSTLE!
IS IT RUFFIANS? THUGS? HAVE THEY COME FOR ME?!
STAY CALM. IT CAN PROBABLY SMELL FEAR.
OH. HUH, SORRY. GUESS I'M JUST A LITTLE BIT... JUMPY.
PROBABLY BEST IF WE AVOID RUFFIANS AND THUGS, THOUGH.
ARE YOU HUNGRY? I KNOW A GREAT PLACE FOR LUNCH.
OH? WHERE?
OH, DON'T WORRY -- YOU'LL KNOW IT WHEN YOU SMELL IT!

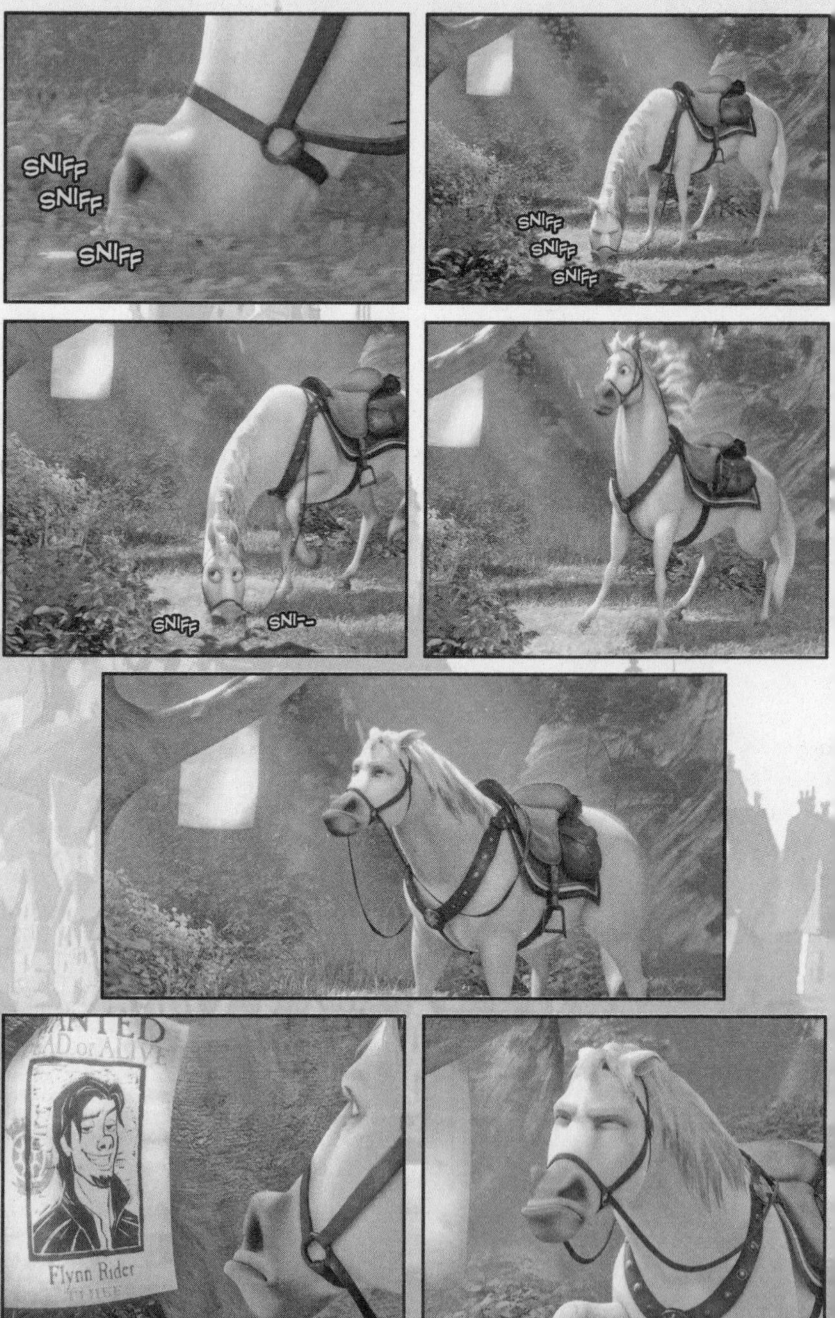
SNIFF
SNIFF
SNIFF
SNIFF
SNIFF
SNIFF
SNIFF
SNI-
Flynn Rider

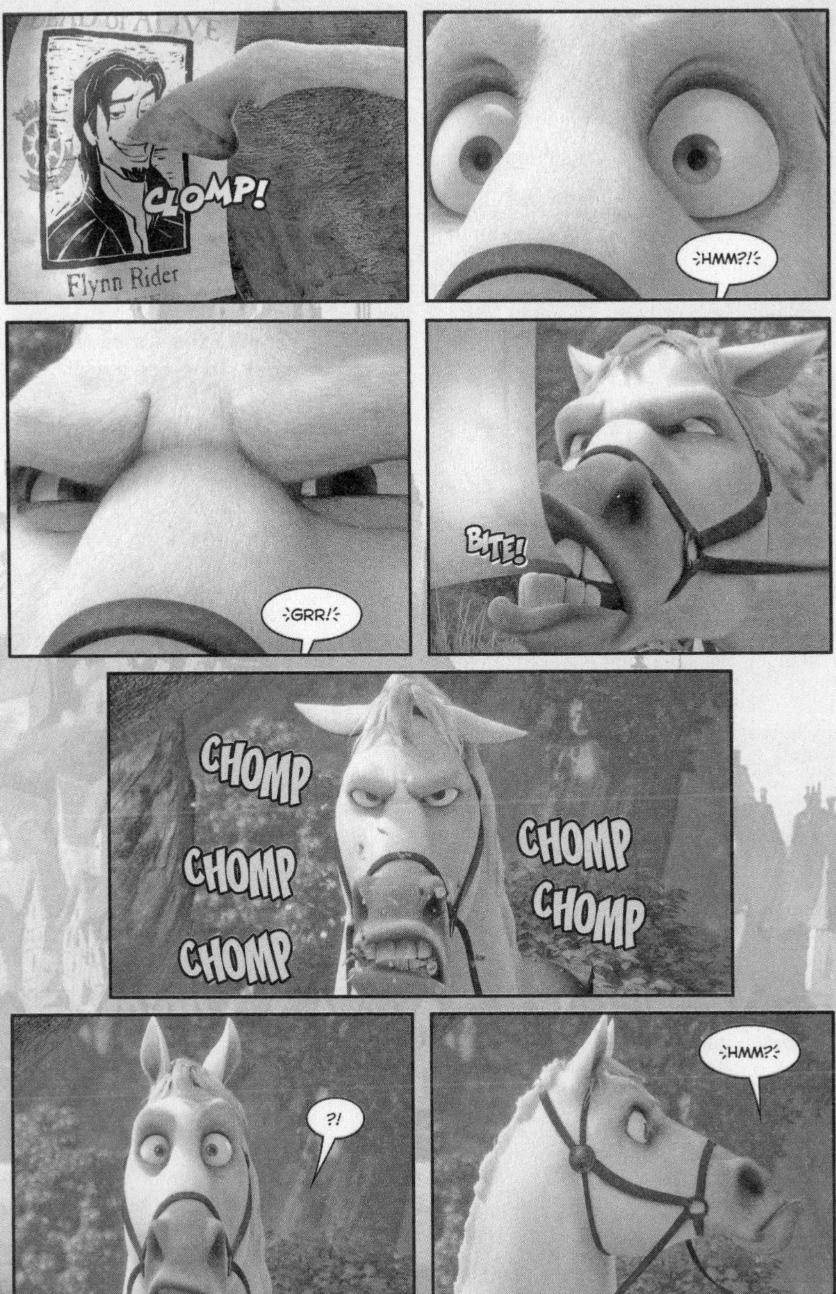
Flynn Rider
CLOMP!
HMM?!
GRR!
BITE!
CHOMP
CHOMP
CHOMP
CHOMP
CHOMP
?!
HMM?

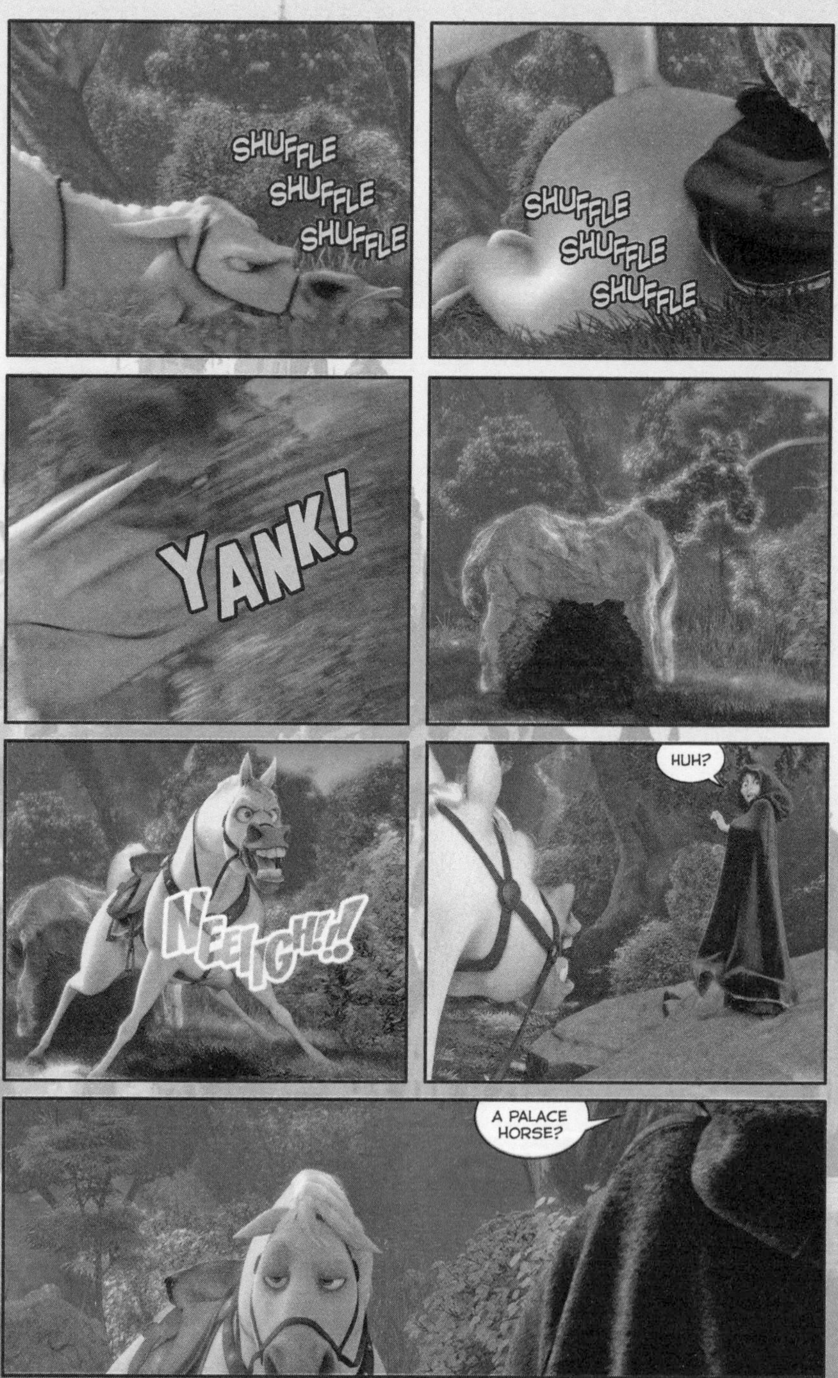
SHUFFLE
SHUFFLE
SHUFFLE
SHUFFLE
SHUFFLE
SHUFFLE
YANK!
NEEIGH!!!
HUH?
A PALACE HORSE?

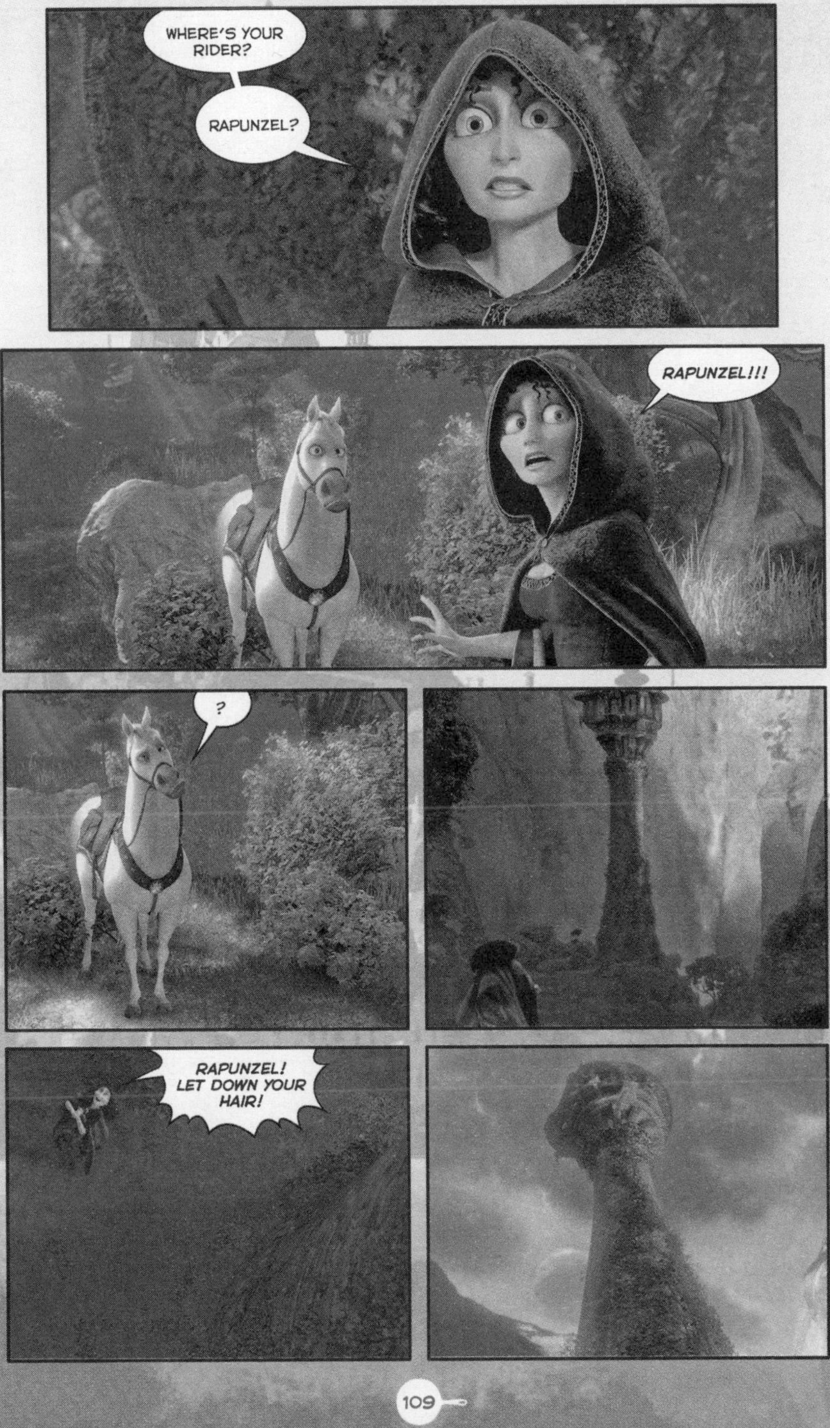
WHERE'S YOUR RIDER?
RAPUNZEL?
RAPUNZEL!!!
?
RAPUNZEL! LET DOWN YOUR HAIR!

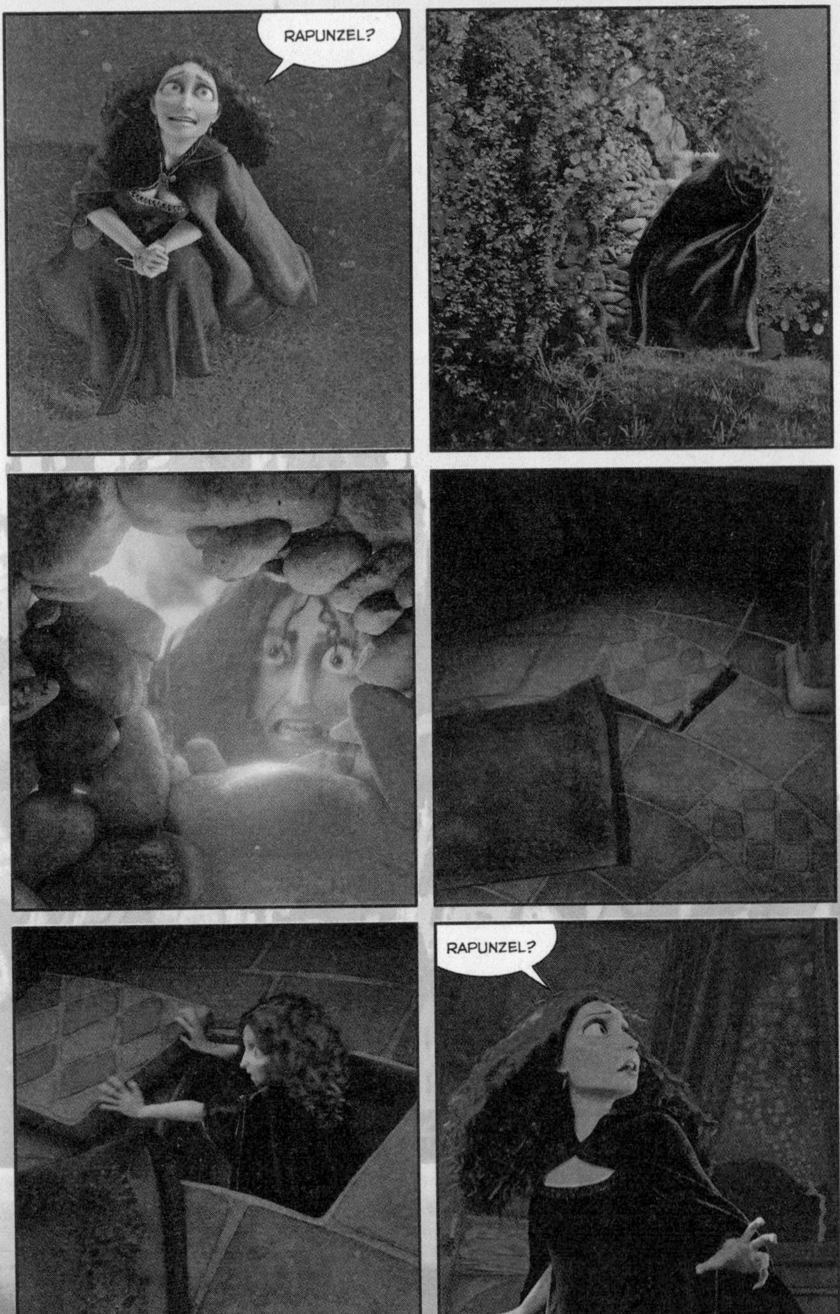
RAPUNZEL?
RAPUNZEL?

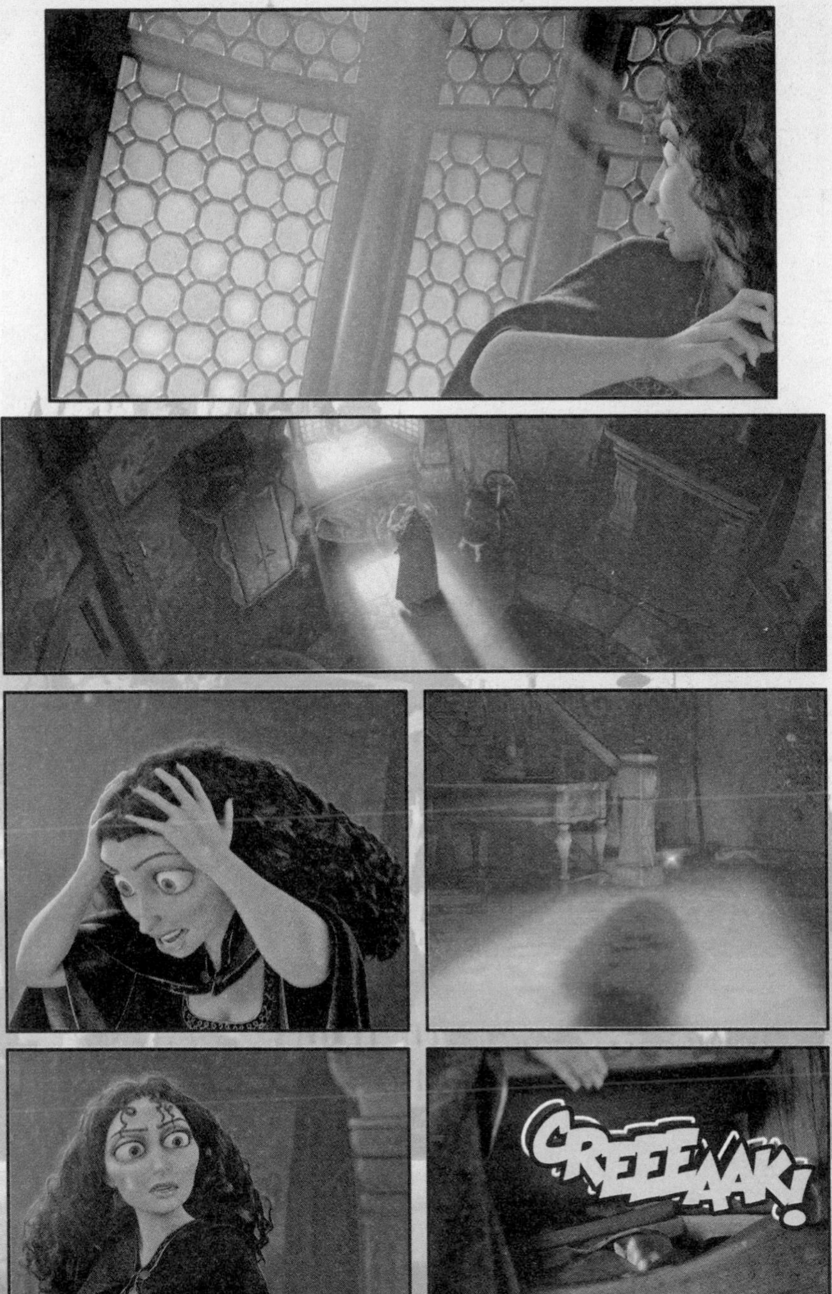
CREEEAAK!

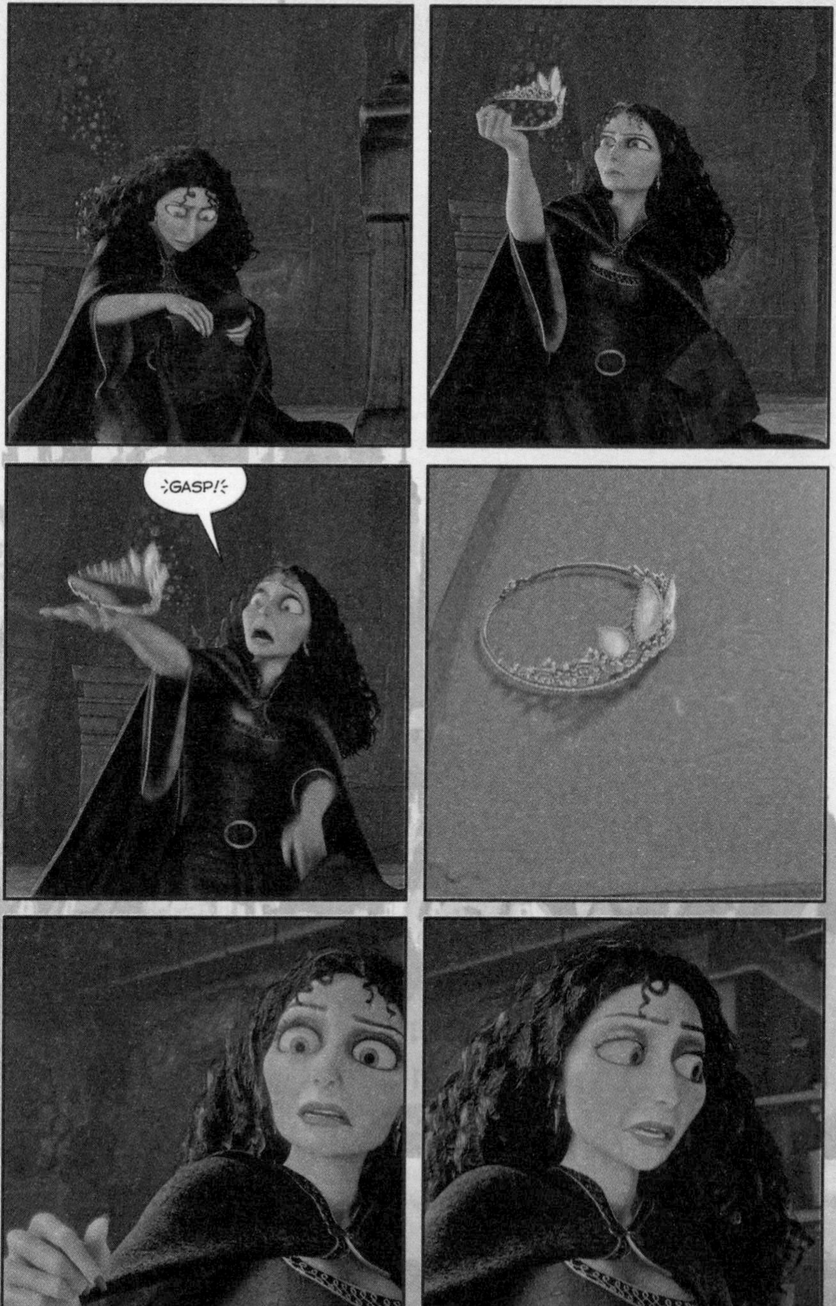
GASP!

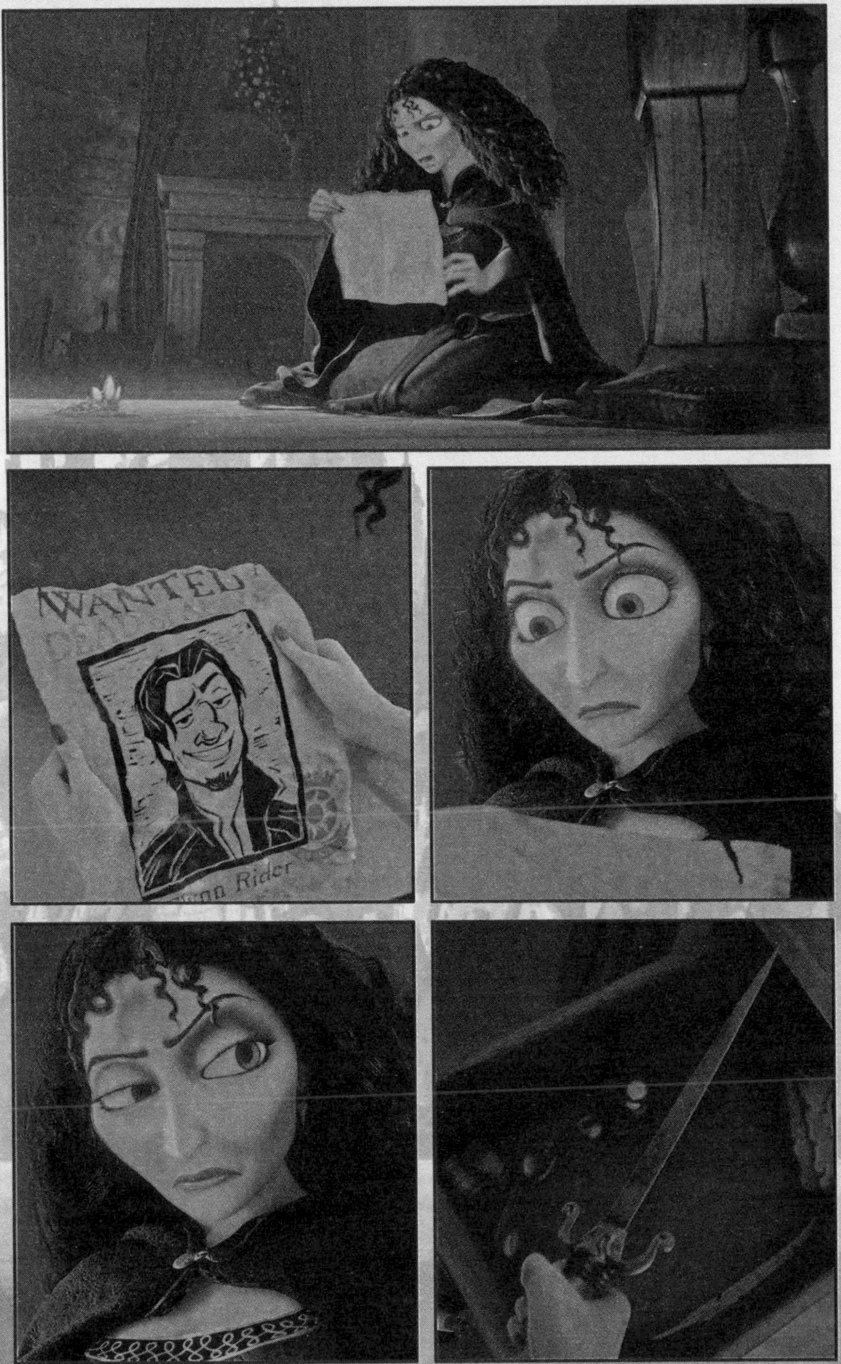
WANTED
Rider

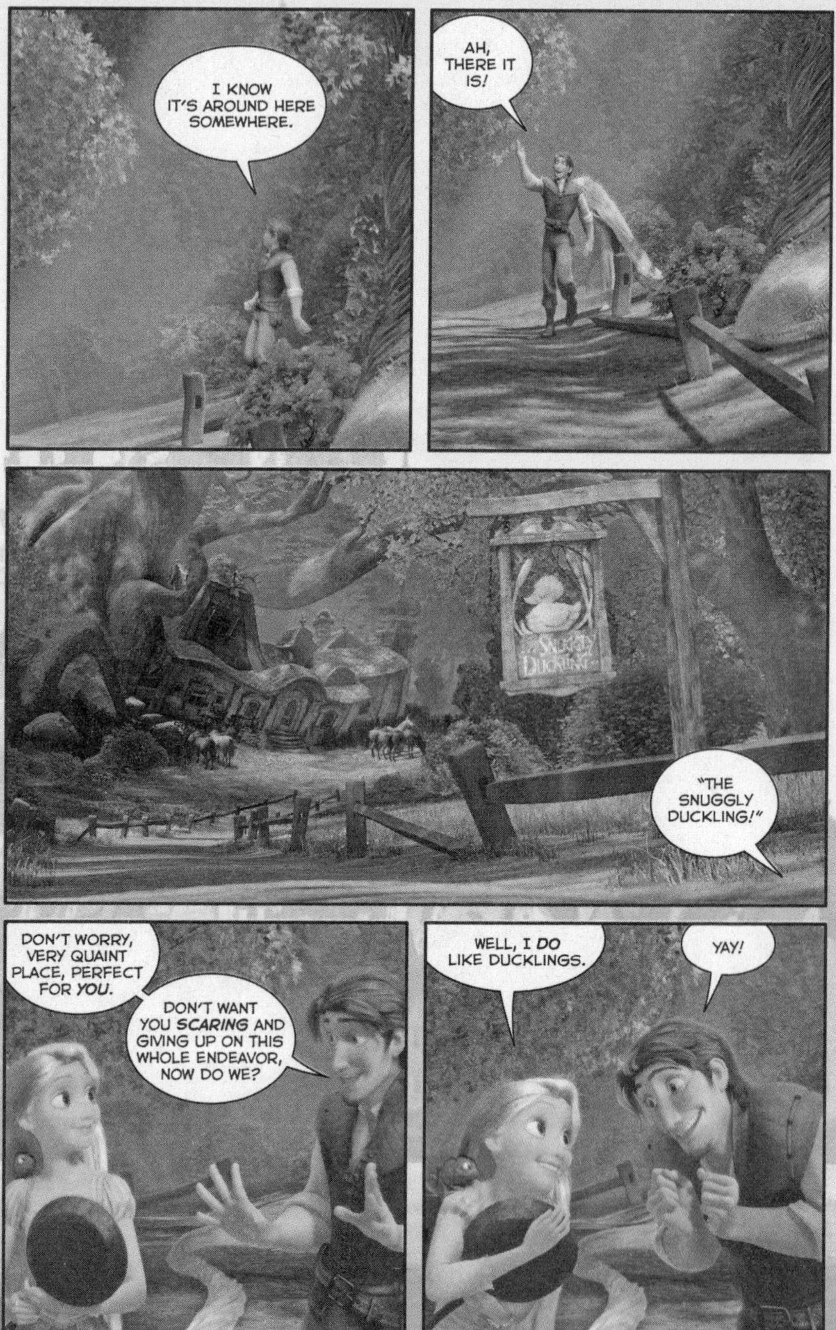
I KNOW IT'S AROUND HERE SOMEWHERE.
AH, THERE IT IS!
"THE SNUGGLY DUCKLING!"
DON'T WORRY, VERY QUAINT PLACE, PERFECT FOR *YOU*.
DON'T WANT YOU *SCARING* AND GIVING UP ON THIS WHOLE ENDEAVOR, NOW DO WE?
WELL, I *DO* LIKE DUCKLINGS.
YAY!

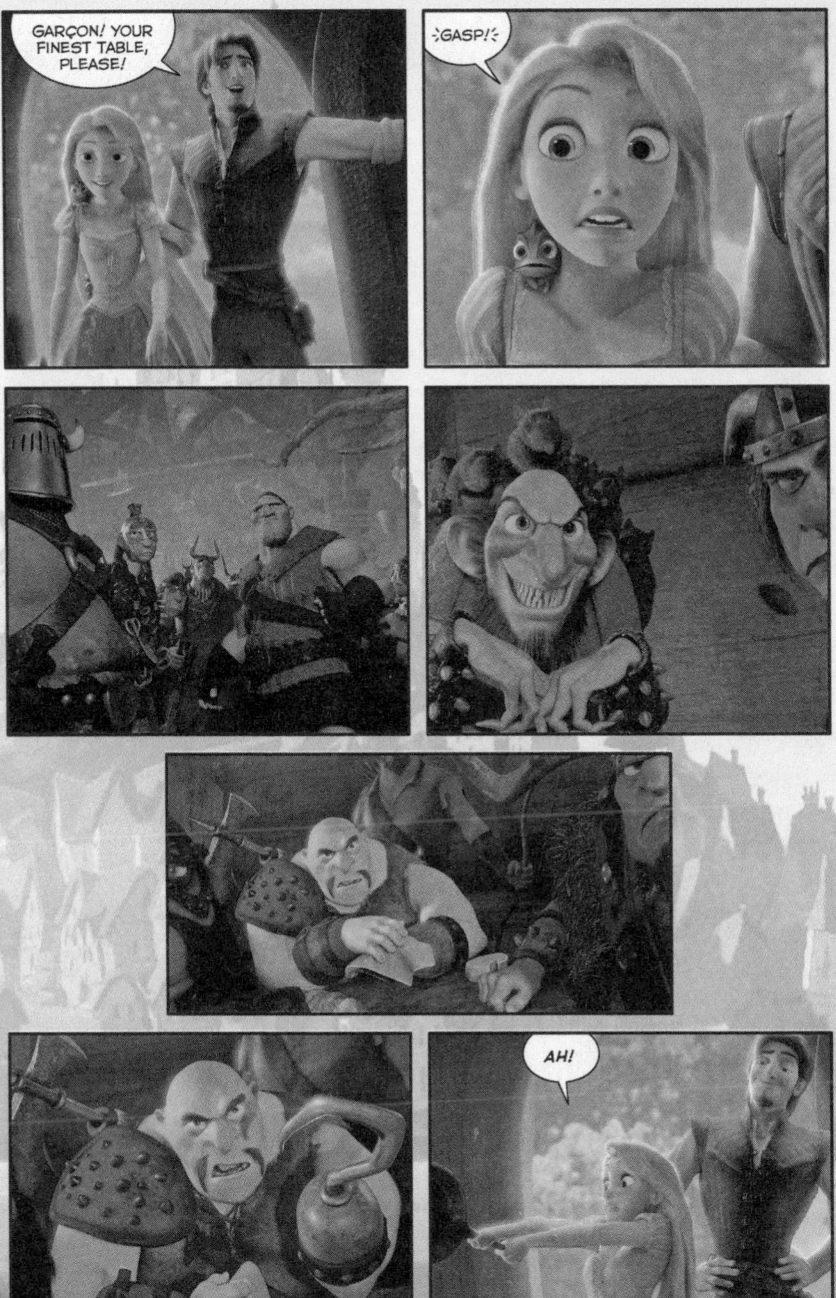
GARÇON! YOUR FINEST TABLE, PLEASE!
GASP!
AH!

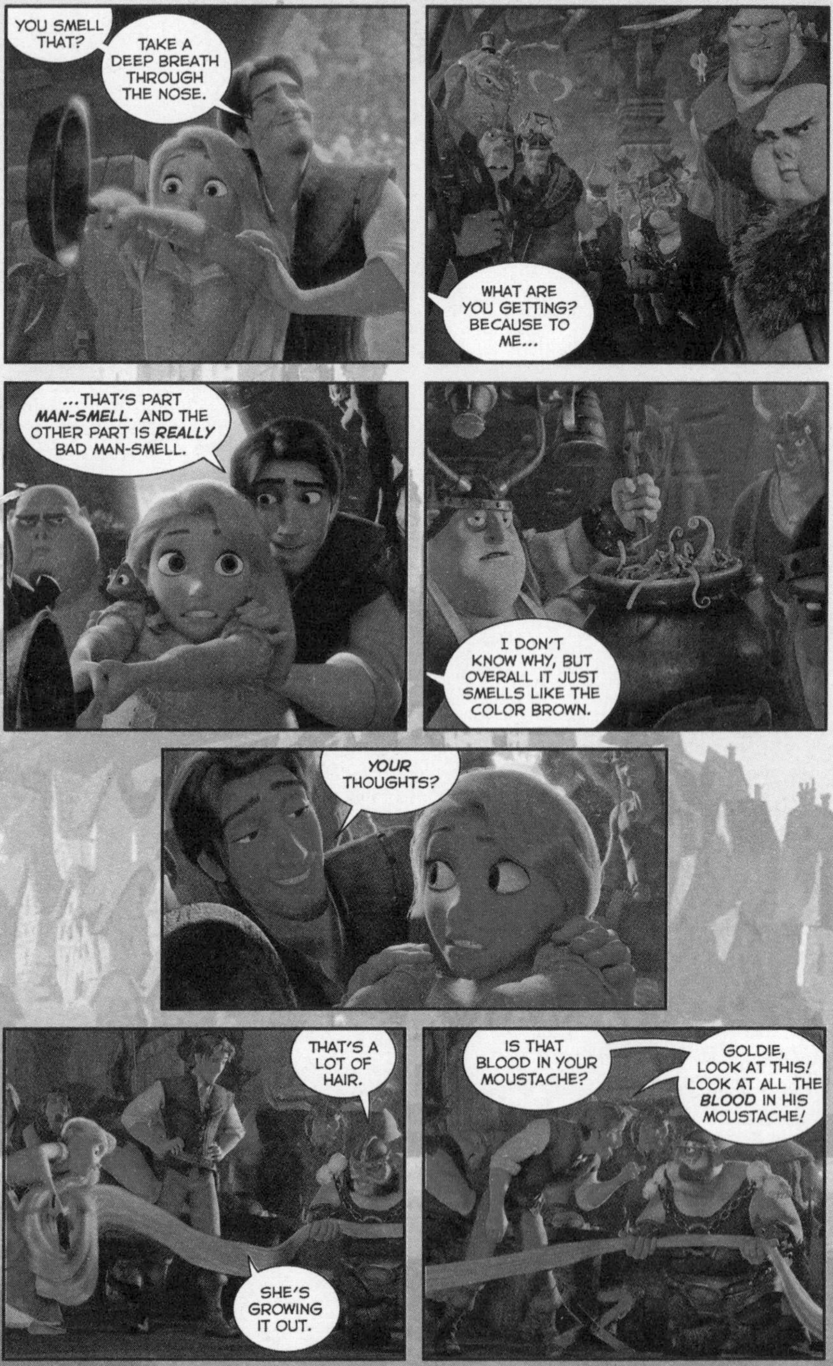
YOU SMELL THAT?
TAKE A DEEP BREATH THROUGH THE NOSE.
WHAT ARE YOU GETTING? BECAUSE TO ME...
...THAT'S PART MAN-SMELL. AND THE OTHER PART IS REALLY BAD MAN-SMELL.
I DON'T KNOW WHY, BUT OVERALL IT JUST SMELLS LIKE THE COLOR BROWN.
YOUR THOUGHTS?
THAT'S A LOT OF HAIR.
SHE'S GROWING IT OUT.
IS THAT BLOOD IN YOUR MOUSTACHE?
GOLDIE, LOOK AT THIS! LOOK AT ALL THE BLOOD IN HIS MOUSTACHE!

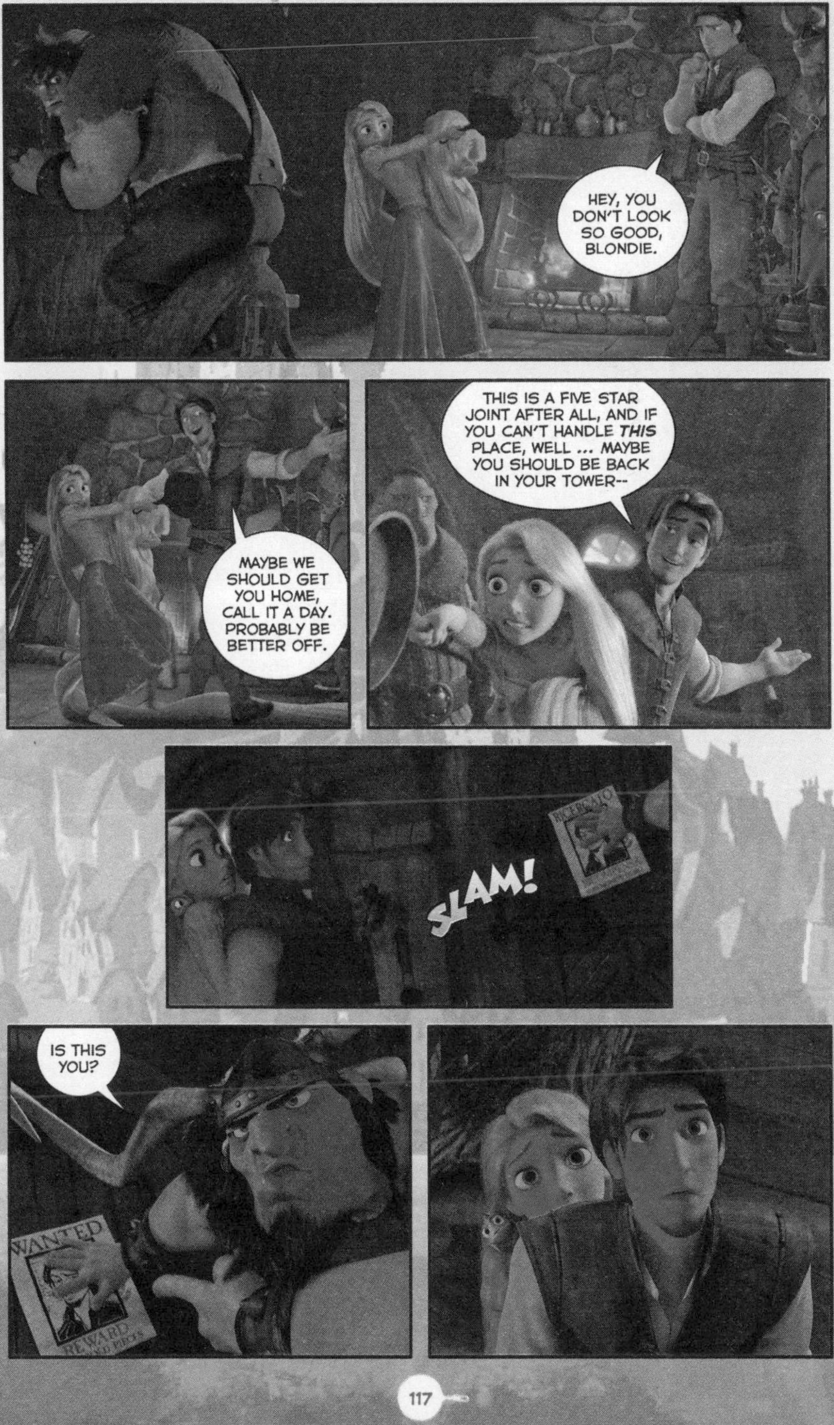
HEY, YOU DON'T LOOK SO GOOD, BLONDIE.
MAYBE WE SHOULD GET YOU HOME, CALL IT A DAY. PROBABLY BE BETTER OFF.
THIS IS A FIVE STAR JOINT AFTER ALL, AND IF YOU CAN'T HANDLE *THIS* PLACE, WELL ... MAYBE YOU SHOULD BE BACK IN YOUR TOWER--
SLAM!
IS THIS YOU?
WANTED
REWARD

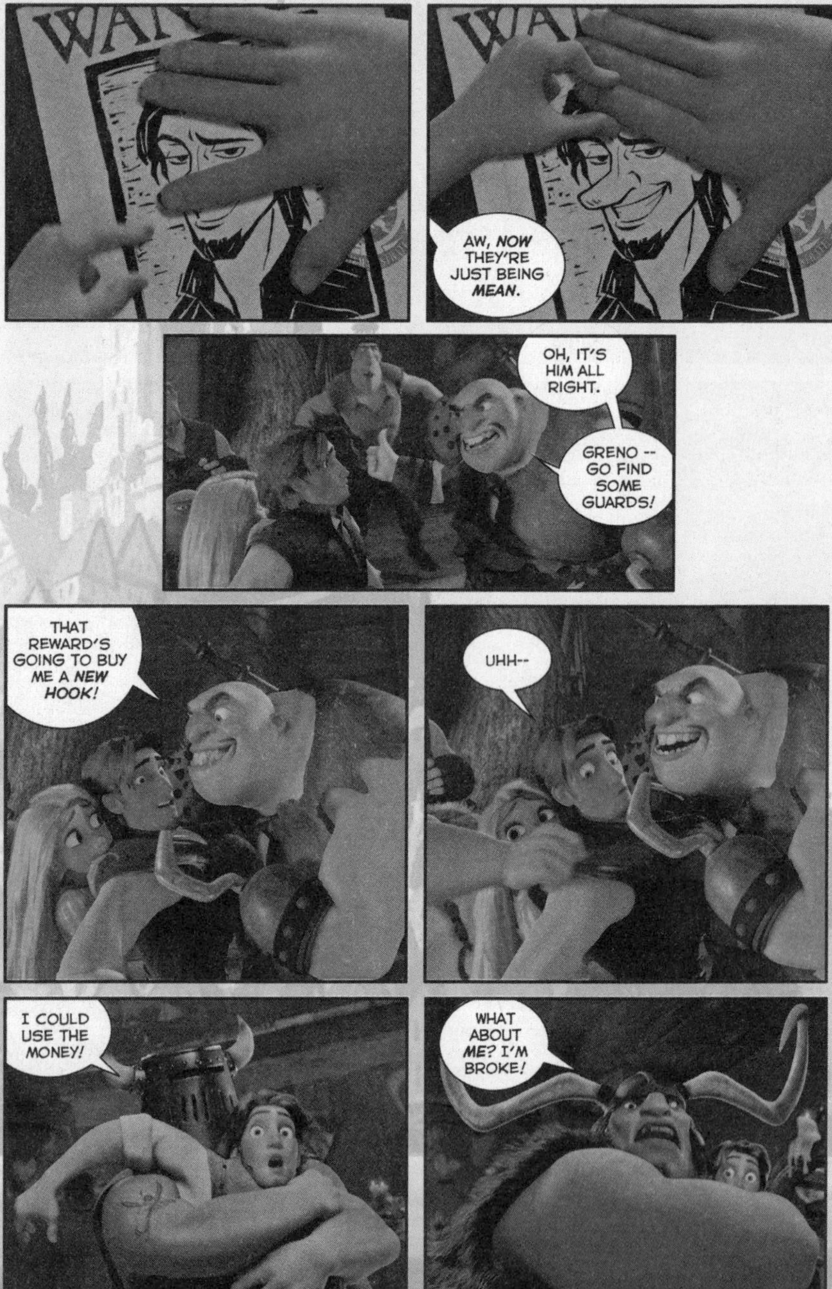
AW, NOW THEY'RE JUST BEING MEAN.
OH, IT'S HIM ALL RIGHT.
GRENO -- GO FIND SOME GUARDS!
THAT REWARD'S GOING TO BUY ME A NEW HOOK!
UHH--
I COULD USE THE MONEY!
WHAT ABOUT ME? I'M BROKE!

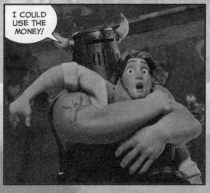

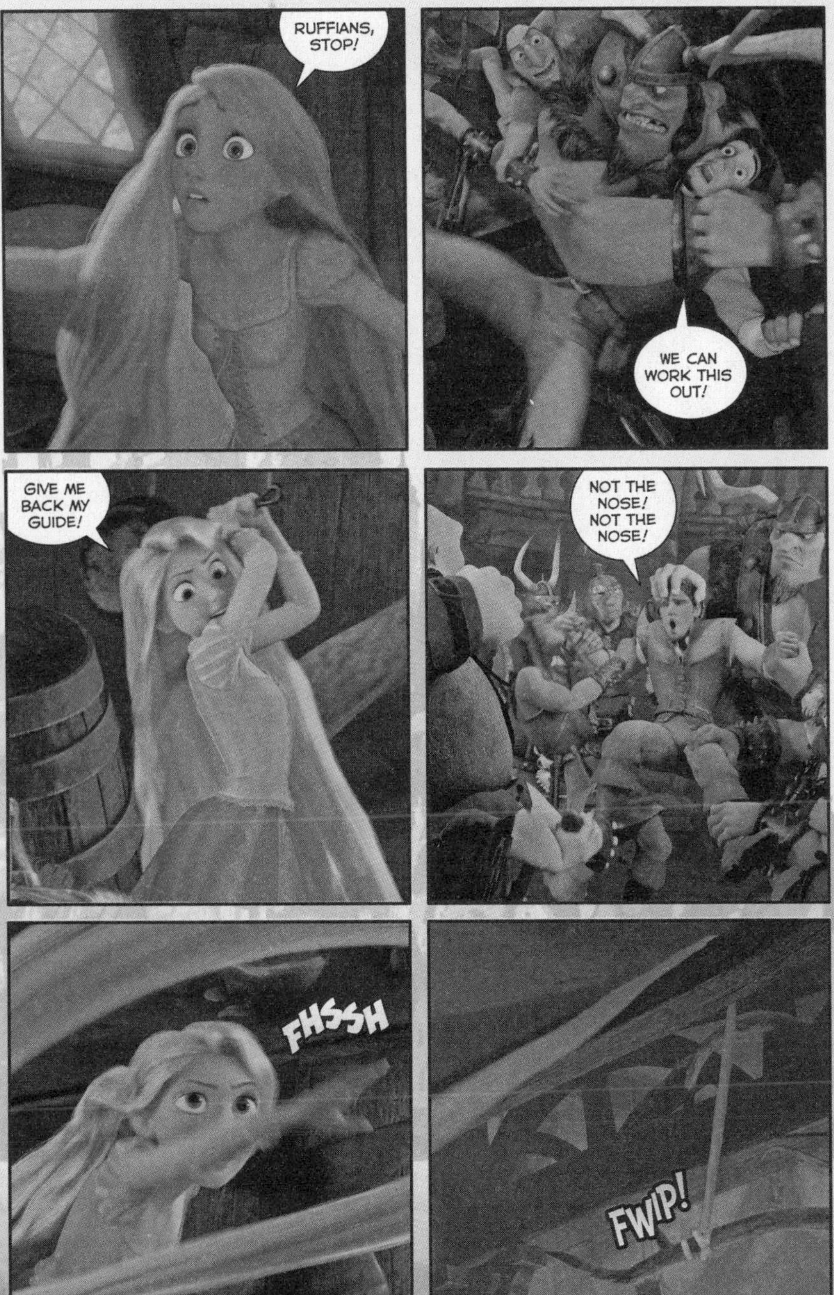
RUFFIANS, STOP!
WE CAN WORK THIS OUT!
GIVE ME BACK MY GUIDE!
NOT THE NOSE! NOT THE NOSE!
FHSSH
FWIP!

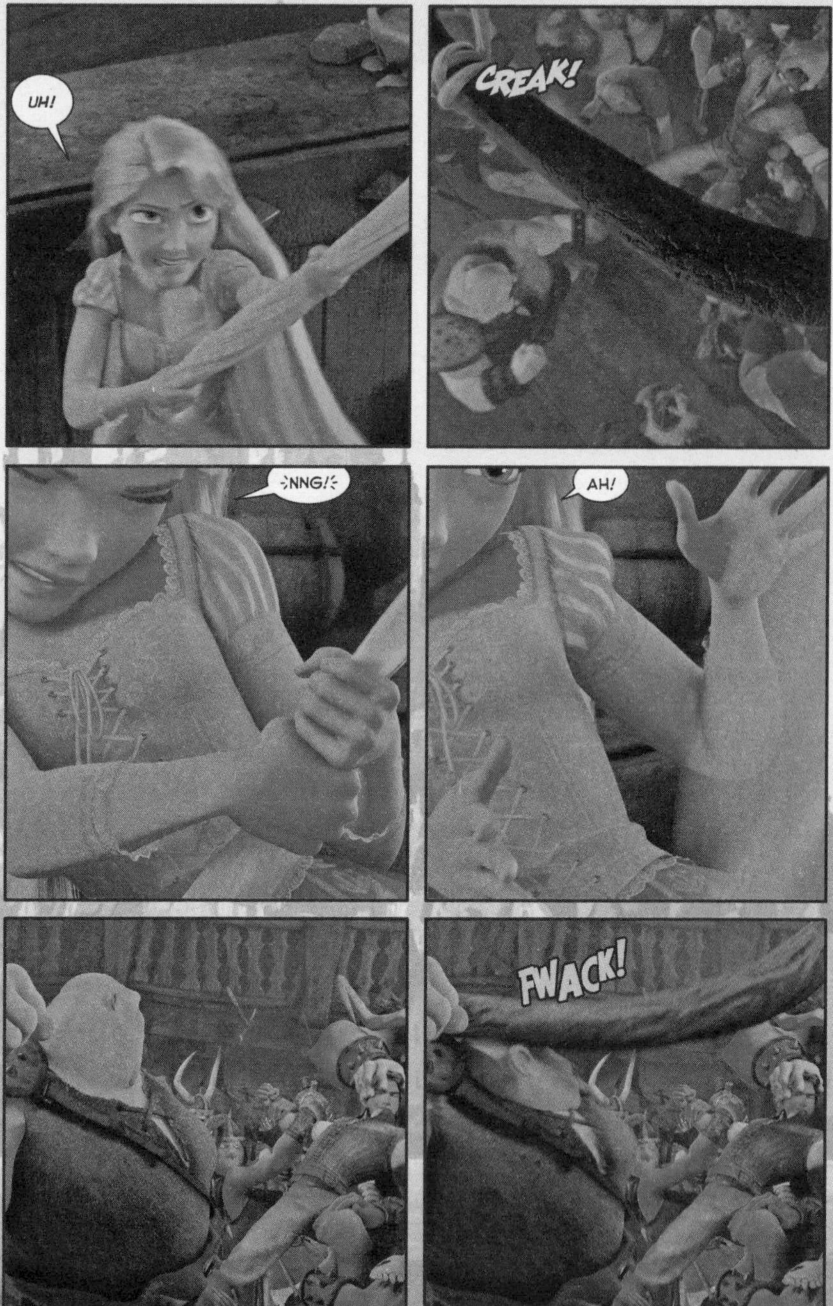
UH!
CREAK!
NNG!
AH!
FWACK!

PUT HIM DOWN!

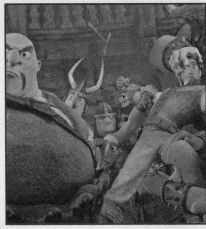

WHOA! OKAY!

I DON'T KNOW WHERE I AM, AND I NEED HIM TO TAKE ME TO SEE THE LANTERNS BECAUSE I'VE BEEN *DREAMING* ABOUT THEM MY *ENTIRE LIFE!*

FIND YOUR HUMANITY! HAVEN'T ANY OF *YOU* EVER HAD A *DREAM?*

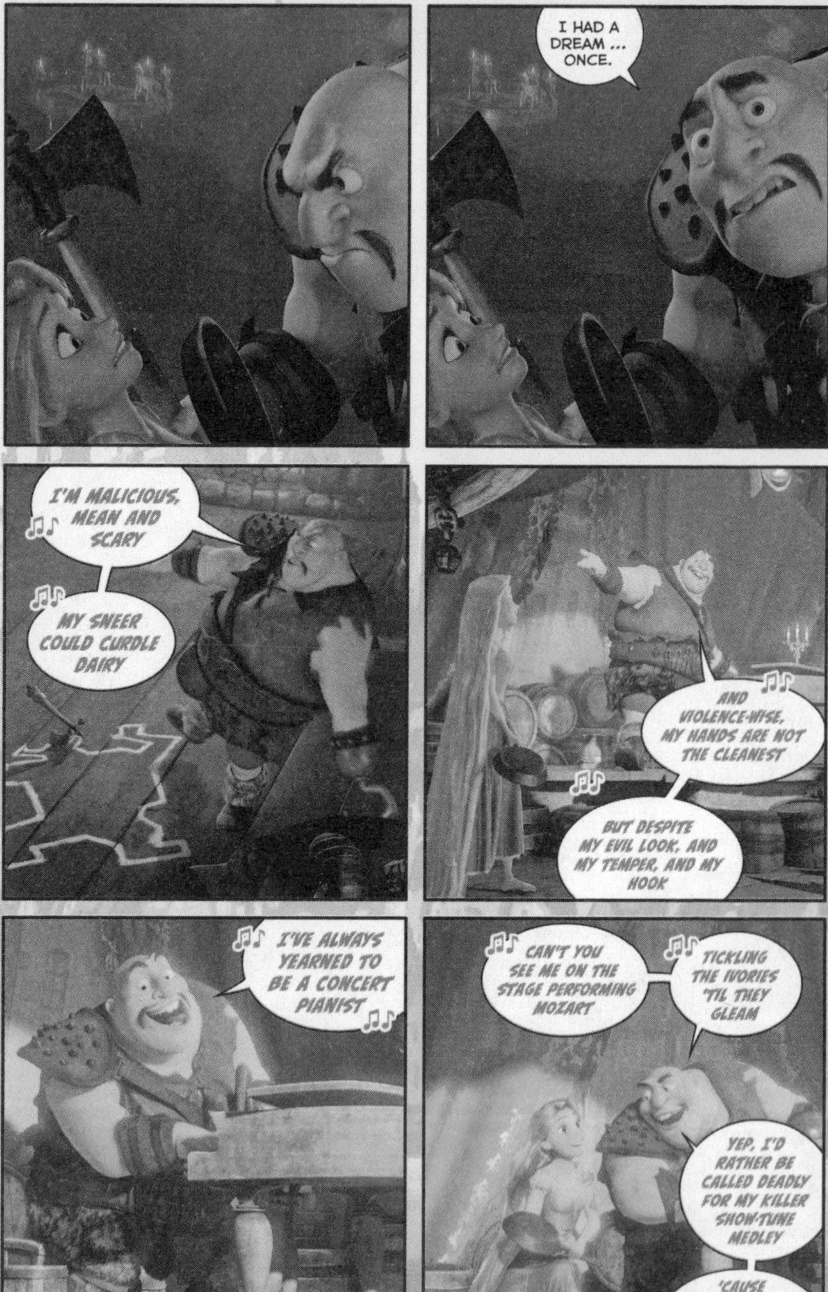
I HAD A DREAM ... ONCE.
I'M MALICIOUS, MEAN AND SCARY
MY SNEER COULD CURDLE DAIRY
AND VIOLENCE-WISE, MY HANDS ARE NOT THE CLEANEST
BUT DESPITE MY EVIL LOOK, AND MY TEMPER, AND MY HOOK
I'VE ALWAYS YEARNED TO BE A CONCERT PIANIST
CAN'T YOU SEE ME ON THE STAGE PERFORMING MOZART
TICKLING THE IVORIES 'TIL THEY GLEAM
YEP, I'D RATHER BE CALLED DEADLY FOR MY KILLER SHOW-TUNE MEDLEY
'CAUSE WAY DOWN DEEP INSIDE I'VE GOT A DREAM

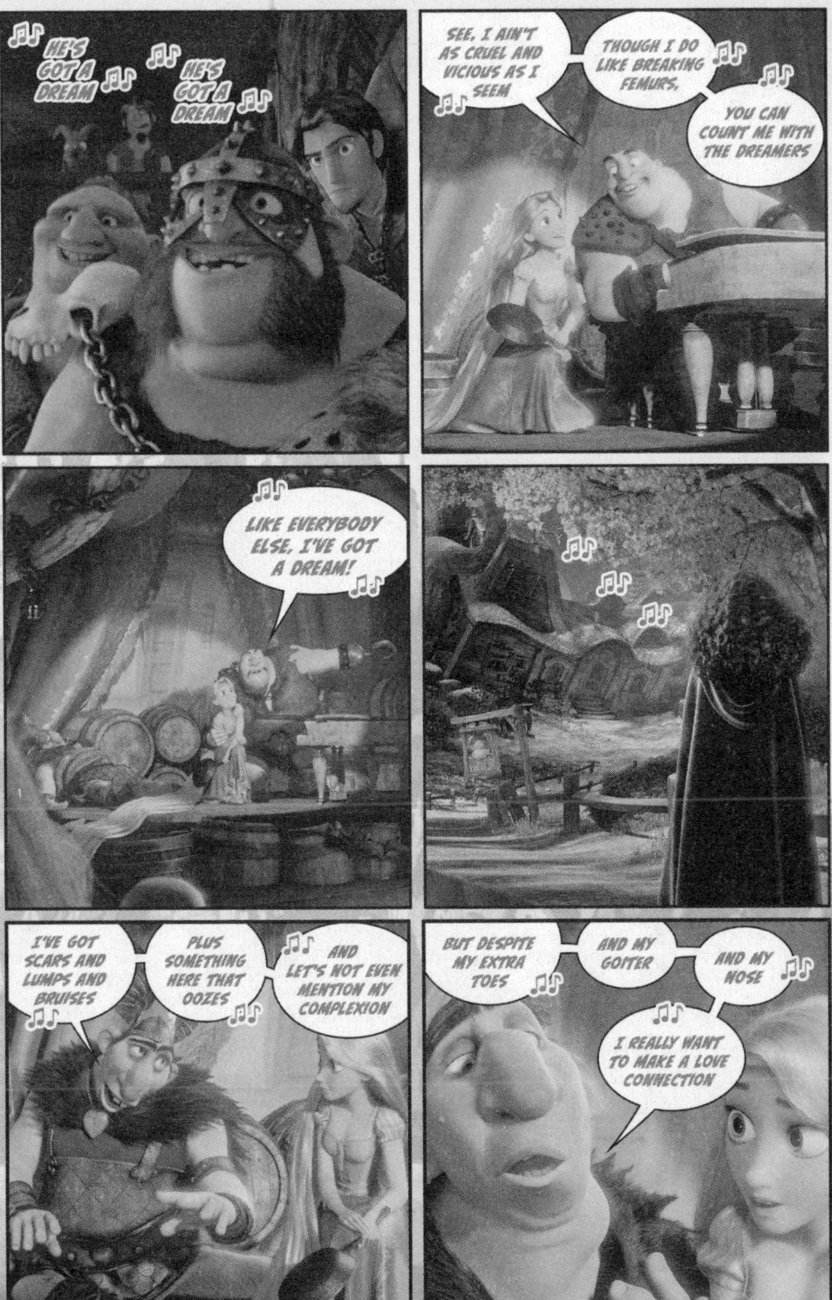
HE'S GOT A DREAM
HE'S GOT A DREAM
SEE, I AIN'T AS CRUEL AND VICIOUS AS I SEEM
THOUGH I DO LIKE BREAKING FEMURS,
YOU CAN COUNT ME WITH THE DREAMERS
LIKE EVERYBODY ELSE, I'VE GOT A DREAM!
I'VE GOT SCARS AND LUMPS AND BRUISES
PLUS SOMETHING HERE THAT OOZES
AND LET'S NOT EVEN MENTION MY COMPLEXION
BUT DESPITE MY EXTRA TOES
AND MY GOITER
AND MY NOSE
I REALLY WANT TO MAKE A LOVE CONNECTION

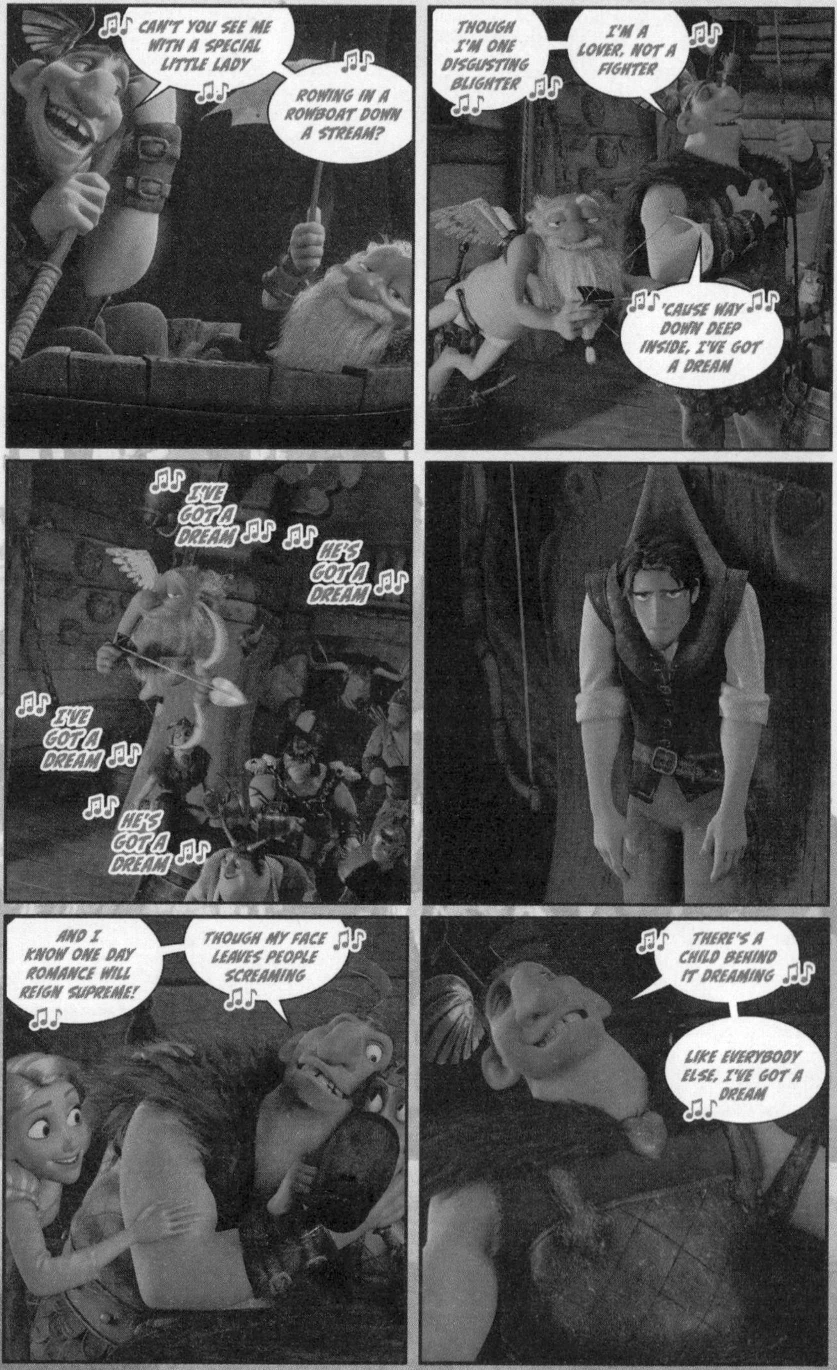
CAN'T YOU SEE ME WITH A SPECIAL LITTLE LADY
ROWING IN A ROWBOAT DOWN A STREAM?
THOUGH I'M ONE DISGUSTING BLIGHTER
I'M A LOVER, NOT A FIGHTER
'CAUSE WAY DOWN DEEP INSIDE, I'VE GOT A DREAM
I'VE GOT A DREAM
HE'S GOT A DREAM
I'VE GOT A DREAM
HE'S GOT A DREAM
AND I KNOW ONE DAY ROMANCE WILL REIGN SUPREME!
THOUGH MY FACE LEAVES PEOPLE SCREAMING
THERE'S A CHILD BEHIND IT DREAMING
LIKE EVERYBODY ELSE, I'VE GOT A DREAM

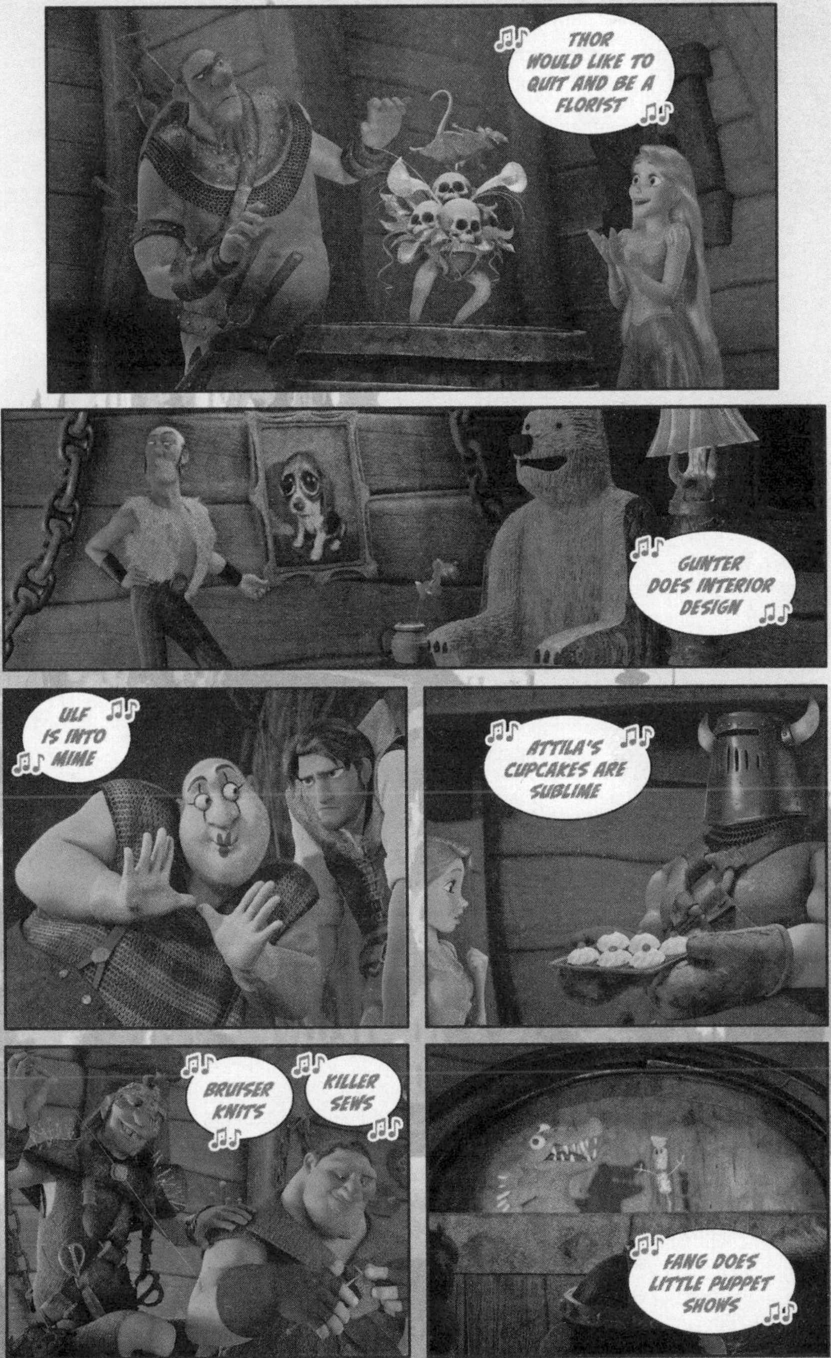
THOR WOULD LIKE TO QUIT AND BE A FLORIST
GUNTER DOES INTERIOR DESIGN
ULF IS INTO MIME
ATTILA'S CUPCAKES ARE SUBLIME
BRUISER KNITS
KILLER SEWS
FANG DOES LITTLE PUPPET SHOWS

TING!

♪ AND VLADIMIR COLLECTS CERAMIC UNICORNS! ♪

WHAT ABOUT YOU?

I'M SORRY, ME?

WHAT'S YOUR DREAM?

NO, NO, NO. SORRY, BOYS -- I DON'T SING.

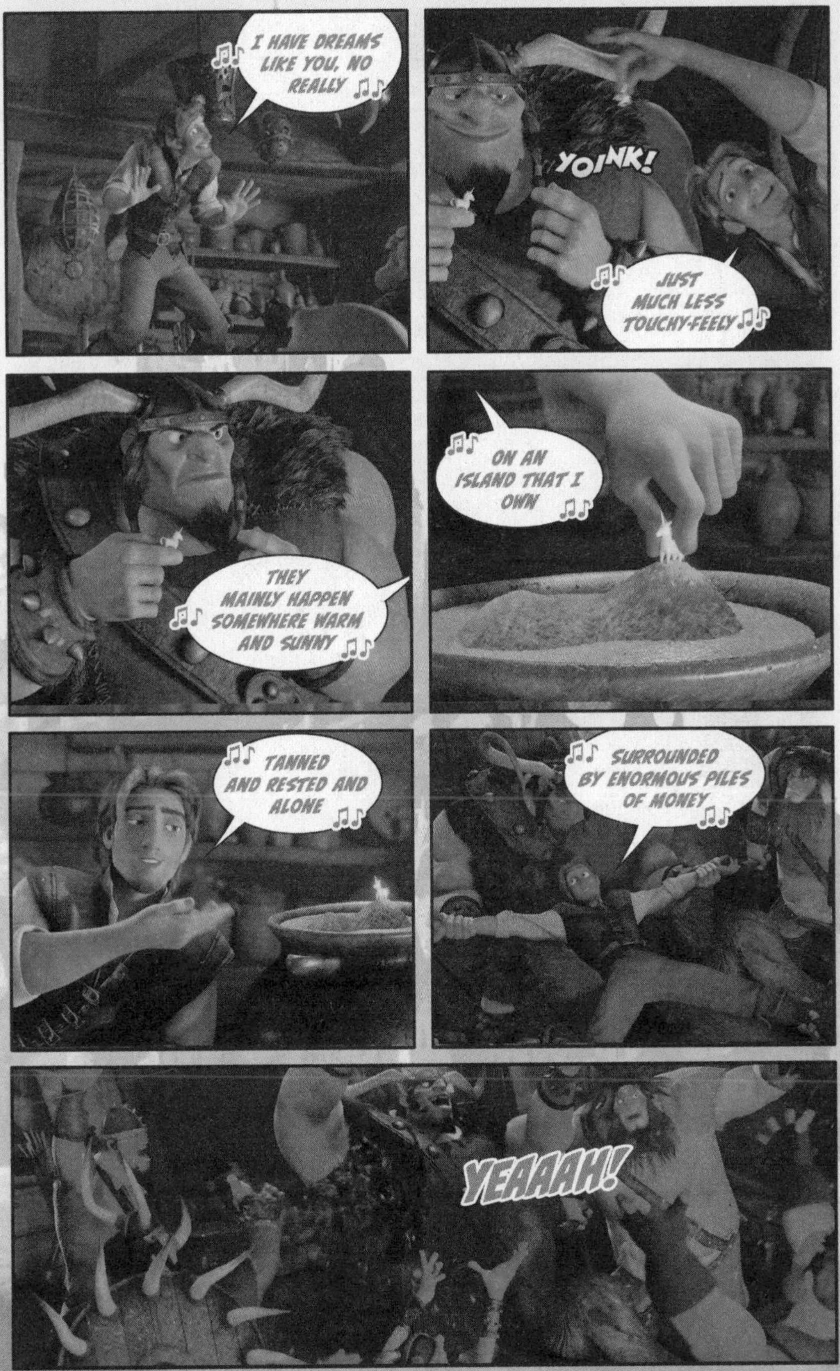
I HAVE DREAMS LIKE YOU, NO REALLY
YOINK!
JUST MUCH LESS TOUCHY-FEELY
THEY MAINLY HAPPEN SOMEWHERE WARM AND SUNNY
ON AN ISLAND THAT I OWN
TANNED AND RESTED AND ALONE
SURROUNDED BY ENORMOUS PILES OF MONEY
YEAAAH!

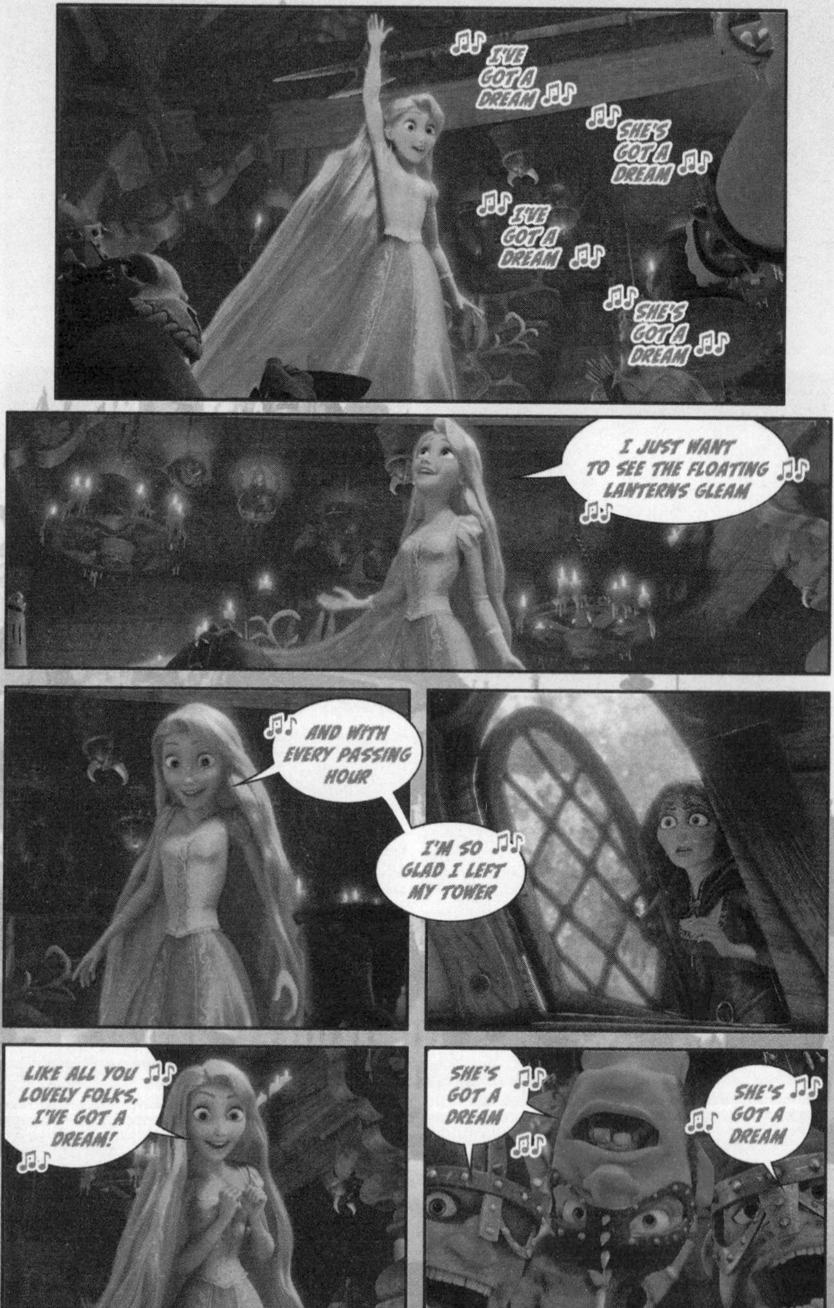
I'VE GOT A DREAM
SHE'S GOT A DREAM
I'VE GOT A DREAM
SHE'S GOT A DREAM
I JUST WANT TO SEE THE FLOATING LANTERNS GLEAM
AND WITH EVERY PASSING HOUR
I'M SO GLAD I LEFT MY TOWER
LIKE ALL YOU LOVELY FOLKS, I'VE GOT A DREAM!
SHE'S GOT A DREAM
SHE'S GOT A DREAM

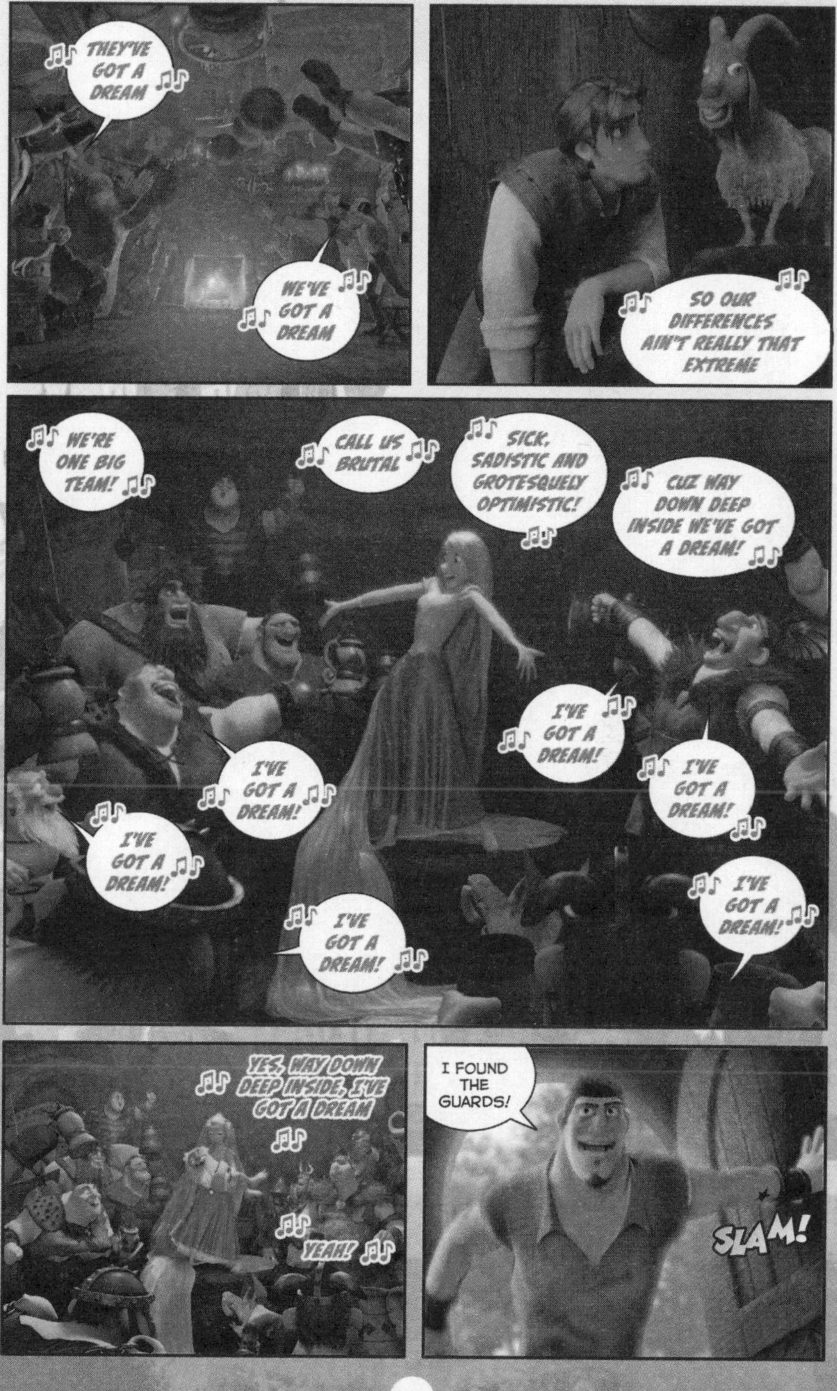
THEY'VE GOT A DREAM
WE'VE GOT A DREAM
SO OUR DIFFERENCES AIN'T REALLY THAT EXTREME
WE'RE ONE BIG TEAM!
CALL US BRUTAL
SICK, SADISTIC AND GROTESQUELY OPTIMISTIC!
CUZ WAY DOWN DEEP INSIDE WE'VE GOT A DREAM!
I'VE GOT A DREAM!
I'VE GOT A DREAM!
I'VE GOT A DREAM!
I'VE GOT A DREAM!
I'VE GOT A DREAM!
I'VE GOT A DREAM!
YES, WAY DOWN DEEP INSIDE, I'VE GOT A DREAM
YEAH!
I FOUND THE GUARDS!
SLAM!

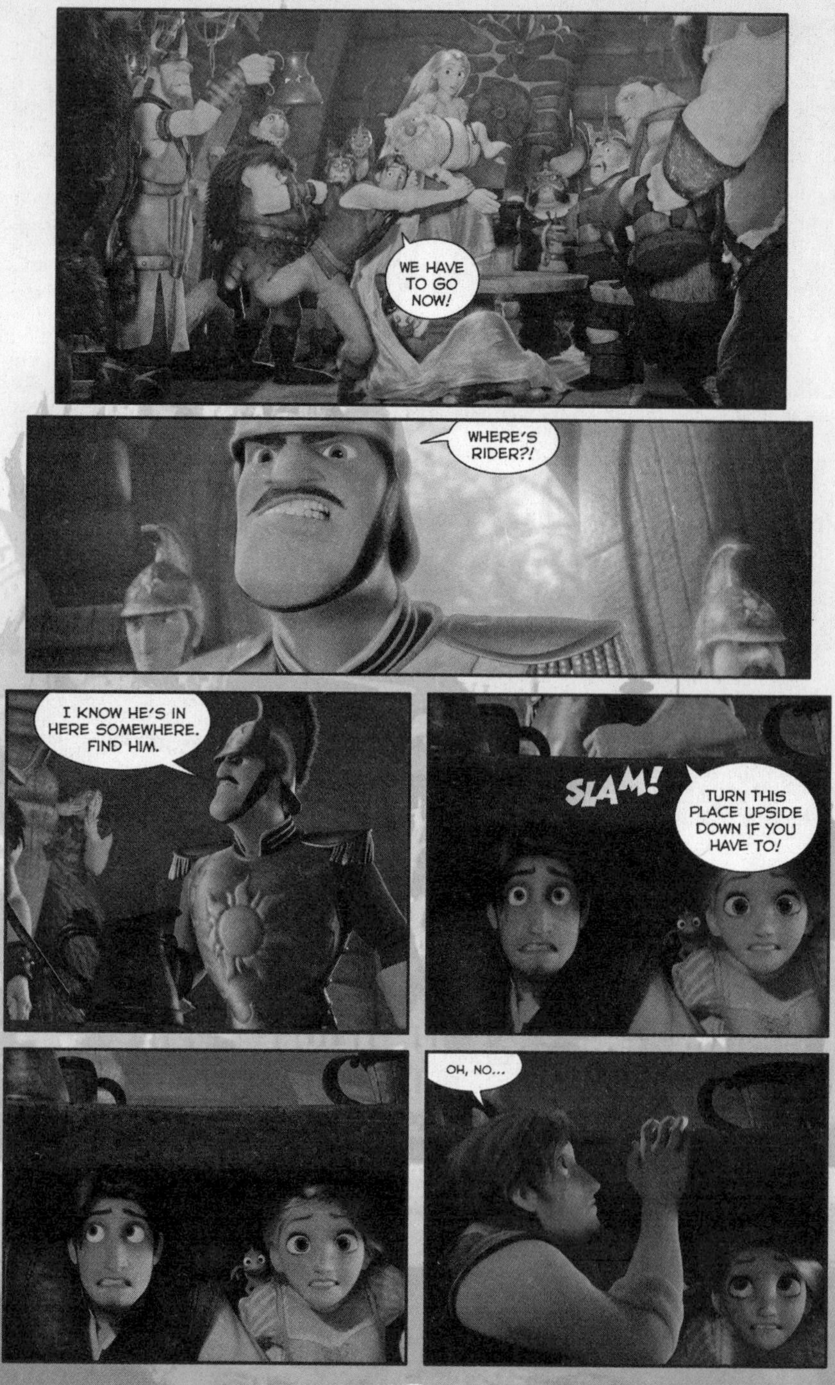
WE HAVE TO GO NOW!
WHERE'S RIDER?!
I KNOW HE'S IN HERE SOMEWHERE. FIND HIM.
SLAM!
TURN THIS PLACE UPSIDE DOWN IF YOU HAVE TO!
OH, NO...

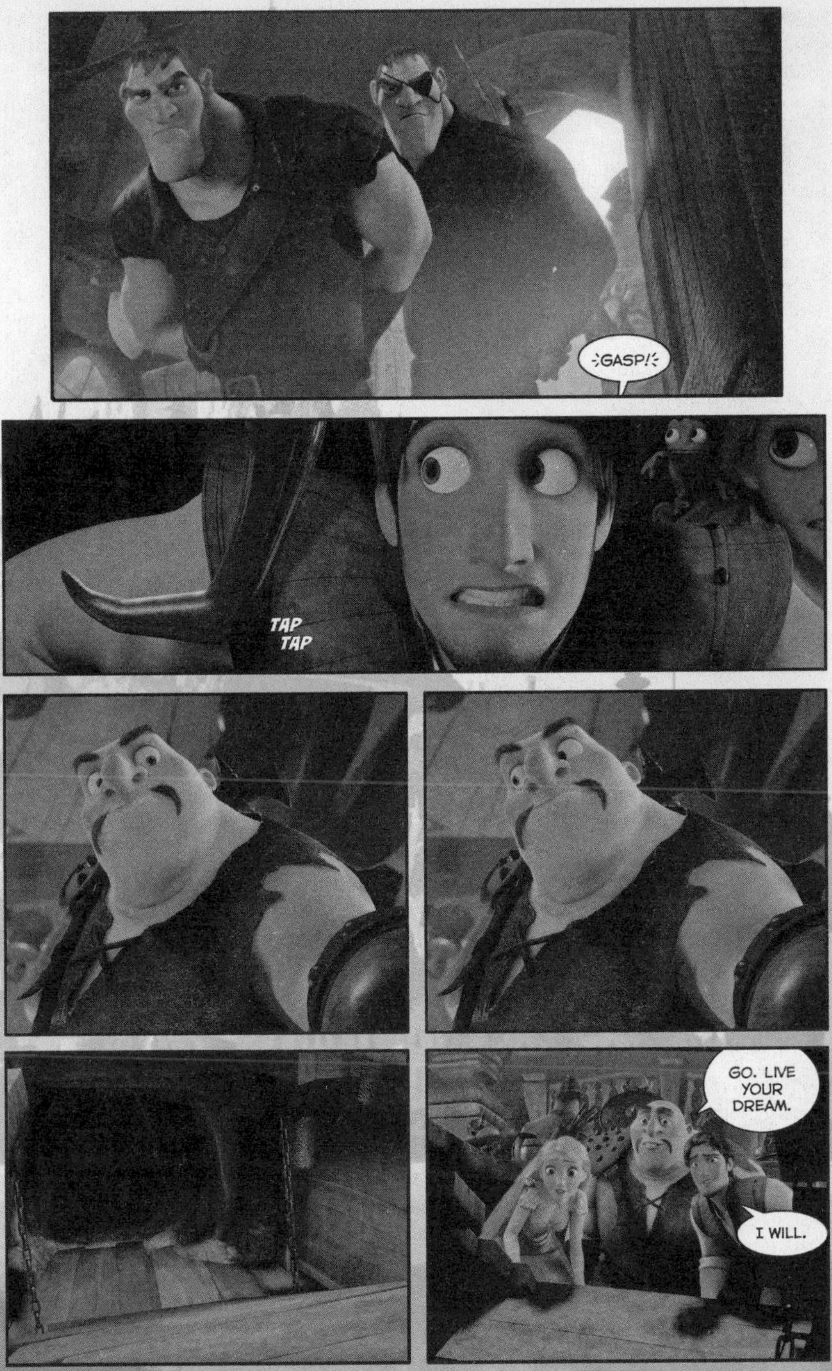
GASP!
TAP
TAP
GO. LIVE YOUR DREAM.
I WILL.

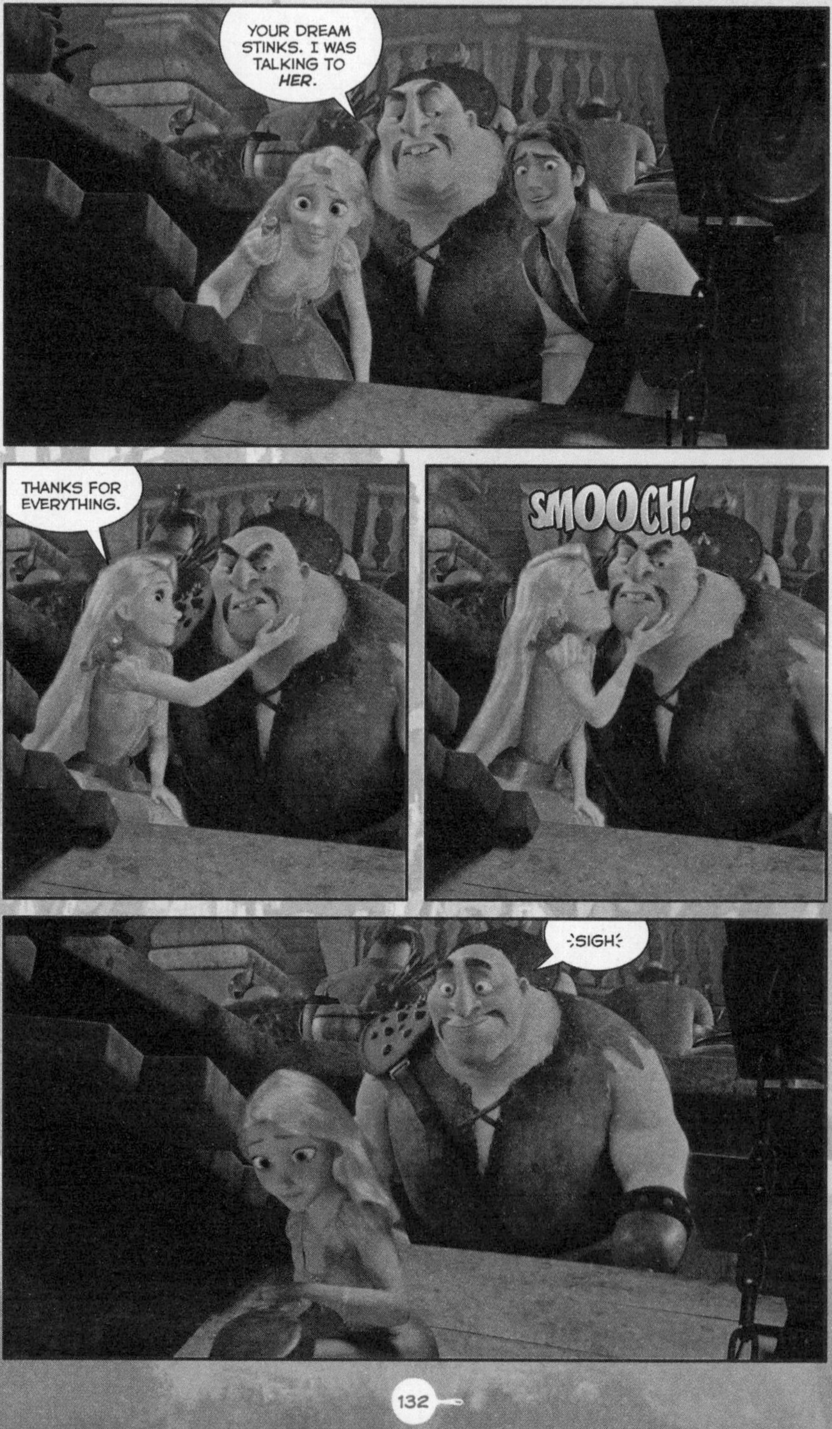
YOUR DREAM STINKS. I WAS TALKING TO *HER*.
THANKS FOR EVERYTHING.
SMOOCH!
SIGH

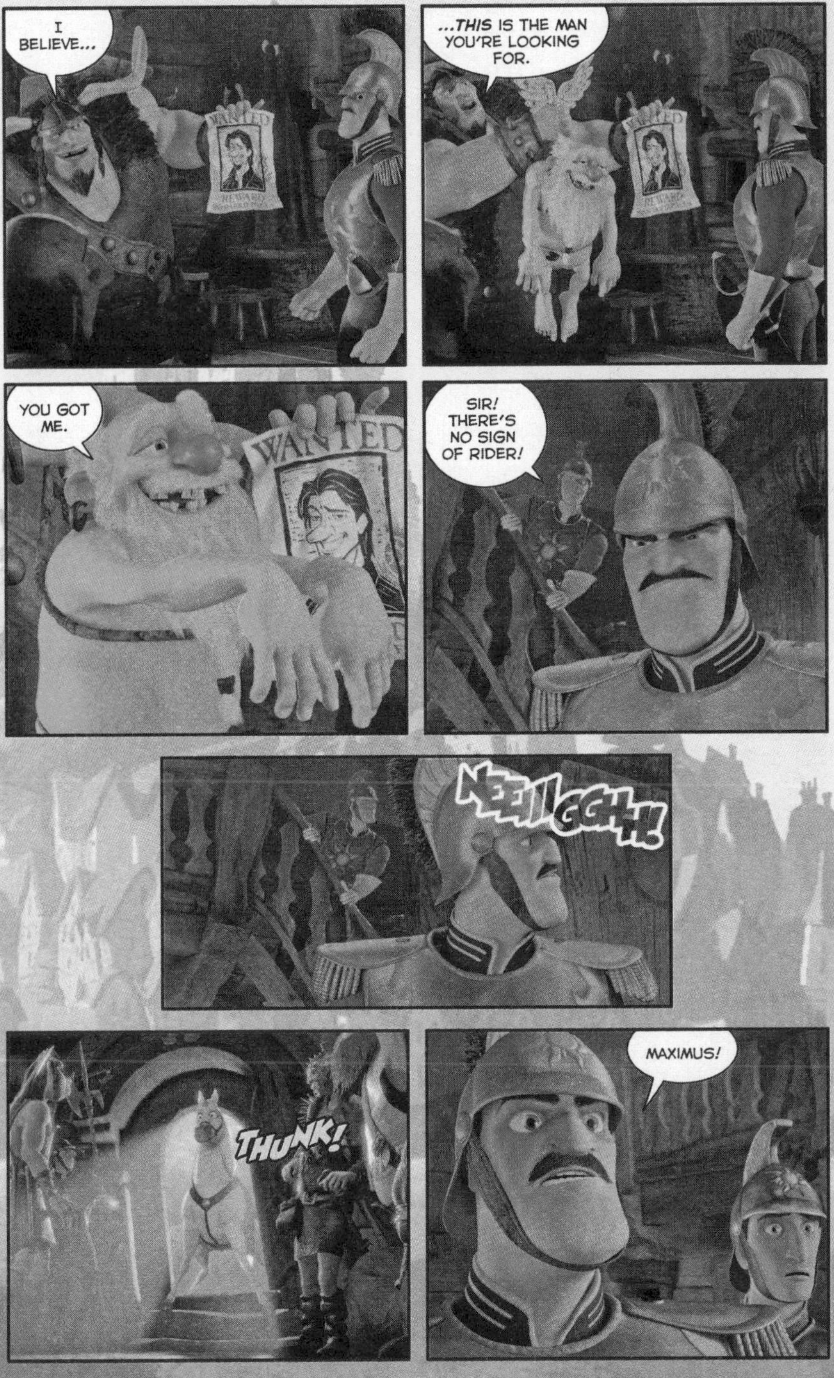
I BELIEVE...
...THIS IS THE MAN YOU'RE LOOKING FOR.
YOU GOT ME.
SIR! THERE'S NO SIGN OF RIDER!
NEEIIGGHH!
THUNK!
MAXIMUS!

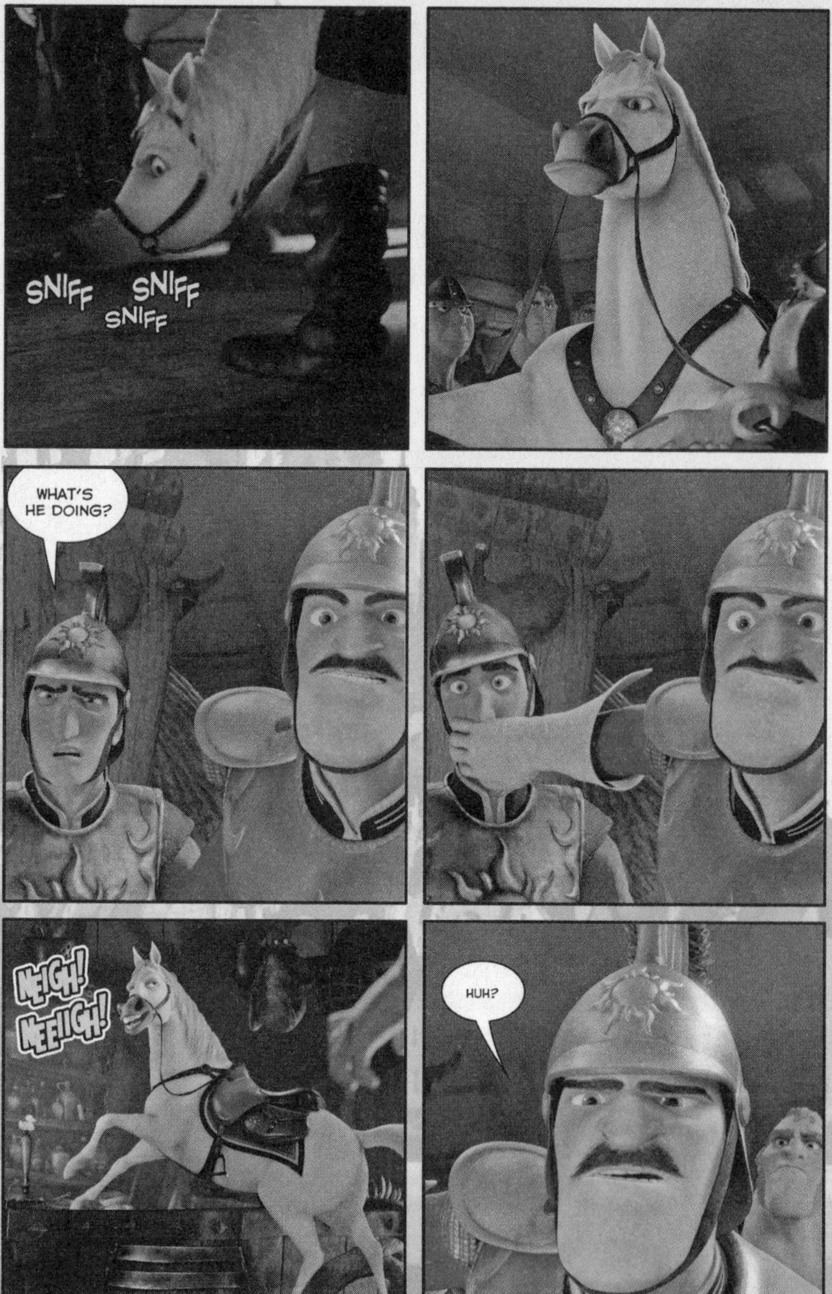
SNIFF SNIFF
SNIFF
WHAT'S HE DOING?
NEIGH! NEEIIGH!
HUH?

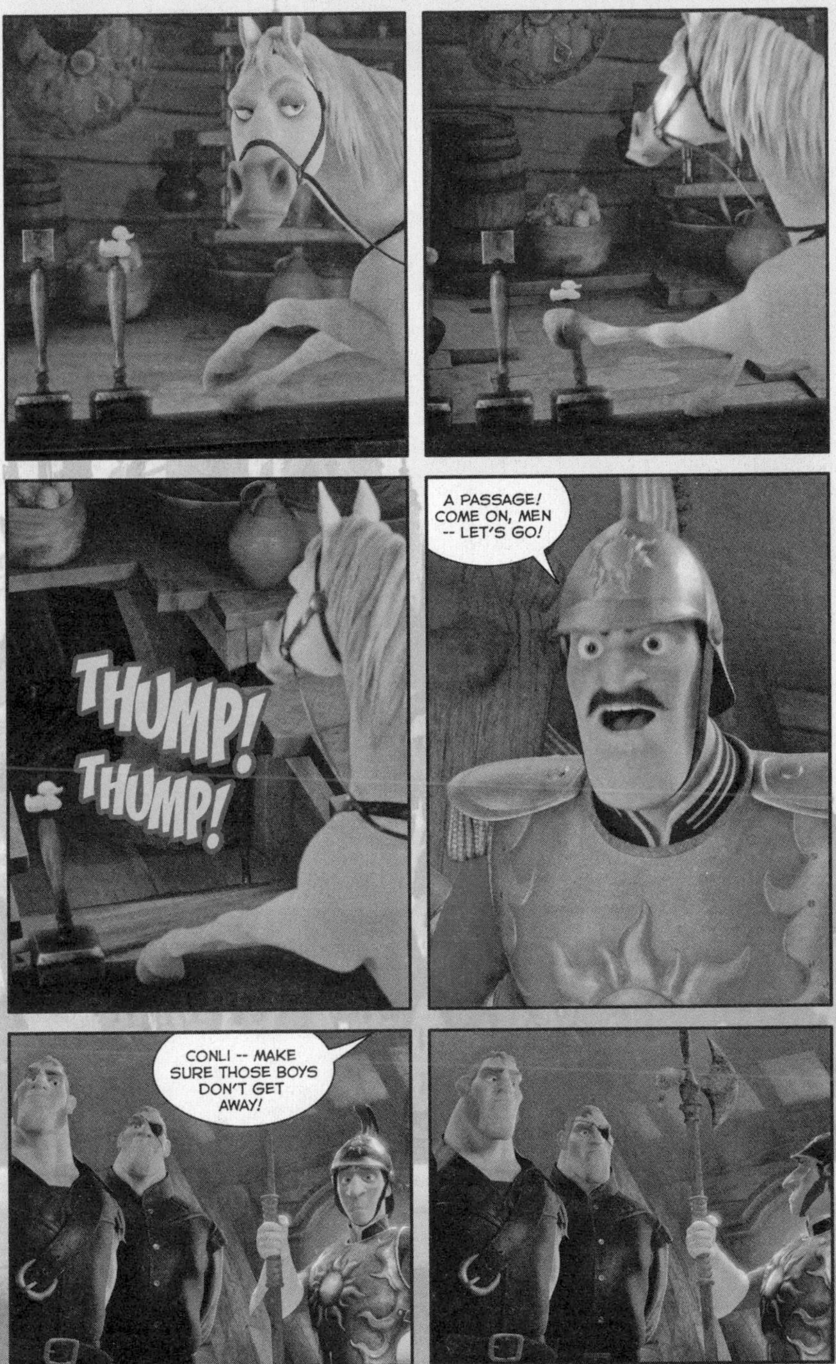
THUMP!
THUMP!
A PASSAGE! COME ON, MEN -- LET'S GO!
CONLI -- MAKE SURE THOSE BOYS DON'T GET AWAY!

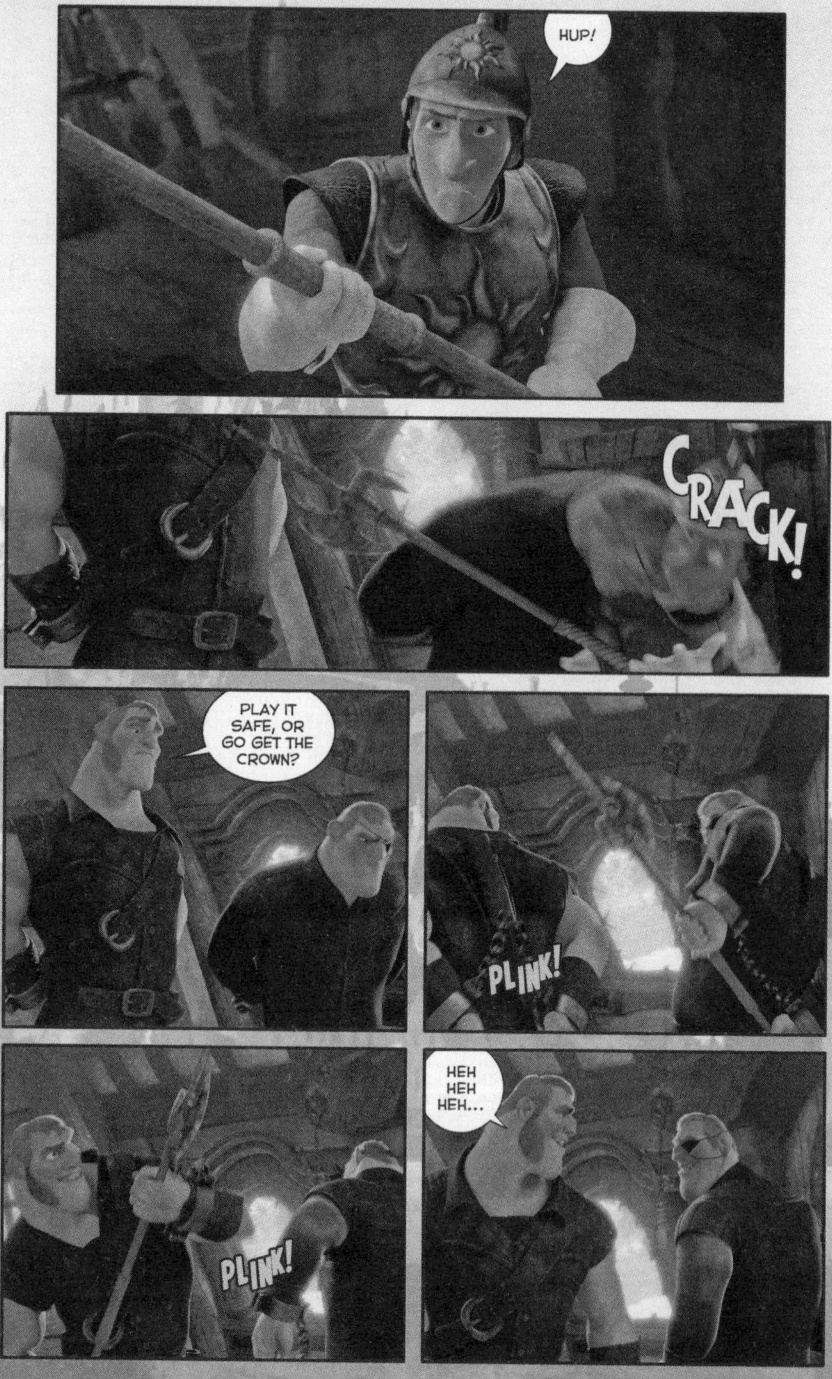
HUP!
CRACK!
PLAY IT SAFE, OR GO GET THE CROWN?
PLINK!
PLINK!
HEH HEH HEH...

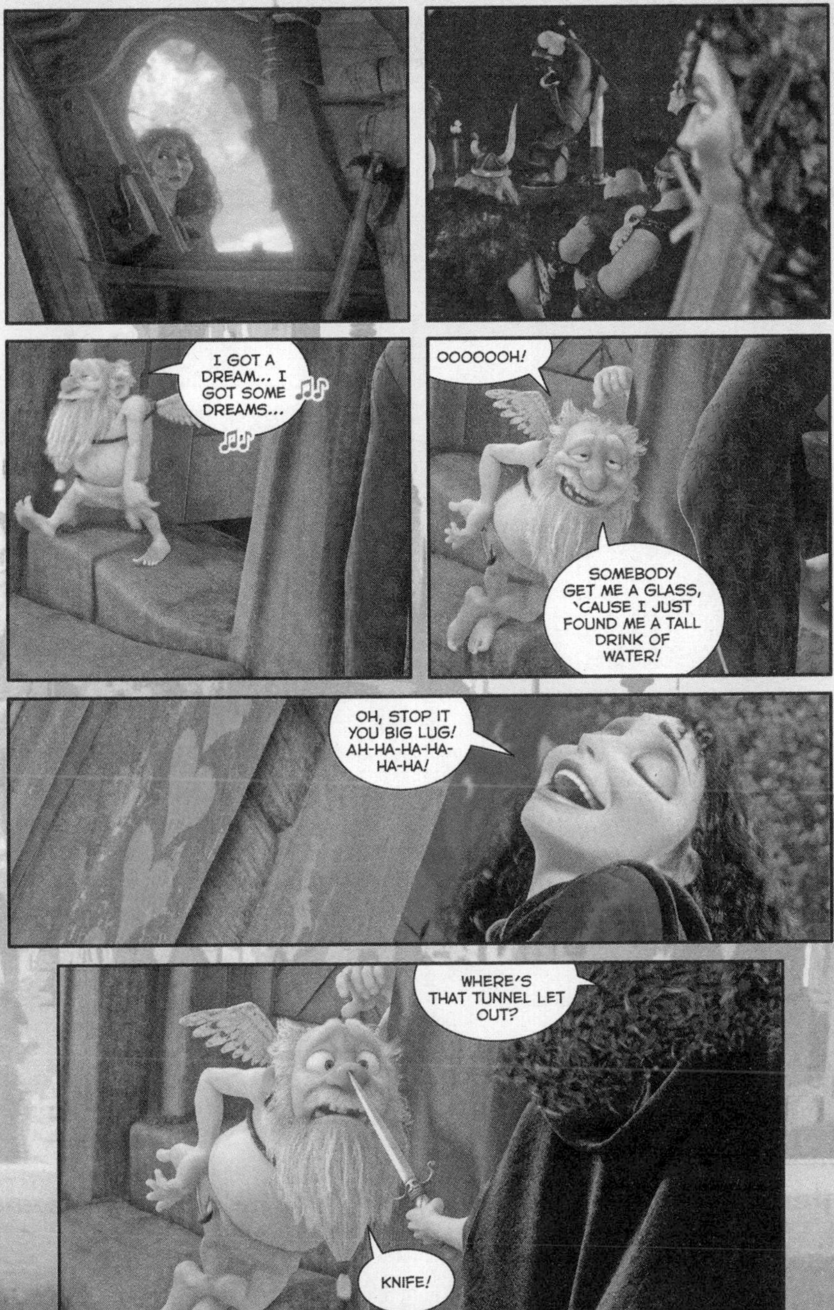
I GOT A DREAM... I GOT SOME DREAMS...
OOOOOOH!
SOMEBODY GET ME A GLASS, 'CAUSE I JUST FOUND ME A TALL DRINK OF WATER!
OH, STOP IT YOU BIG LUG! AH-HA-HA-HA-HA-HA!
WHERE'S THAT TUNNEL LET OUT?
KNIFE!

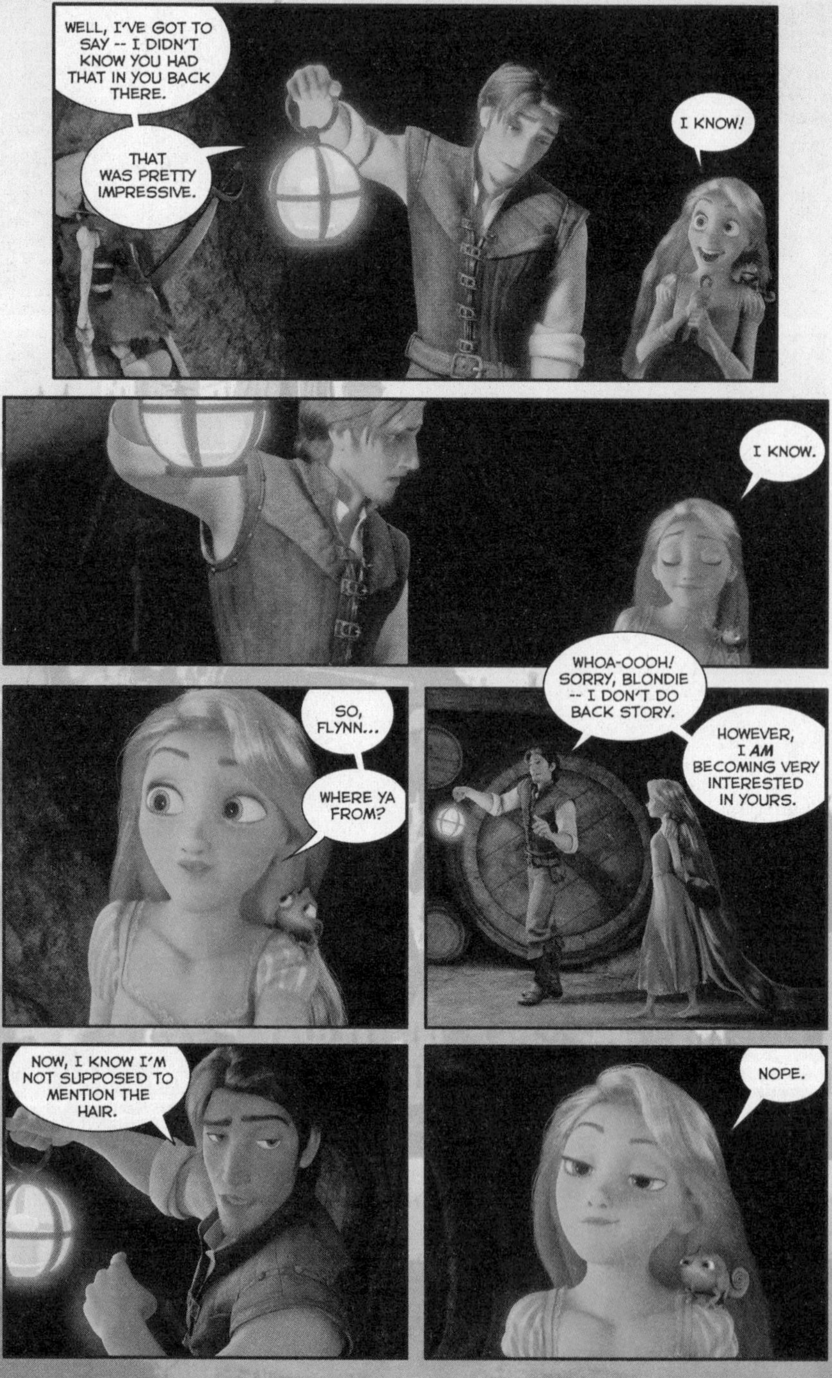
WELL, I'VE GOT TO SAY -- I DIDN'T KNOW YOU HAD THAT IN YOU BACK THERE.
THAT WAS PRETTY IMPRESSIVE.
I KNOW!
I KNOW.
SO, FLYNN...
WHERE YA FROM?
WHOA-OOOH! SORRY, BLONDIE -- I DON'T DO BACK STORY.
HOWEVER, I *AM* BECOMING VERY INTERESTED IN YOURS.
NOW, I KNOW I'M NOT SUPPOSED TO MENTION THE HAIR.
NOPE.

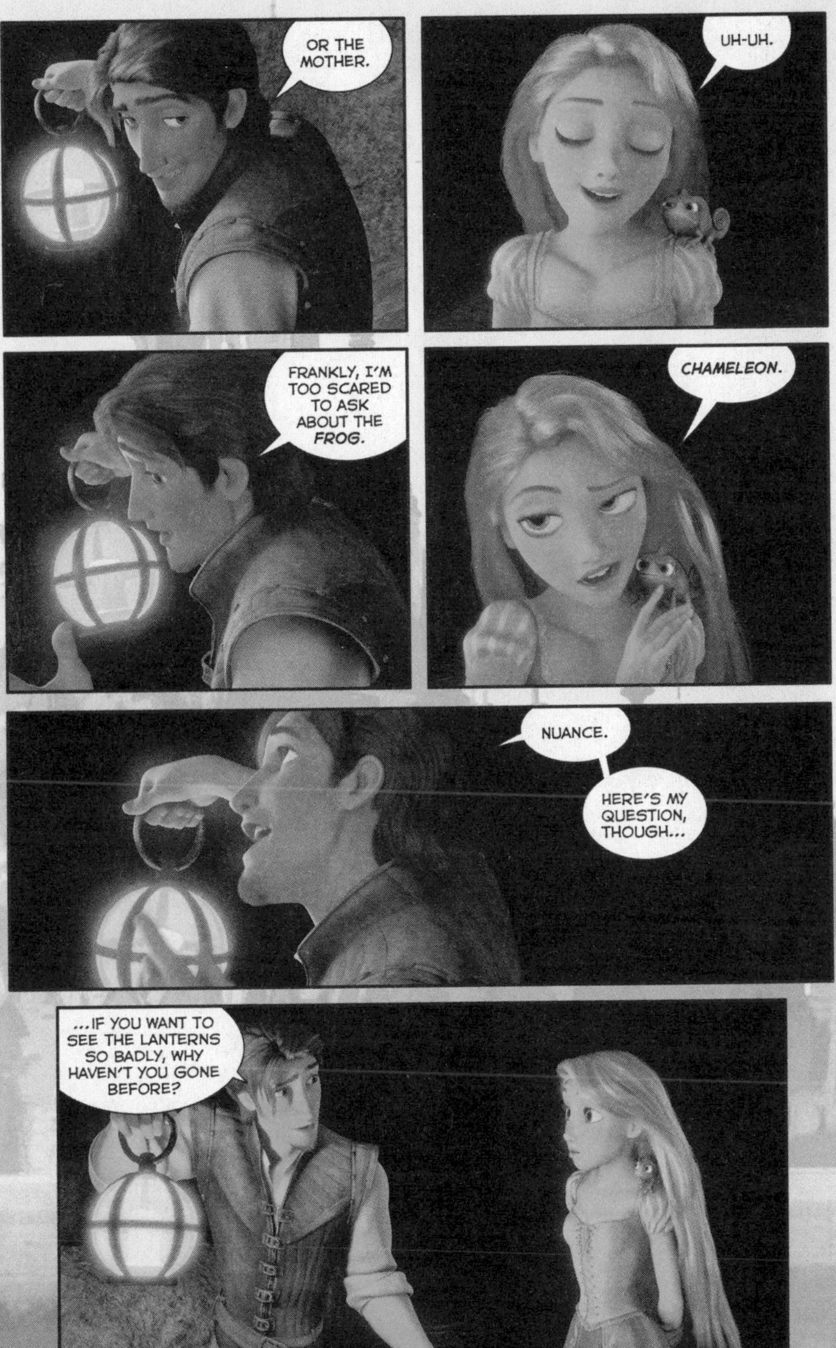
OR THE MOTHER.
UH-UH.
FRANKLY, I'M TOO SCARED TO ASK ABOUT THE *FROG*.
*CHAMELEON*.
NUANCE.
HERE'S MY QUESTION, THOUGH...
...IF YOU WANT TO SEE THE LANTERNS SO BADLY, WHY HAVEN'T YOU GONE BEFORE?

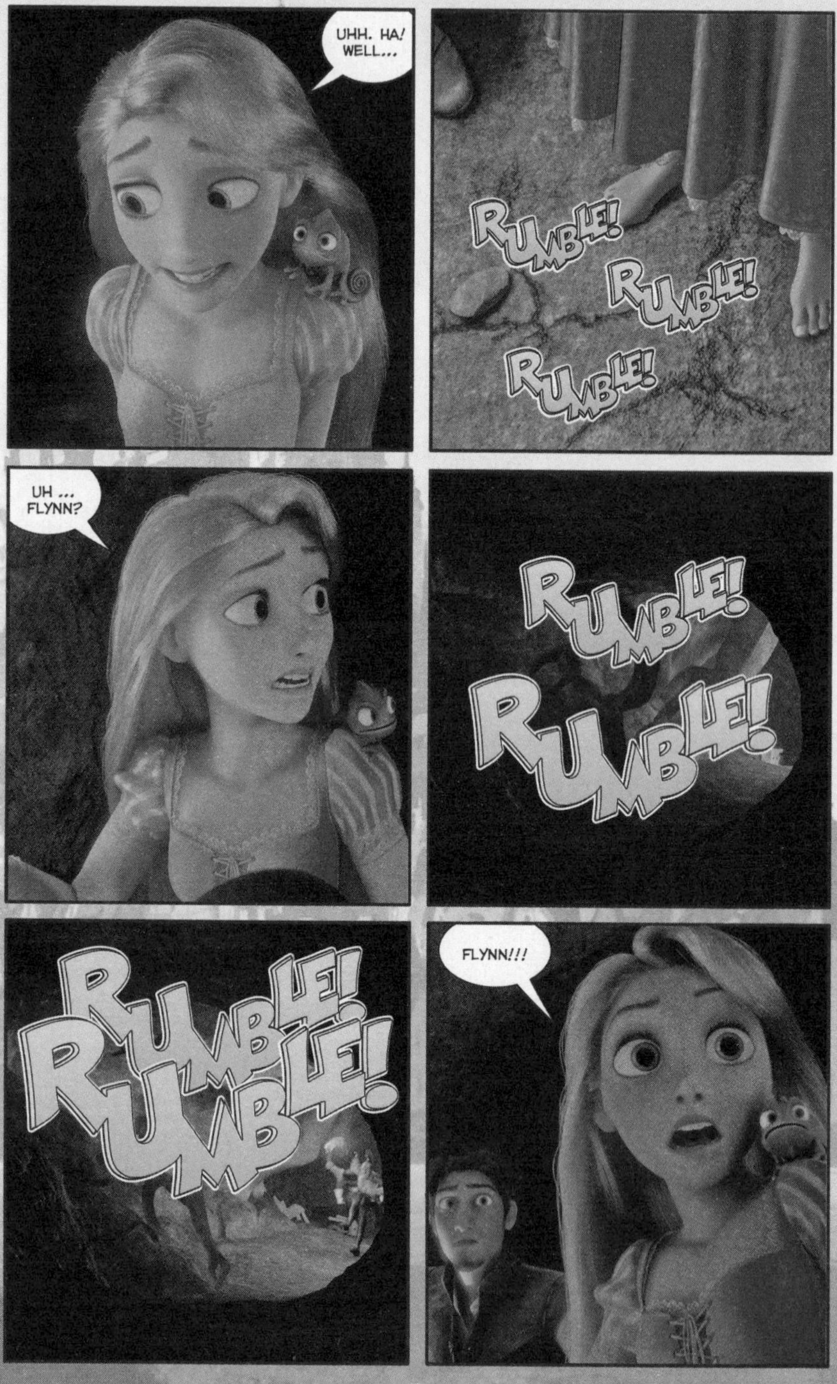
UHH. HA! WELL...
RUMBLE!
RUMBLE!
RUMBLE!
UH ... FLYNN?
RUMBLE!
RUMBLE!
RUMBLE!
RUMBLE!
FLYNN!!!

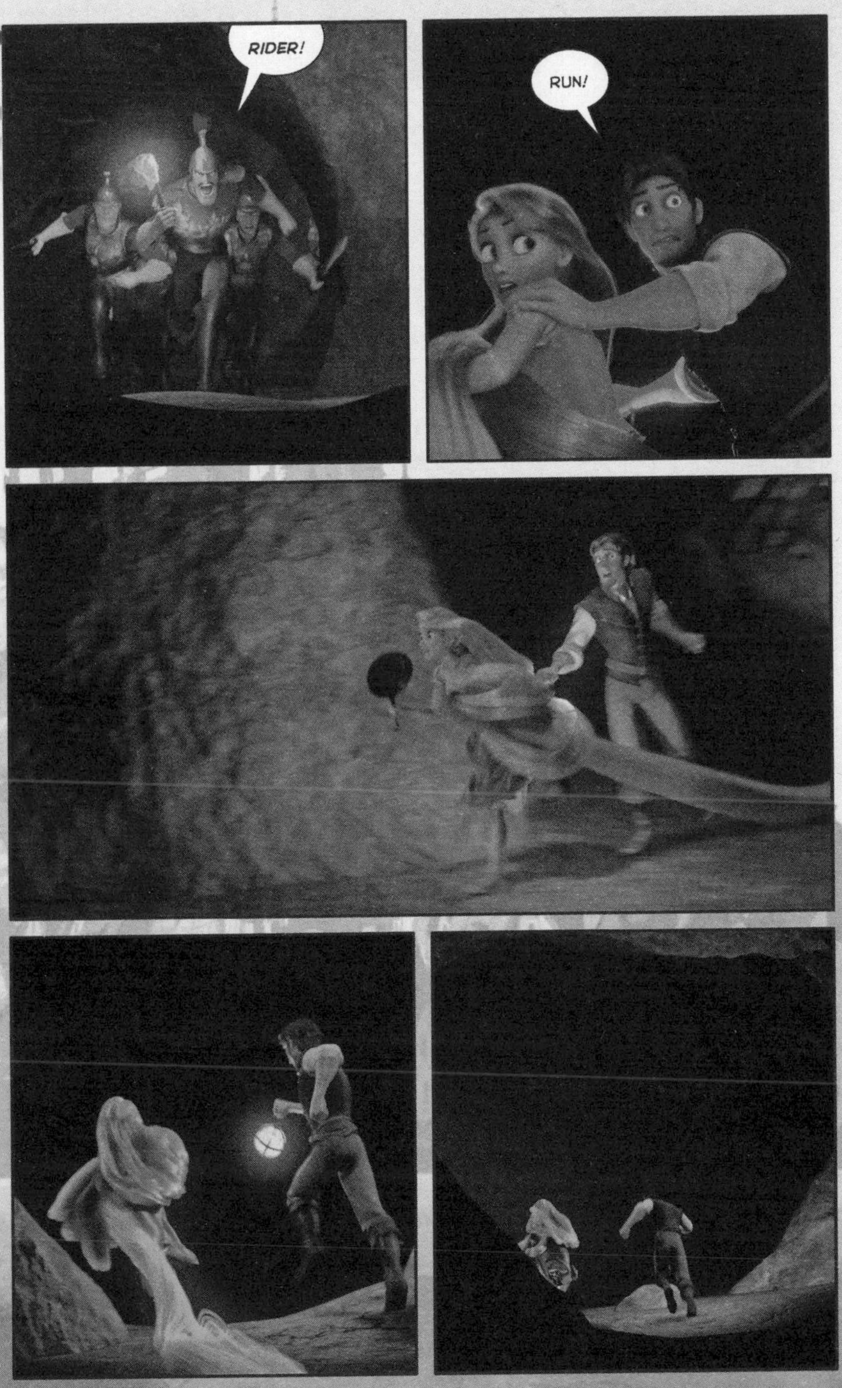
RIDER!
RUN!

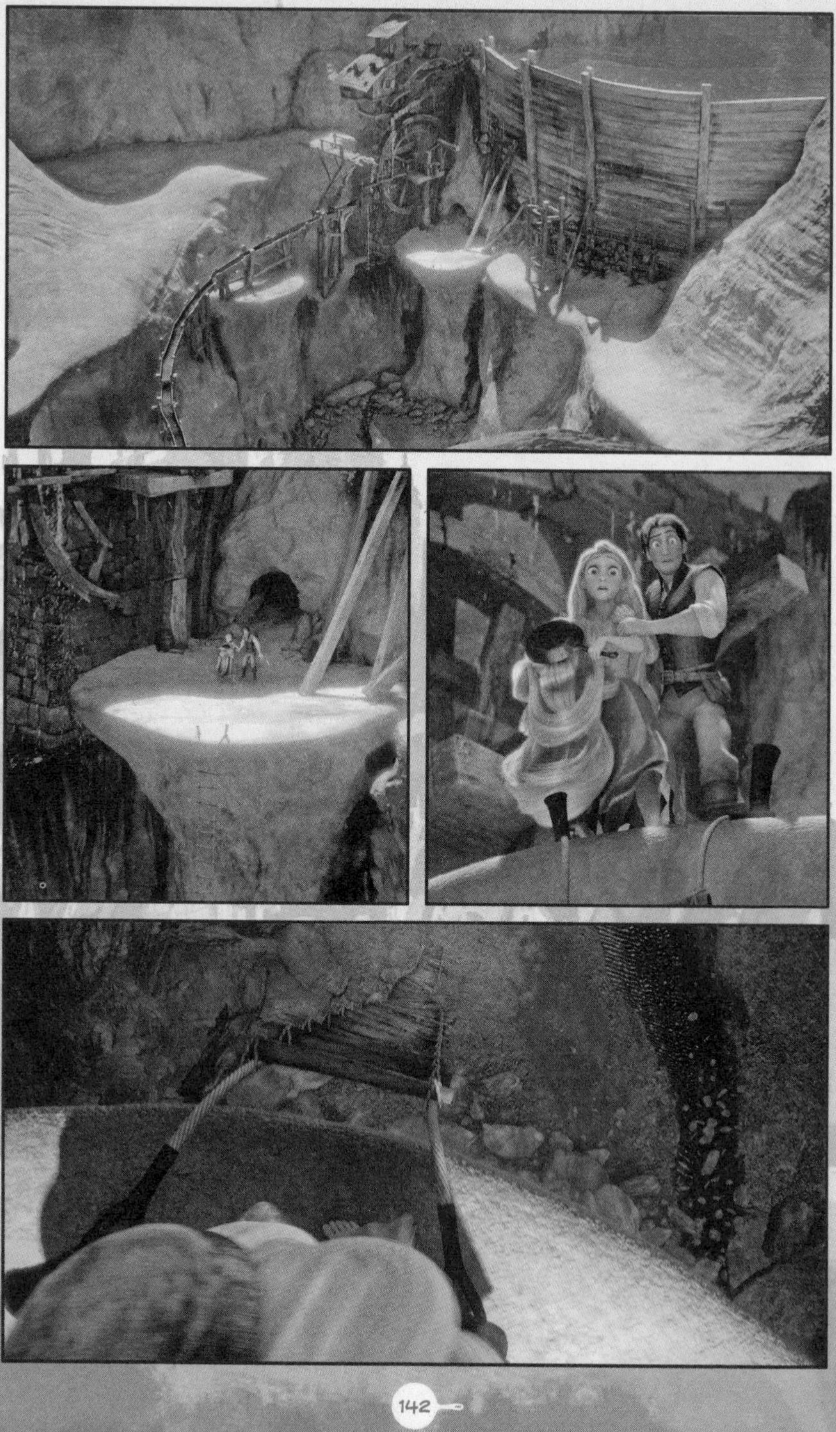

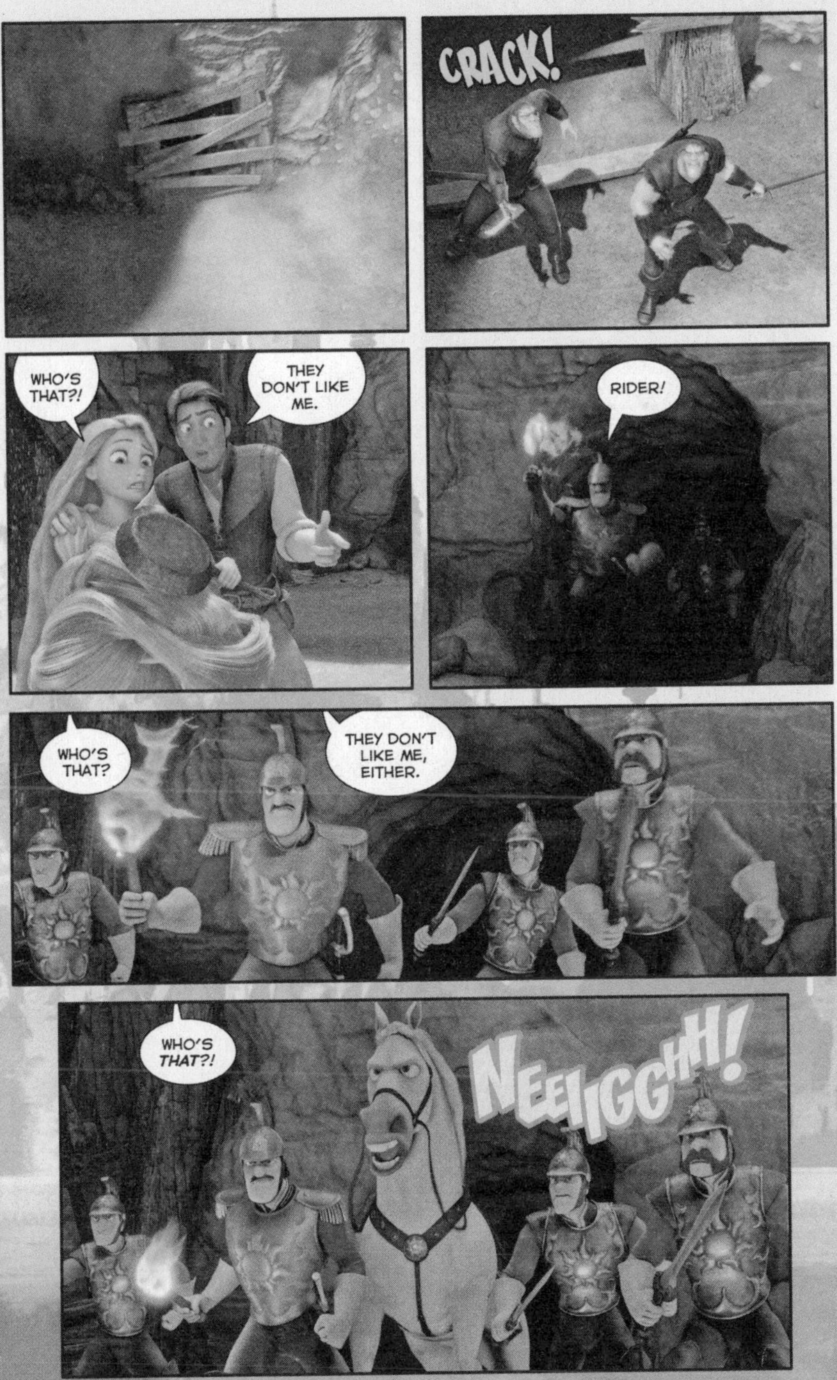
CRACK!
WHO'S THAT?!
THEY DON'T LIKE ME.
RIDER!
WHO'S THAT?
THEY DON'T LIKE ME, EITHER.
WHO'S THAT?!
NEEIIGGHH!

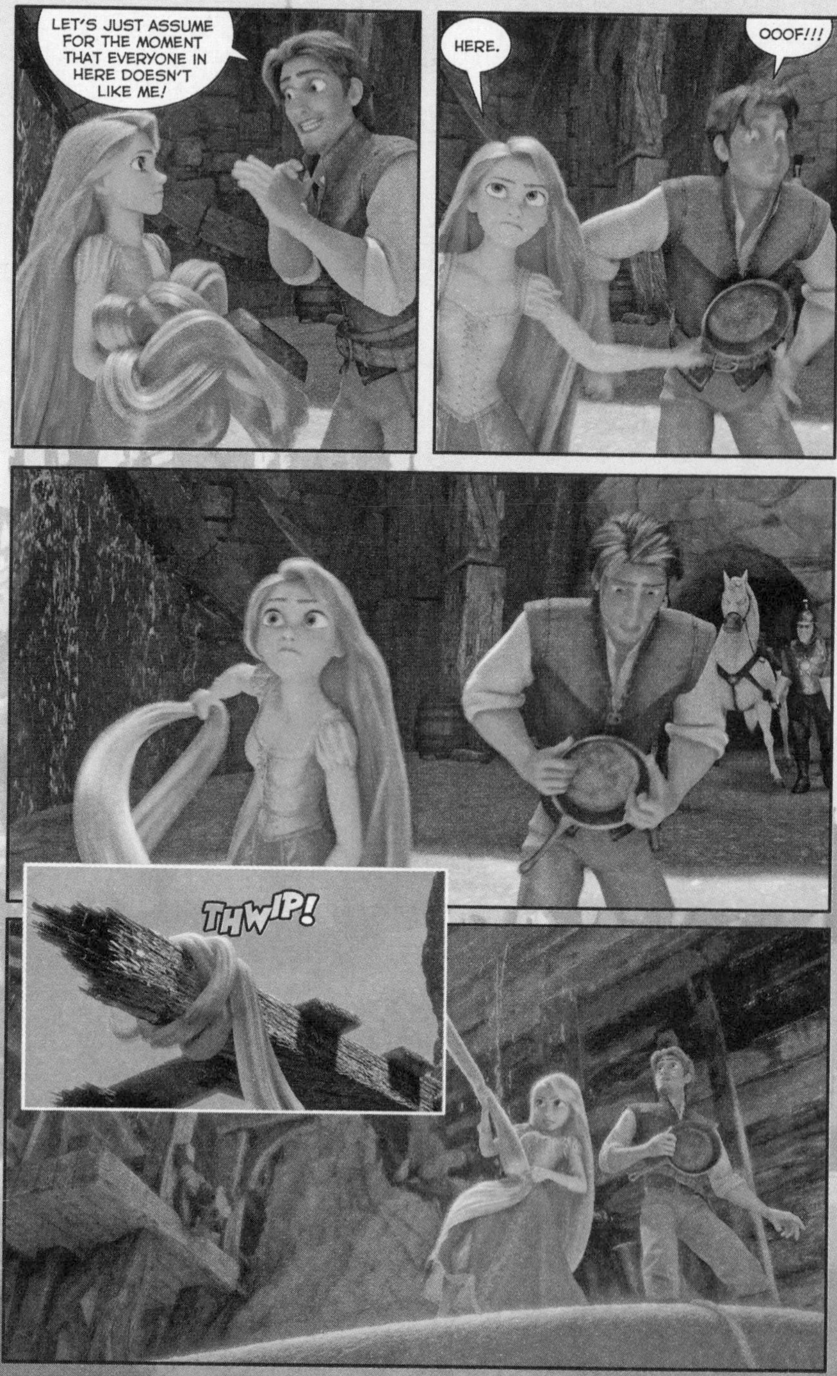
LET'S JUST ASSUME FOR THE MOMENT THAT EVERYONE IN HERE DOESN'T LIKE ME!
HERE.
OOOF!!!
THWIP!

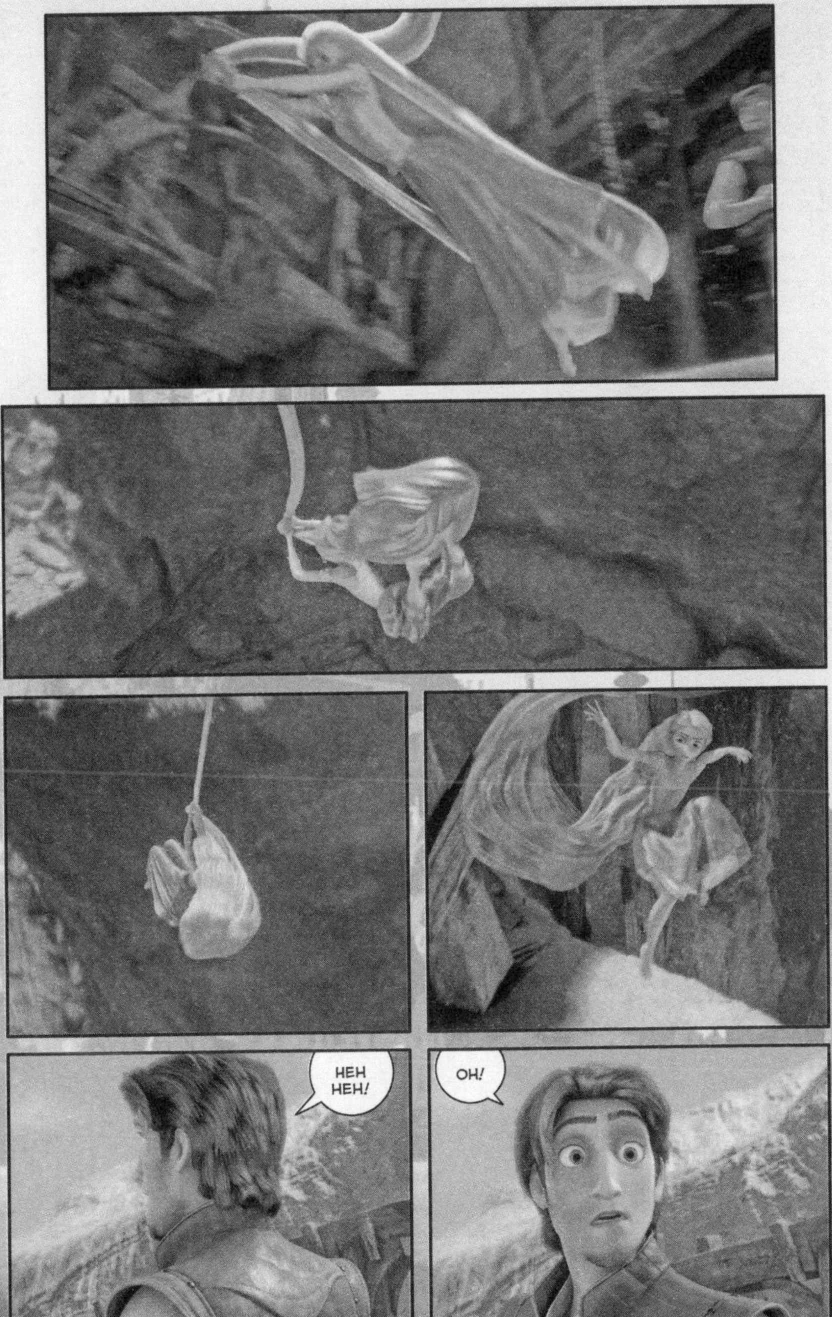
HEH HEH!
OH!

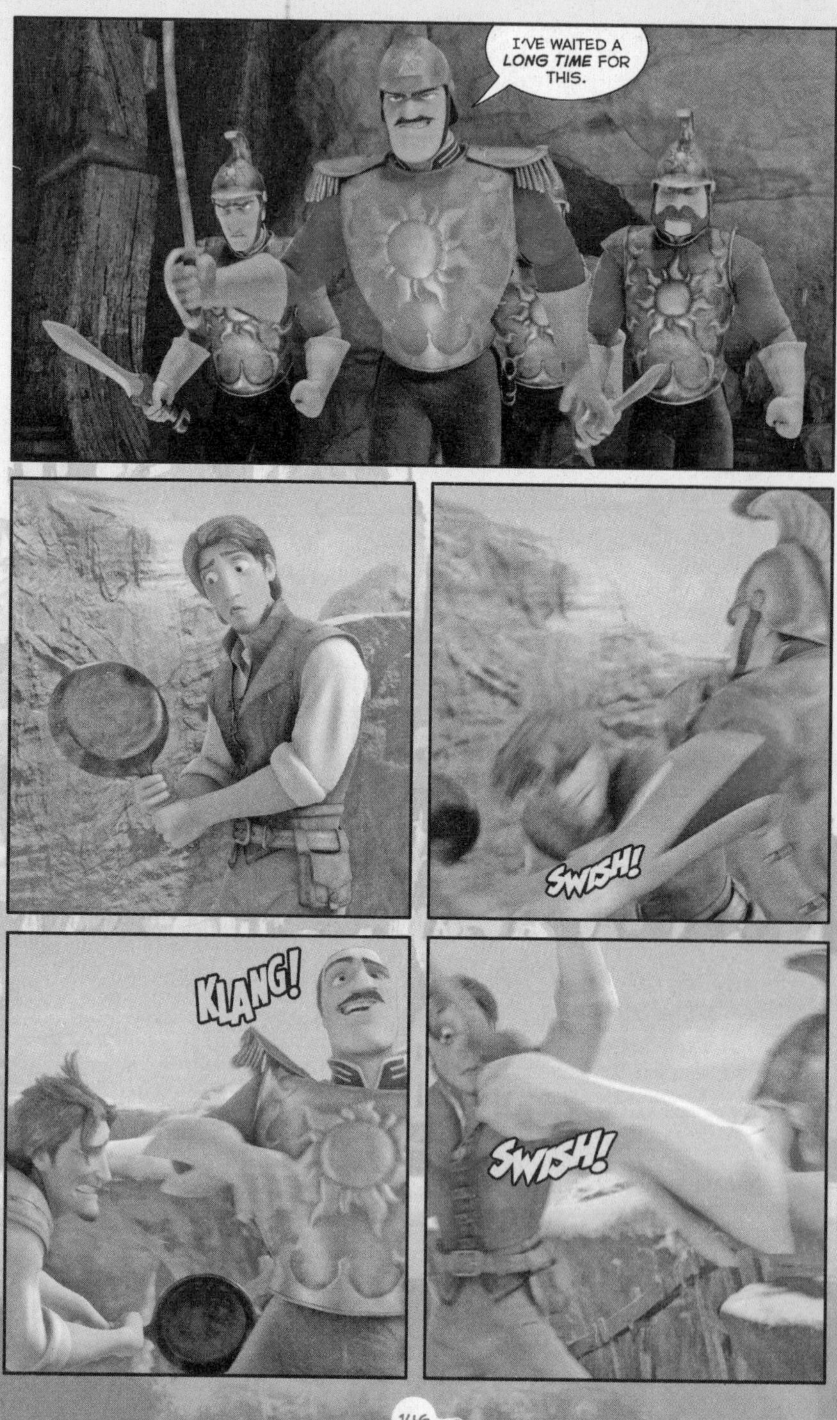
I'VE WAITED A *LONG TIME* FOR THIS.
SWISH!
KLANG!
SWISH!

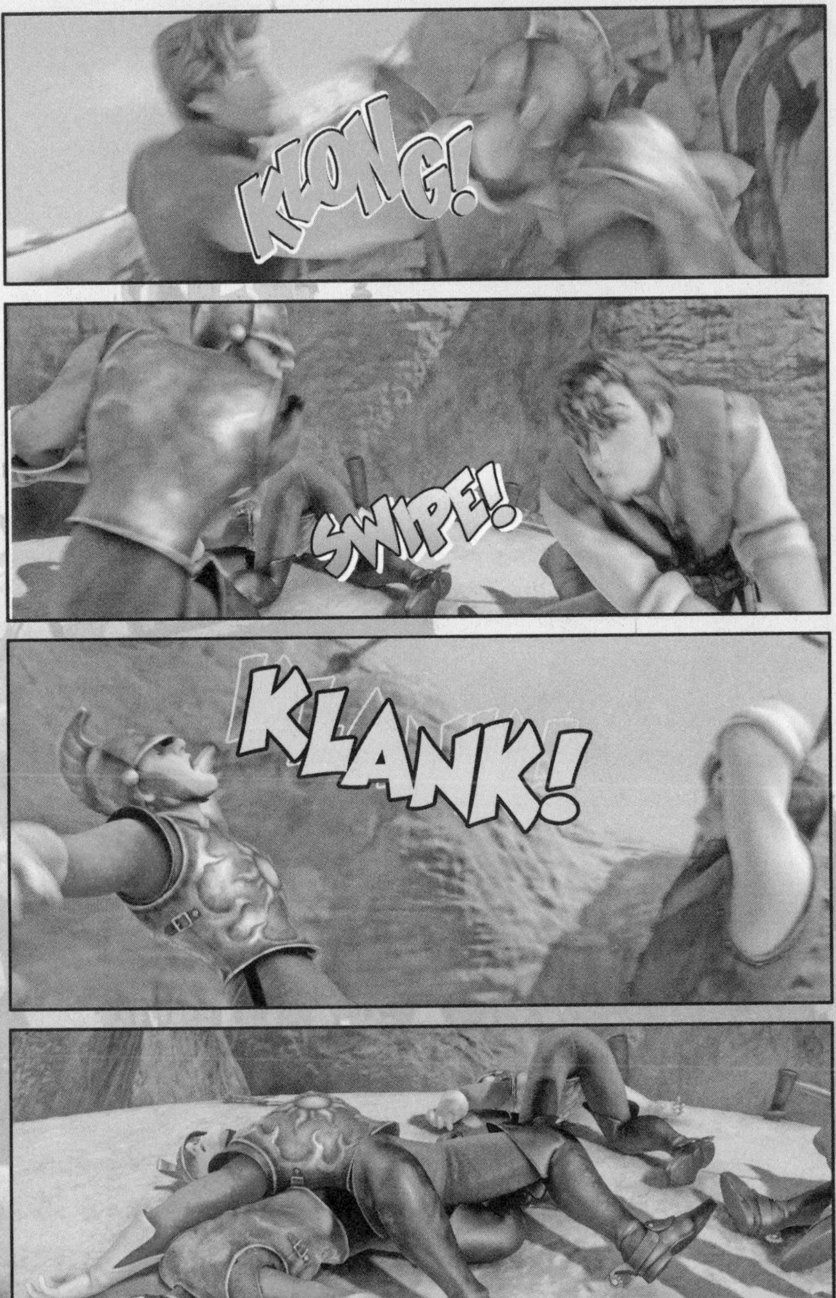
KLONG!
SWIPE!
KLANK!

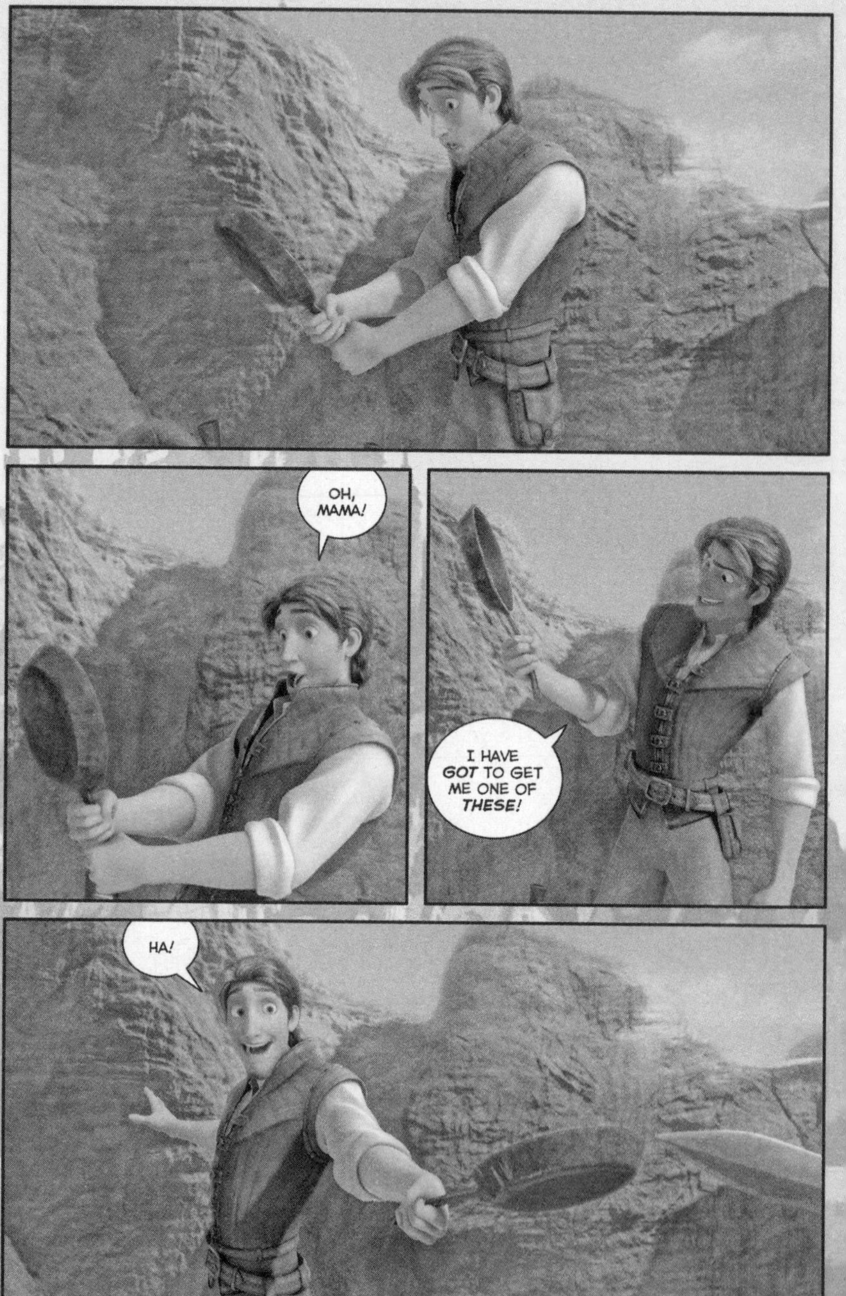
OH, MAMA!
I HAVE GOT TO GET ME ONE OF THESE!
HA!

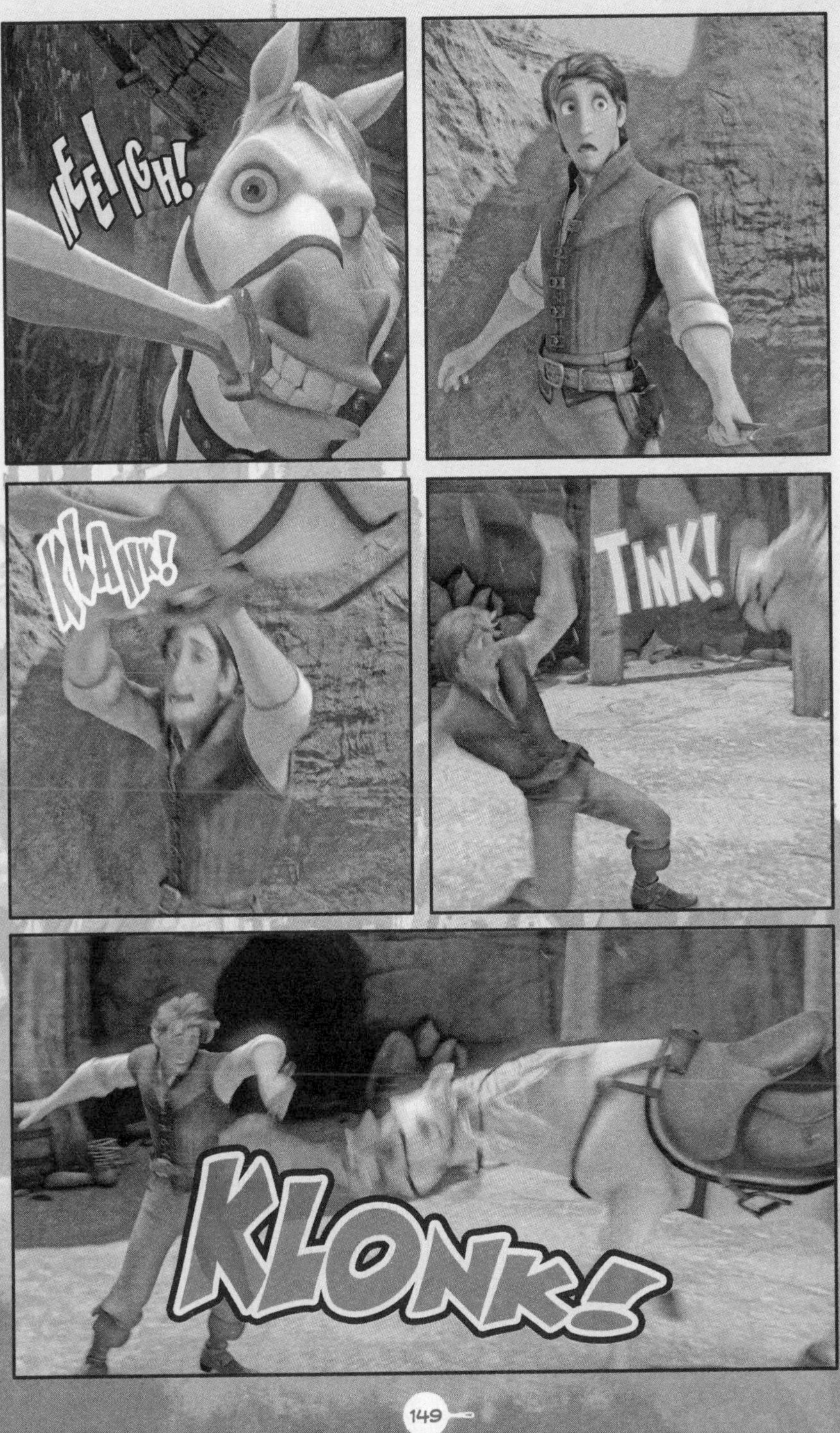
NEEIGH!
KLANK!
TINK!
KLONK!

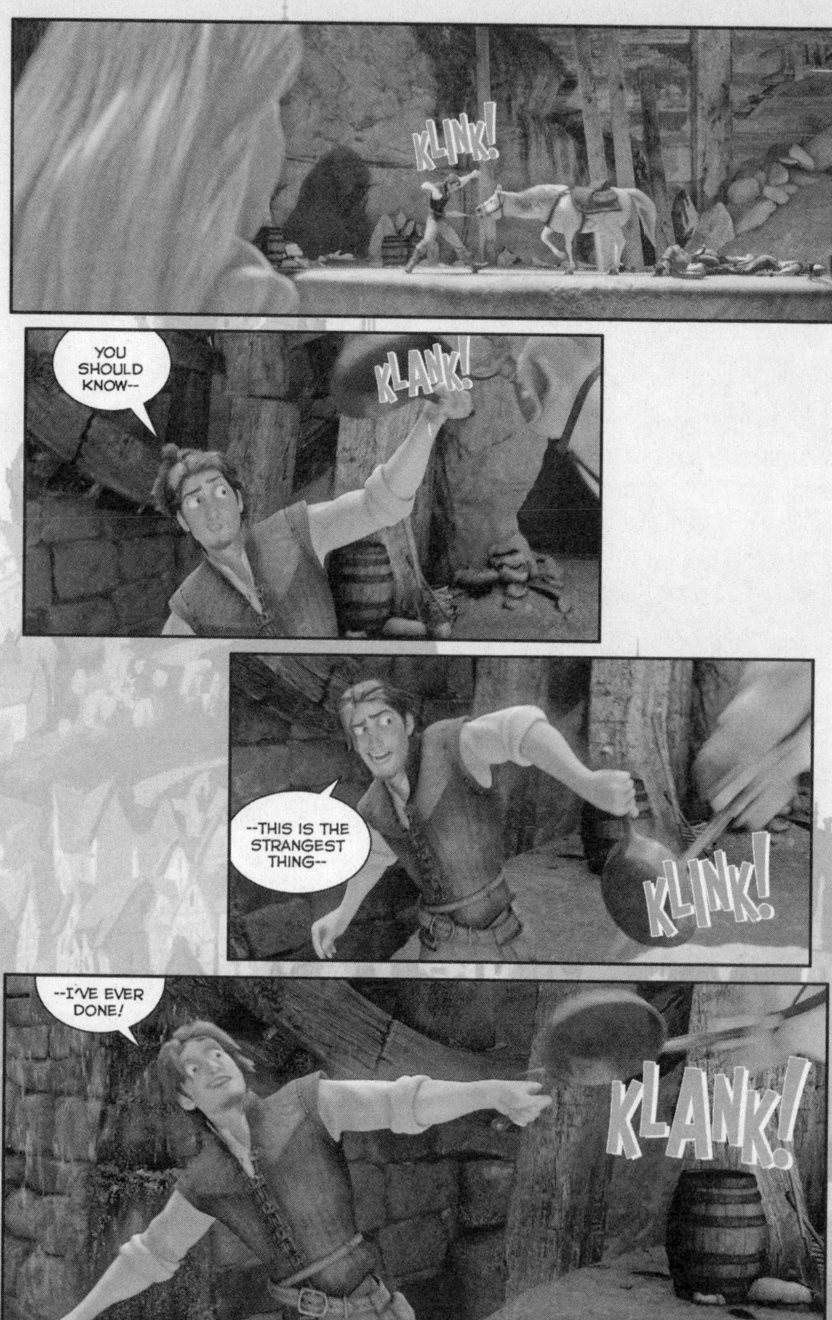
KLINK!
YOU SHOULD KNOW--
KLANK!
--THIS IS THE STRANGEST THING--
KLINK!
--I'VE EVER DONE!
KLANK!

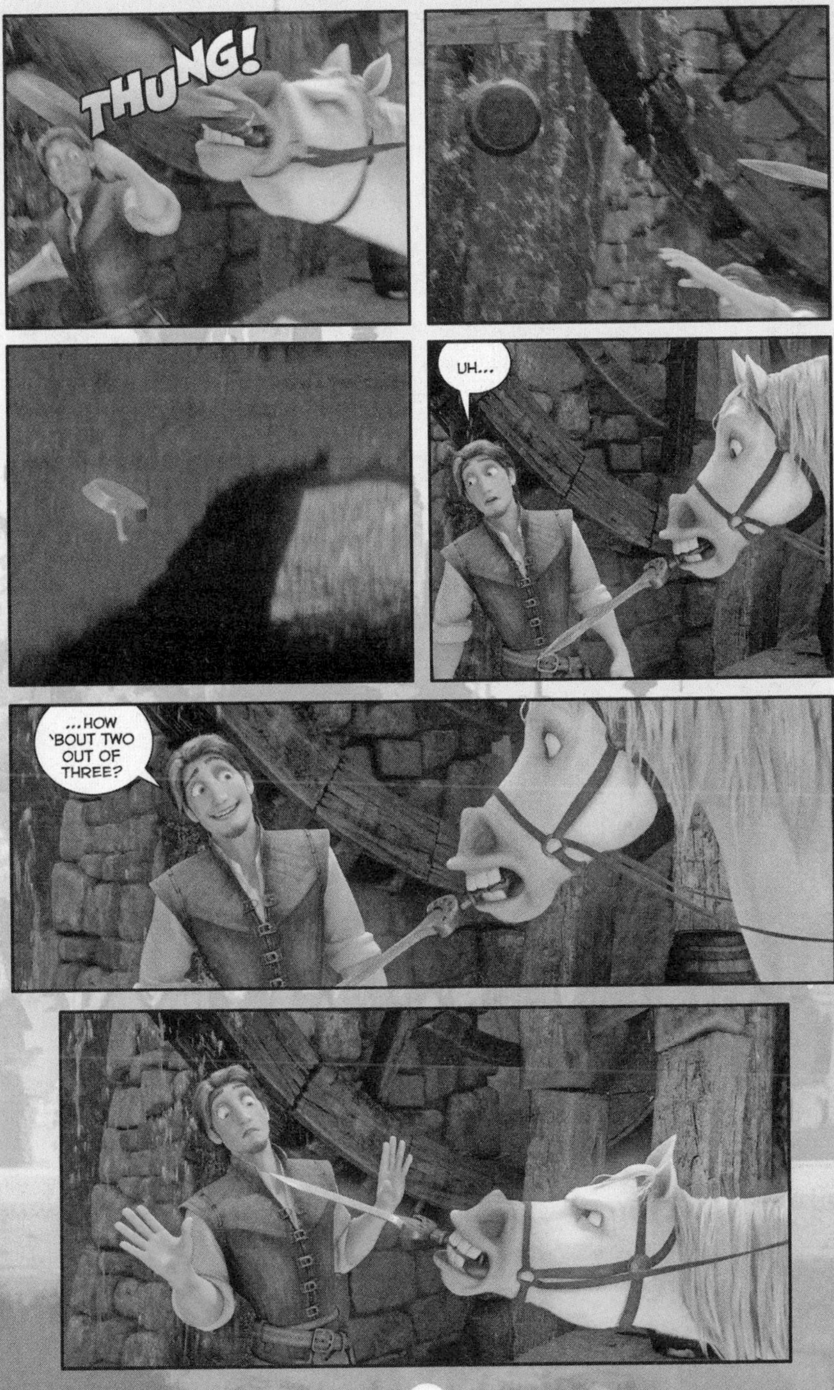
THUNG!
UH...
...HOW 'BOUT TWO OUT OF THREE?

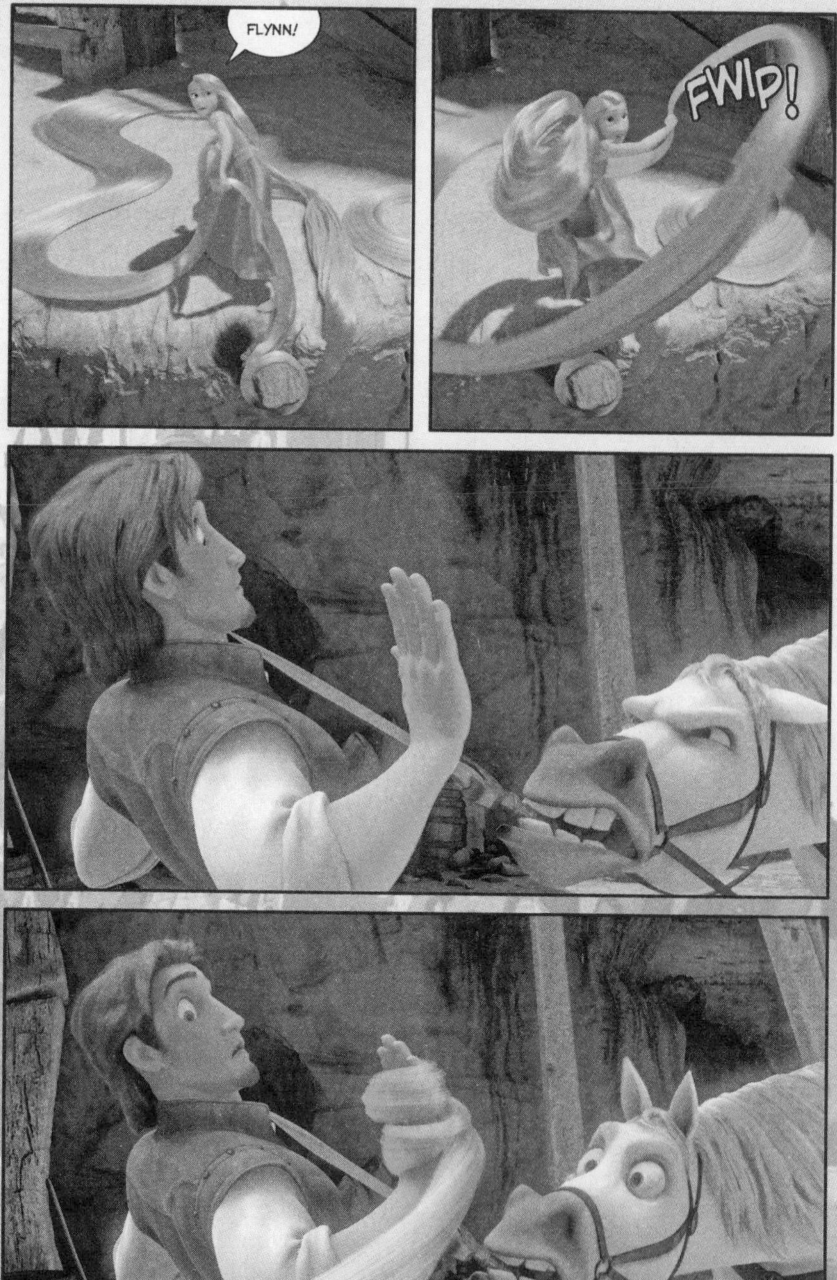
FLYNN!
FWIP!

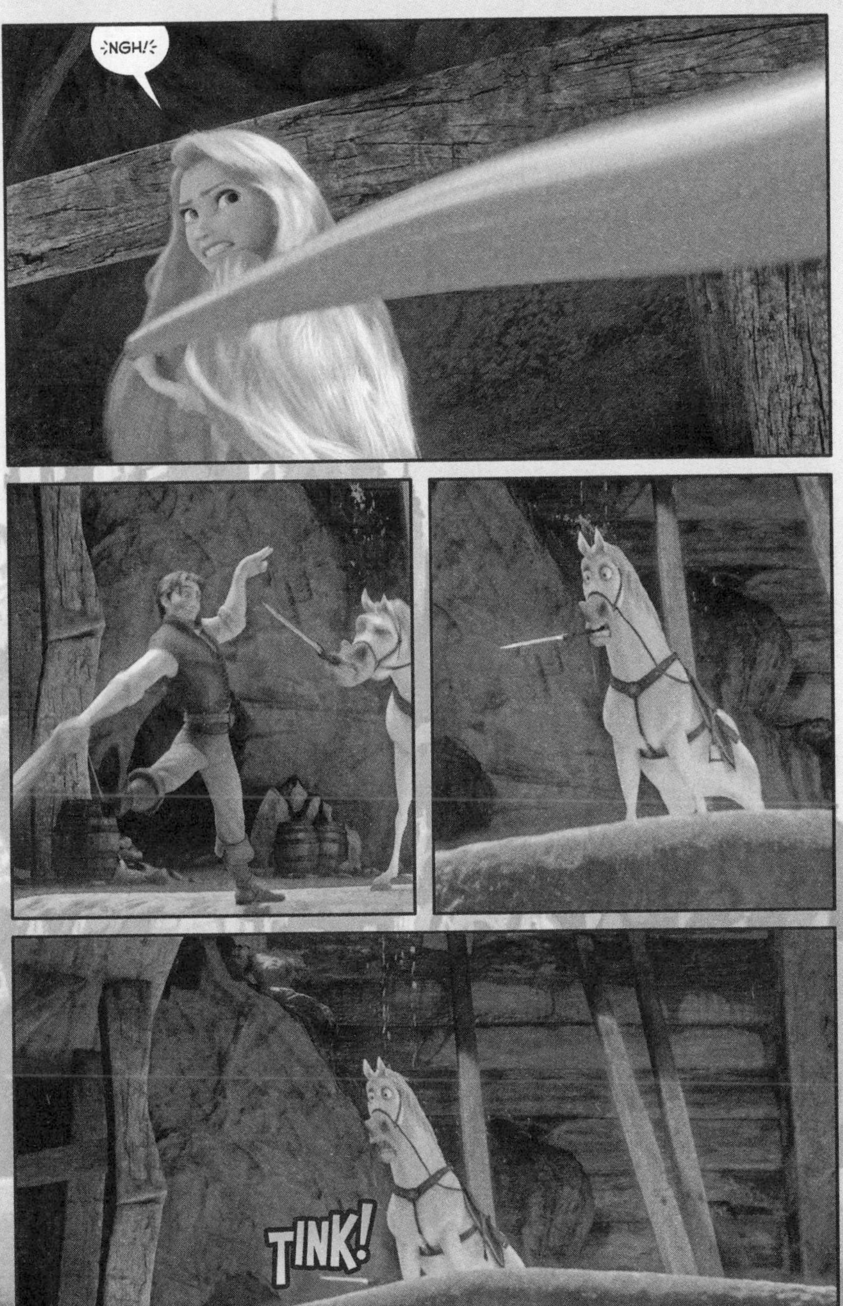
NGH!
TINK!

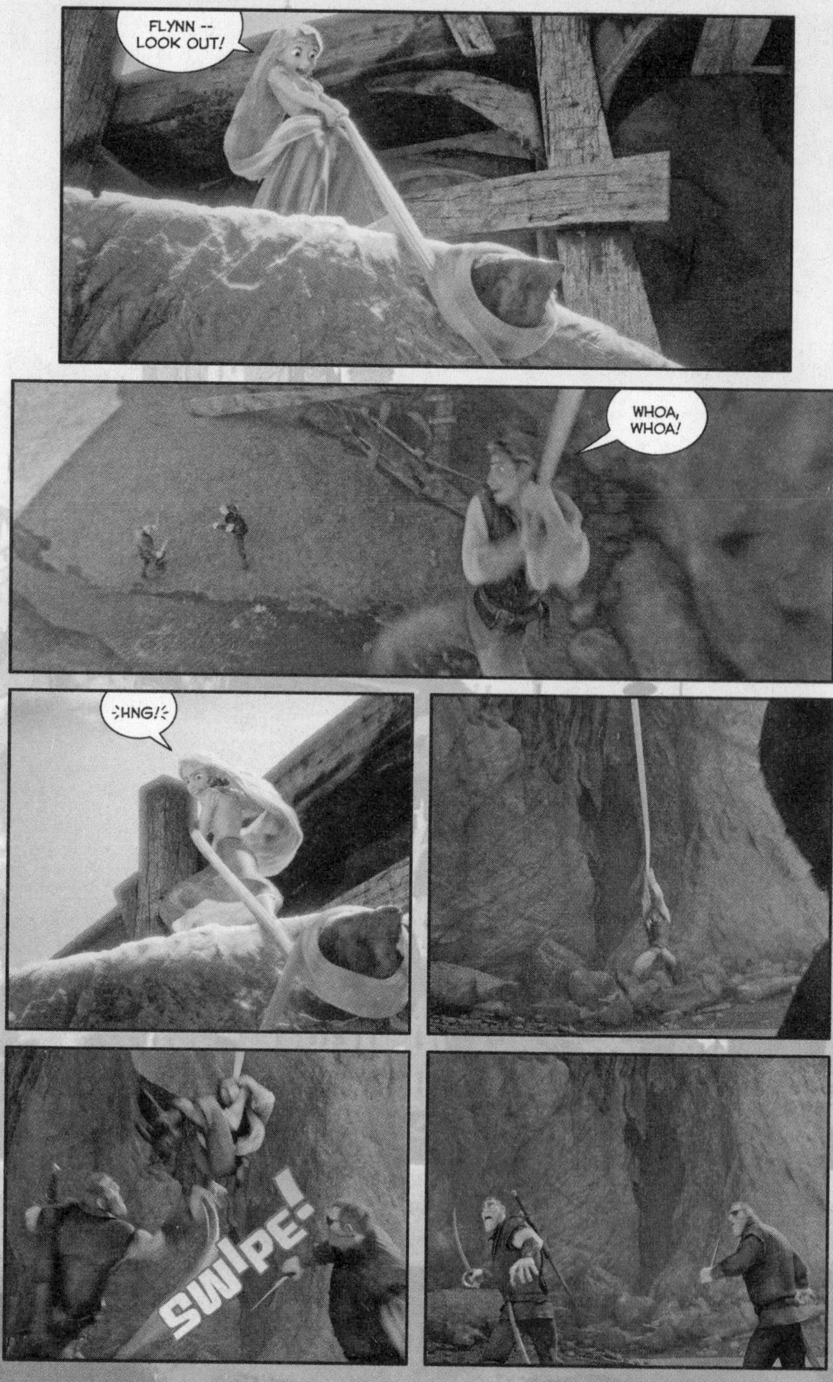
FLYNN -- LOOK OUT!
WHOA, WHOA!
HNG!
SWIPE!

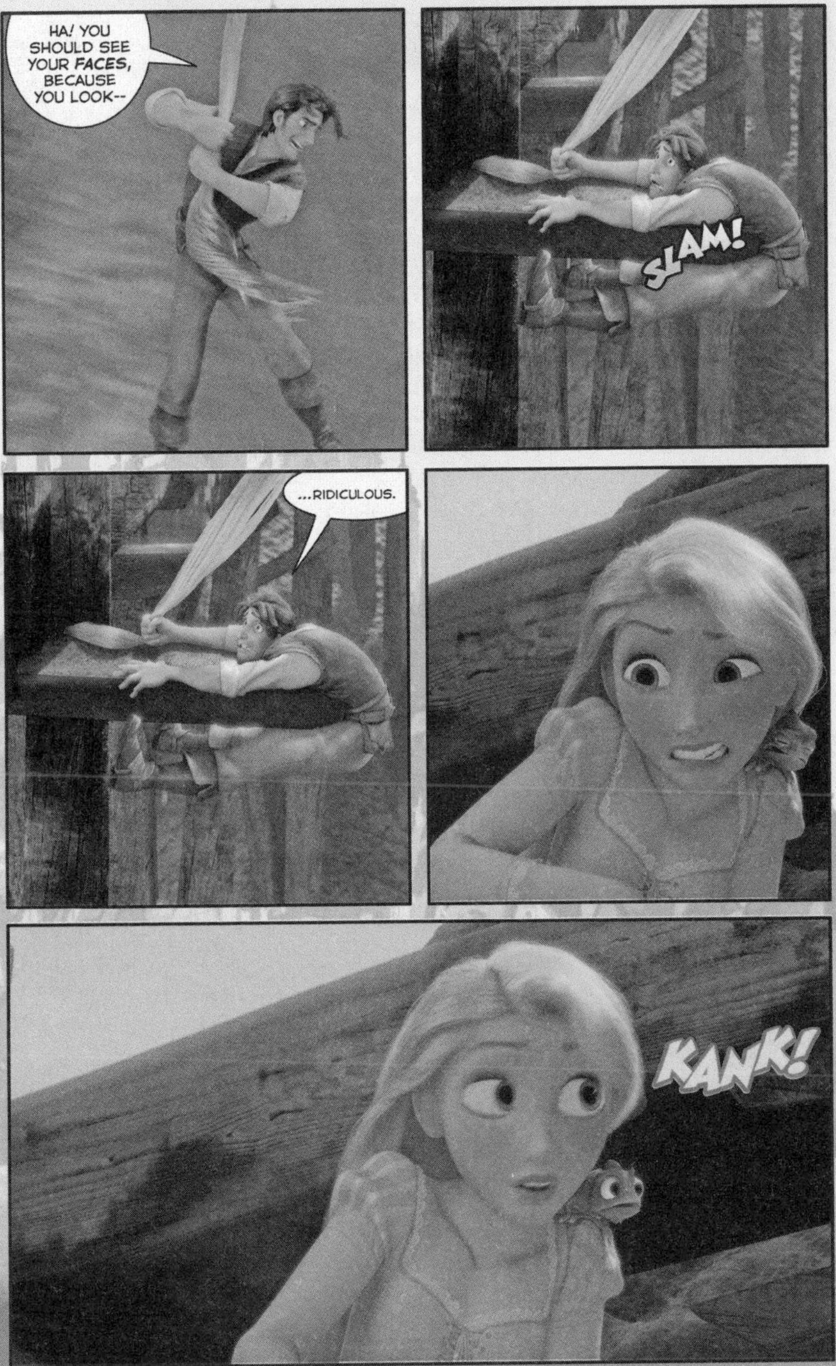
HA! YOU SHOULD SEE YOUR *FACES*, BECAUSE YOU LOOK--
SLAM!
...RIDICULOUS.
KANK!

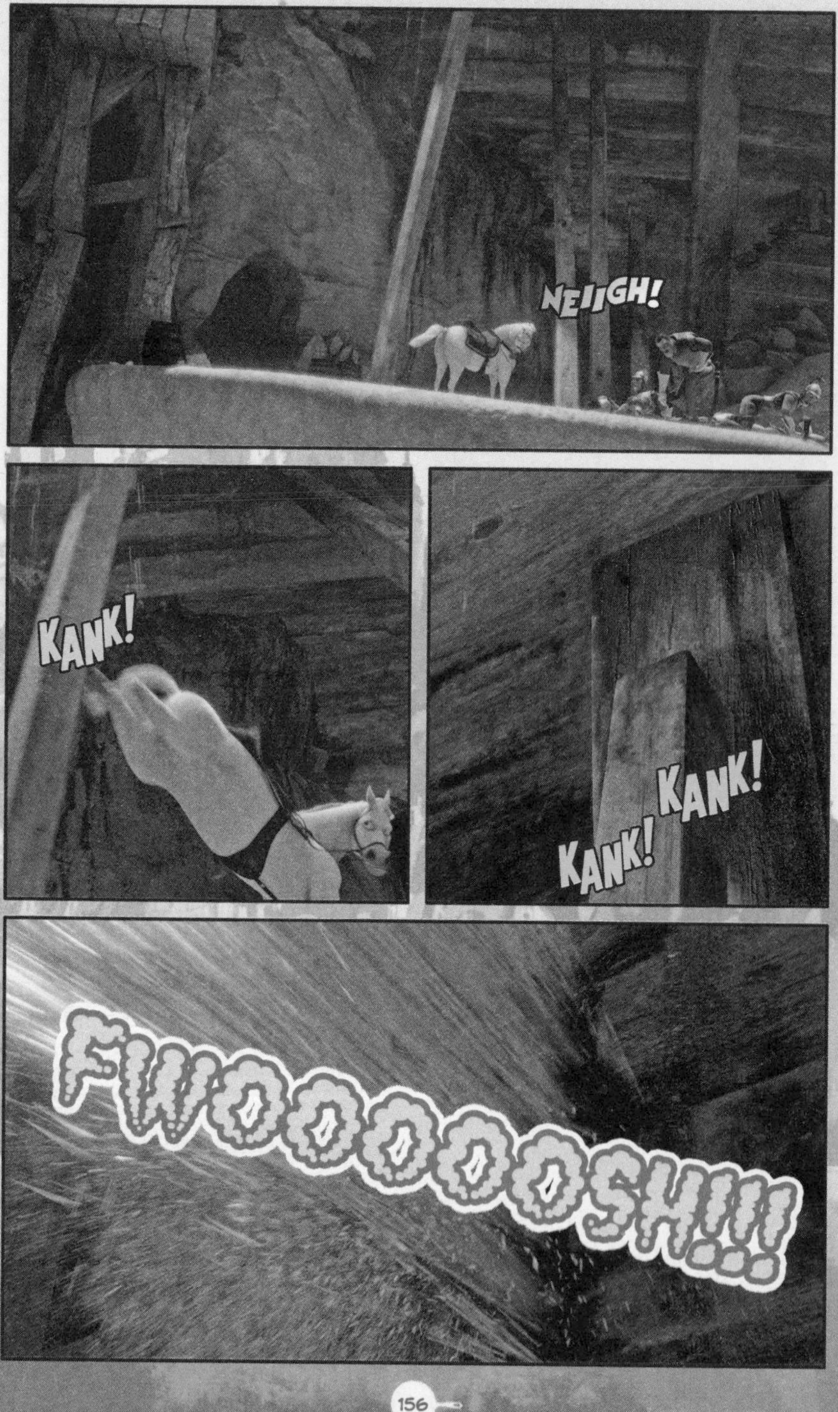
NEIIGH!
KANK!
KANK!
KANK!
FWOOOOOOSH!!!

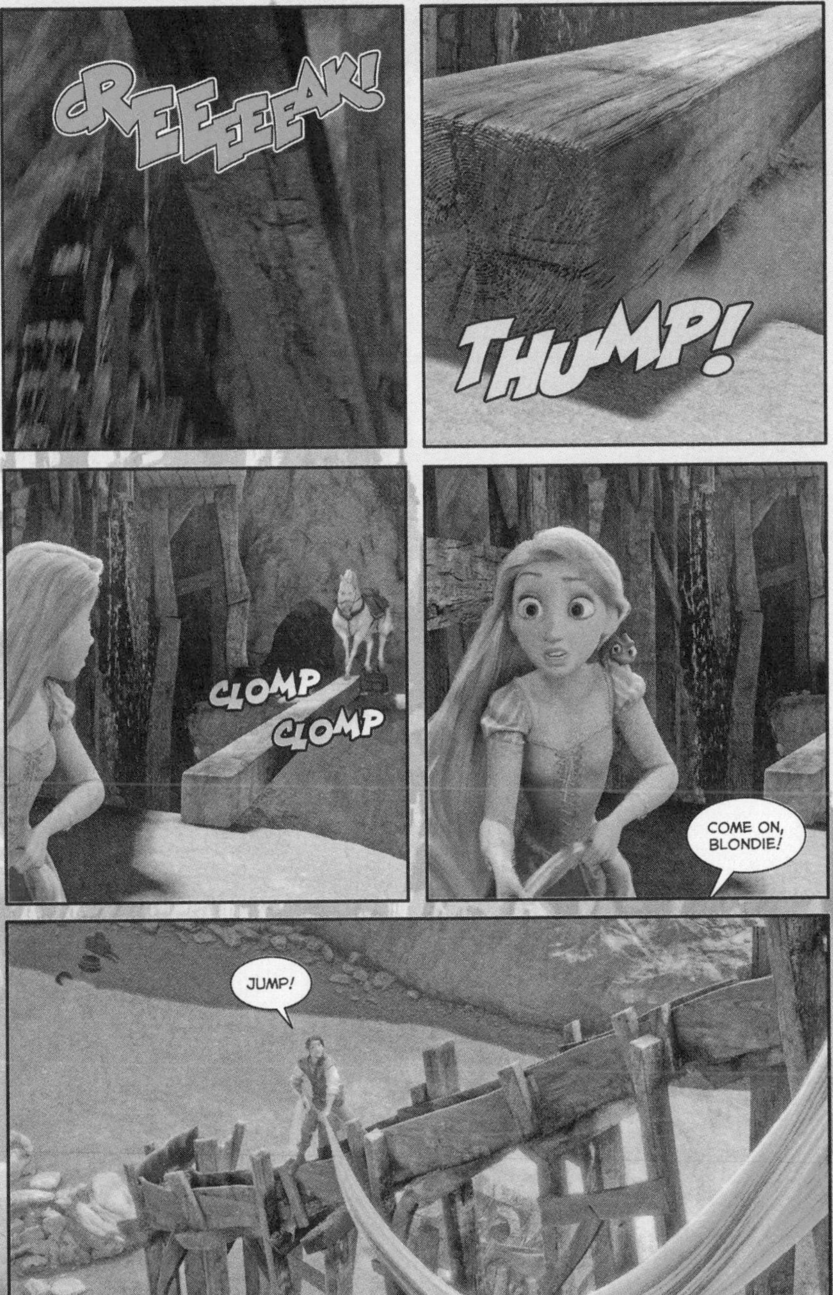
CREEEEEAK!
THUMP!
CLOMP
CLOMP
COME ON, BLONDIE!
JUMP!

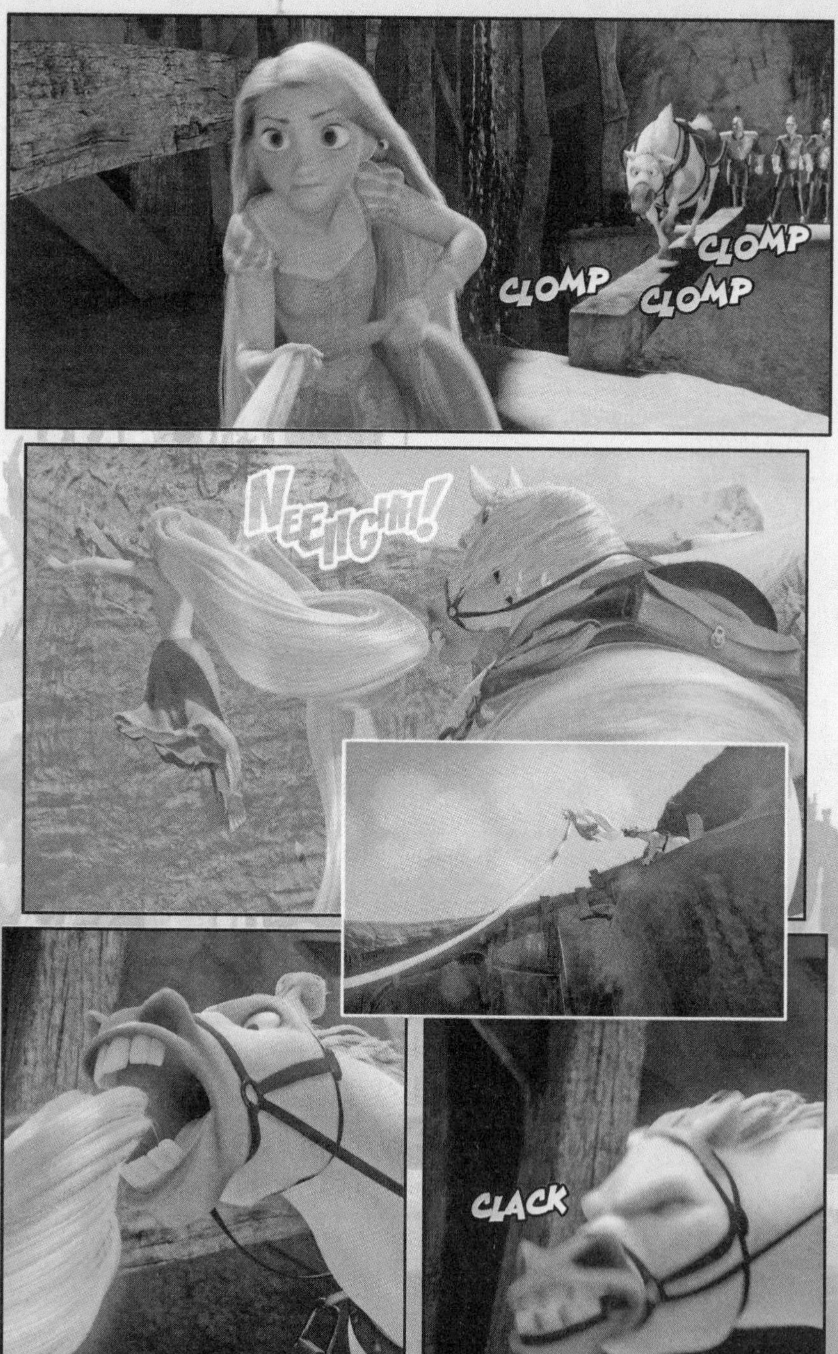
CLOMP
CLOMP
CLOMP
NEEIIGHH!
CLACK

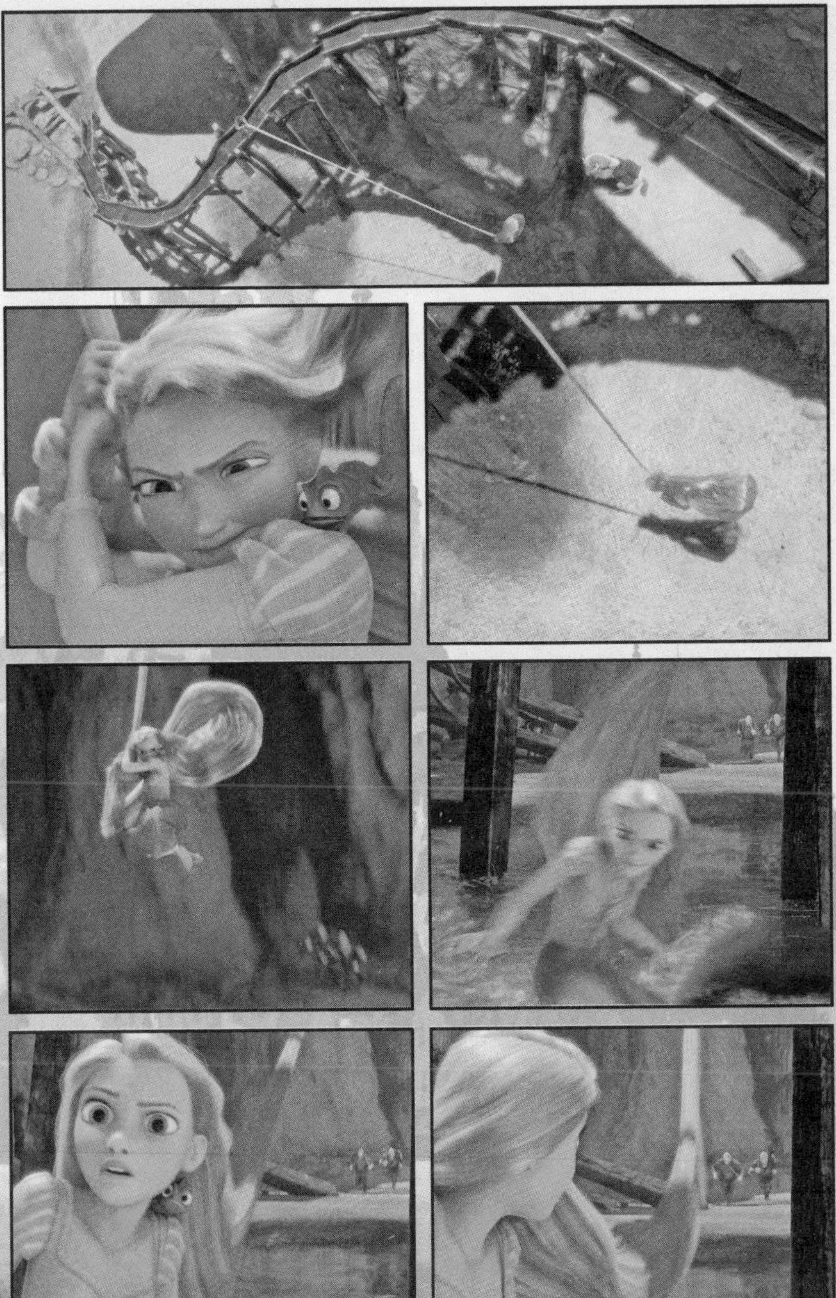

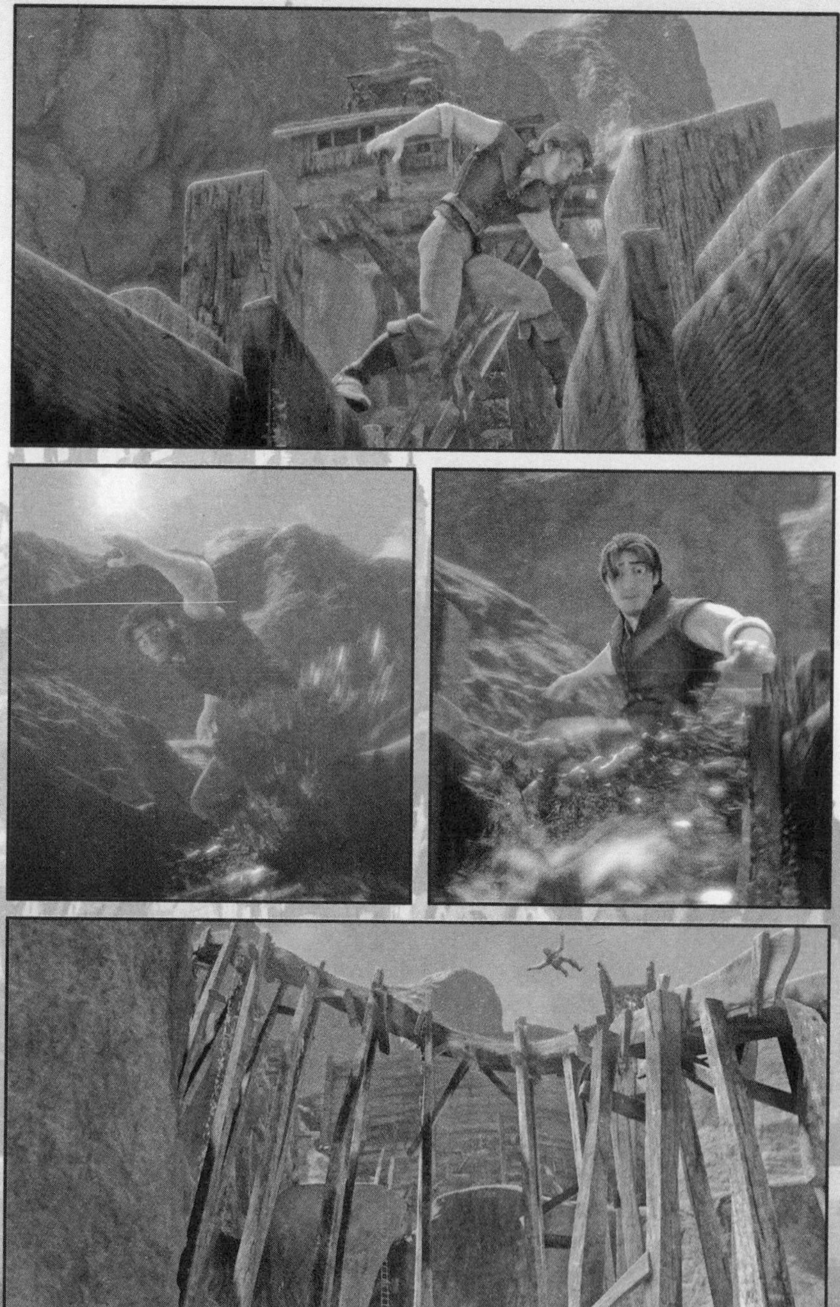

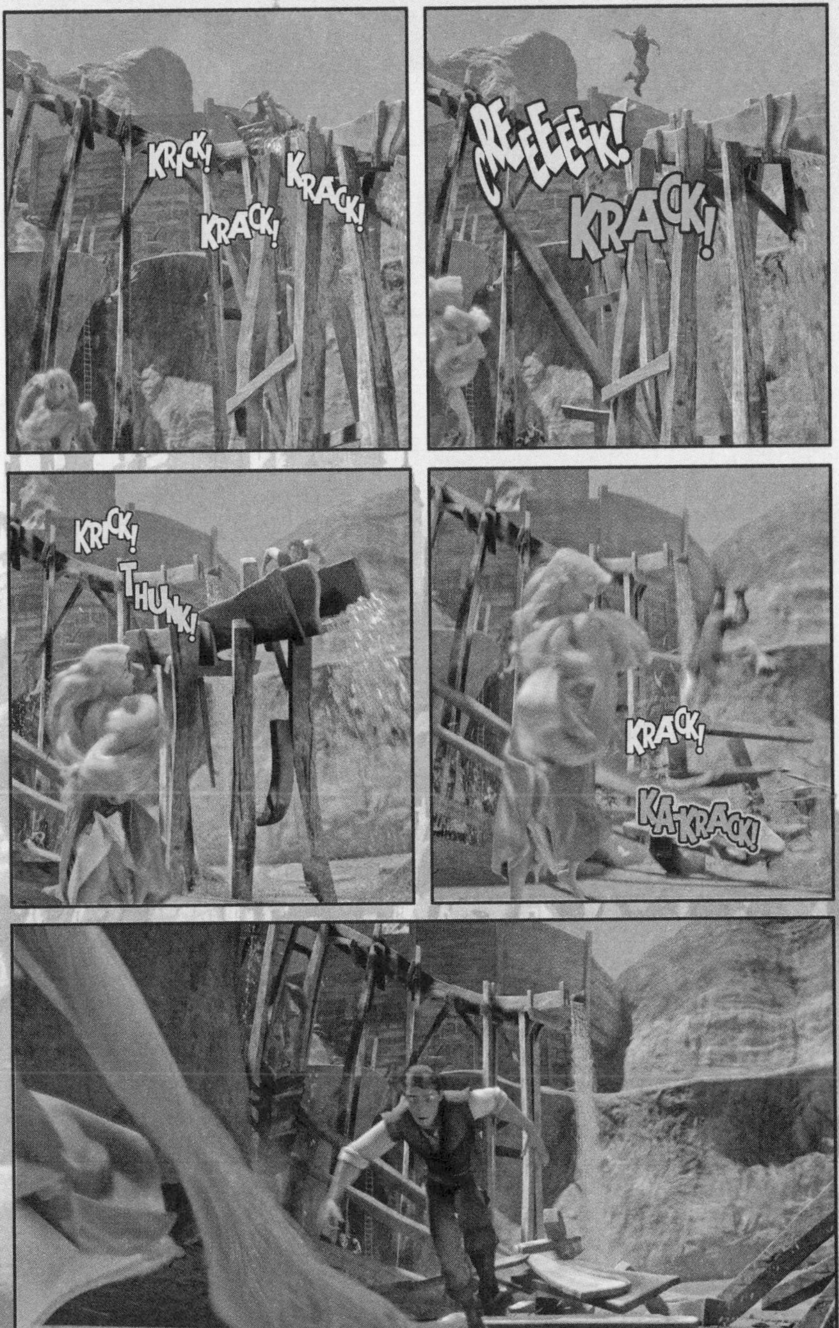
KRICK!
KRACK!
KRACK!
CREEEEEK!
KRACK!
KRICK!
THUNK!
KRACK!
KA-KRACK!

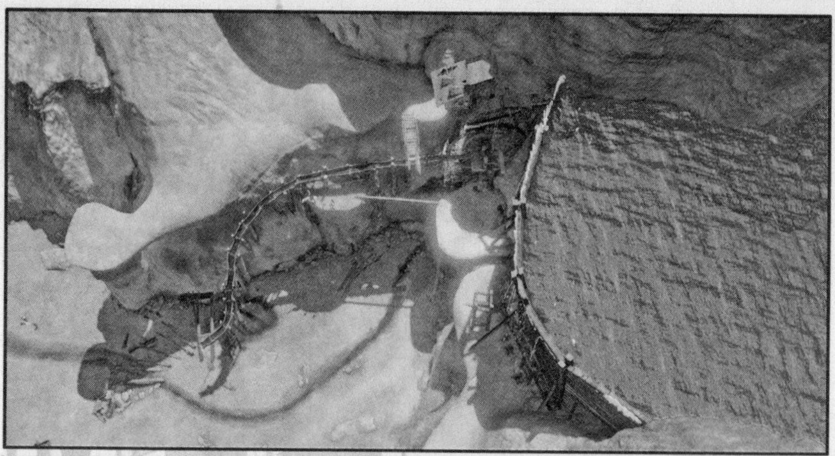

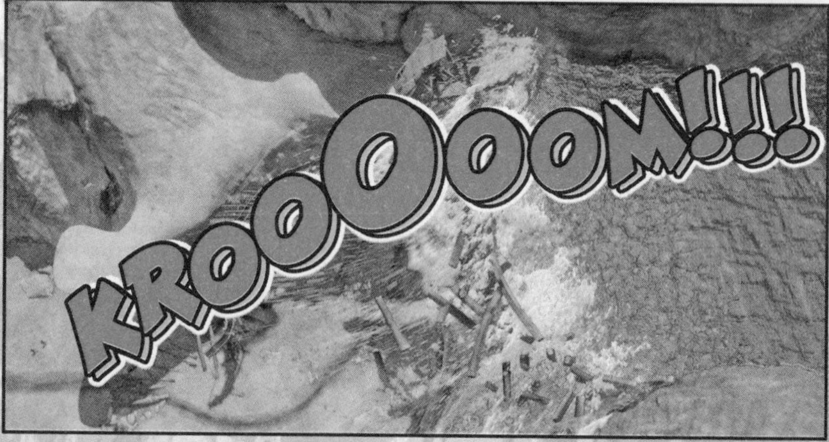
KROOOOOOM!!!!

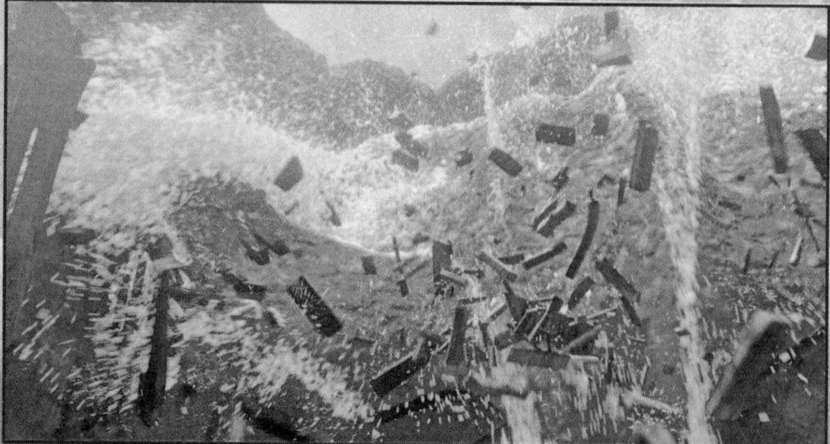

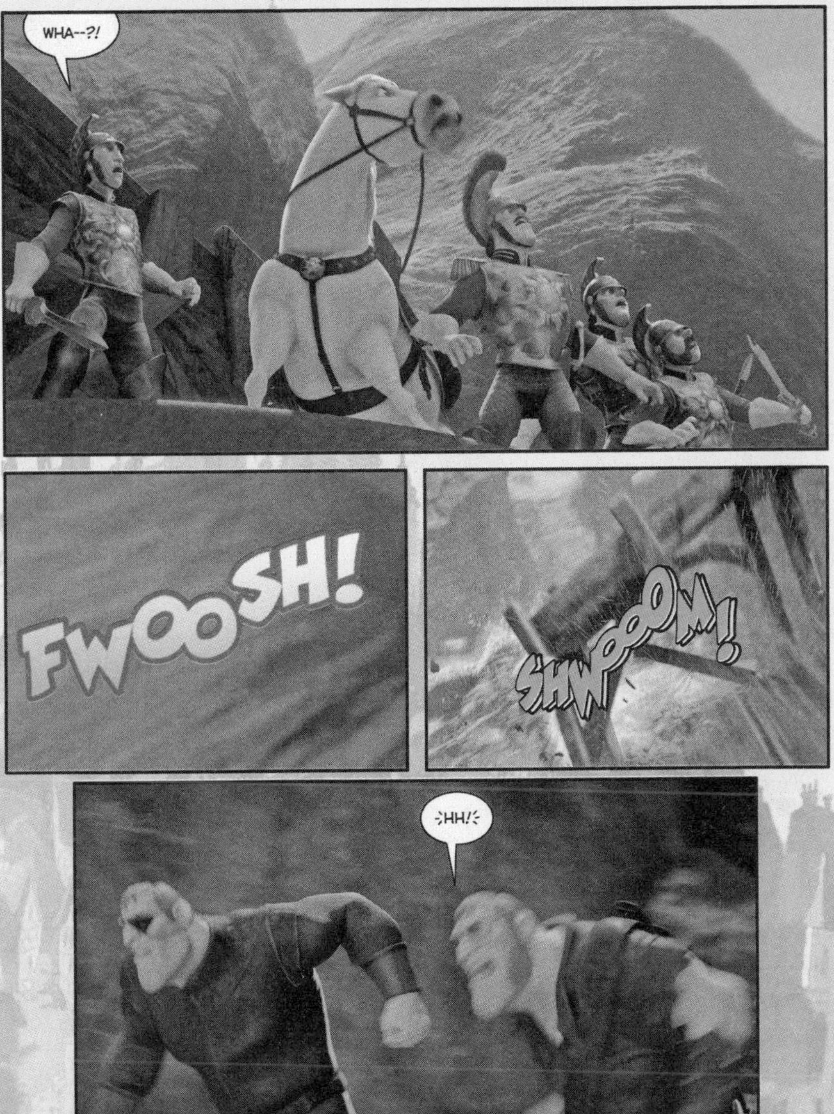
WHA--?!
FWOOSH!
SHWOOOOM!
HH!
FWOOSH!

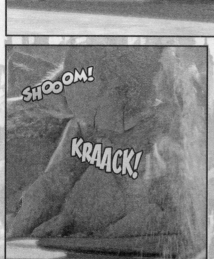

SHOOOM!

KRAACK!

KROOOM!

SHWOOOSH!

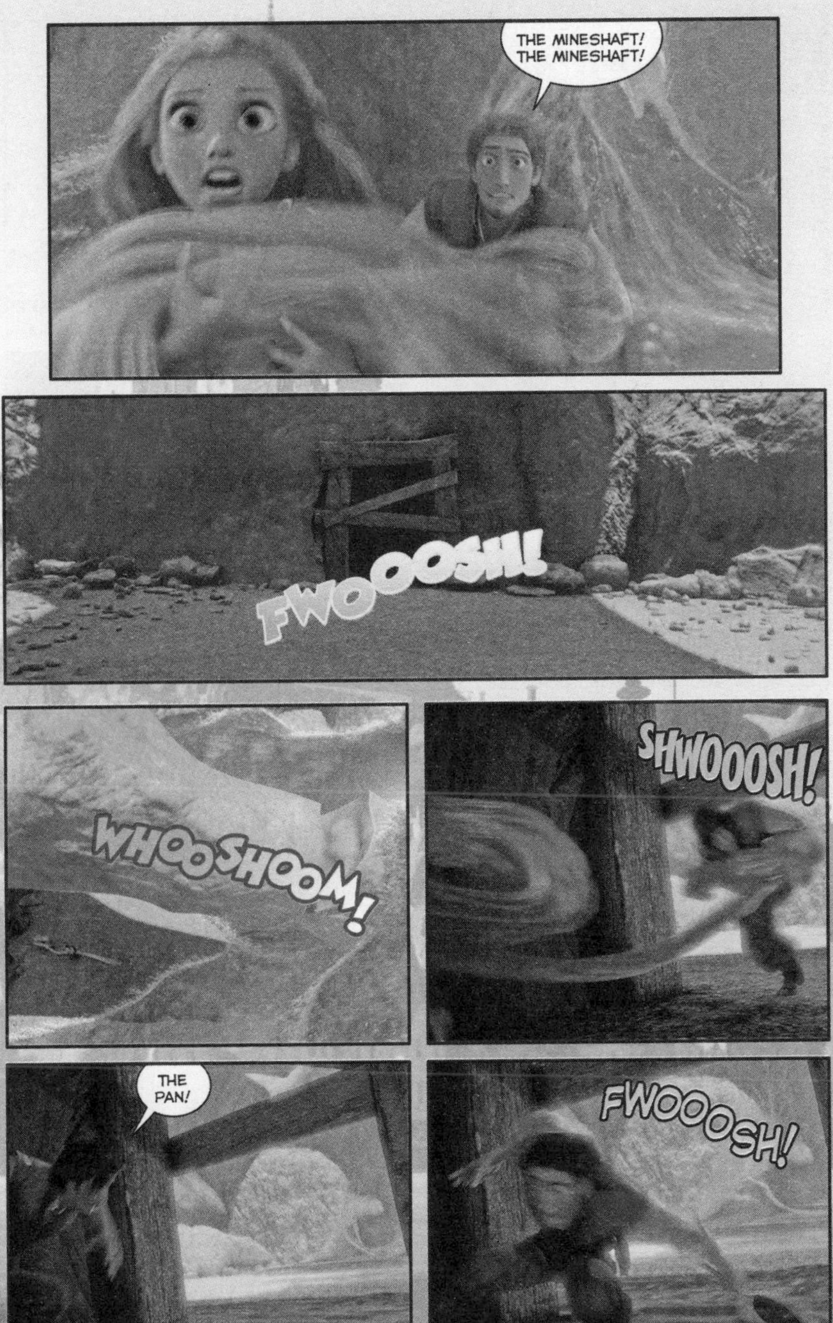
THE MINESHAFT! THE MINESHAFT!
FWOOOSH!
WHOOSHOOM!
SHWOOOOSH!
THE PAN!
FWOOOOSH!

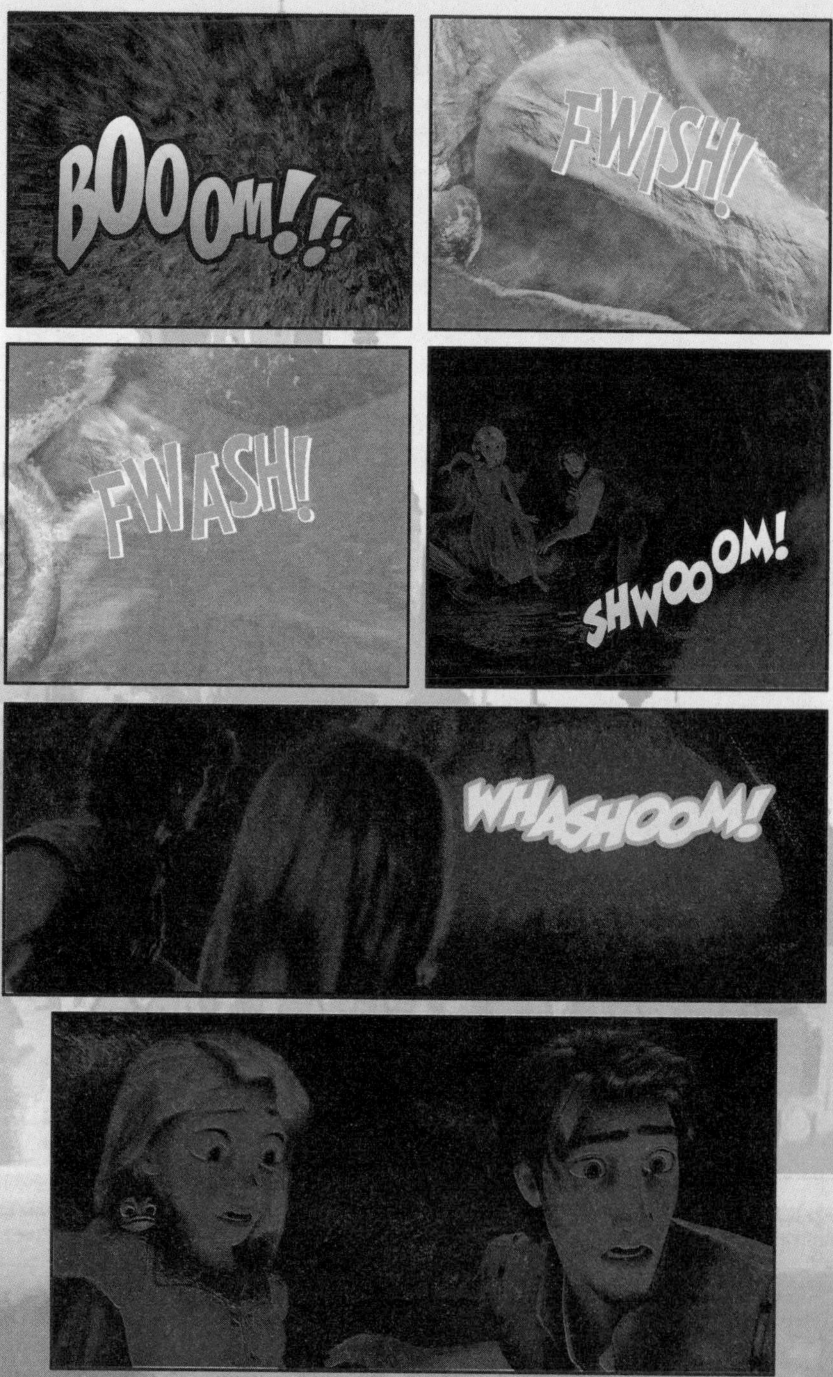
BOOOM!!!
FWISH!
FWASH!
SHWOOOM!
WHASHOOOM!

SPLOOSH!

‑GASP!‑

IT'S NO USE --
I CAN'T SEE
ANYTHING.

IT'S PITCH
BLACK DOWN
THERE.

‑NNNGG!‑

‑GAH!‑

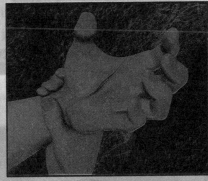

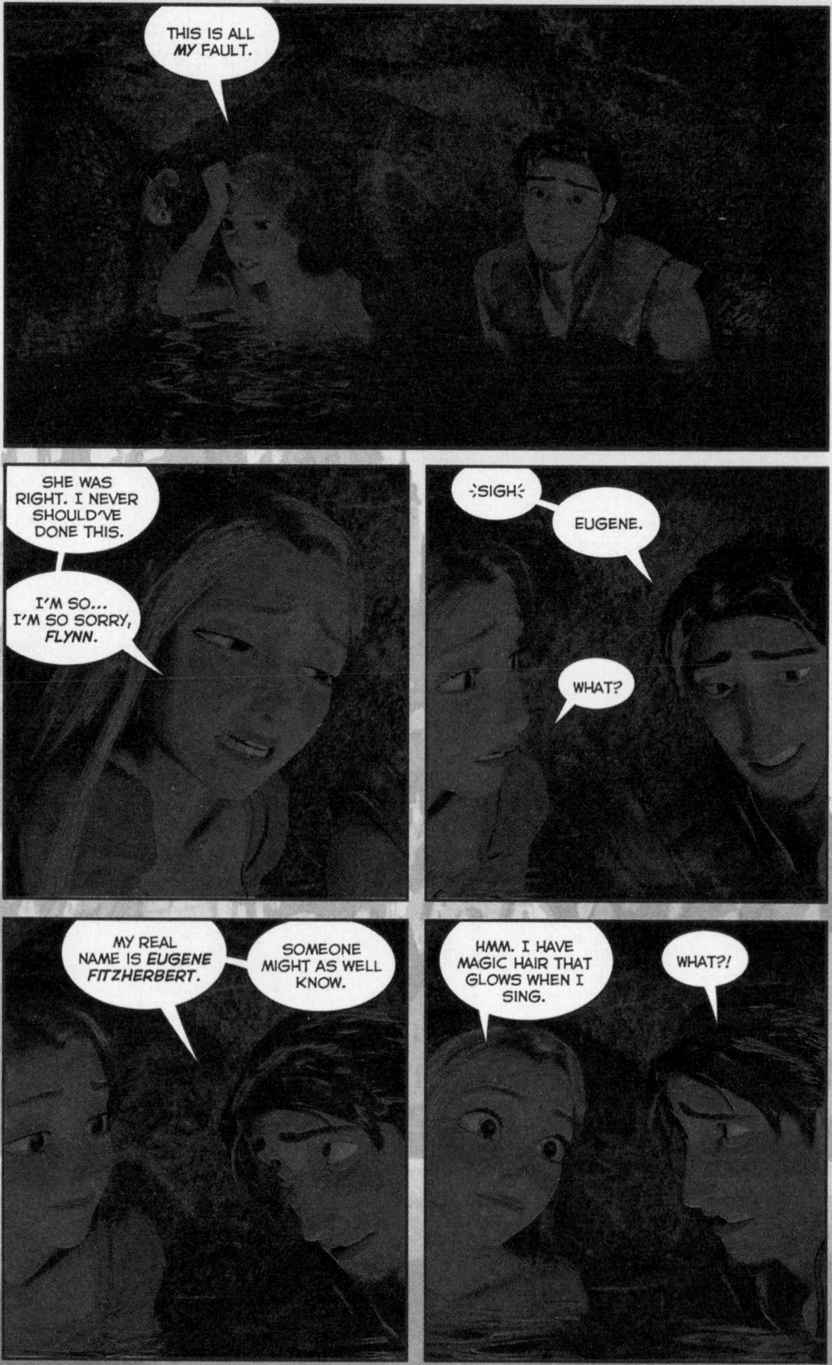
THIS IS ALL *MY* FAULT.
SHE WAS RIGHT. I NEVER SHOULD'VE DONE THIS.
I'M SO... I'M SO SORRY, *FLYNN*.
-SIGH-
EUGENE.
WHAT?
MY REAL NAME IS *EUGENE FITZHERBERT*.
SOMEONE MIGHT AS WELL KNOW.
HMM. I HAVE MAGIC HAIR THAT GLOWS WHEN I SING.
WHAT?!

I HAVE *MAGIC HAIR* THAT GLOWS WHEN I *SING!*

♫♪ FLOWER, GLEAM AND GLOW

♫♪ LET YOUR POWER SHINE

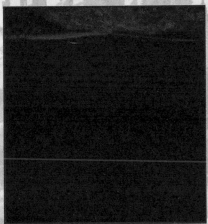

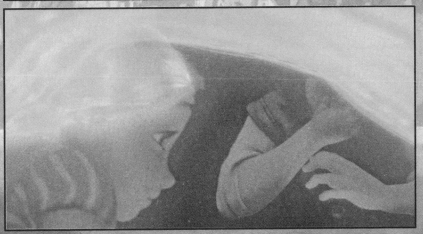

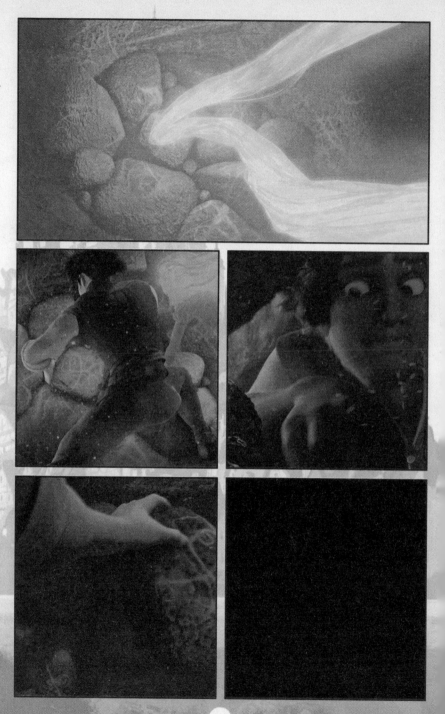

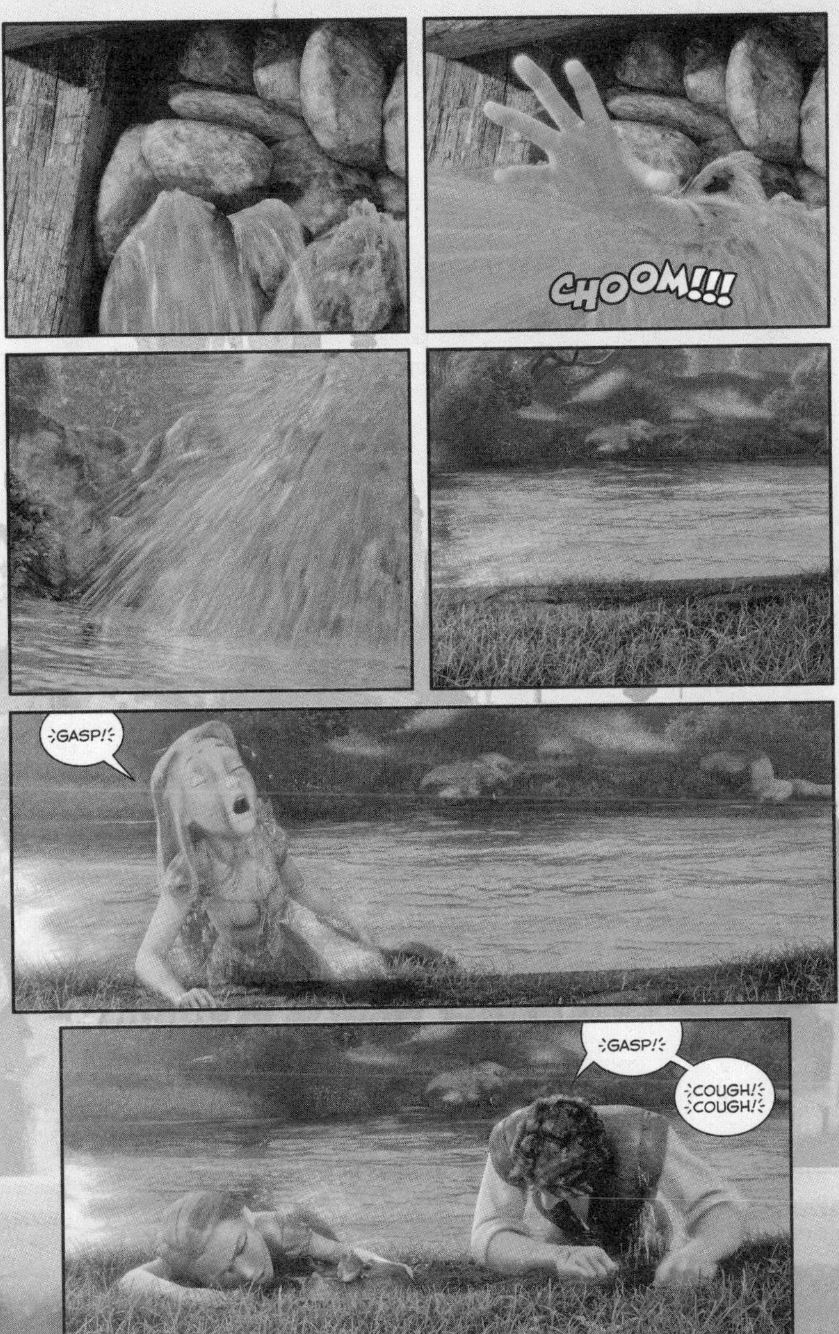
CHOOM!!!
GASP!
GASP!
COUGH! COUGH!

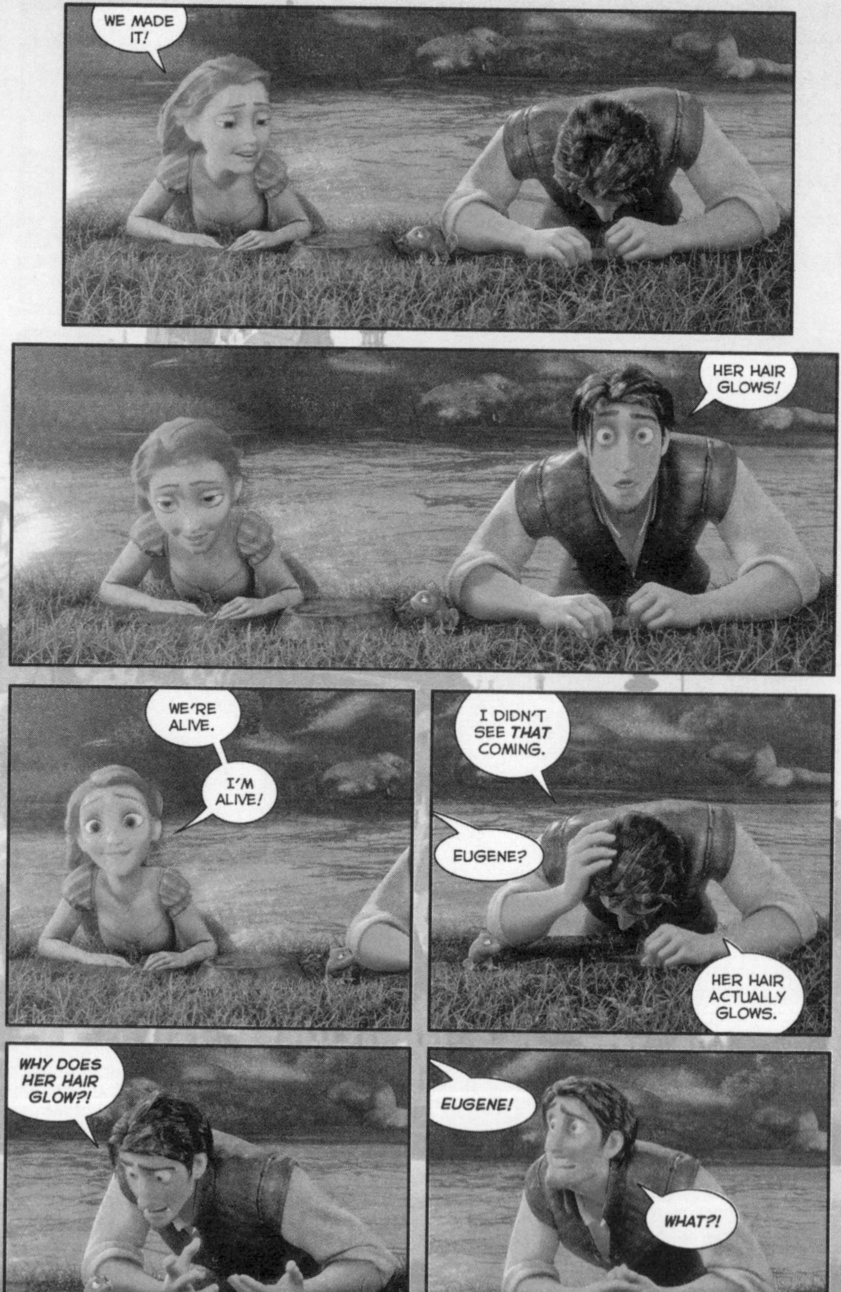
WE MADE IT!
HER HAIR GLOWS!
WE'RE ALIVE.
I'M ALIVE!
I DIDN'T SEE THAT COMING.
EUGENE?
HER HAIR ACTUALLY GLOWS.
WHY DOES HER HAIR GLOW?!
EUGENE!
WHAT?!

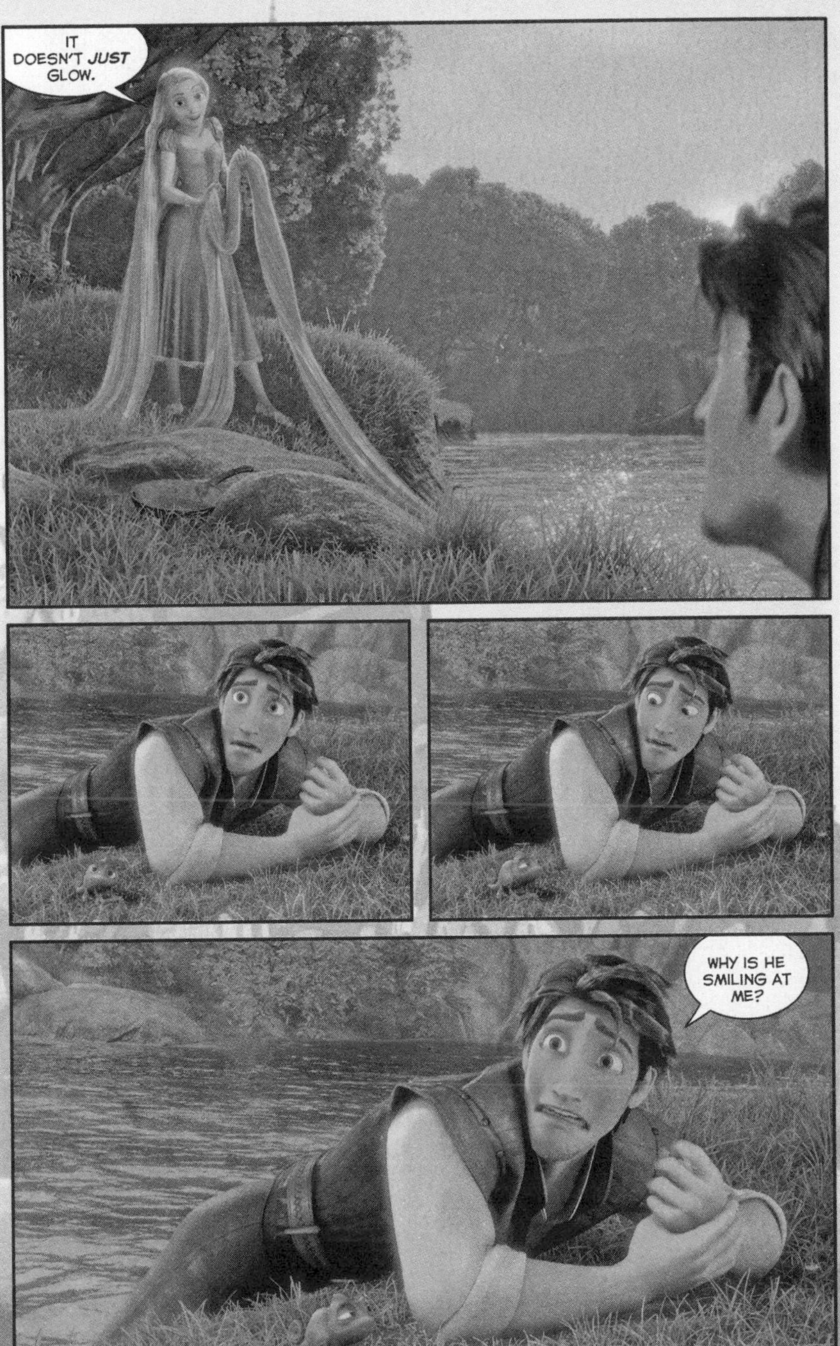
IT DOESN'T *JUST* GLOW.
WHY IS HE SMILING AT ME?

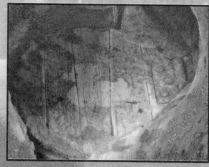

:COUGH!:
:COUGH!:
:COUGH!:

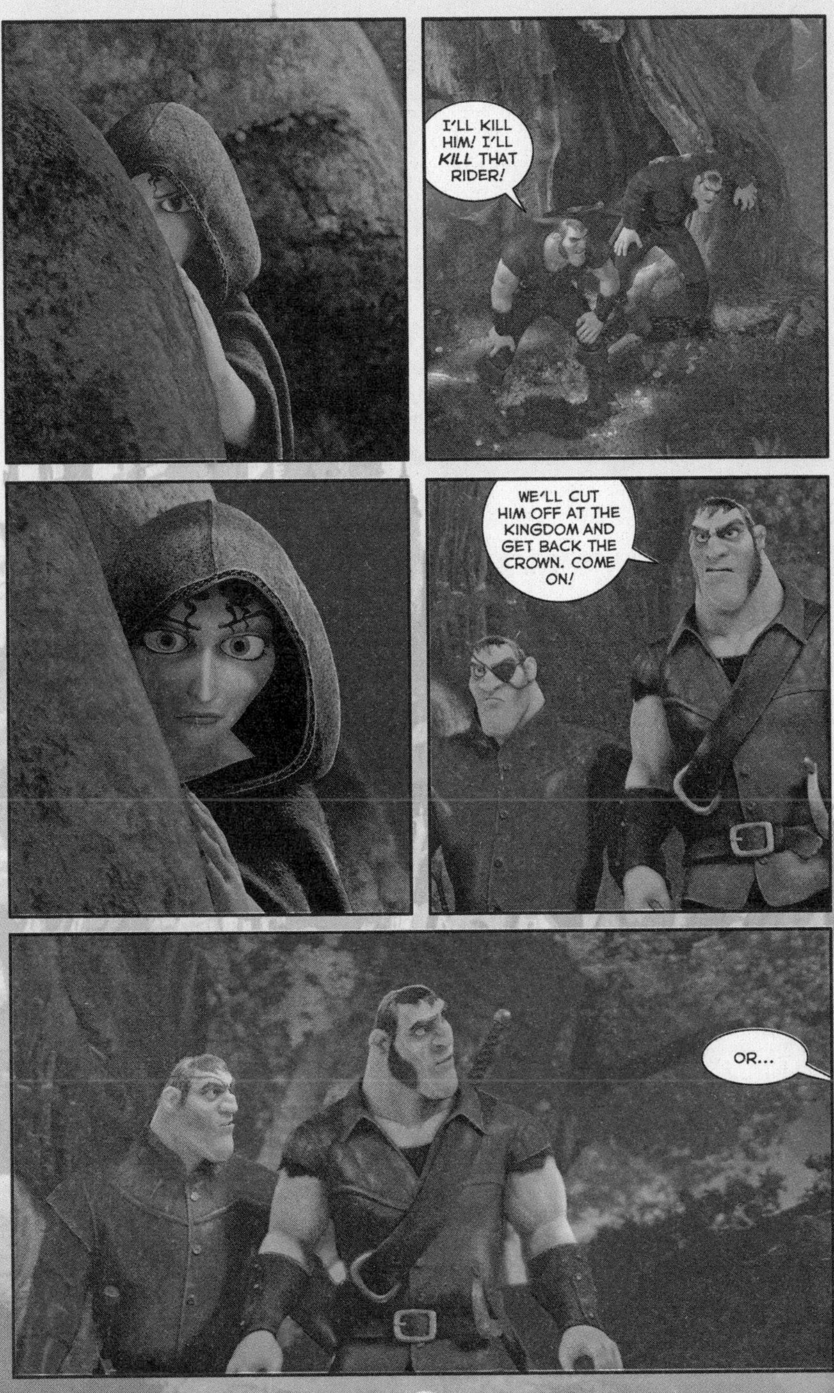
I'LL KILL HIM! I'LL KILL THAT RIDER!
WE'LL CUT HIM OFF AT THE KINGDOM AND GET BACK THE CROWN. COME ON!
OR...

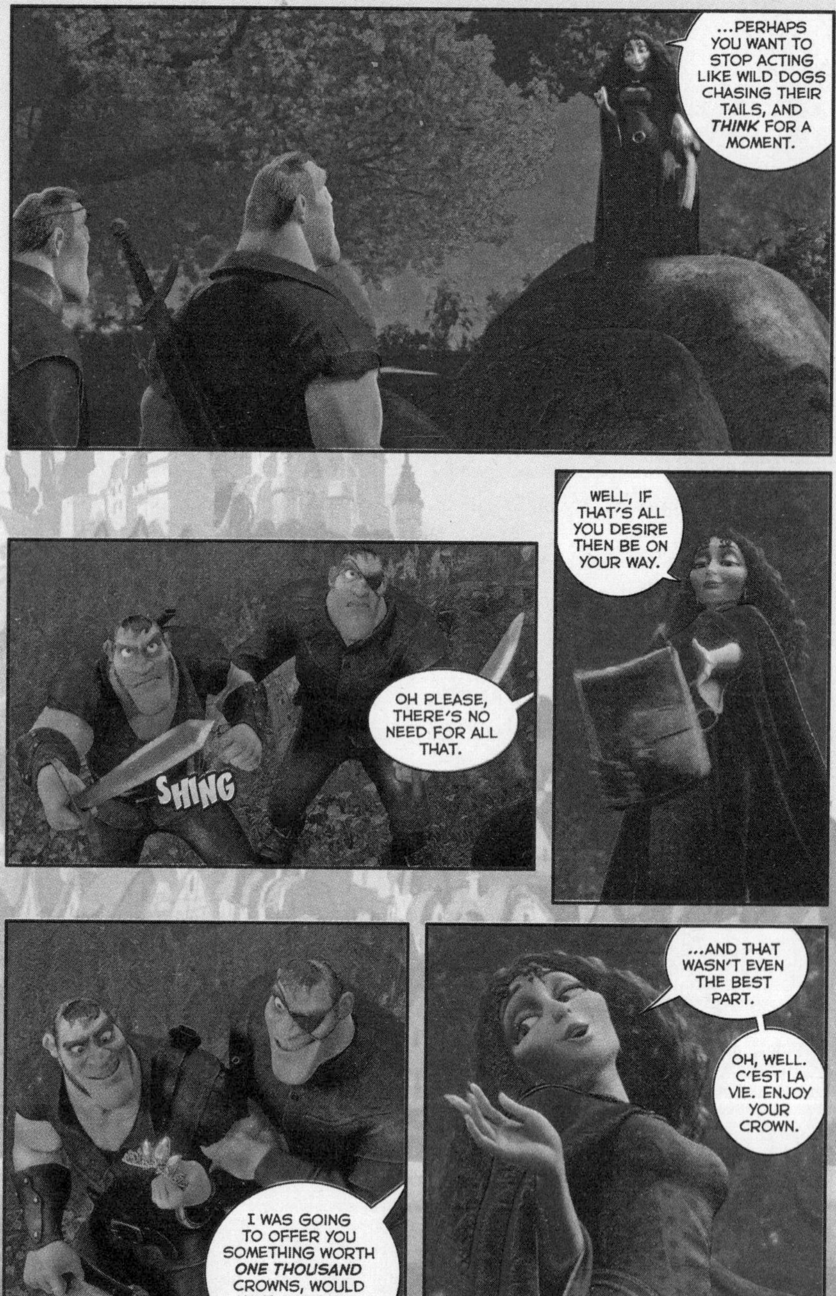
...PERHAPS YOU WANT TO STOP ACTING LIKE WILD DOGS CHASING THEIR TAILS, AND *THINK* FOR A MOMENT.
SHING
OH PLEASE, THERE'S NO NEED FOR ALL THAT.
WELL, IF THAT'S ALL YOU DESIRE THEN BE ON YOUR WAY.
I WAS GOING TO OFFER YOU SOMETHING WORTH *ONE THOUSAND* CROWNS, WOULD HAVE MADE YOU RICH BEYOND BELIEF...
...AND THAT WASN'T EVEN THE BEST PART.
OH, WELL. C'EST LA VIE. ENJOY YOUR CROWN.

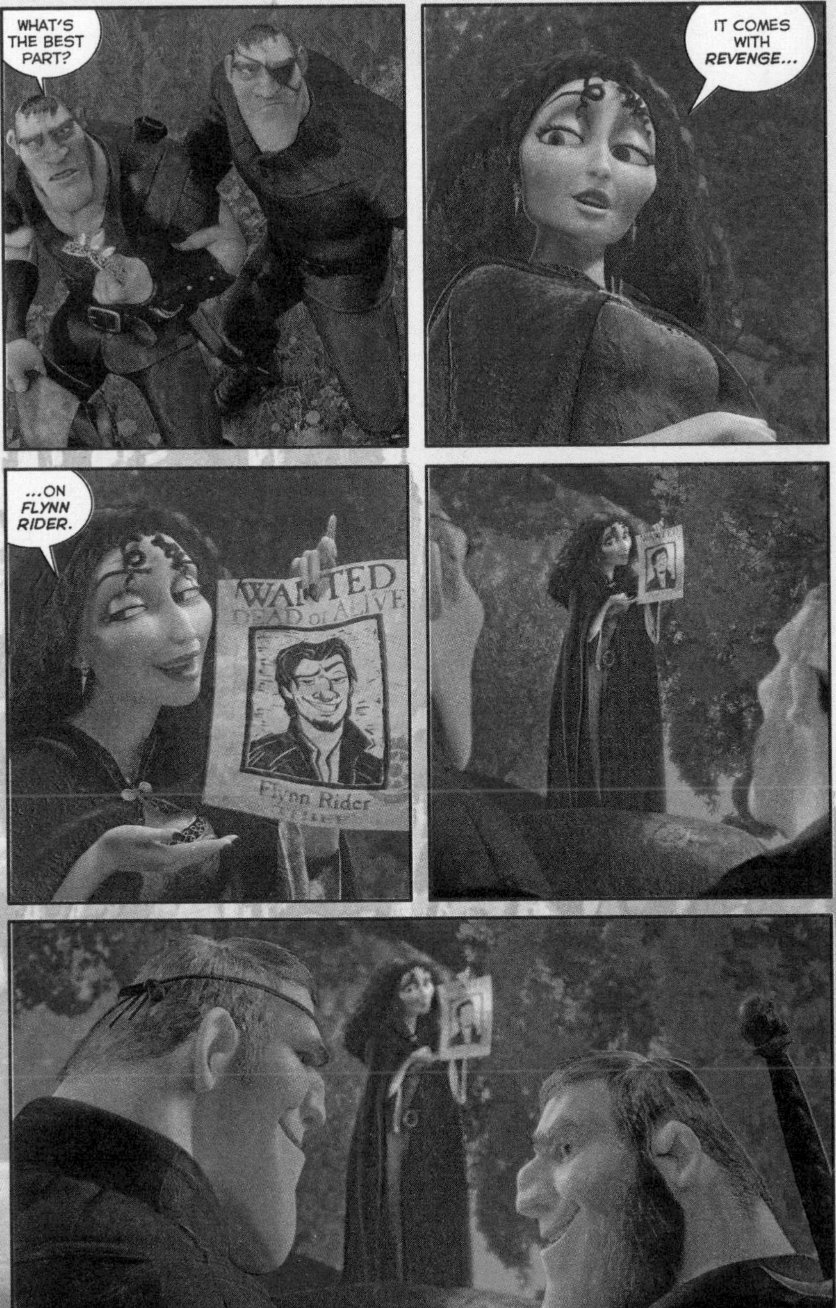
WHAT'S THE BEST PART?
IT COMES WITH REVENGE...
...ON FLYNN RIDER.
WANTED
DEAD or ALIVE
Flynn Rider

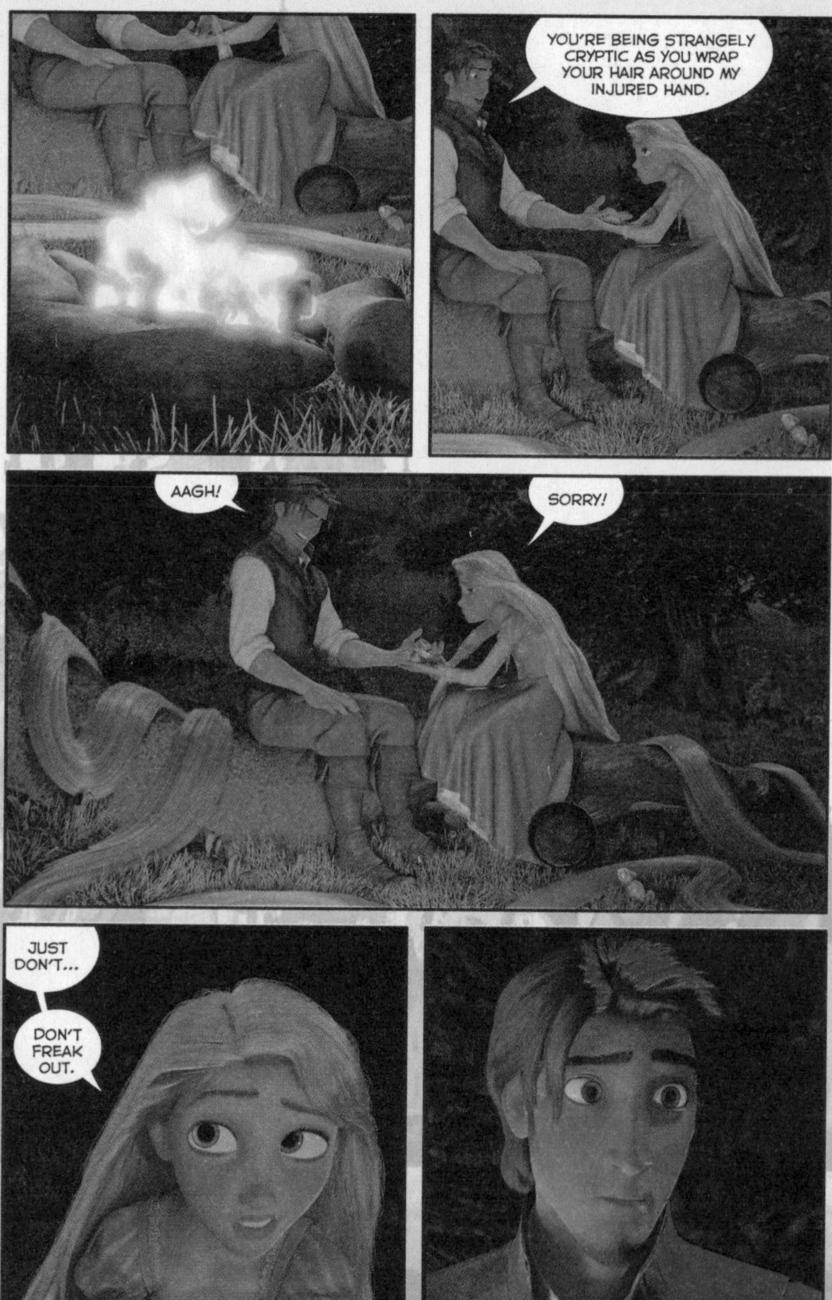
YOU'RE BEING STRANGELY CRYPTIC AS YOU WRAP YOUR HAIR AROUND MY INJURED HAND.
AAGH!
SORRY!
JUST DON'T...
DON'T FREAK OUT.

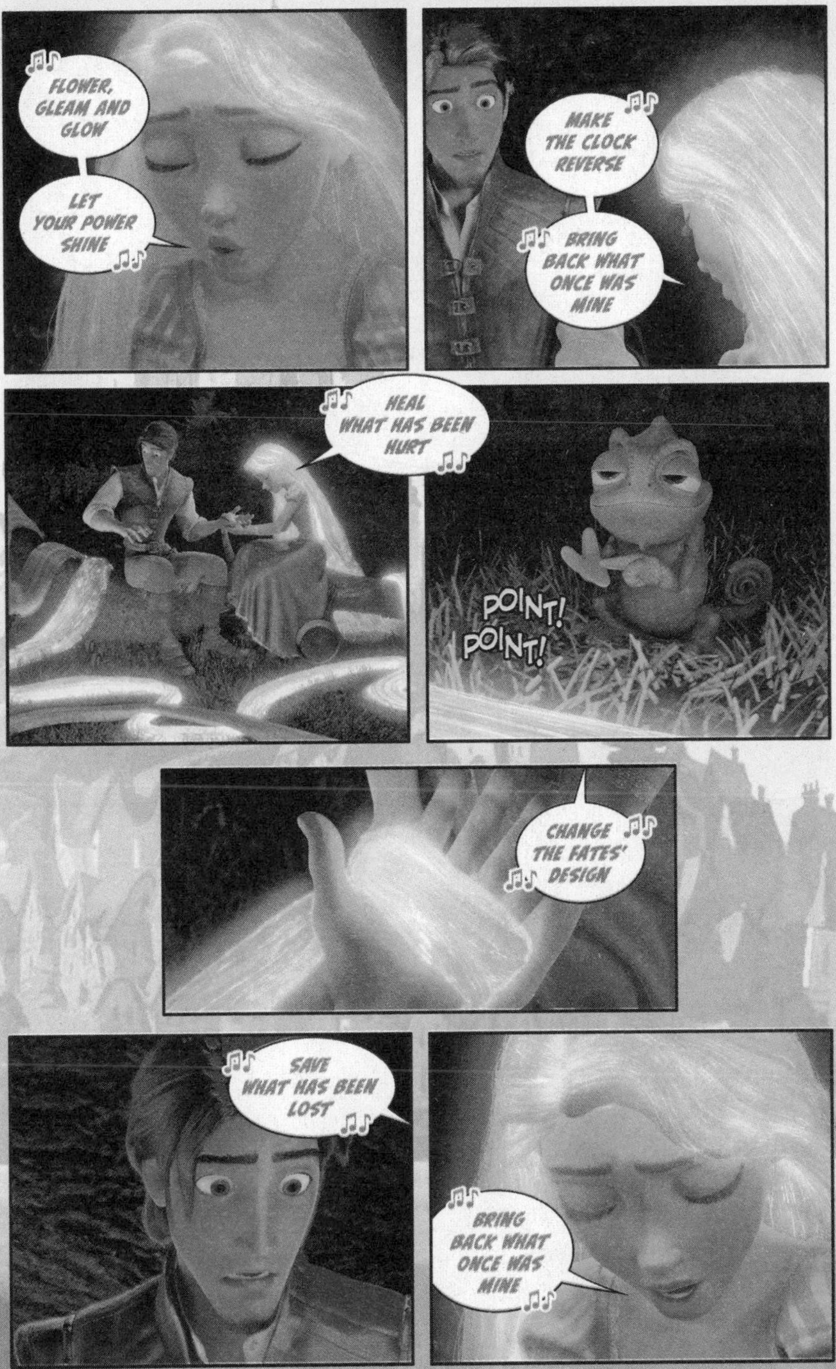
FLOWER, GLEAM AND GLOW
LET YOUR POWER SHINE
MAKE THE CLOCK REVERSE
BRING BACK WHAT ONCE WAS MINE
HEAL WHAT HAS BEEN HURT
POINT! POINT!
CHANGE THE FATES' DESIGN
SAVE WHAT HAS BEEN LOST
BRING BACK WHAT ONCE WAS MINE

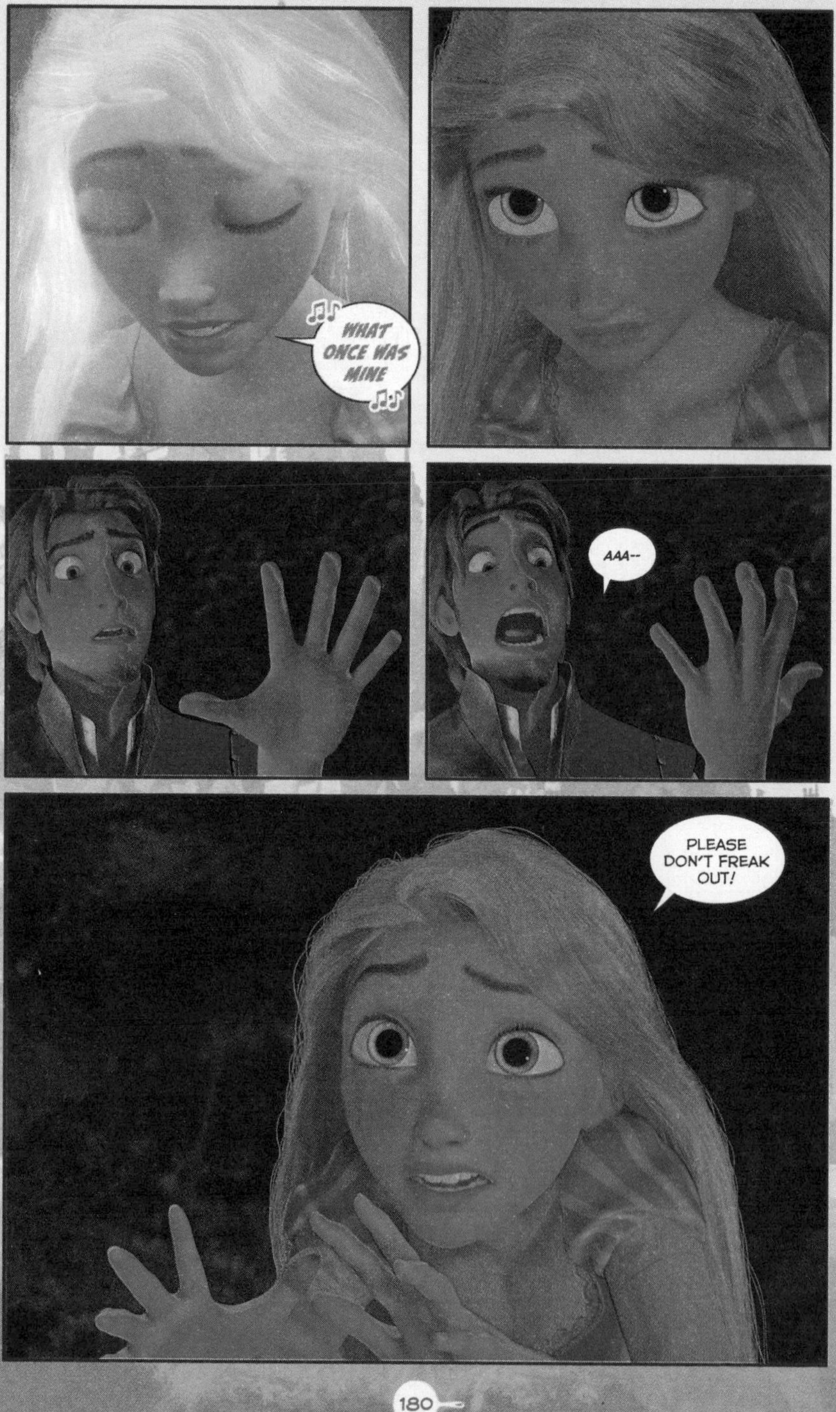
WHAT ONCE WAS MINE
AAA--
PLEASE DON'T FREAK OUT!

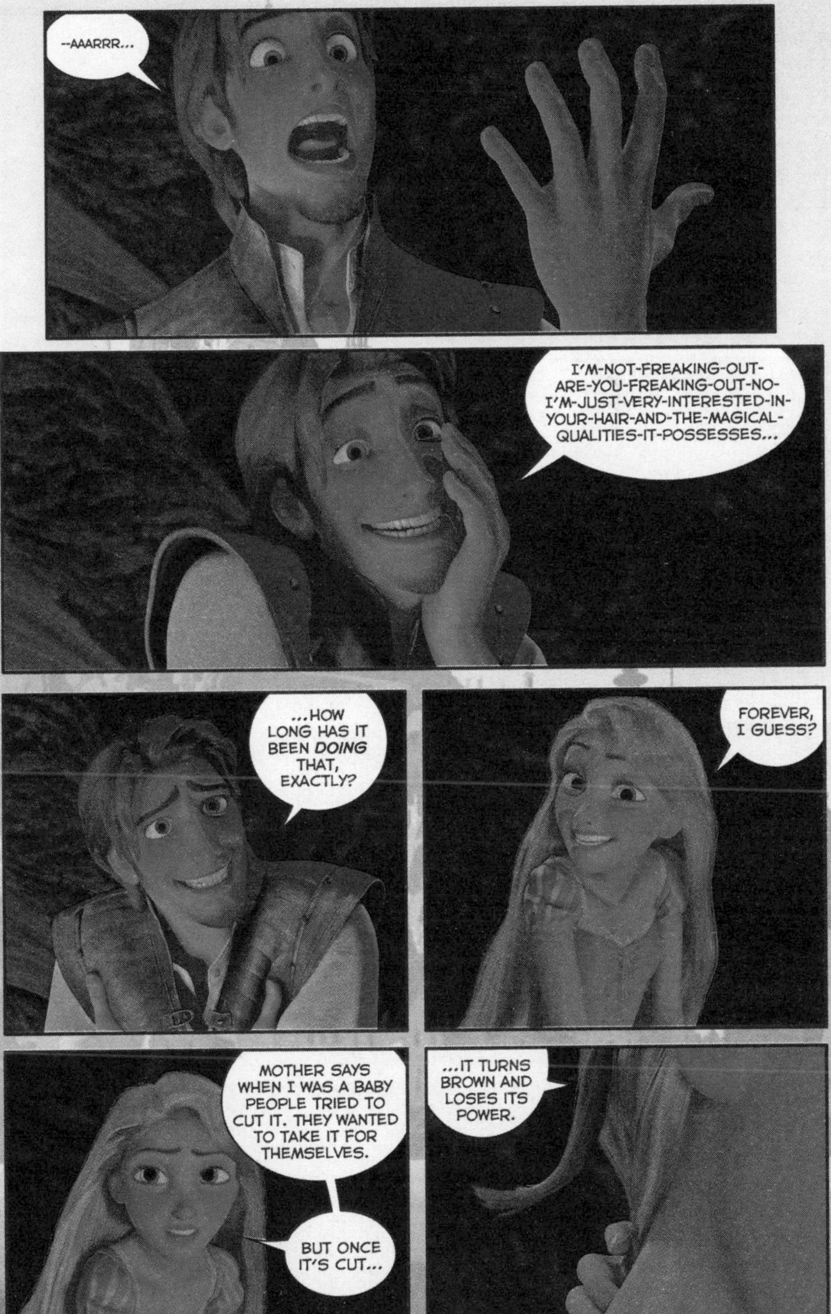
--AAARRR...
I'M-NOT-FREAKING-OUT-ARE-YOU-FREAKING-OUT-NO-I'M-JUST-VERY-INTERESTED-IN-YOUR-HAIR-AND-THE-MAGICAL-QUALITIES-IT-POSSESSES...
...HOW LONG HAS IT BEEN *DOING* THAT, EXACTLY?
FOREVER, I GUESS?
MOTHER SAYS WHEN I WAS A BABY PEOPLE TRIED TO CUT IT. THEY WANTED TO TAKE IT FOR THEMSELVES.
BUT ONCE IT'S CUT...
...IT TURNS BROWN AND LOSES ITS POWER.

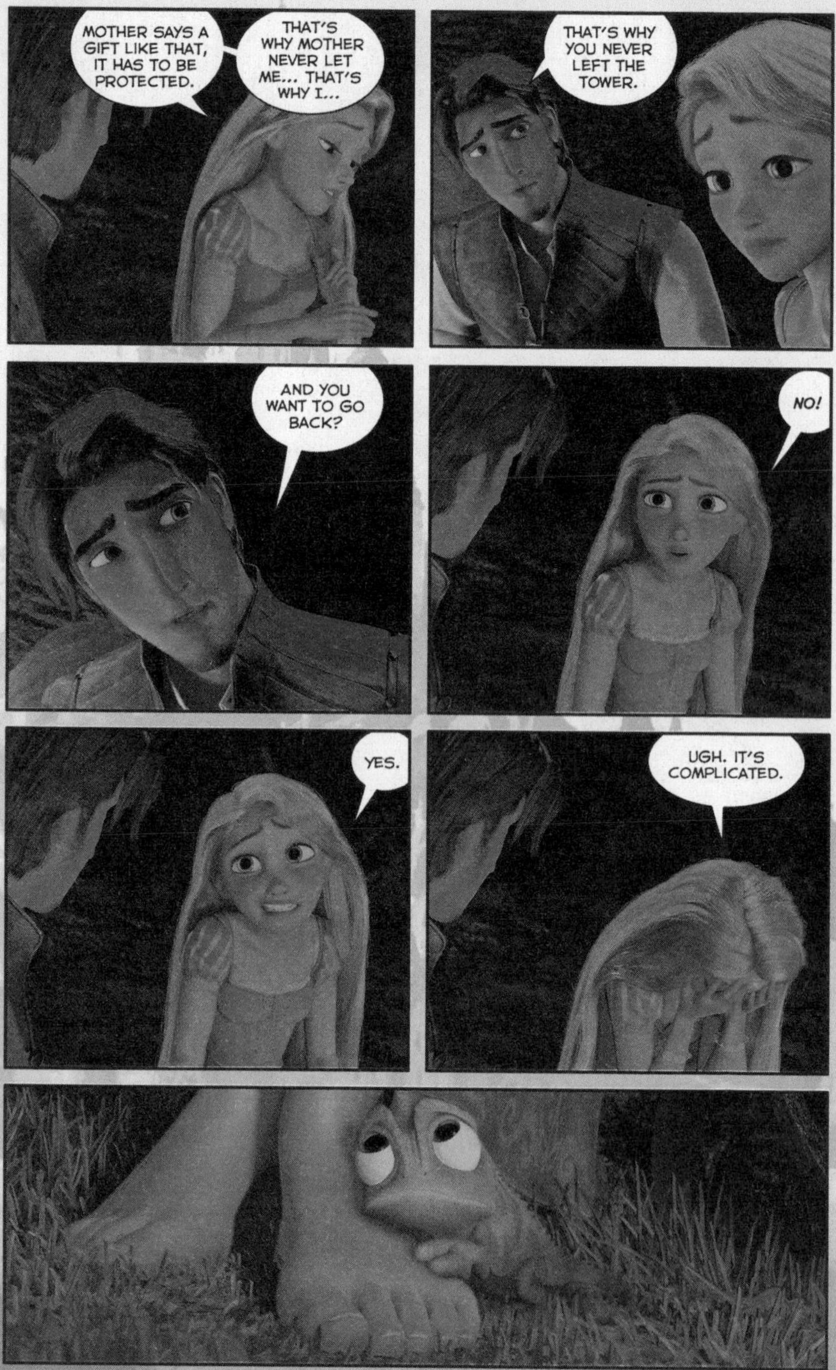
MOTHER SAYS A GIFT LIKE THAT, IT HAS TO BE PROTECTED.
THAT'S WHY MOTHER NEVER LET ME... THAT'S WHY I...
THAT'S WHY YOU NEVER LEFT THE TOWER.
AND YOU WANT TO GO BACK?
NO!
YES.
UGH. IT'S COMPLICATED.

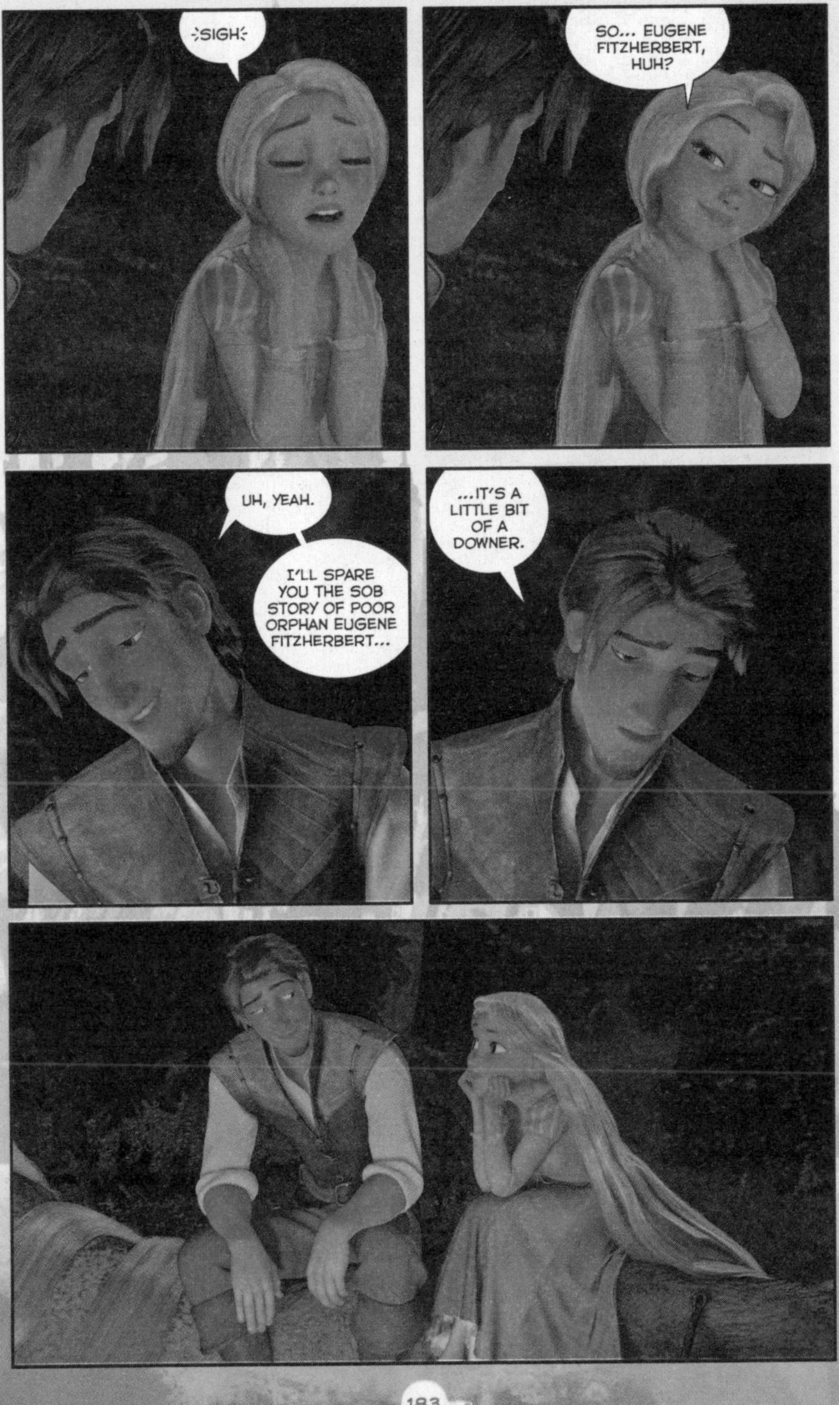
SIGH
SO... EUGENE FITZHERBERT, HUH?
UH, YEAH.
I'LL SPARE YOU THE SOB STORY OF POOR ORPHAN EUGENE FITZHERBERT...
...IT'S A LITTLE BIT OF A DOWNER.

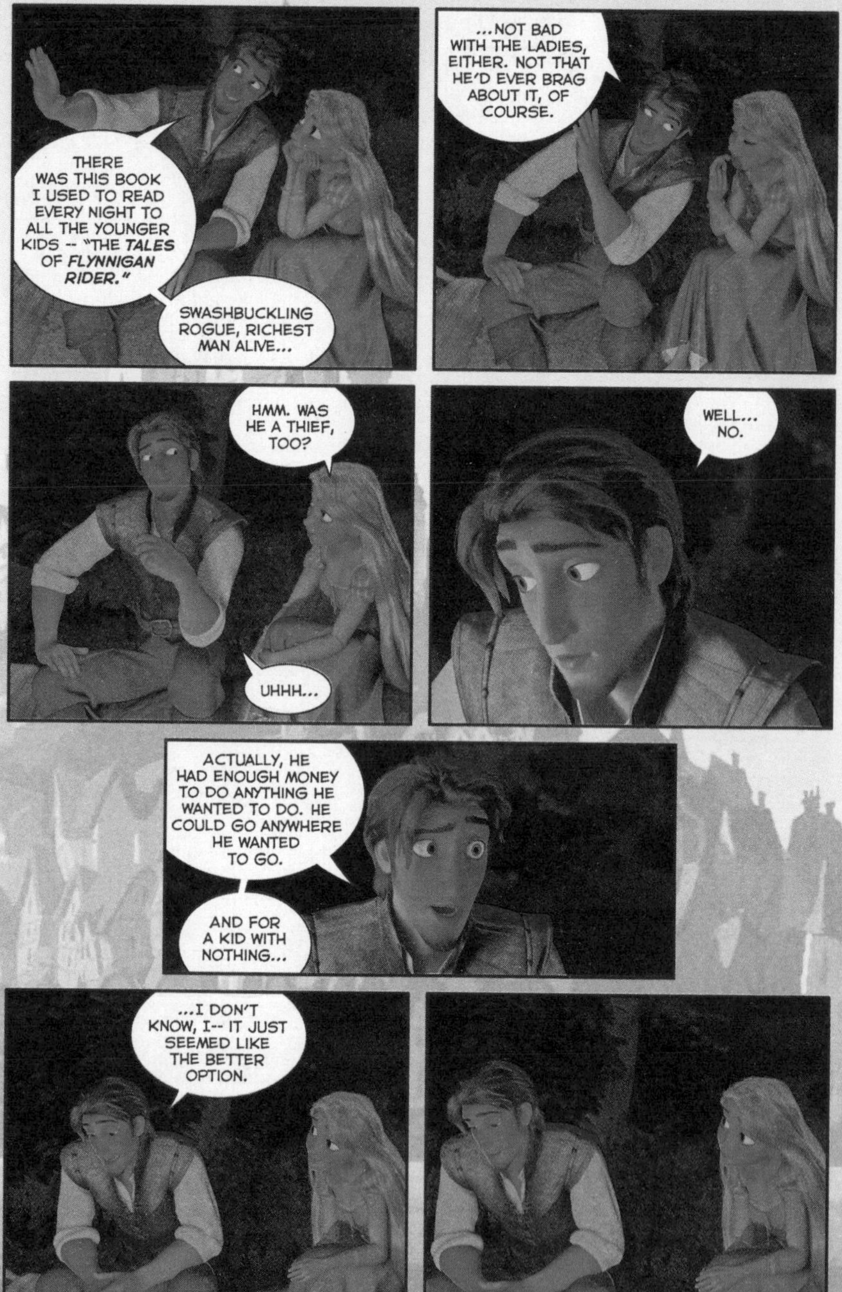
THERE WAS THIS BOOK I USED TO READ EVERY NIGHT TO ALL THE YOUNGER KIDS -- "THE *TALES* OF *FLYNNIGAN RIDER.*"
SWASHBUCKLING ROGUE, RICHEST MAN ALIVE...
...NOT BAD WITH THE LADIES, EITHER. NOT THAT HE'D EVER BRAG ABOUT IT, OF COURSE.
HMM. WAS HE A THIEF, TOO?
UHHH...
WELL... NO.
ACTUALLY, HE HAD ENOUGH MONEY TO DO ANYTHING HE WANTED TO DO. HE COULD GO ANYWHERE HE WANTED TO GO.
AND FOR A KID WITH NOTHING...
...I DON'T KNOW, I-- IT JUST SEEMED LIKE THE BETTER OPTION.

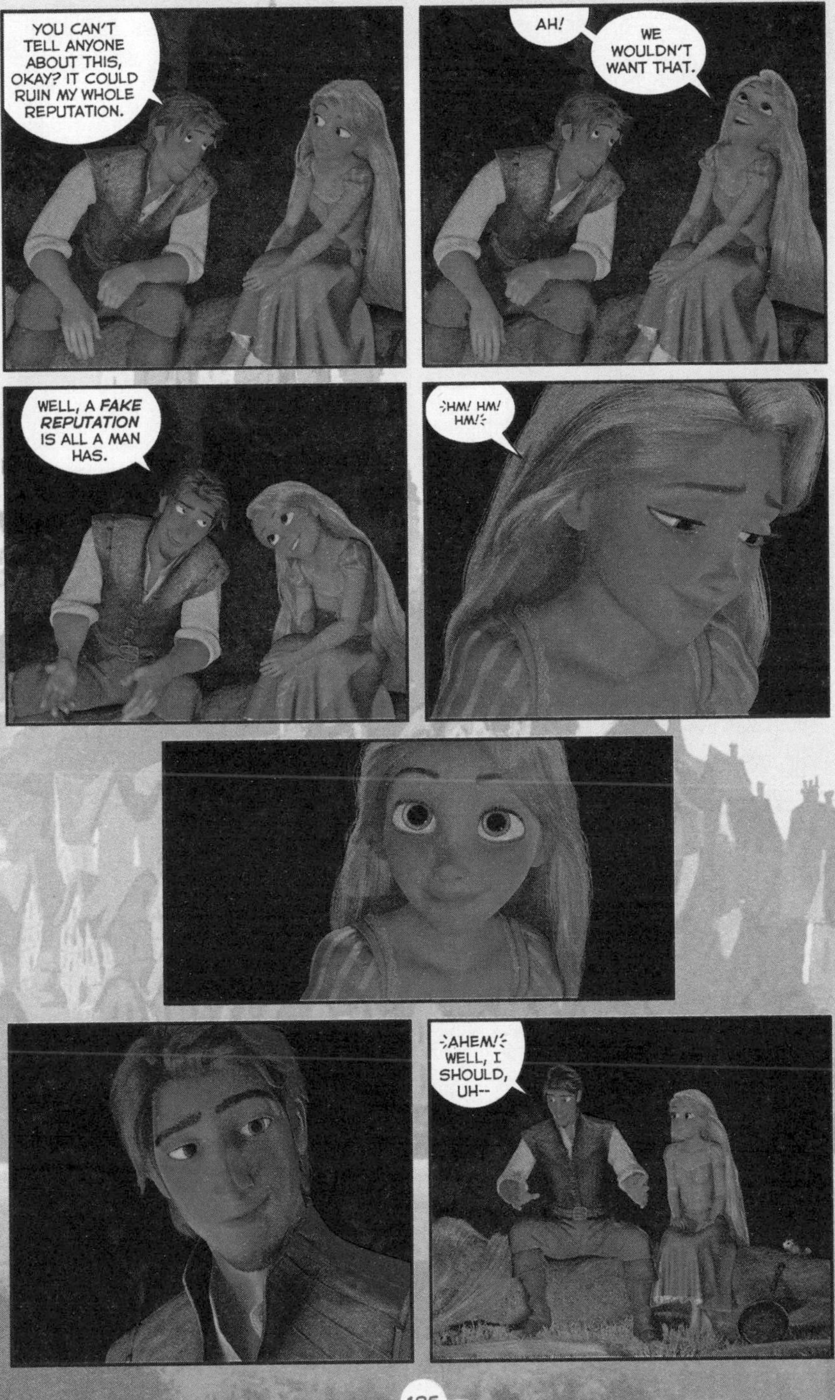
YOU CAN'T TELL ANYONE ABOUT THIS, OKAY? IT COULD RUIN MY WHOLE REPUTATION.
AH!
WE WOULDN'T WANT THAT.
WELL, A *FAKE REPUTATION* IS ALL A MAN HAS.
HM! HM! HM!
AHEM! WELL, I SHOULD, UH--

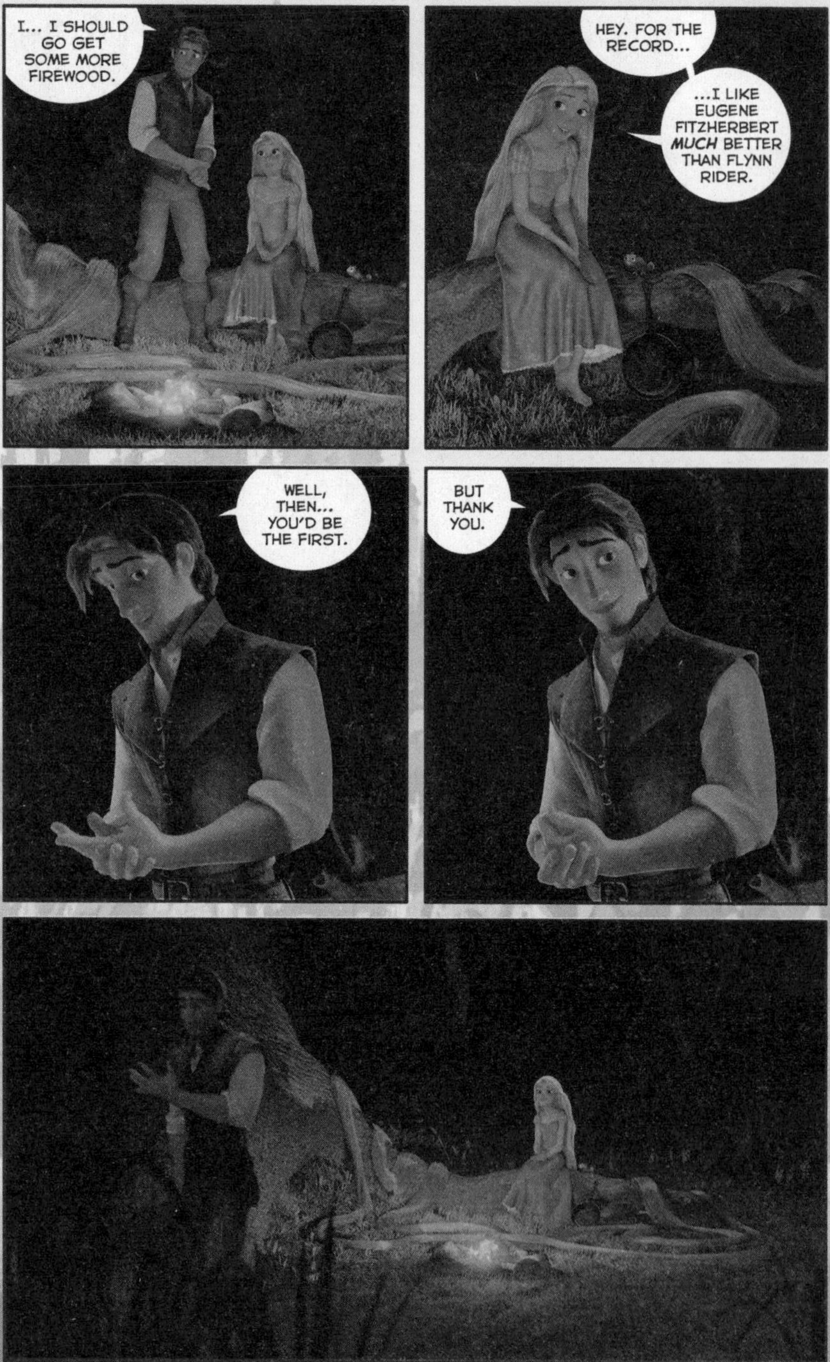
I... I SHOULD GO GET SOME MORE FIREWOOD.
HEY. FOR THE RECORD...
...I LIKE EUGENE FITZHERBERT *MUCH* BETTER THAN FLYNN RIDER.
WELL, THEN... YOU'D BE THE FIRST.
BUT THANK YOU.

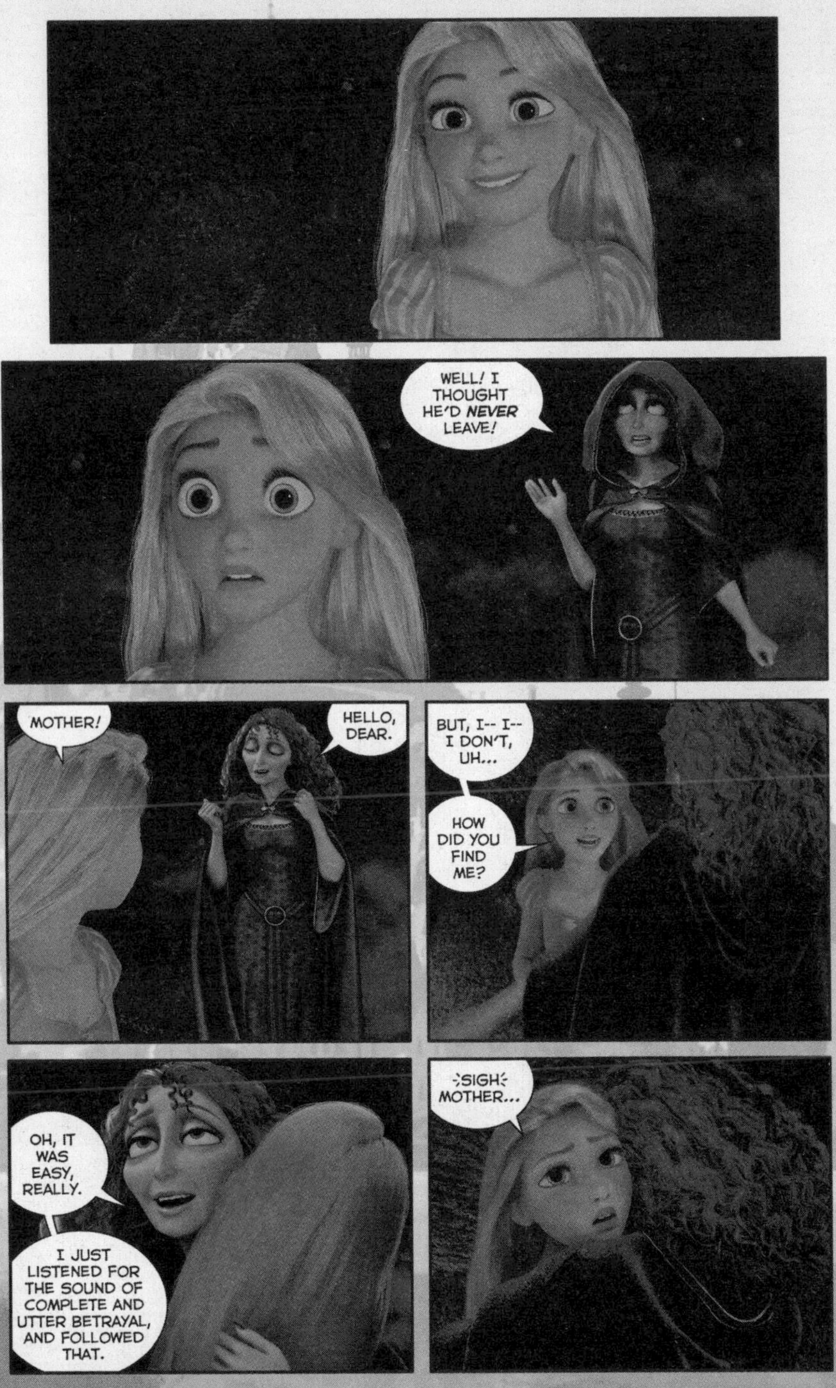
WELL! I THOUGHT HE'D *NEVER* LEAVE!
MOTHER!
HELLO, DEAR.
BUT, I-- I-- I DON'T, UH...
HOW DID YOU FIND ME?
OH, IT WAS EASY, REALLY.
I JUST LISTENED FOR THE SOUND OF COMPLETE AND UTTER BETRAYAL, AND FOLLOWED THAT.
SIGH MOTHER...

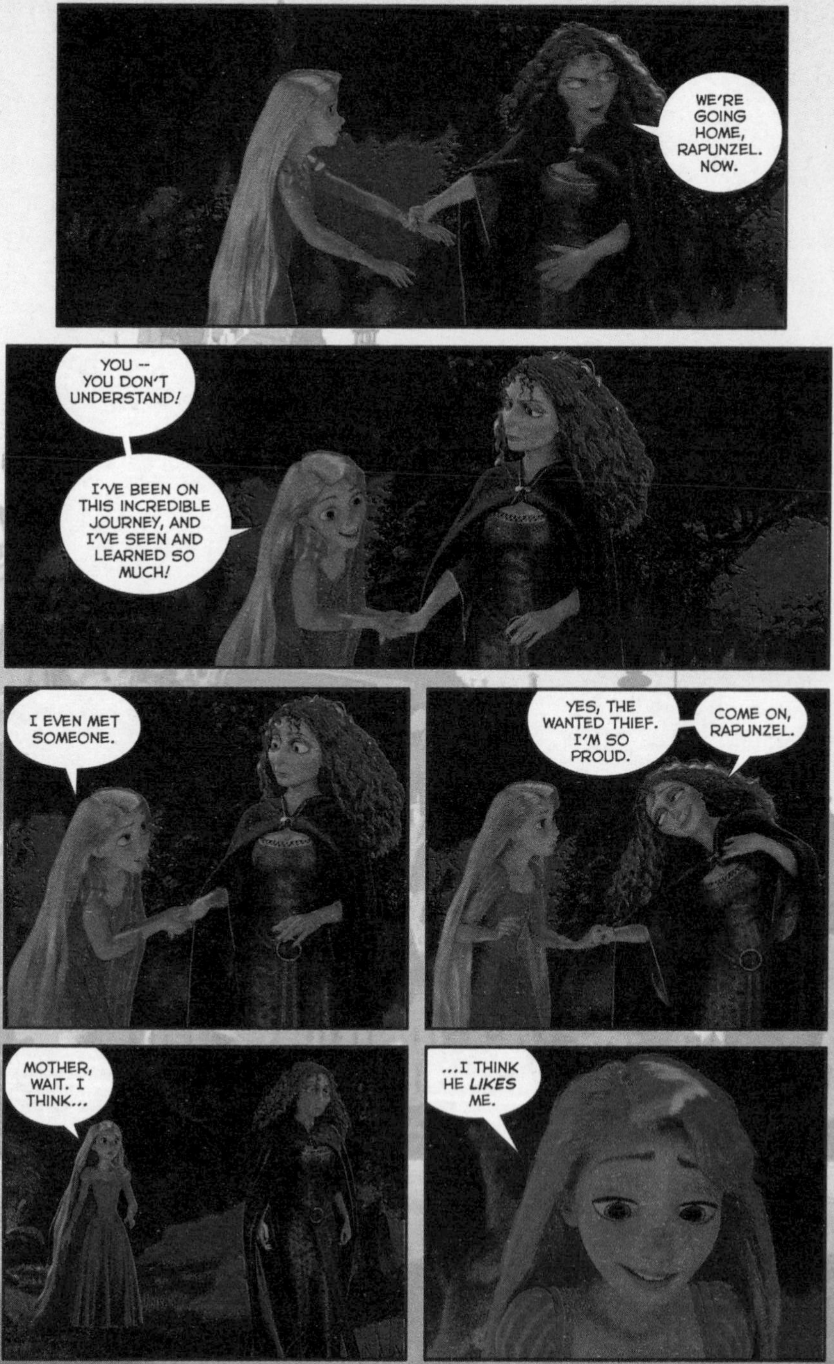
WE'RE GOING HOME, RAPUNZEL. NOW.
YOU -- YOU DON'T UNDERSTAND!
I'VE BEEN ON THIS INCREDIBLE JOURNEY, AND I'VE SEEN AND LEARNED SO MUCH!
I EVEN MET SOMEONE.
YES, THE WANTED THIEF. I'M SO PROUD.
COME ON, RAPUNZEL.
MOTHER, WAIT. I THINK...
...I THINK HE *LIKES* ME.

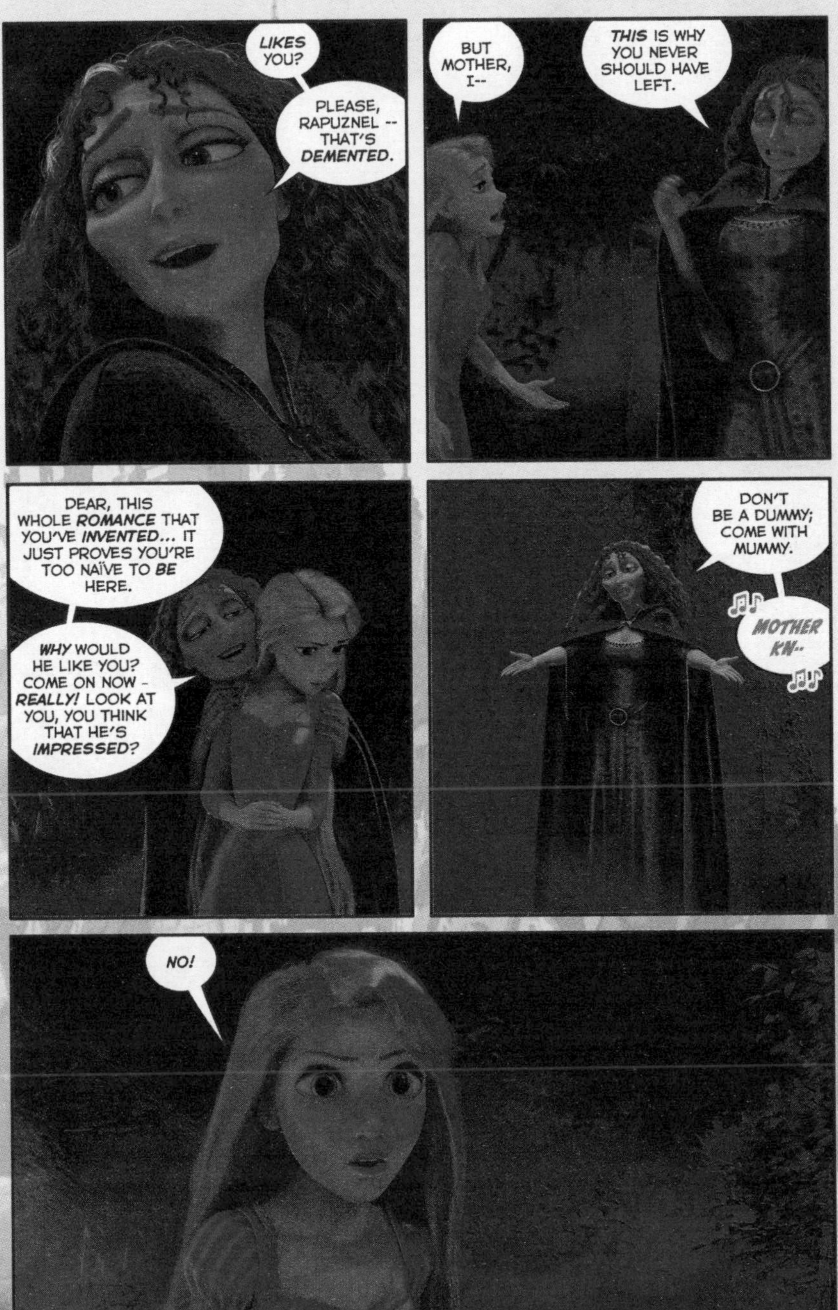

LIKES YOU?
PLEASE, RAPUZNEL -- THAT'S DEMENTED.
BUT MOTHER, I--
THIS IS WHY YOU NEVER SHOULD HAVE LEFT.
DEAR, THIS WHOLE ROMANCE THAT YOU'VE INVENTED... IT JUST PROVES YOU'RE TOO NAÏVE TO BE HERE.
WHY WOULD HE LIKE YOU? COME ON NOW - REALLY! LOOK AT YOU, YOU THINK THAT HE'S IMPRESSED?
DON'T BE A DUMMY; COME WITH MUMMY.
MOTHER KN-
NO!

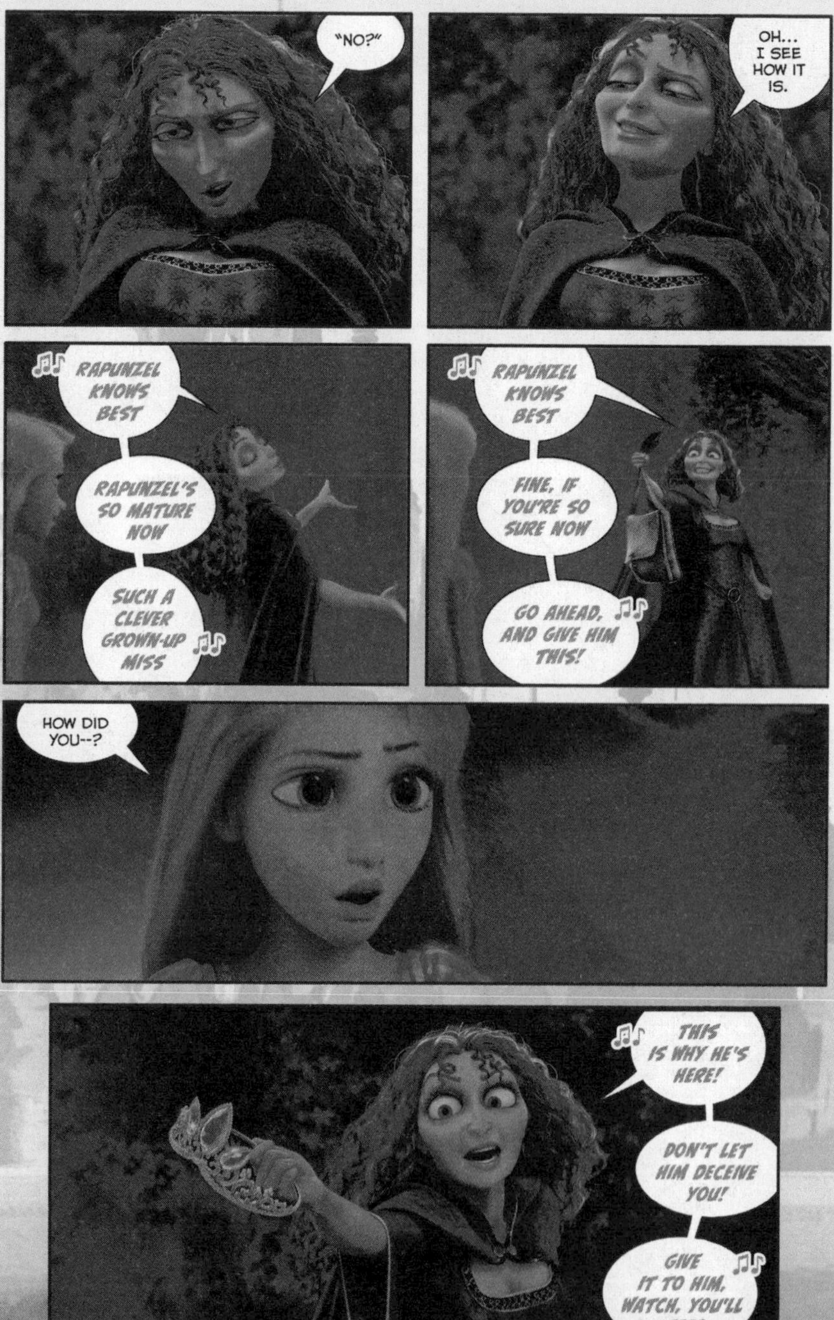
"NO?"
OH... I SEE HOW IT IS.
RAPUNZEL KNOWS BEST
RAPUNZEL'S SO MATURE NOW
SUCH A CLEVER GROWN-UP MISS
RAPUNZEL KNOWS BEST
FINE, IF YOU'RE SO SURE NOW
GO AHEAD, AND GIVE HIM THIS!
HOW DID YOU--?
THIS IS WHY HE'S HERE!
DON'T LET HIM DECEIVE YOU!
GIVE IT TO HIM, WATCH, YOU'LL SEE!

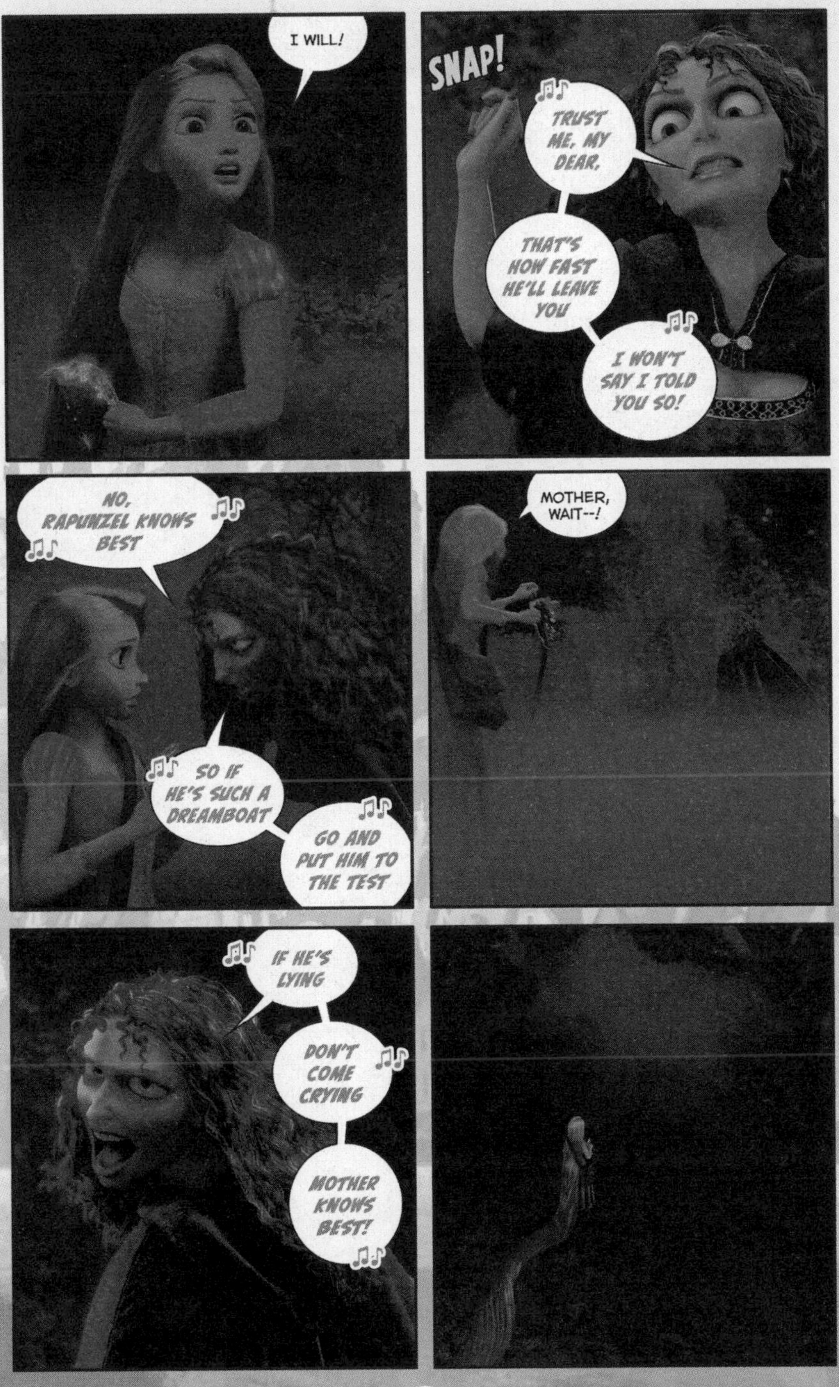
I WILL!
SNAP!
TRUST ME, MY DEAR,
THAT'S HOW FAST HE'LL LEAVE YOU
I WON'T SAY I TOLD YOU SO!
NO, RAPUNZEL KNOWS BEST
SO IF HE'S SUCH A DREAMBOAT
GO AND PUT HIM TO THE TEST
MOTHER, WAIT--!
IF HE'S LYING
DON'T COME CRYING
MOTHER KNOWS BEST!

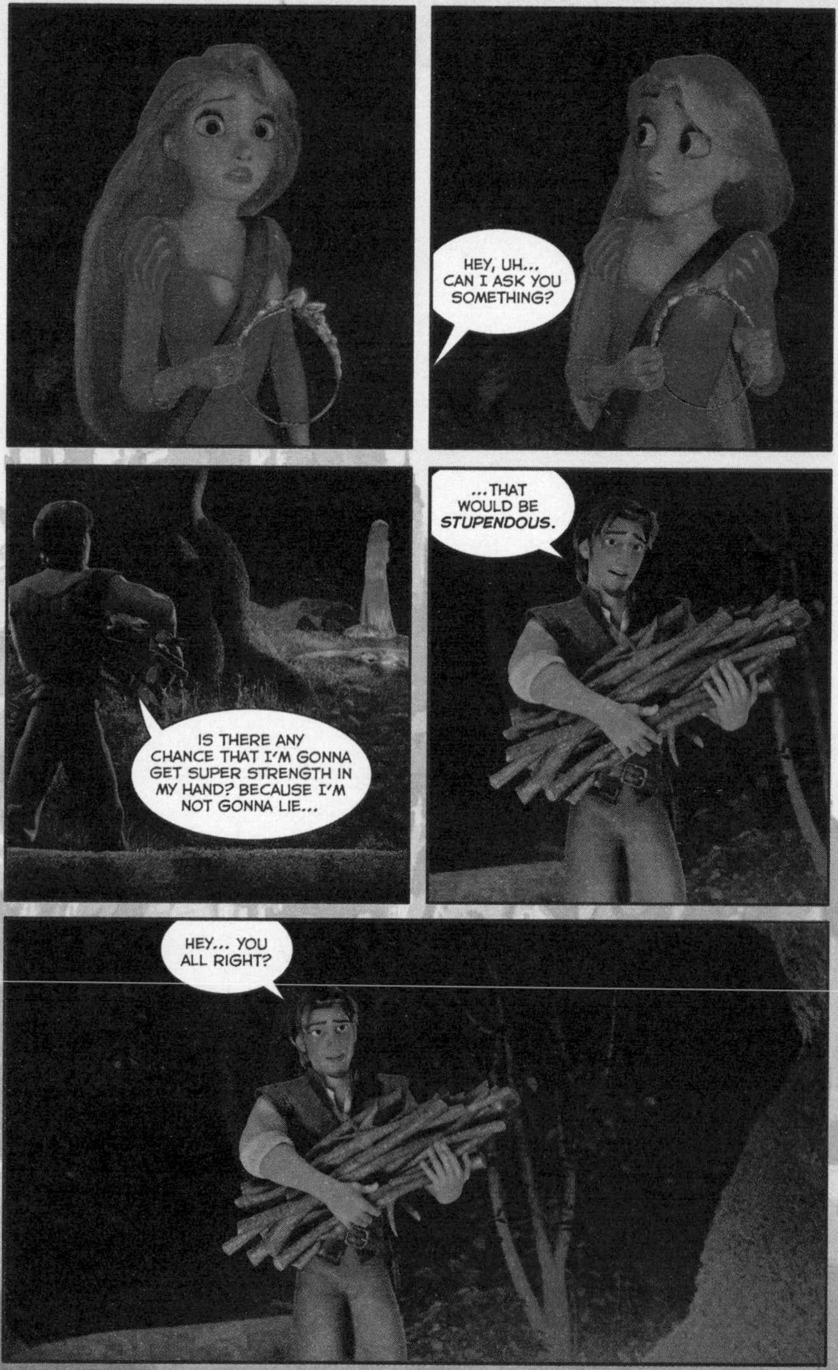
HEY, UH... CAN I ASK YOU SOMETHING?
IS THERE ANY CHANCE THAT I'M GONNA GET SUPER STRENGTH IN MY HAND? BECAUSE I'M NOT GONNA LIE...
...THAT WOULD BE *STUPENDOUS*.
HEY... YOU ALL RIGHT?

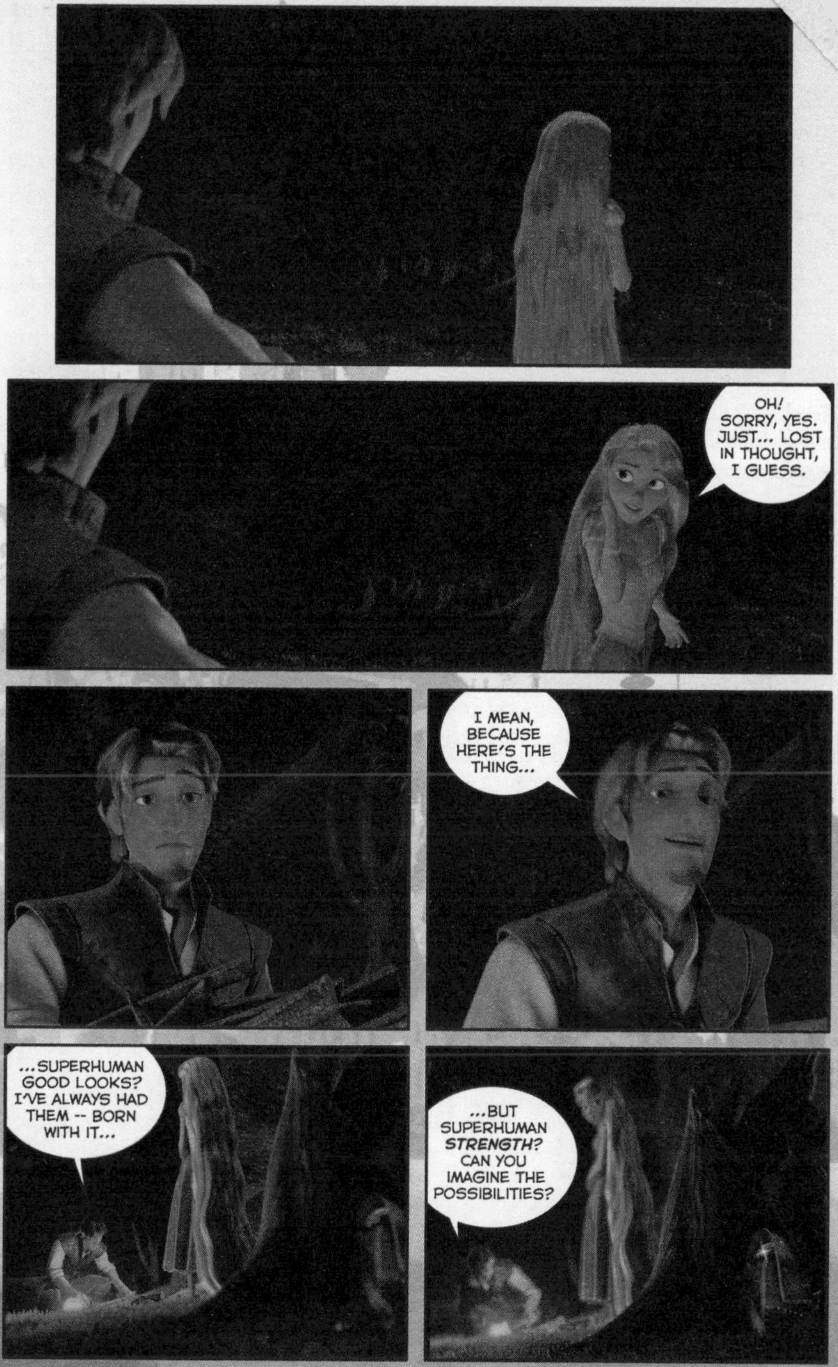
OH! SORRY, YES. JUST... LOST IN THOUGHT, I GUESS.
I MEAN, BECAUSE HERE'S THE THING...
...SUPERHUMAN GOOD LOOKS? I'VE ALWAYS HAD THEM -- BORN WITH IT...
...BUT SUPERHUMAN *STRENGTH?* CAN YOU IMAGINE THE POSSIBILITIES?

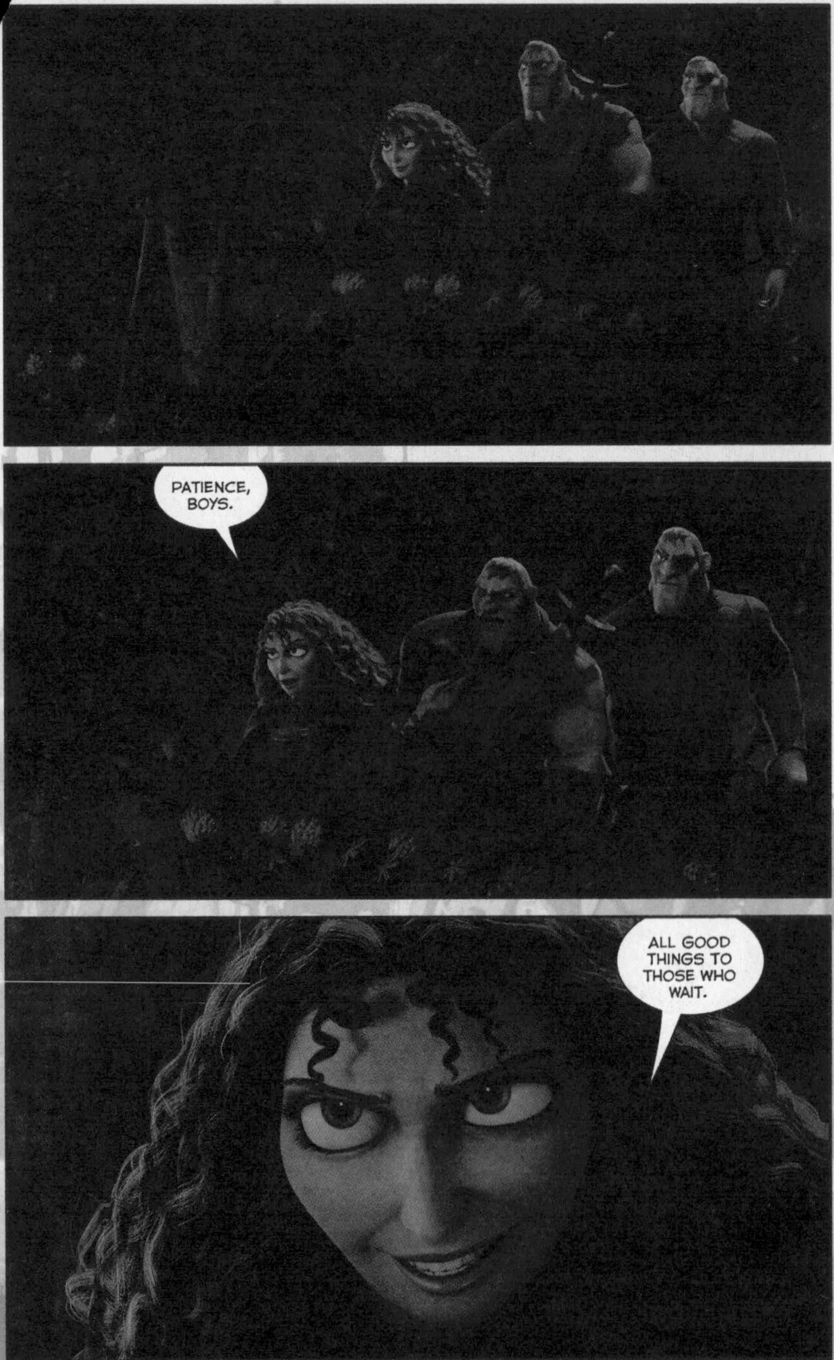
PATIENCE, BOYS.
ALL GOOD THINGS TO THOSE WHO WAIT.

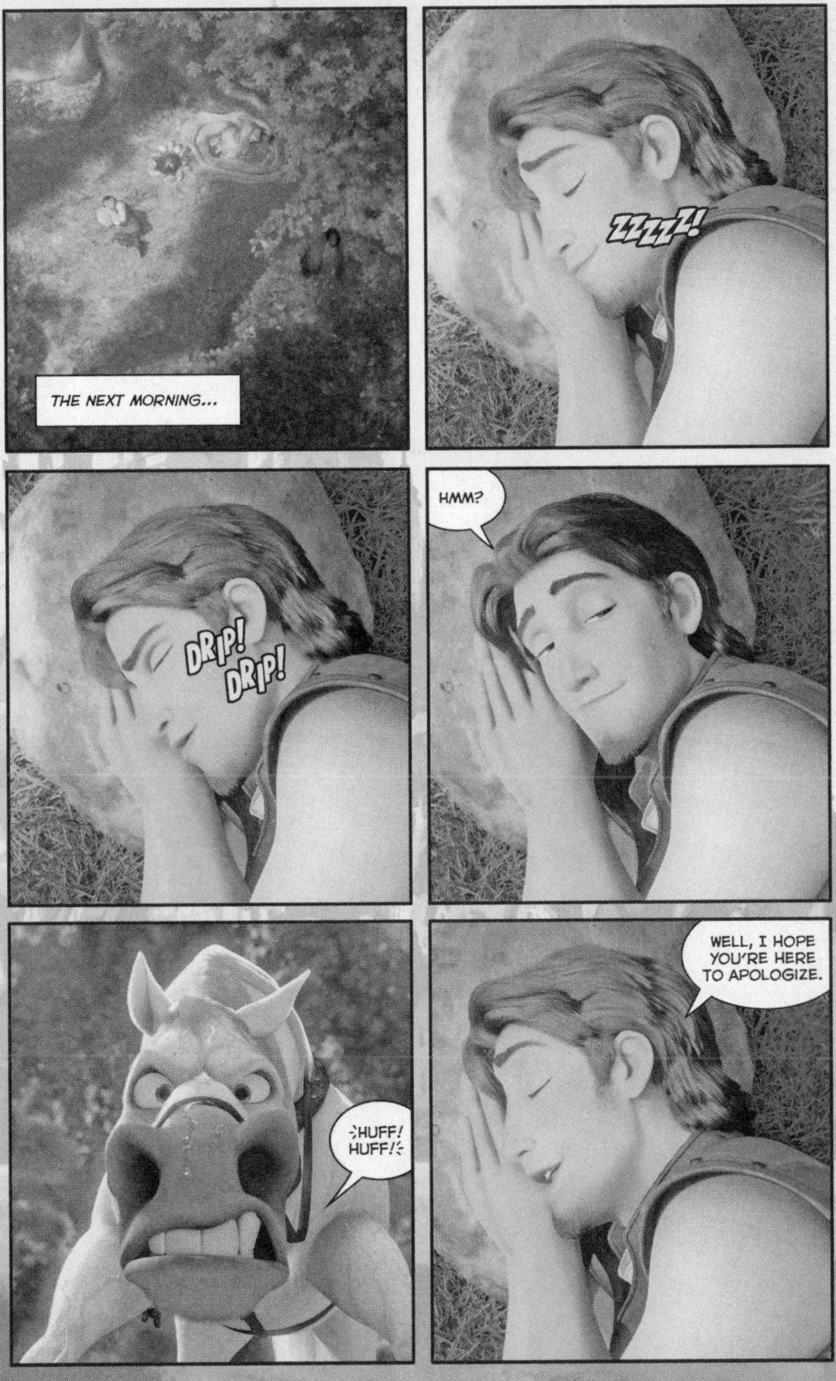
THE NEXT MORNING...
ZZZZZ!
DRIP! DRIP!
HMM?
HUFF! HUFF!
WELL, I HOPE YOU'RE HERE TO APOLOGIZE.

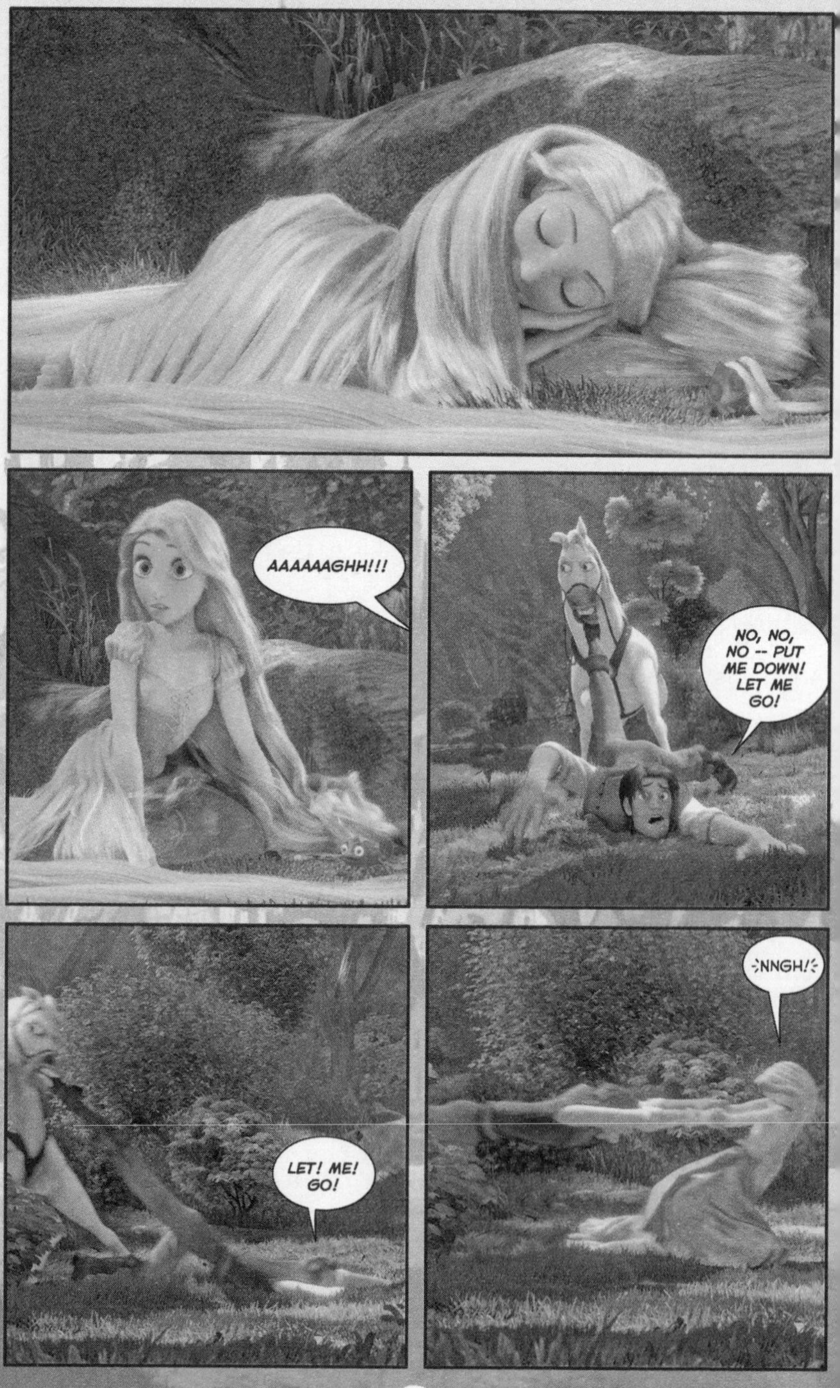
AAAAAAGHH!!!
NO, NO, NO -- PUT ME DOWN! LET ME GO!
LET! ME! GO!
NNGH!

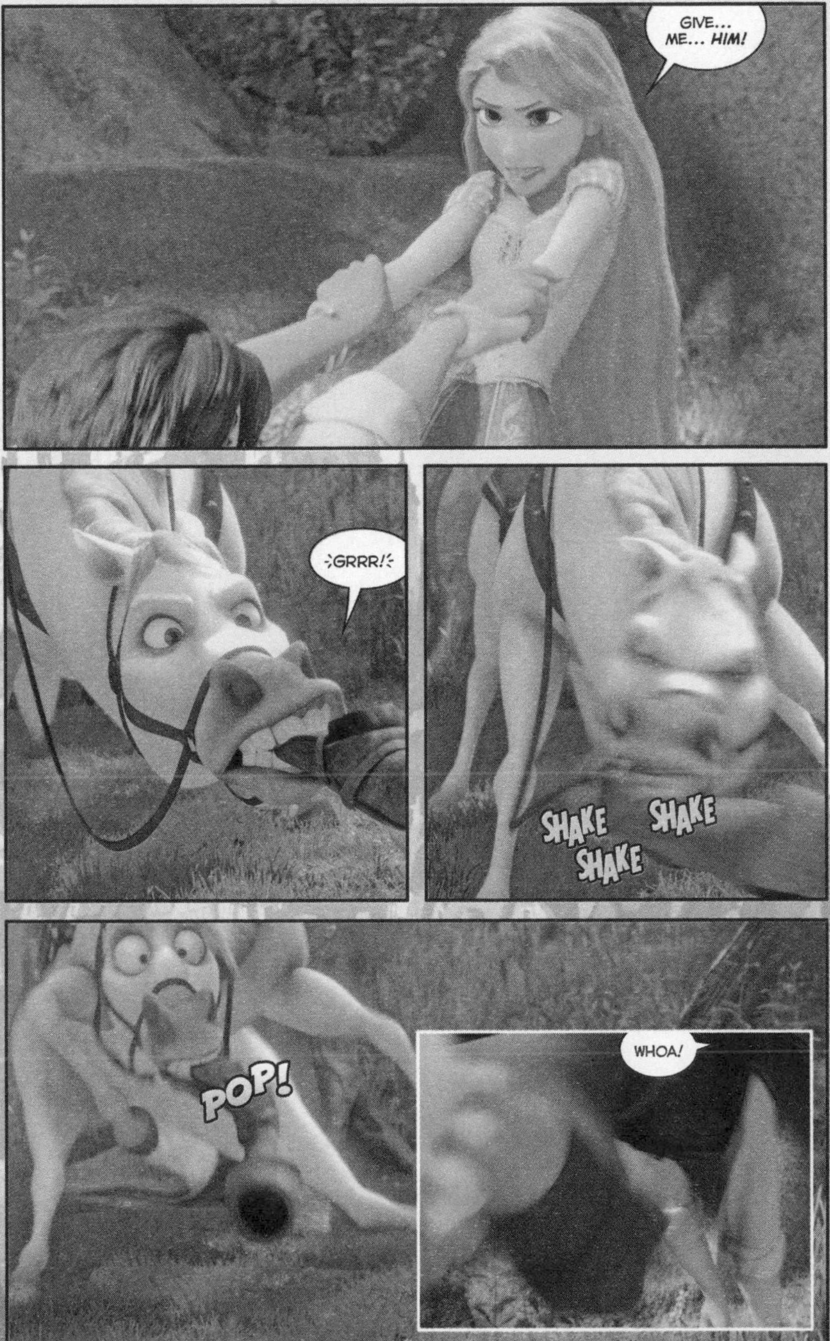
GIVE... ME... HIM!
GRRR!
SHAKE
SHAKE
SHAKE
POP!
WHOA!

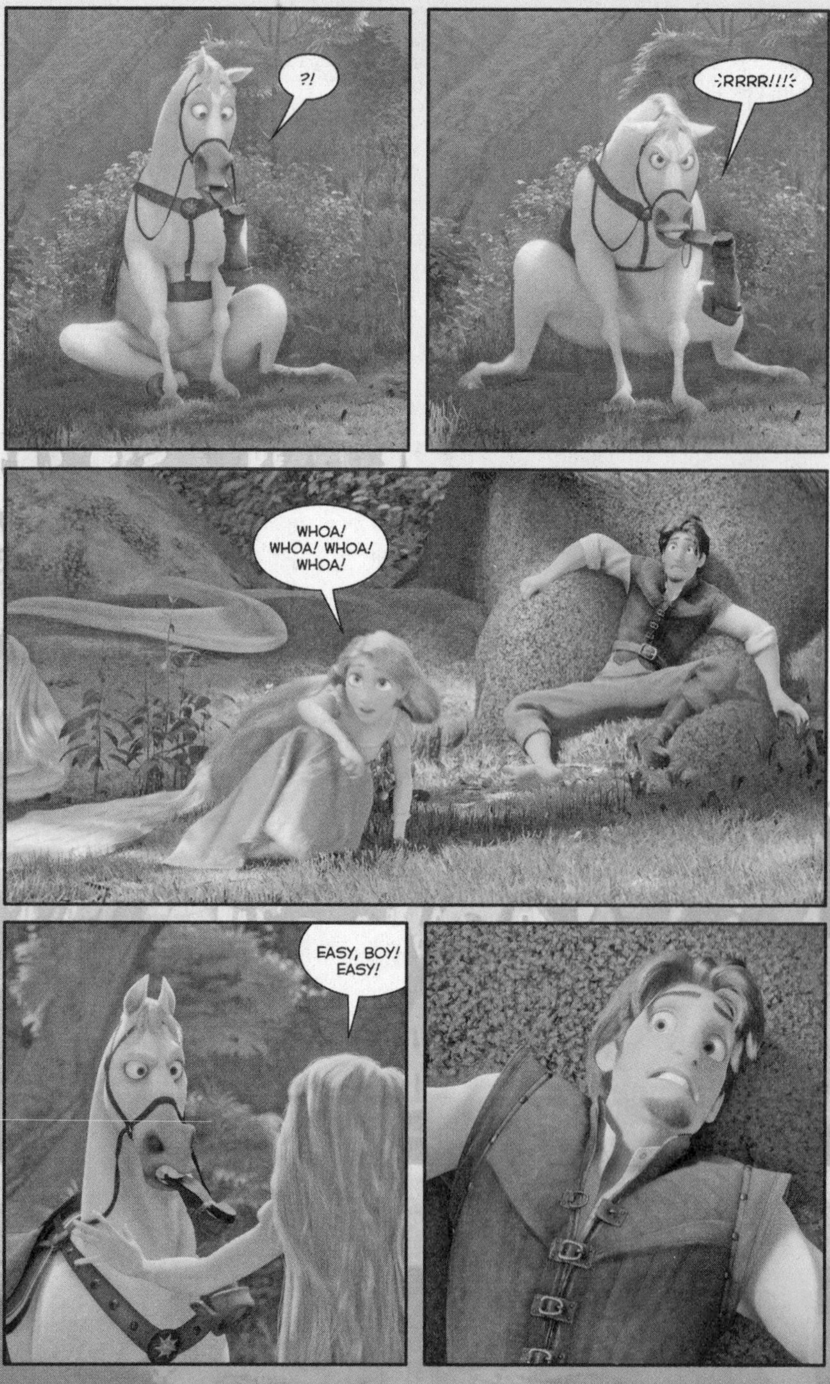
?!
RRRR!!!
WHOA! WHOA! WHOA! WHOA!
EASY, BOY! EASY!

SETTLE DOWN! WHOA! WHOA!
EASY, BOY. EASY.
!!!!
THAT'S IT.

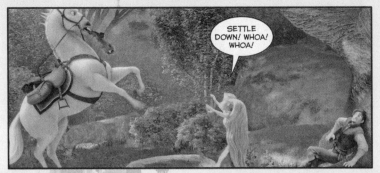

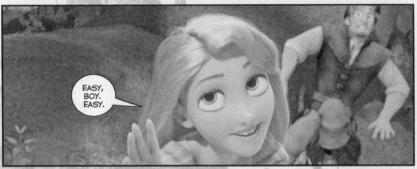

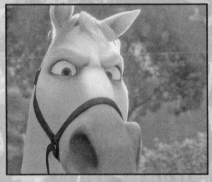

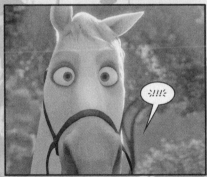

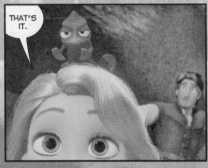

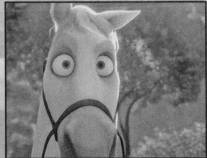

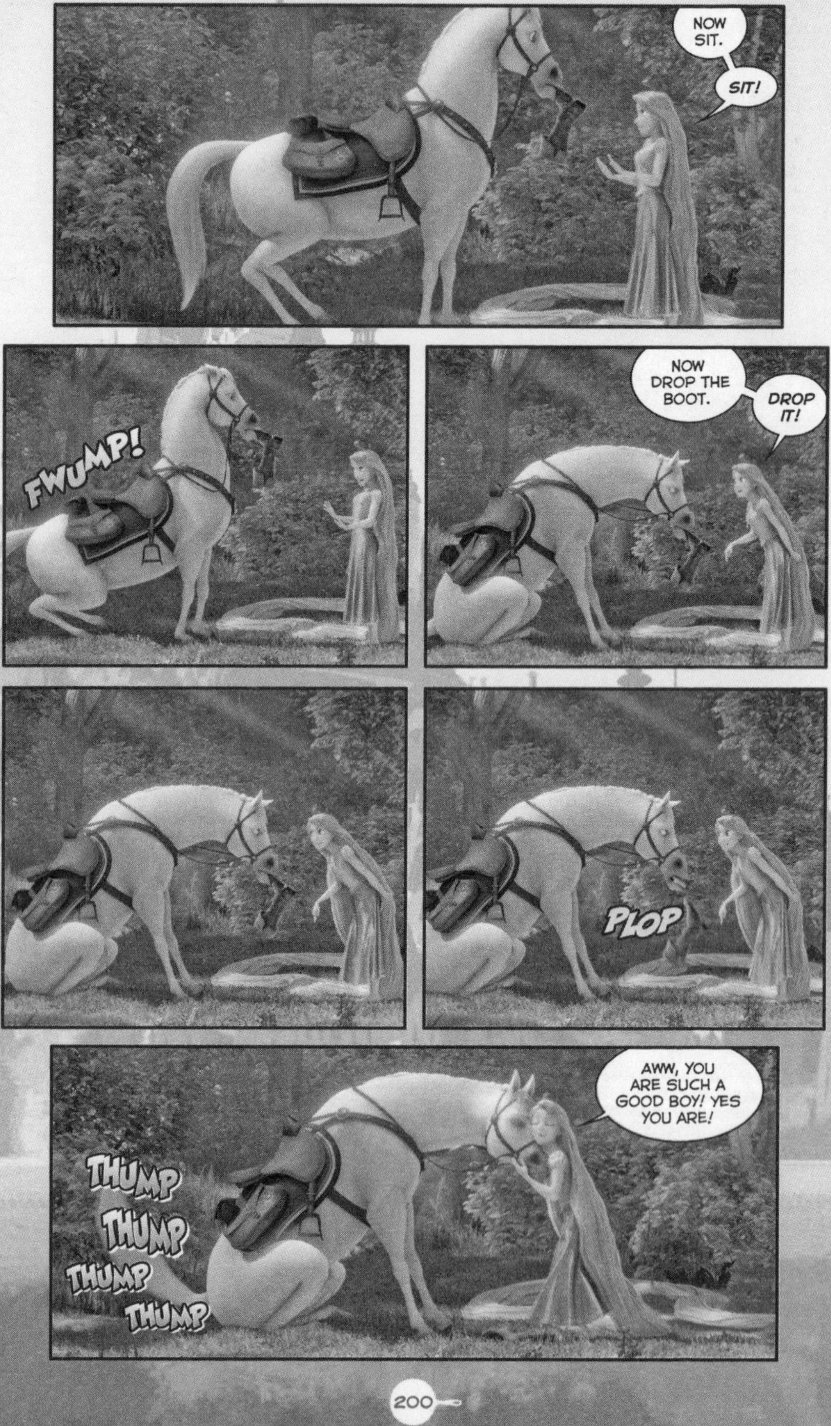
NOW SIT.
SIT!
FWUMP!
NOW DROP THE BOOT.
DROP IT!
PLOP
AWW, YOU ARE SUCH A GOOD BOY! YES YOU ARE!
THUMP
THUMP
THUMP
THUMP

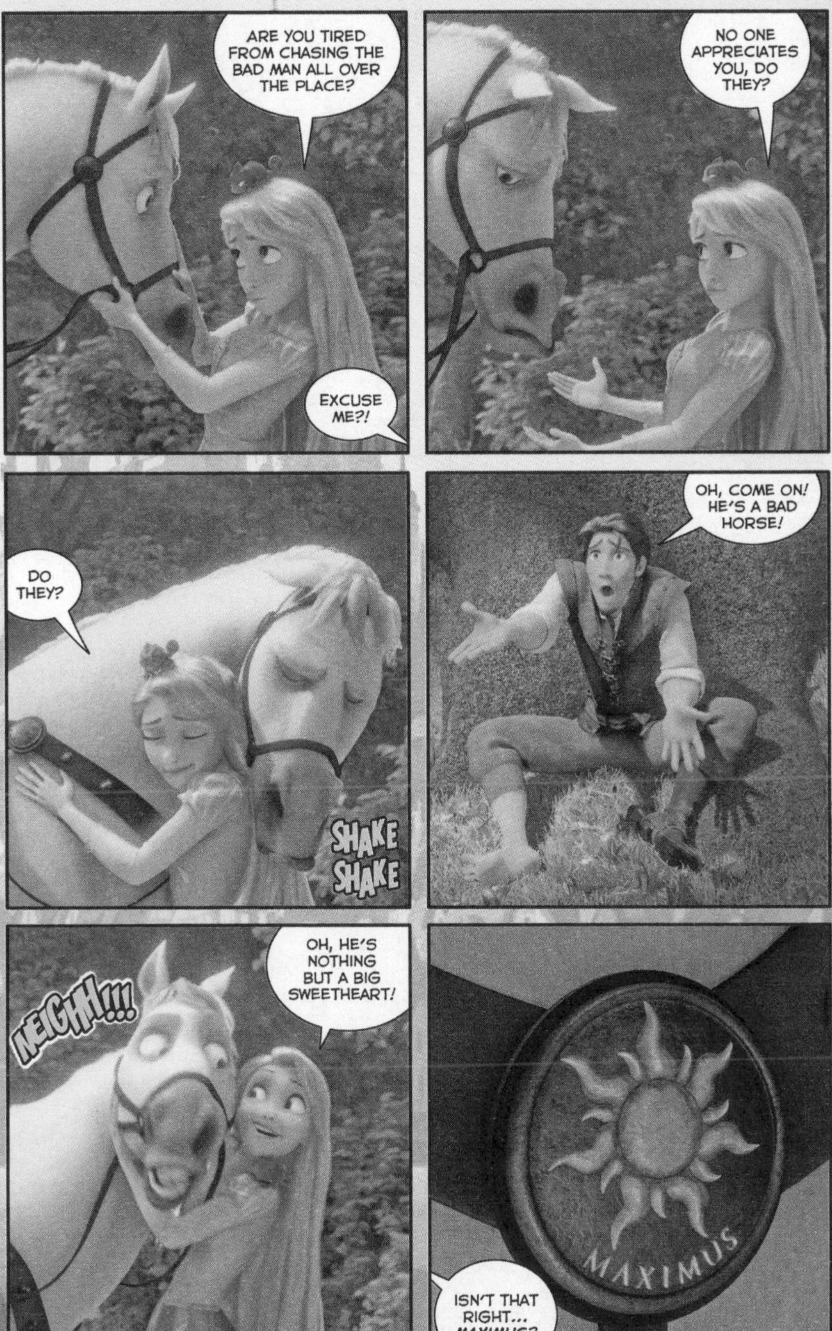
ARE YOU TIRED FROM CHASING THE BAD MAN ALL OVER THE PLACE?
EXCUSE ME?!
NO ONE APPRECIATES YOU, DO THEY?
DO THEY?
SHAKE SHAKE
OH, COME ON! HE'S A BAD HORSE!
NEIGHH!!!
OH, HE'S NOTHING BUT A BIG SWEETHEART!
MAXIMUS
ISN'T THAT RIGHT... *MAXIMUS*?

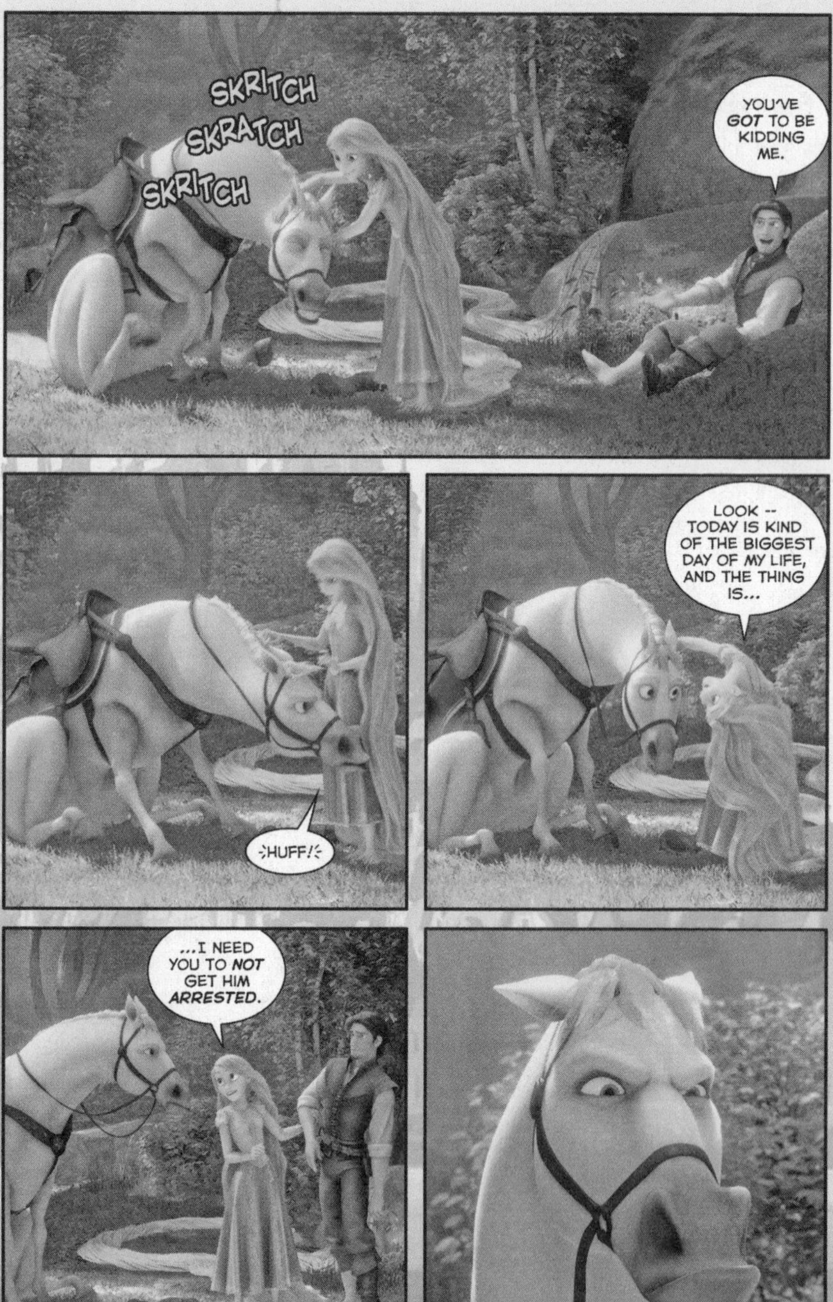
SKRITCH
SKRATCH
SKRITCH
YOU'VE GOT TO BE KIDDING ME.
HUFF!
LOOK -- TODAY IS KIND OF THE BIGGEST DAY OF MY LIFE, AND THE THING IS...
...I NEED YOU TO NOT GET HIM ARRESTED.

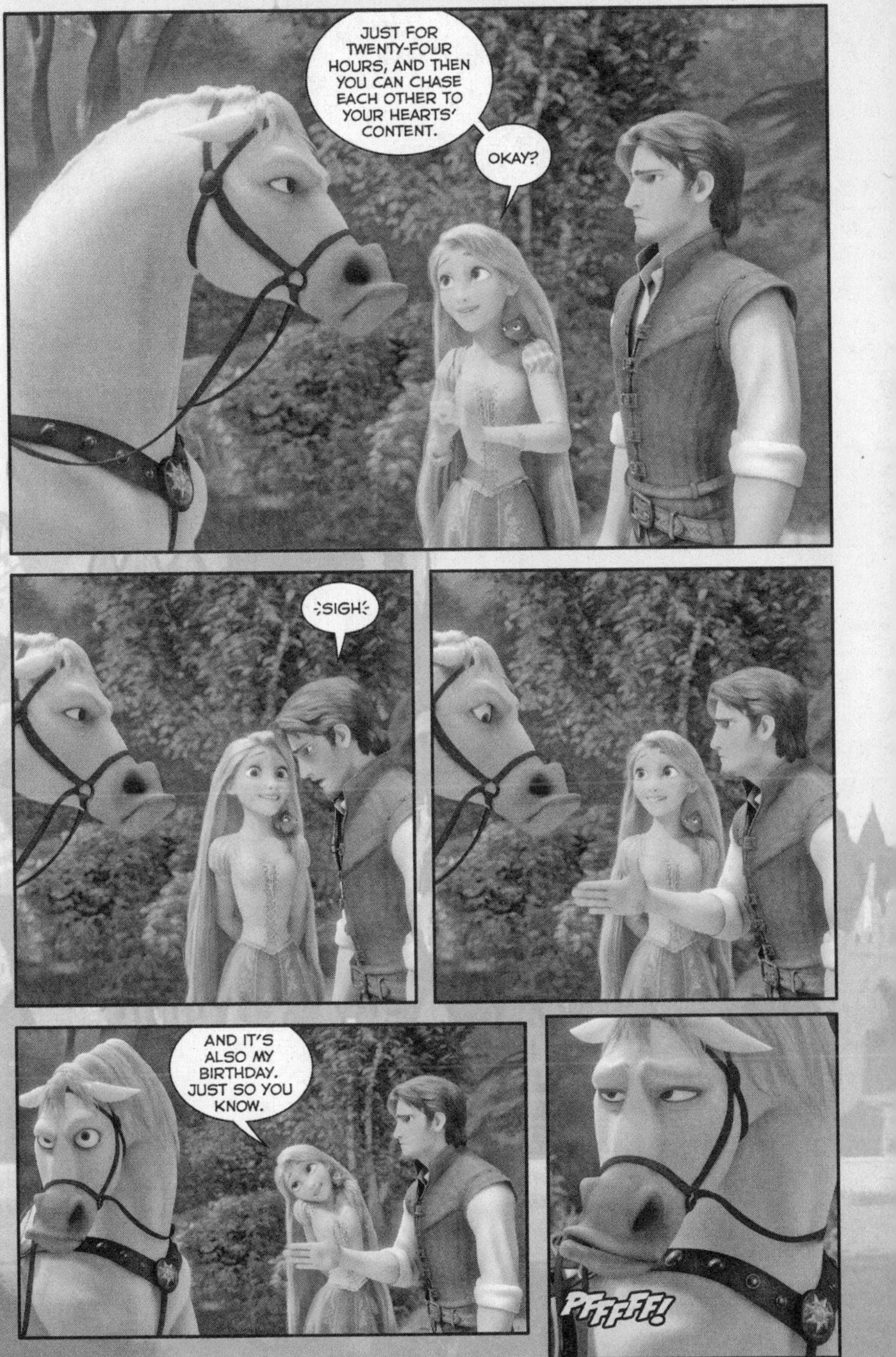
JUST FOR TWENTY-FOUR HOURS, AND THEN YOU CAN CHASE EACH OTHER TO YOUR HEARTS' CONTENT.
OKAY?
SIGH
AND IT'S ALSO MY BIRTHDAY. JUST SO YOU KNOW.
PFFFFFF!

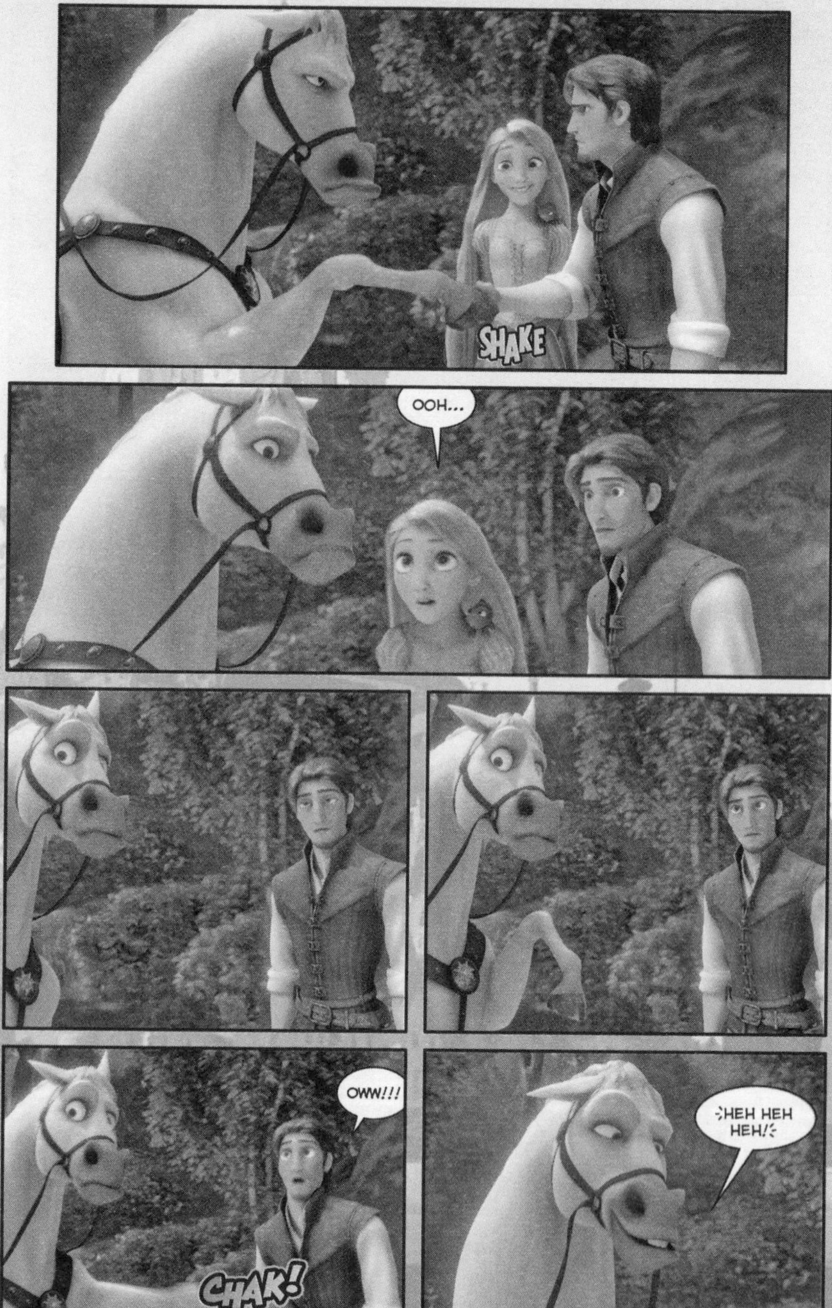
SHAKE
OOH...
OWW!!!
CHAK!
HEH HEH HEH!

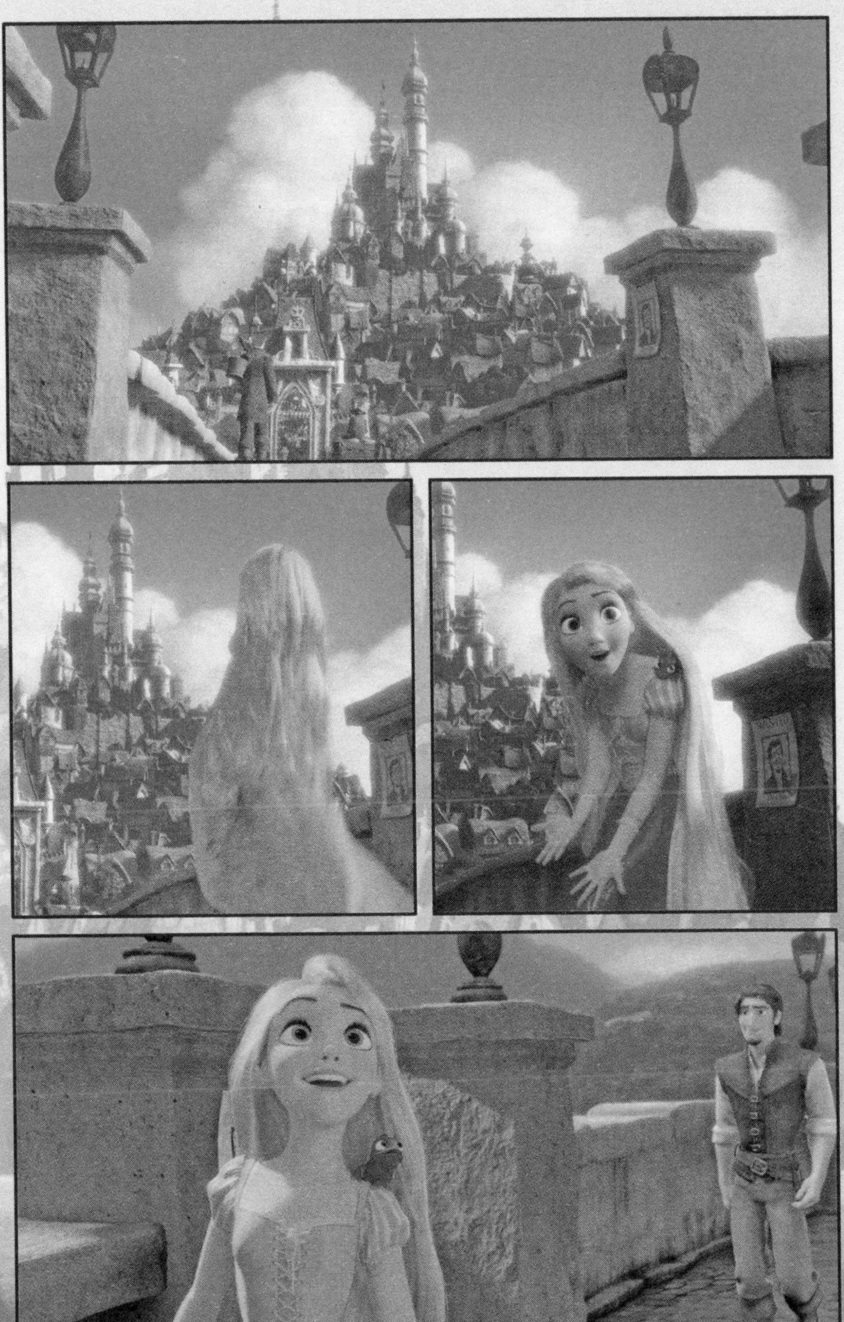

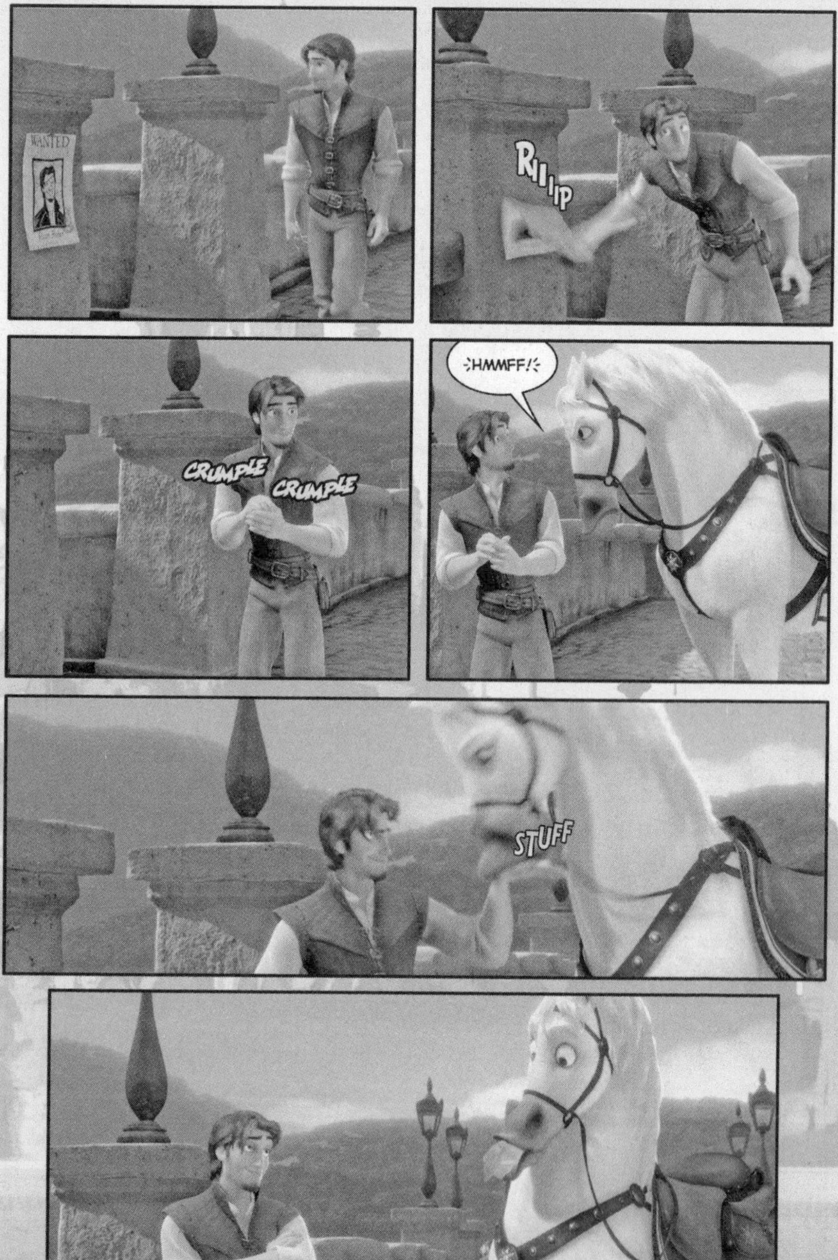
WANTED
RIIIIP
CRUMPLE
CRUMPLE
HMMFF!
STUFF

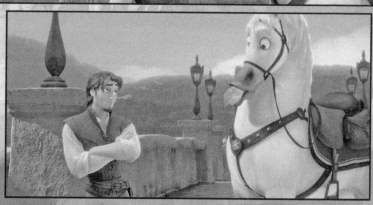

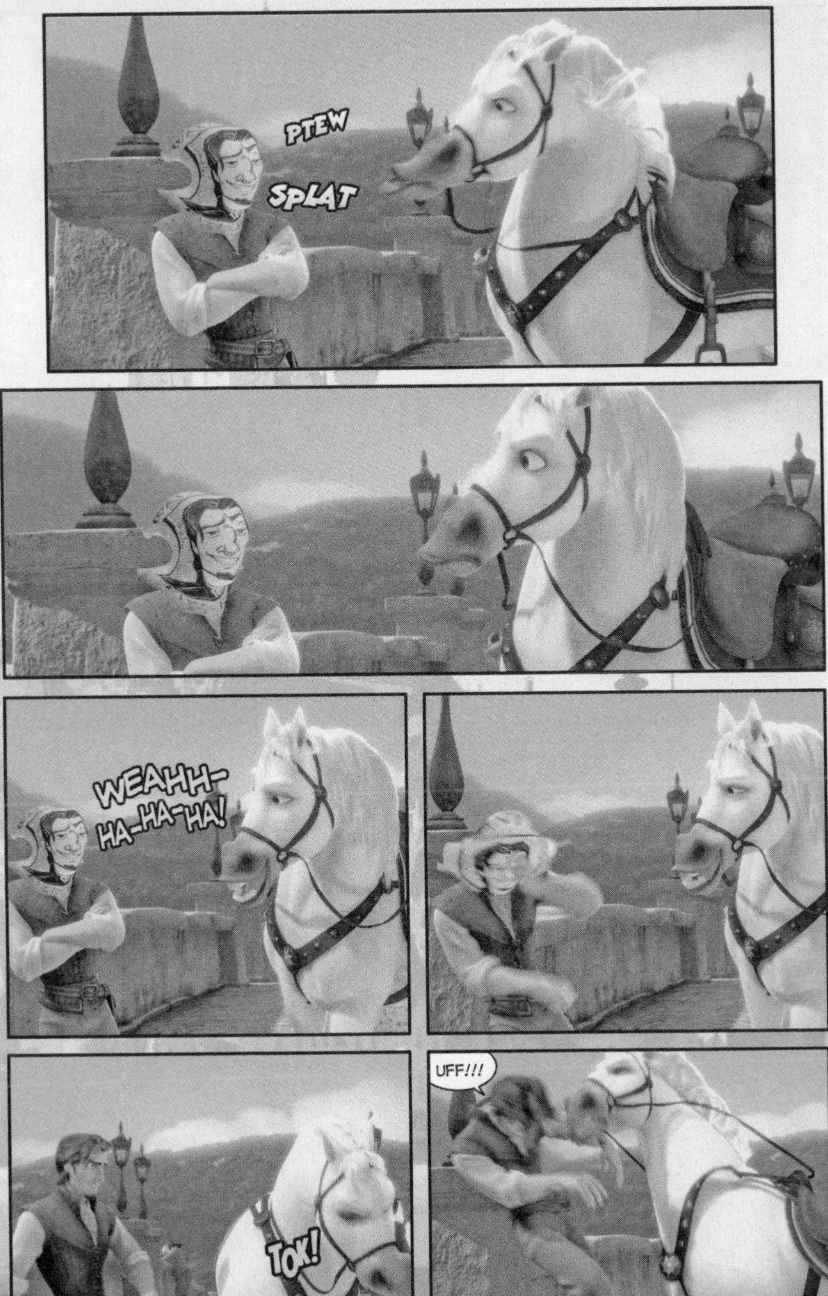
PTEW
SPLAT
WEAHH-HA-HA-HA!
UFF!!!
TOK!

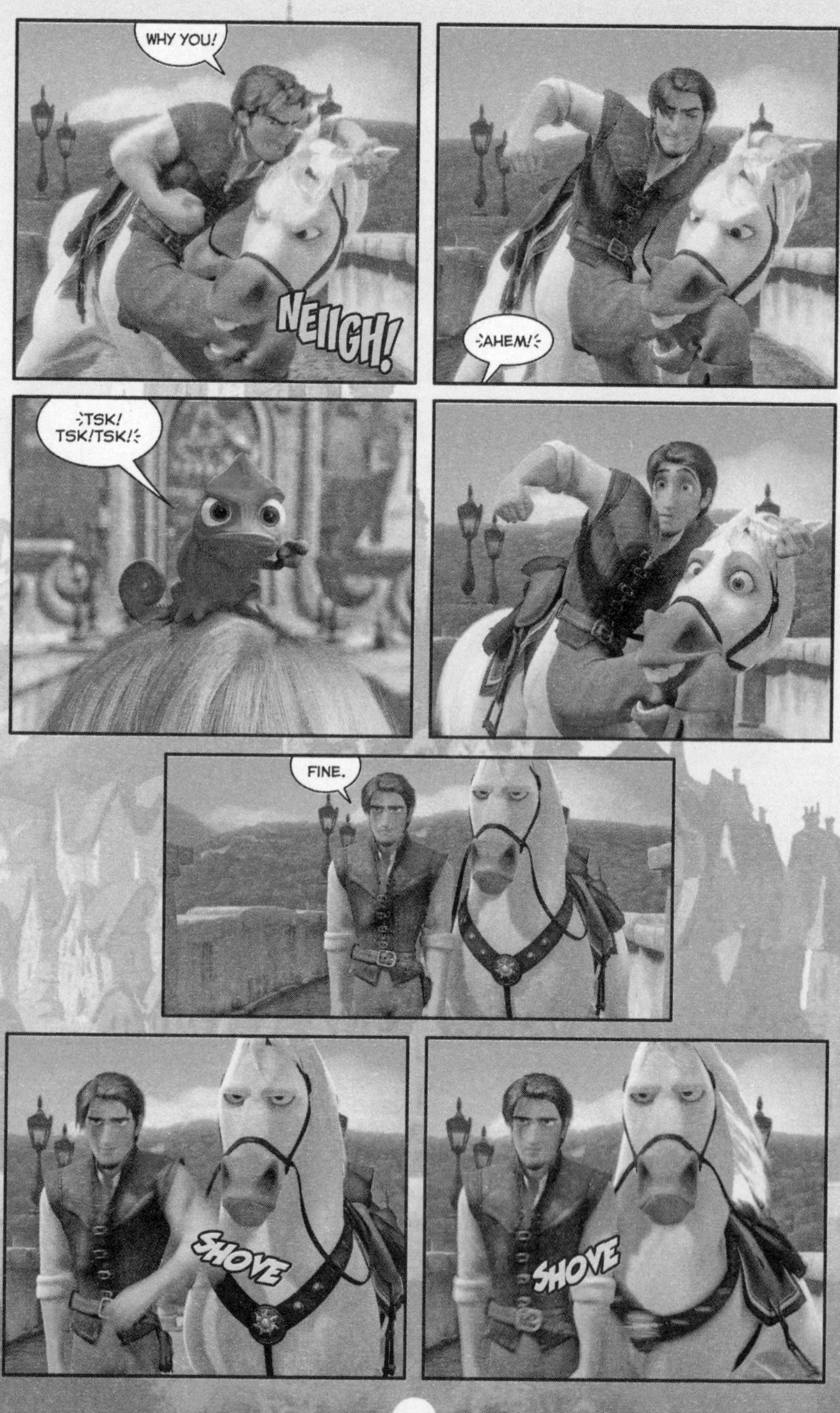
WHY YOU!
NEIIGH!
AHEM!
TSK! TSK! TSK!
FINE.
SHOVE
SHOVE

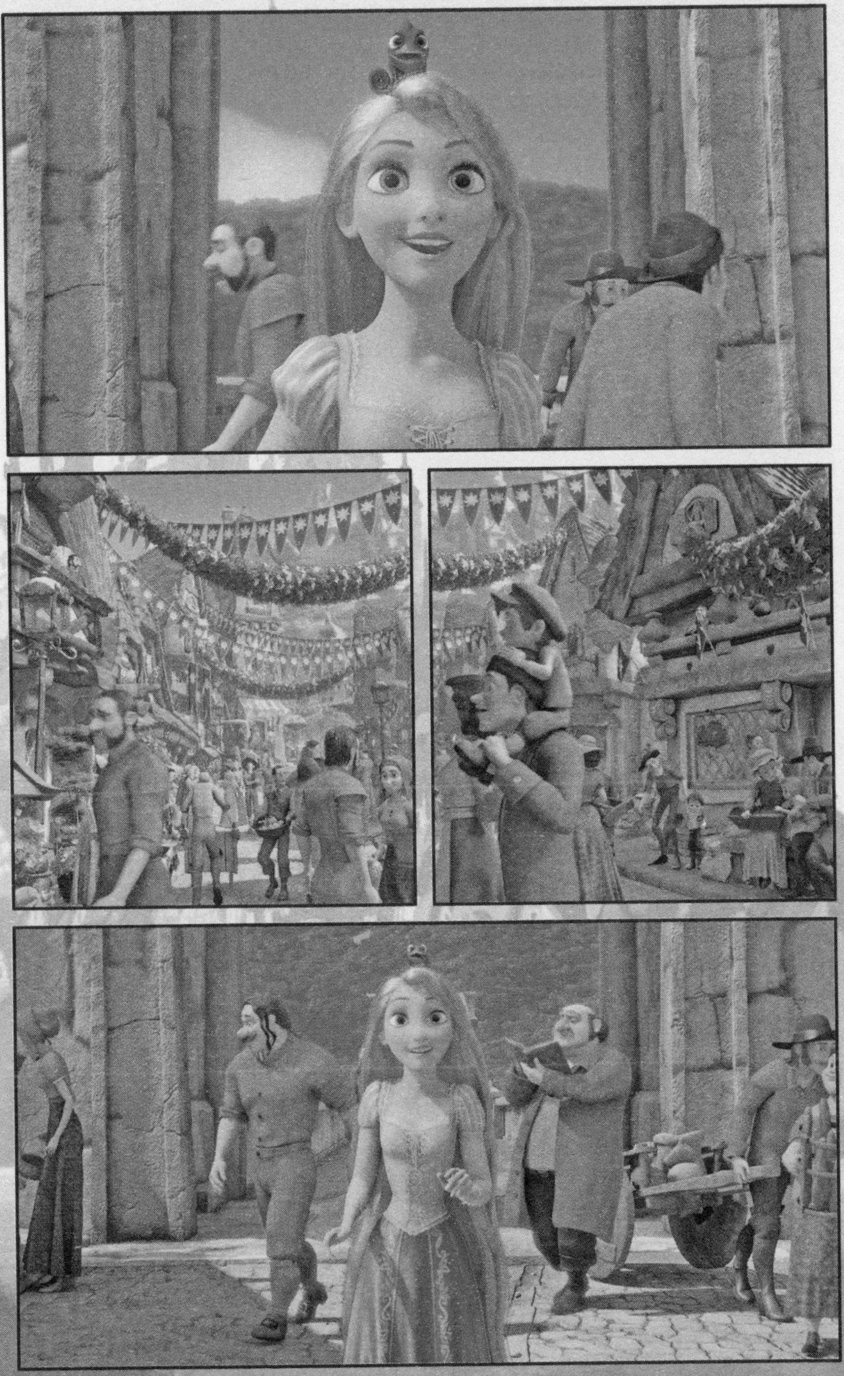

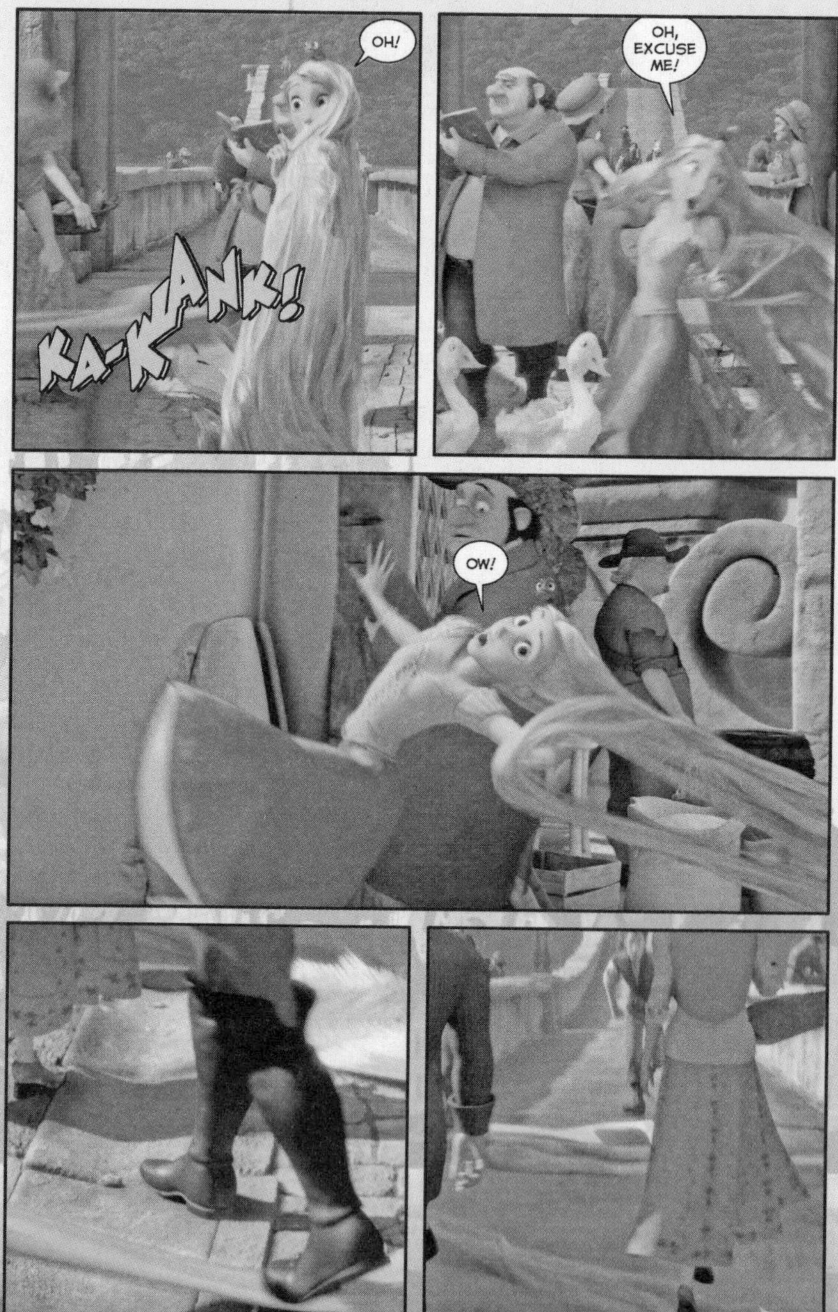
OH!
KA-KLANK!
OH, EXCUSE ME!
OW!

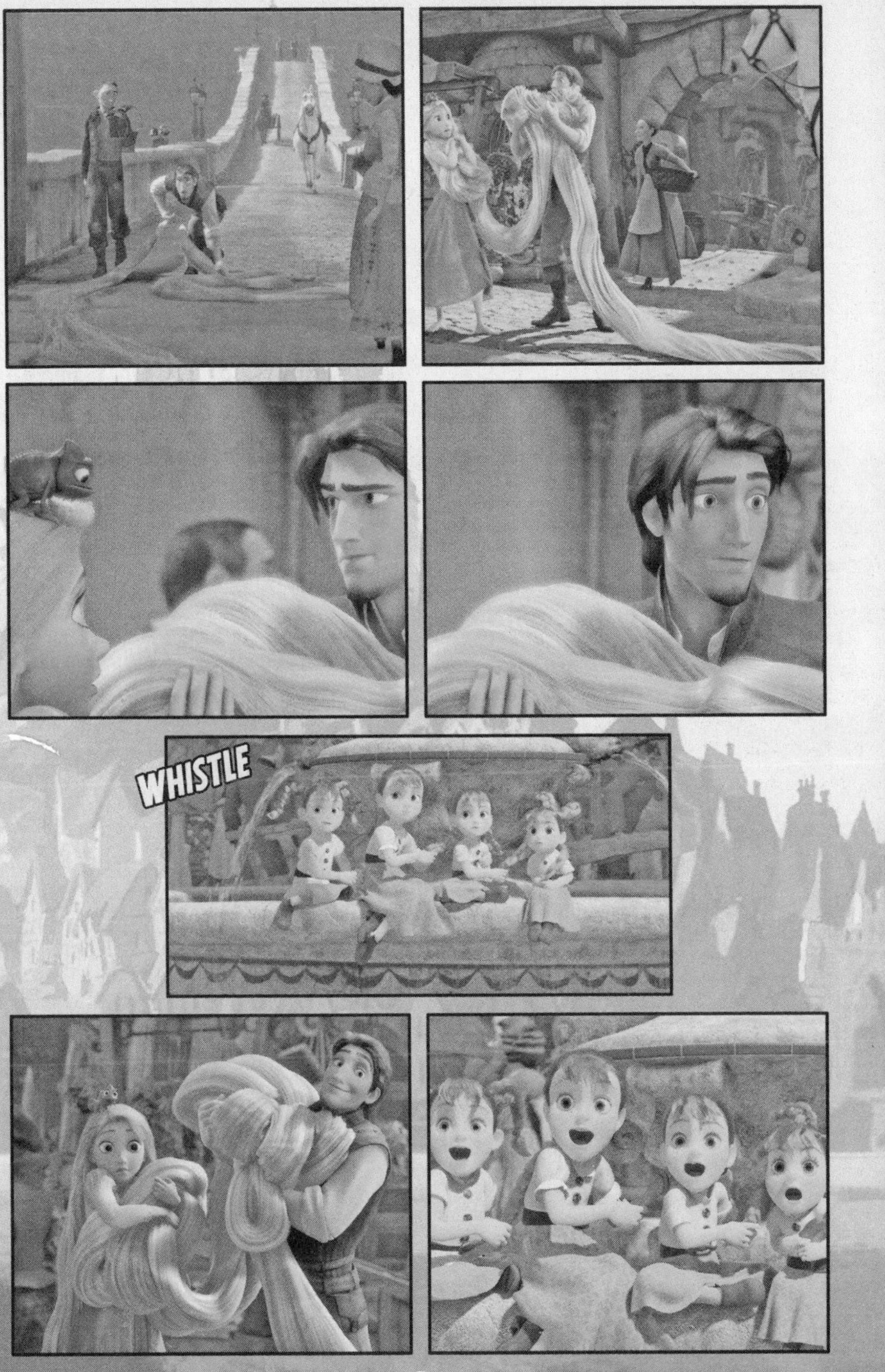
WHISTLE

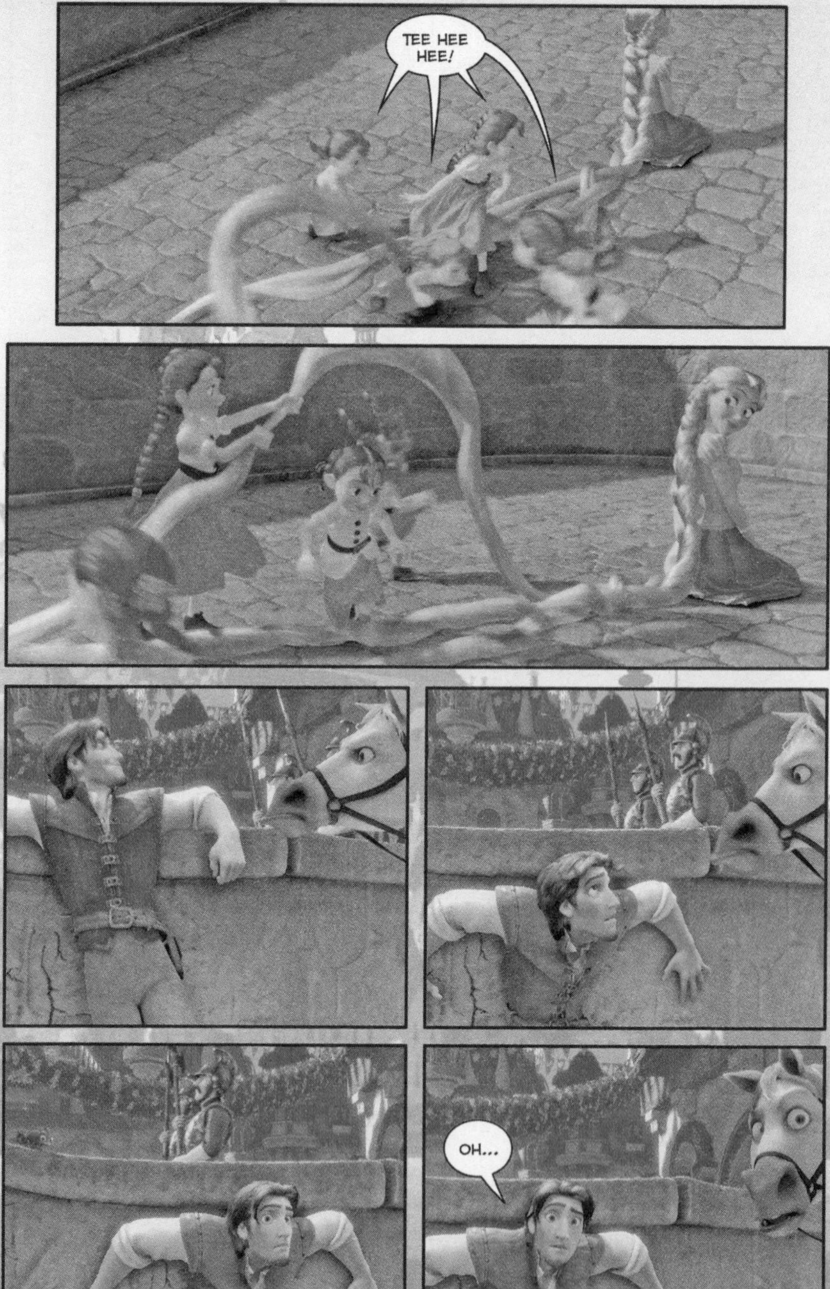
TEE HEE HEE!
OH...

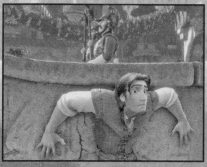

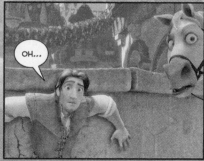

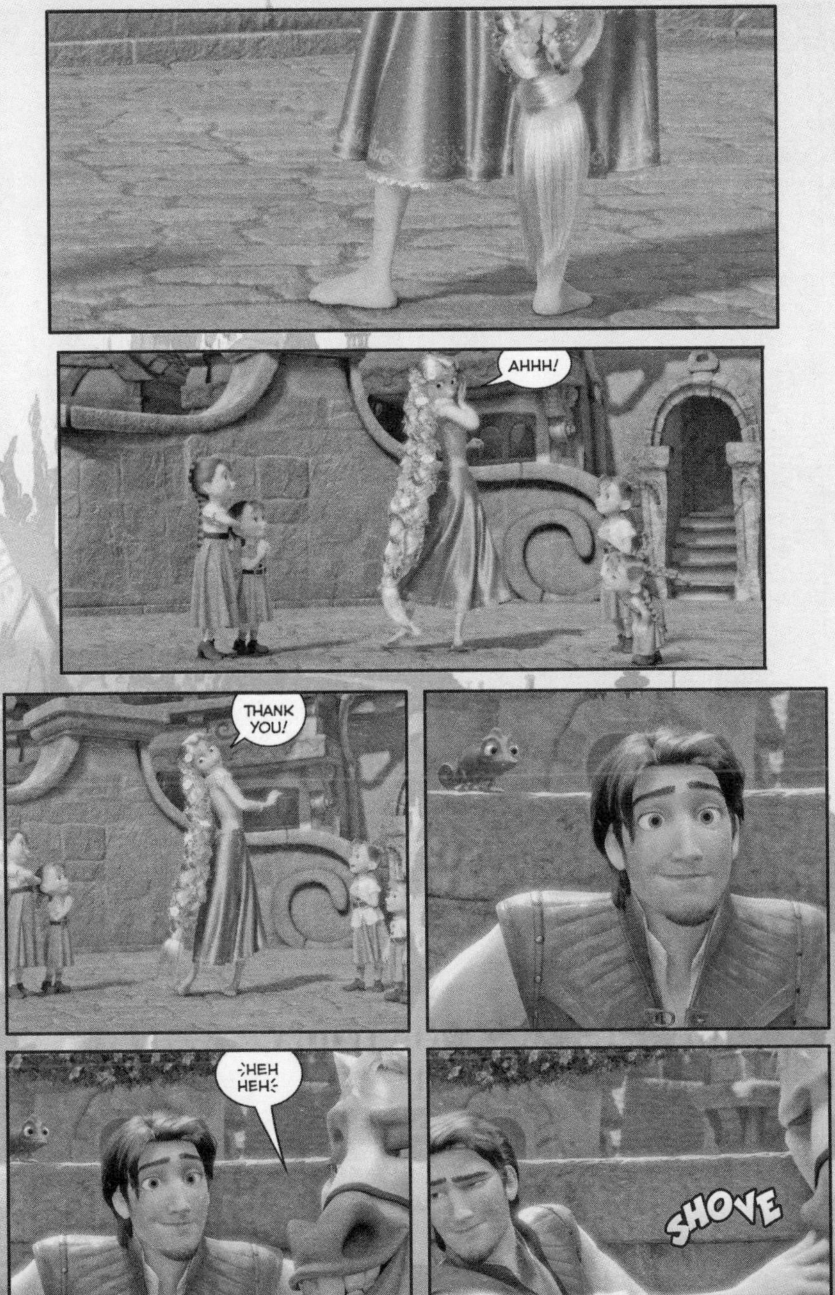
AHHH!
THANK YOU!
HEH HEH
SHOVE

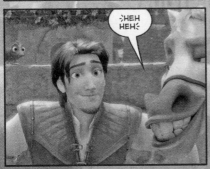

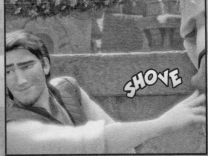

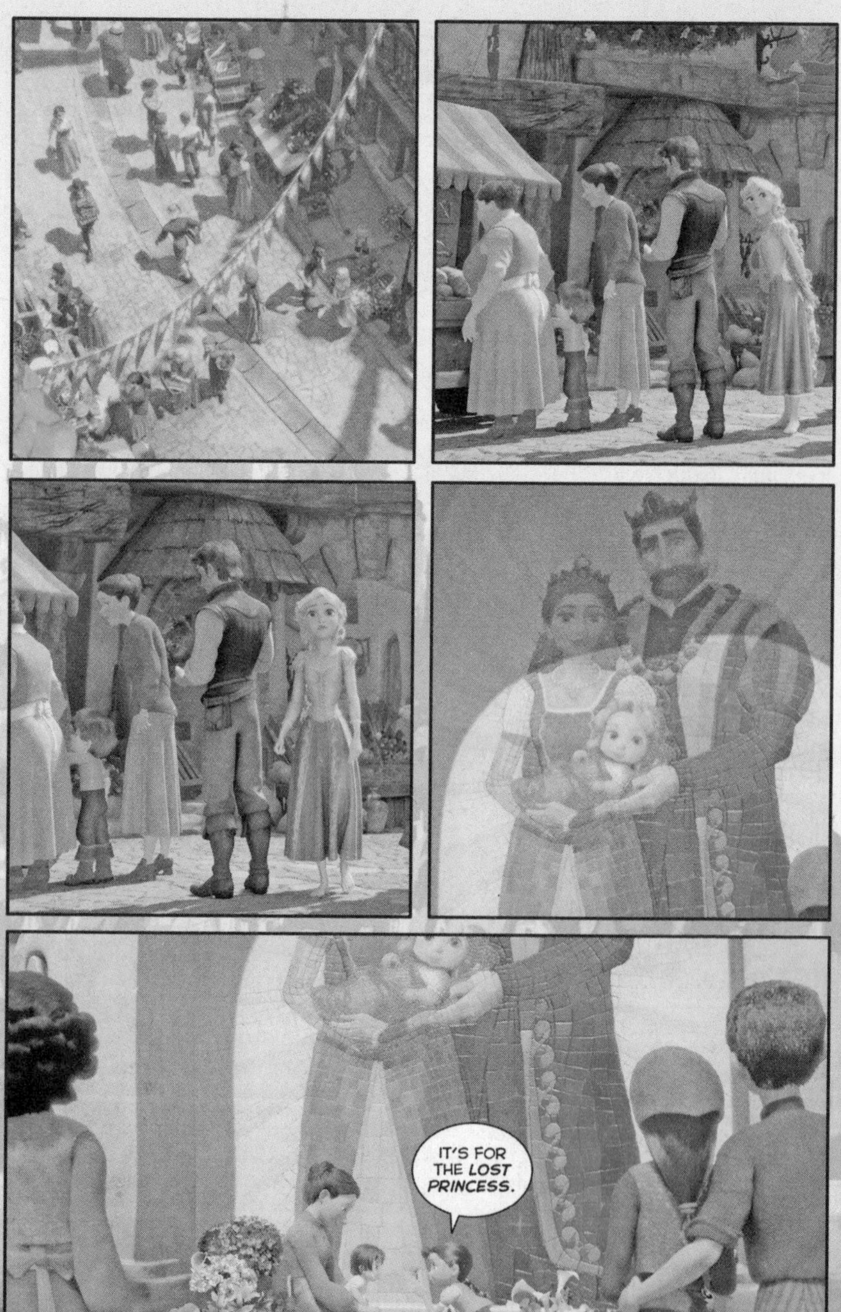
IT'S FOR THE *LOST PRINCESS*.

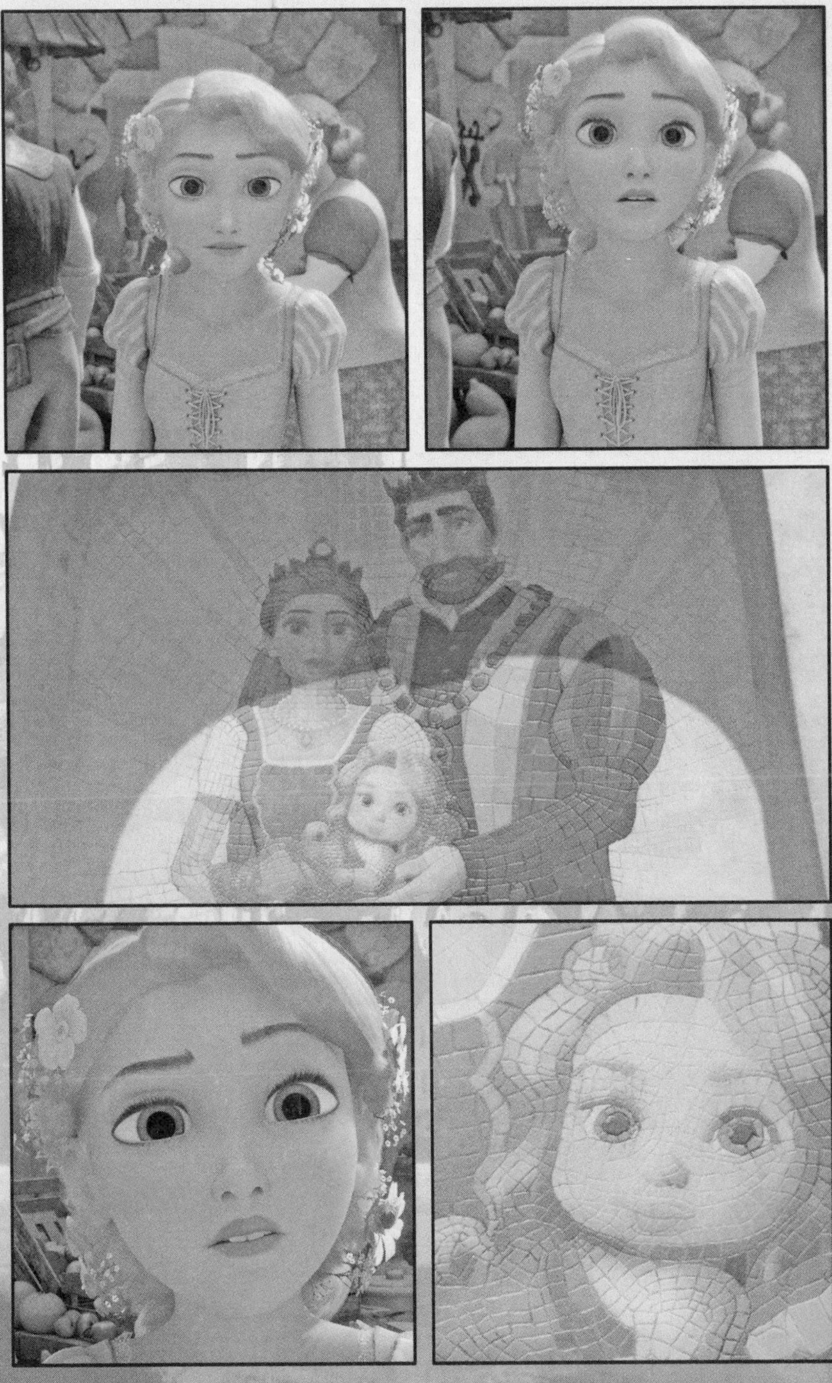

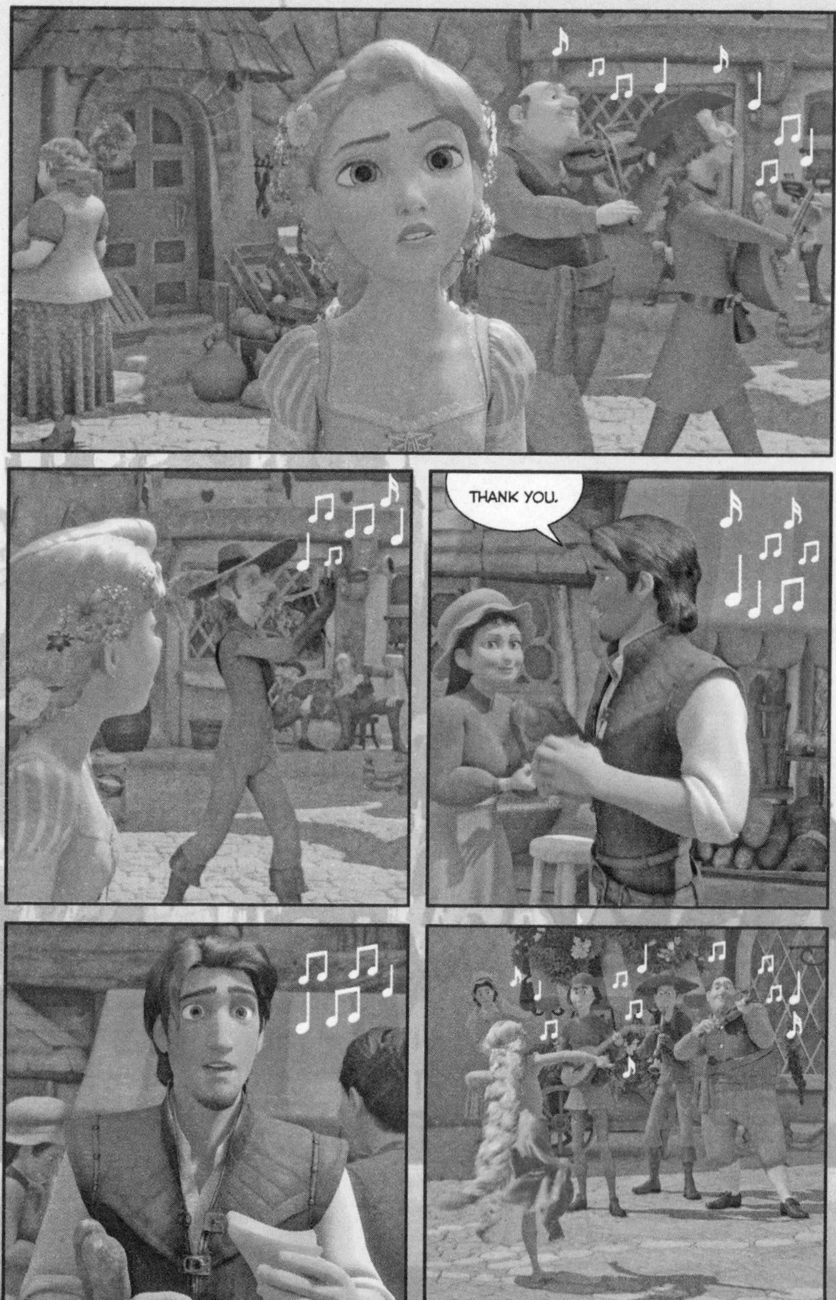
THANK YOU.

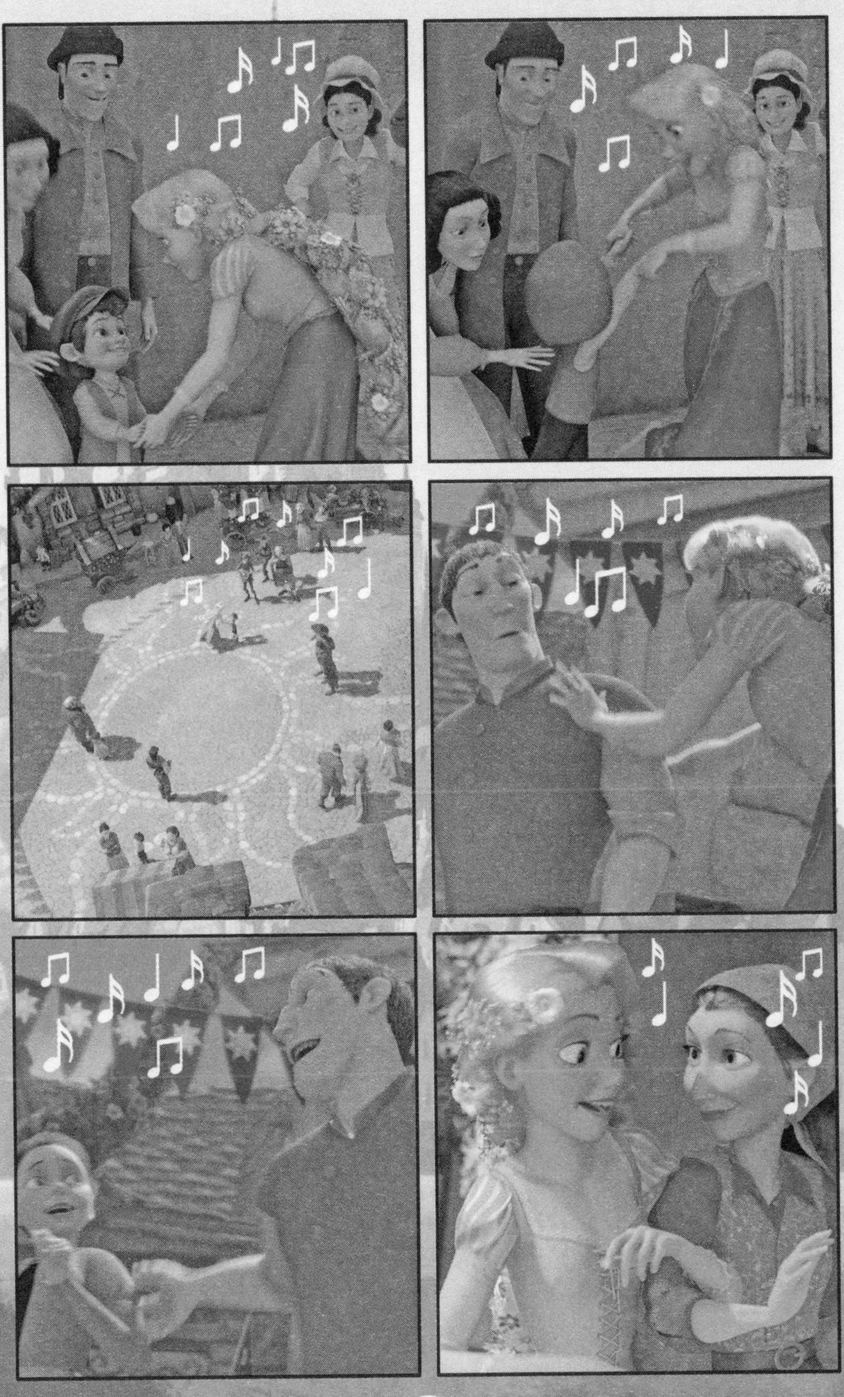

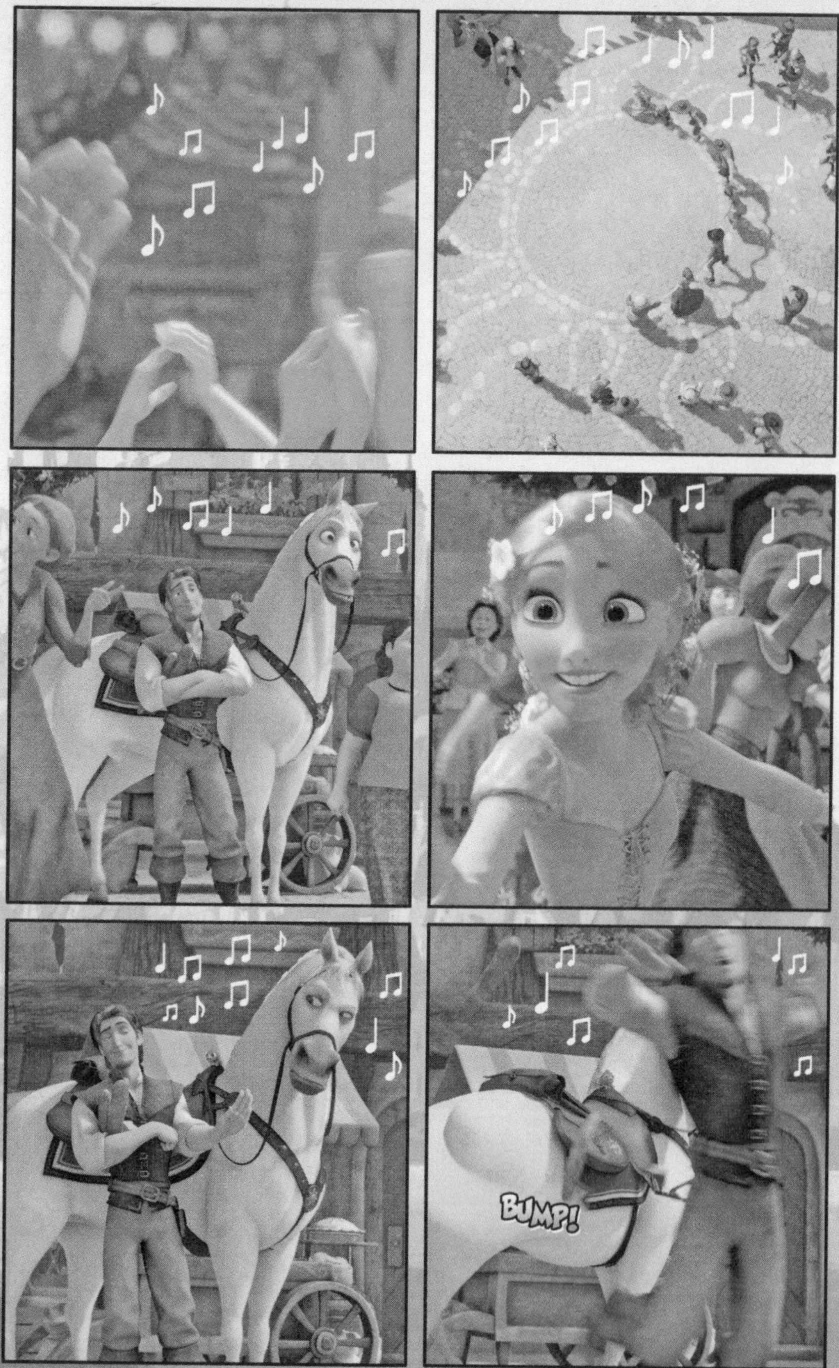
BUMP!

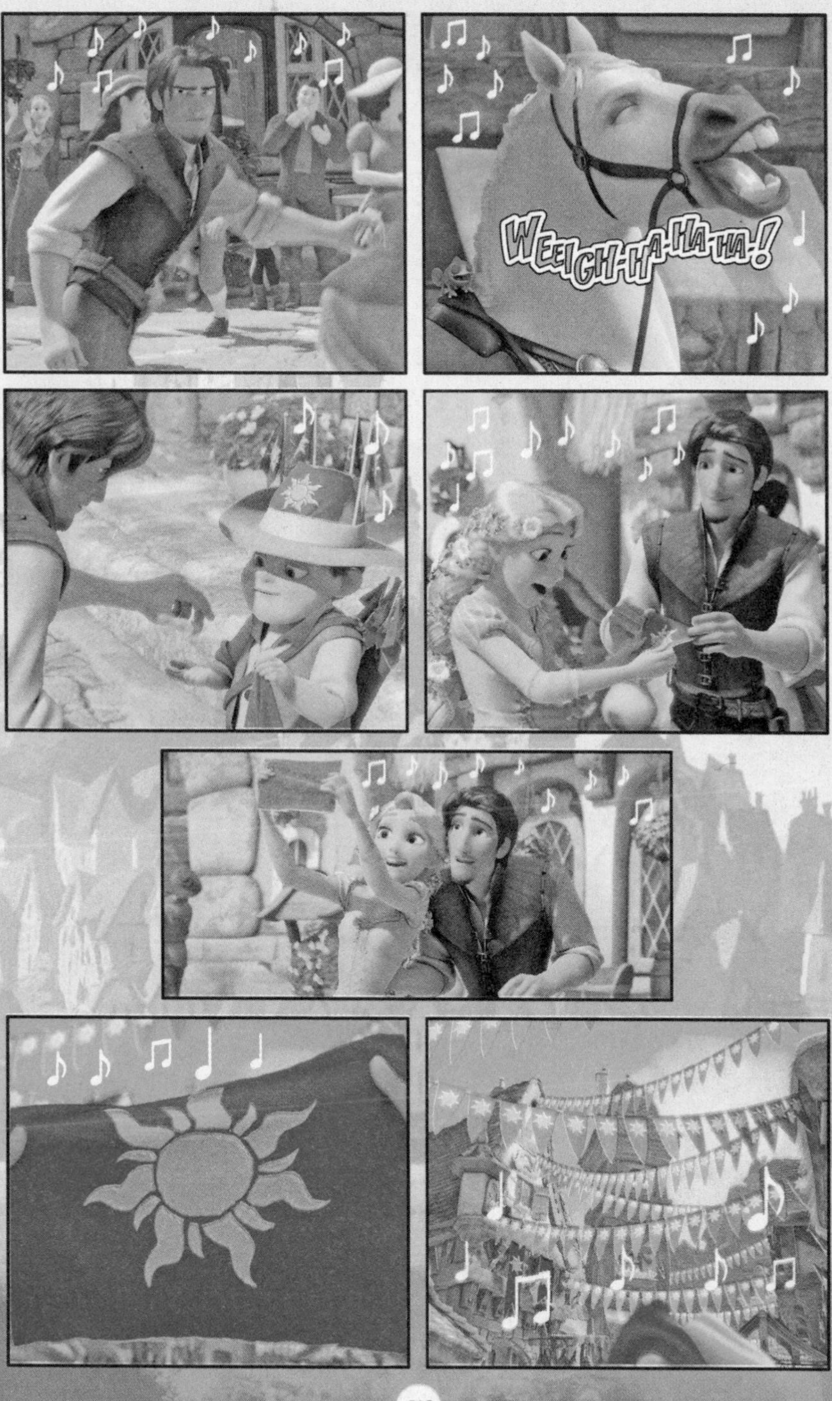
WEEIGH-HA-HA-HA!

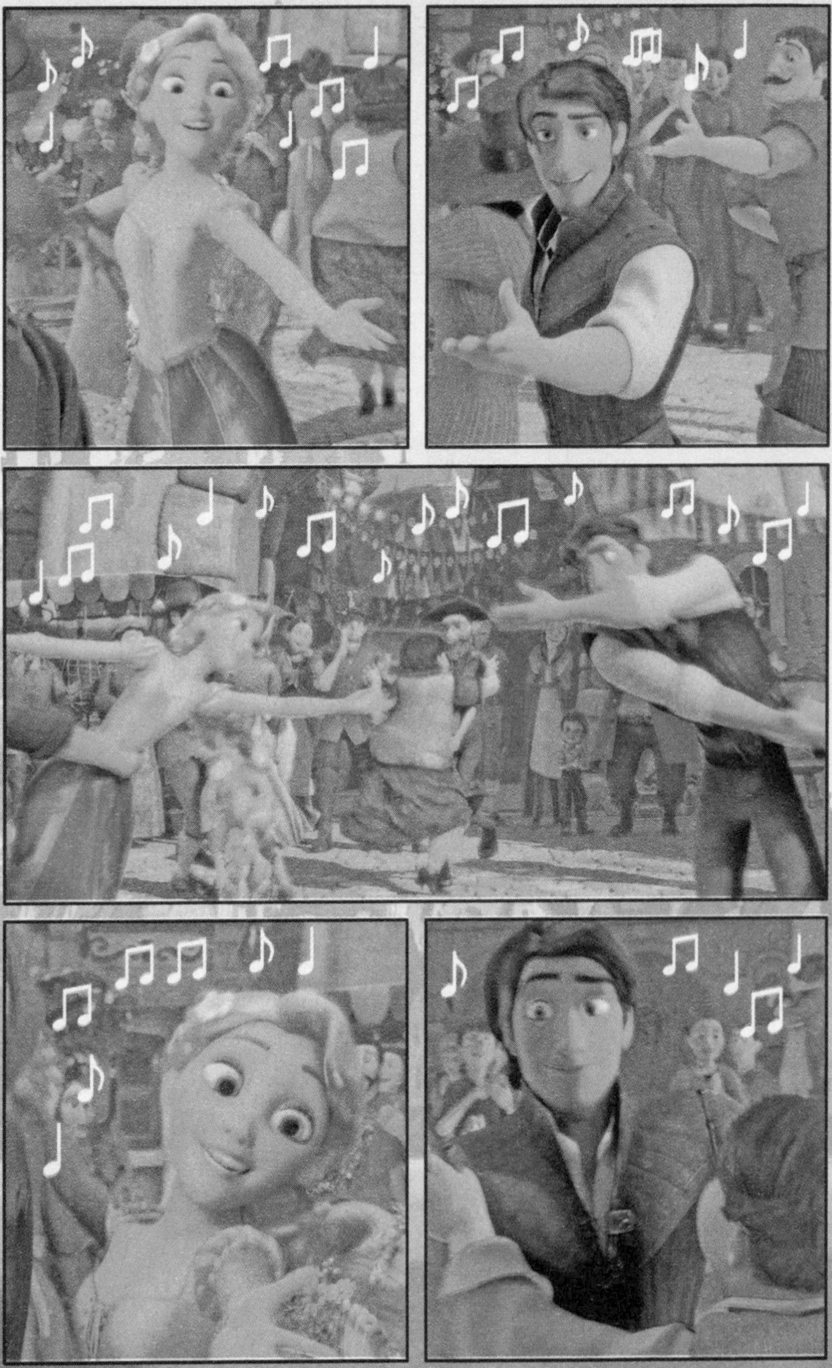

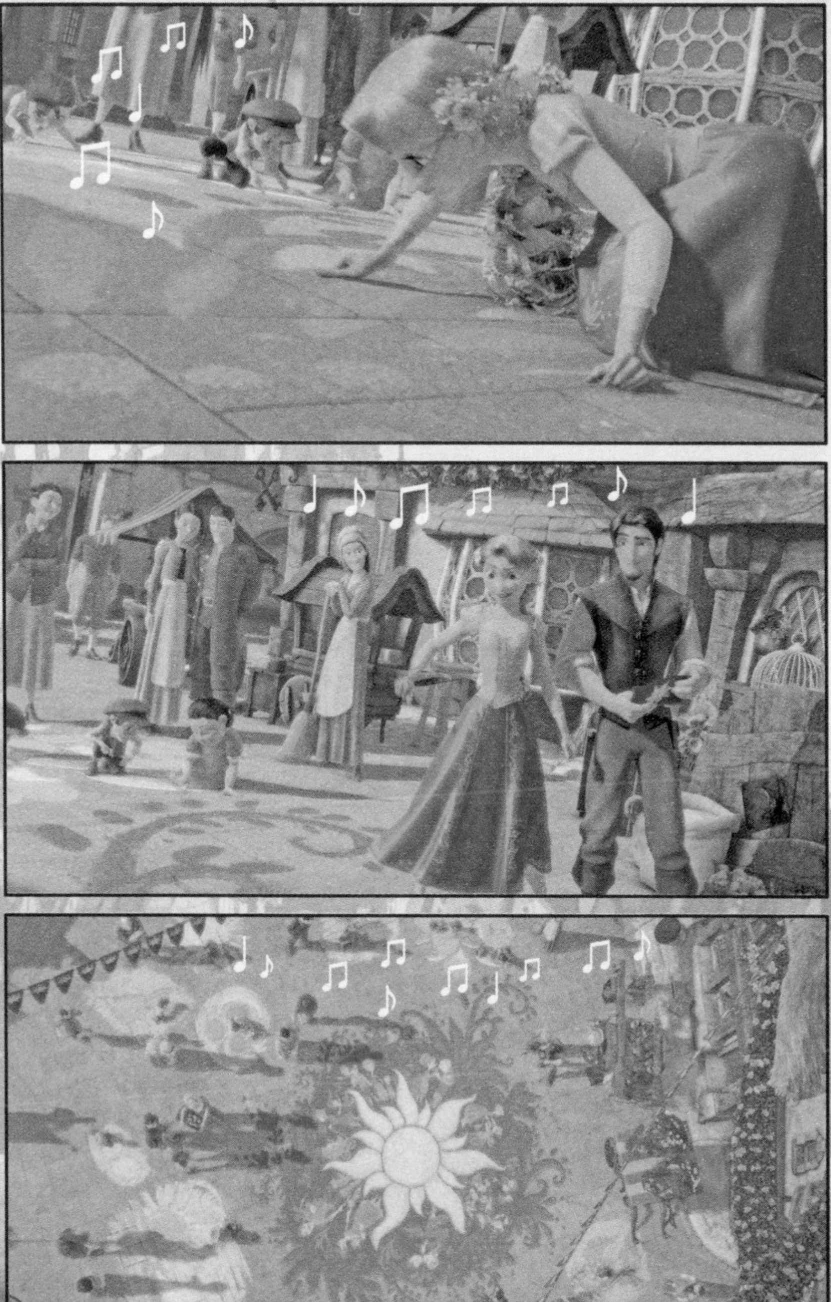

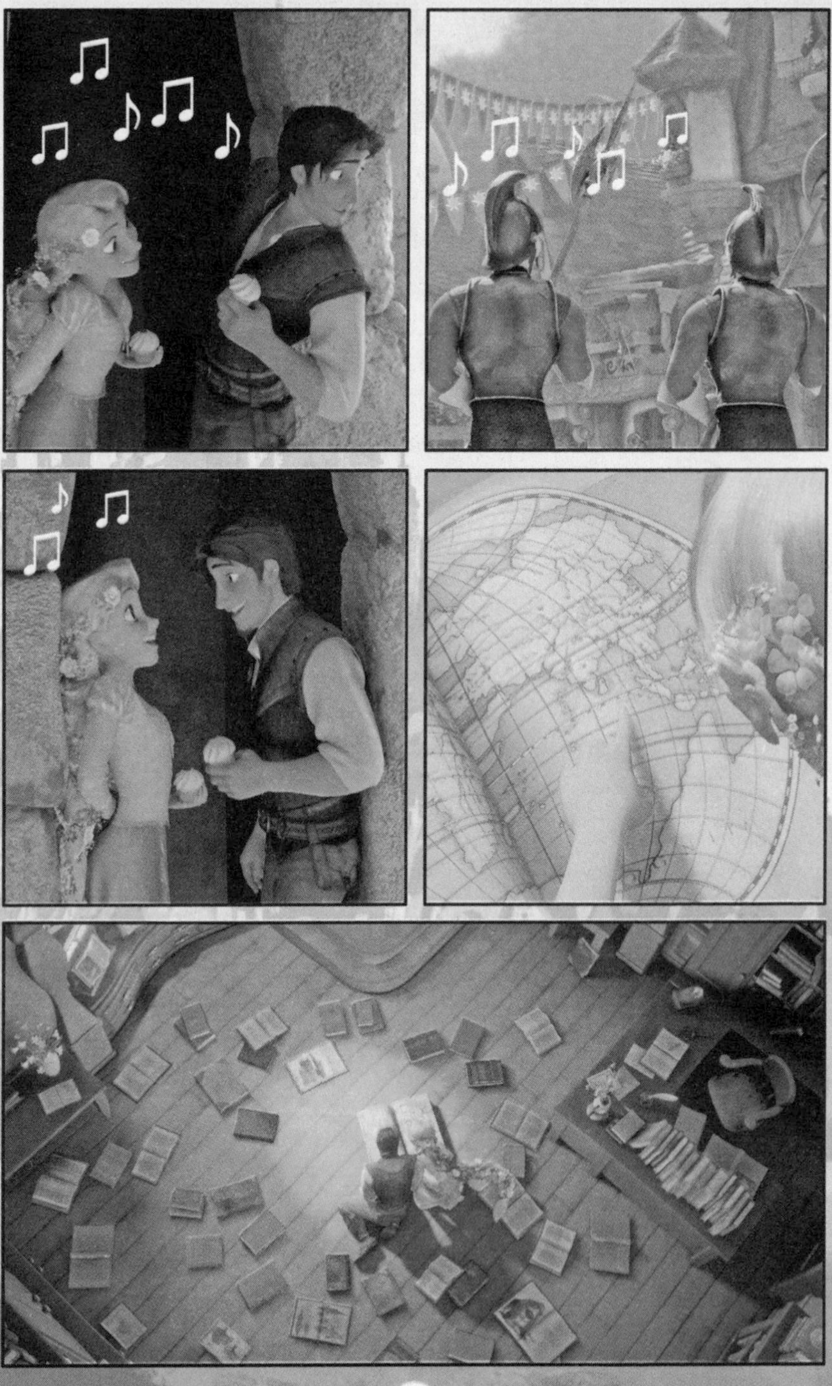

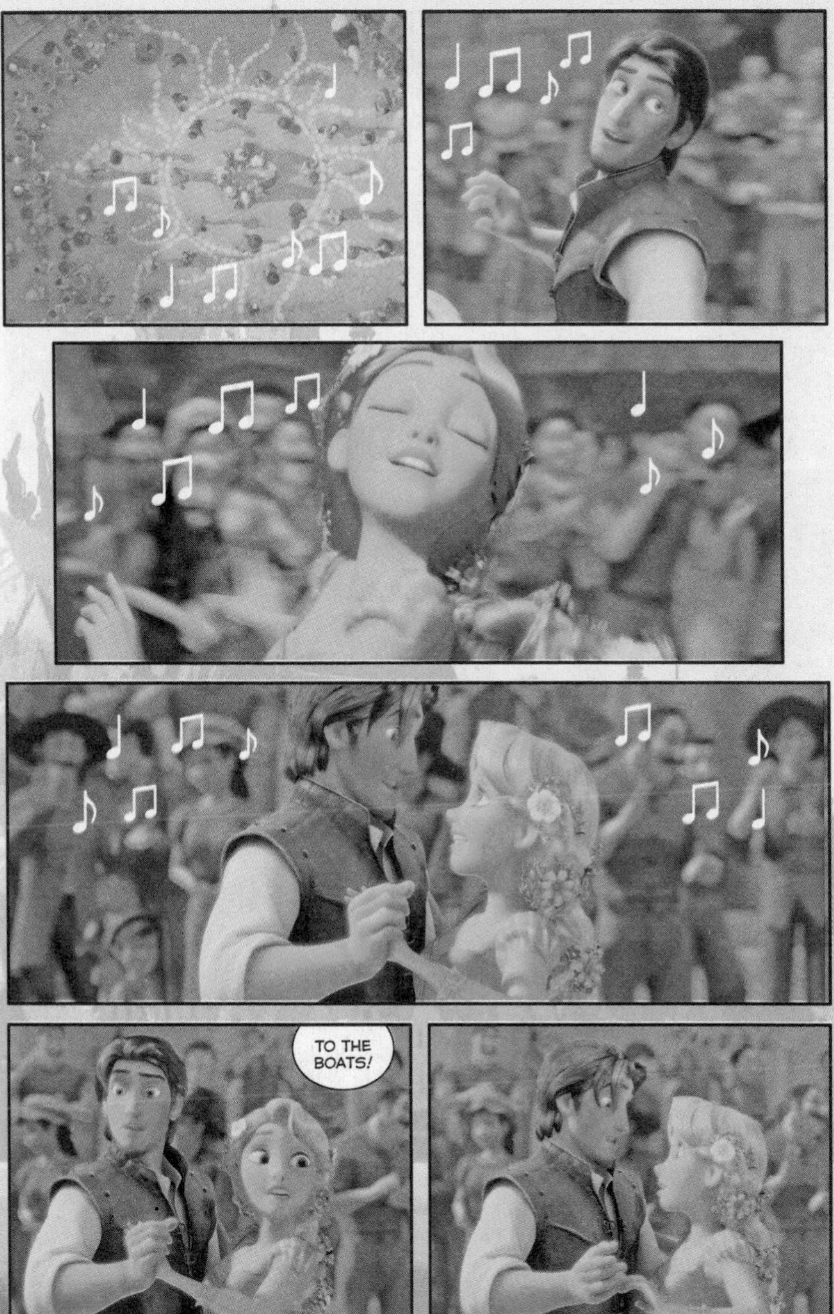
TO THE BOATS!

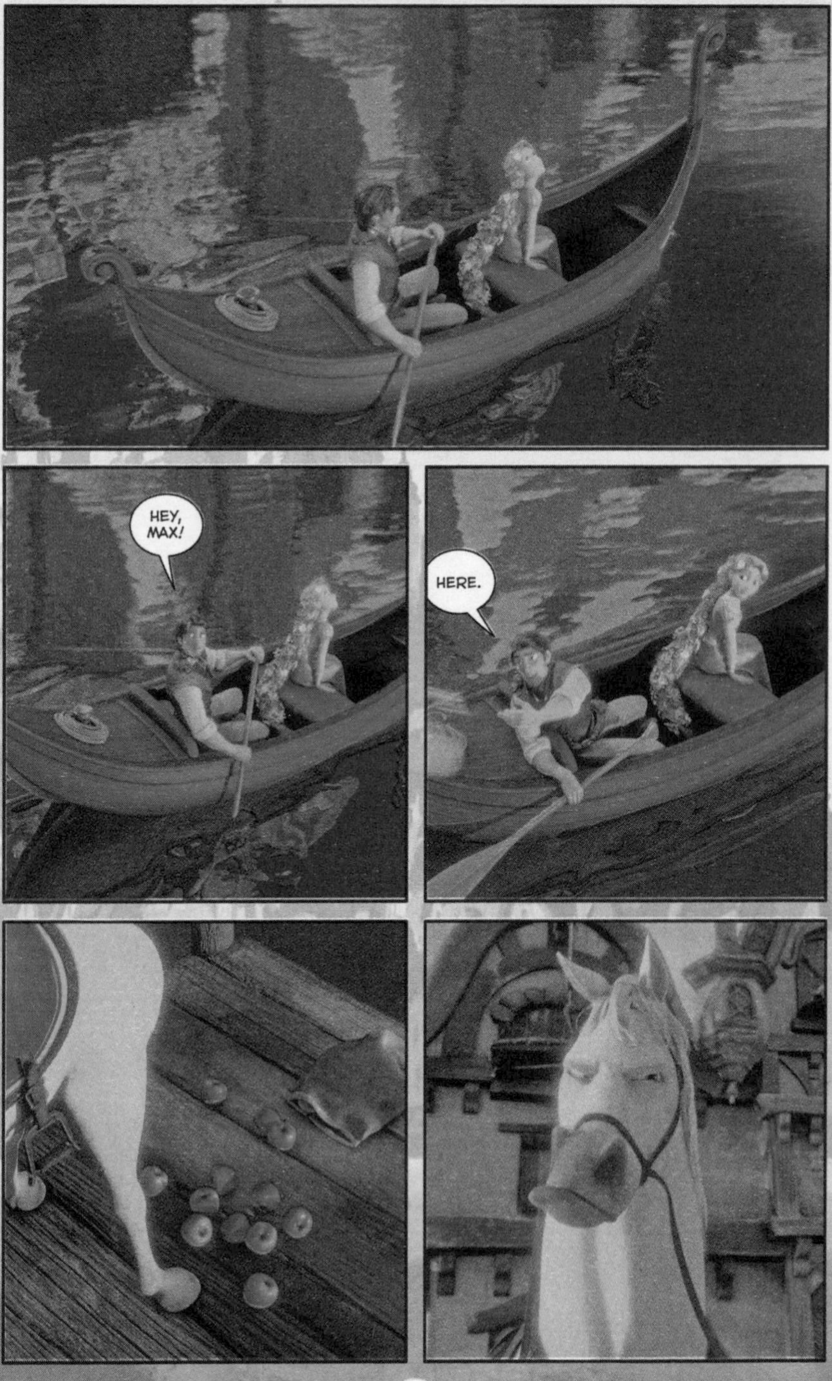
HEY, MAX!
HERE.

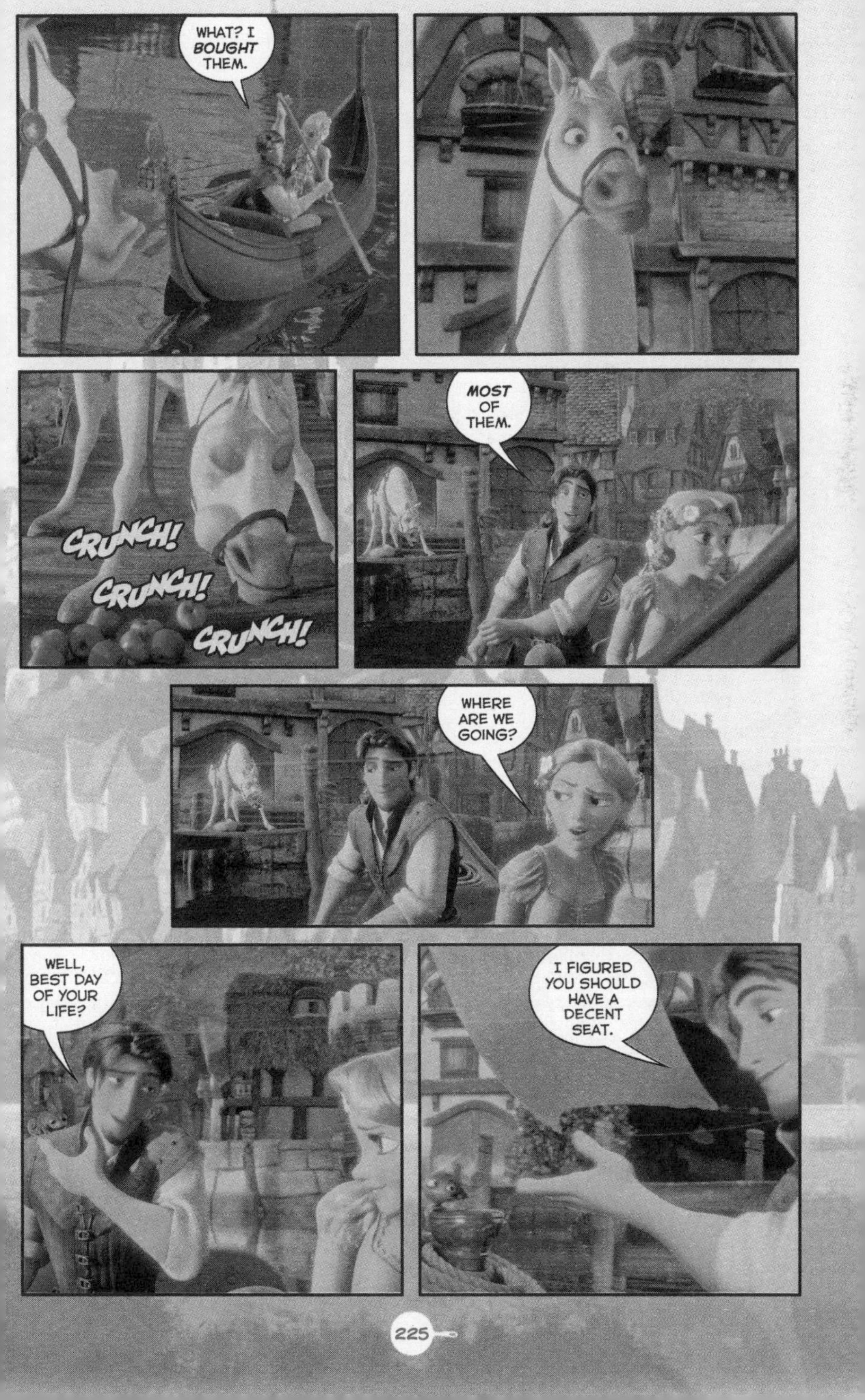
WHAT? I BOUGHT THEM.
CRUNCH!
CRUNCH!
CRUNCH!
MOST OF THEM.
WHERE ARE WE GOING?
WELL, BEST DAY OF YOUR LIFE?
I FIGURED YOU SHOULD HAVE A DECENT SEAT.

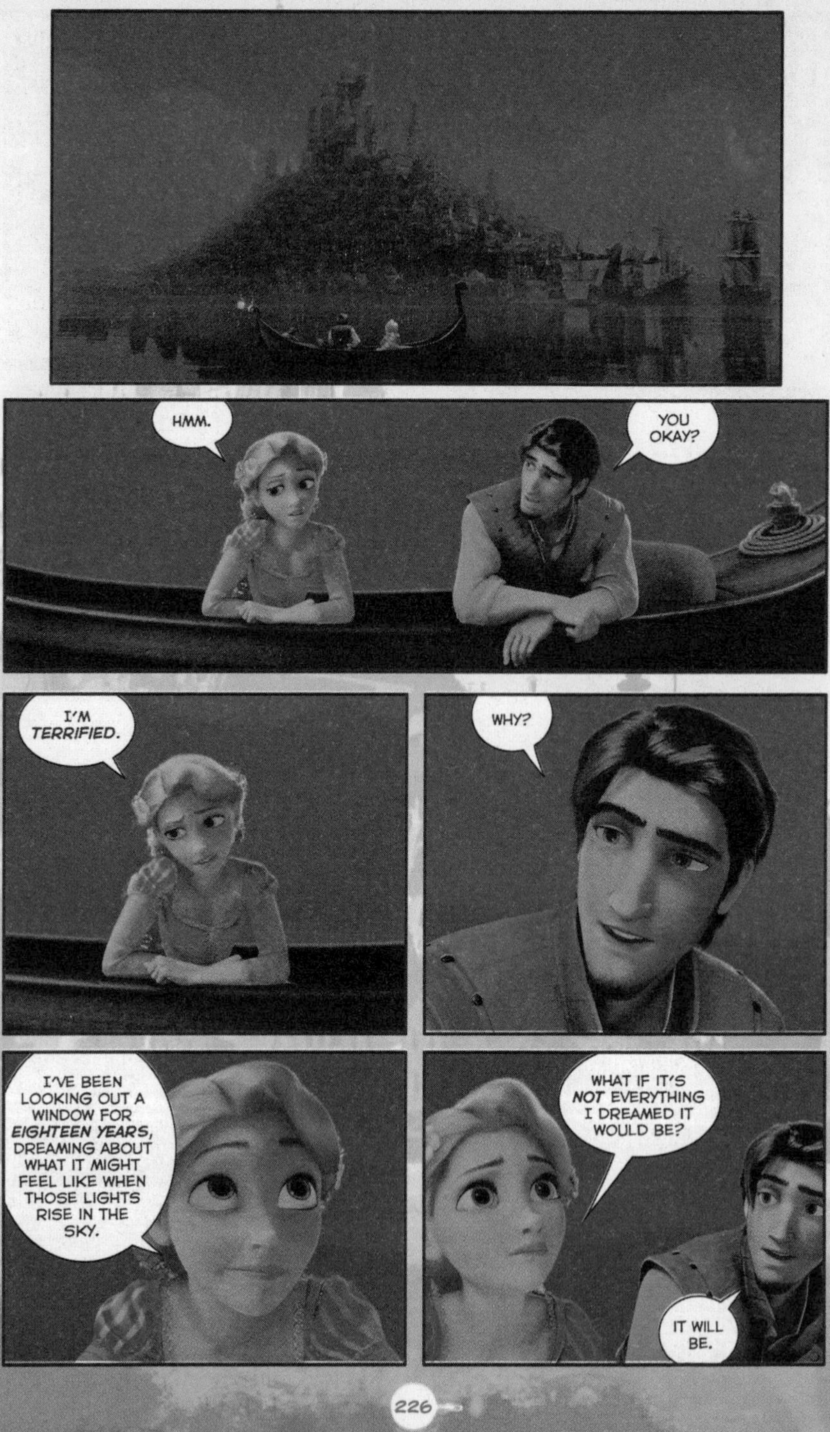
HMM.
YOU OKAY?
I'M *TERRIFIED*.
WHY?
I'VE BEEN LOOKING OUT A WINDOW FOR *EIGHTEEN YEARS*, DREAMING ABOUT WHAT IT MIGHT FEEL LIKE WHEN THOSE LIGHTS RISE IN THE SKY.
WHAT IF IT'S *NOT* EVERYTHING I DREAMED IT WOULD BE?
IT WILL BE.

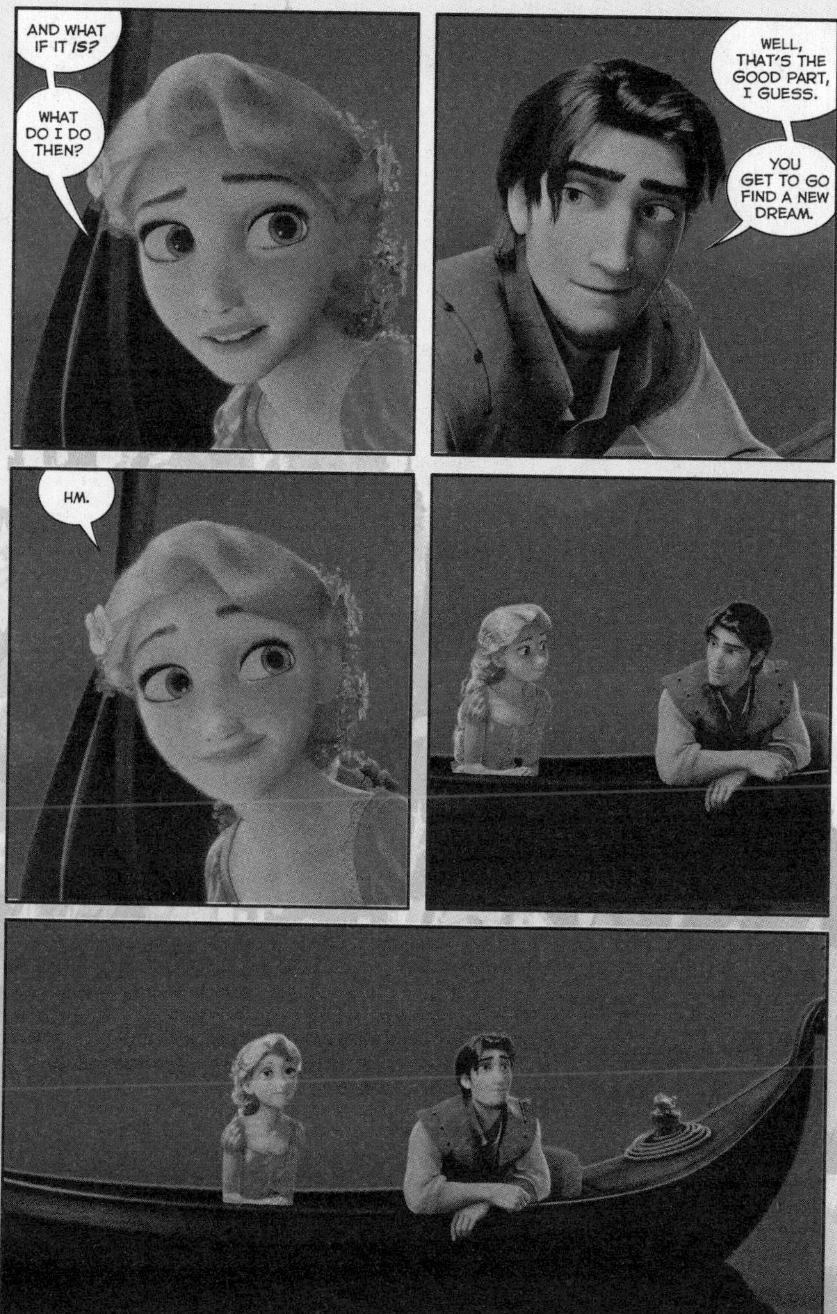
AND WHAT IF IT *IS?*
WHAT DO I DO THEN?
WELL, THAT'S THE GOOD PART, I GUESS.
YOU GET TO GO FIND A NEW DREAM.
HM.

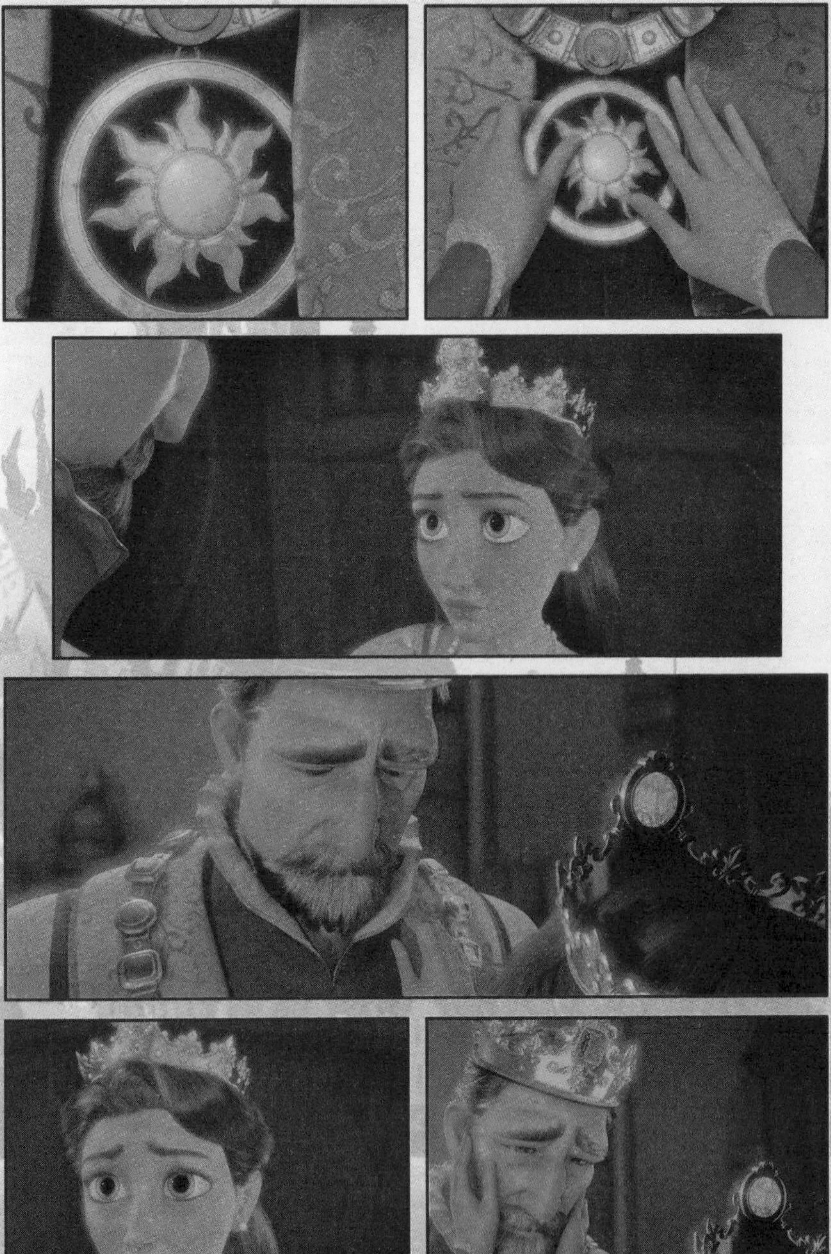

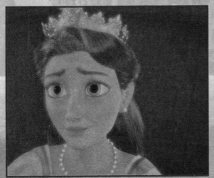

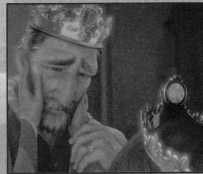

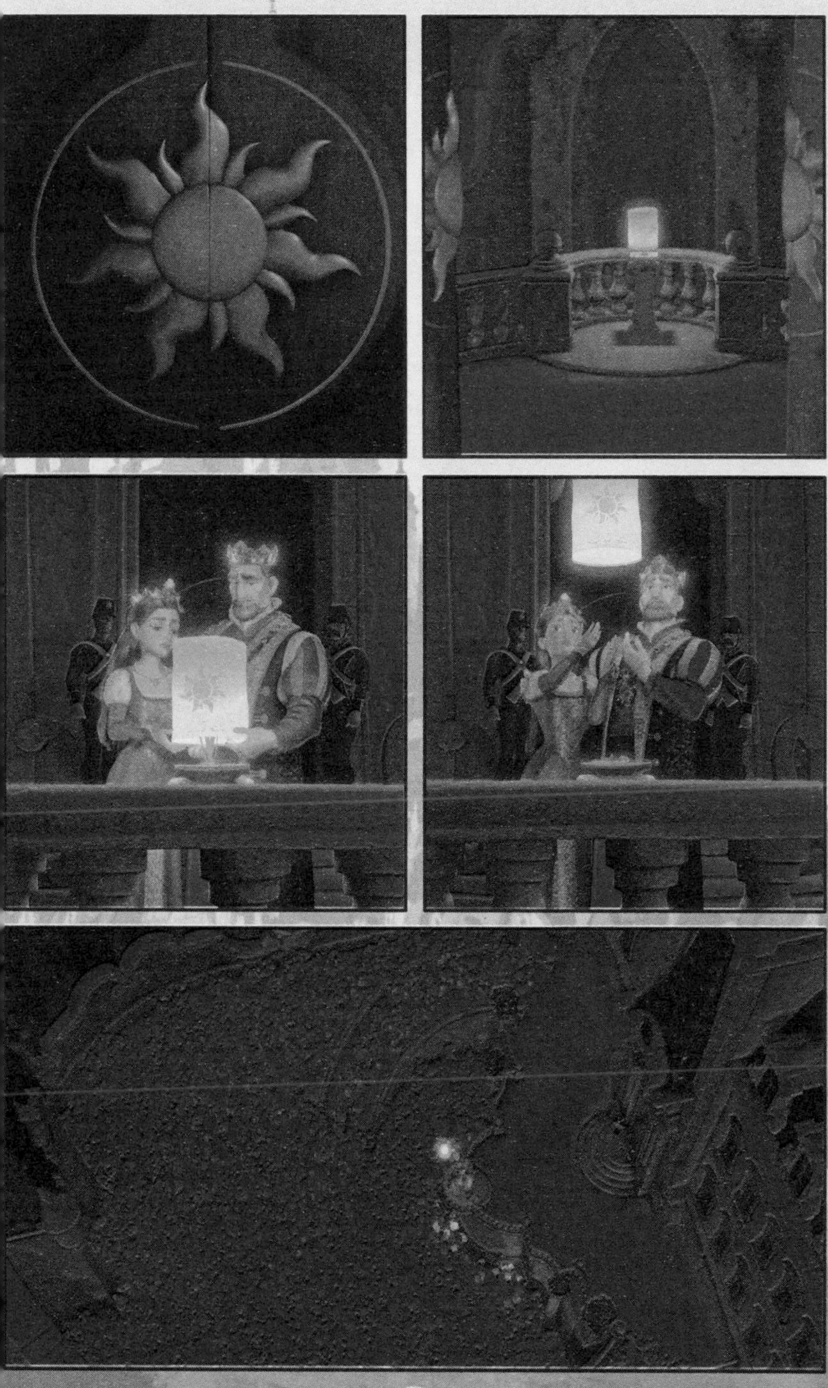

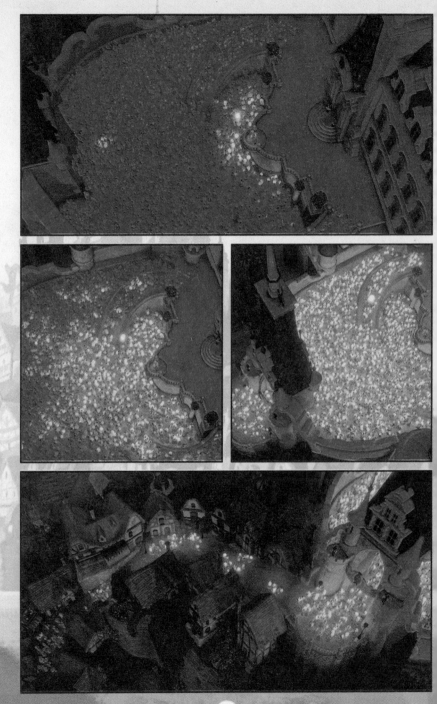

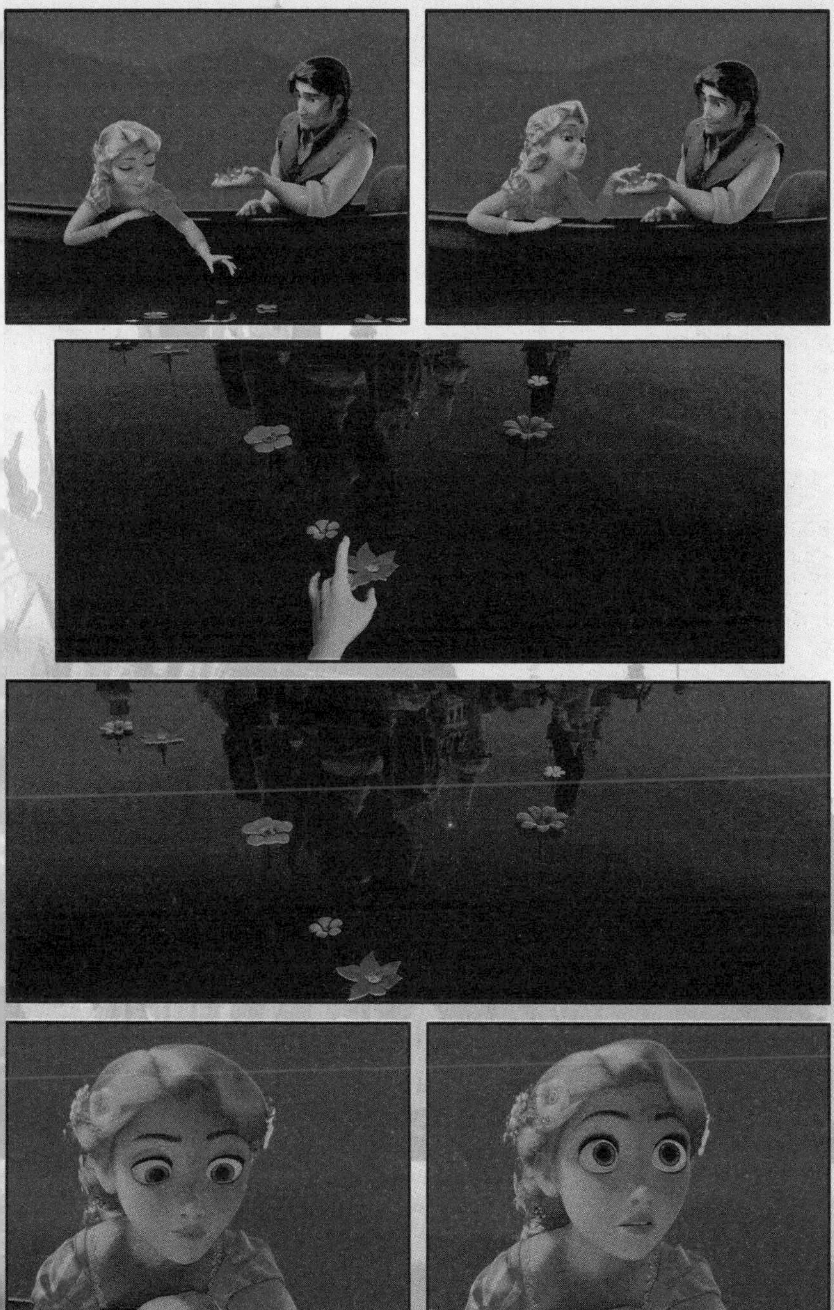

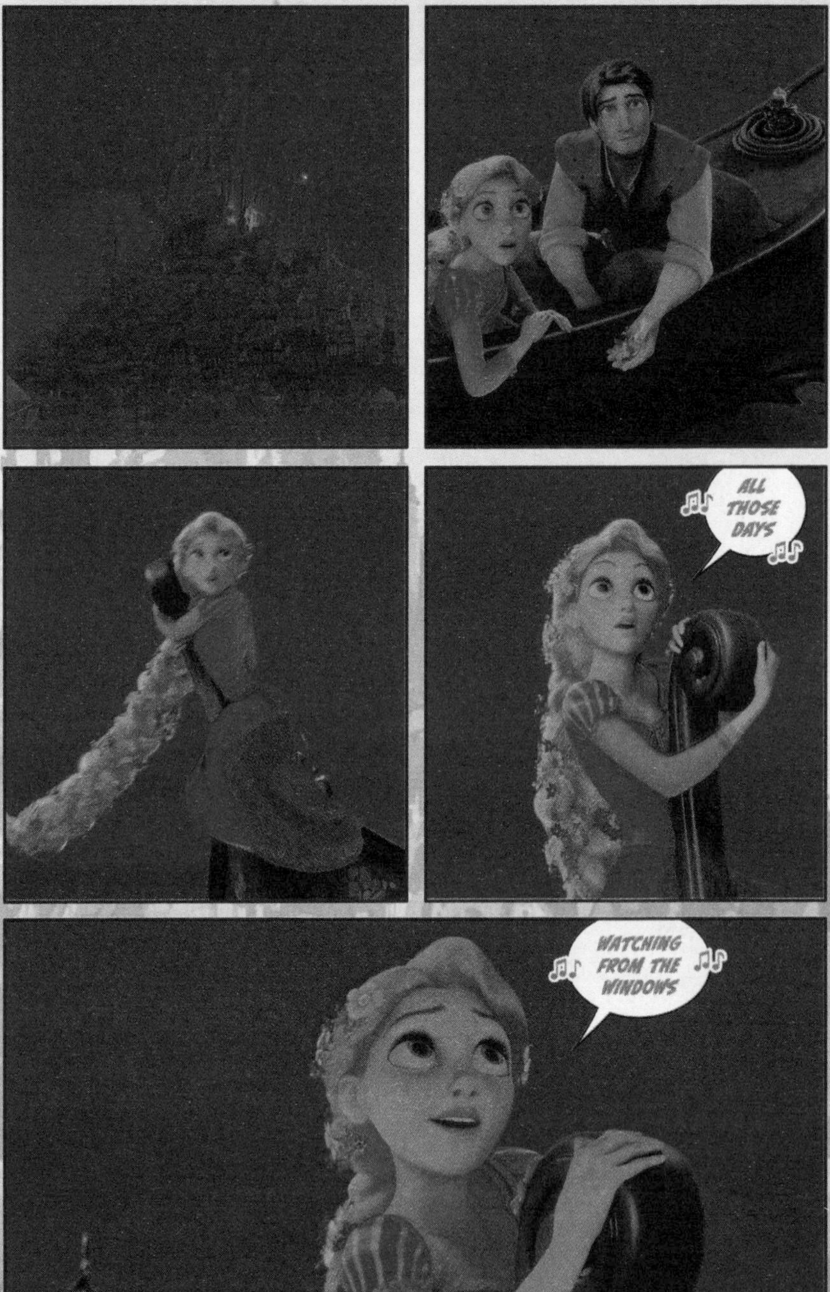
ALL THOSE DAYS
WATCHING FROM THE WINDOWS

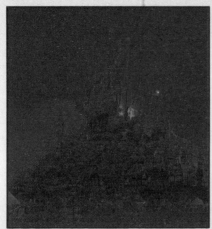

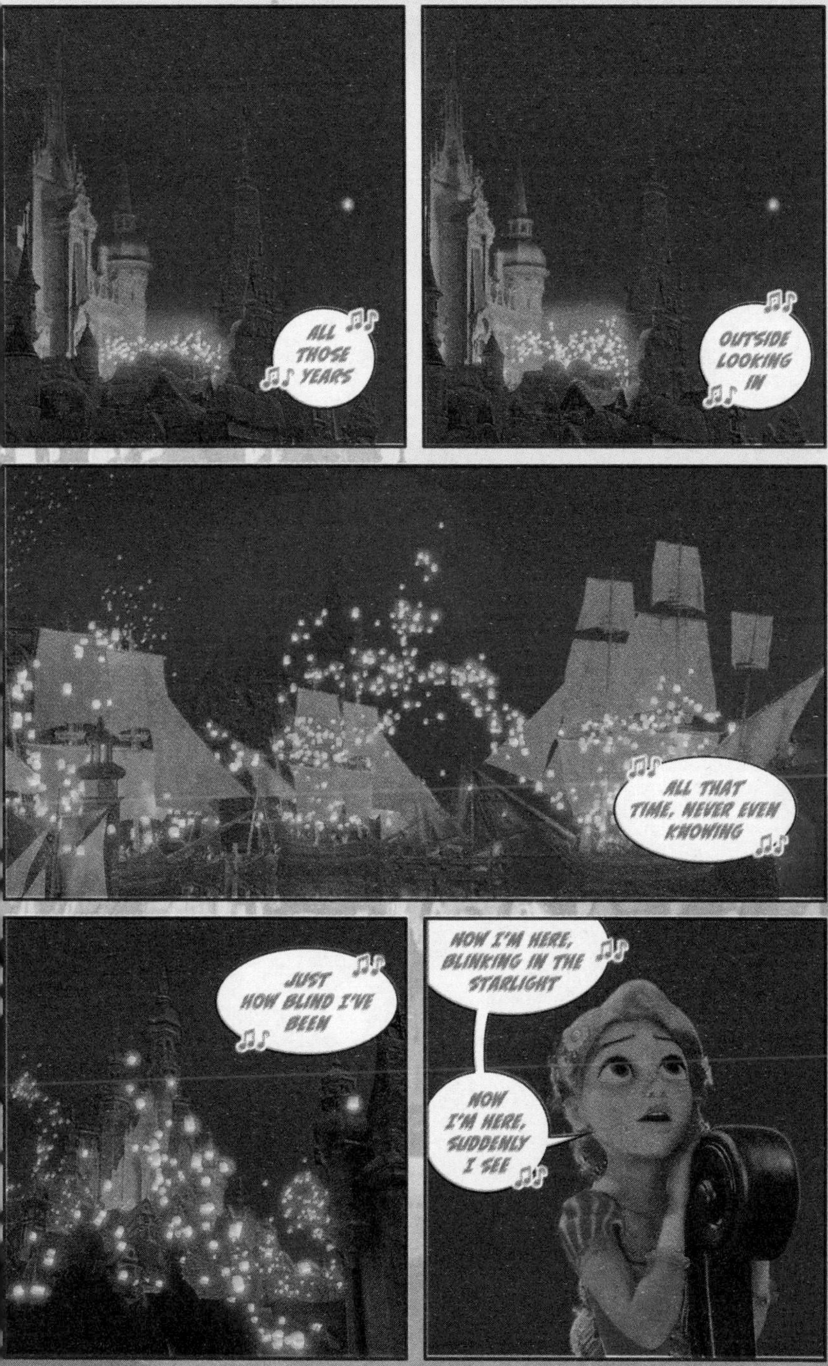
ALL THOSE YEARS
OUTSIDE LOOKING IN
ALL THAT TIME, NEVER EVEN KNOWING
JUST HOW BLIND I'VE BEEN
NOW I'M HERE, BLINKING IN THE STARLIGHT
NOW I'M HERE, SUDDENLY I SEE

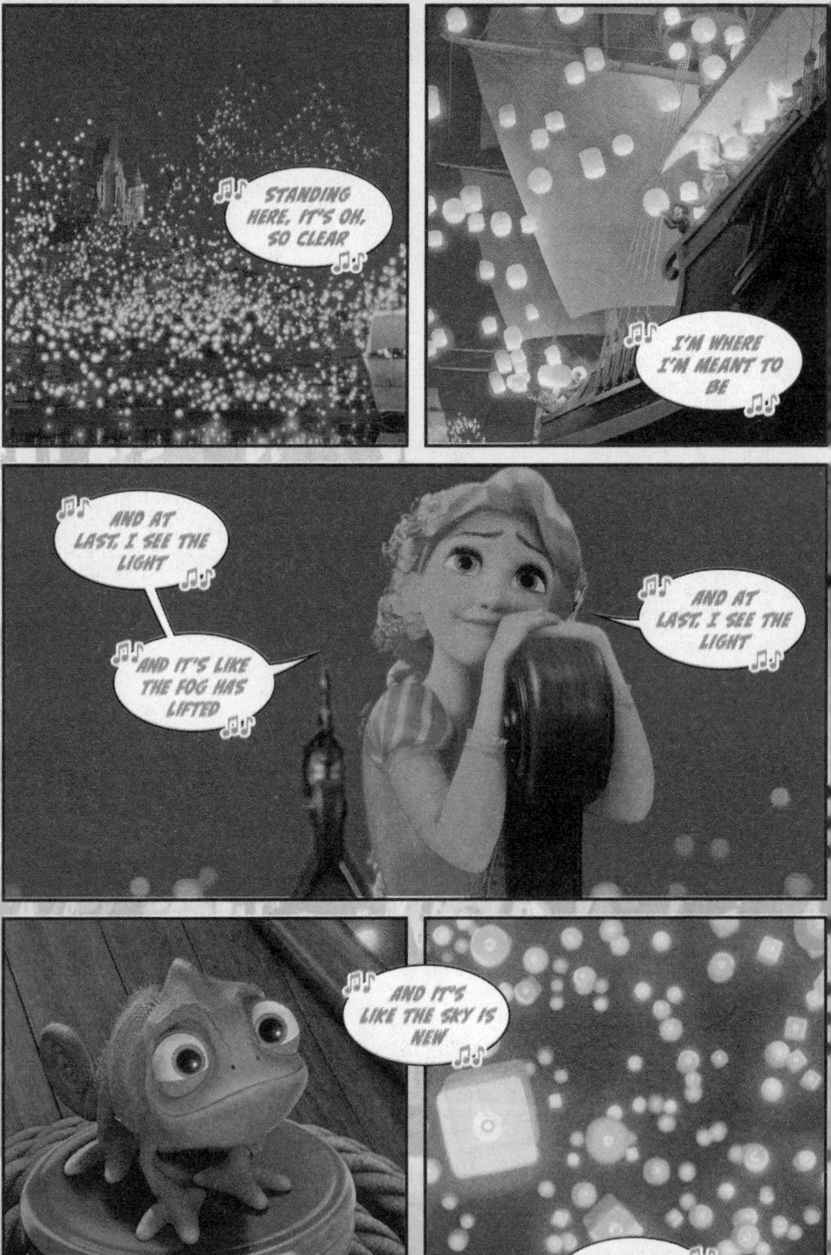
STANDING HERE, IT'S OH, SO CLEAR
I'M WHERE I'M MEANT TO BE
AND AT LAST, I SEE THE LIGHT
AND IT'S LIKE THE FOG HAS LIFTED
AND AT LAST, I SEE THE LIGHT
AND IT'S LIKE THE SKY IS NEW
AND IT'S WARM AND REAL AND BRIGHT

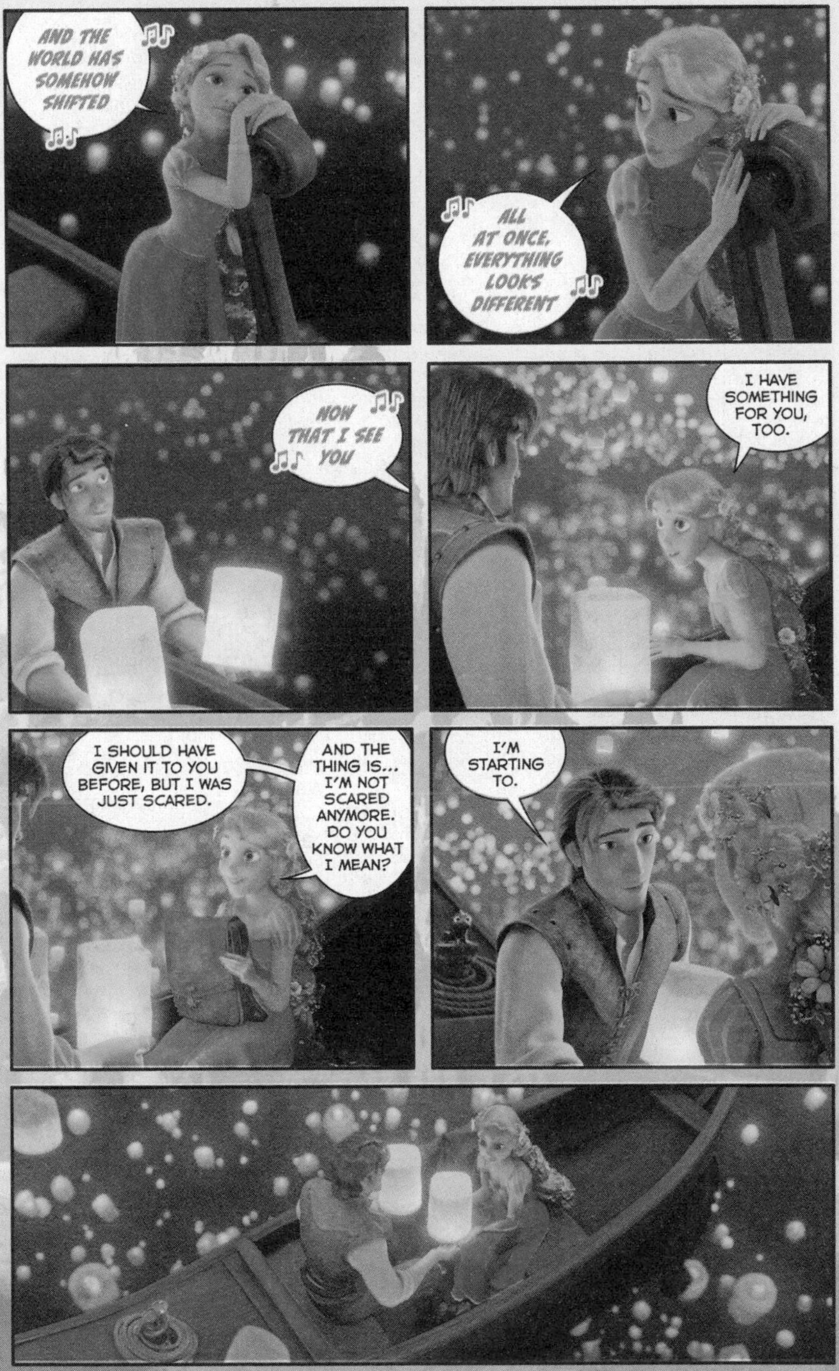
AND THE WORLD HAS SOMEHOW SHIFTED
ALL AT ONCE, EVERYTHING LOOKS DIFFERENT
NOW THAT I SEE YOU
I HAVE SOMETHING FOR YOU, TOO.
I SHOULD HAVE GIVEN IT TO YOU BEFORE, BUT I WAS JUST SCARED.
AND THE THING IS... I'M NOT SCARED ANYMORE. DO YOU KNOW WHAT I MEAN?
I'M STARTING TO.

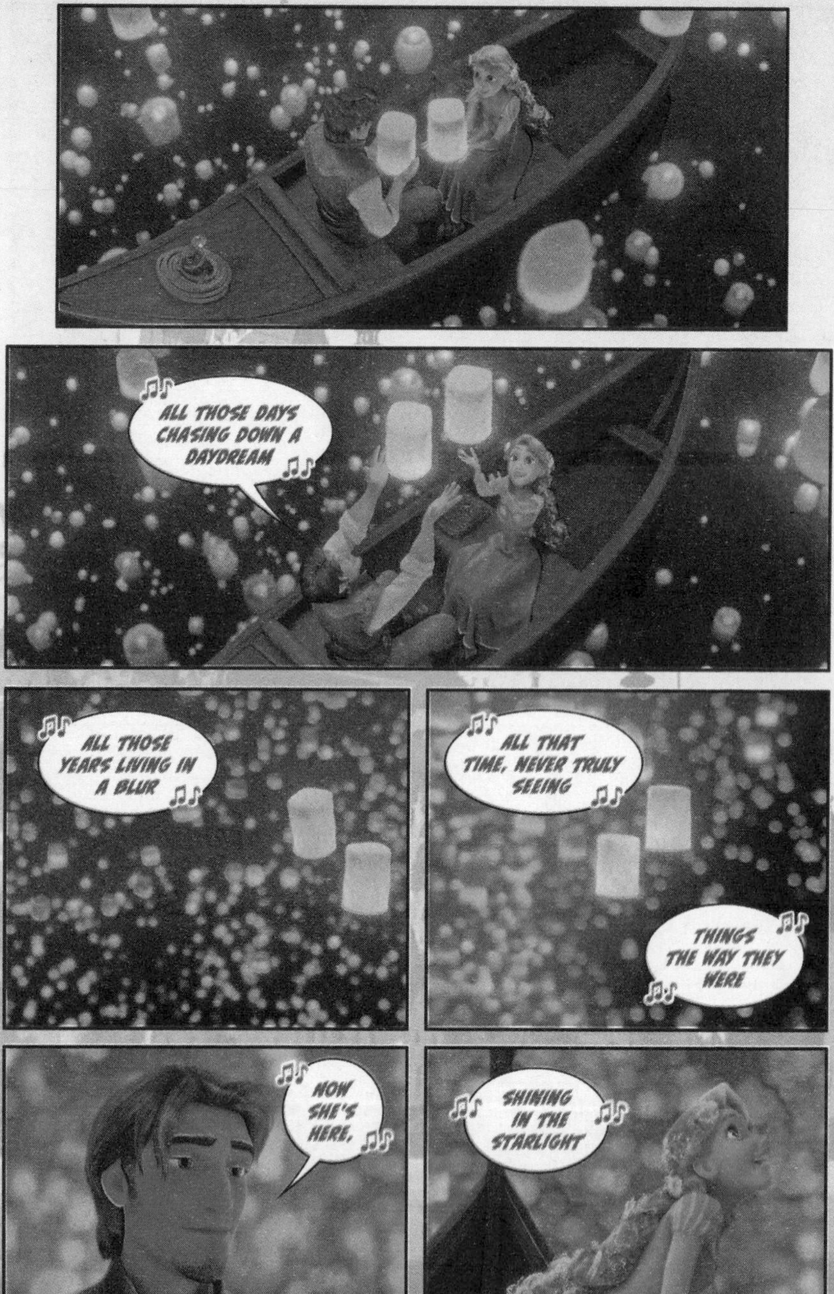

ALL THOSE DAYS CHASING DOWN A DAYDREAM
ALL THOSE YEARS LIVING IN A BLUR
ALL THAT TIME, NEVER TRULY SEEING
THINGS THE WAY THEY WERE
NOW SHE'S HERE,
SHINING IN THE STARLIGHT

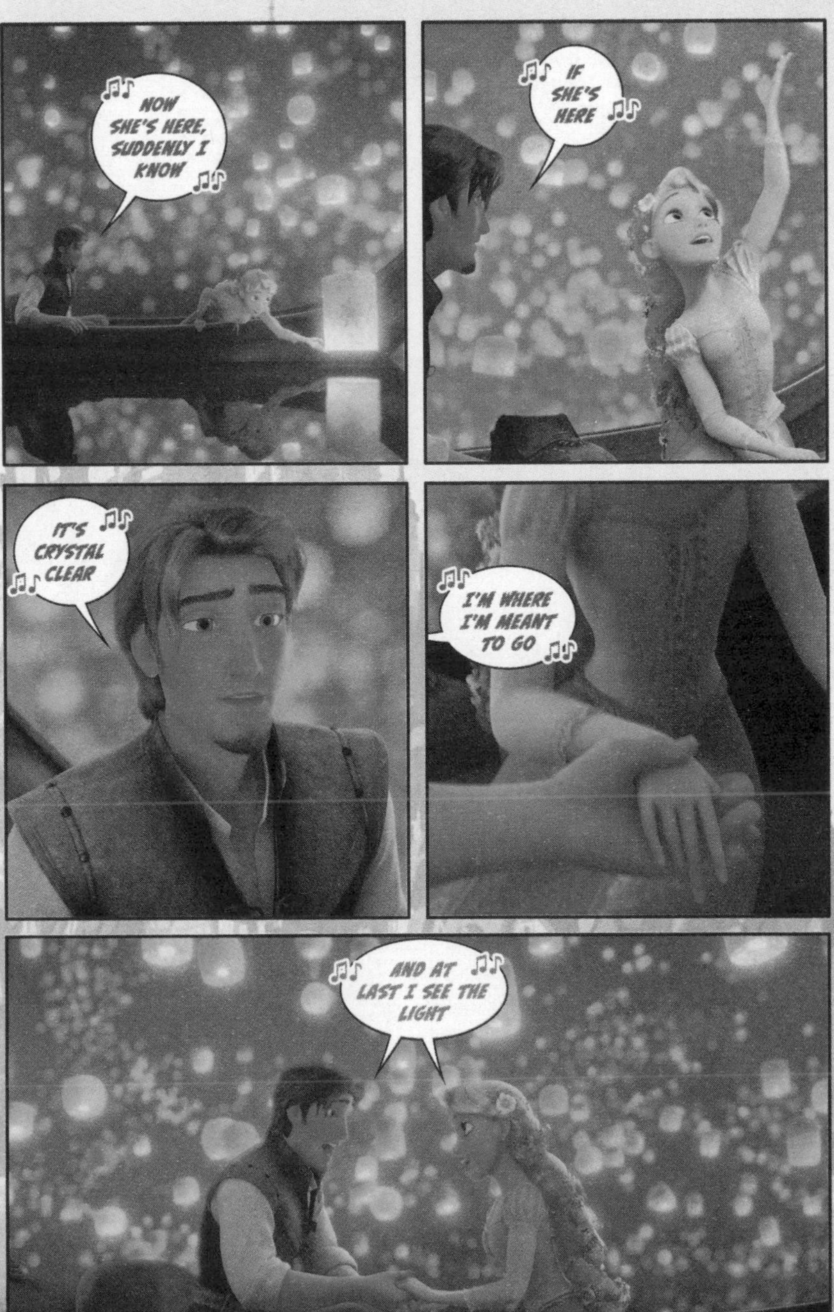
NOW SHE'S HERE, SUDDENLY I KNOW
IF SHE'S HERE
IT'S CRYSTAL CLEAR
I'M WHERE I'M MEANT TO GO
AND AT LAST I SEE THE LIGHT

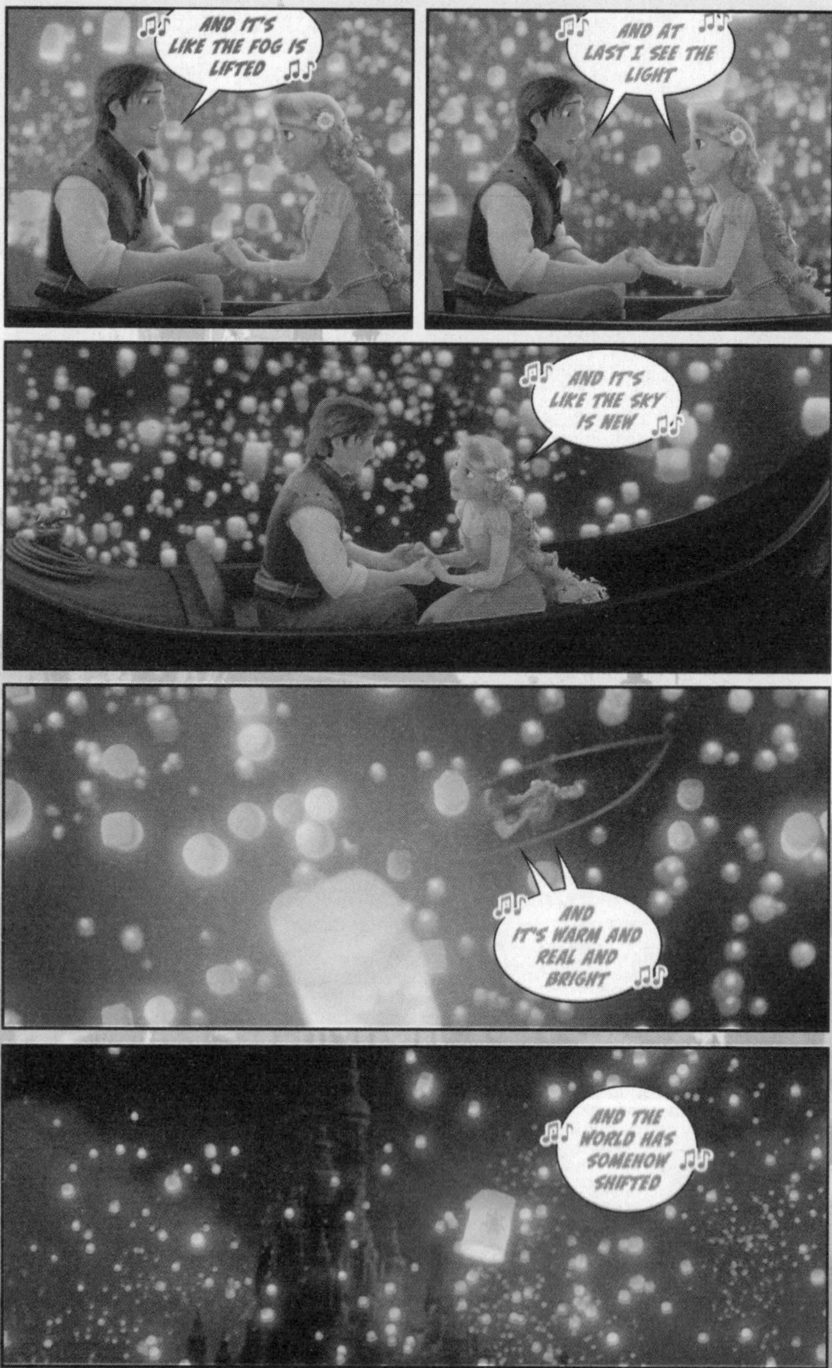
AND IT'S LIKE THE FOG IS LIFTED
AND AT LAST I SEE THE LIGHT
AND IT'S LIKE THE SKY IS NEW
AND IT'S WARM AND REAL AND BRIGHT
AND THE WORLD HAS SOMEHOW SHIFTED

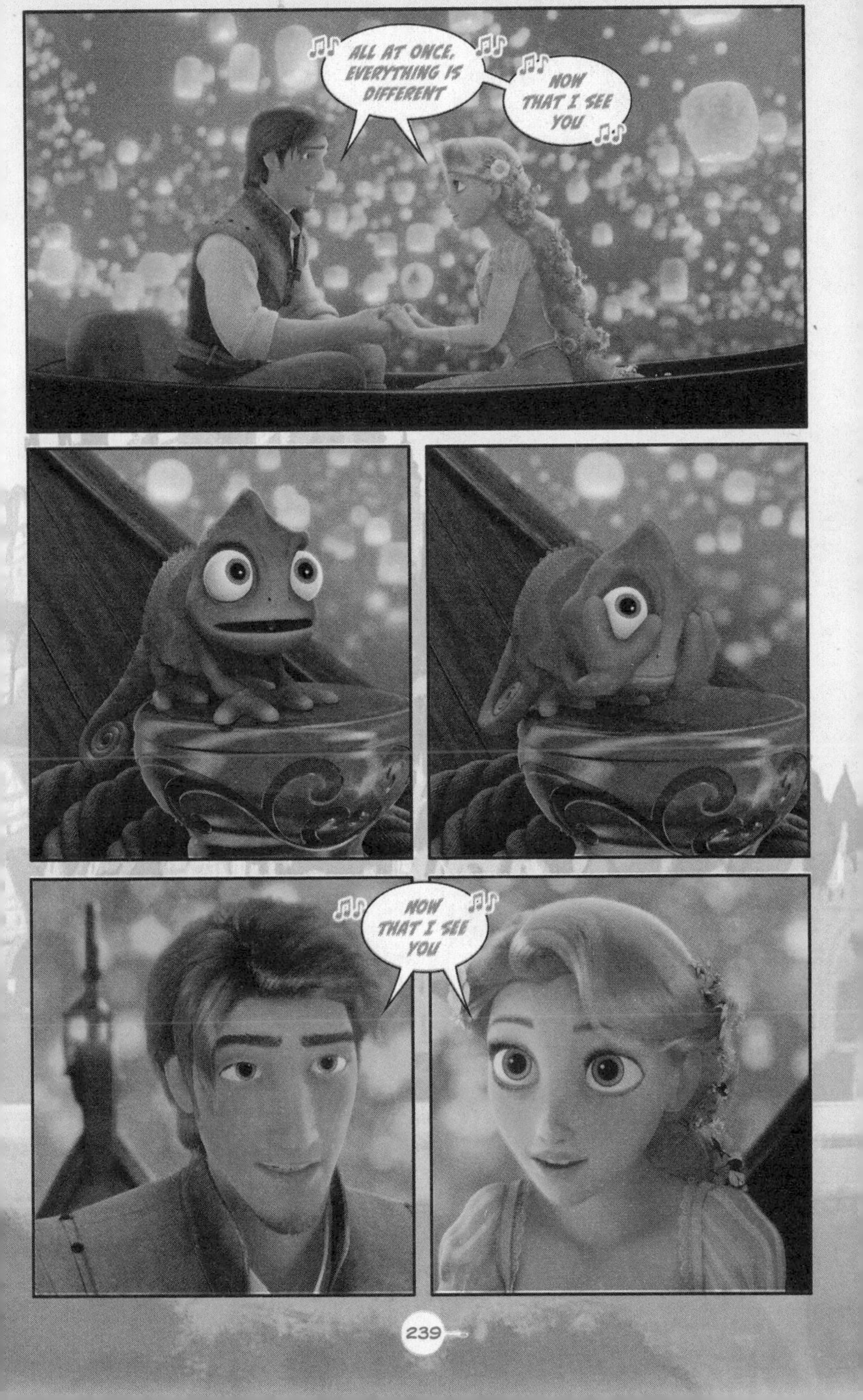
ALL AT ONCE, EVERYTHING IS DIFFERENT
NOW THAT I SEE YOU
NOW THAT I SEE YOU

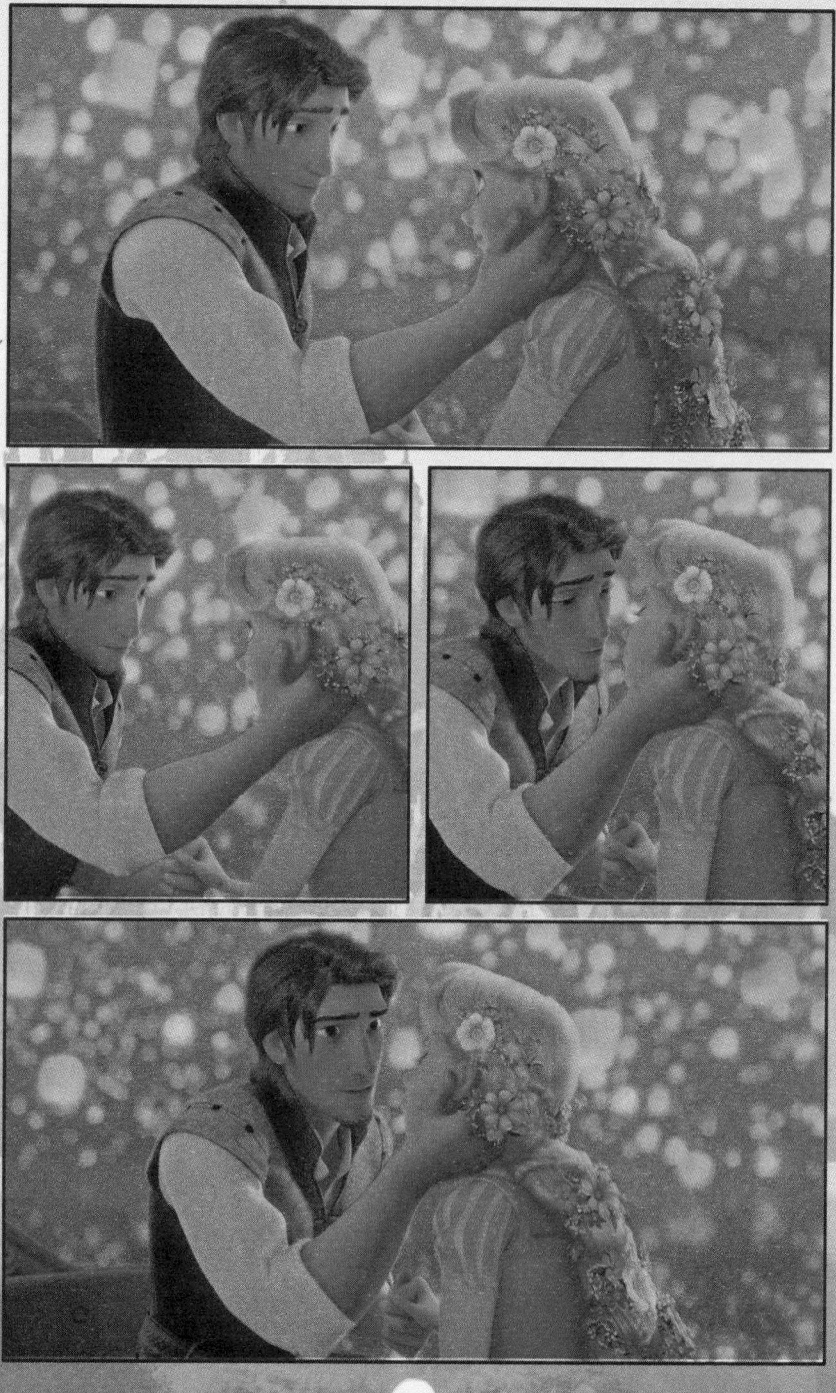

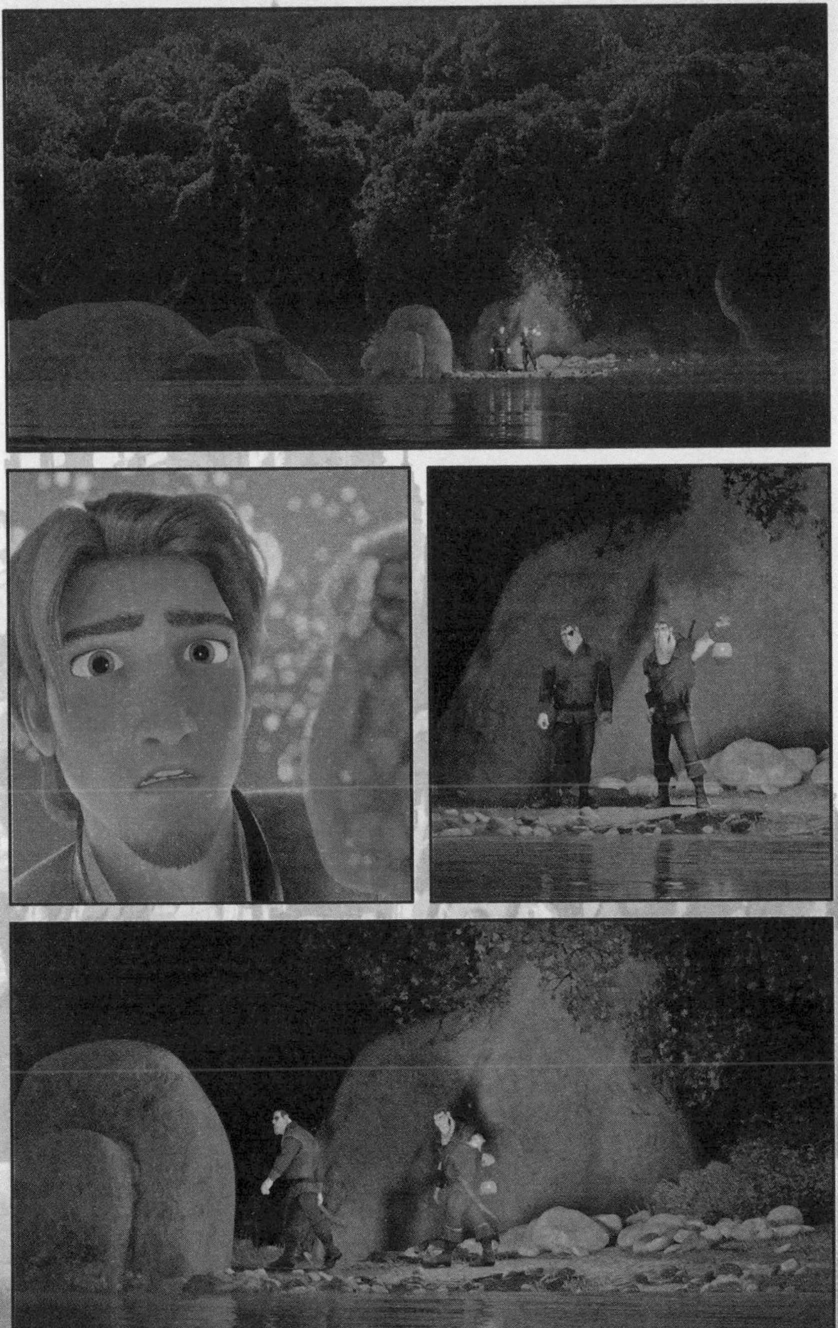

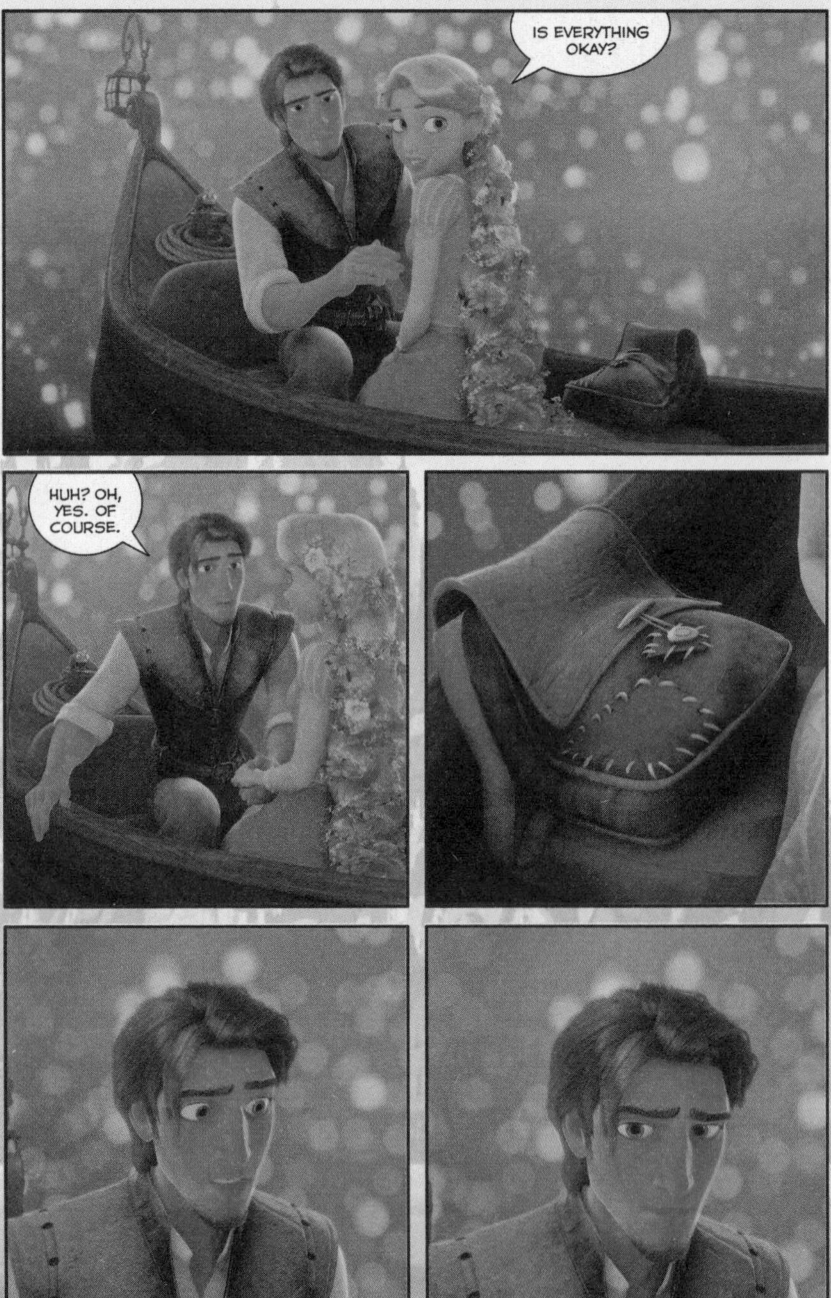
IS EVERYTHING OKAY?
HUH? OH, YES. OF COURSE.

I'M SORRY -- EVERYTHING'S FINE.

THERE'S JUST SOMETHING I HAVE TO TAKE CARE OF.

OKAY...

OKAY.

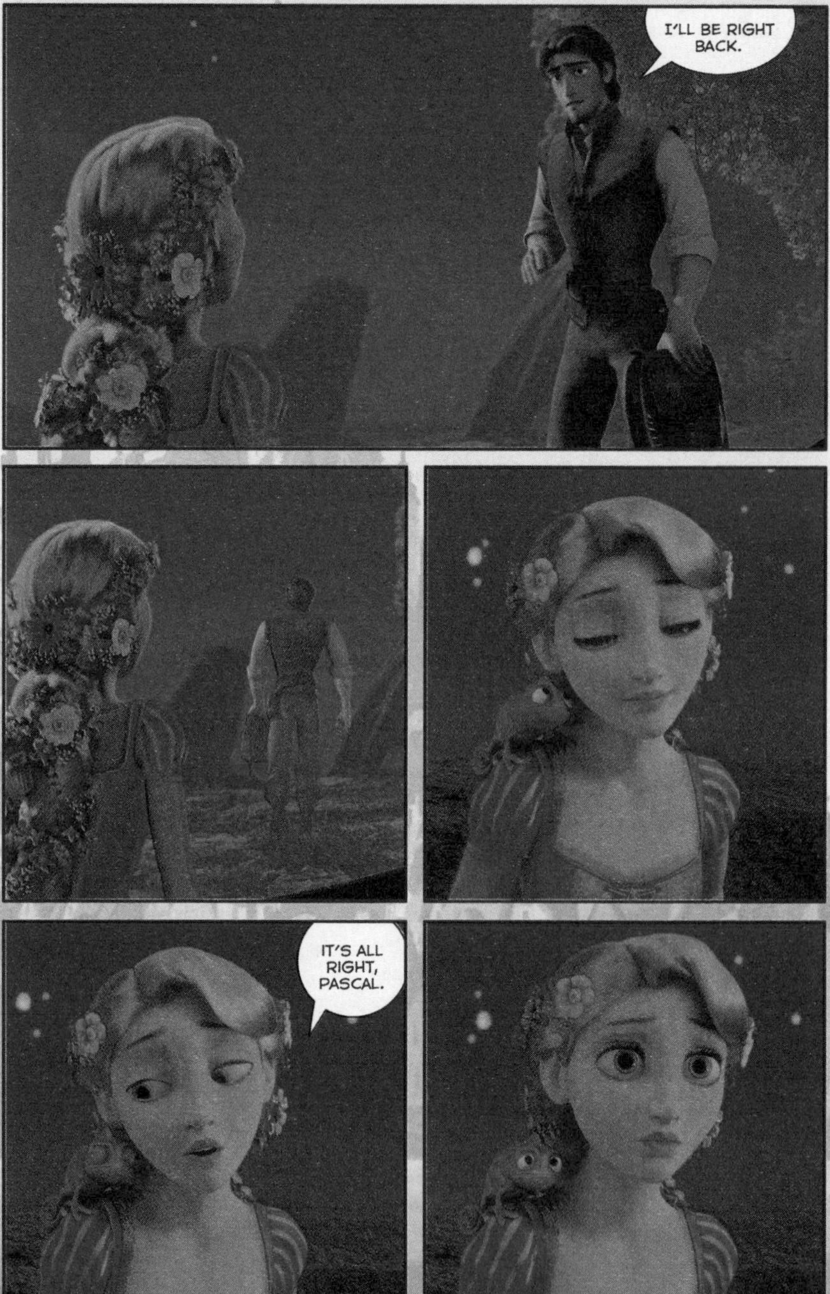
I'LL BE RIGHT BACK.
IT'S ALL RIGHT, PASCAL.

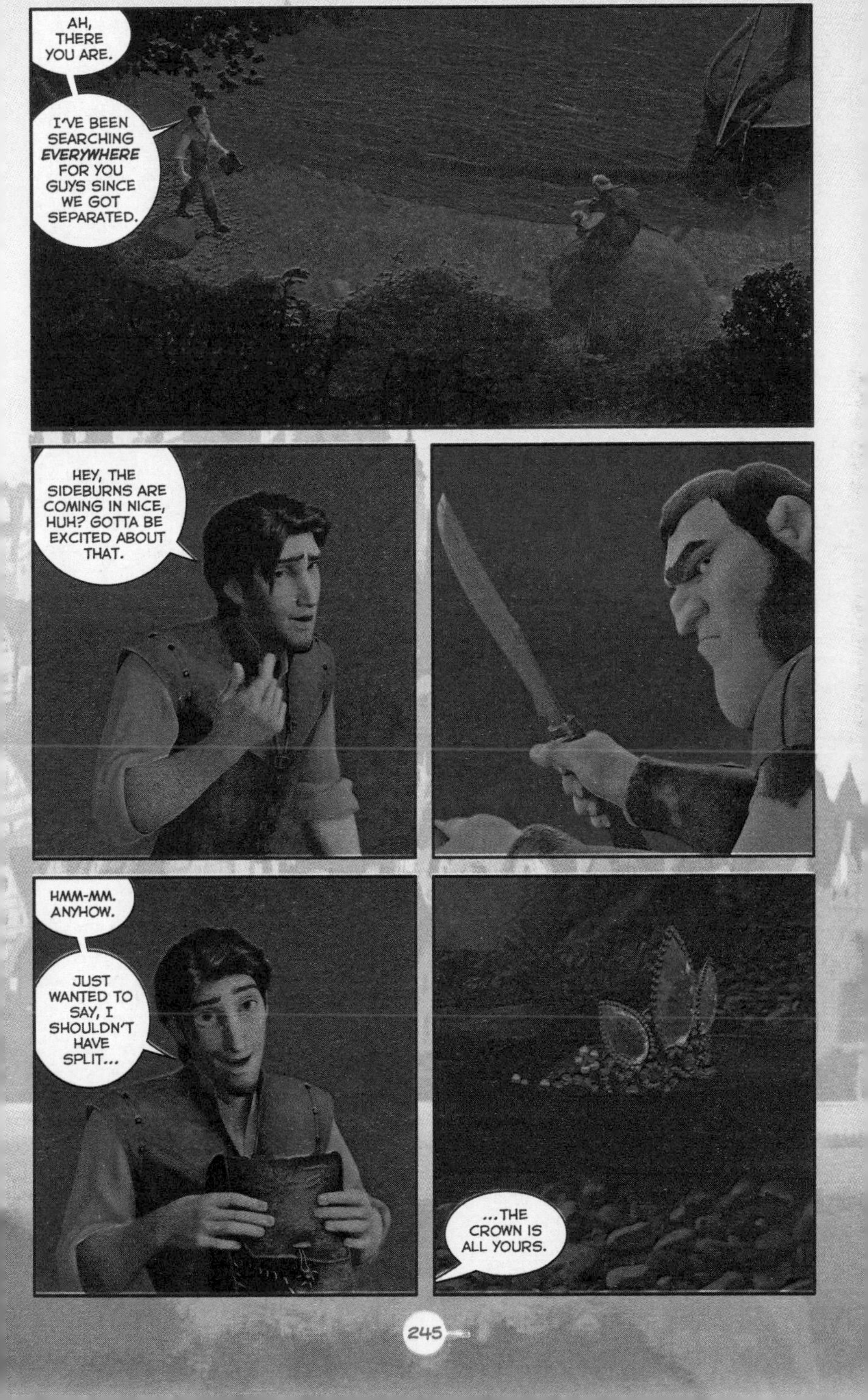
AH, THERE YOU ARE.
I'VE BEEN SEARCHING ***EVERYWHERE*** FOR YOU GUYS SINCE WE GOT SEPARATED.
HEY, THE SIDEBURNS ARE COMING IN NICE, HUH? GOTTA BE EXCITED ABOUT THAT.
HMM-MM. ANYHOW.
JUST WANTED TO SAY, I SHOULDN'T HAVE SPLIT...
...THE CROWN IS ALL YOURS.

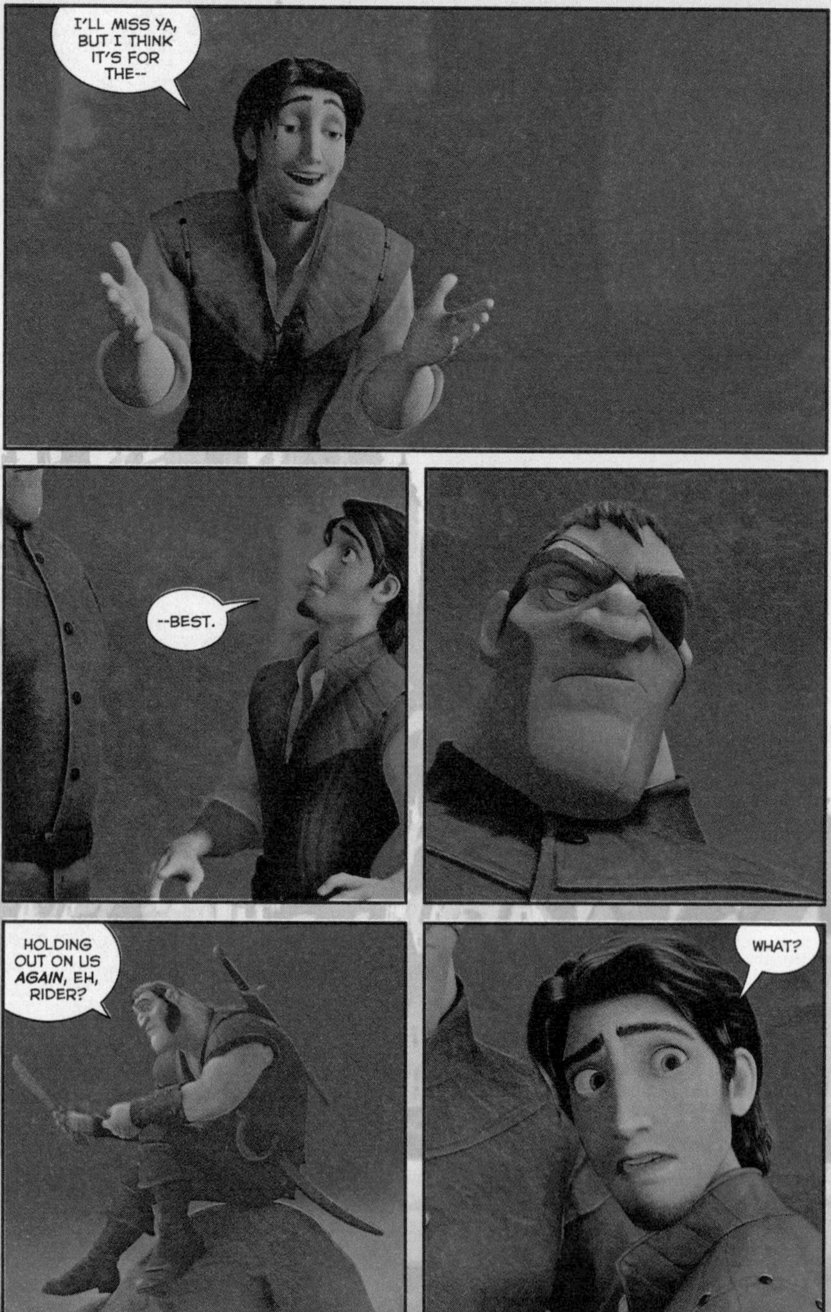
I'LL MISS YA, BUT I THINK IT'S FOR THE--
--BEST.
HOLDING OUT ON US *AGAIN*, EH, RIDER?
WHAT?

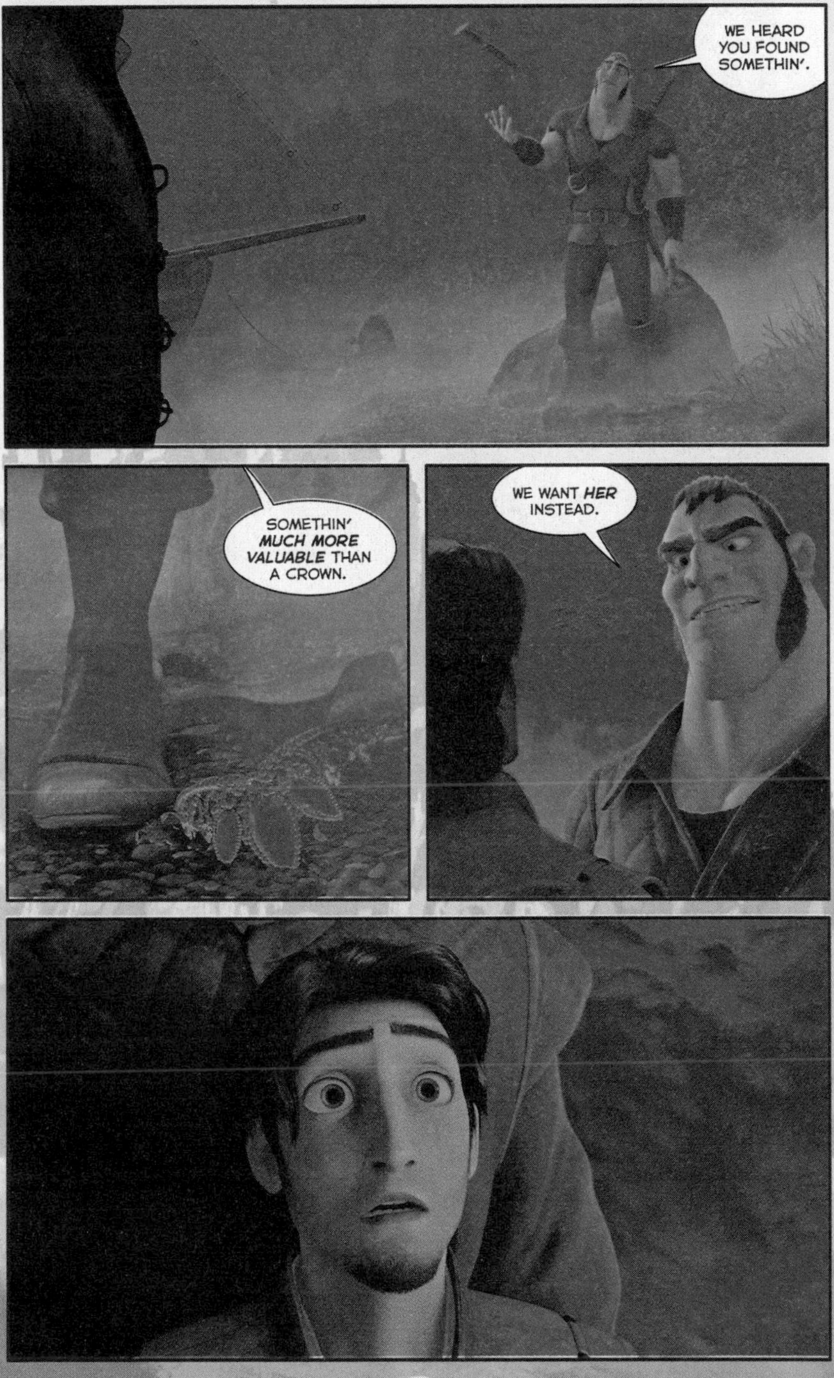
WE HEARD YOU FOUND SOMETHIN'.
SOMETHIN' *MUCH MORE VALUABLE* THAN A CROWN.
WE WANT *HER* INSTEAD.

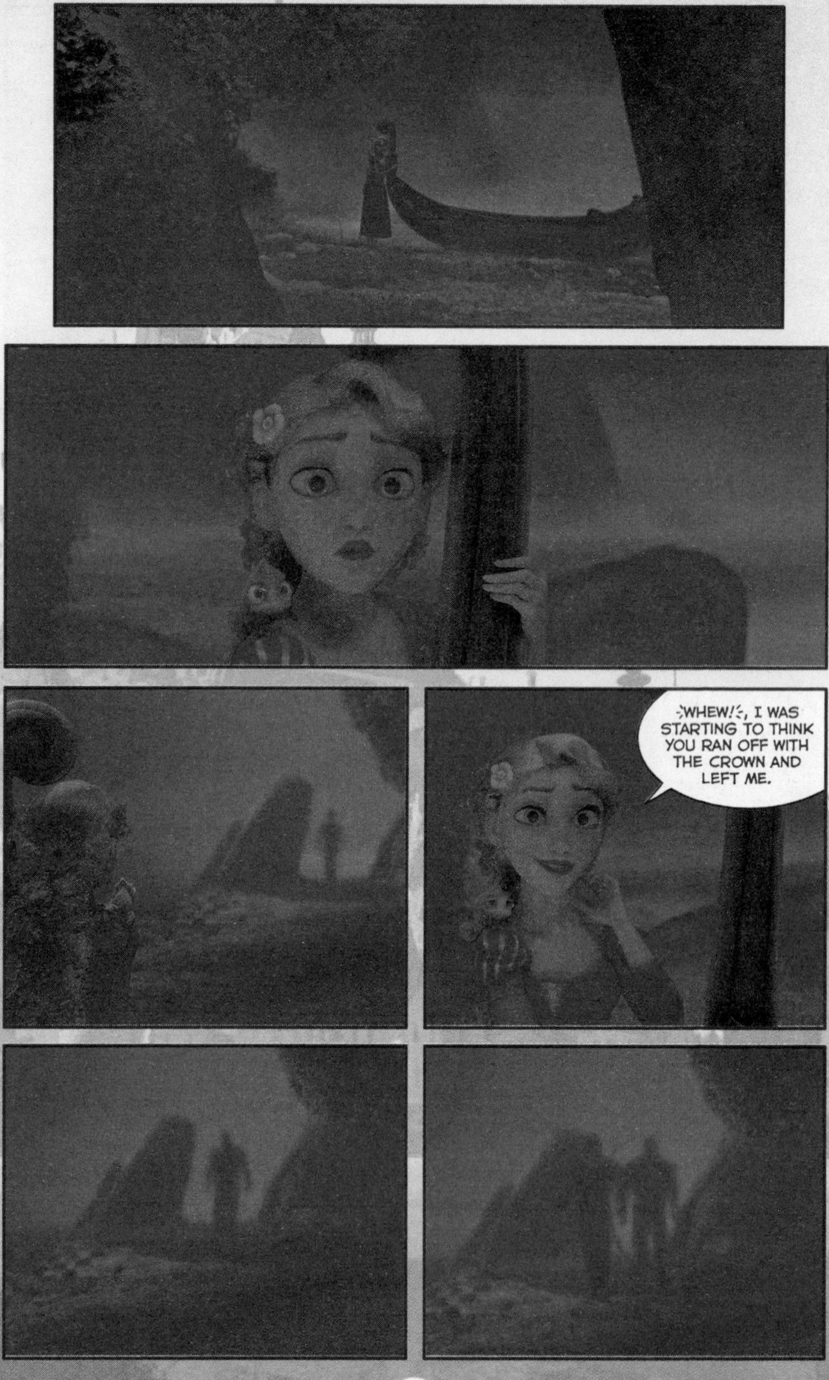
WHEW!, I WAS STARTING TO THINK YOU RAN OFF WITH THE CROWN AND LEFT ME.

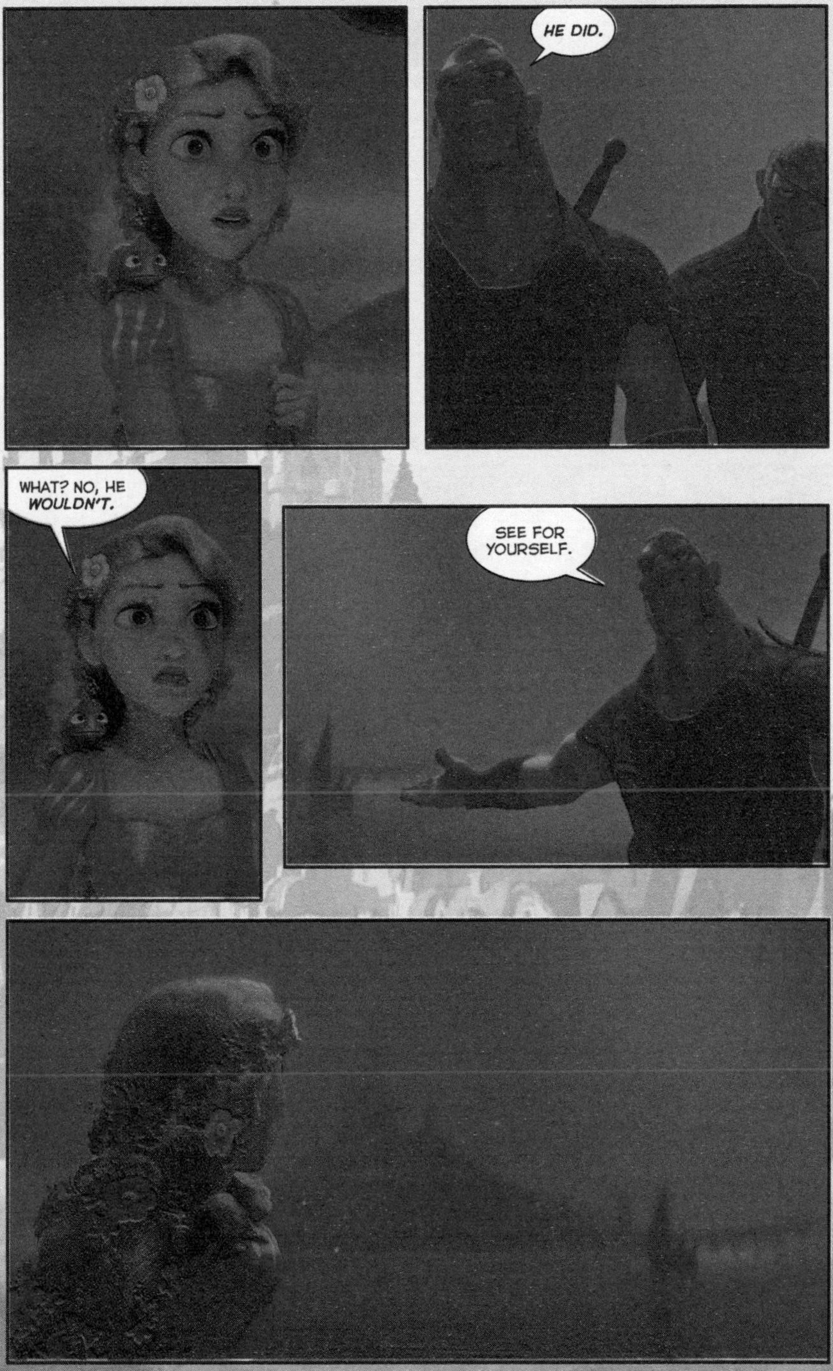
HE DID.
WHAT? NO, HE *WOULDN'T.*
SEE FOR YOURSELF.

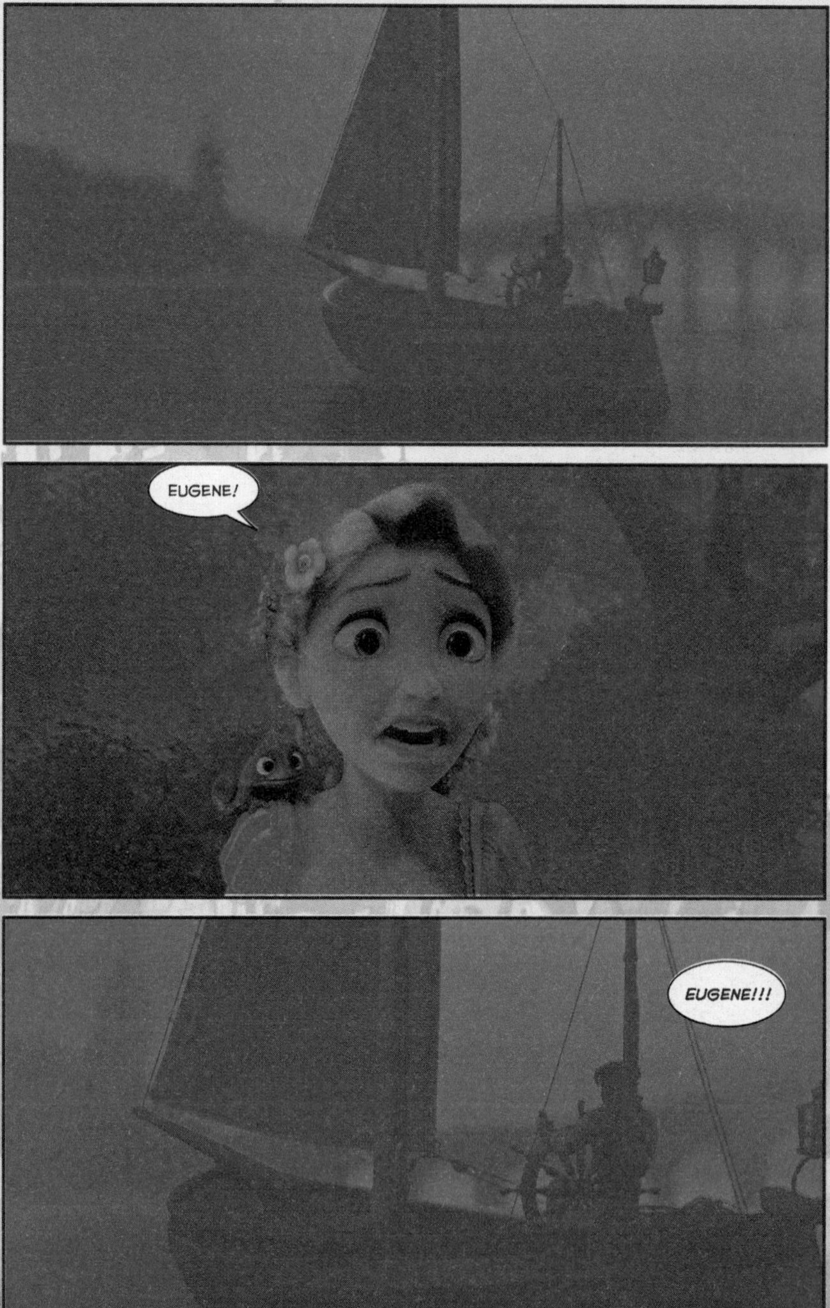
EUGENE!
EUGENE!!!

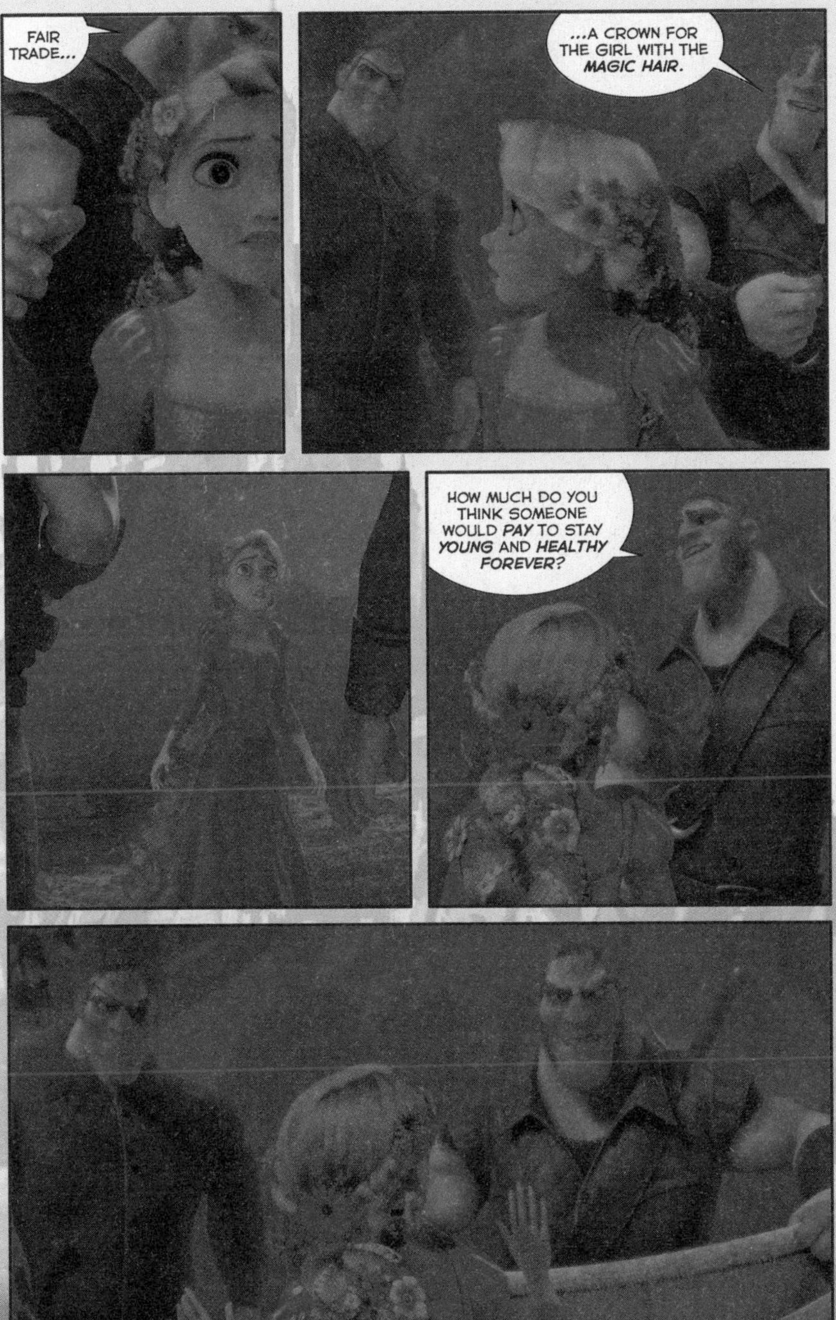
FAIR TRADE...
...A CROWN FOR THE GIRL WITH THE *MAGIC HAIR*.
HOW MUCH DO YOU THINK SOMEONE WOULD *PAY* TO STAY *YOUNG* AND *HEALTHY FOREVER*?

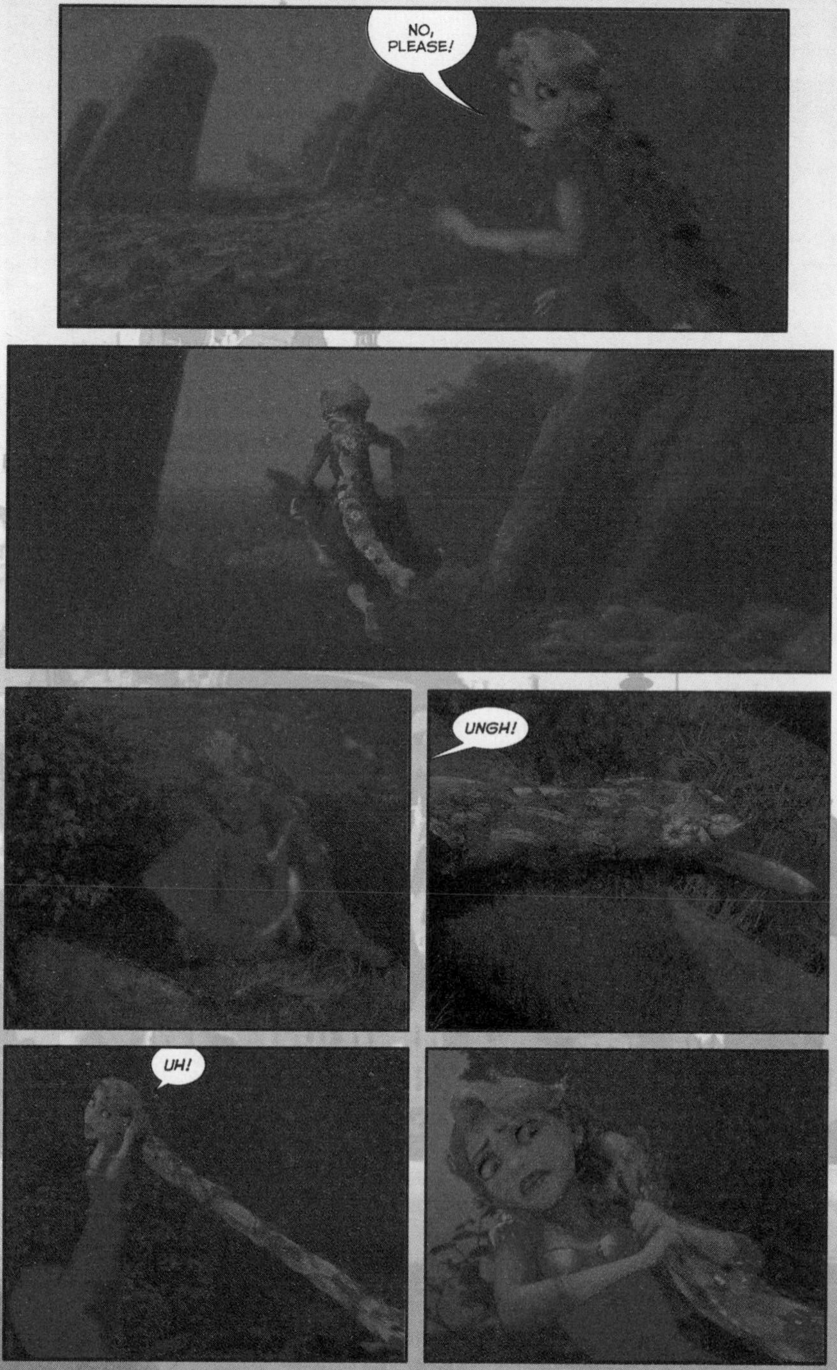
NO, PLEASE!
UNGH!
UH!

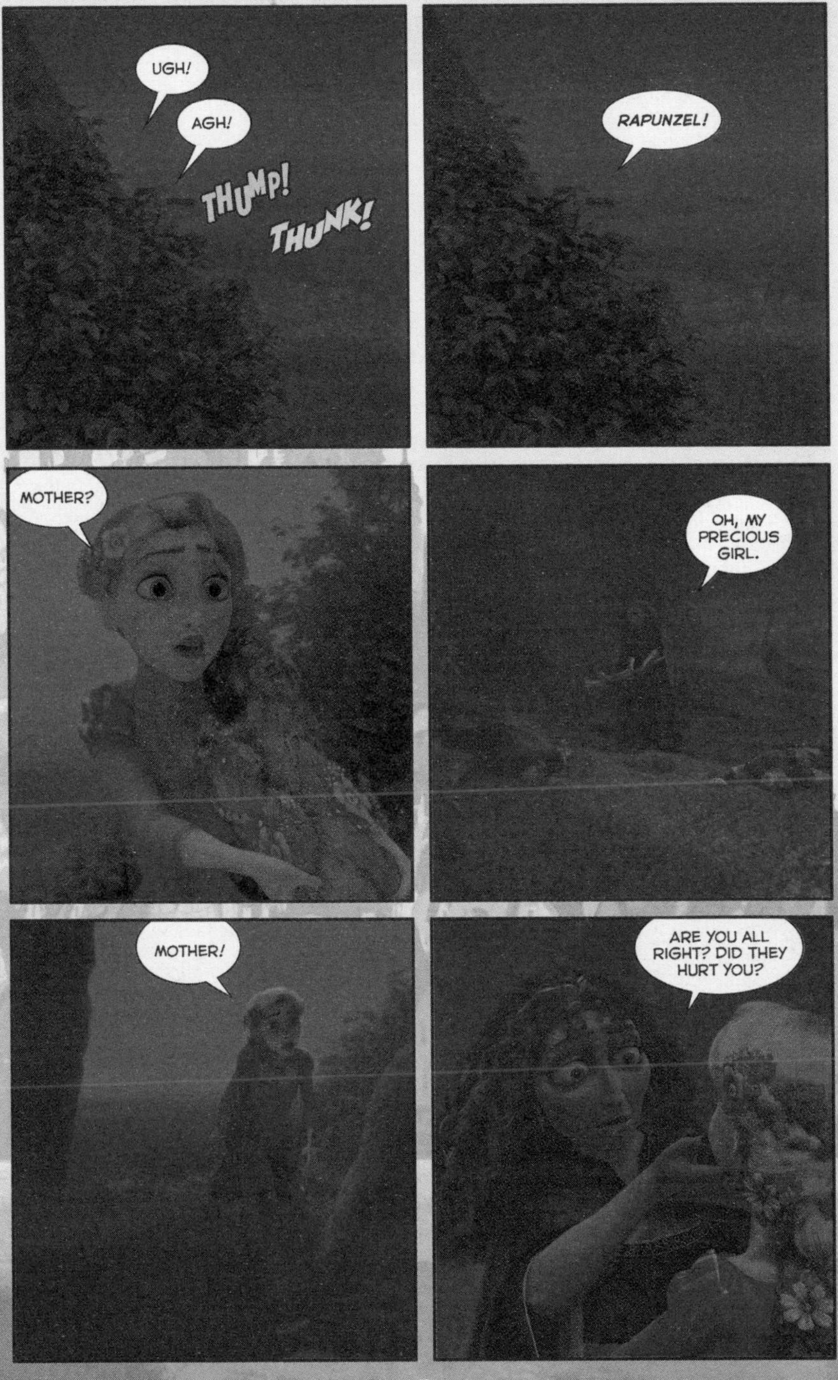
UGH!
AGH!
THUMP!
THUNK!
RAPUNZEL!
MOTHER?
OH, MY PRECIOUS GIRL.
MOTHER!
ARE YOU ALL RIGHT? DID THEY HURT YOU?

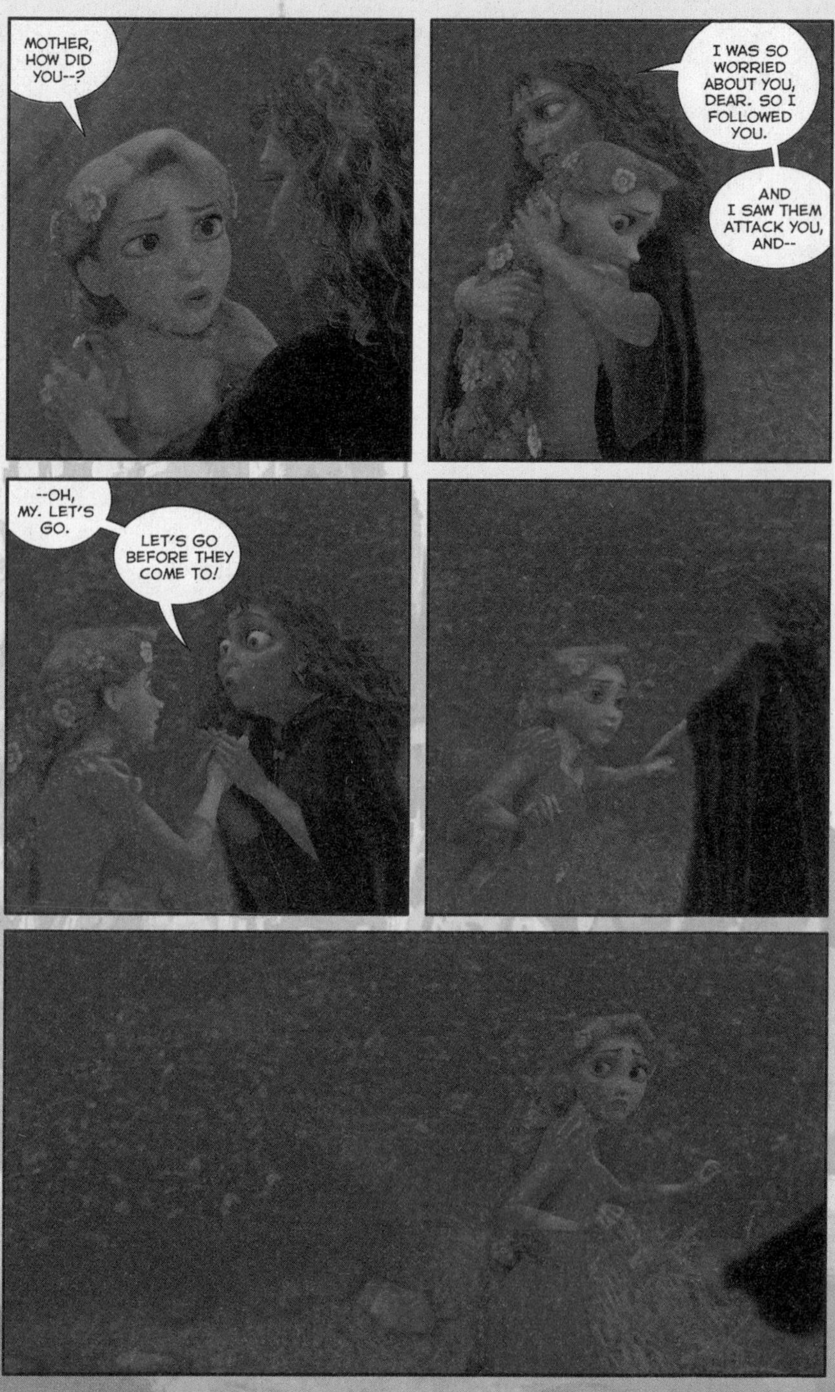
MOTHER, HOW DID YOU--?
I WAS SO WORRIED ABOUT YOU, DEAR. SO I FOLLOWED YOU.
AND I SAW THEM ATTACK YOU, AND--
--OH, MY. LET'S GO.
LET'S GO BEFORE THEY COME TO!

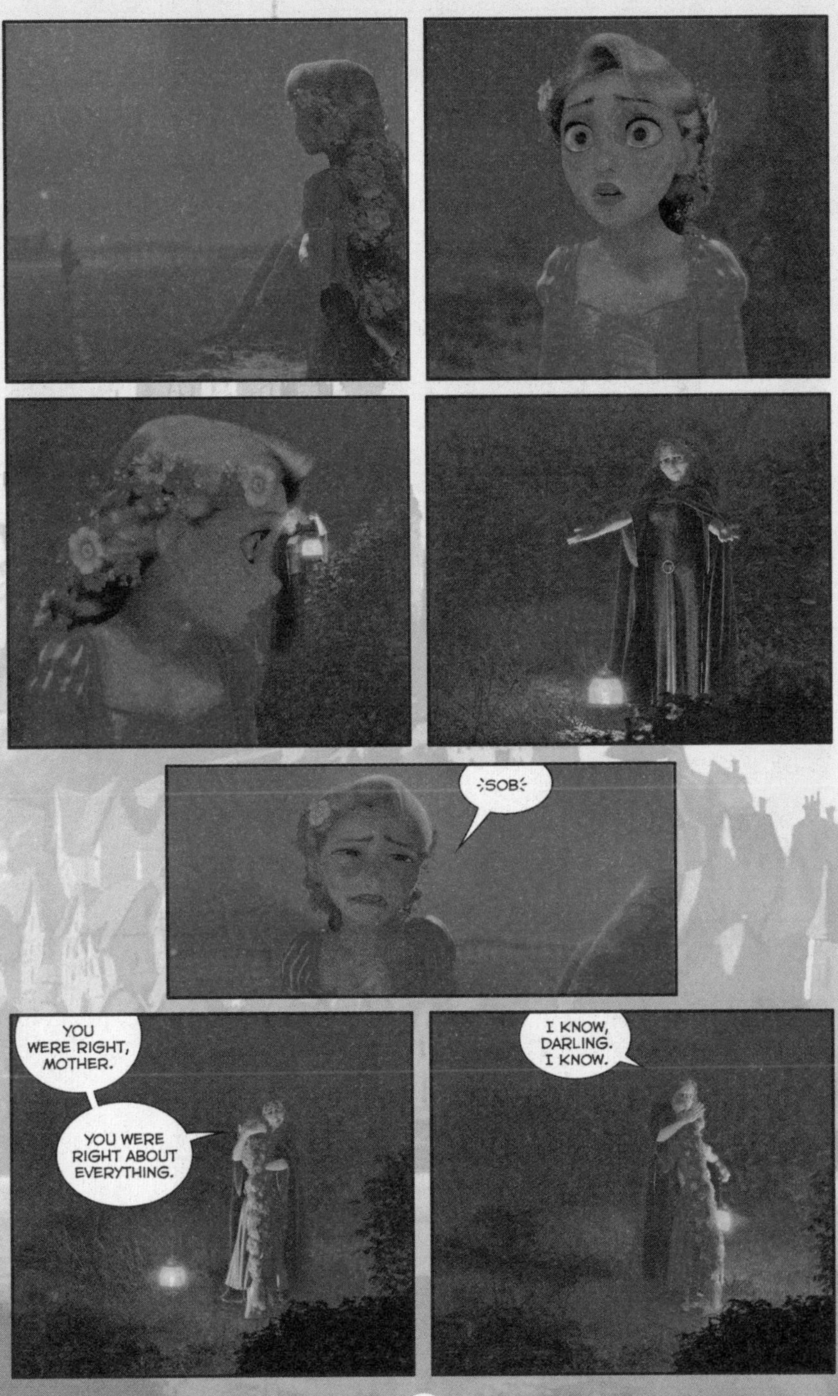
·SOB·
YOU WERE RIGHT, MOTHER.
YOU WERE RIGHT ABOUT EVERYTHING.
I KNOW, DARLING. I KNOW.

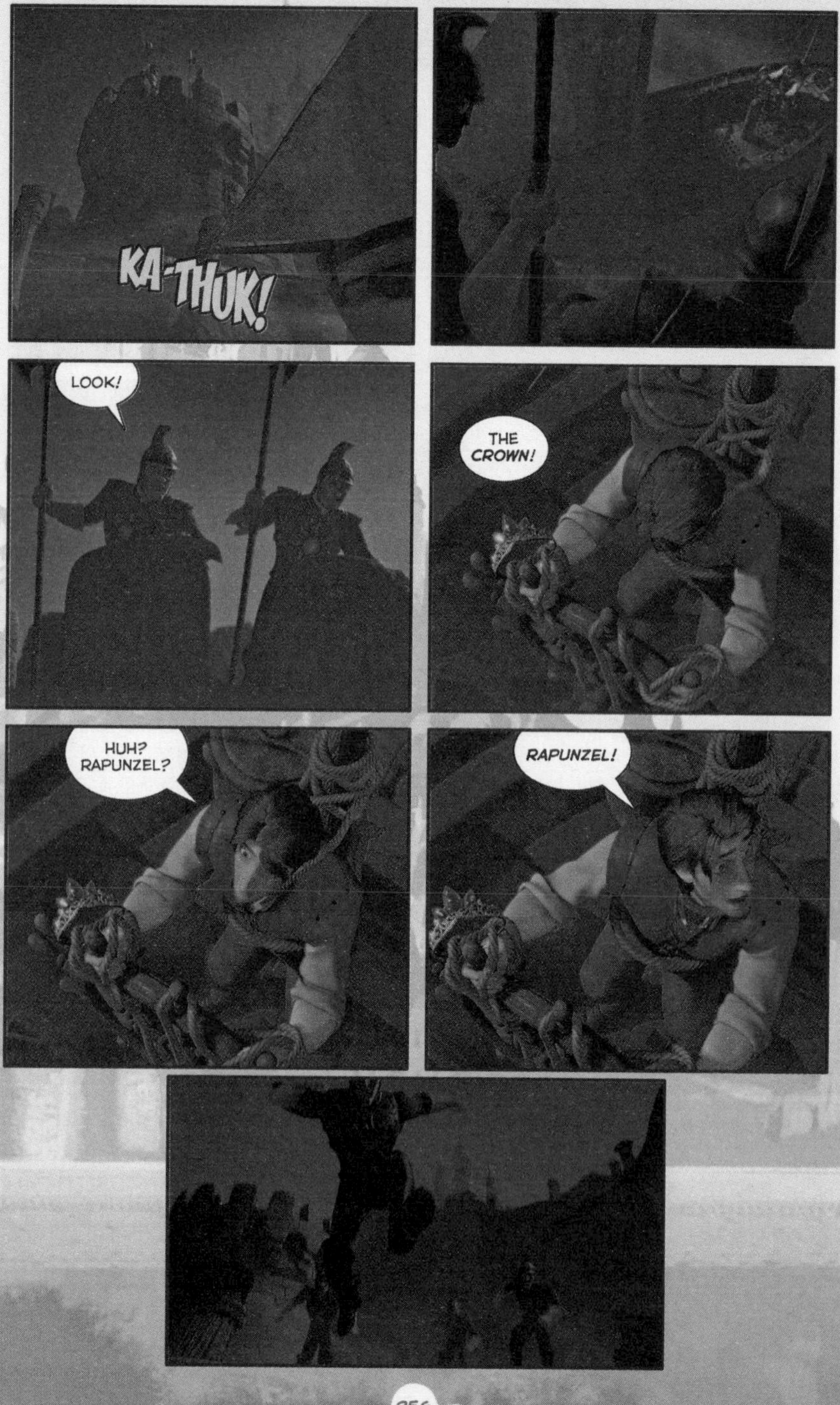
KA-THUK!
LOOK!
THE CROWN!
HUH? RAPUNZEL?
RAPUNZEL!

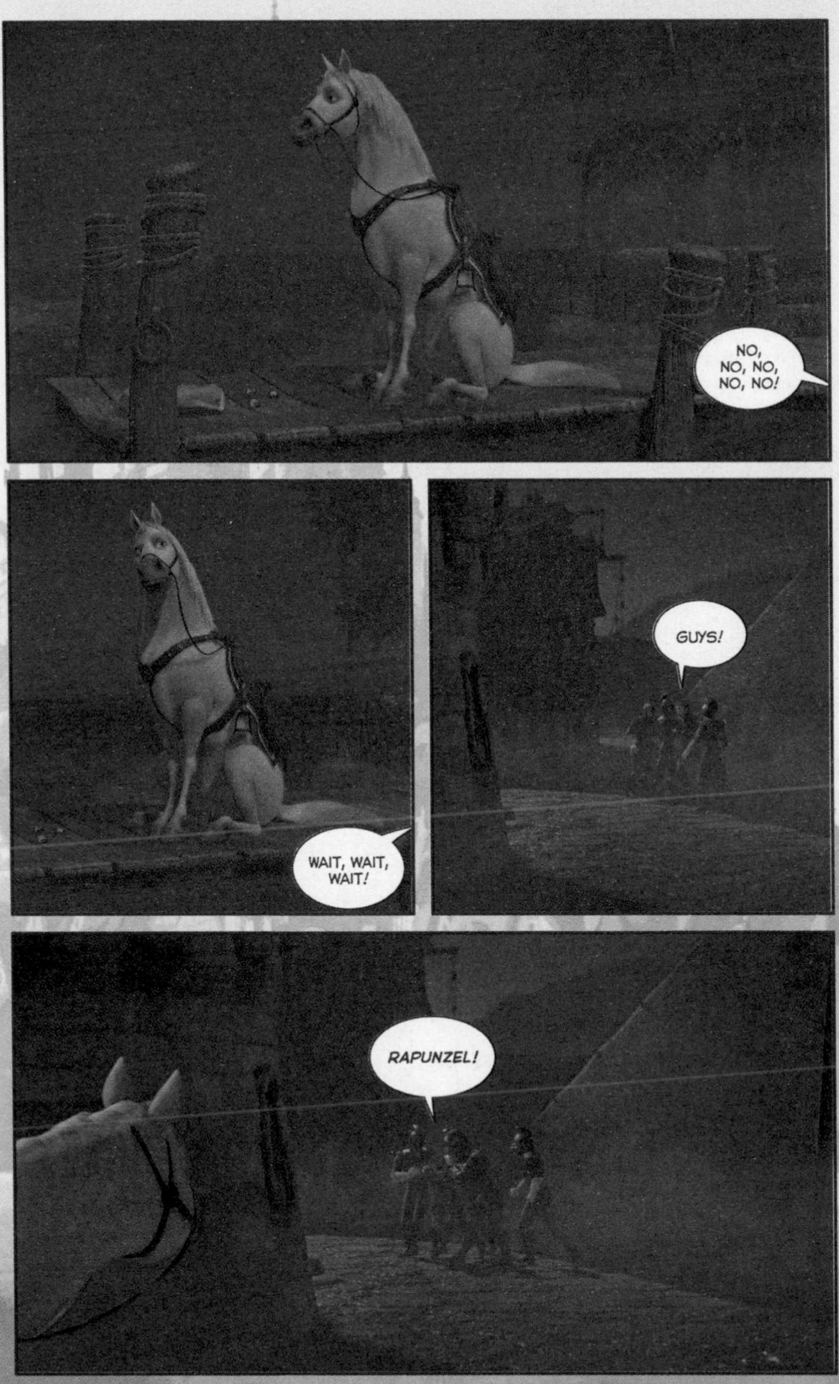
NO, NO, NO, NO, NO!
WAIT, WAIT, WAIT!
GUYS!
RAPUNZEL!

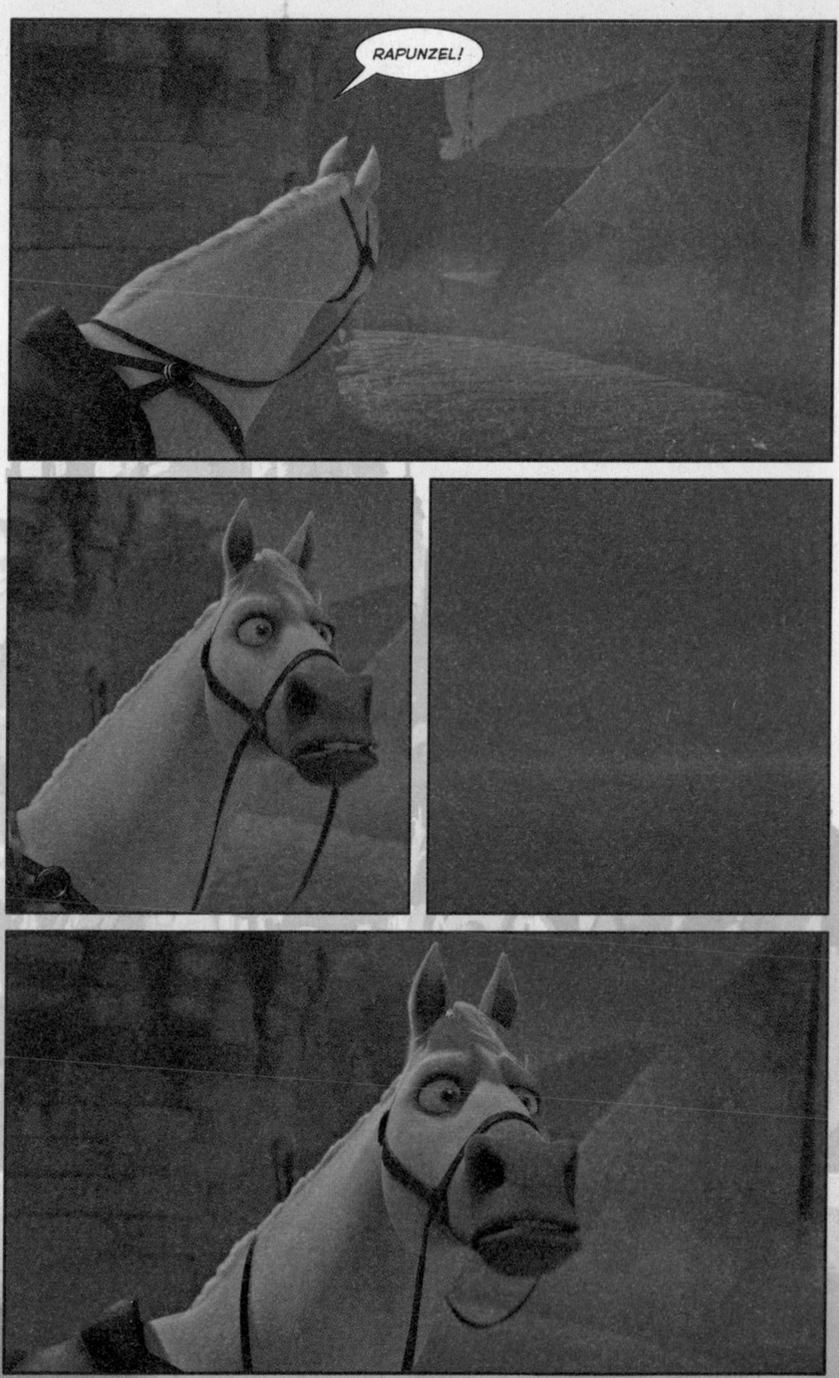
RAPUNZEL!

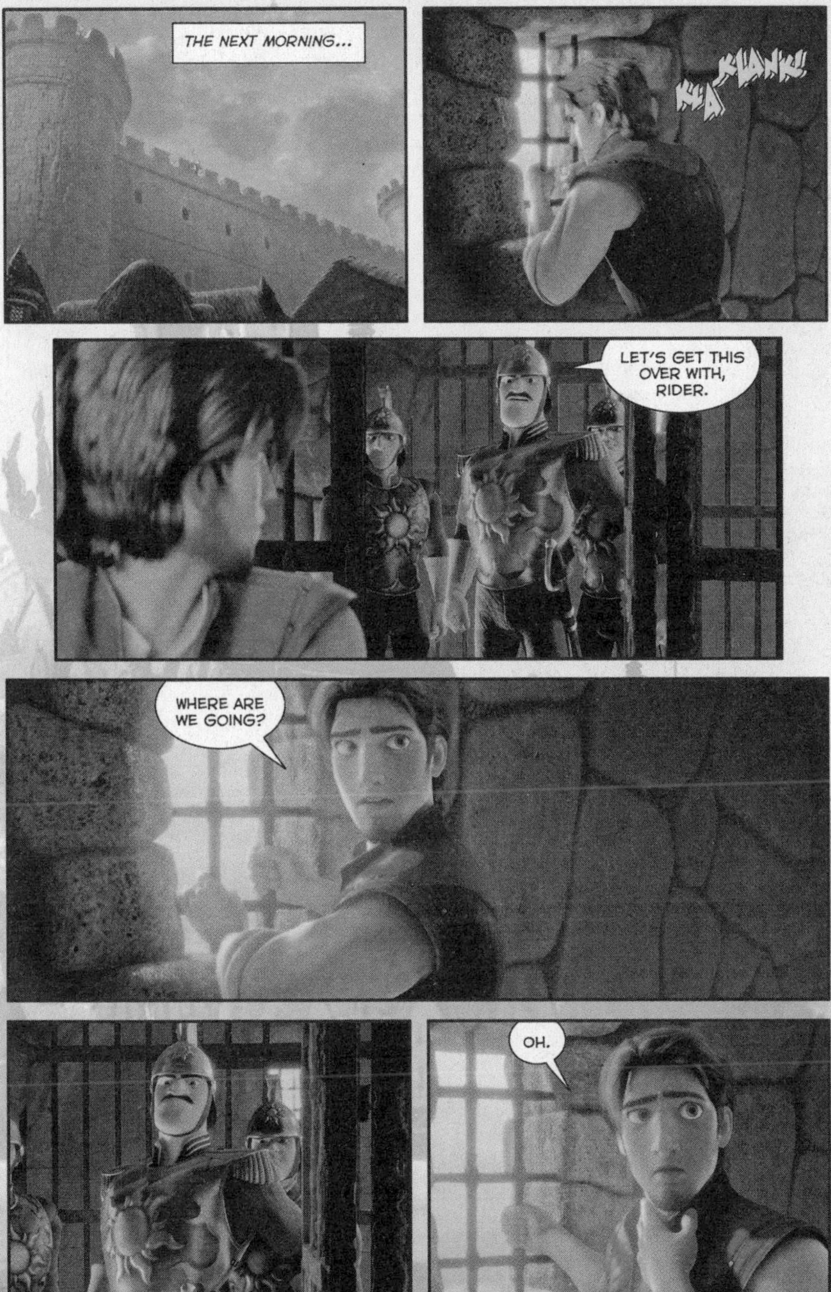
THE NEXT MORNING...
KLANK! KLANK!
LET'S GET THIS OVER WITH, RIDER.
WHERE ARE WE GOING?
OH.

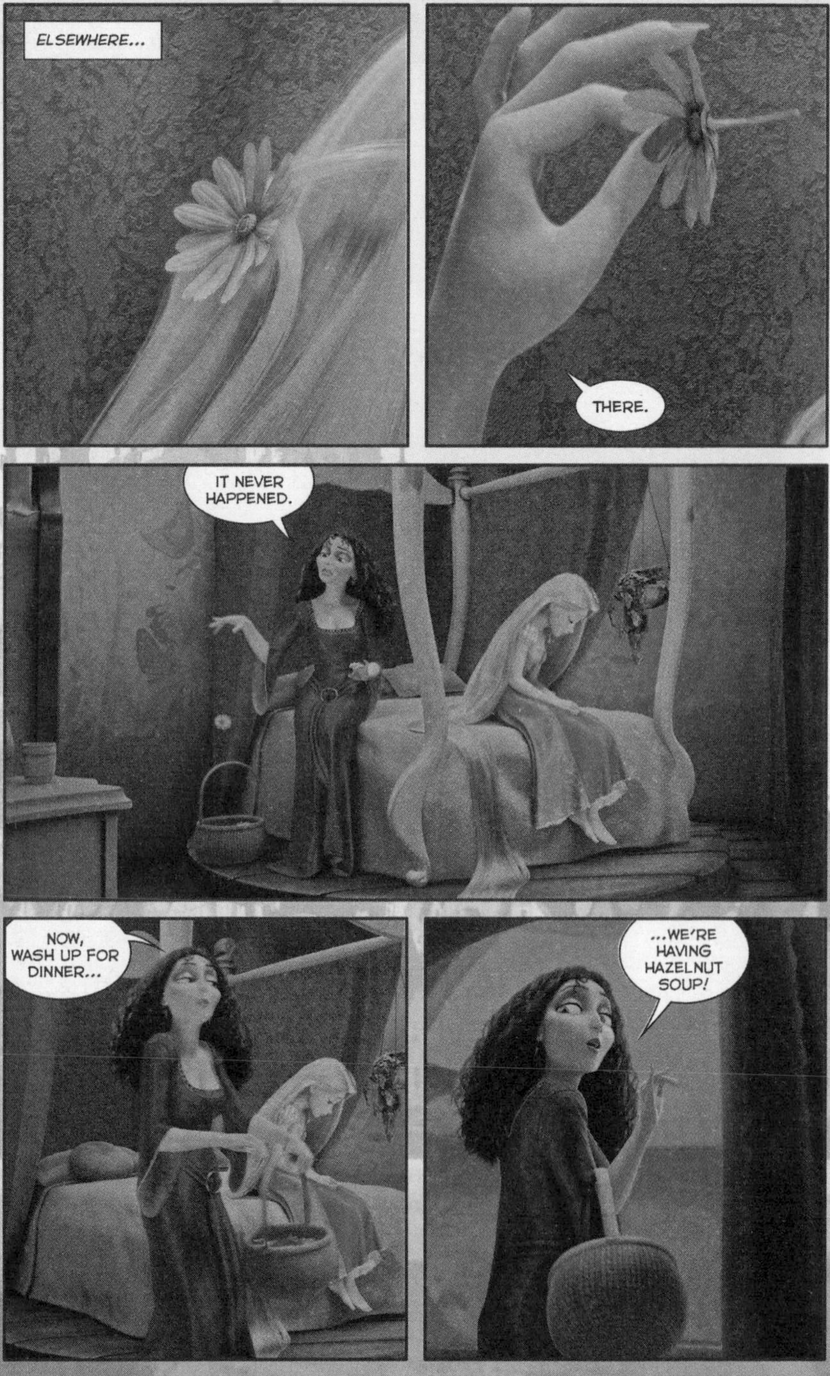
ELSEWHERE...
THERE.
IT NEVER HAPPENED.
NOW, WASH UP FOR DINNER...
...WE'RE HAVING HAZELNUT SOUP!

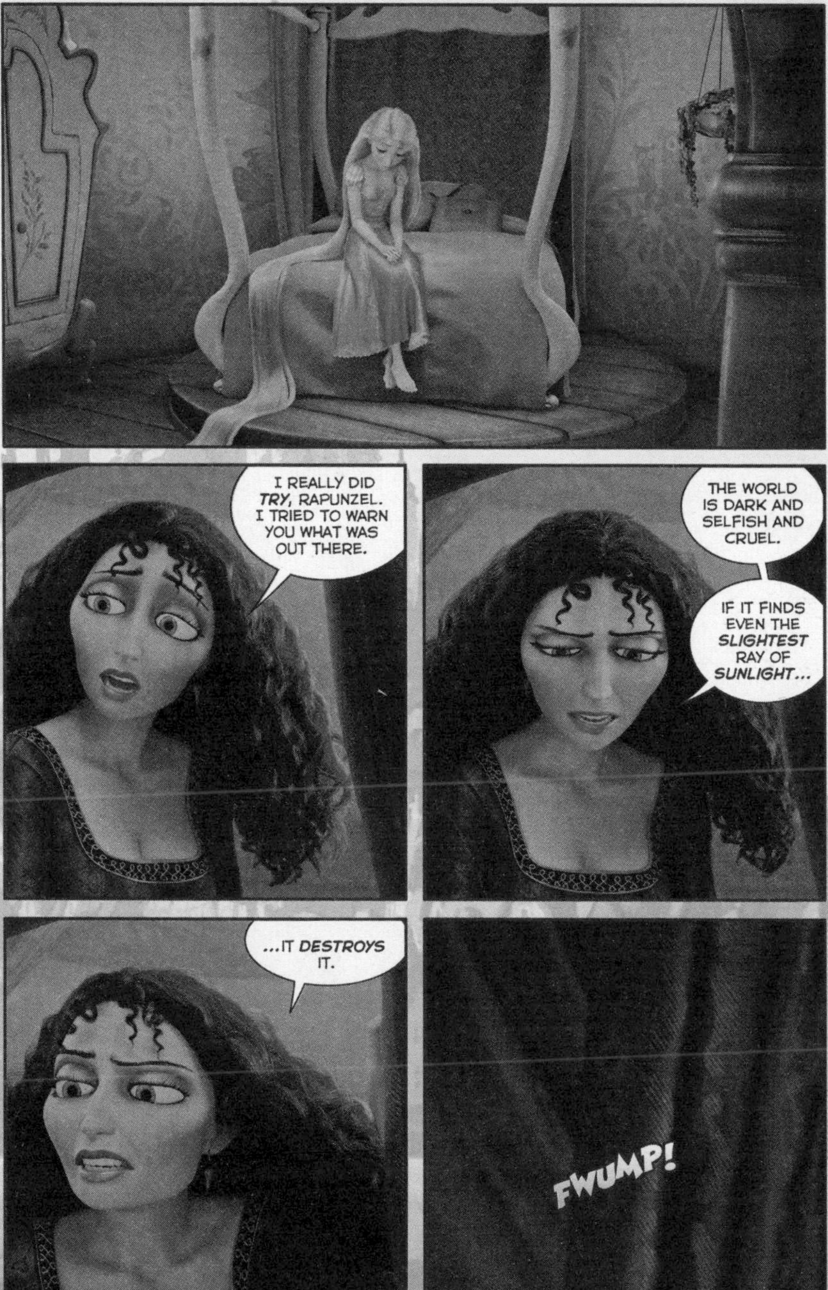
I REALLY DID TRY, RAPUNZEL. I TRIED TO WARN YOU WHAT WAS OUT THERE.
THE WORLD IS DARK AND SELFISH AND CRUEL.
IF IT FINDS EVEN THE SLIGHTEST RAY OF SUNLIGHT...
...IT DESTROYS IT.
FWUMP!

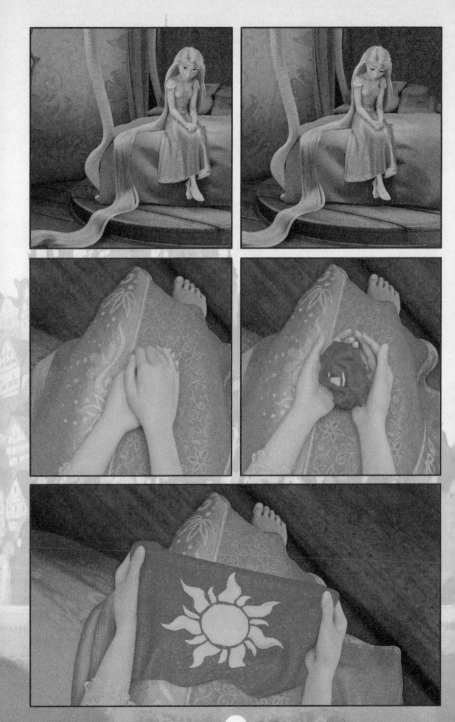

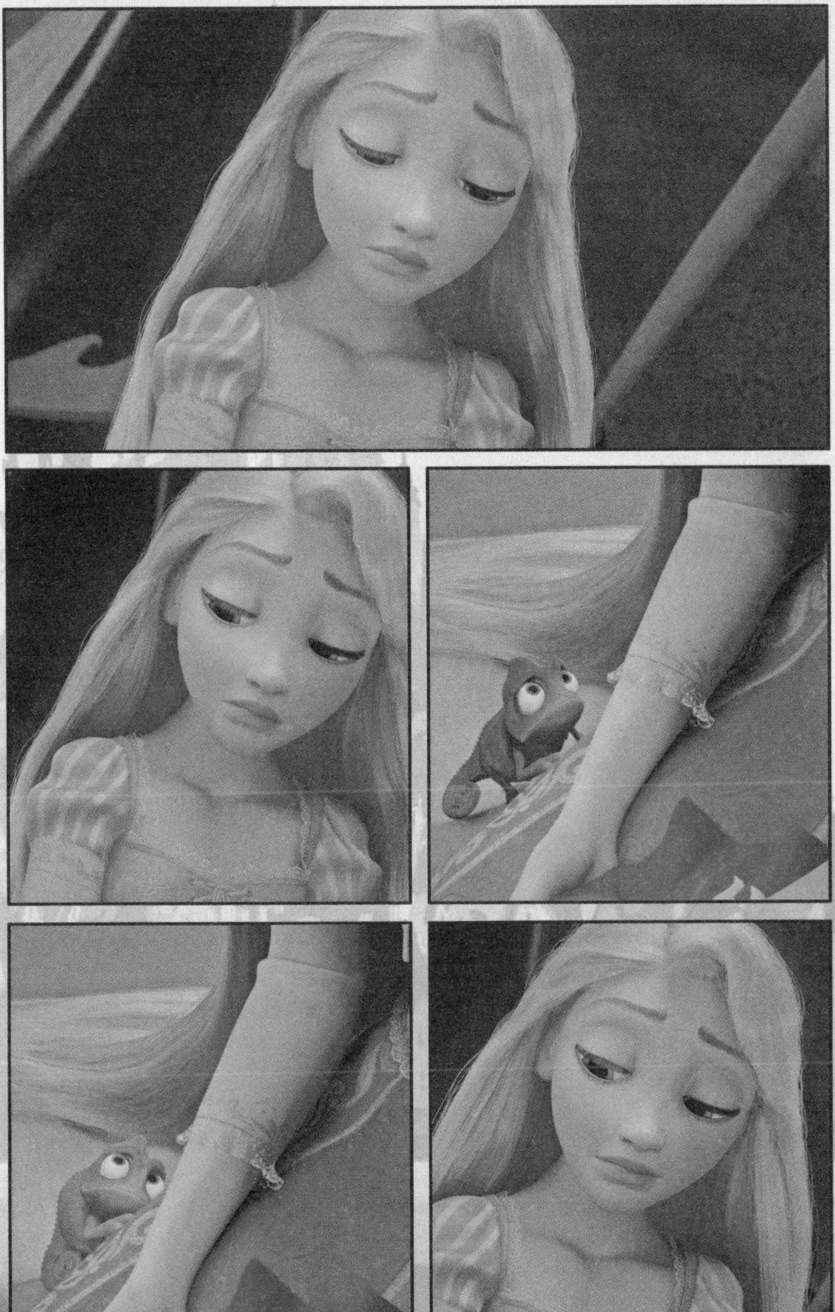

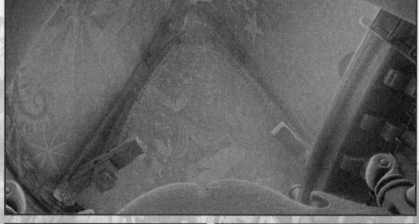

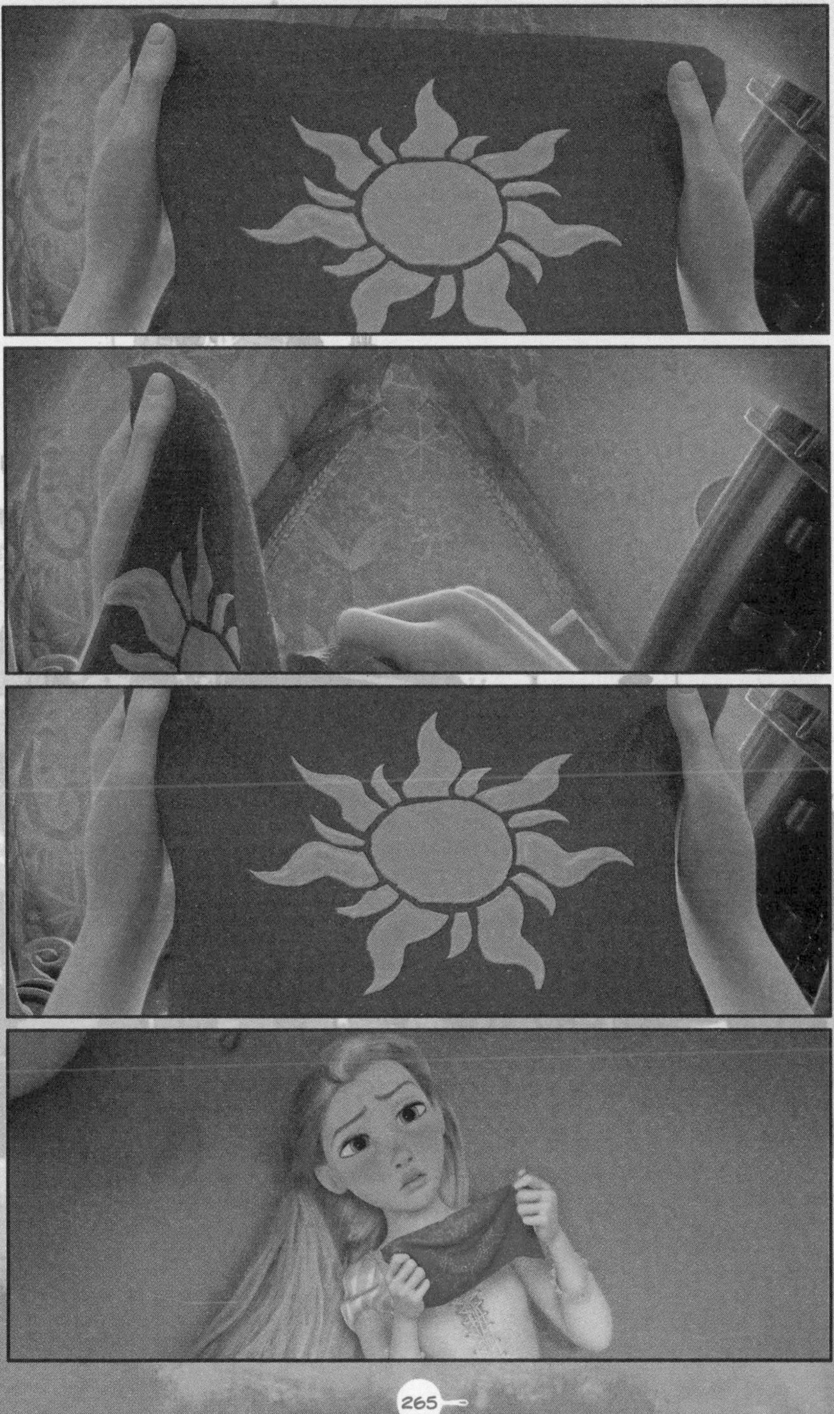

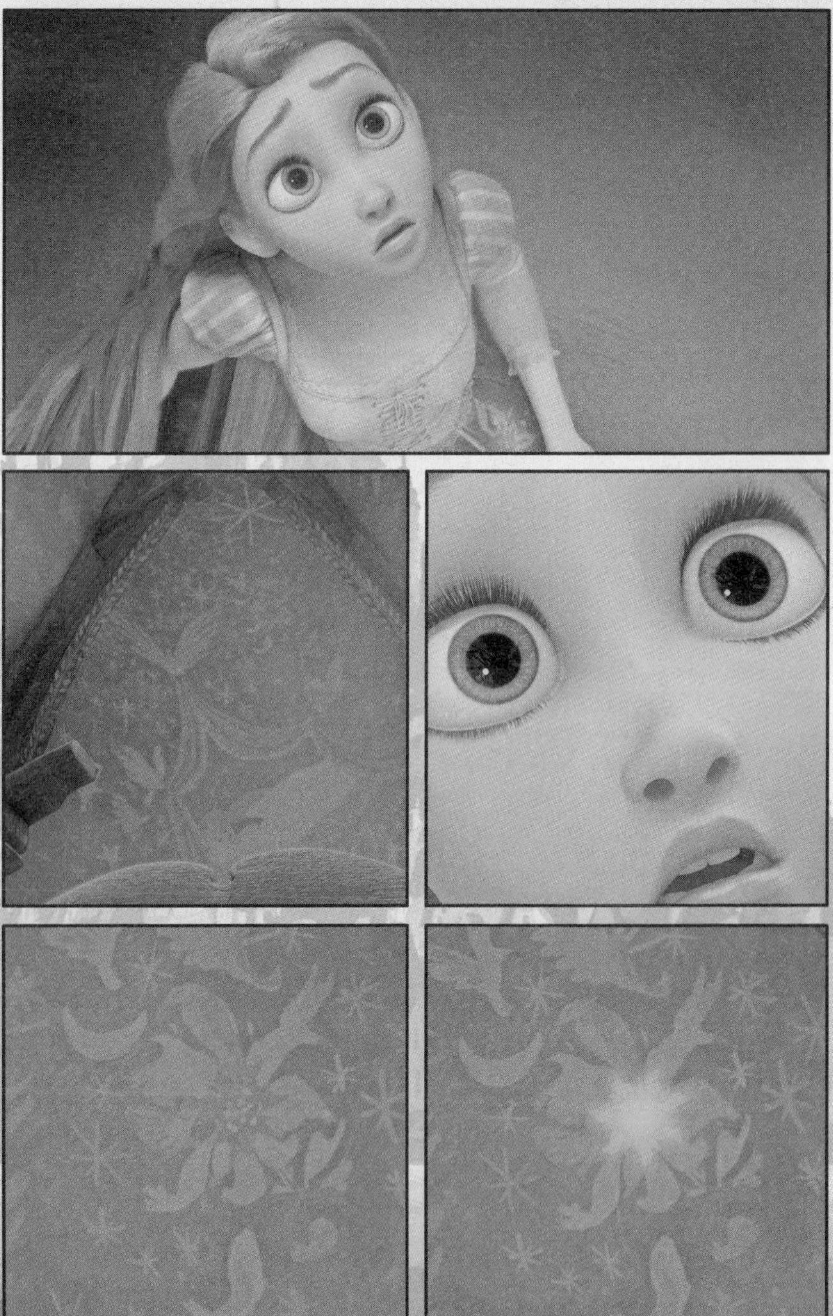

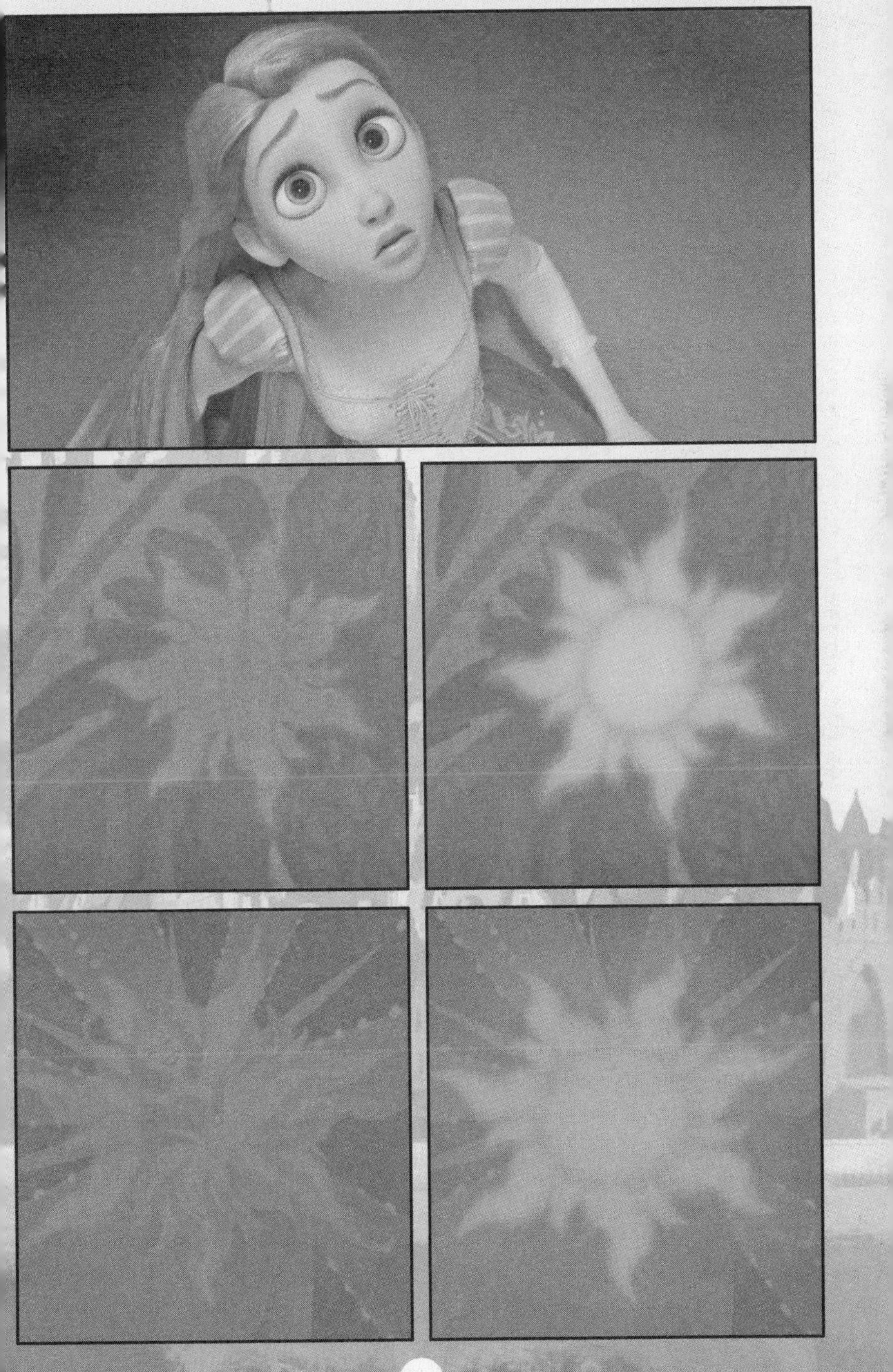

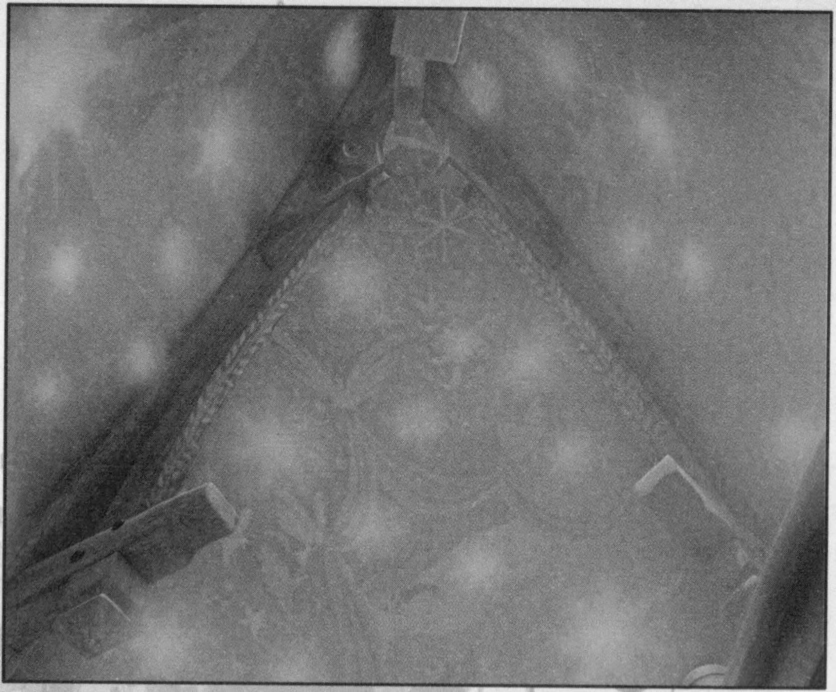

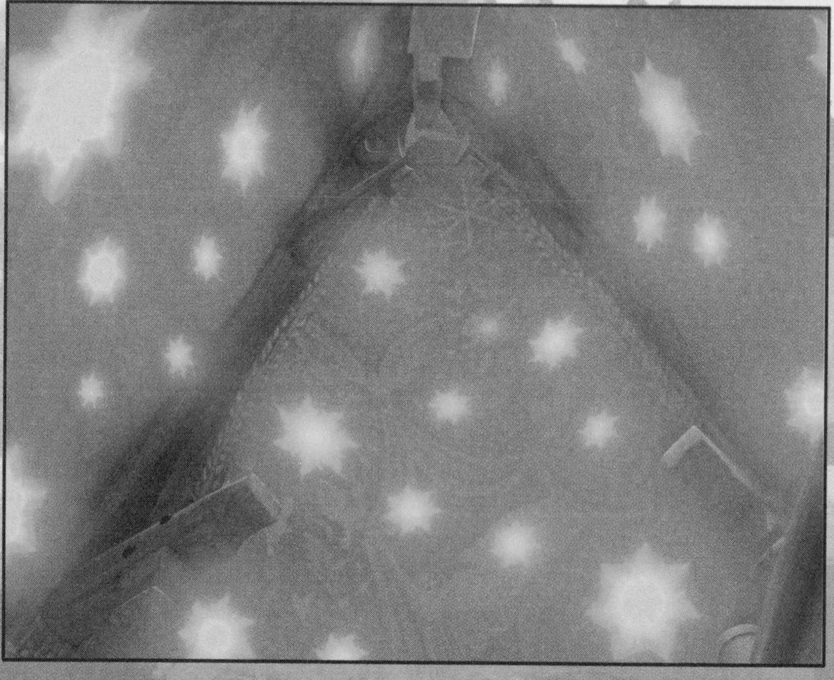

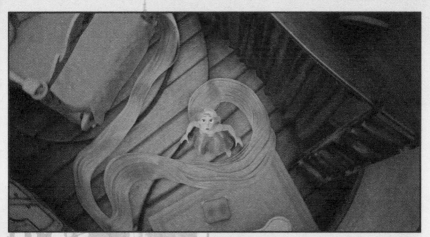

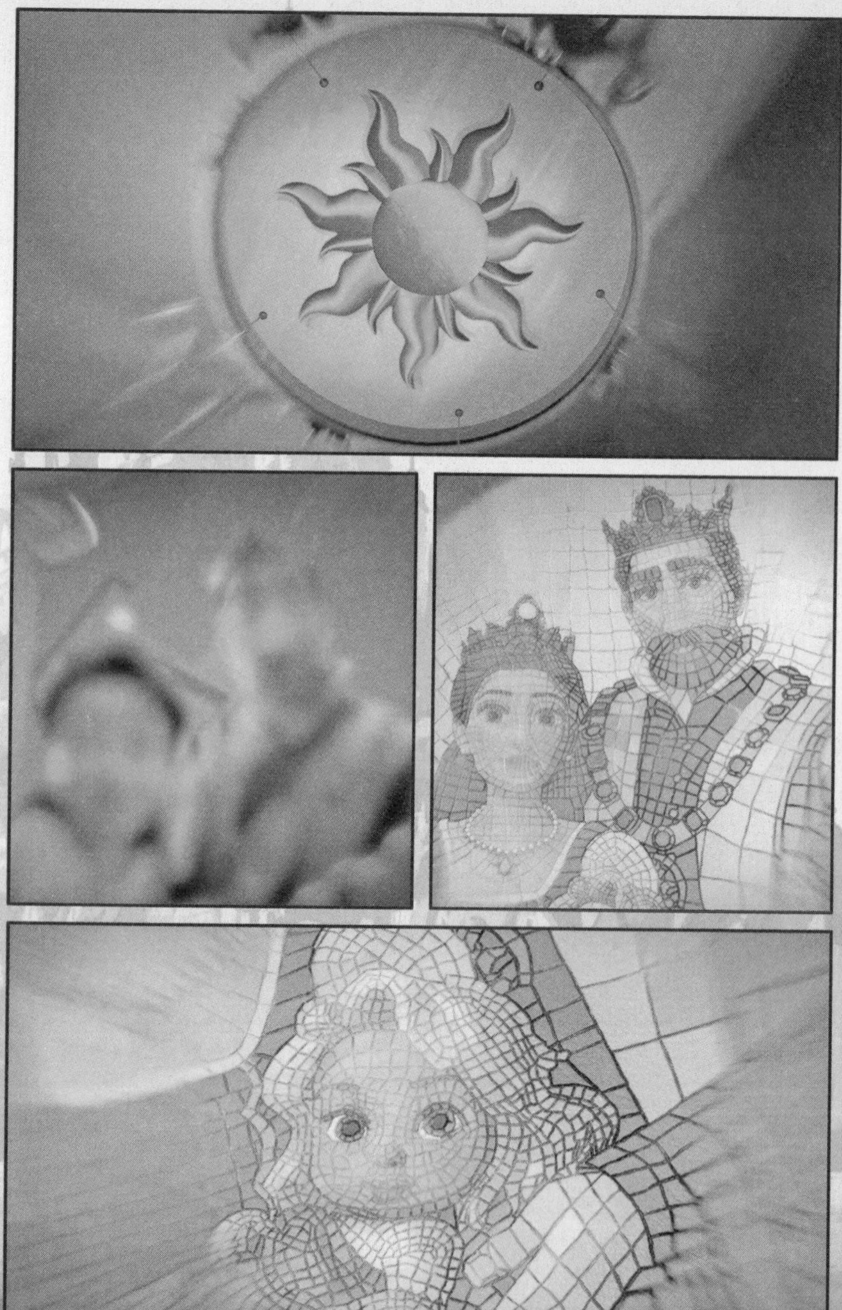

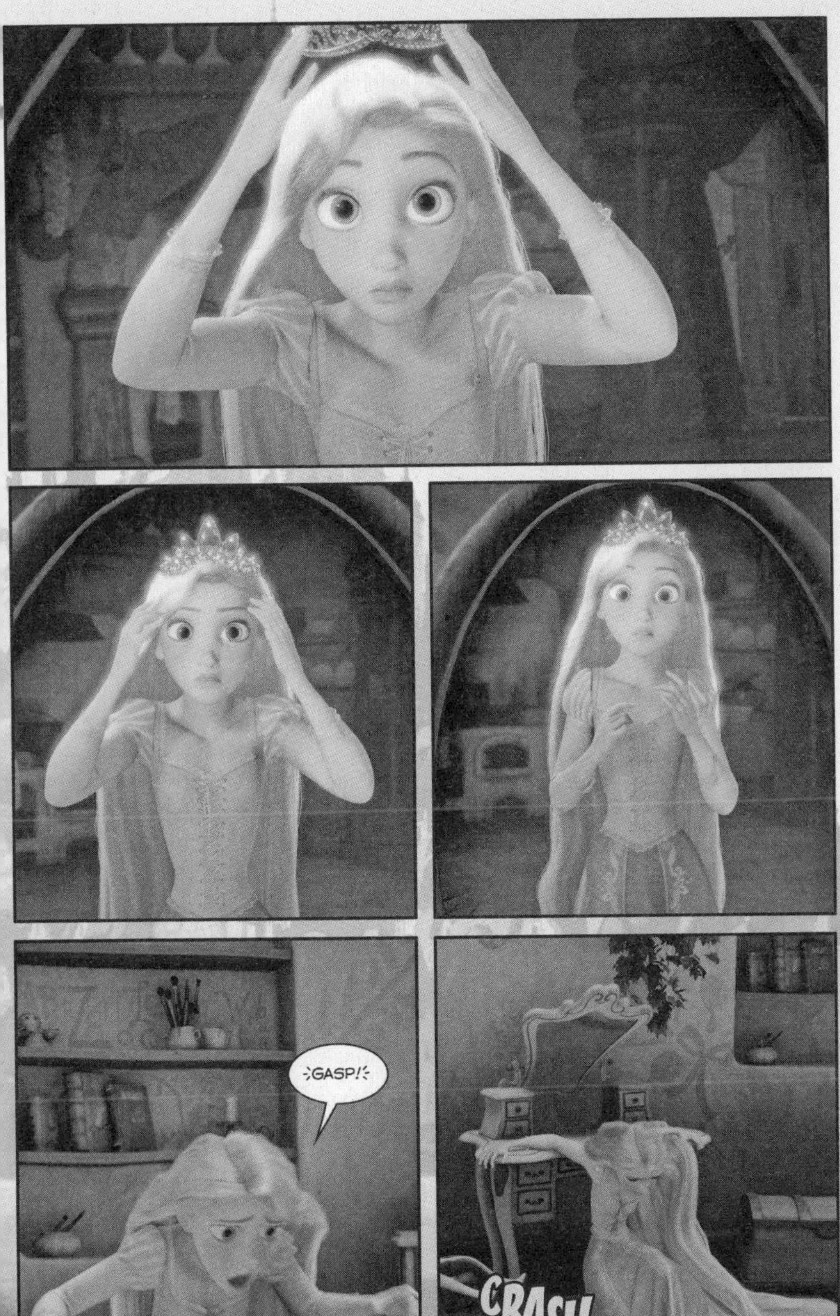
GASP!
CRASH

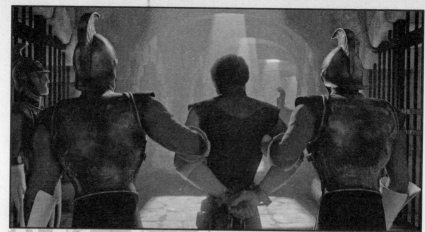

CHAK!

CHOK!

HOW DID YOU KNOW ABOUT HER?! TELL ME NOW!

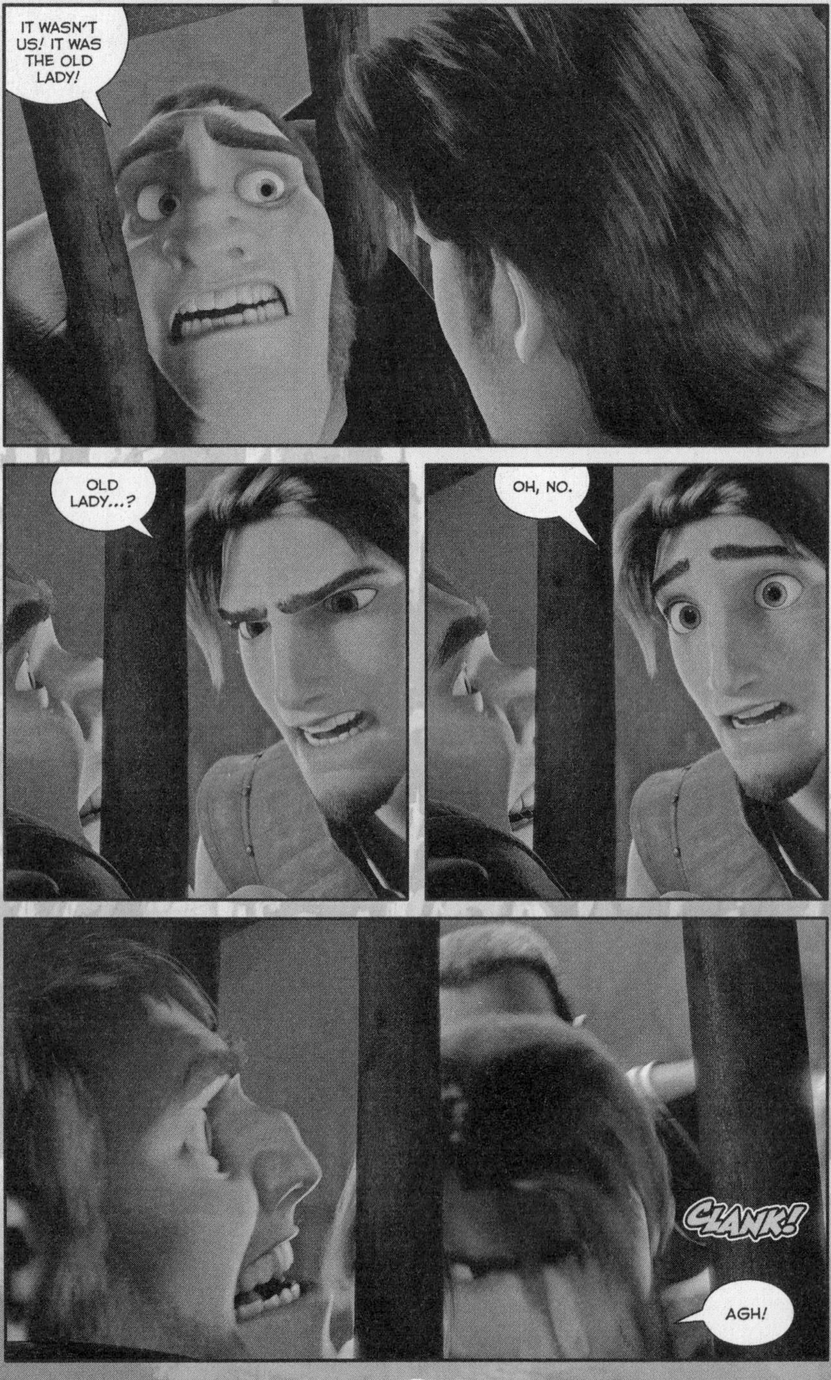
IT WASN'T US! IT WAS THE OLD LADY!
OLD LADY...?
OH, NO.
CLANK!
AGH!

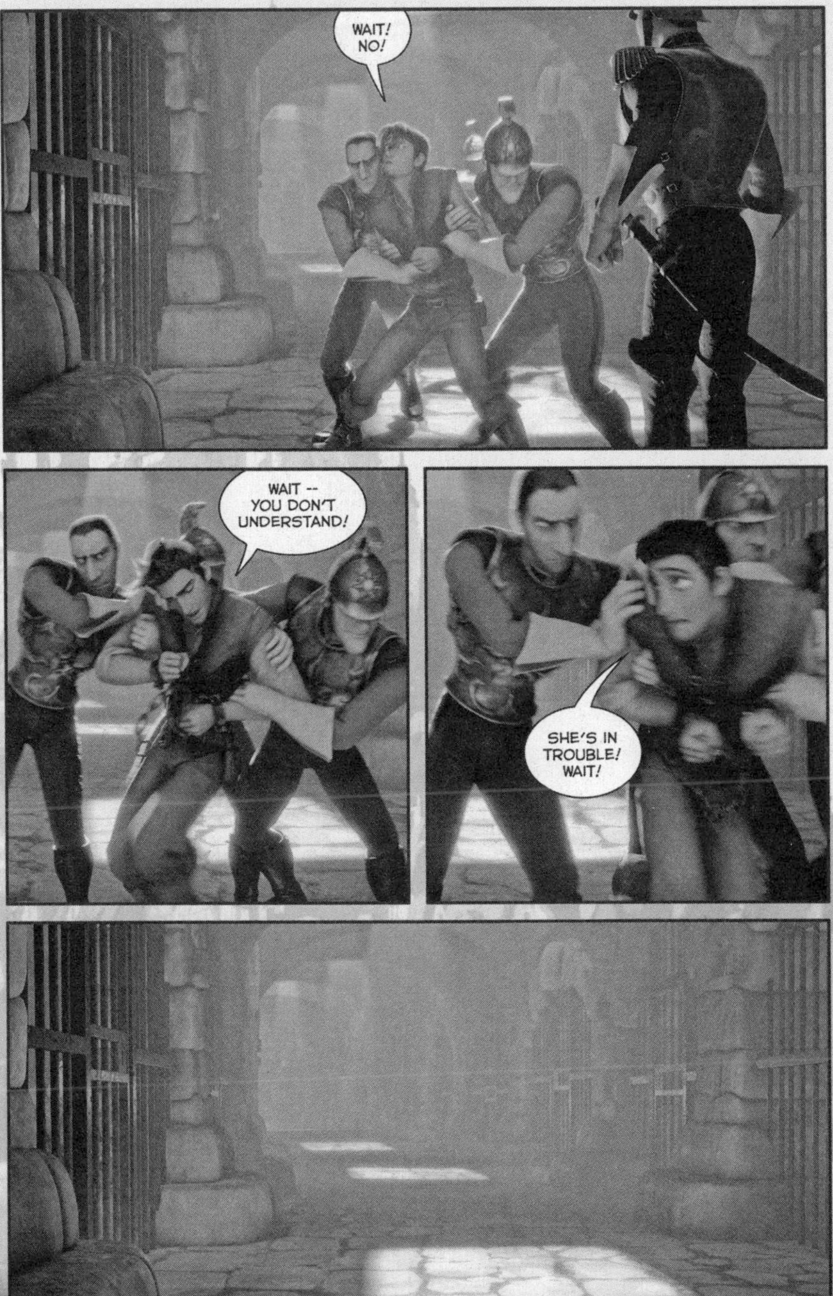
WAIT! NO!
WAIT -- YOU DON'T UNDERSTAND!
SHE'S IN TROUBLE! WAIT!

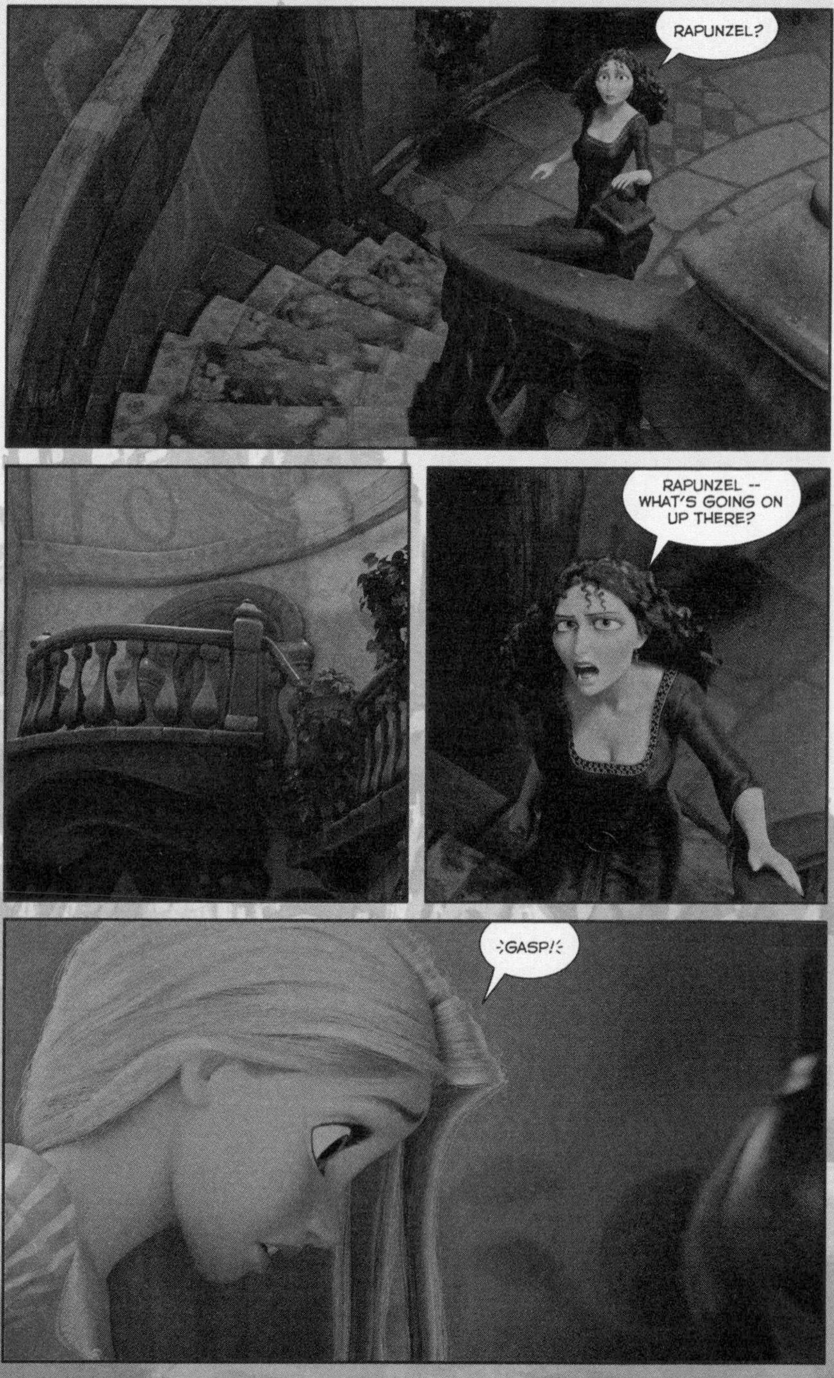
RAPUNZEL?
RAPUNZEL -- WHAT'S GOING ON UP THERE?
-GASP!-

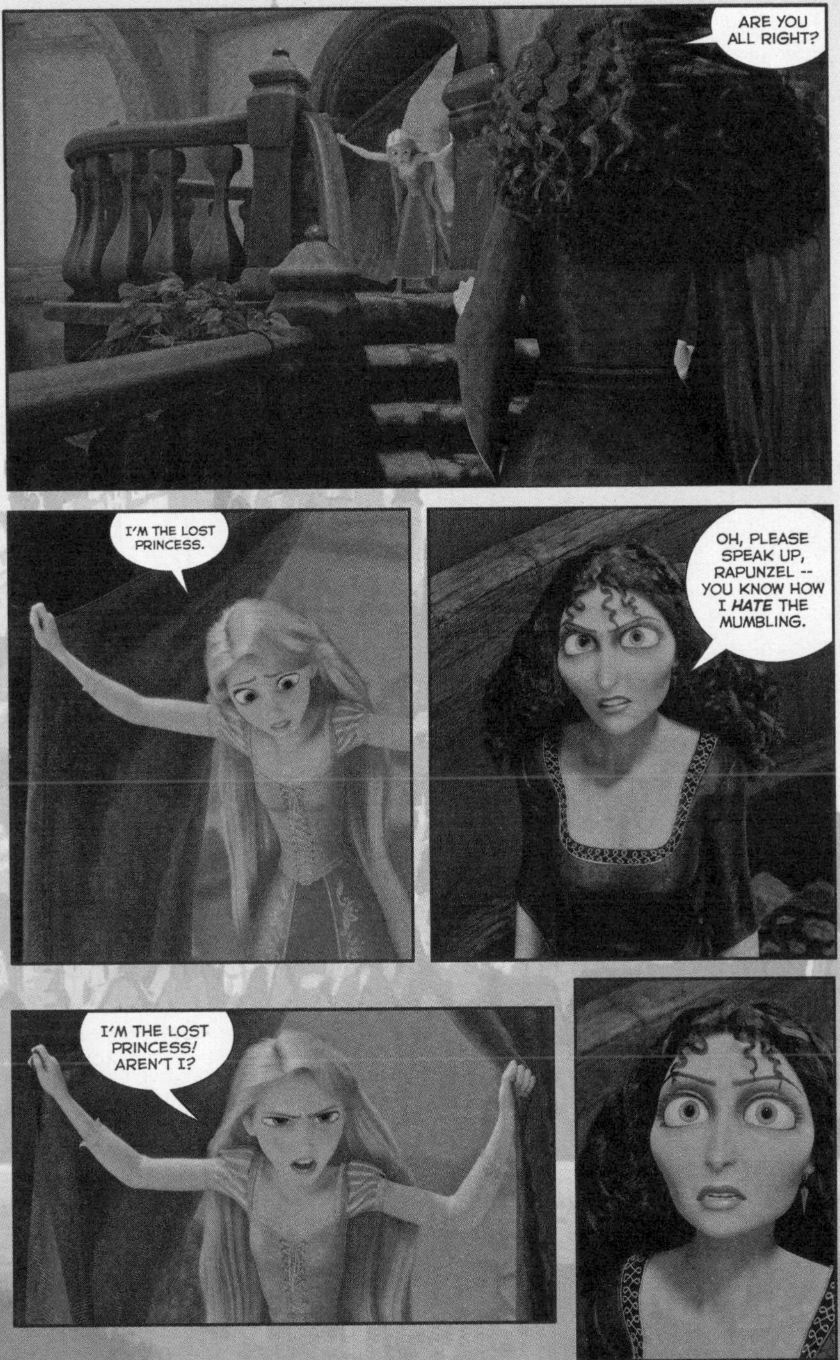
ARE YOU ALL RIGHT?
I'M THE LOST PRINCESS.
OH, PLEASE SPEAK UP, RAPUNZEL -- YOU KNOW HOW I *HATE* THE MUMBLING.
I'M THE LOST PRINCESS! AREN'T I?

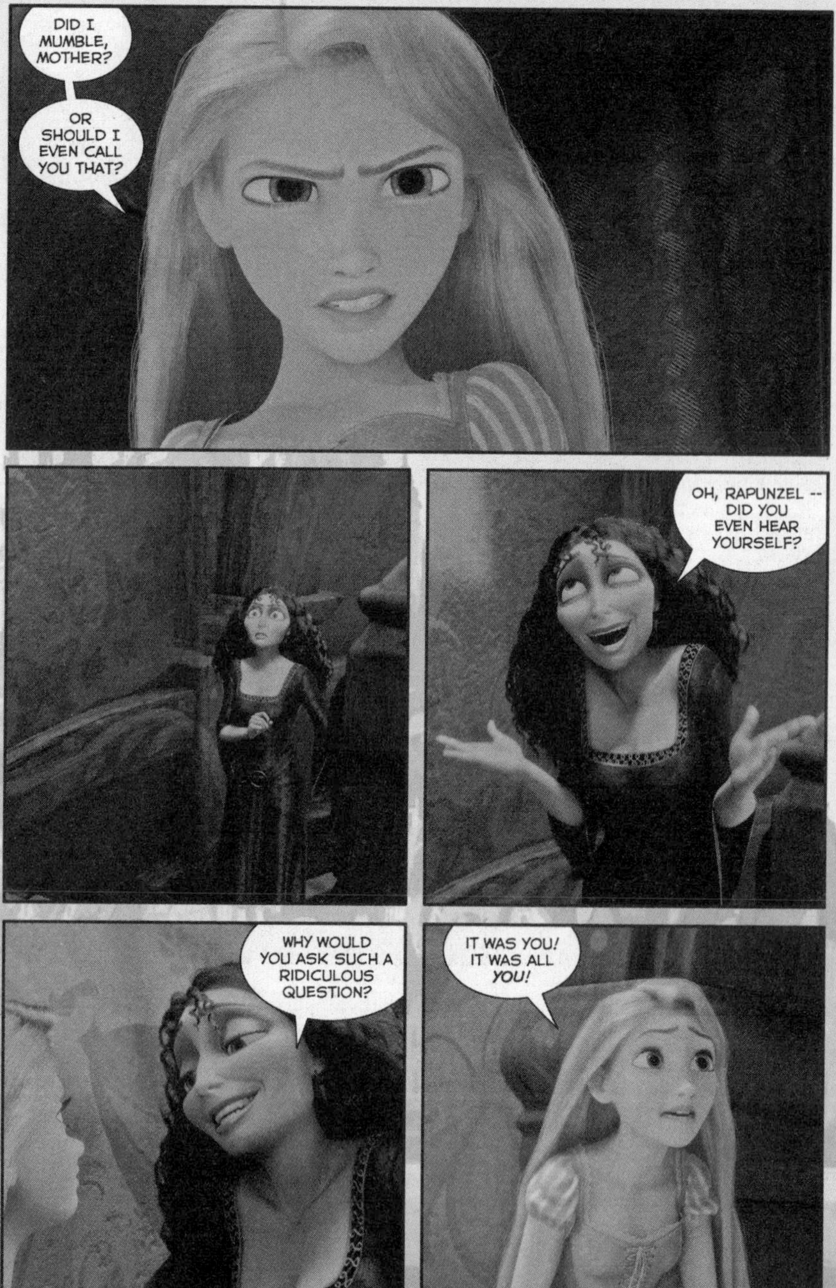
DID I MUMBLE, MOTHER?
OR SHOULD I EVEN CALL YOU THAT?
OH, RAPUNZEL -- DID YOU EVEN HEAR YOURSELF?
WHY WOULD YOU ASK SUCH A RIDICULOUS QUESTION?
IT WAS YOU! IT WAS ALL *YOU!*

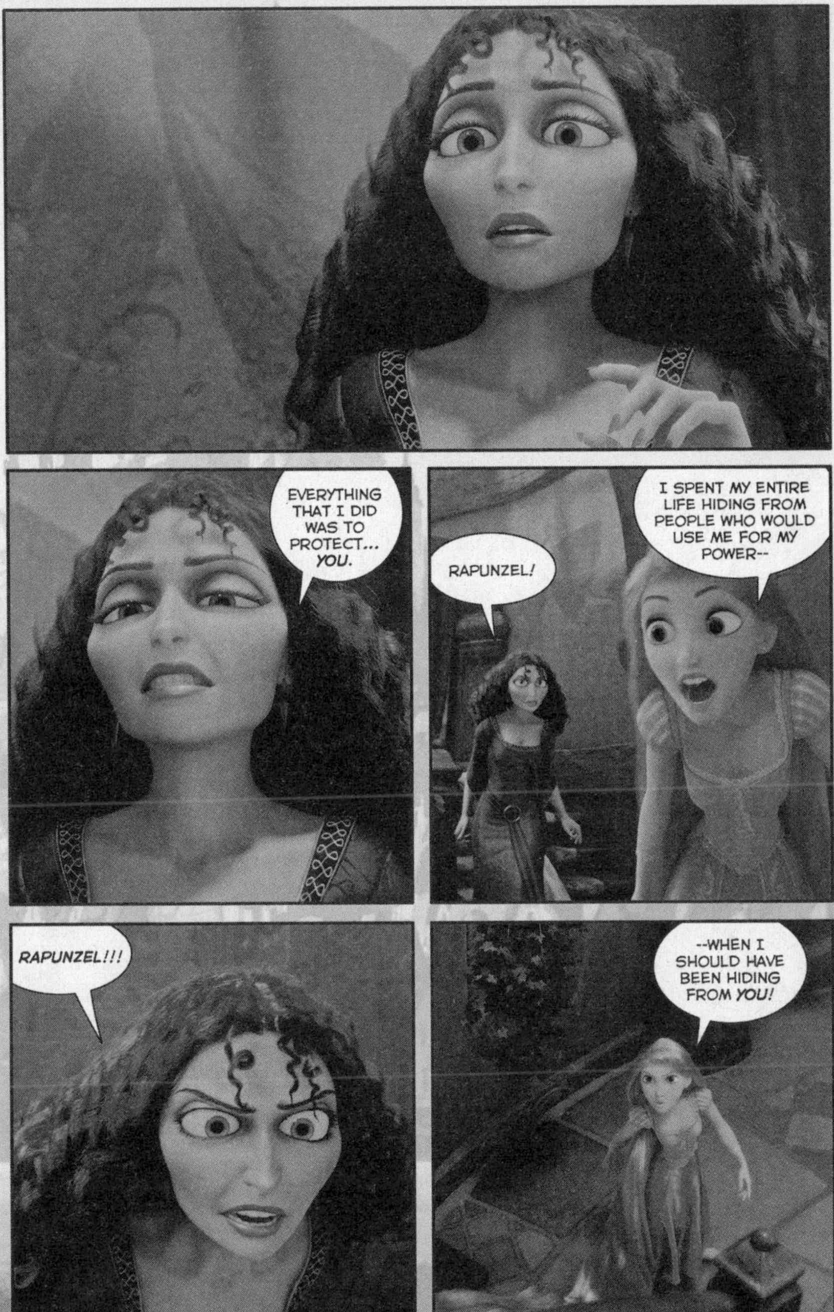
EVERYTHING THAT I DID WAS TO PROTECT... *YOU.*
I SPENT MY ENTIRE LIFE HIDING FROM PEOPLE WHO WOULD USE ME FOR MY POWER--
RAPUNZEL!
*RAPUNZEL!!!*
--WHEN I SHOULD HAVE BEEN HIDING FROM *YOU!*

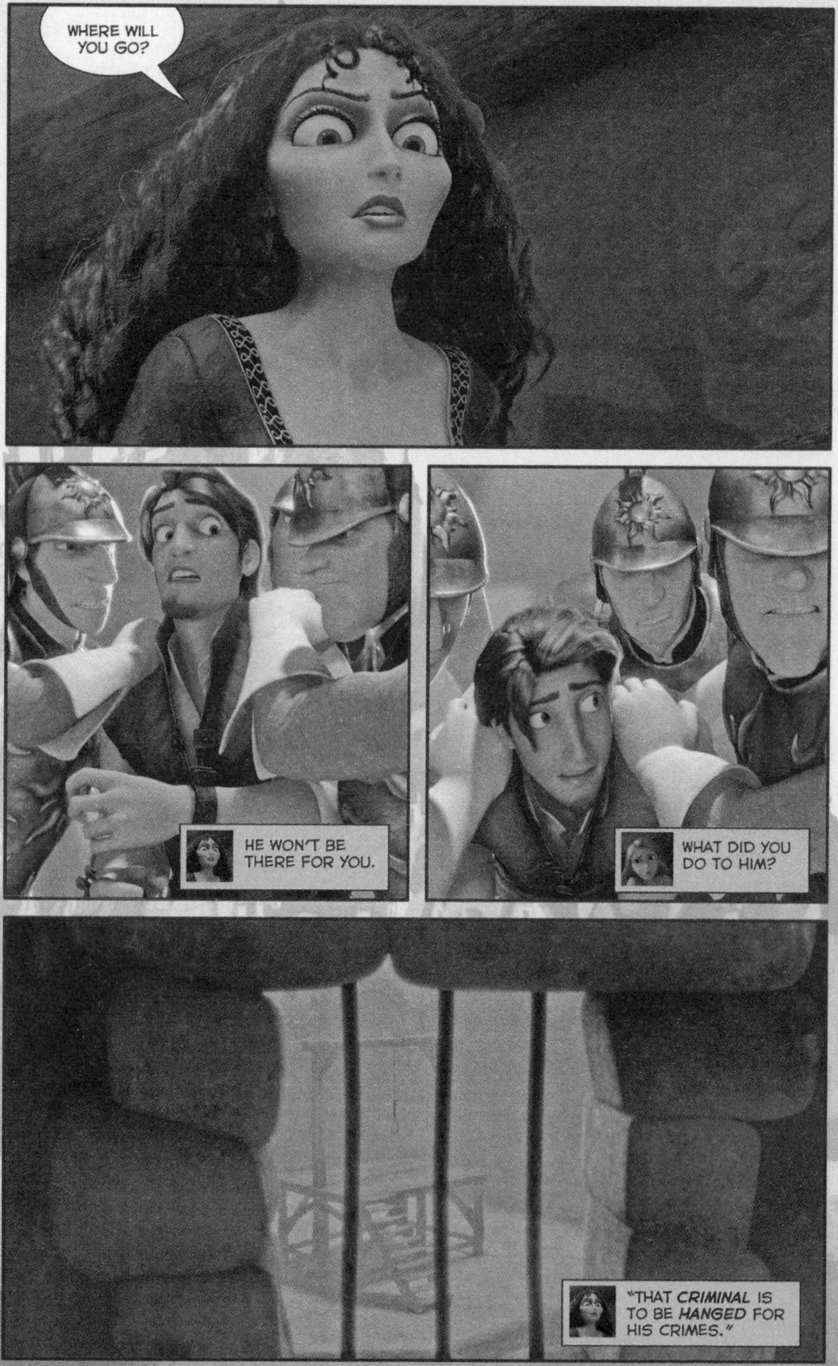

WHERE WILL YOU GO?
HE WON'T BE THERE FOR YOU.
WHAT DID YOU DO TO HIM?
"THAT *CRIMINAL* IS TO BE *HANGED* FOR HIS CRIMES."

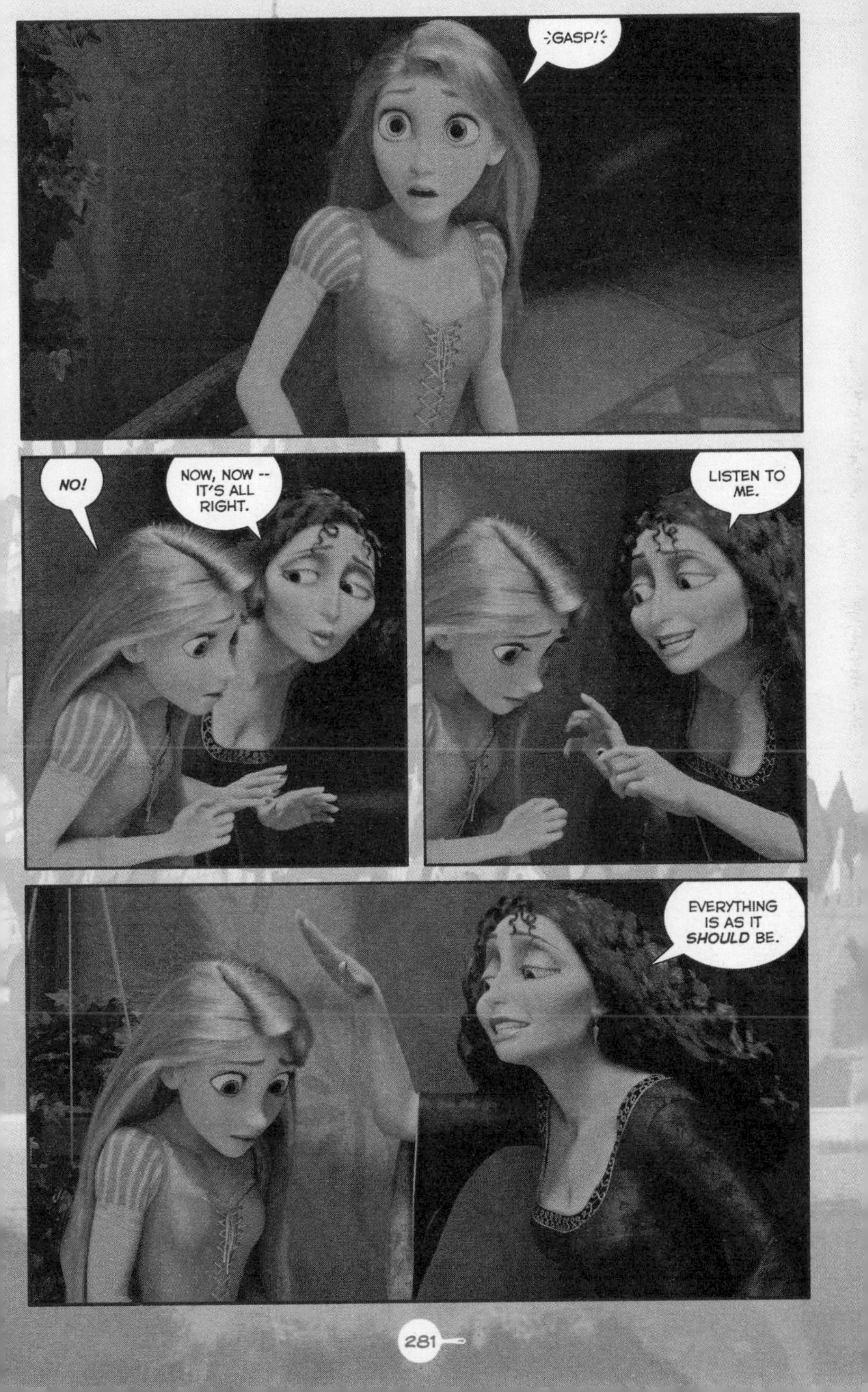
-GASP!-
NO!
NOW, NOW -- IT'S ALL RIGHT.
LISTEN TO ME.
EVERYTHING IS AS IT *SHOULD* BE.

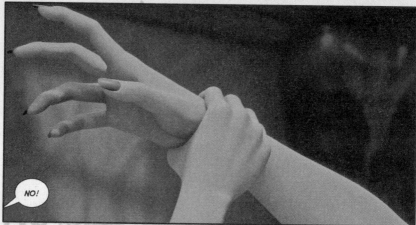

NO!

YOU WERE WRONG ABOUT THE WORLD.

AND YOU WERE WRONG ABOUT *ME*.

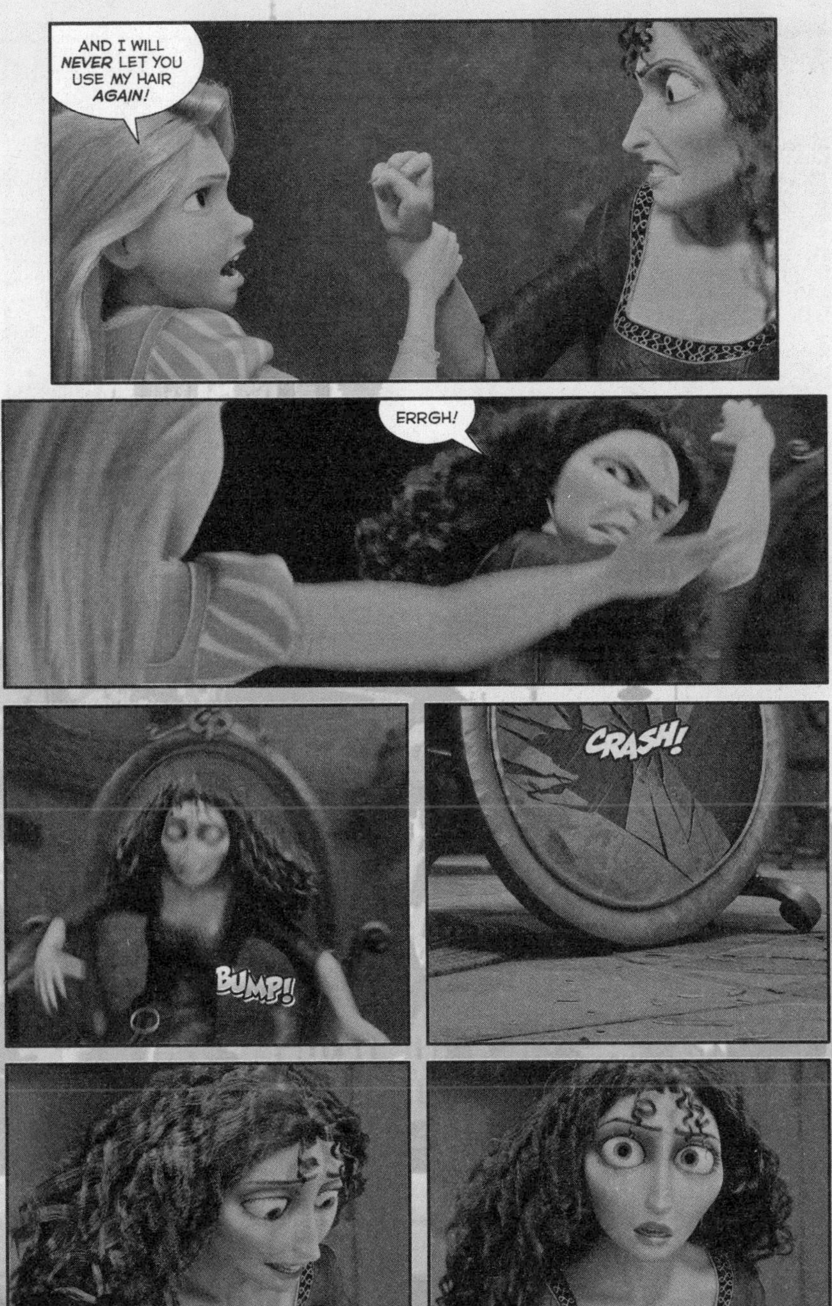
AND I WILL NEVER LET YOU USE MY HAIR AGAIN!
ERRGH!
BUMP!
CRASH!

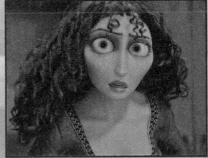

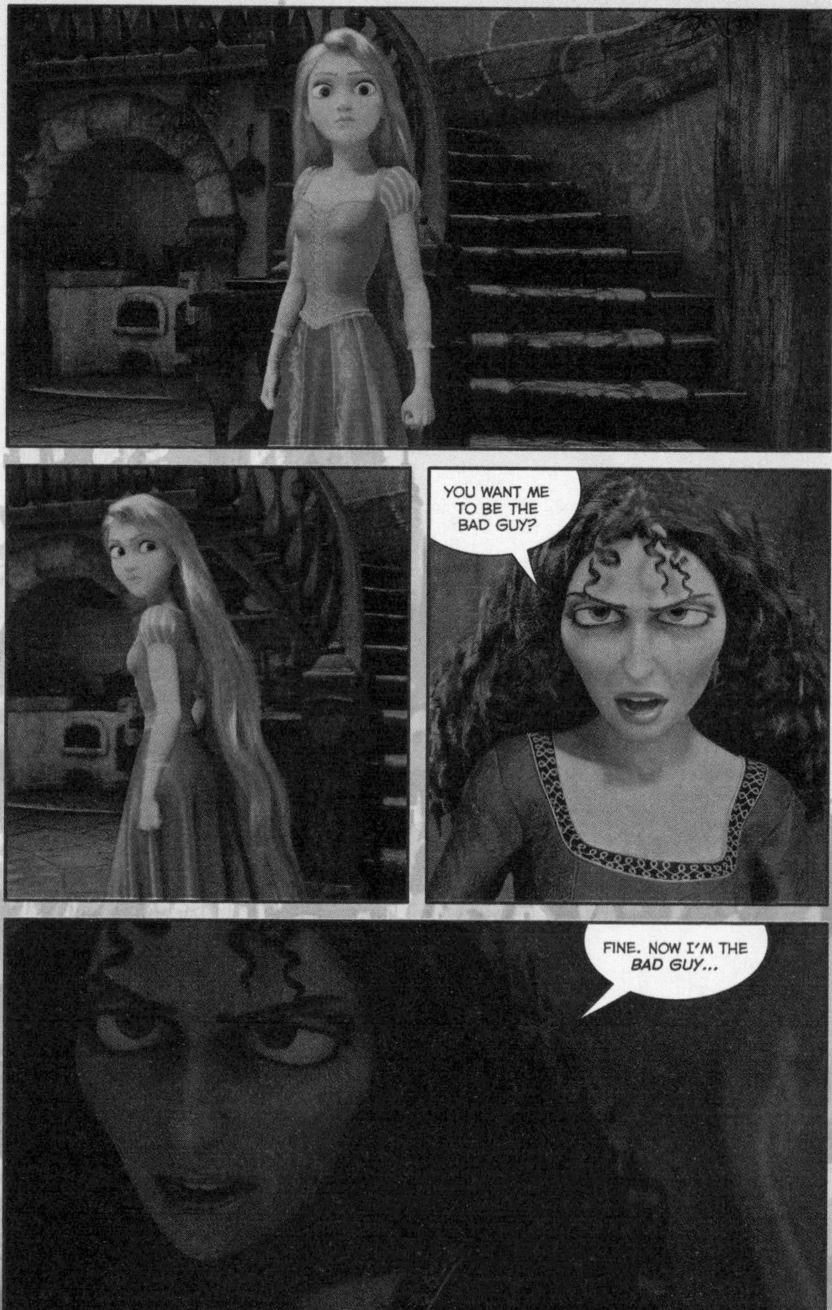
YOU WANT ME TO BE THE BAD GUY?
FINE. NOW I'M THE *BAD GUY*...

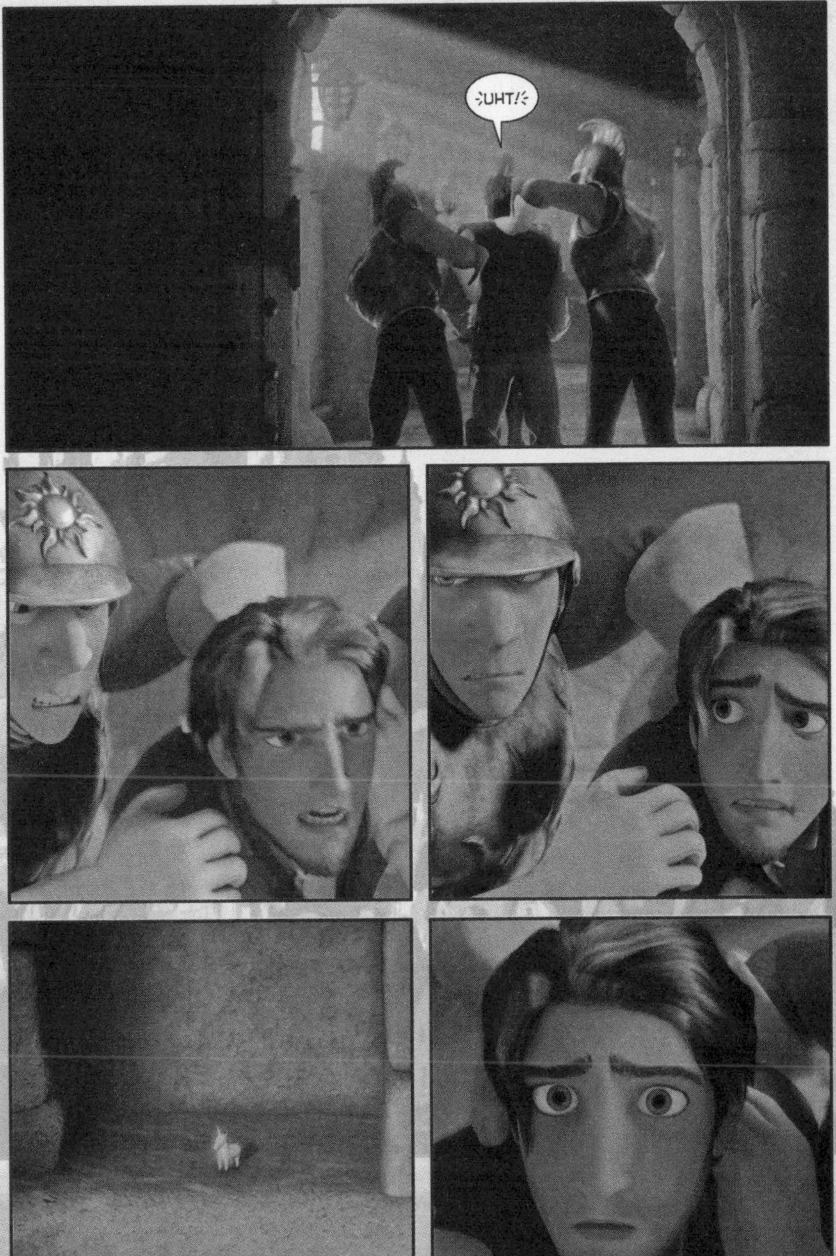
UHT!

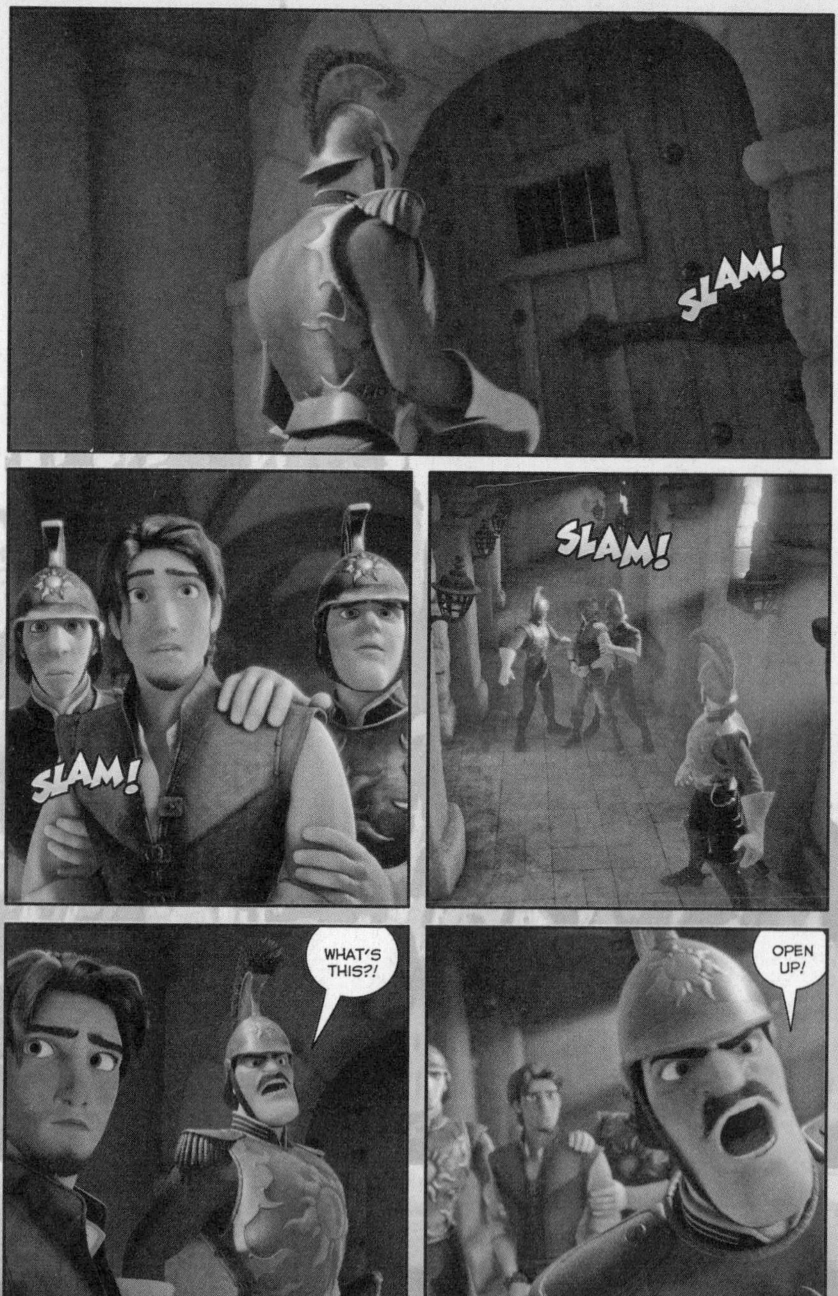
SLAM!
SLAM!
SLAM!
WHAT'S THIS?!
OPEN UP!

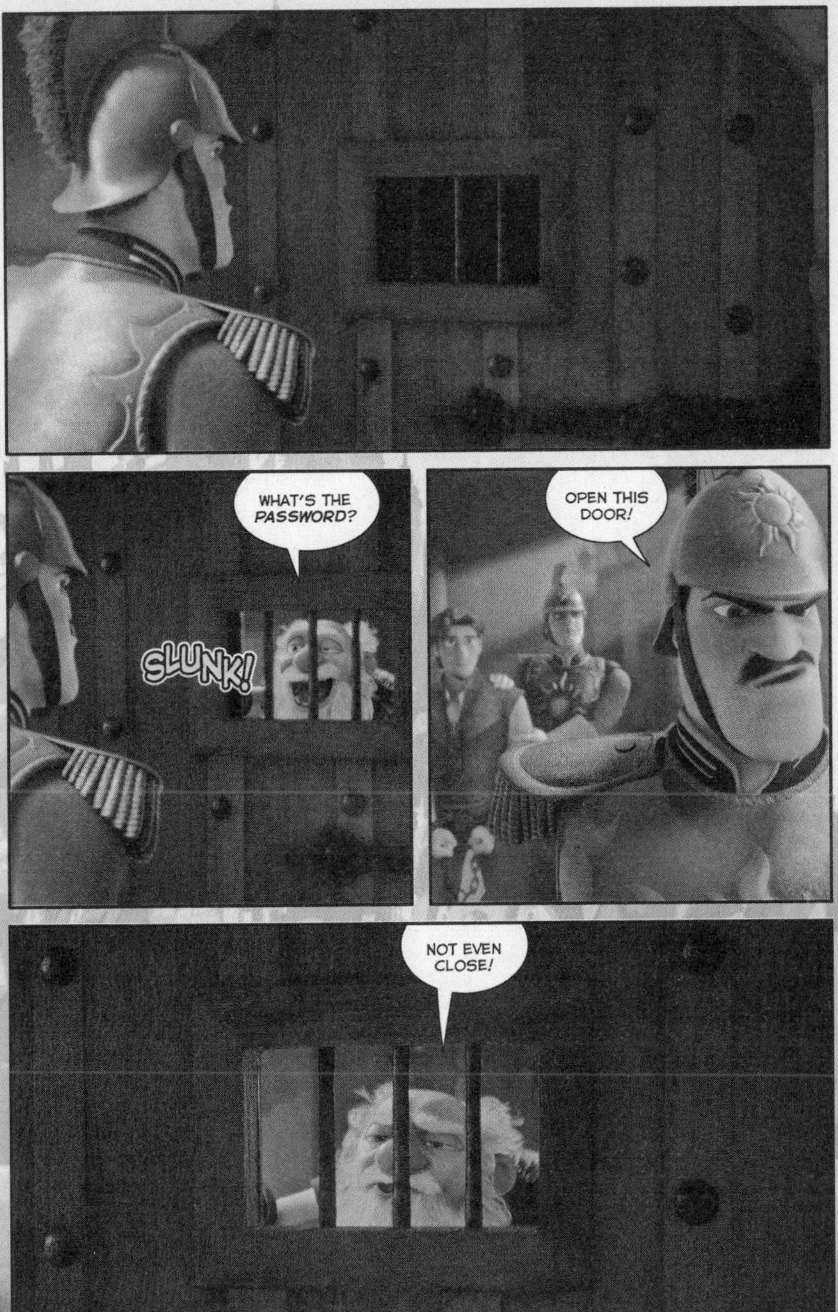
WHAT'S THE PASSWORD?
SLUNK!
OPEN THIS DOOR!
NOT EVEN CLOSE!

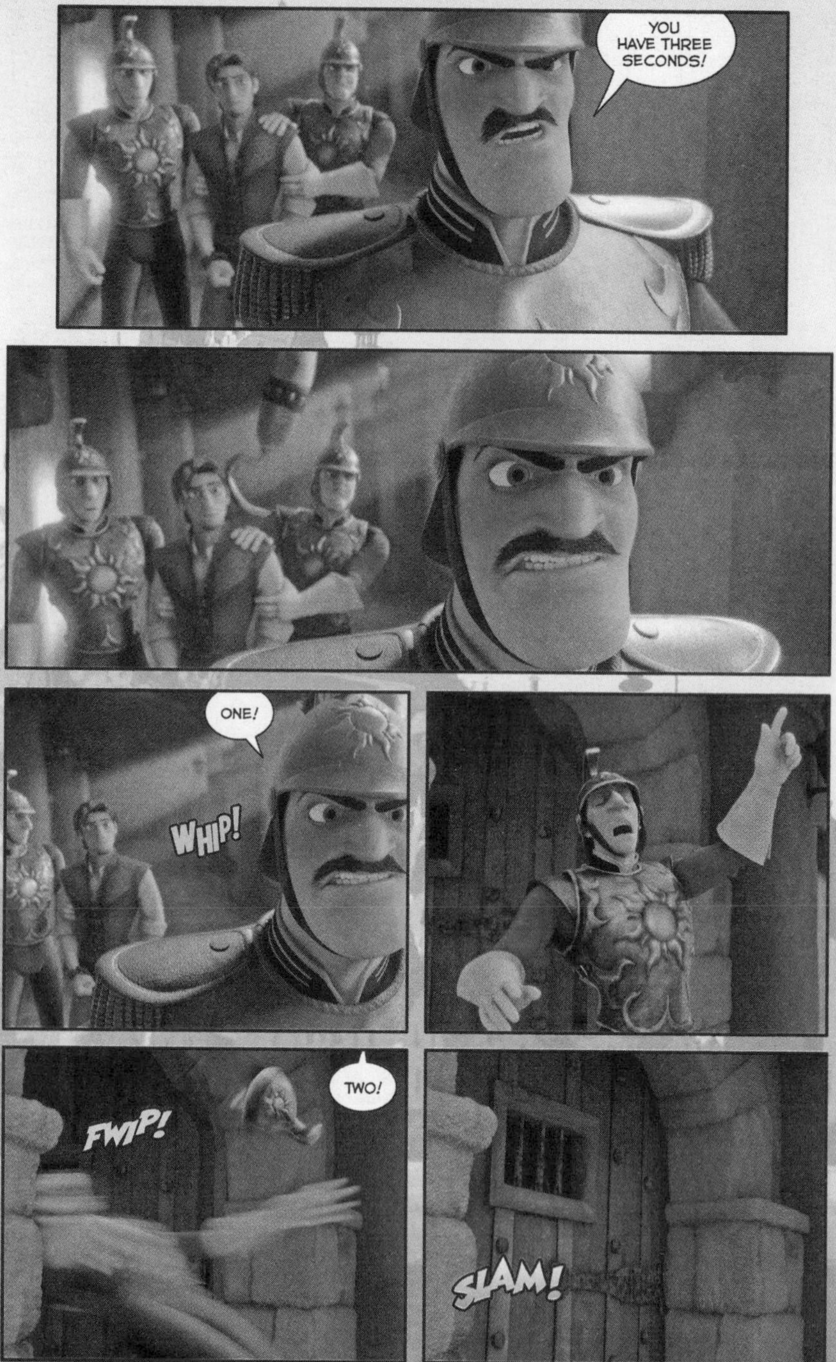
YOU HAVE THREE SECONDS!
ONE!
WHIP!
FWIP!
TWO!
SLAM!

THREE?

KLANG!

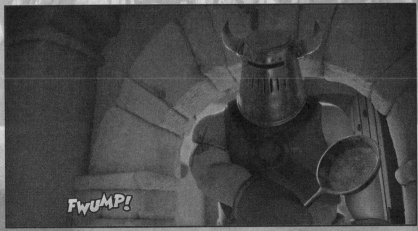

FWUMP!

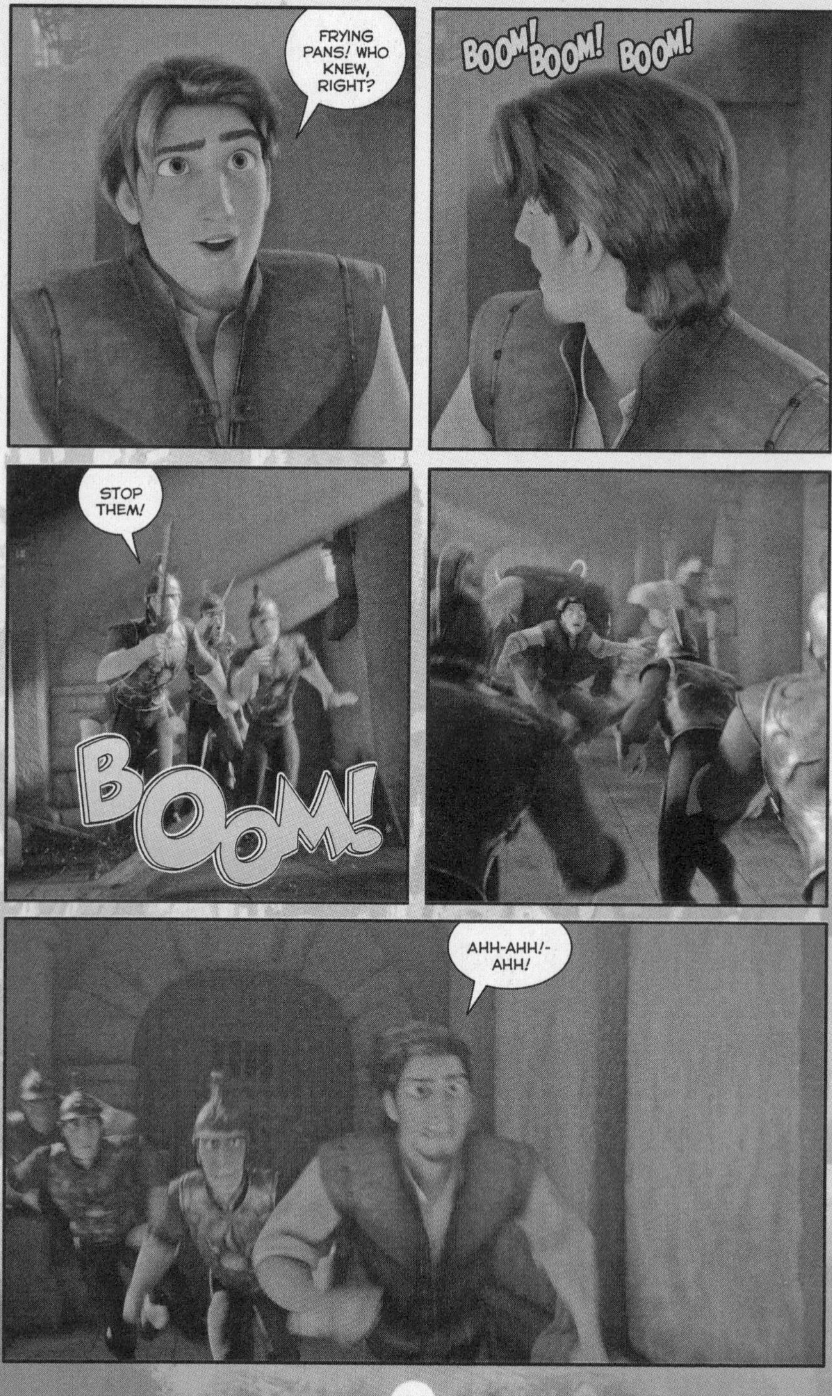
FRYING PANS! WHO KNEW, RIGHT?
BOOM! BOOM! BOOM!
STOP THEM!
BOOM!
AHH-AHH!- AHH!

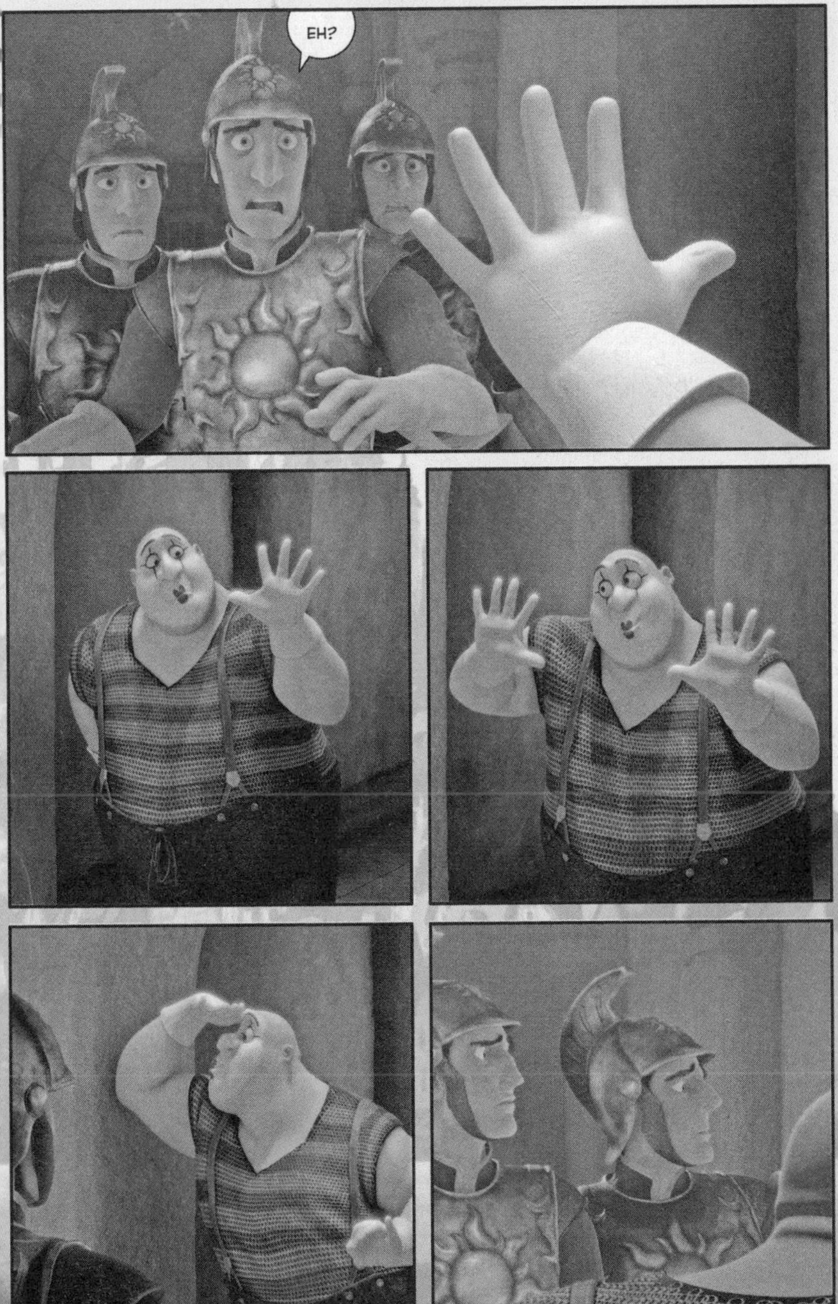
EH?

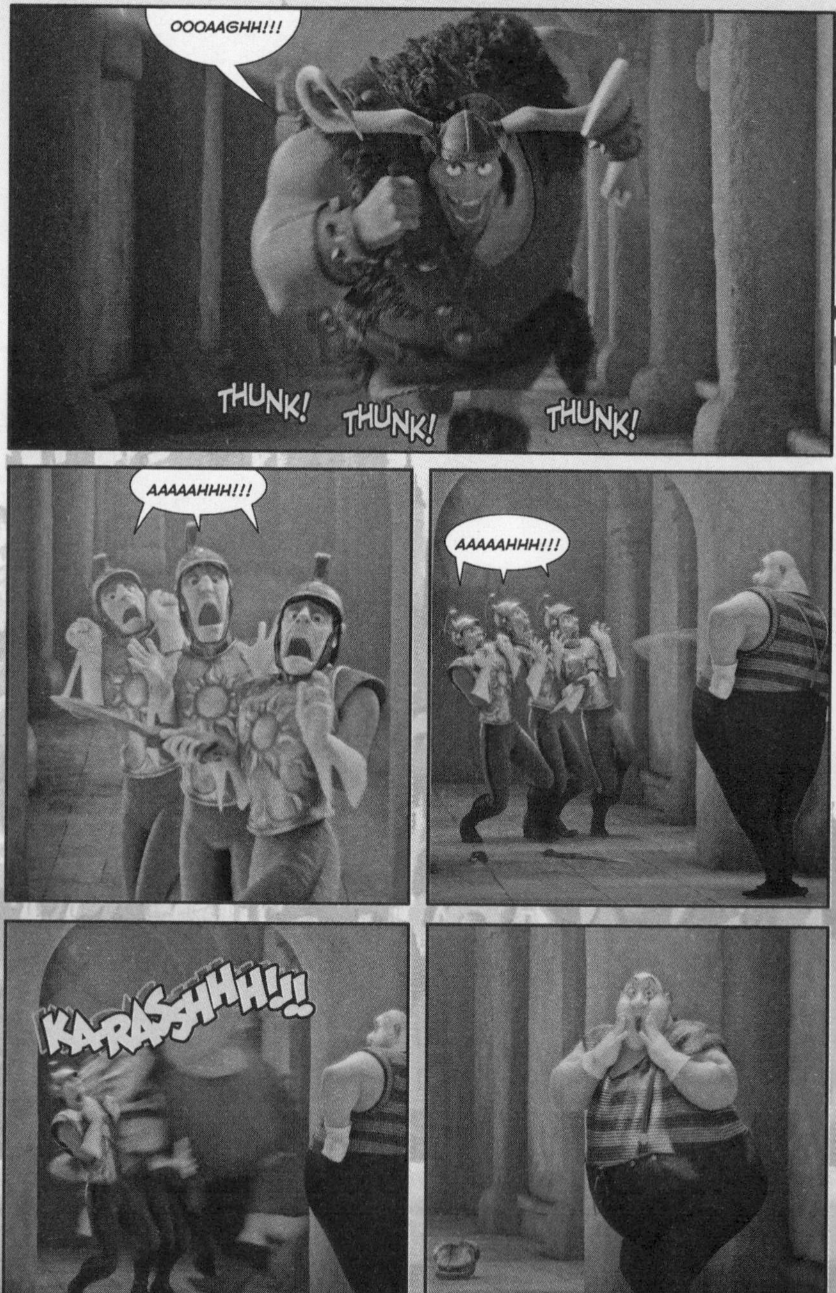
OOOAAGHH!!!
THUNK!
THUNK!
THUNK!
AAAAAHHH!!!
AAAAAHHH!!!
KARASHHH!!!

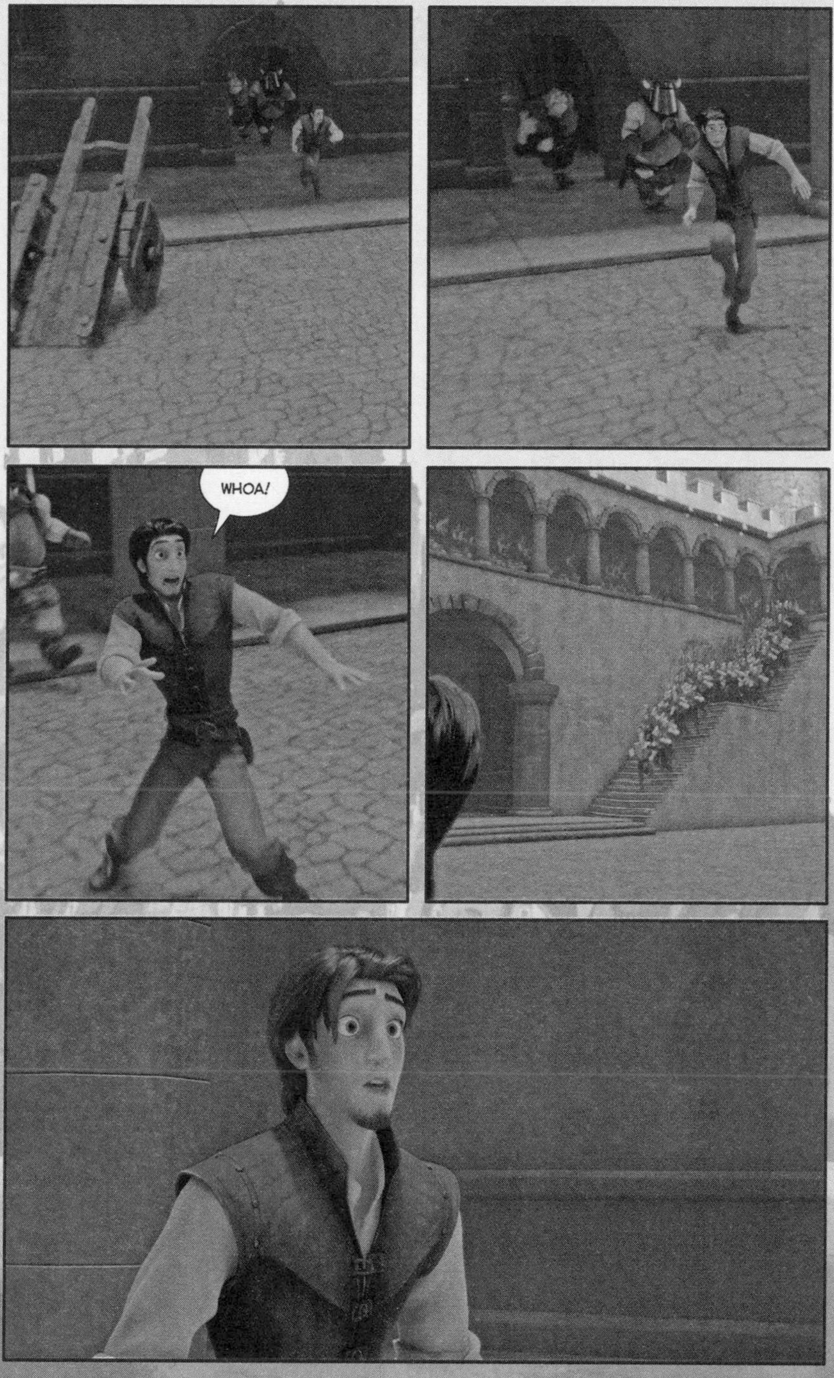
WHOA!

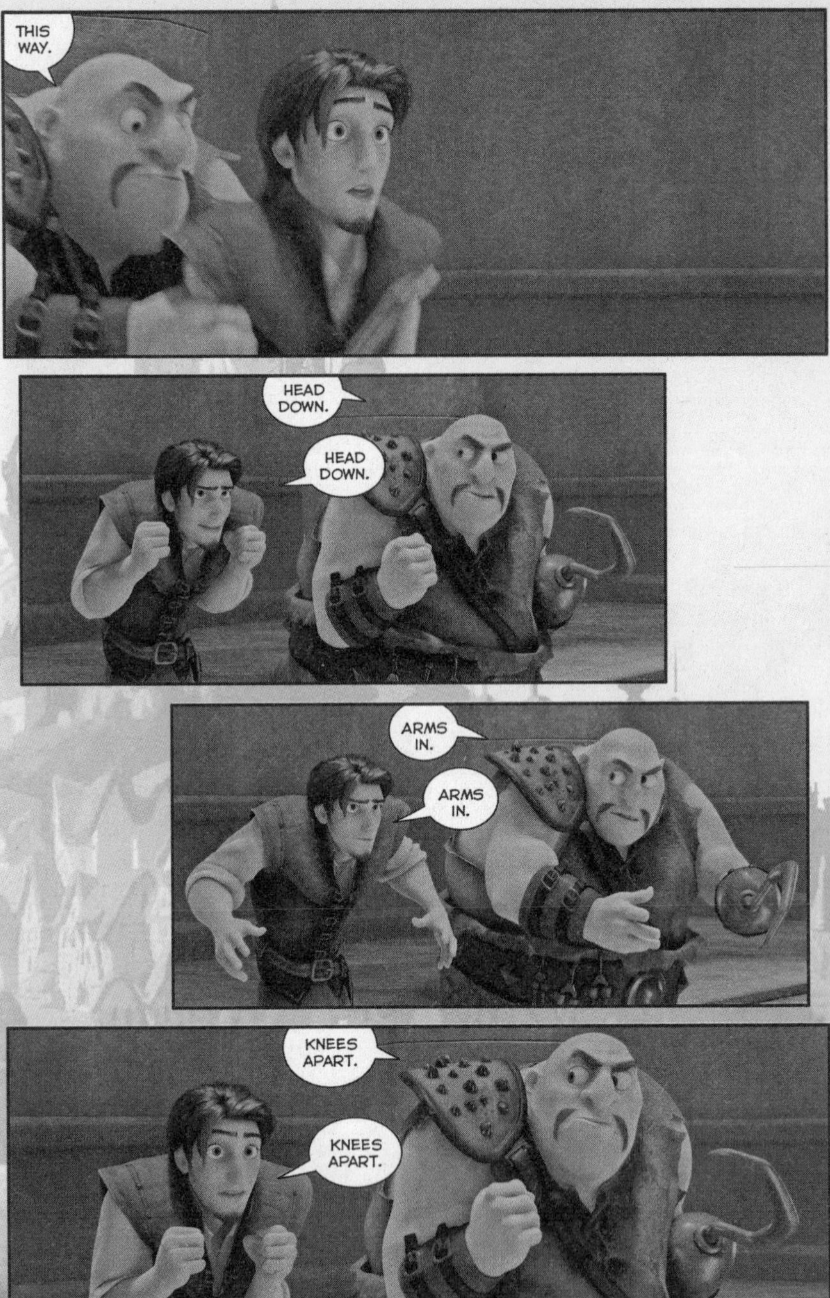
THIS WAY.
HEAD DOWN.
HEAD DOWN.
ARMS IN.
ARMS IN.
KNEES APART.
KNEES APART.

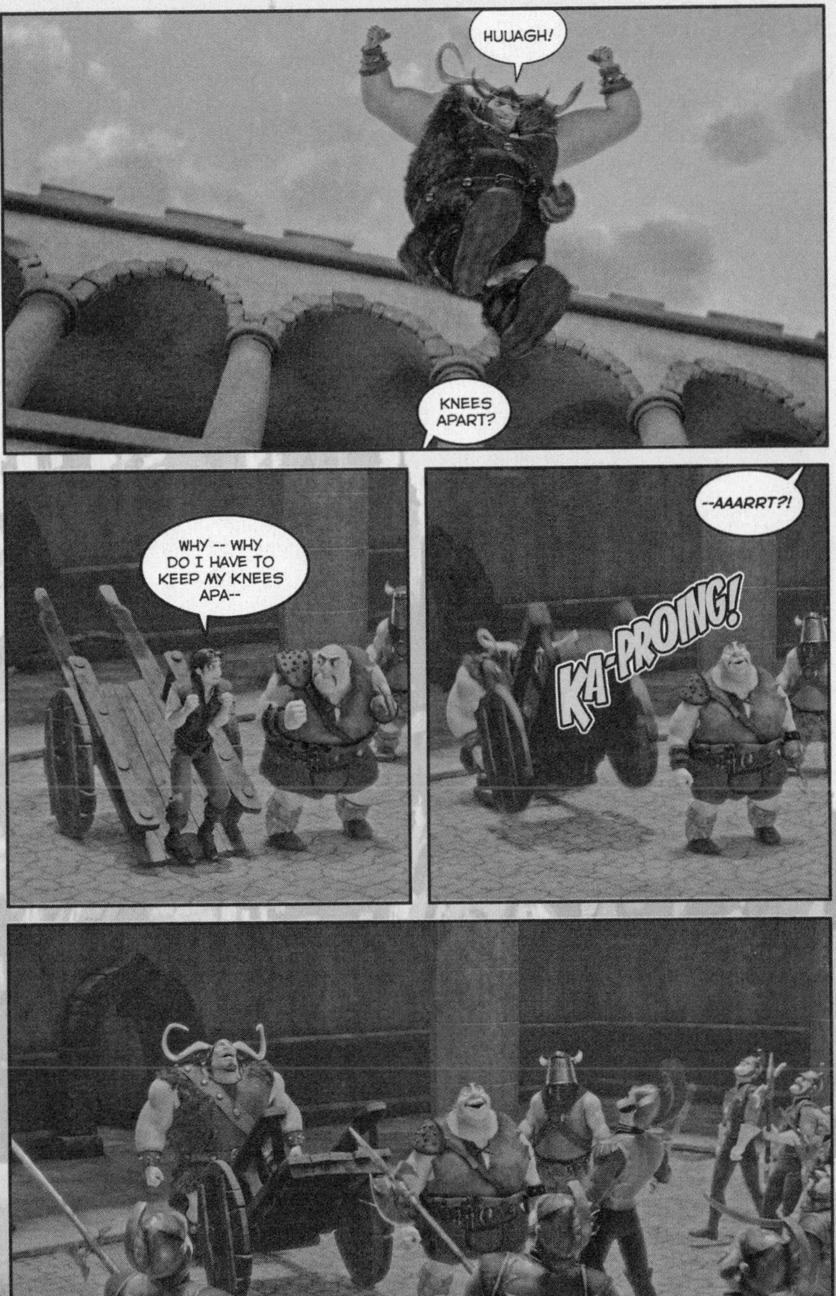
HUUAGH!
KNEES APART?
WHY -- WHY DO I HAVE TO KEEP MY KNEES APA--
--AAARRT?!
KA-PROING!

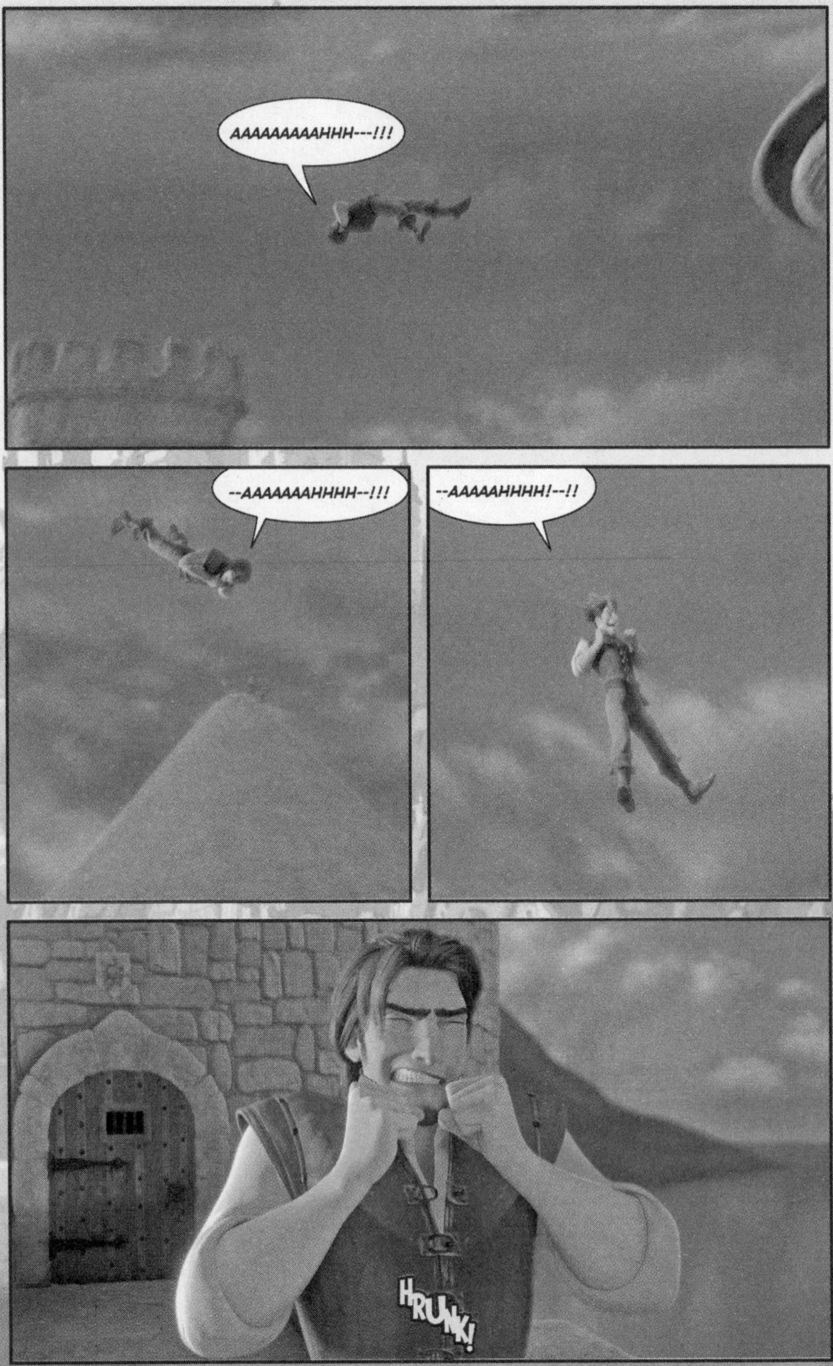
AAAAAAAAAAHHH---!!!
--AAAAAAAAHHHH--!!!
--AAAAAHHHH!--!!
HRUNK!

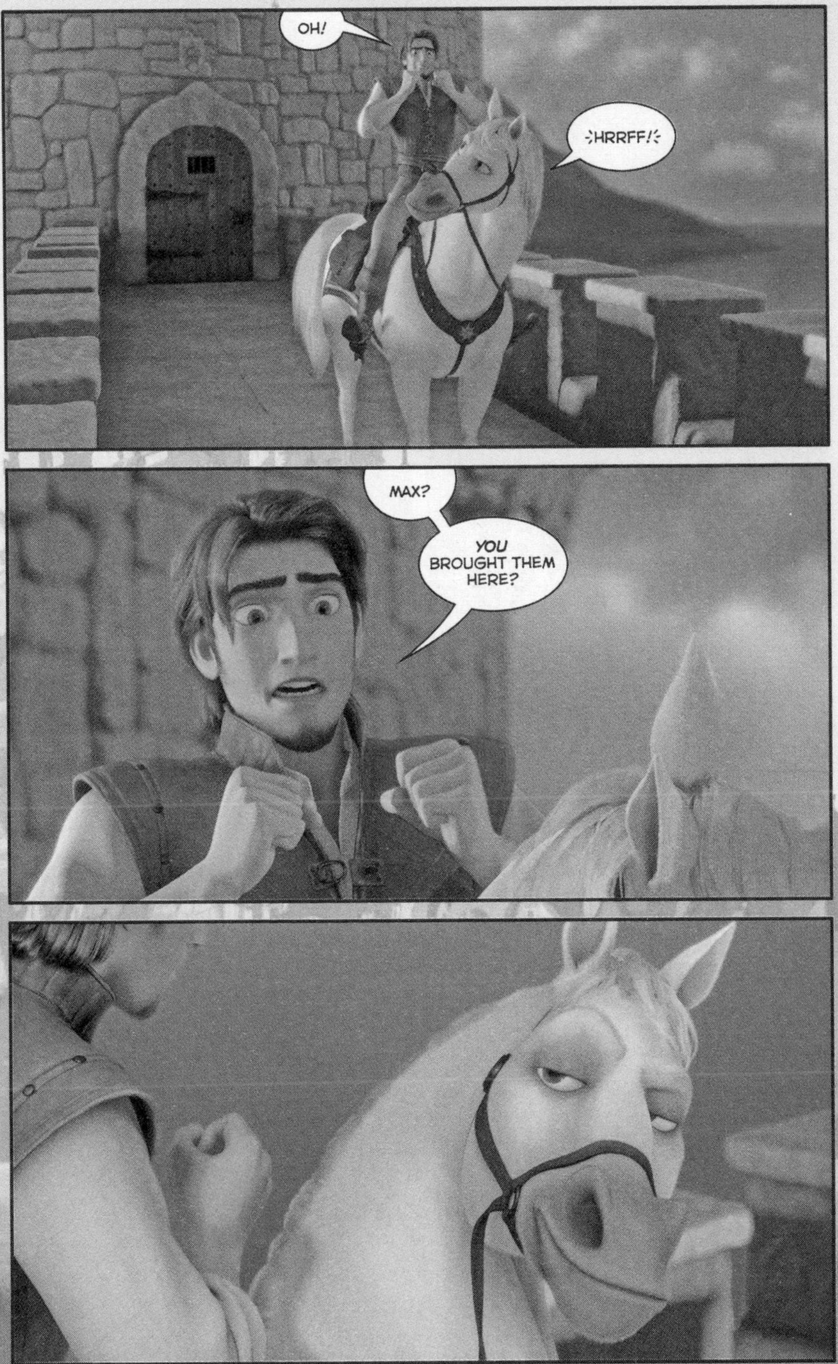
OH!
HRRFF!
MAX?
YOU BROUGHT THEM HERE?

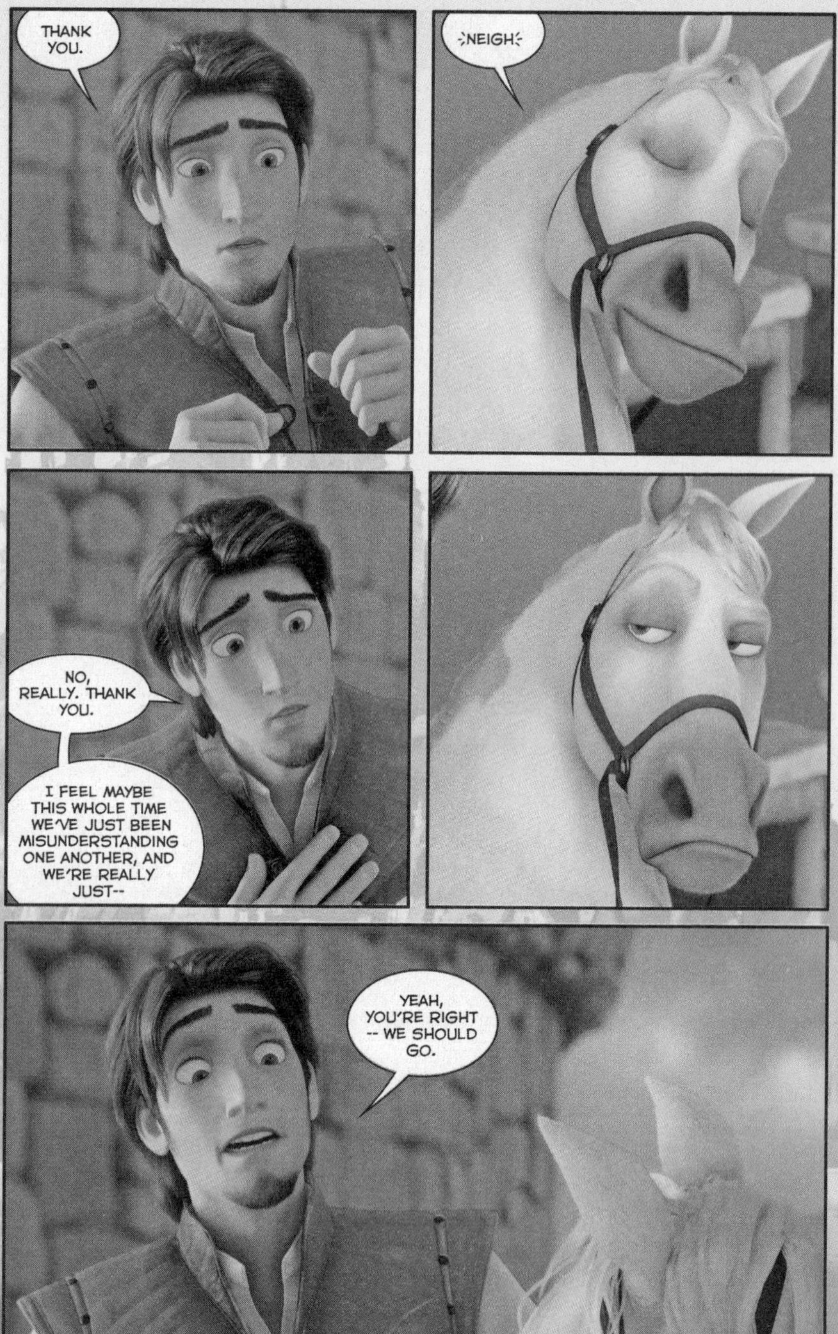
THANK YOU.
NEIGH
NO, REALLY. THANK YOU.
I FEEL MAYBE THIS WHOLE TIME WE'VE JUST BEEN MISUNDERSTANDING ONE ANOTHER, AND WE'RE REALLY JUST--
YEAH, YOU'RE RIGHT -- WE SHOULD GO.

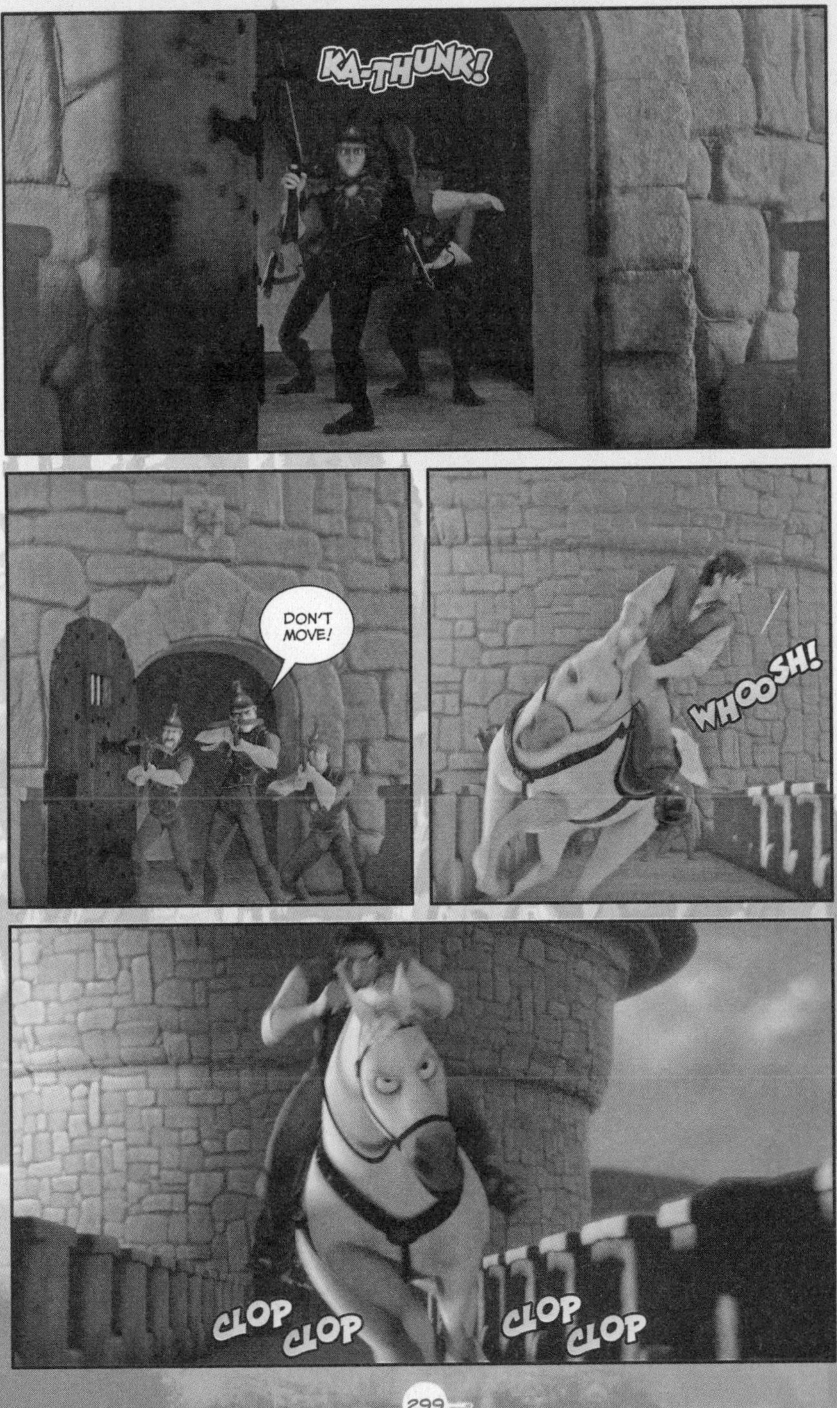
KA-THUNK!
DON'T MOVE!
WHOOSH!
CLOP CLOP
CLOP CLOP

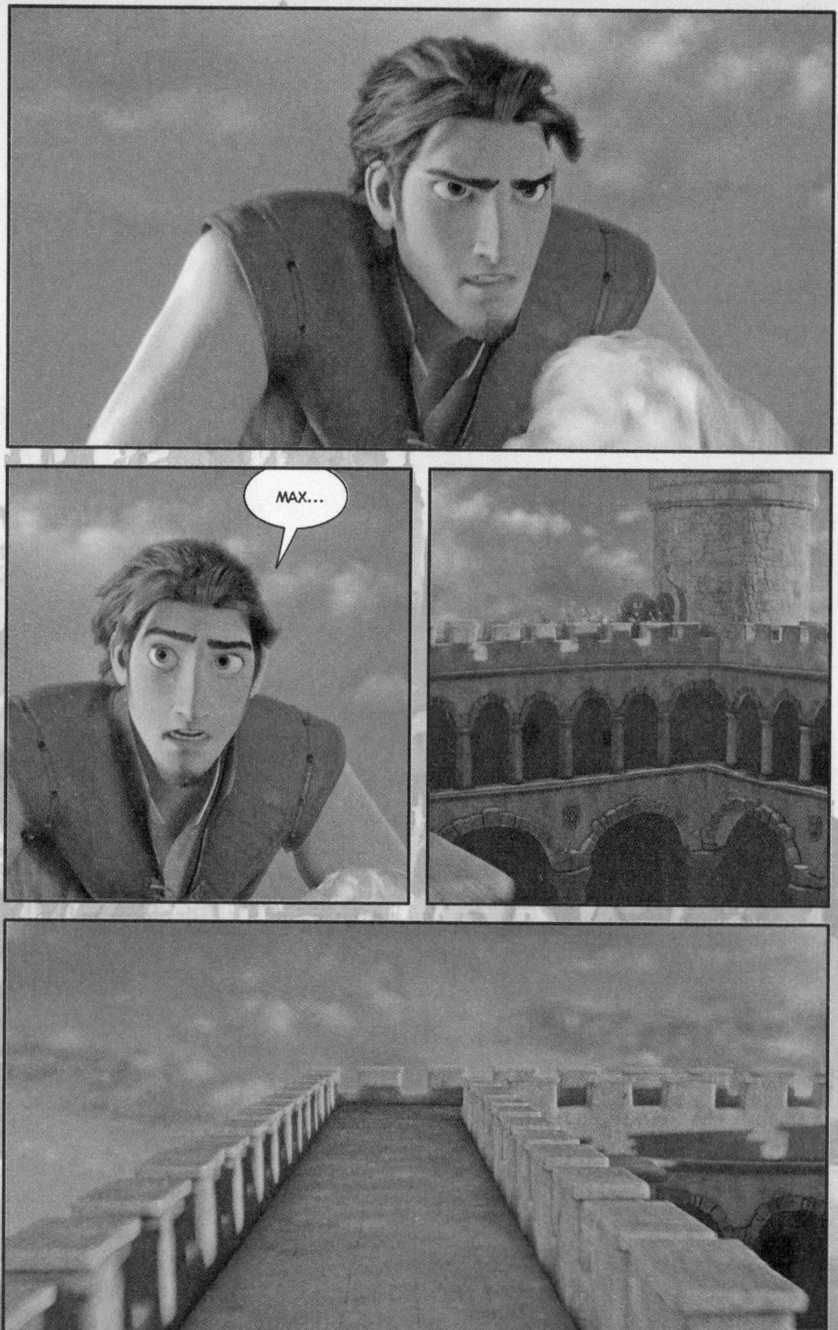
MAX...

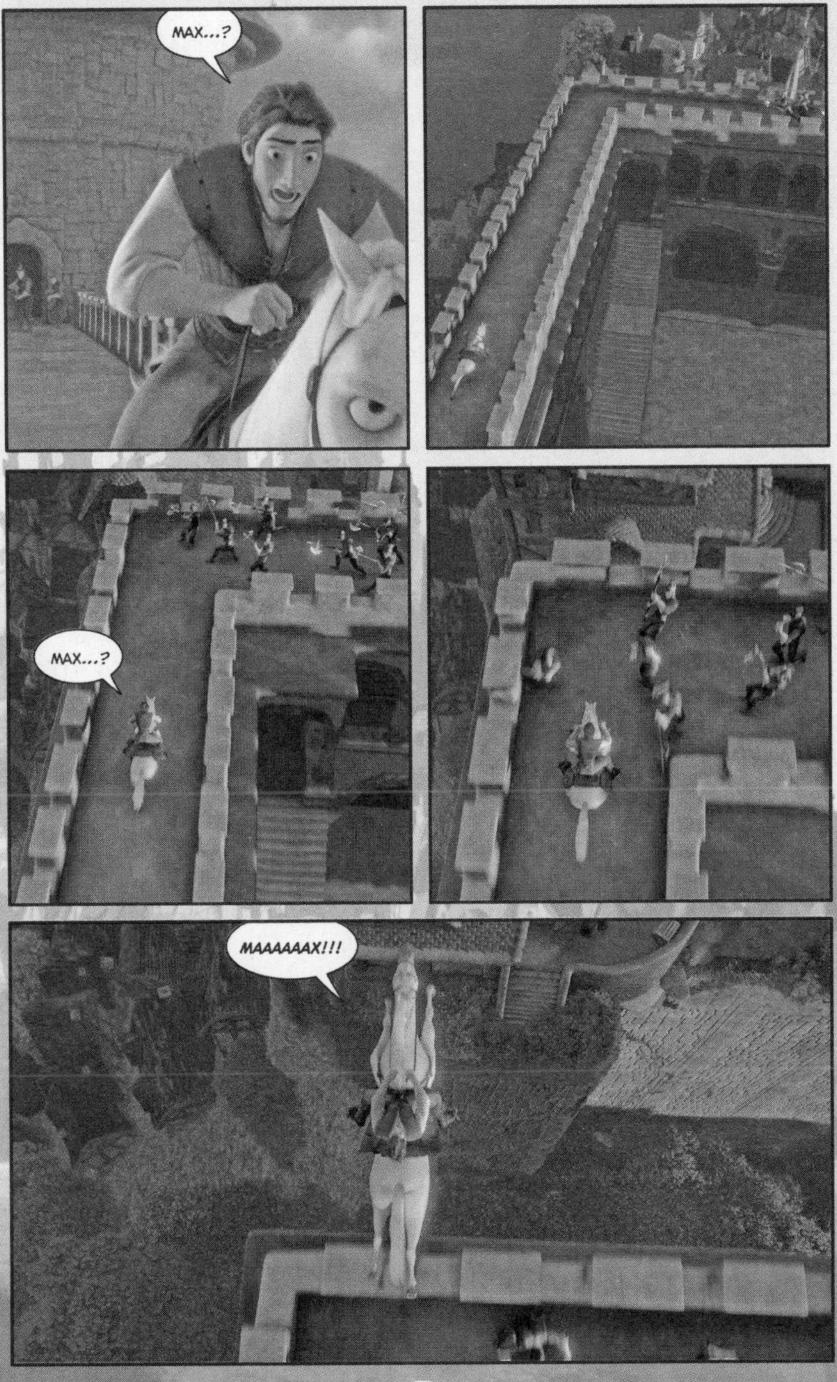
MAX...?
MAX...?
MAAAAAAX!!!

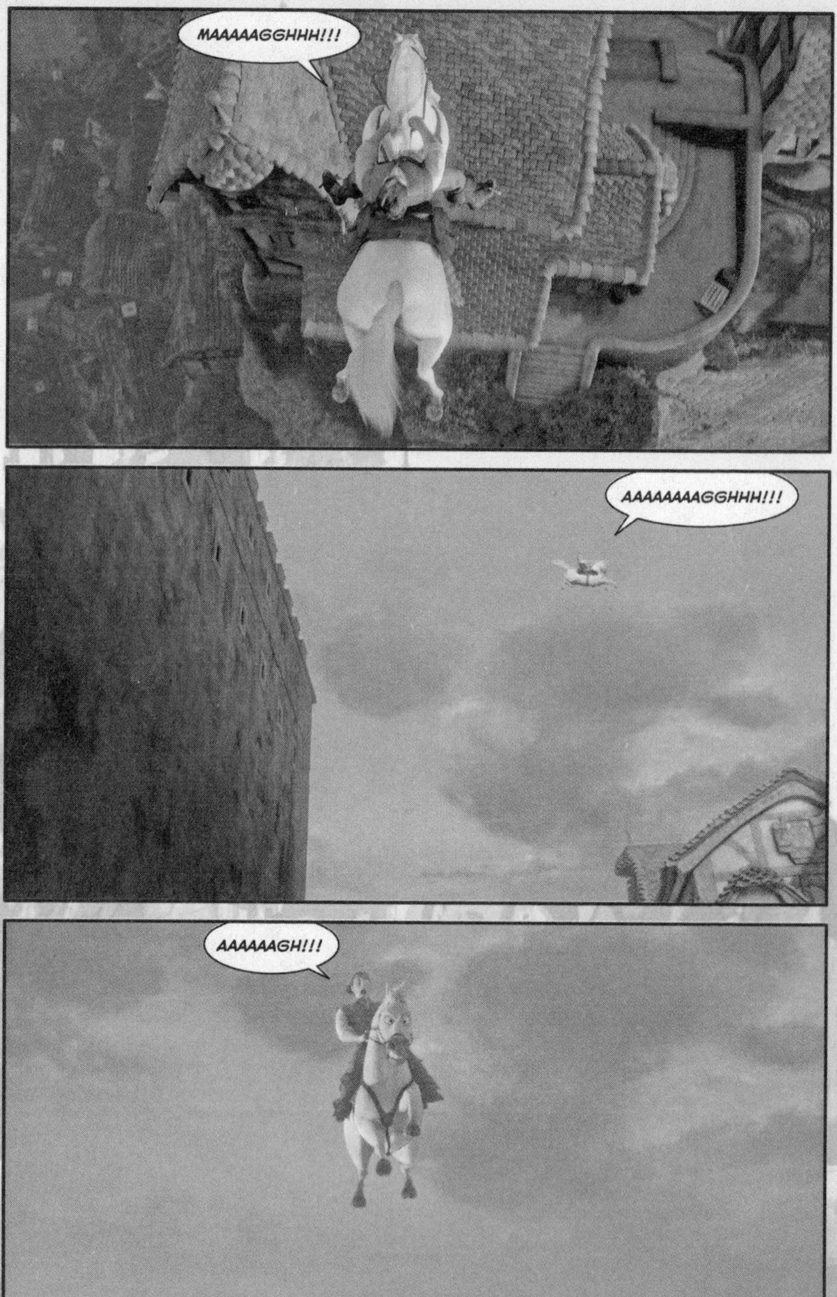
MAAAAAGGHHH!!!
AAAAAAAAGGHHH!!!
AAAAAAGH!!!

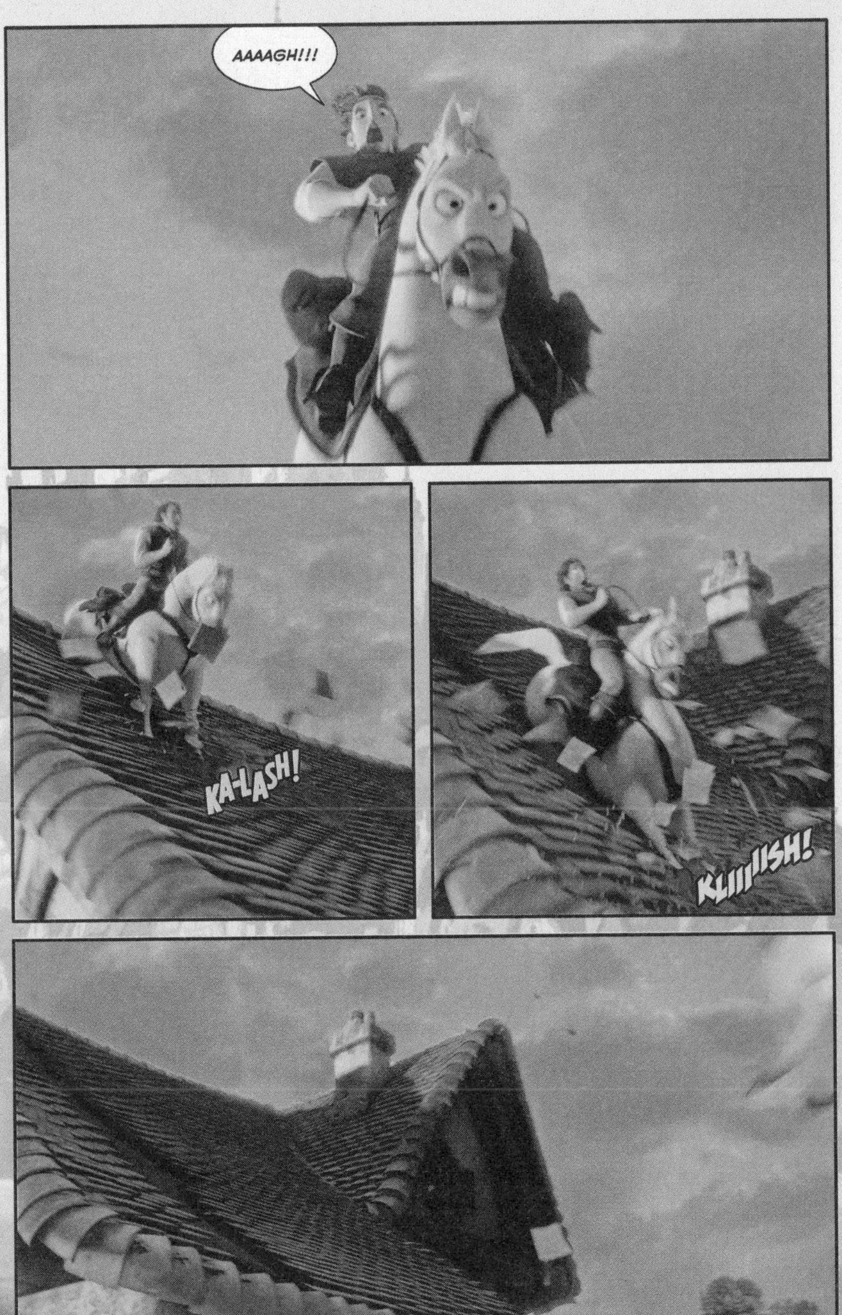
AAAAGH!!!
KA-LASH!
KLIIIIISH!

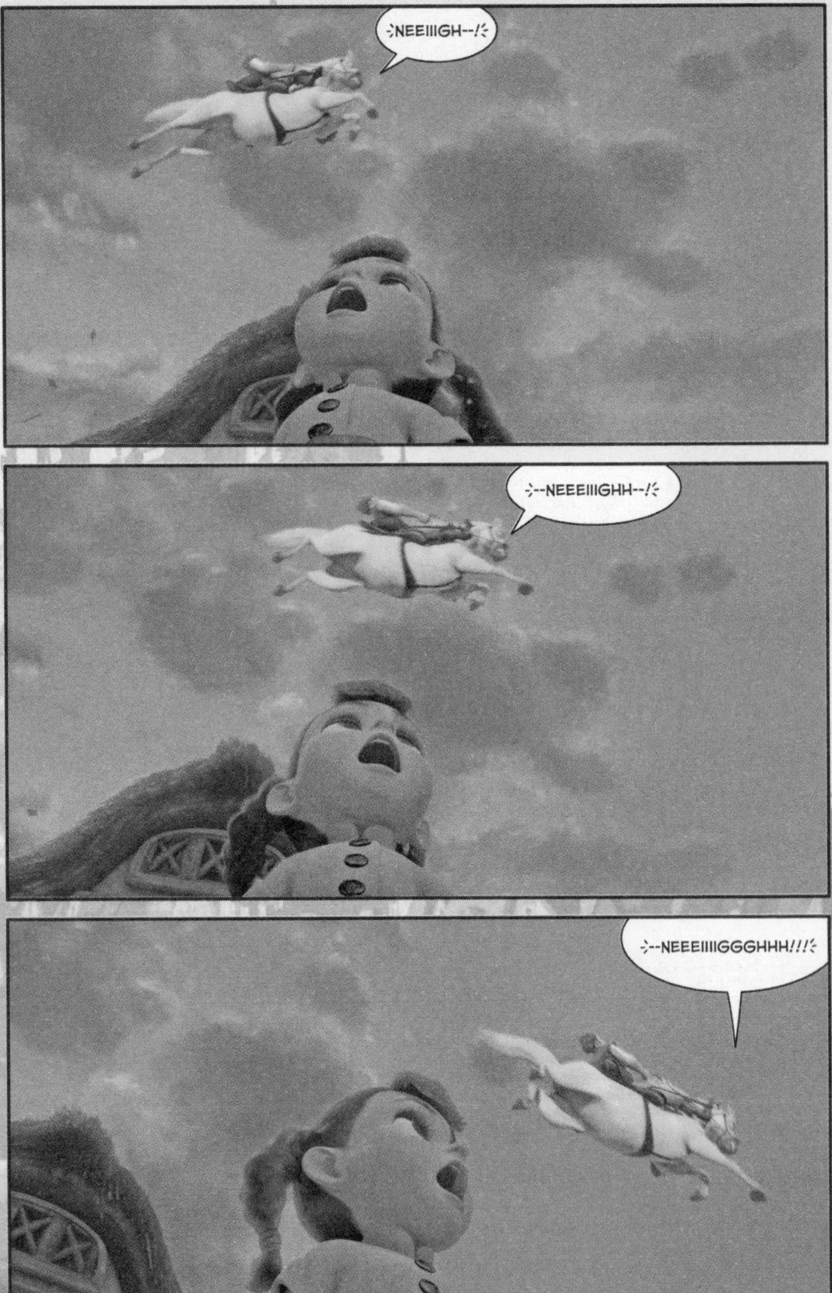
NEEIIIGH--!
--NEEEIIIGHH--!
--NEEEIIIIGGGHHH!!!

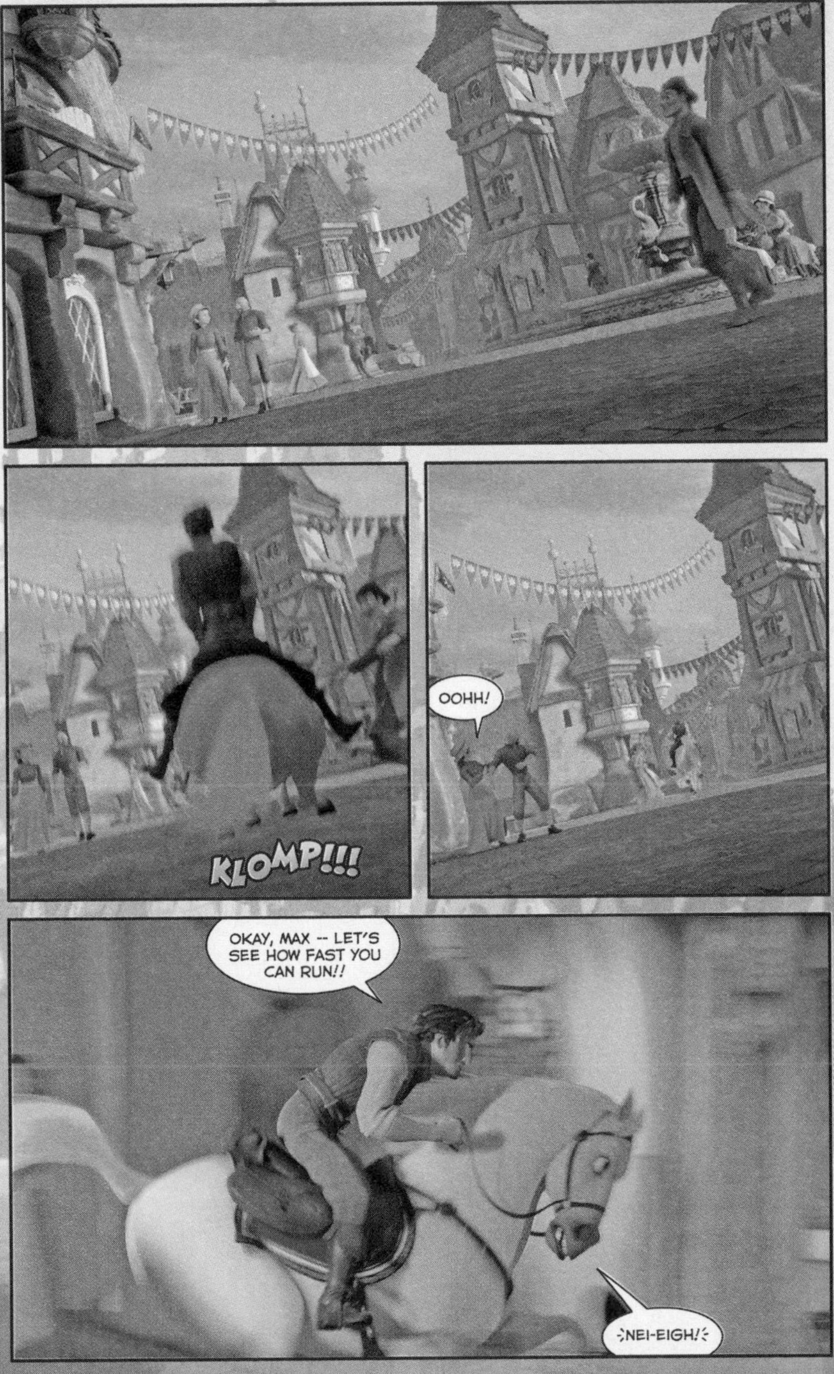
KLOMP!!!
OOHH!
OKAY, MAX -- LET'S SEE HOW FAST YOU CAN RUN!!
NEI-EIGH!

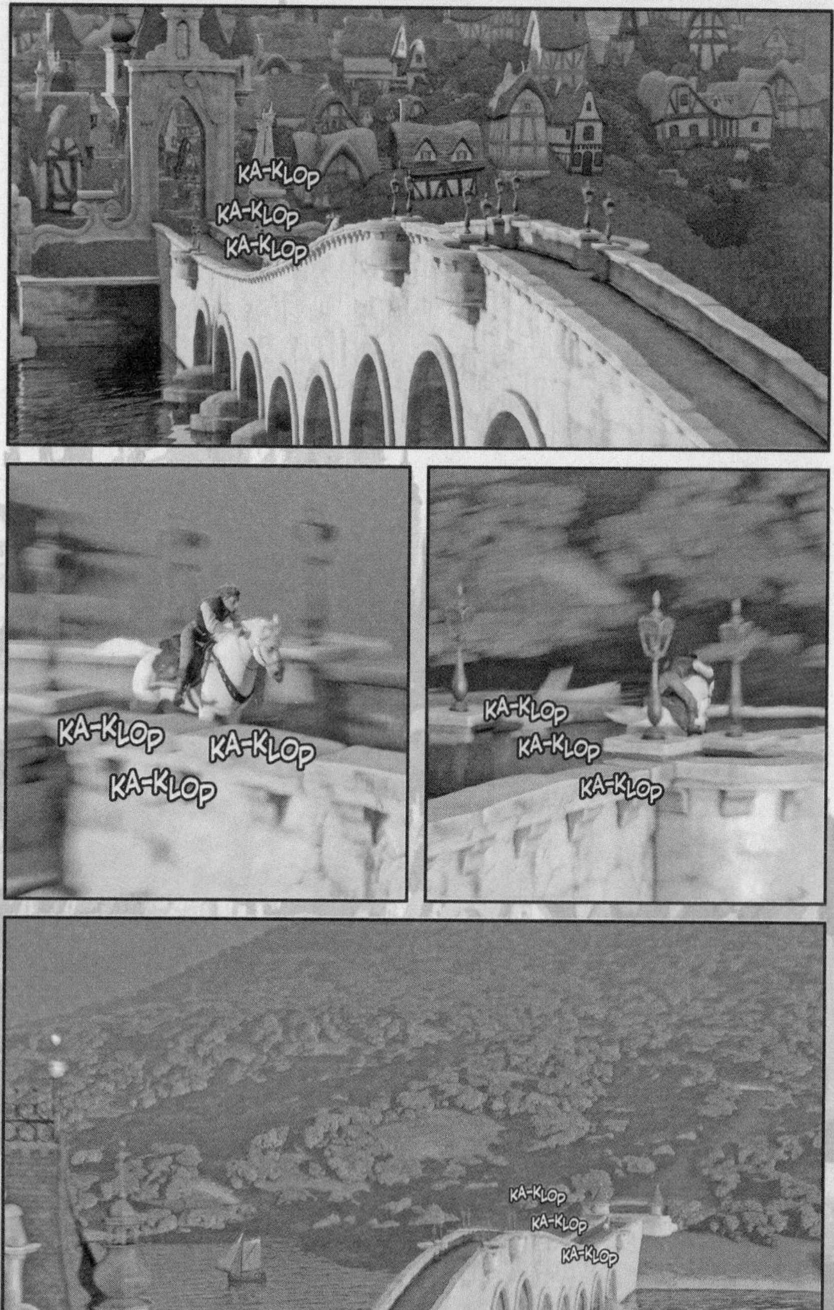
KA-KLOP
KA-KLOP
KA-KLOP
KA-KLOP
KA-KLOP
KA-KLOP
KA-KLOP
KA-KLOP
KA-KLOP
KA-KLOP
KA-KLOP
KA-KLOP

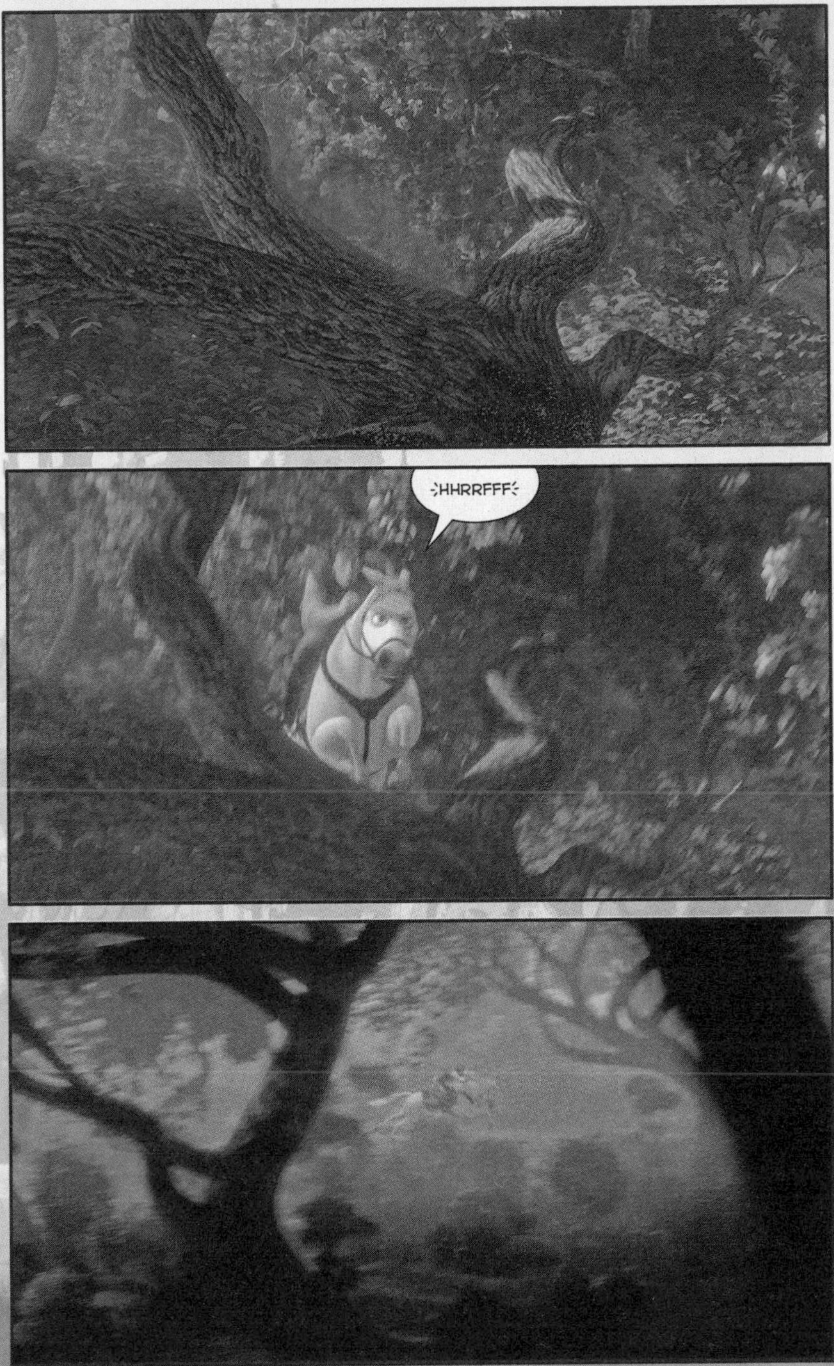
HHRRFFF

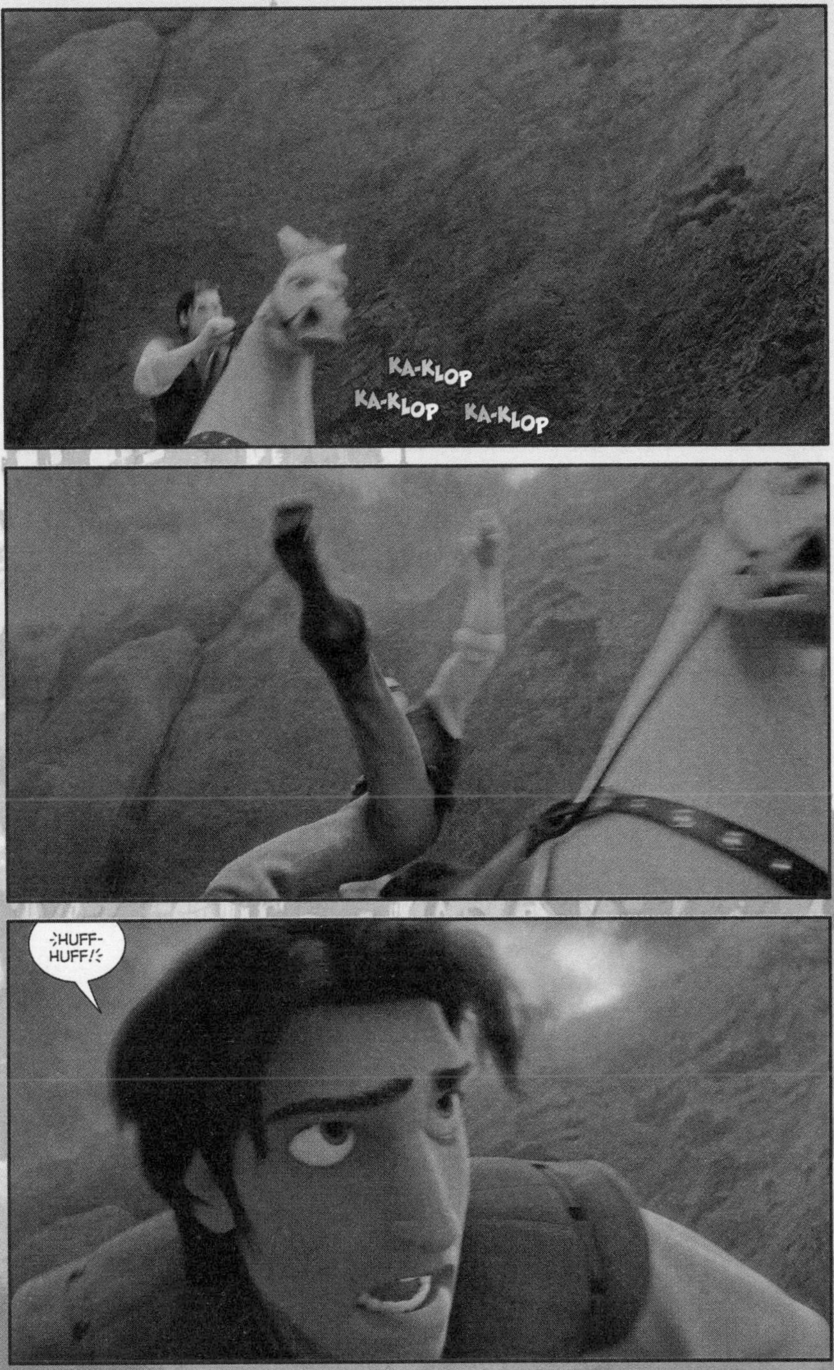
KA-KLOP
KA-KLOP KA-KLOP
HUFF-HUFF!

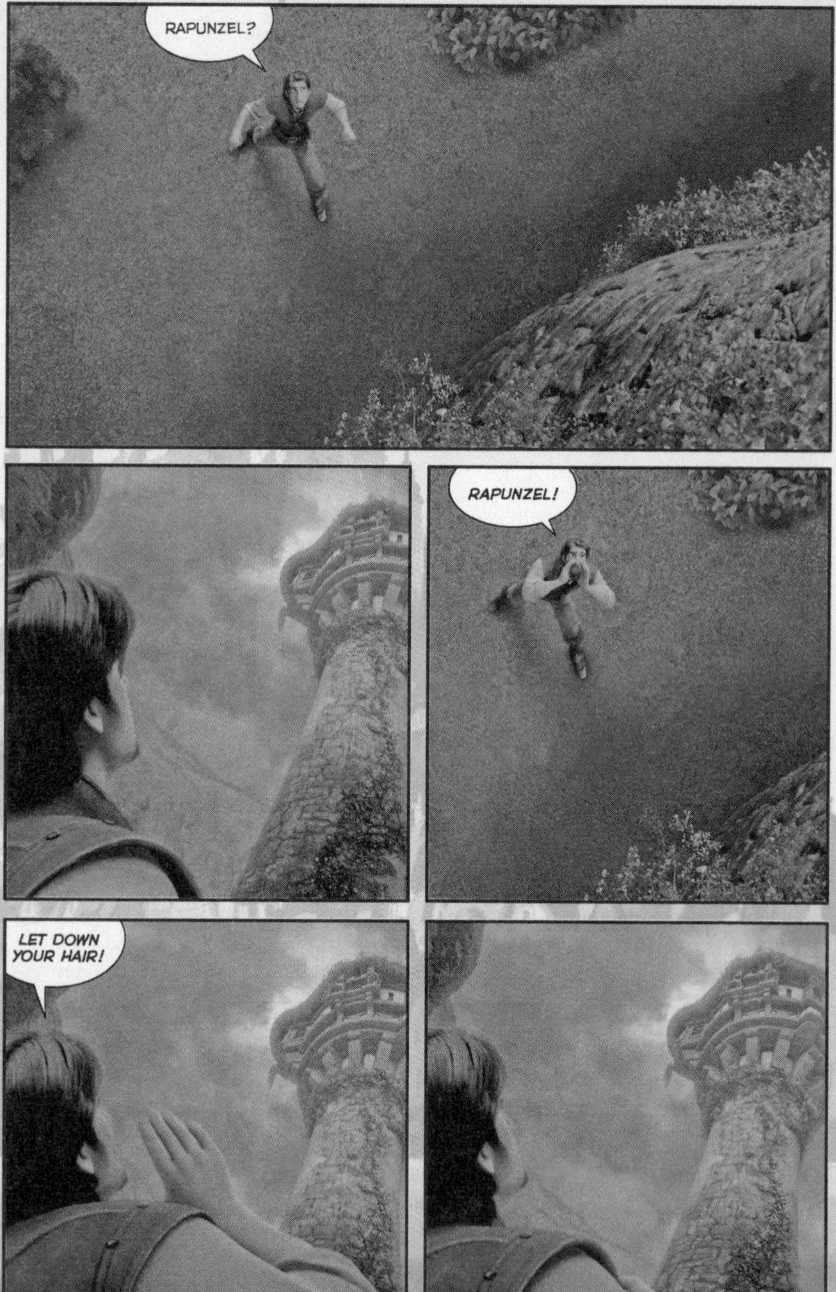
RAPUNZEL?
RAPUNZEL!
LET DOWN YOUR HAIR!

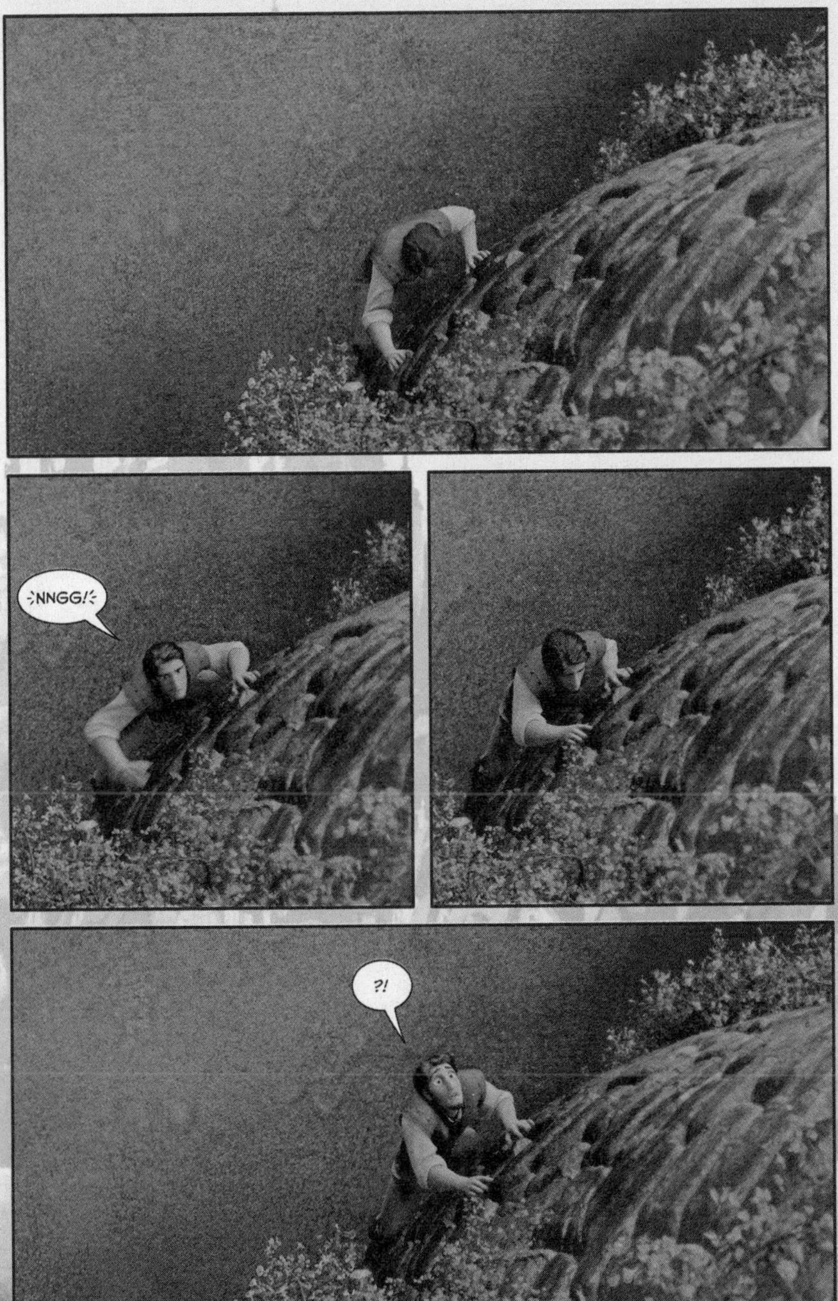
NNGG!
?!

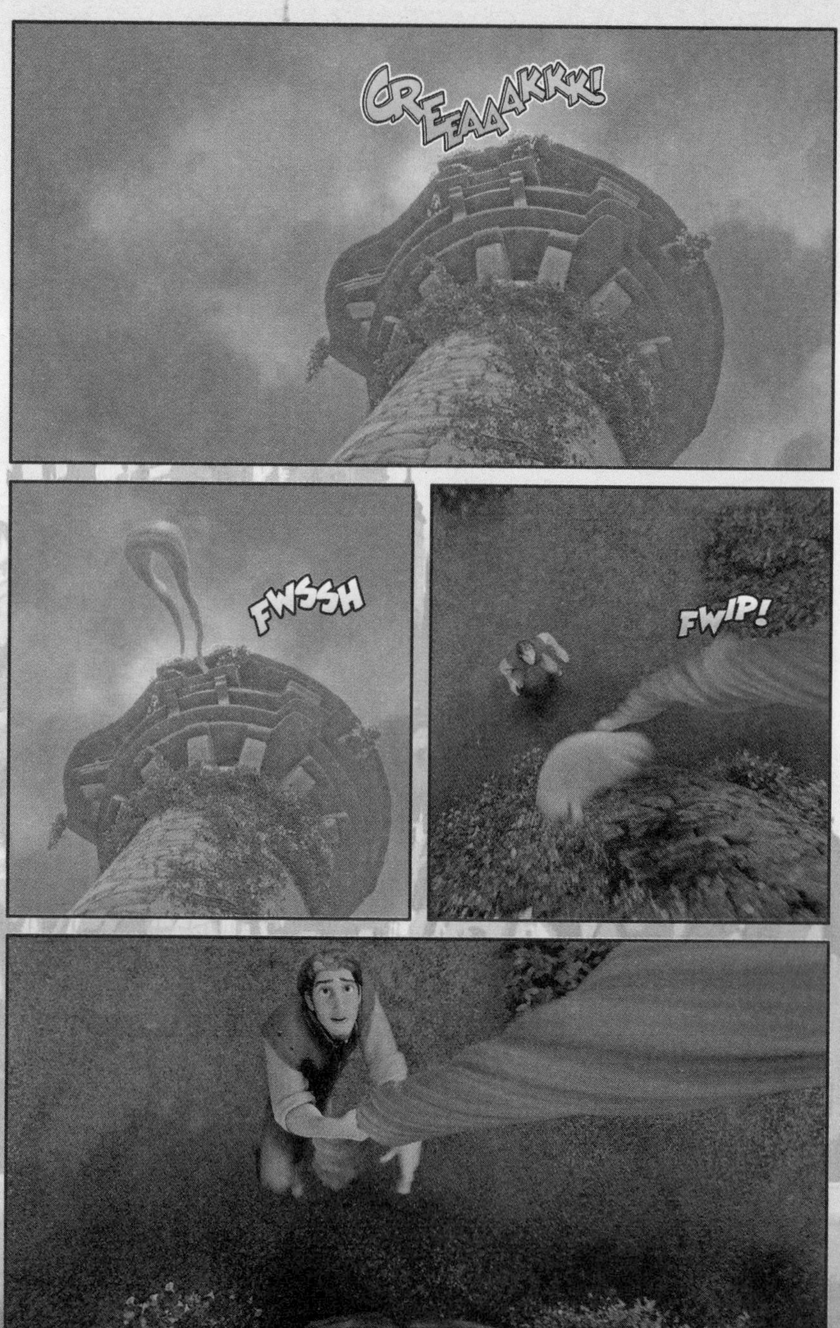
CREEAAAKKK!
FWSSH
FWIP!

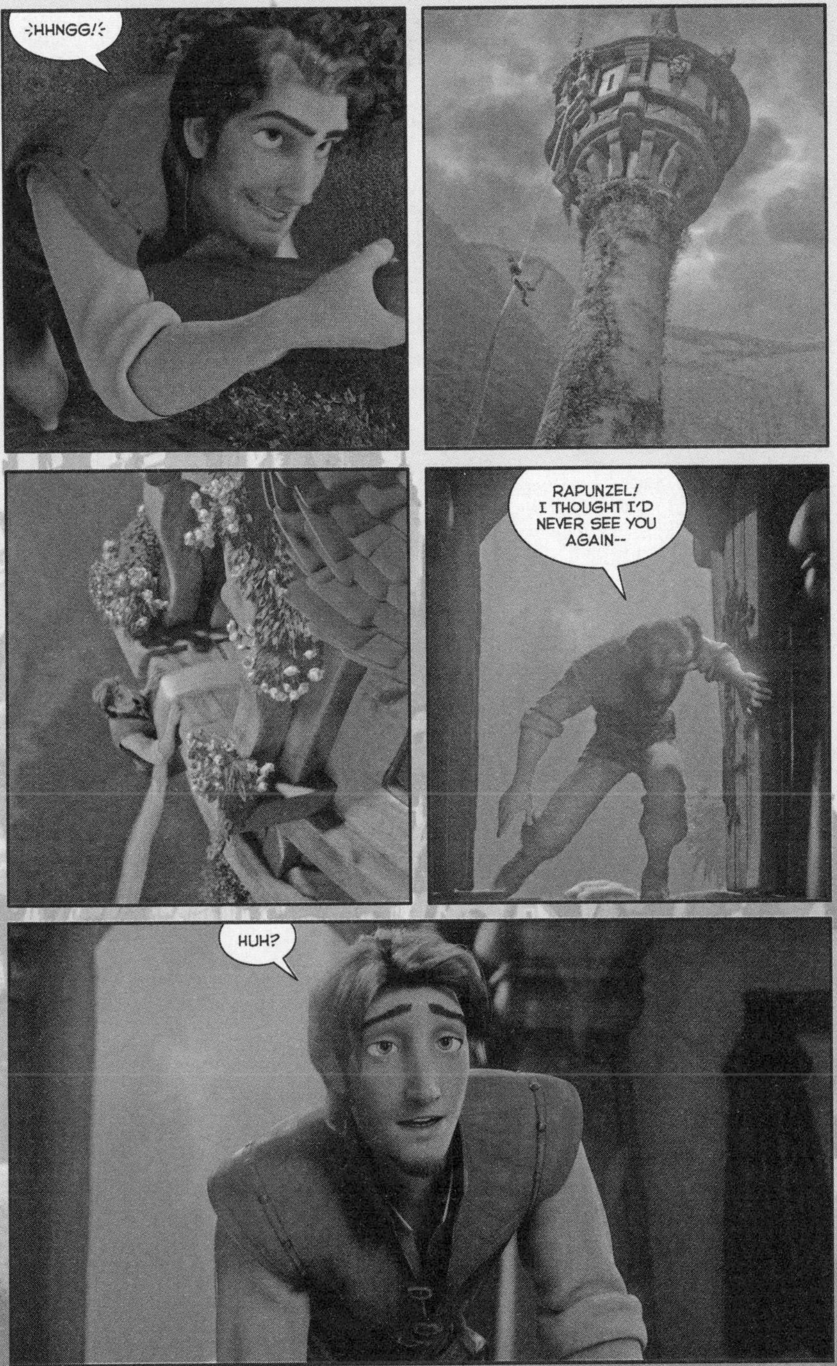
HHNGG!
RAPUNZEL! I THOUGHT I'D NEVER SEE YOU AGAIN--
HUH?

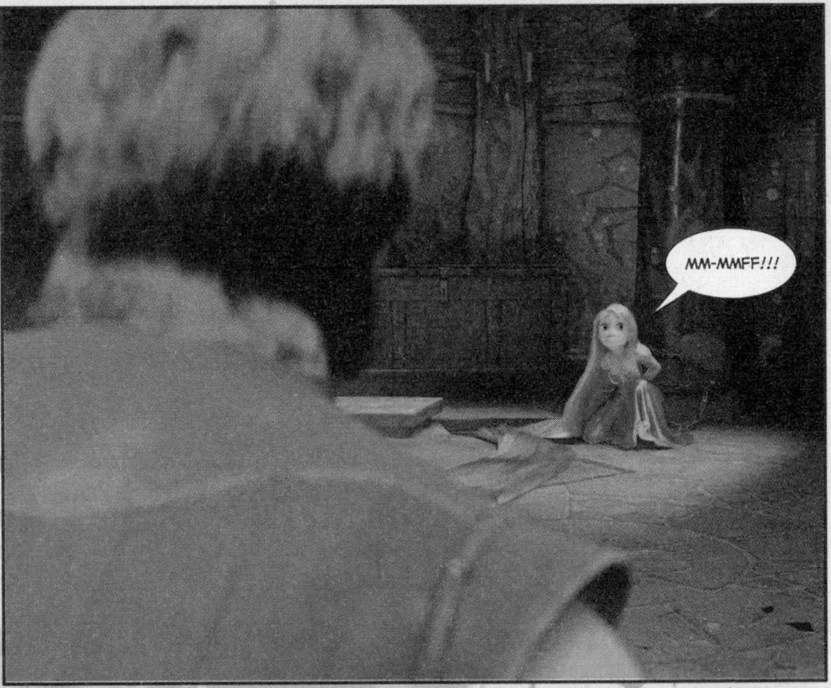
MM-MMFF!!!

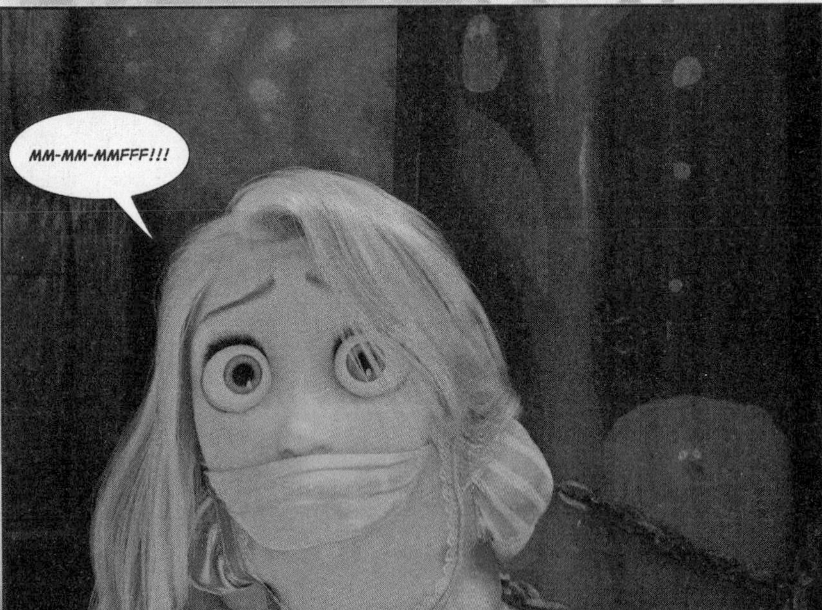
MM-MM-MMFFF!!!

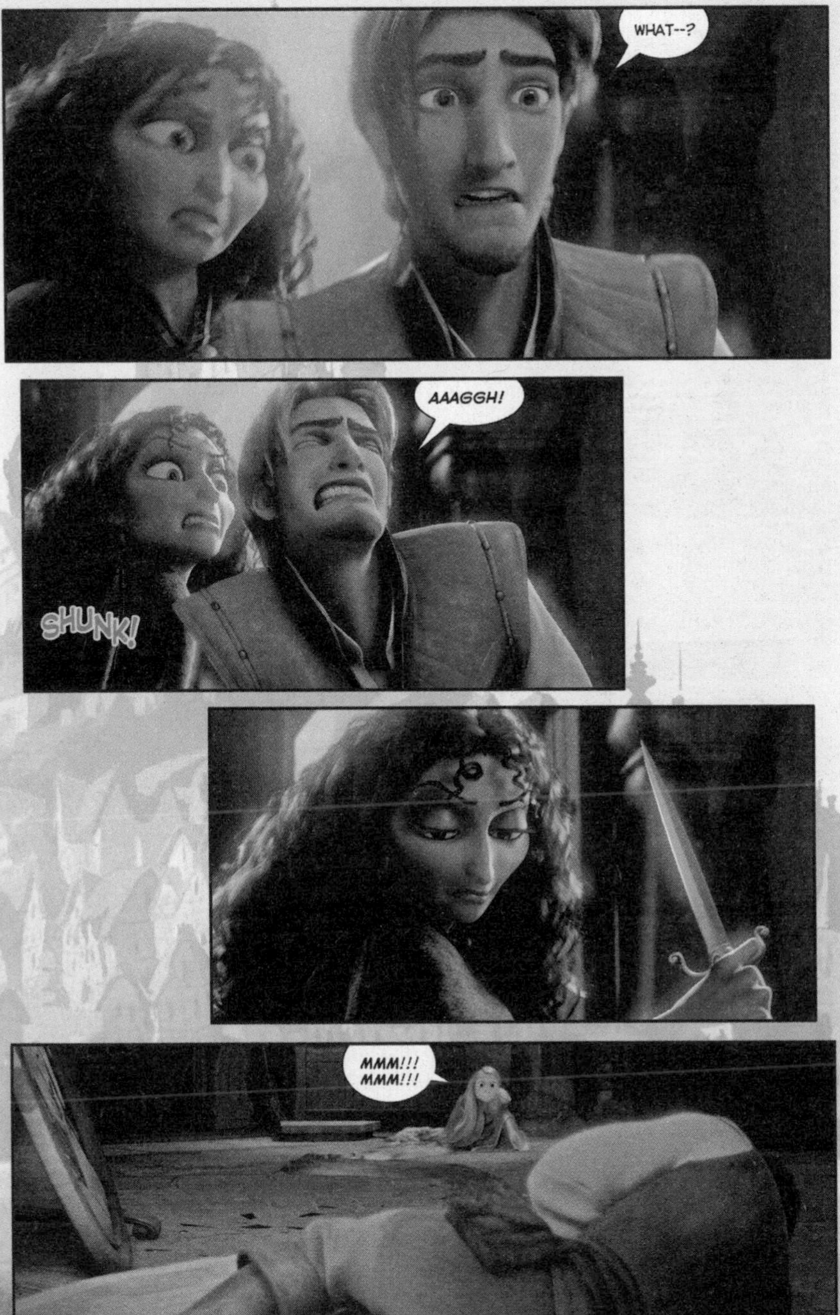
WHAT--?
AAAGGH!
SHUNK!
MMM!!!
MMM!!!

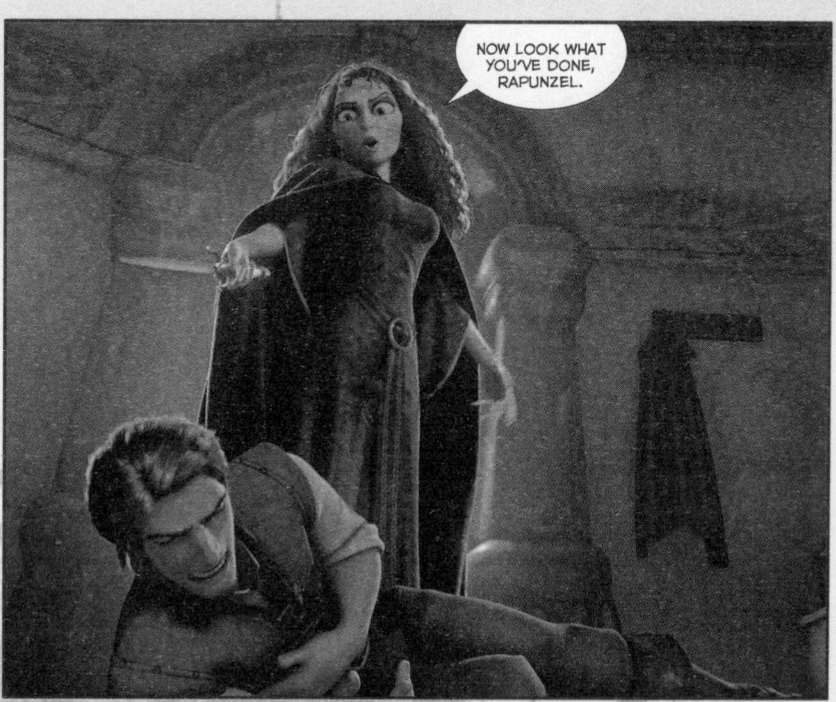
NOW LOOK WHAT YOU'VE DONE, RAPUNZEL.

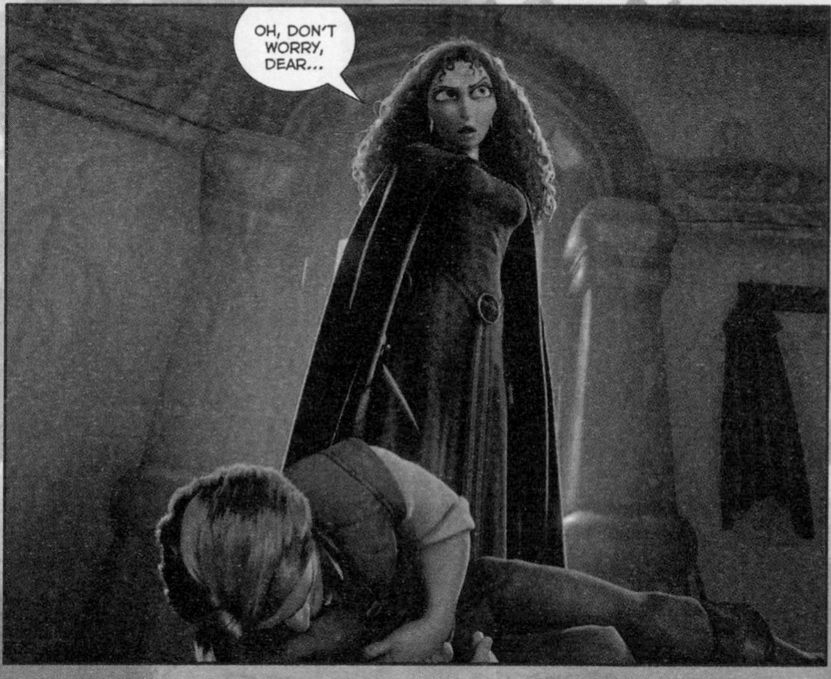
OH, DON'T WORRY, DEAR...

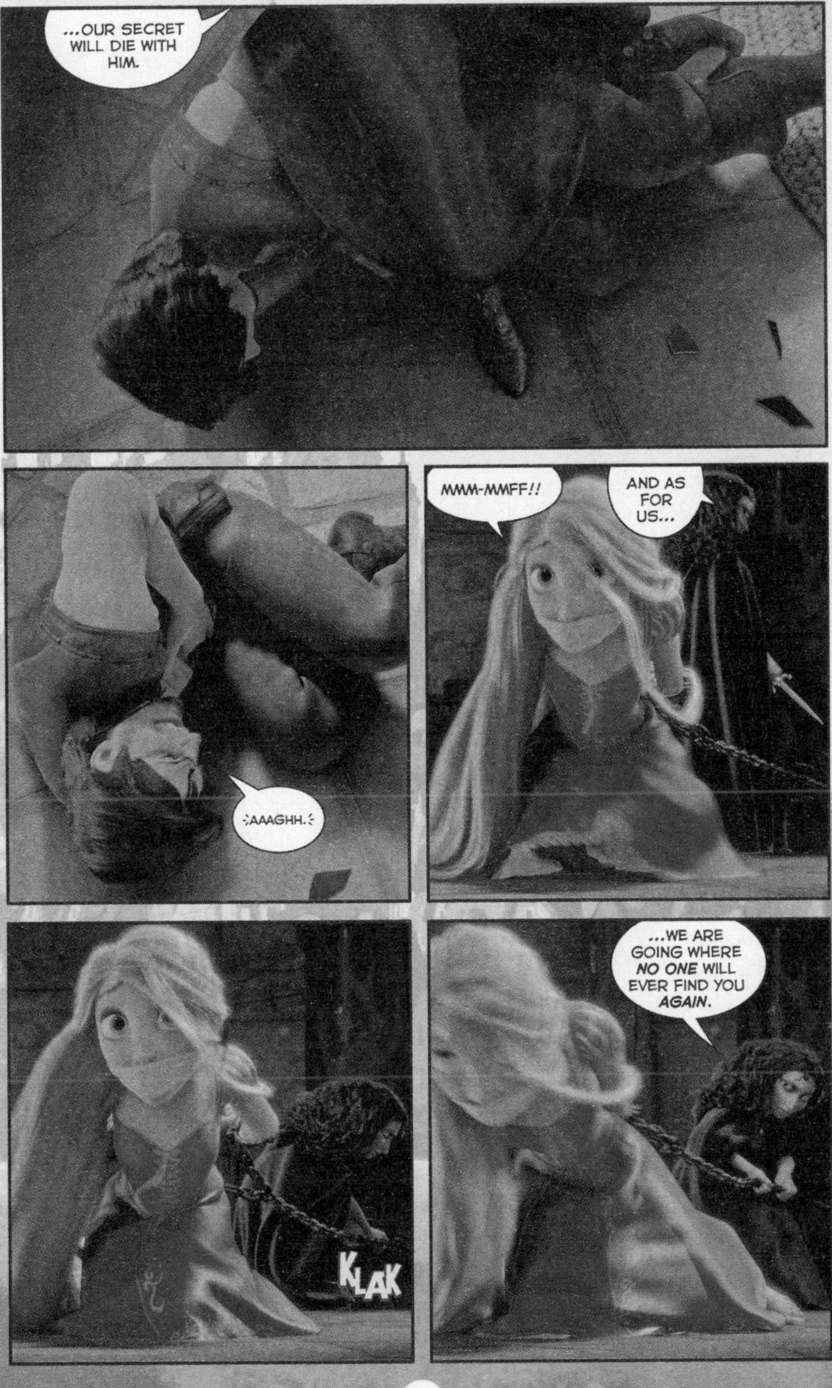
...OUR SECRET WILL DIE WITH HIM.
AAAGHH.
MMM-MMFF!!
AND AS FOR US...
KLAK
...WE ARE GOING WHERE NO ONE WILL EVER FIND YOU AGAIN.

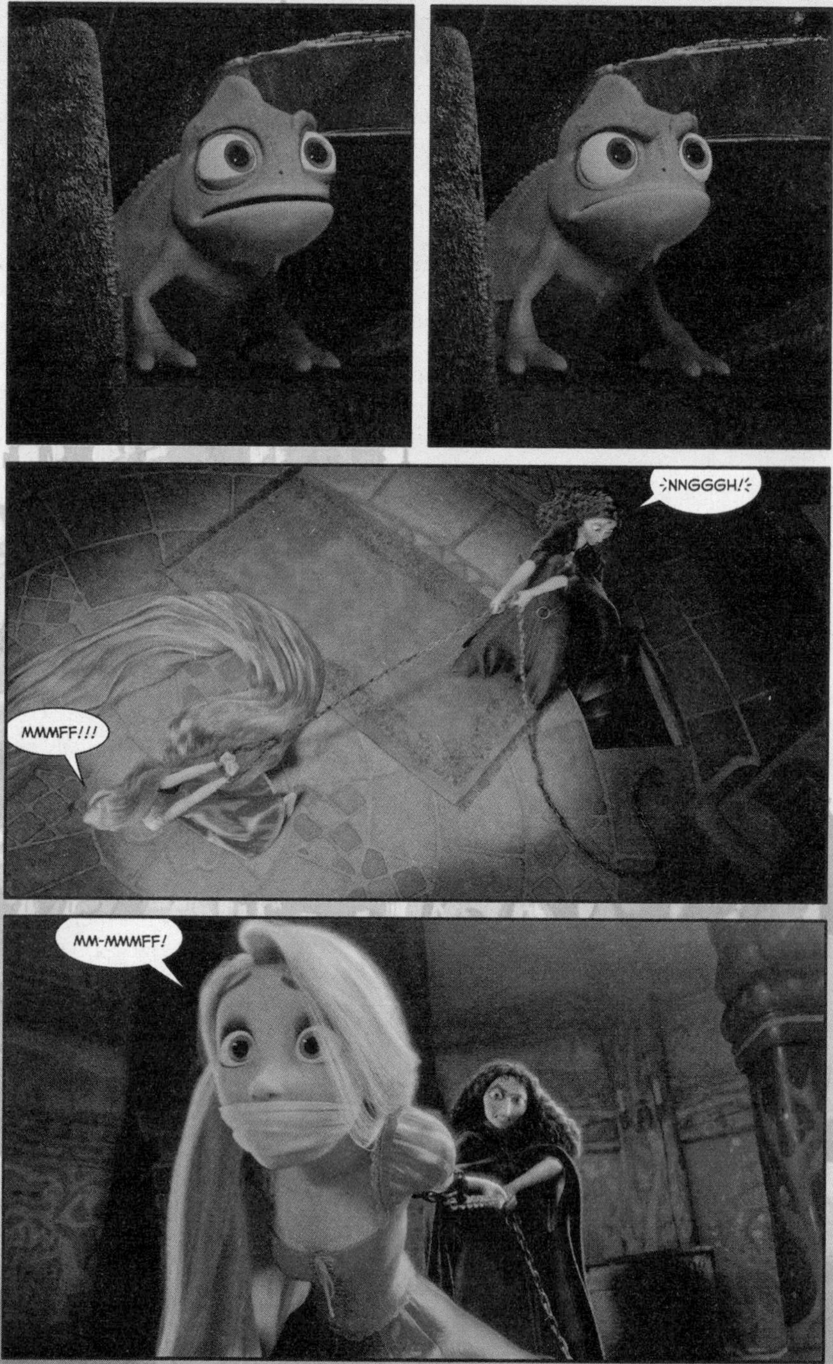
NNGGGH!
MMMFF!!!
MM-MMMFF!

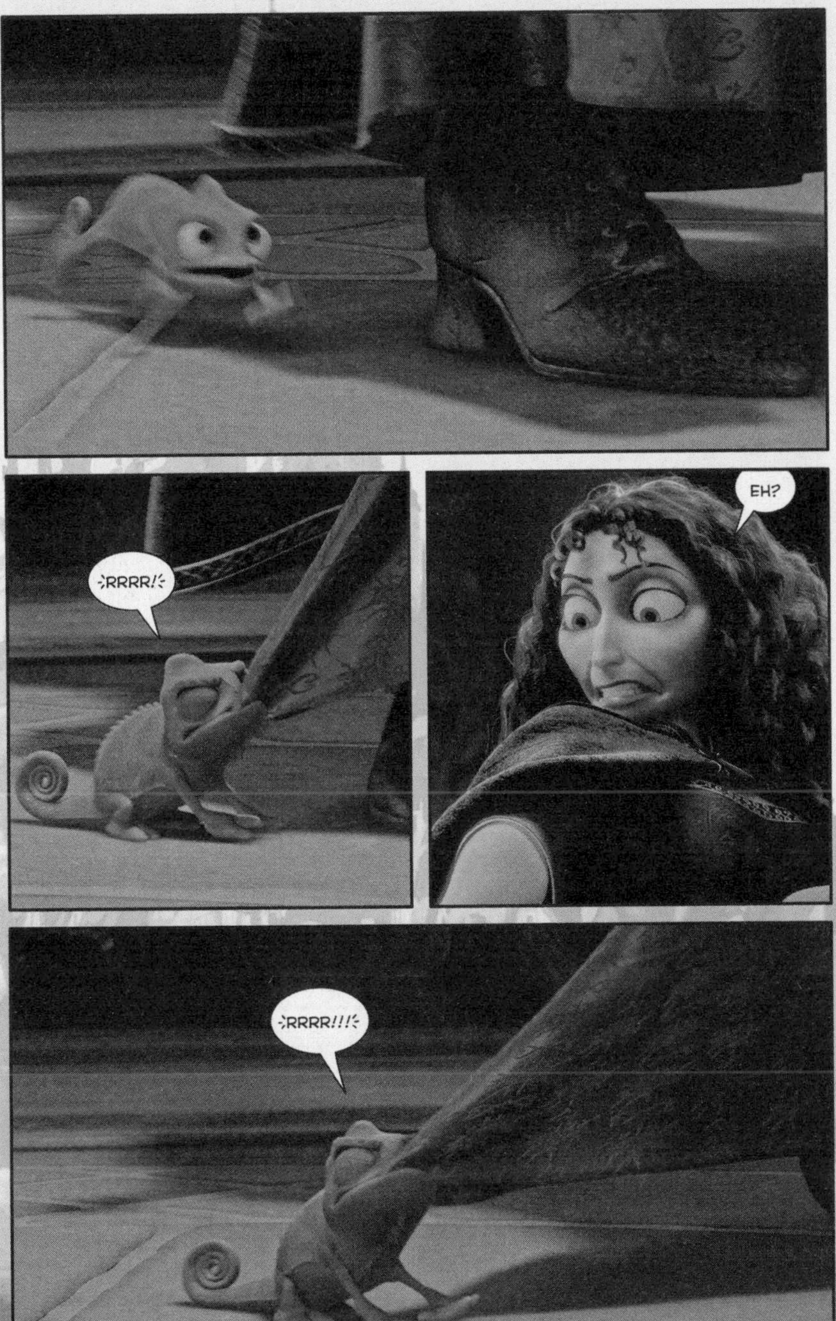
RRRR!
EH?
RRRR!!!

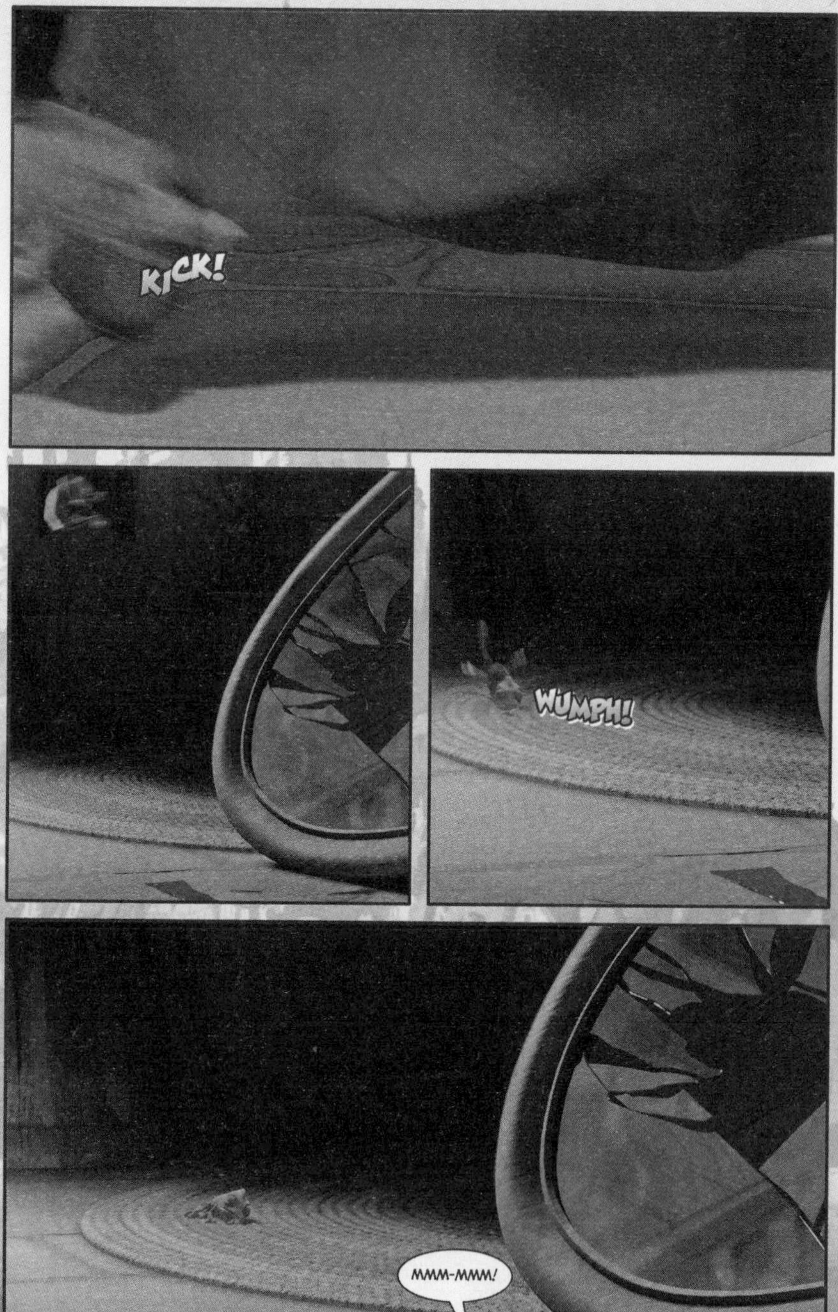
KICK!
WUMPH!
MMM-MMM!

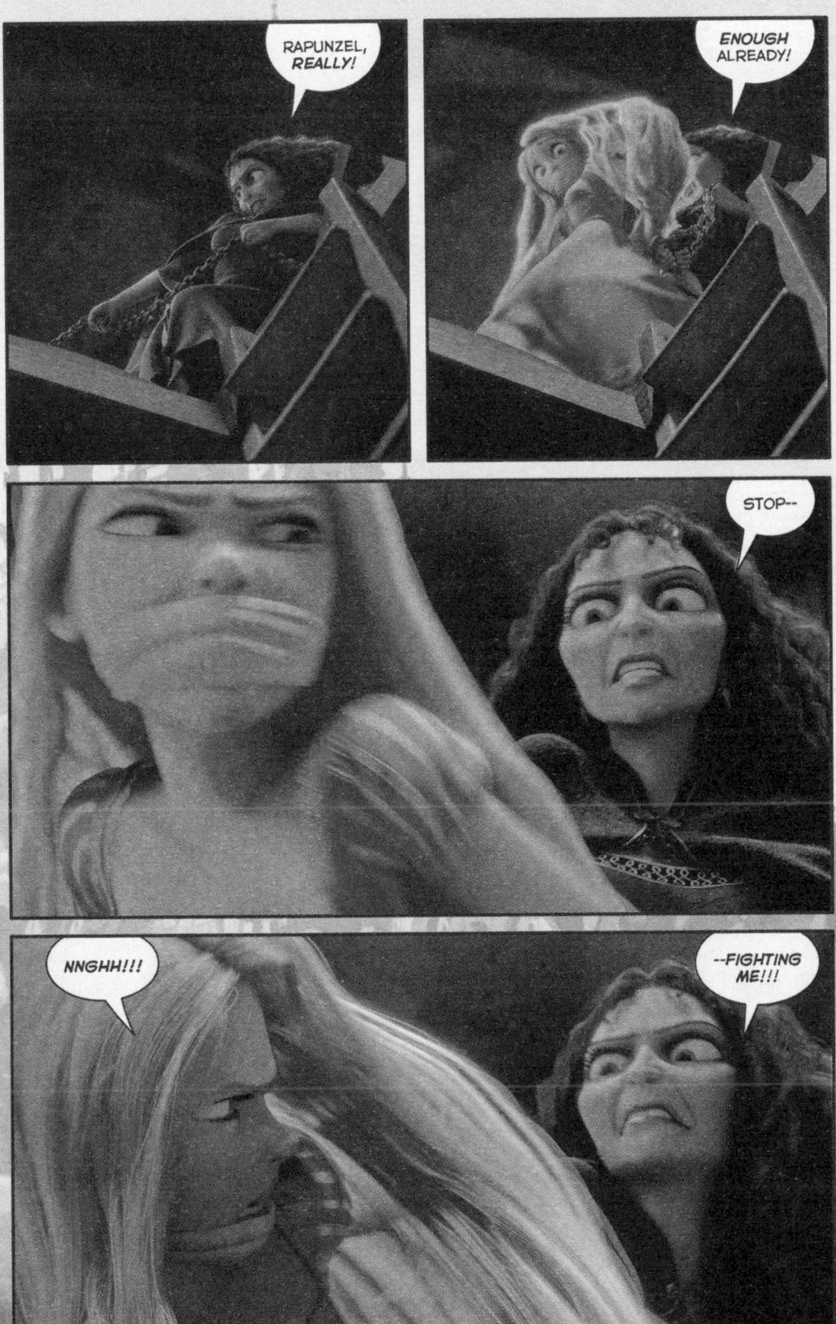
RAPUNZEL, REALLY!
ENOUGH ALREADY!
STOP--
NNGHH!!!
--FIGHTING ME!!!

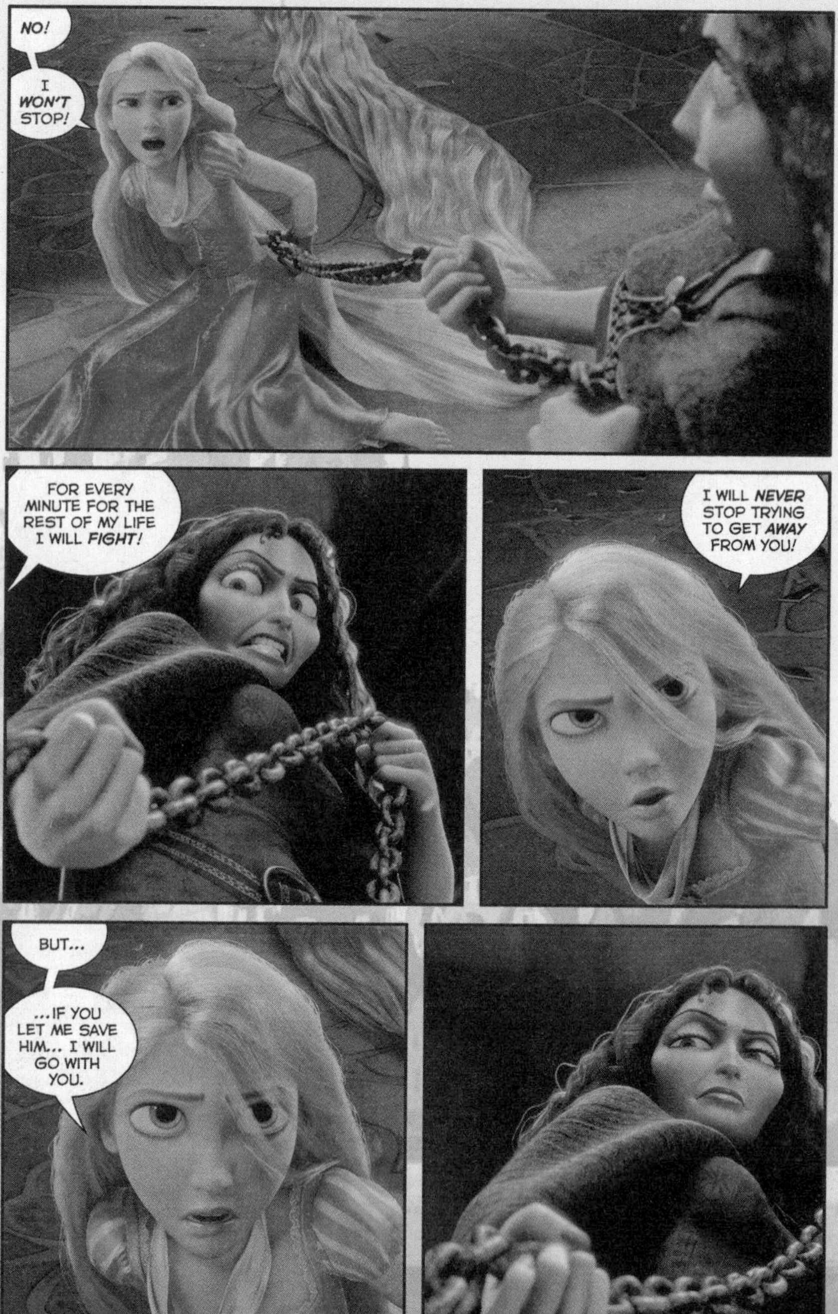
NO!
I WON'T STOP!
FOR EVERY MINUTE FOR THE REST OF MY LIFE I WILL FIGHT!
I WILL NEVER STOP TRYING TO GET AWAY FROM YOU!
BUT...
...IF YOU LET ME SAVE HIM... I WILL GO WITH YOU.

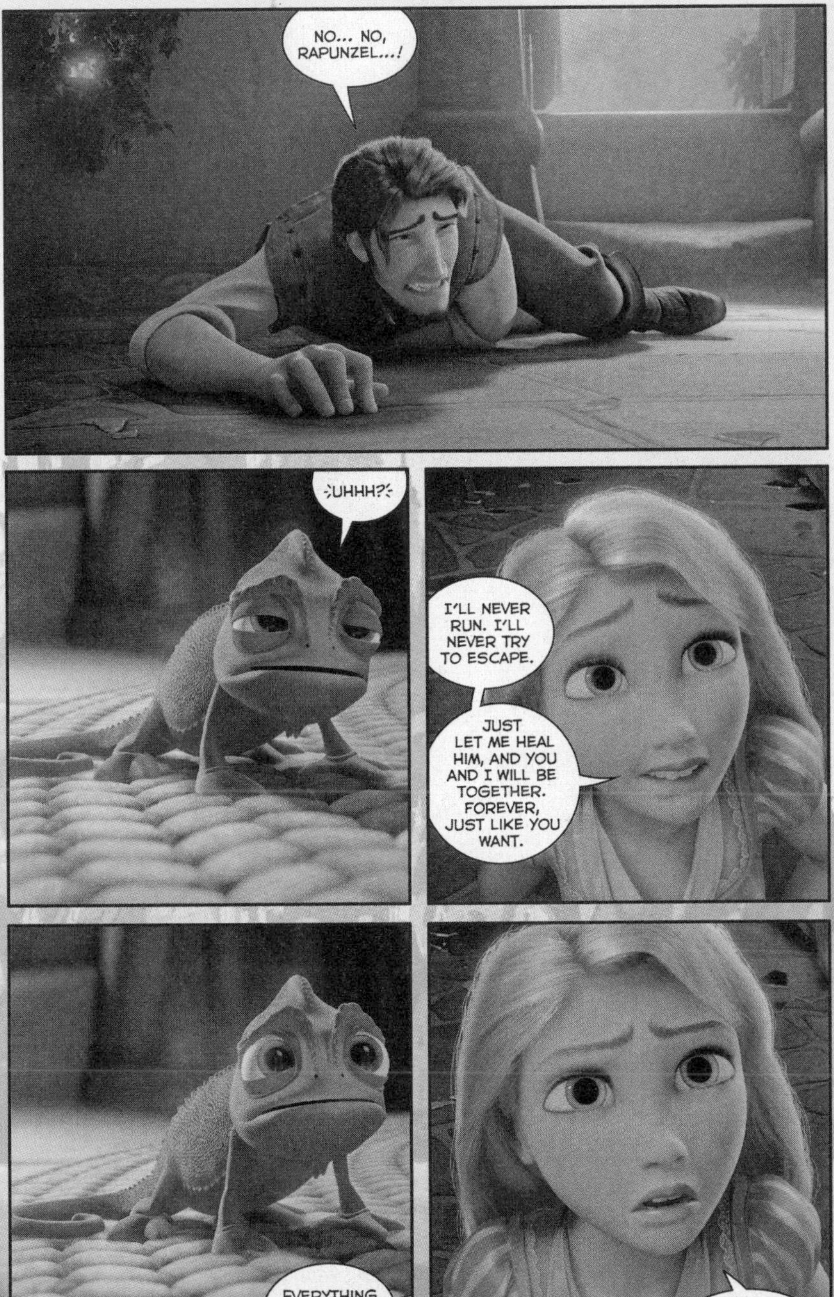
NO... NO, RAPUNZEL...!
UHHH?
I'LL NEVER RUN. I'LL NEVER TRY TO ESCAPE.
JUST LET ME HEAL HIM, AND YOU AND I WILL BE TOGETHER. FOREVER, JUST LIKE YOU WANT.
EVERYTHING WILL BE THE WAY IT WAS...
...I PROMISE.

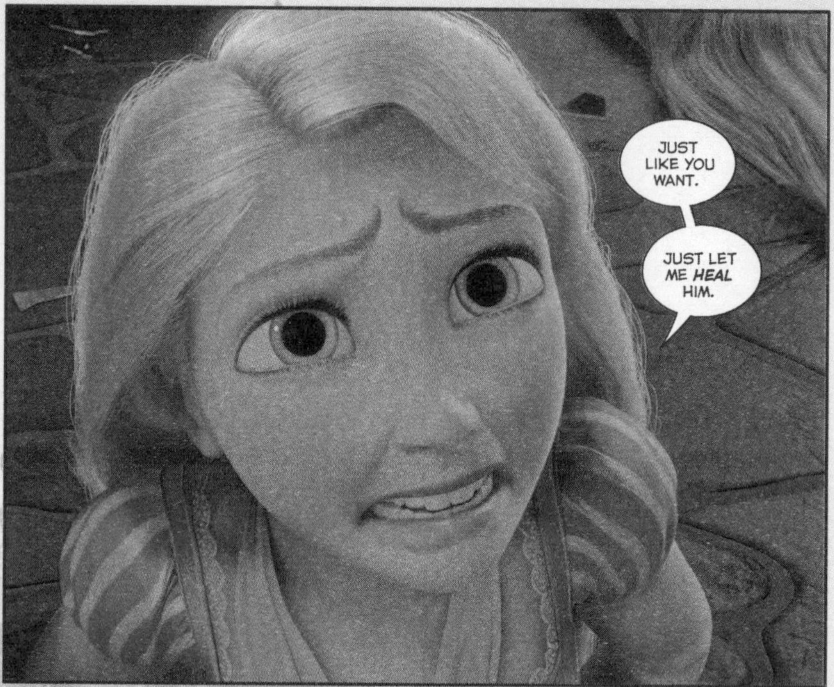
JUST LIKE YOU WANT.
JUST LET ME *HEAL* HIM.

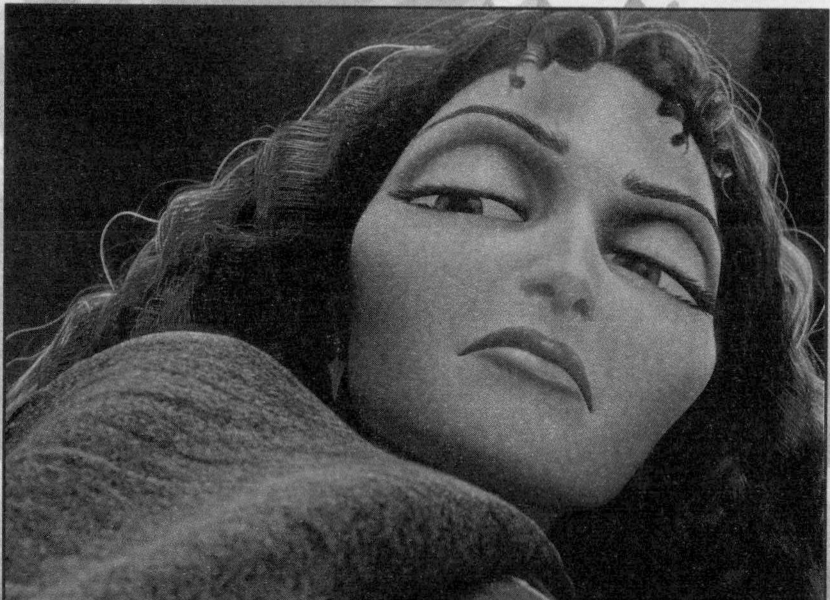

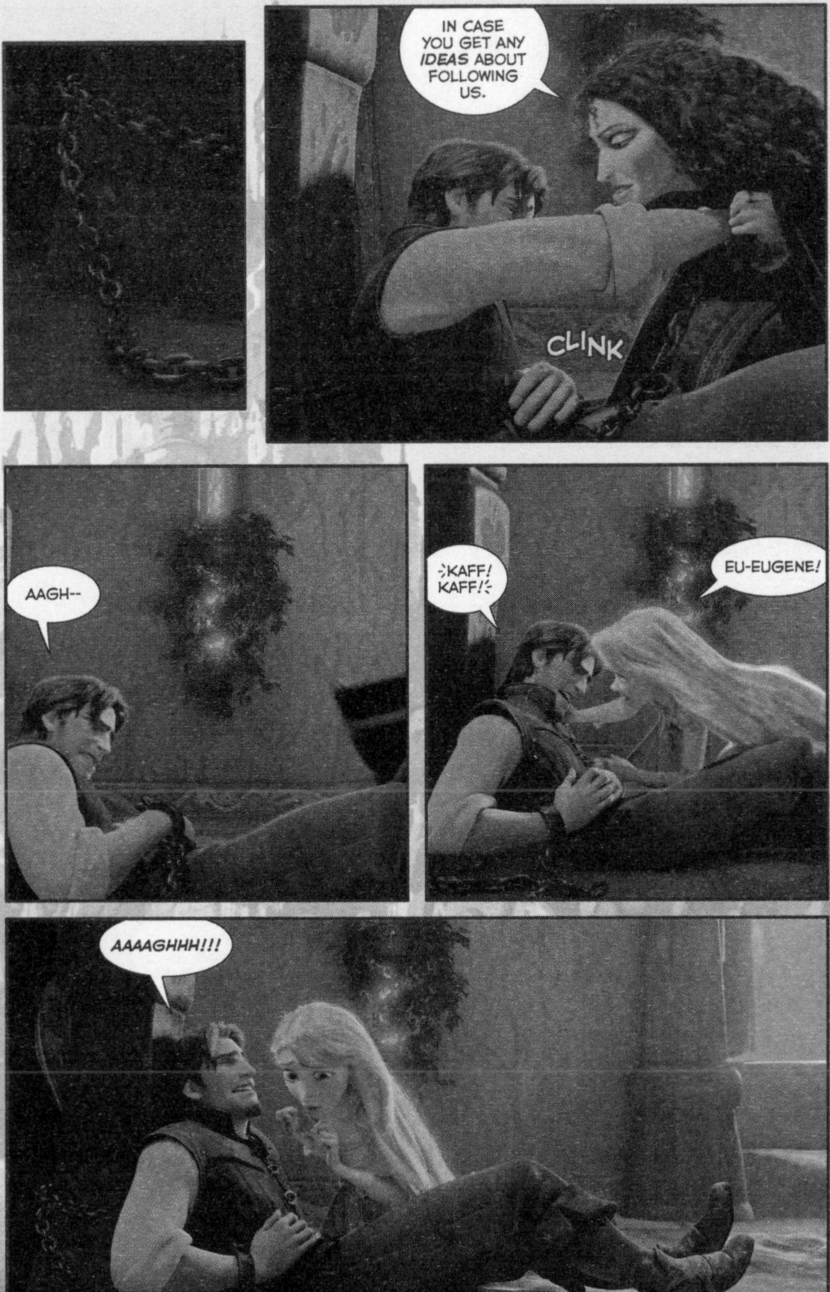
IN CASE YOU GET ANY IDEAS ABOUT FOLLOWING US.
CLINK
AAGH--
KAFF! KAFF!
EU-EUGENE!
AAAAGHHH!!!

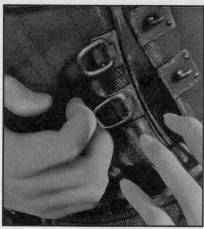

I'M SO SORRY. EVERYTHING'S GOING TO BE OKAY--

NO... RAPUNZEL...

I PROMISE. YOU HAVE TO TRUST ME. JUST BREATHE...

I CAN'T LET YOU DO THIS.

I CAN'T LET YOU DIE.

BUT IF YOU DO THIS... THEN *YOU* WILL DIE.

SHH, SHH, SHH! HEY, IT'S GONNA BE ALL RIGHT.

I'LL BE FINE. IF YOU'RE OKAY, I'LL BE FINE.

RAPUNZEL, WAIT...

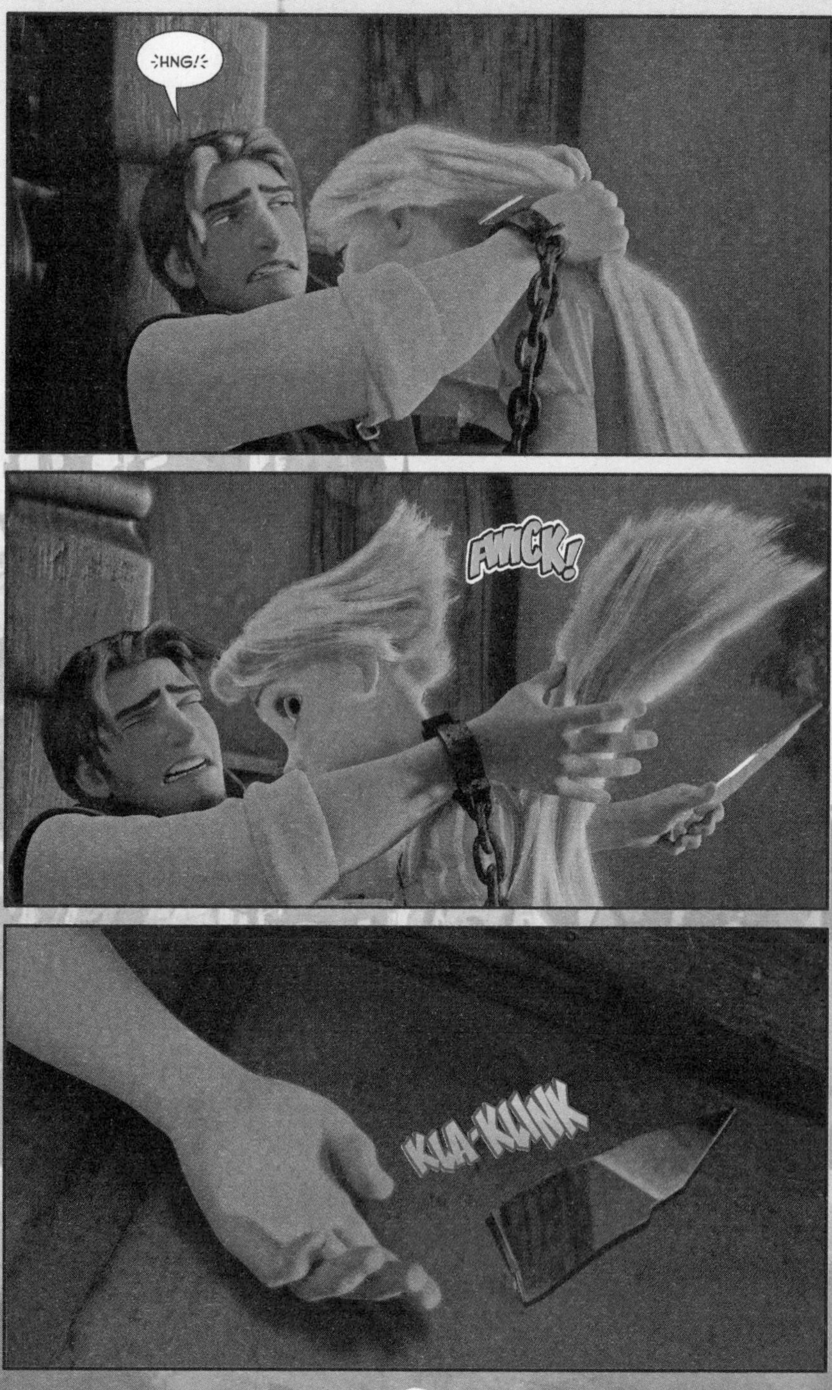
HNG!
FWICK!
KLA-KLINK

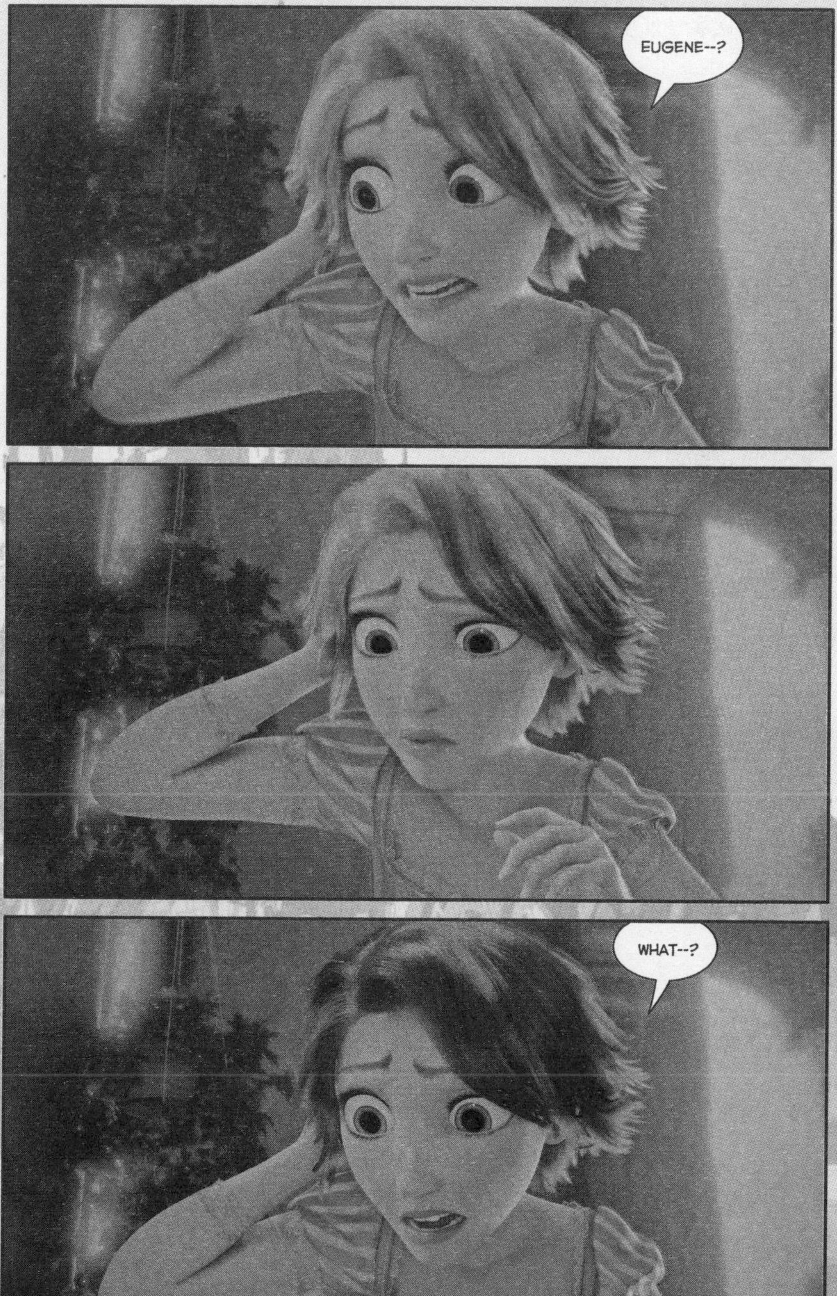
EUGENE--?
WHAT--?

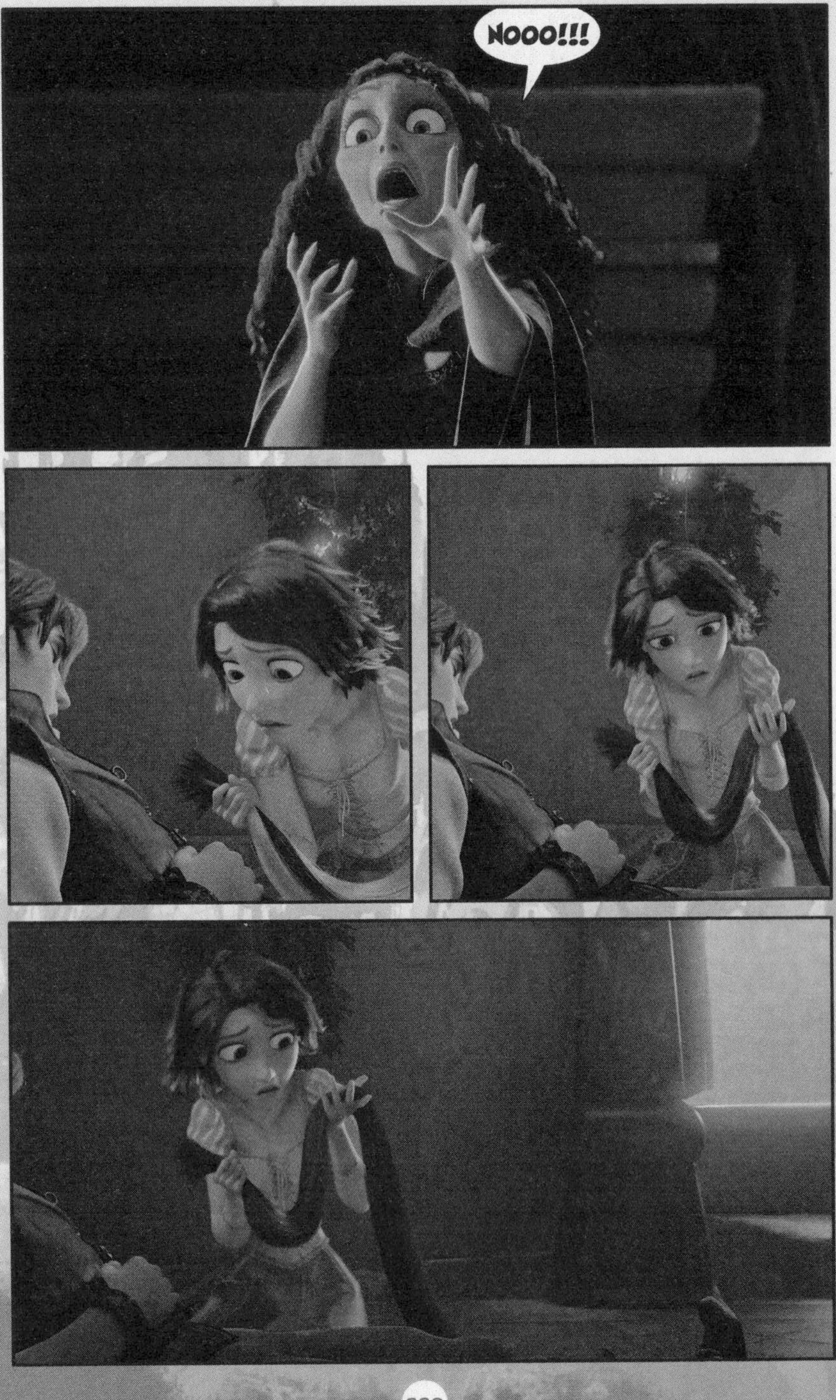
NOOO!!!

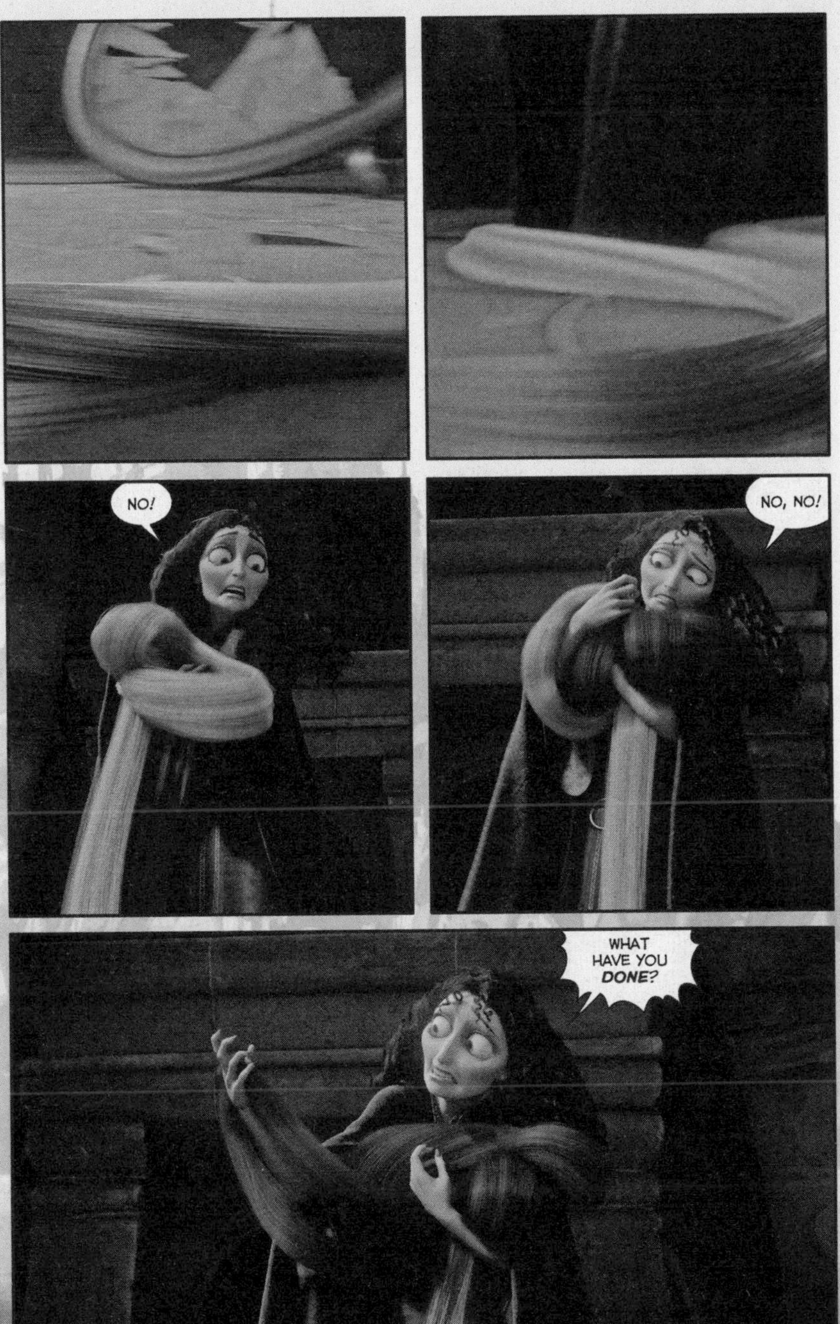
NO!
NO, NO!
WHAT HAVE YOU DONE?

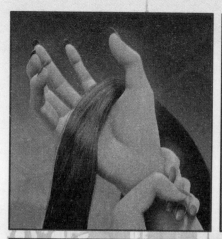

WHAT HAVE YOU DONE?!

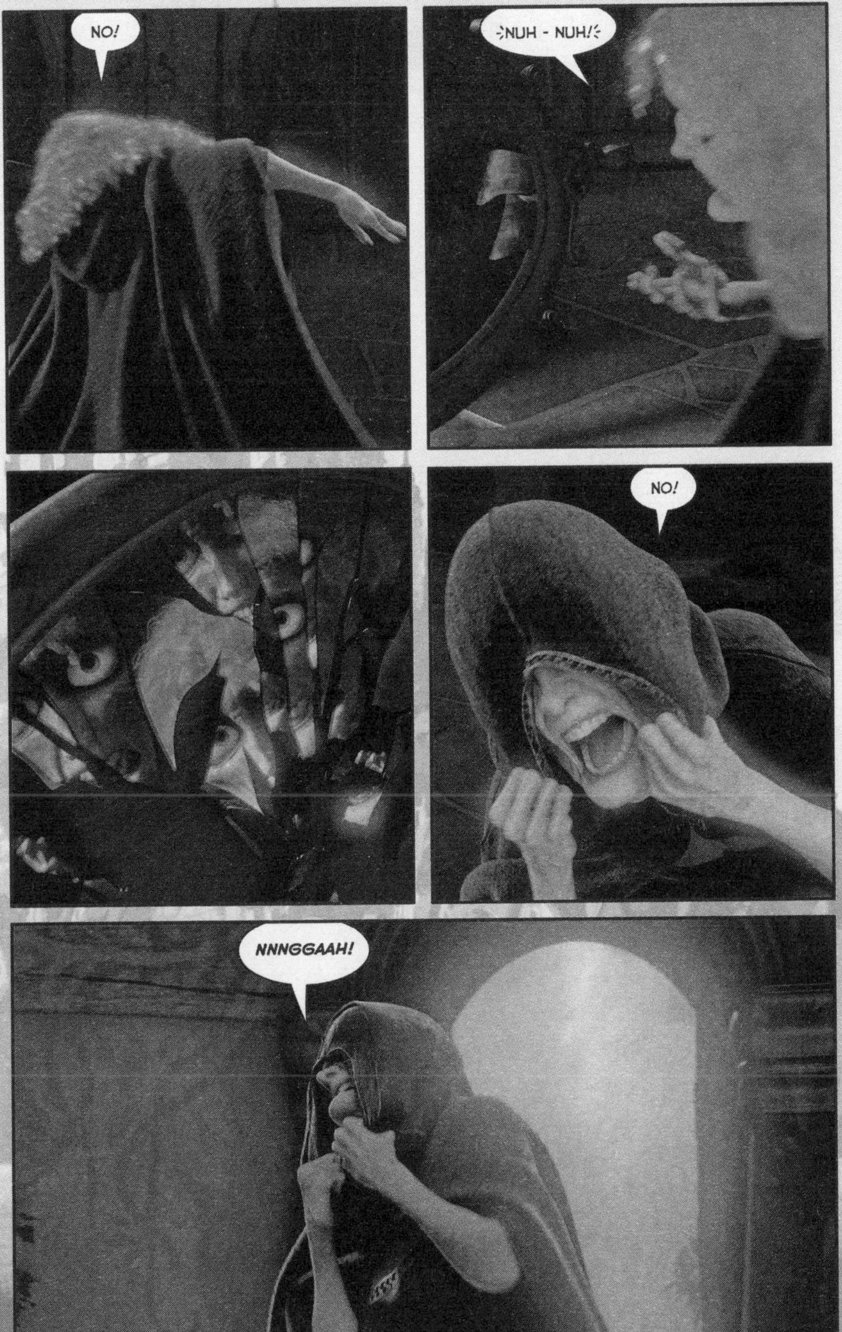
NO!
NUH - NUH!
NO!
NNNGGAAH!

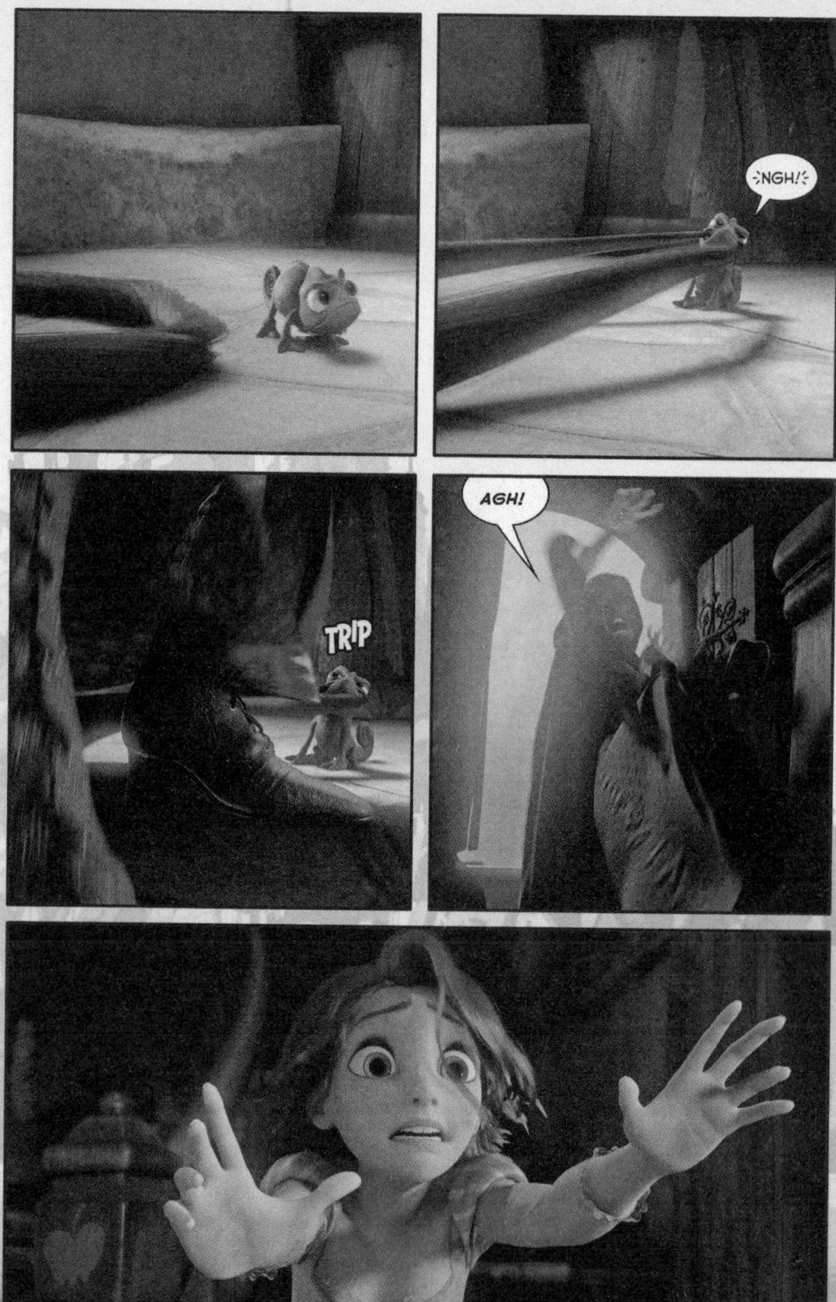
NGH!
TRIP
AGH!

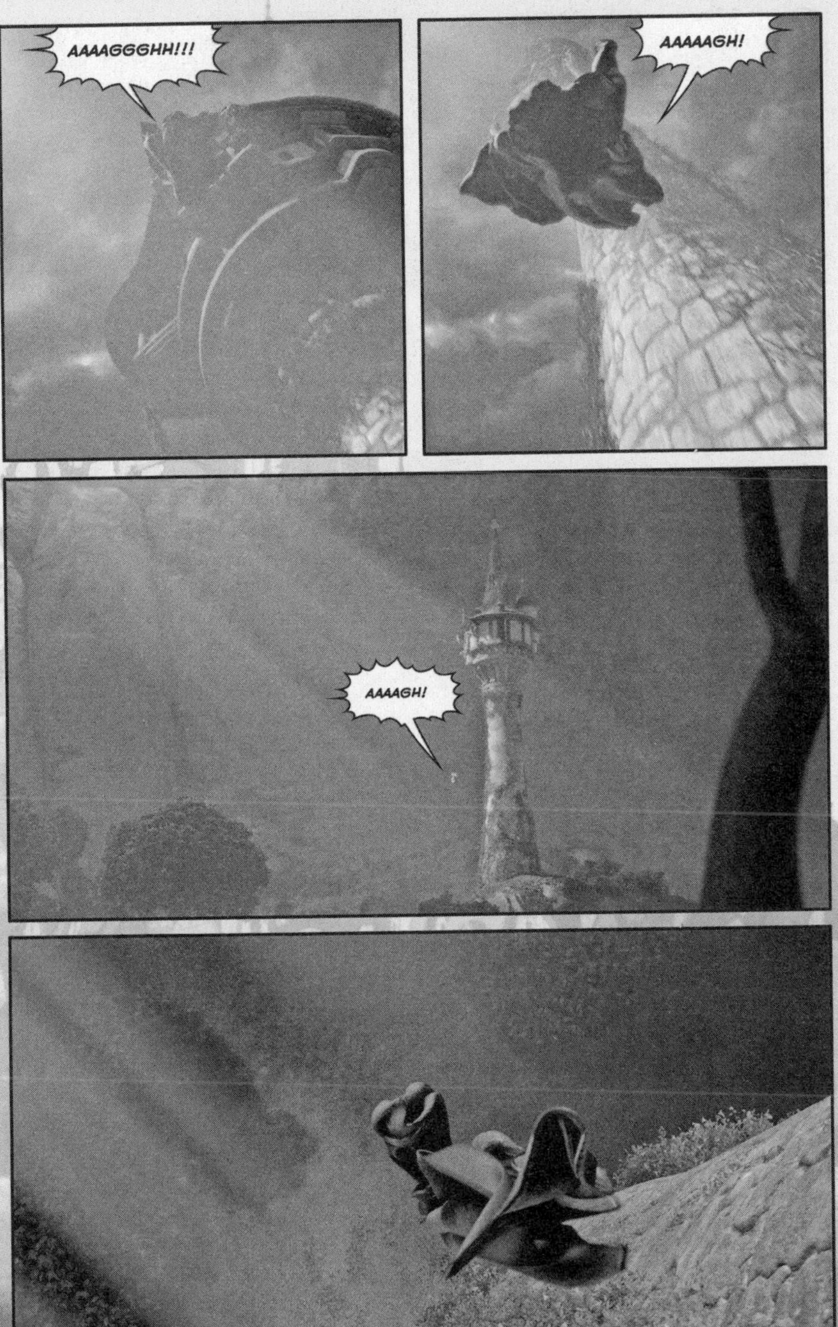
AAAAGGGHH!!!
AAAAAGH!
AAAAGH!

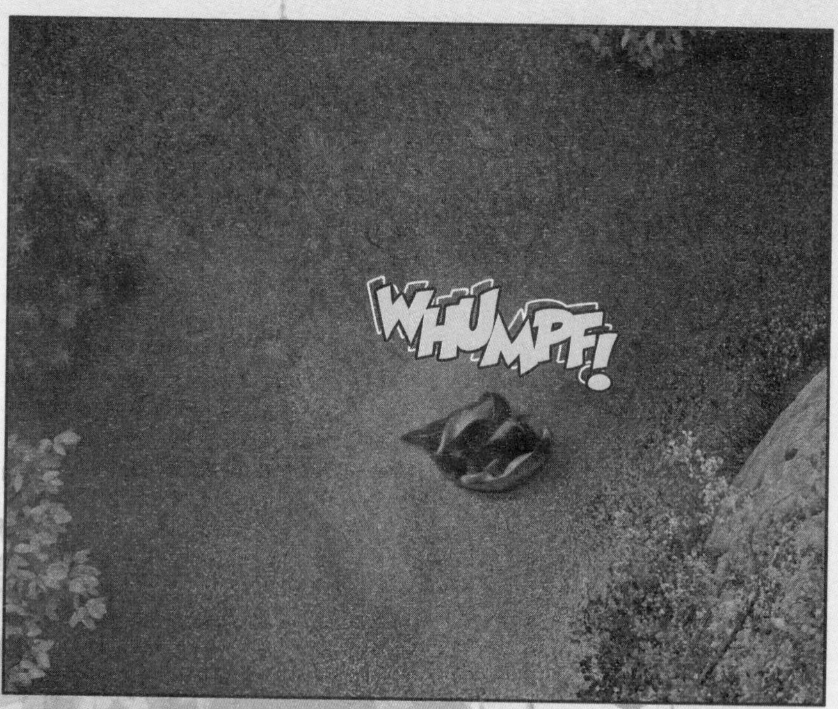
WHUMPF!

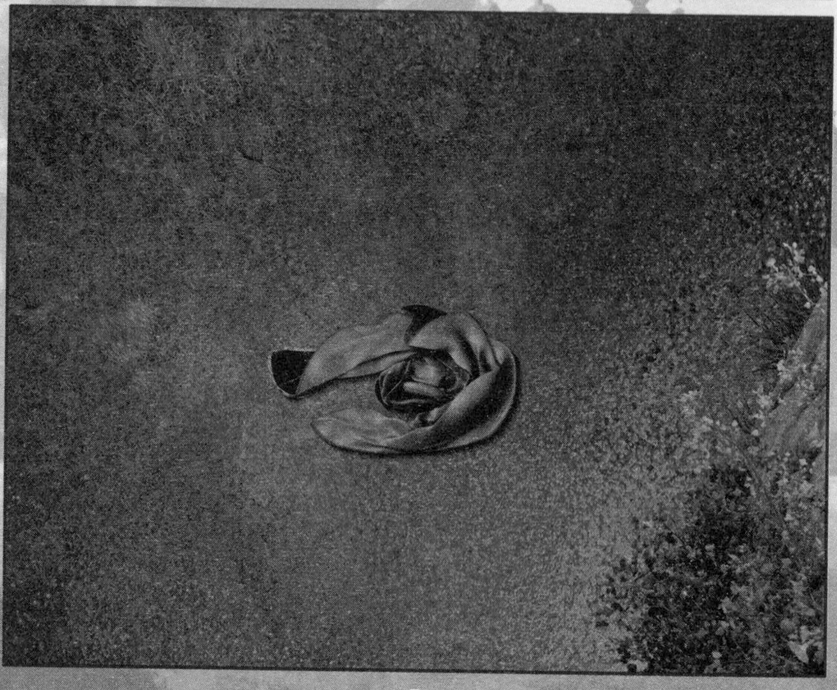

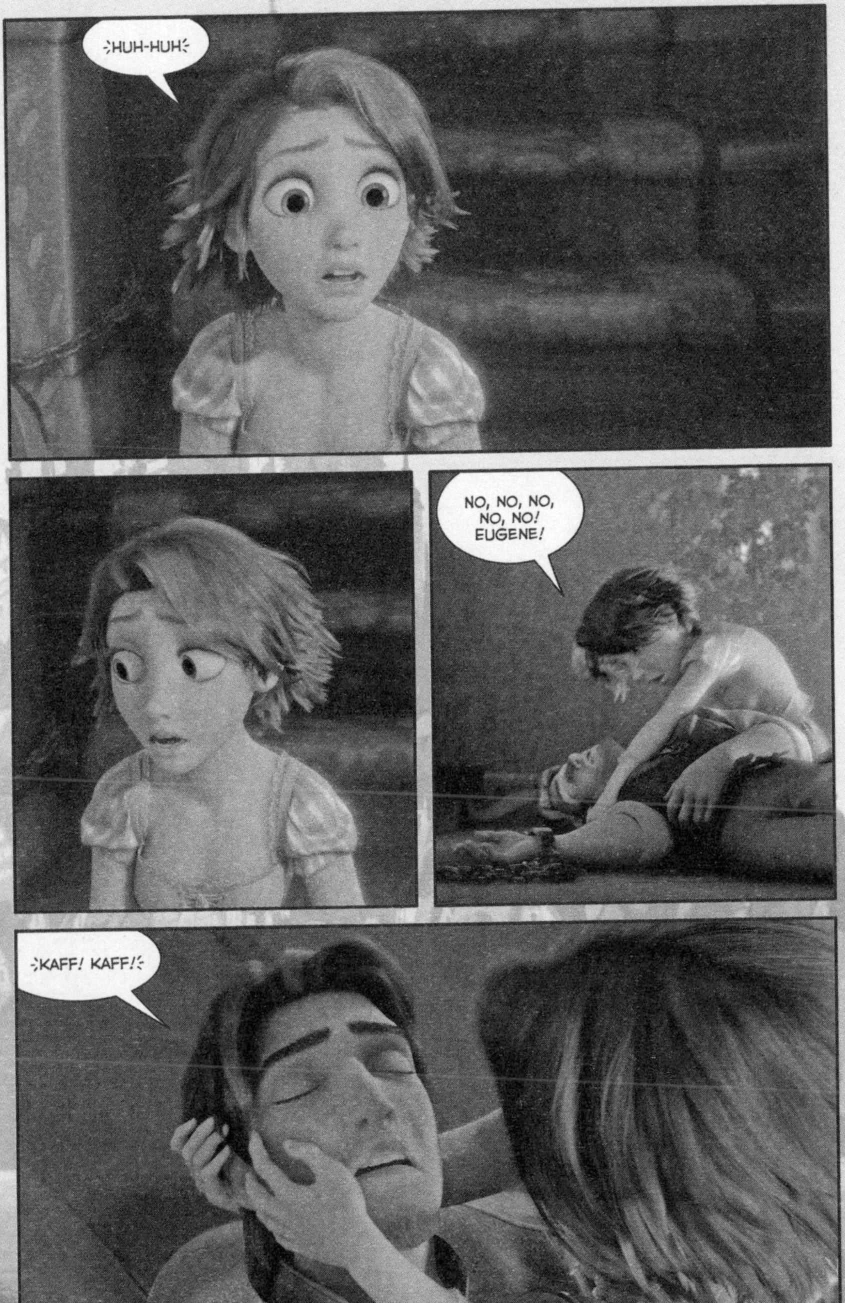
HUH-HUH
NO, NO, NO, NO, NO! EUGENE!
KAFF! KAFF!

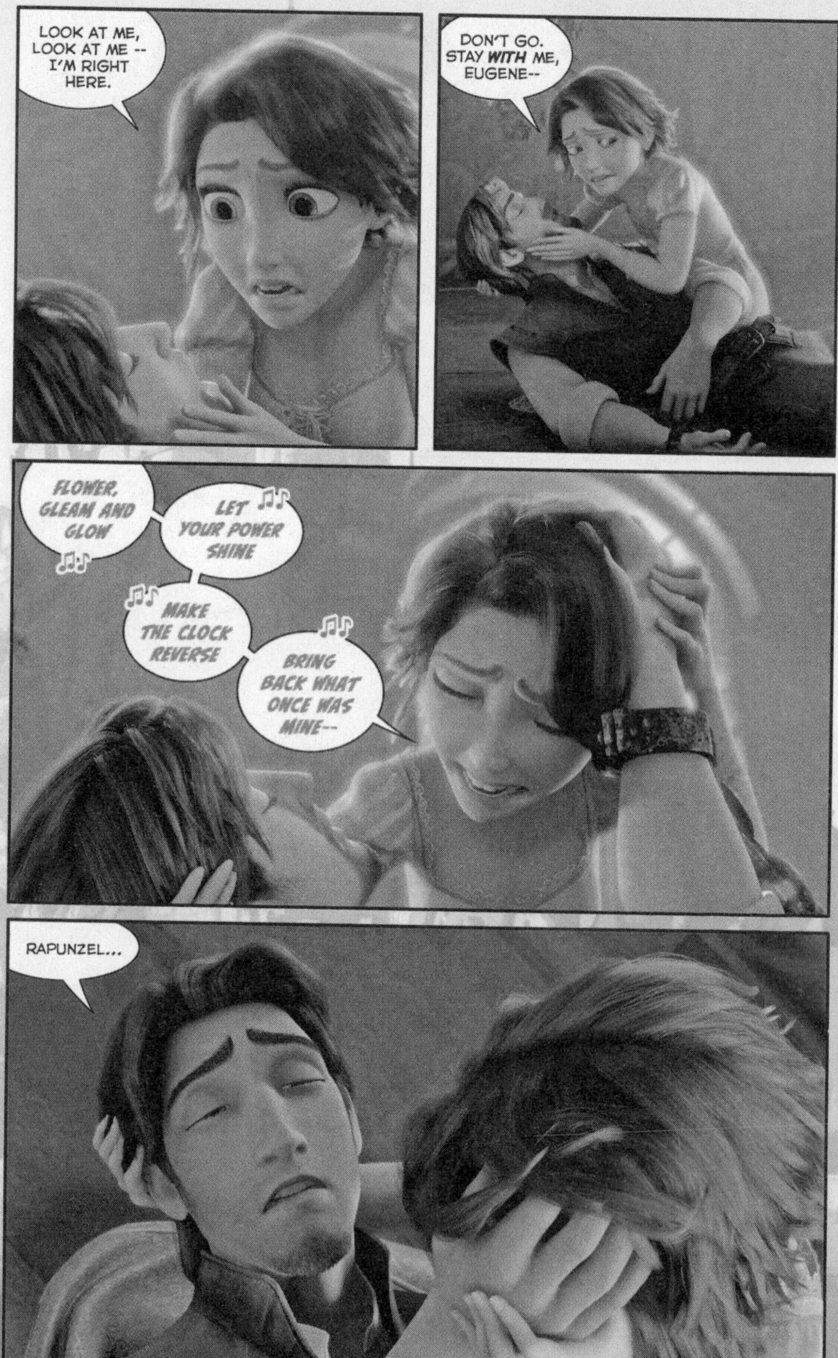
LOOK AT ME, LOOK AT ME -- I'M RIGHT HERE.
DON'T GO. STAY WITH ME, EUGENE--
FLOWER, GLEAM AND GLOW
LET YOUR POWER SHINE
MAKE THE CLOCK REVERSE
BRING BACK WHAT ONCE WAS MINE--
RAPUNZEL...

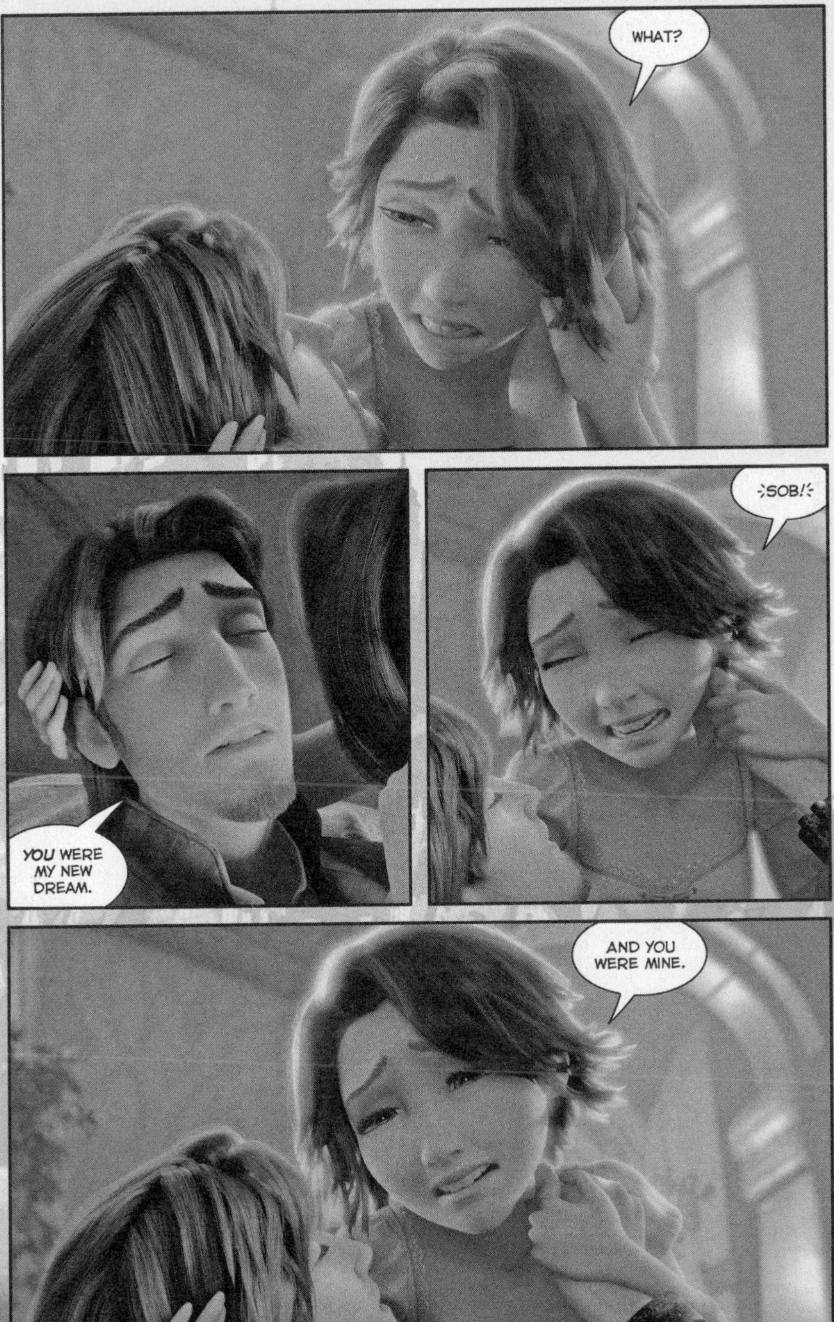
WHAT?
YOU WERE MY NEW DREAM.
SOB!
AND YOU WERE MINE.

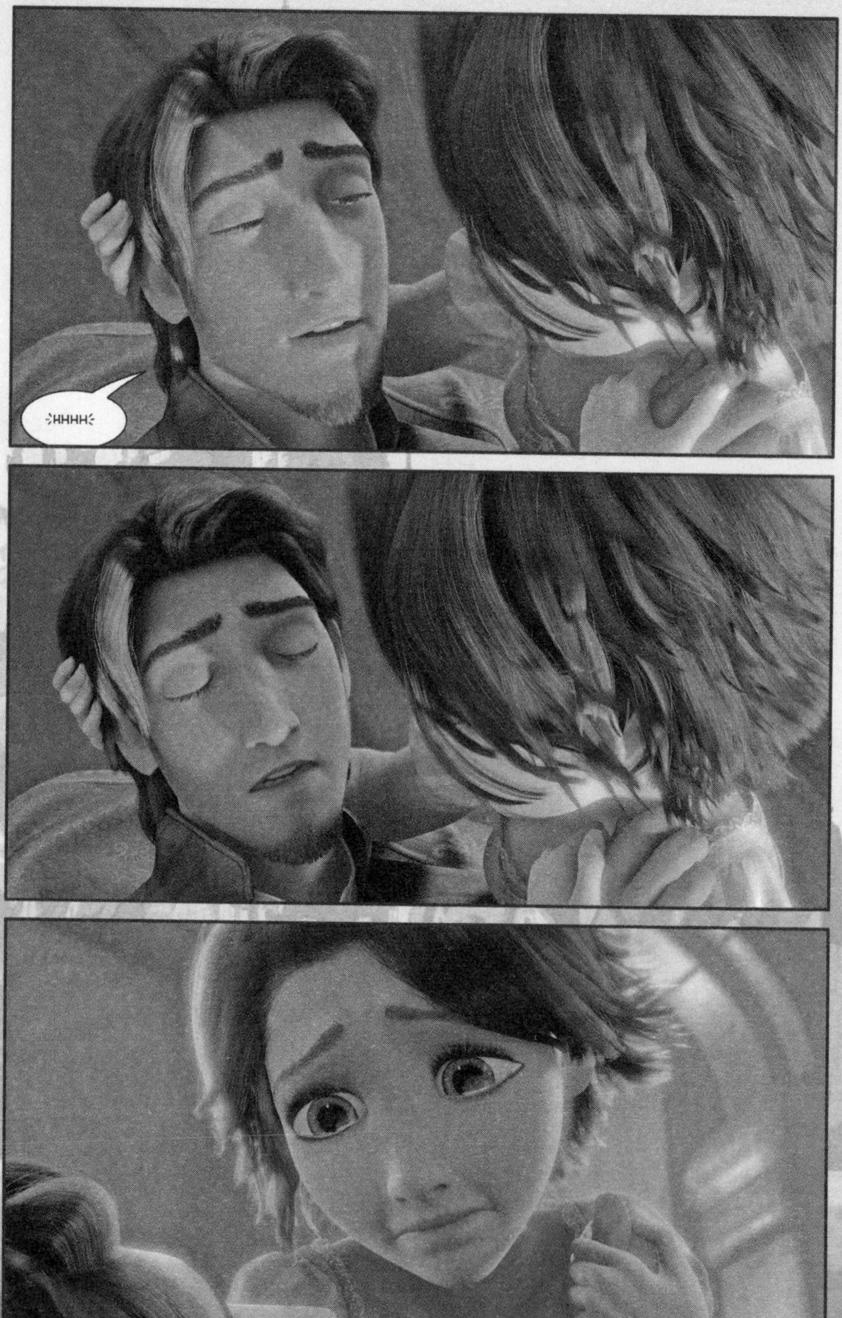
HHHH

HEAL WHAT HAS BEEN HURT
CHANGE THE FATES' DESIGN
SAVE WHAT HAS BEEN LOST
BRING BACK WHAT ONCE WAS MINE
WHAT ONCE WAS MINE
SOB
DRIP!

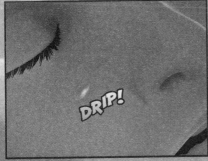

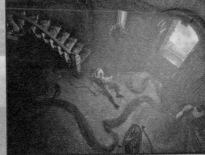

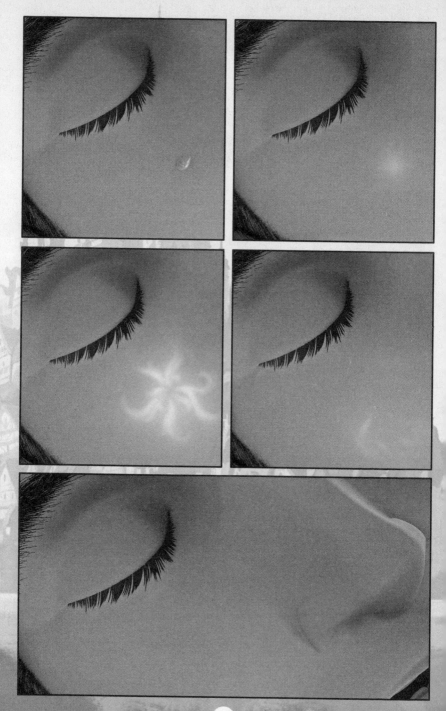

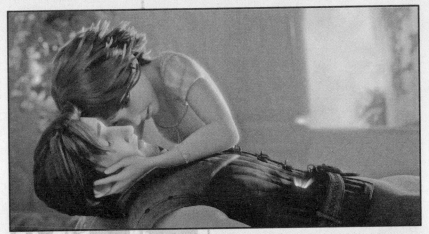

FWOOSH!

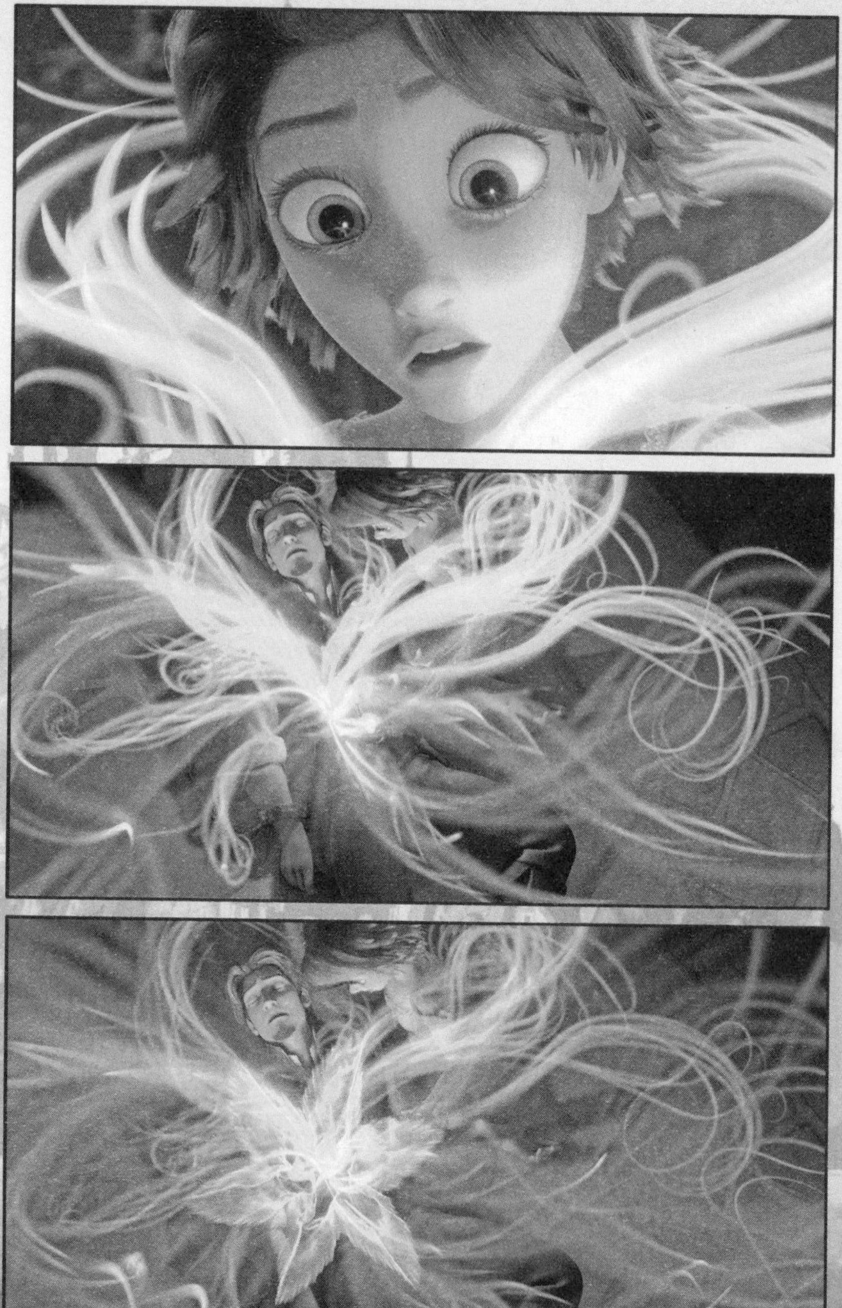

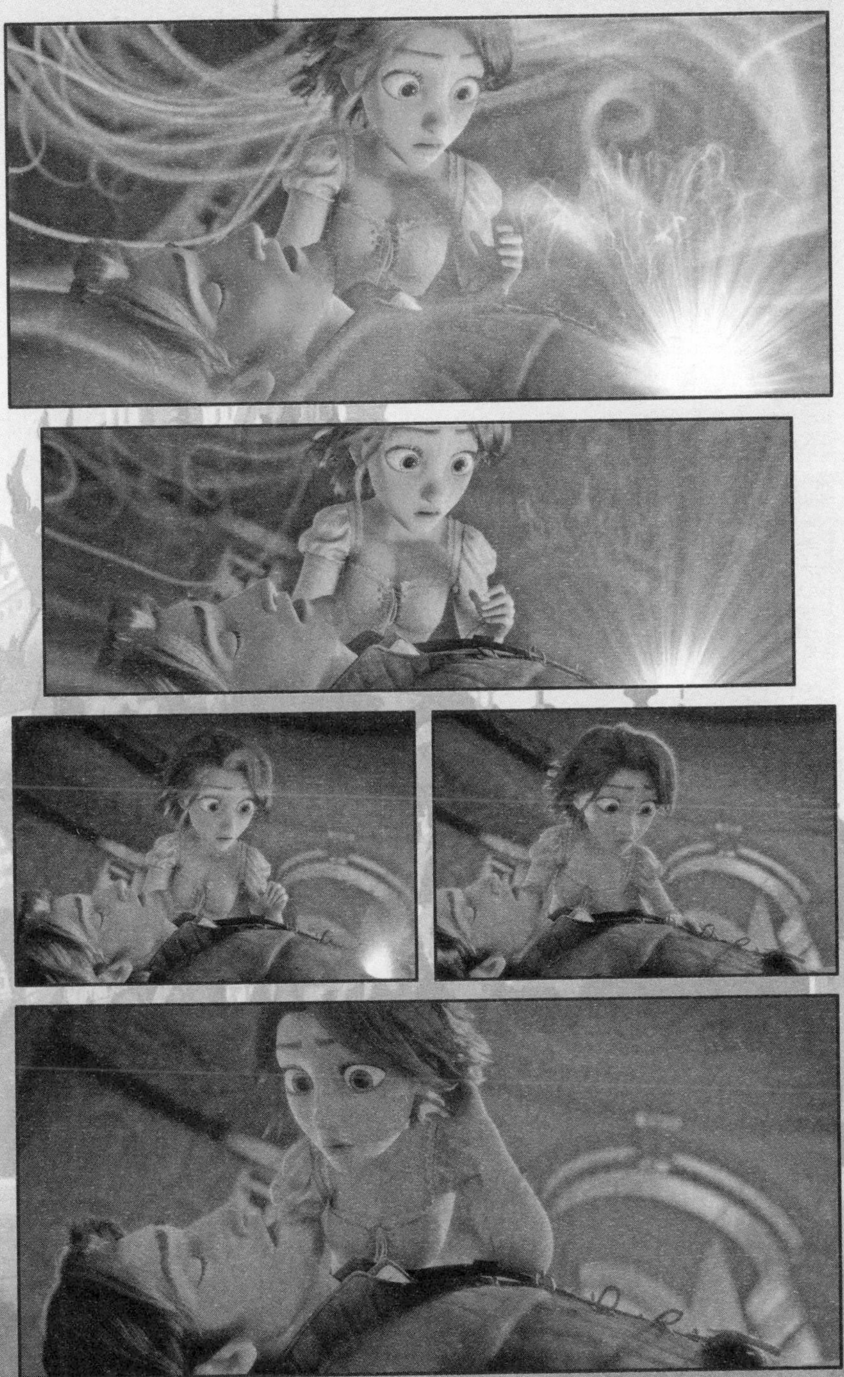

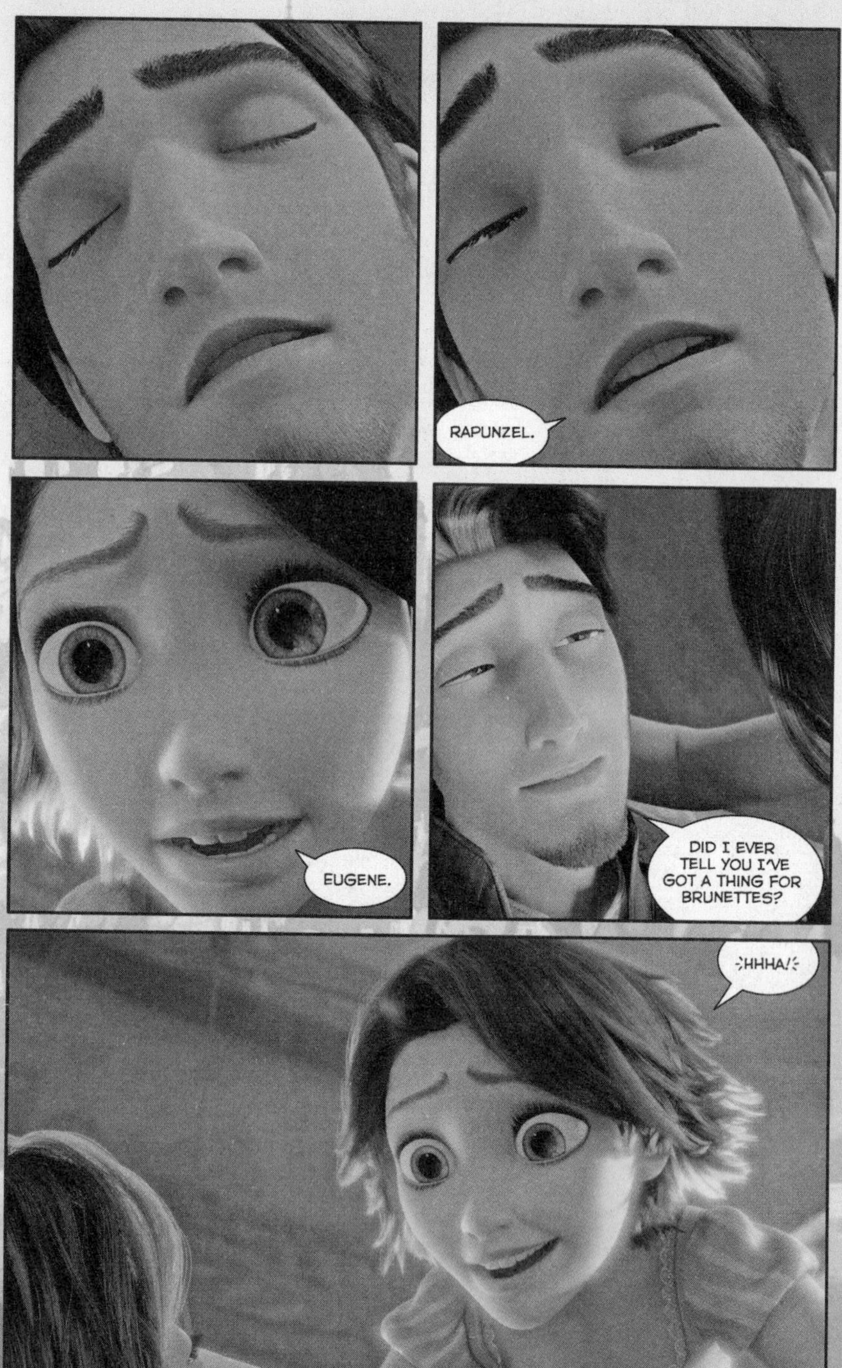
RAPUNZEL.
EUGENE.
DID I EVER TELL YOU I'VE GOT A THING FOR BRUNETTES?
HHHA!

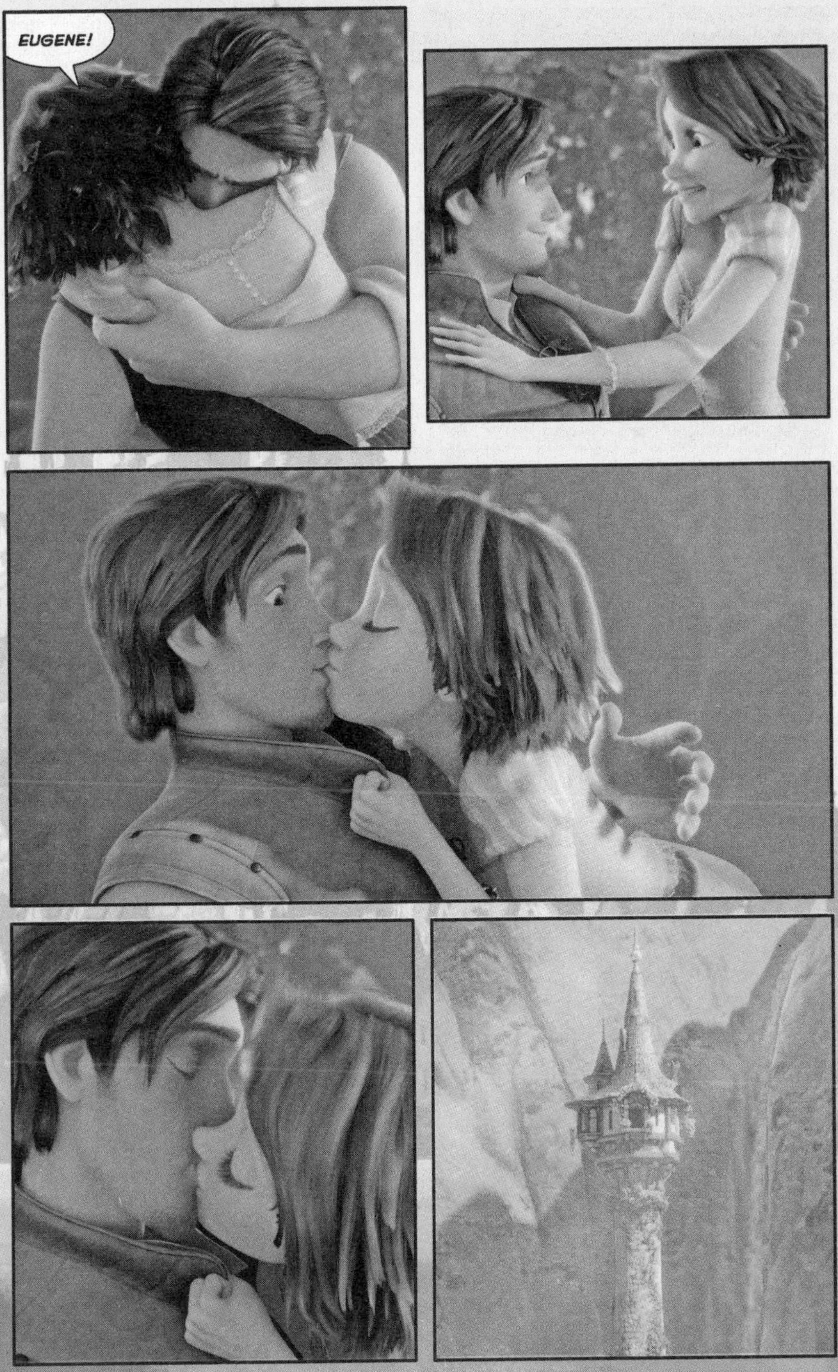
EUGENE!

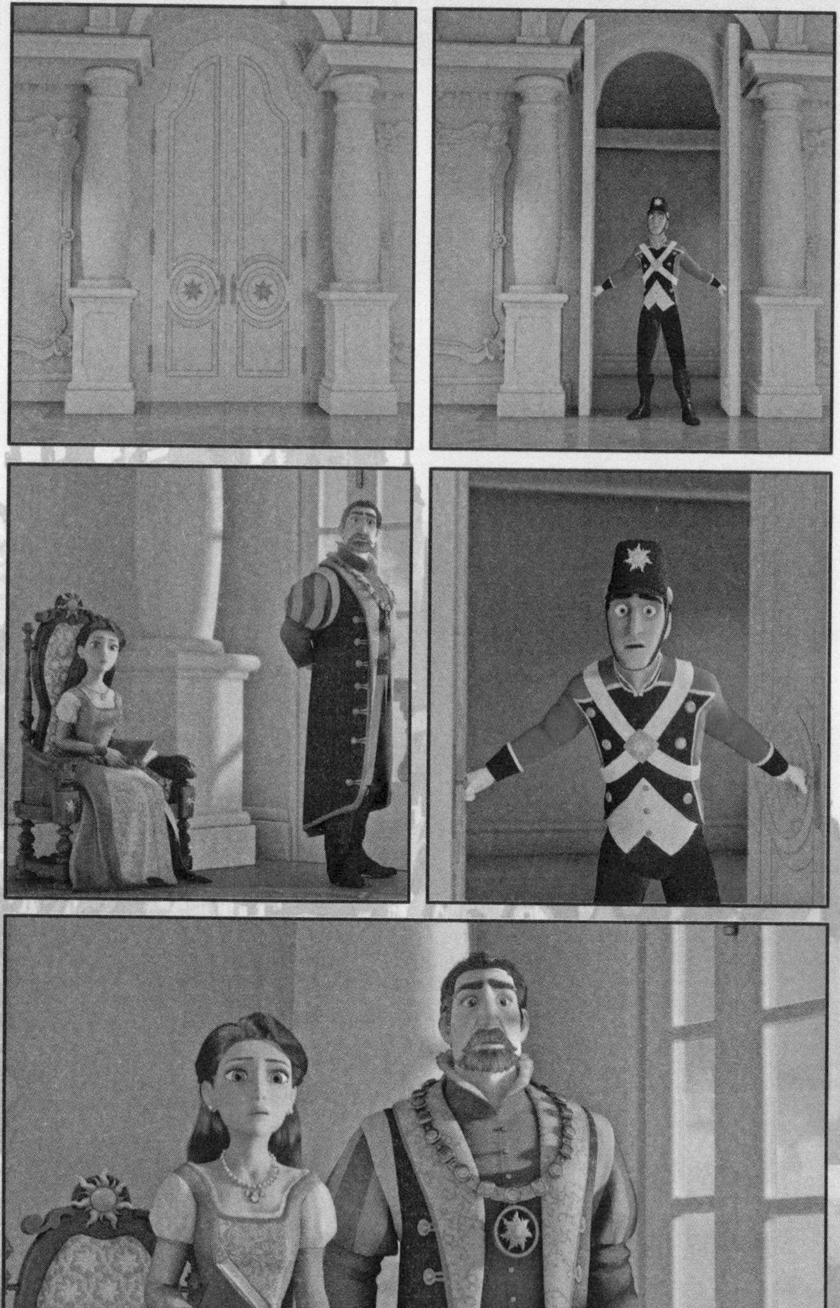

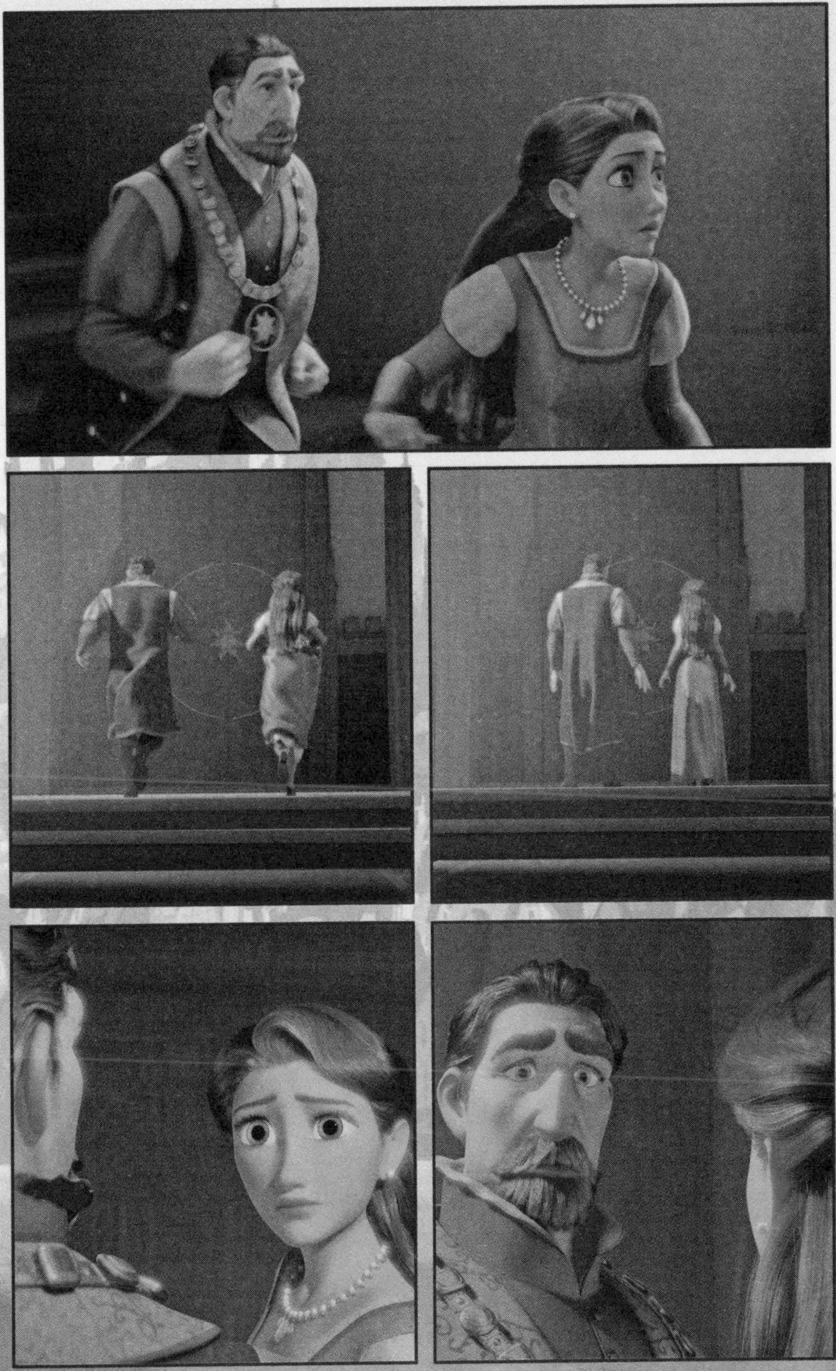

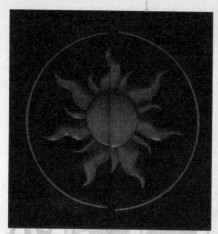

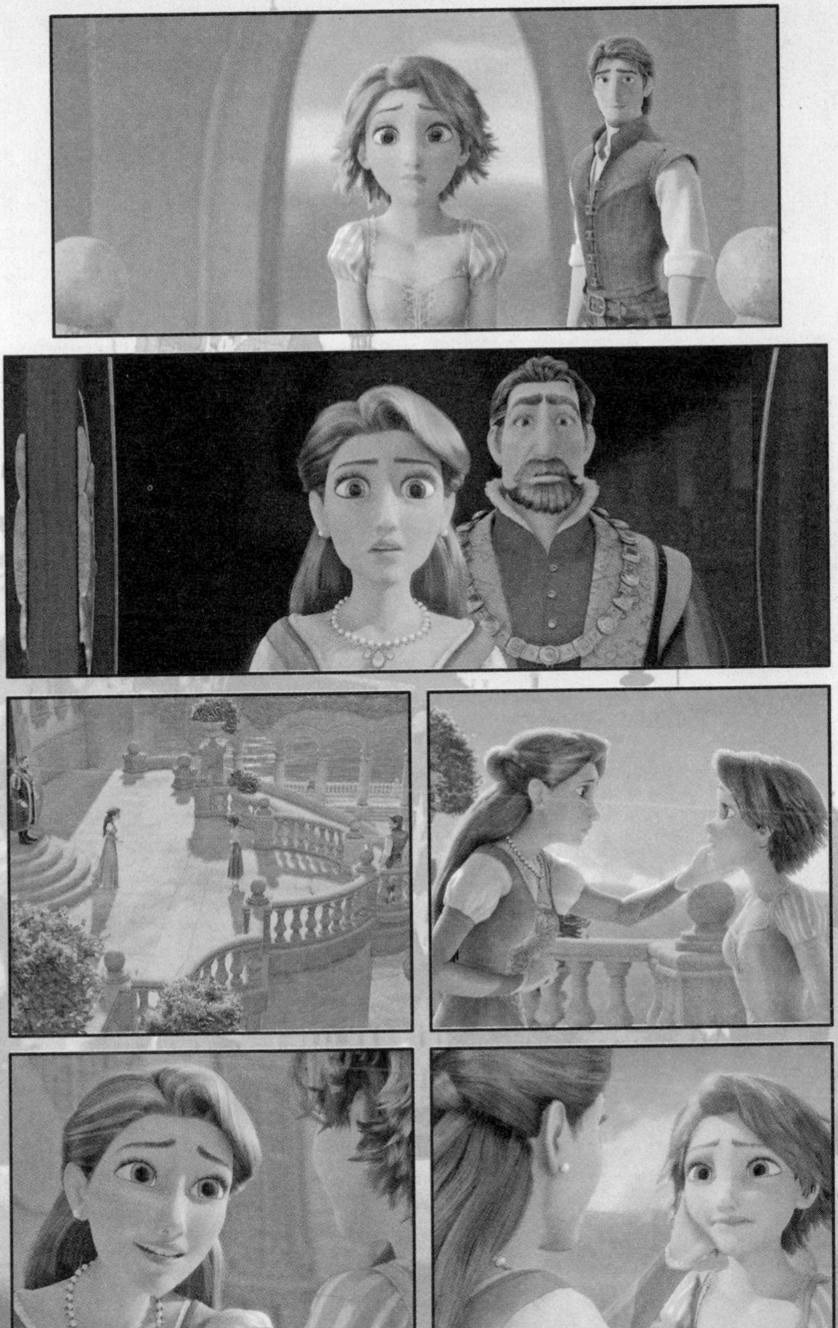

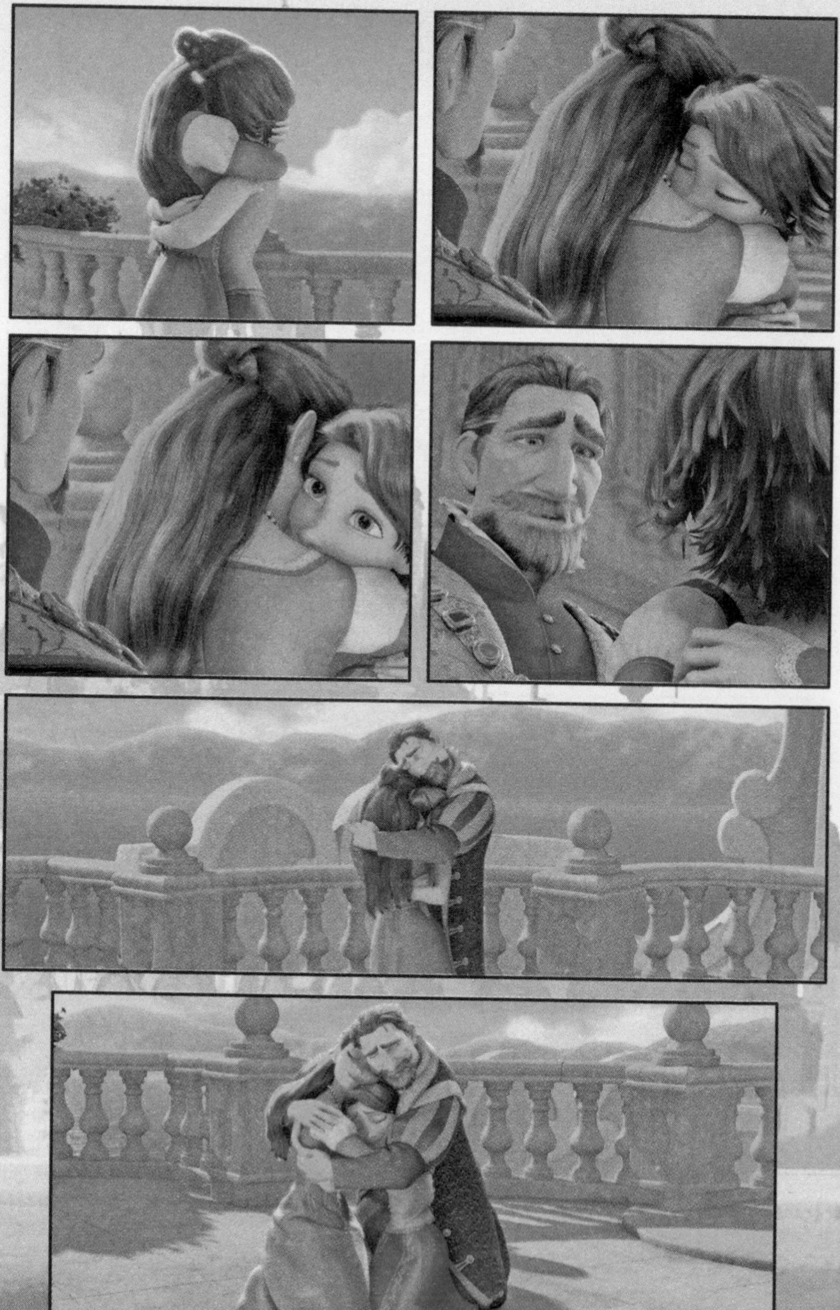

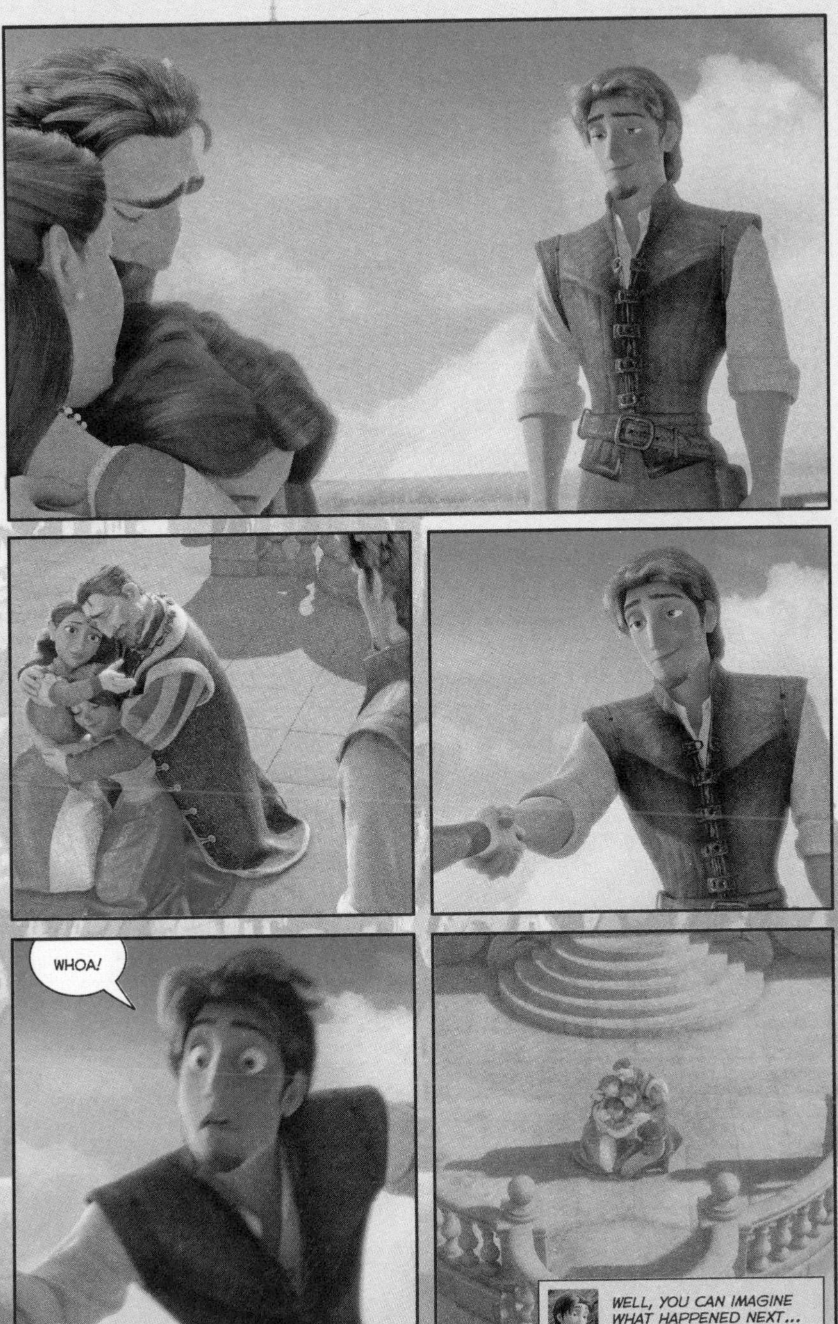
WHOA!
WELL, YOU CAN IMAGINE WHAT HAPPENED NEXT...

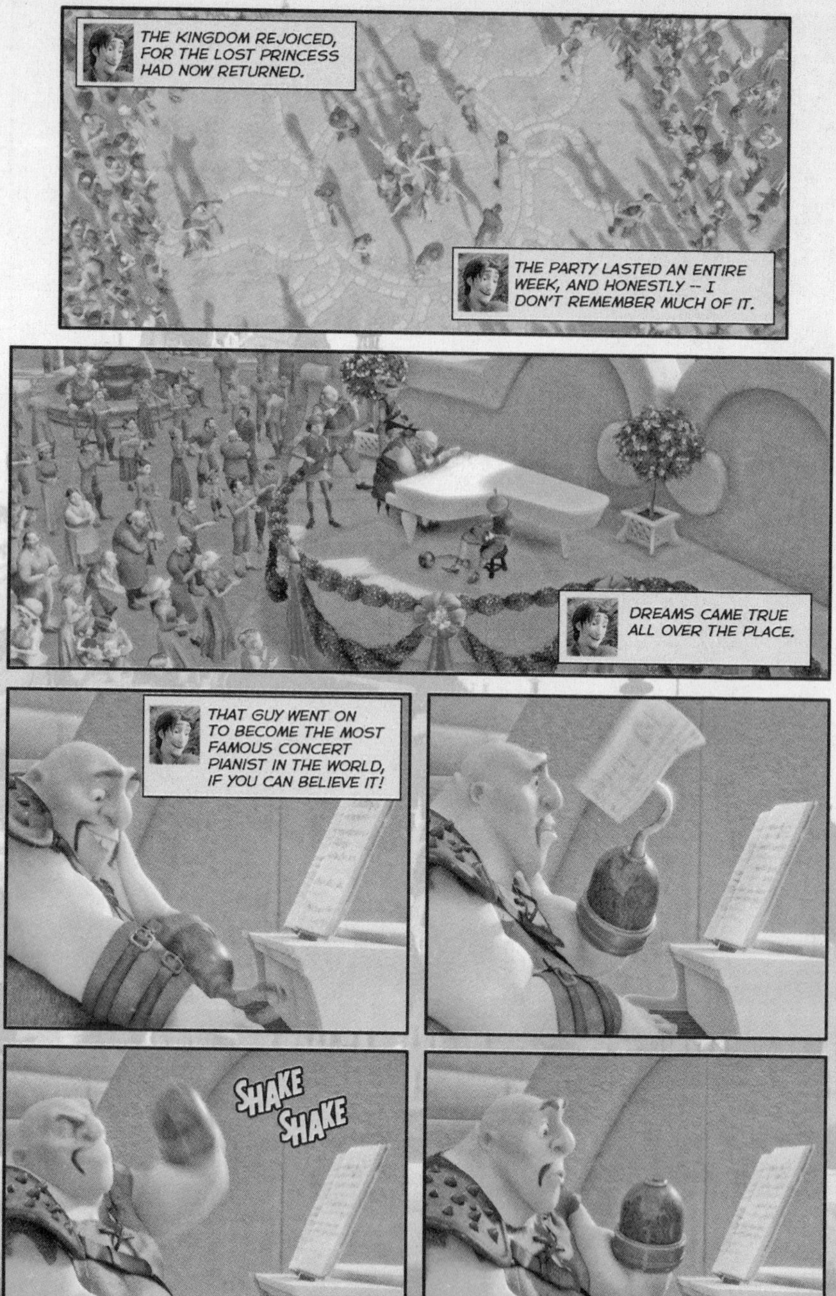
THE KINGDOM REJOICED, FOR THE LOST PRINCESS HAD NOW RETURNED.
THE PARTY LASTED AN ENTIRE WEEK, AND HONESTLY -- I DON'T REMEMBER MUCH OF IT.
DREAMS CAME TRUE ALL OVER THE PLACE.
THAT GUY WENT ON TO BECOME THE MOST FAMOUS CONCERT PIANIST IN THE WORLD, IF YOU CAN BELIEVE IT!
SHAKE
SHAKE

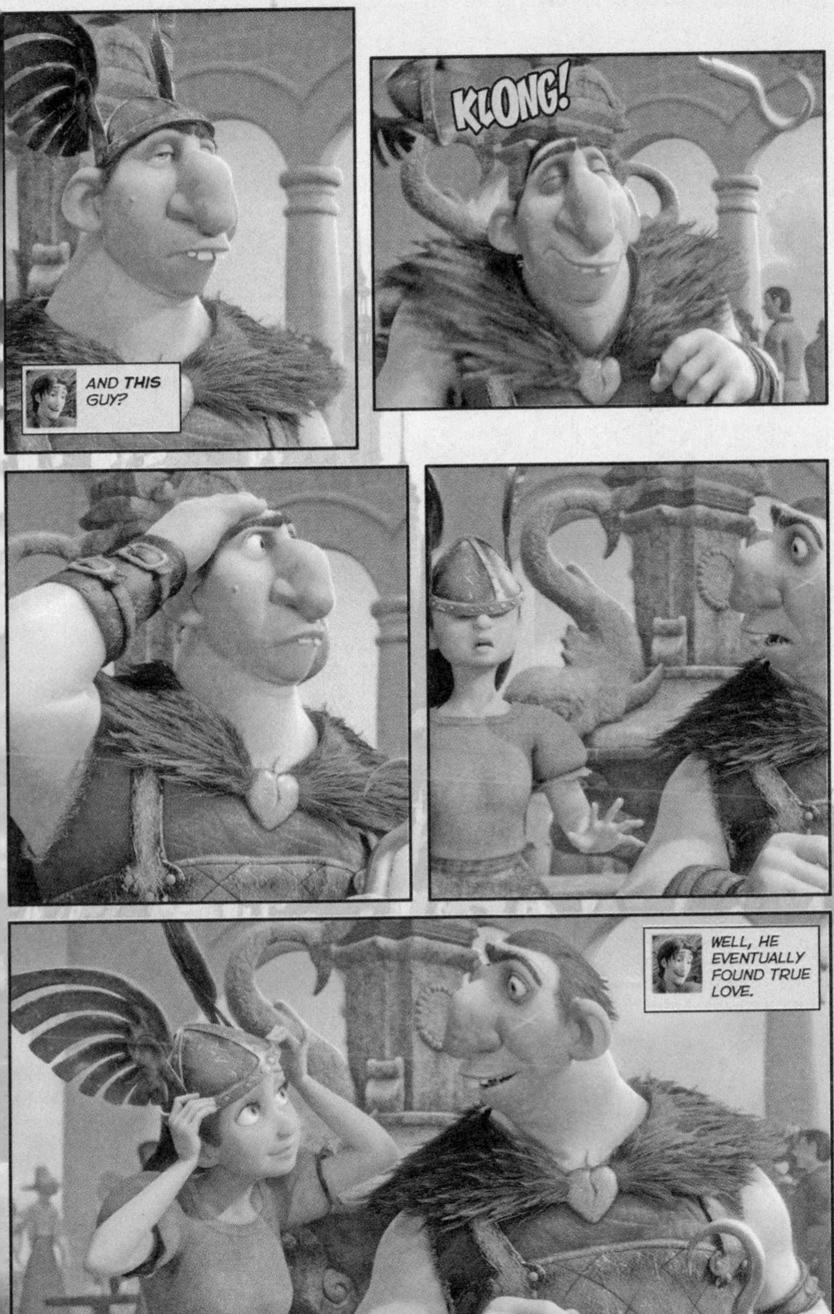
AND THIS GUY?
KLONG!
WELL, HE EVENTUALLY FOUND TRUE LOVE.

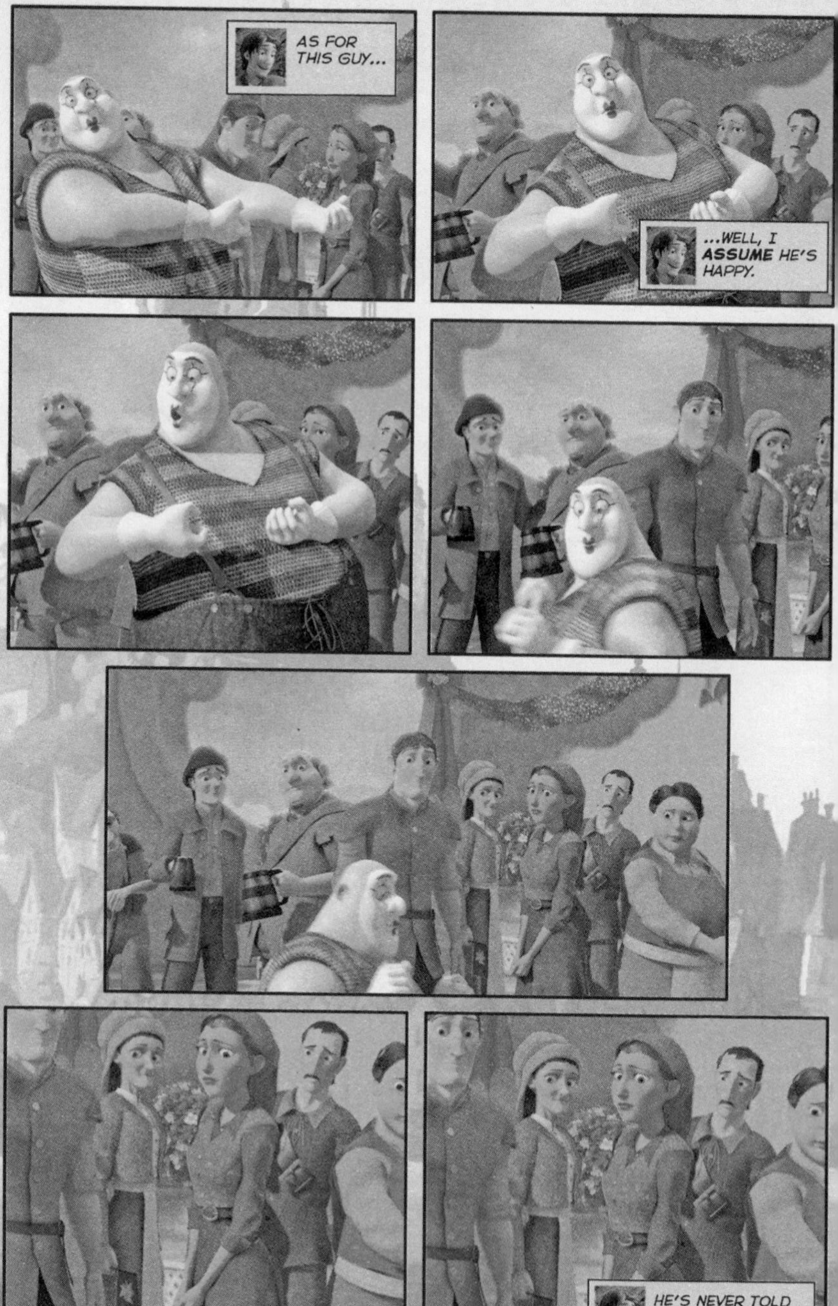
AS FOR THIS GUY...
...WELL, I ASSUME HE'S HAPPY.
HE'S NEVER TOLD ME OTHERWISE.

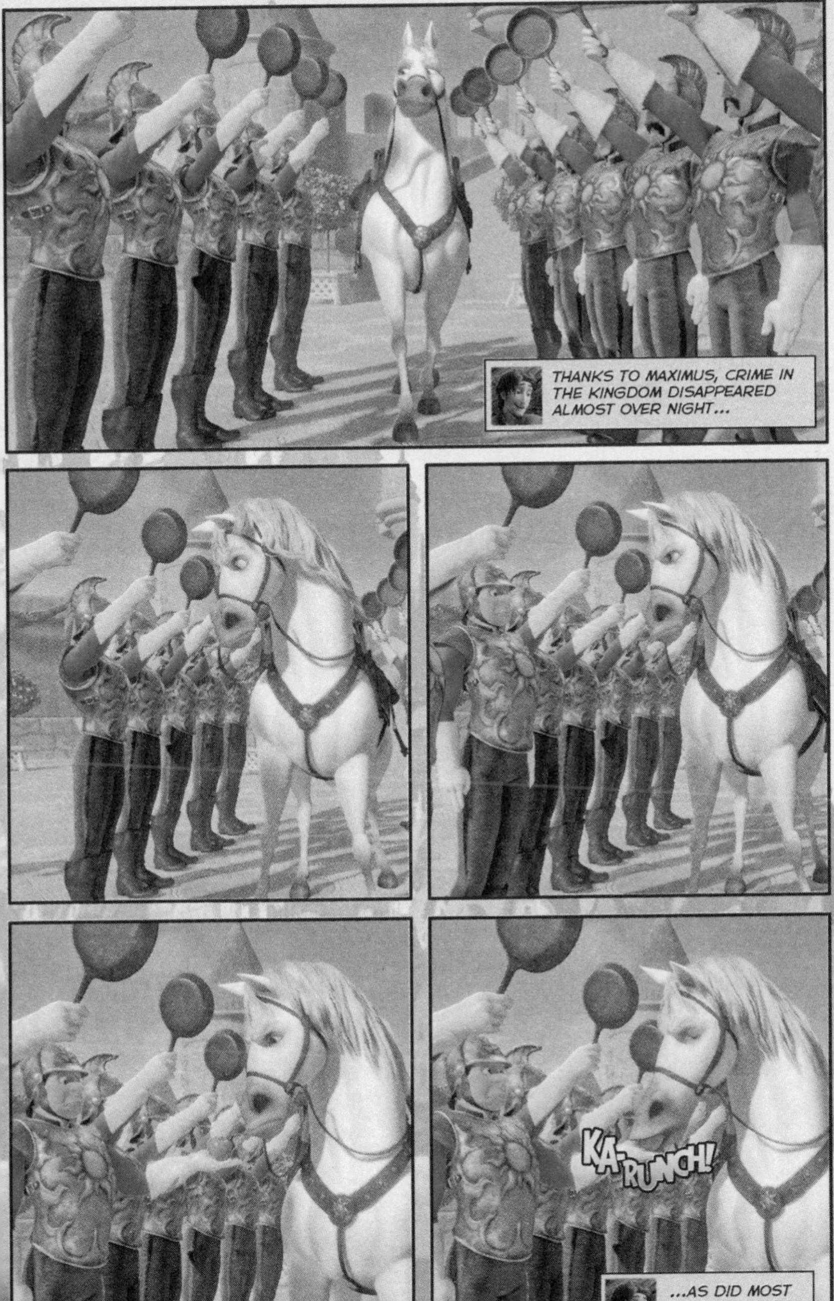
THANKS TO MAXIMUS, CRIME IN THE KINGDOM DISAPPEARED ALMOST OVER NIGHT...
KA-RUNCH!
...AS DID MOST OF THE APPLES.

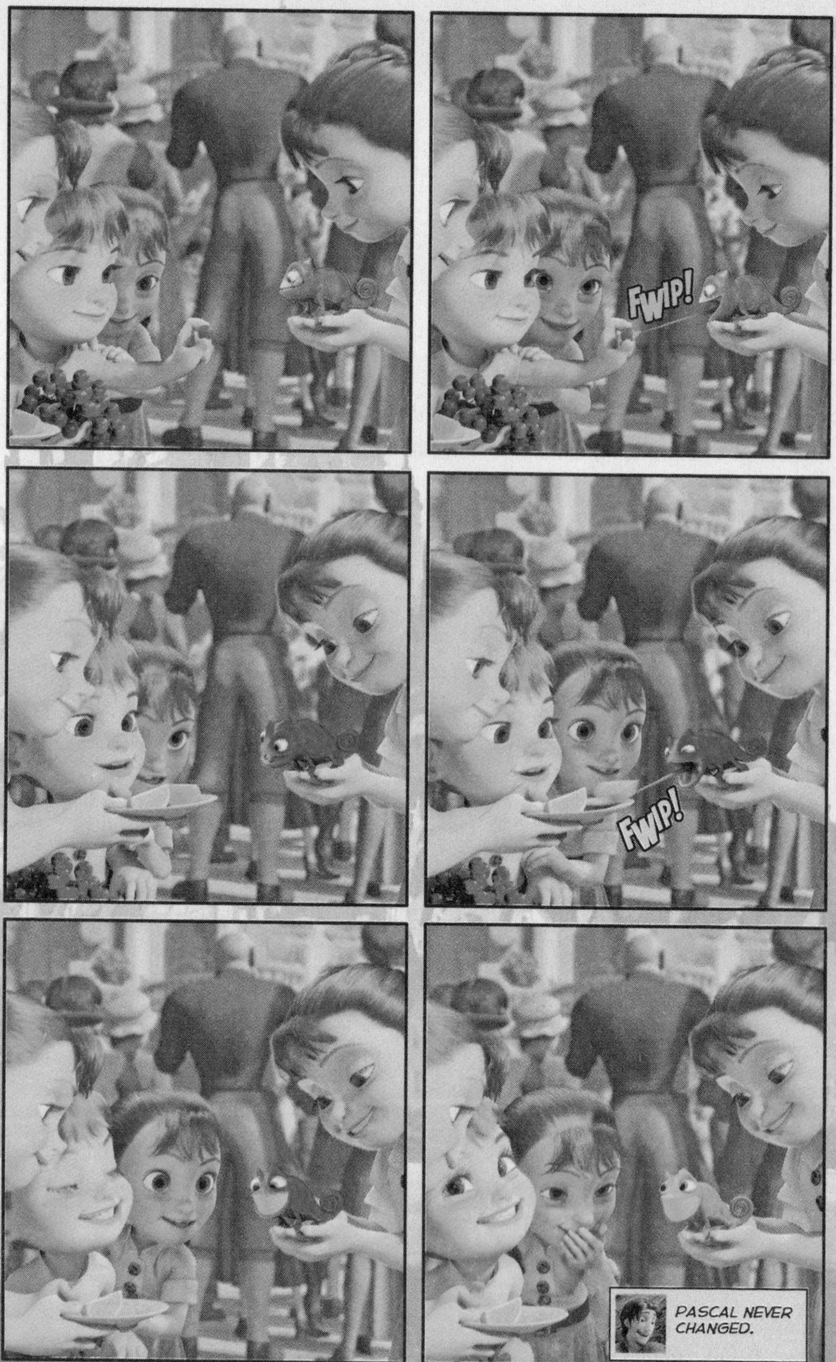
FWIP!
FWIP!
PASCAL NEVER CHANGED.

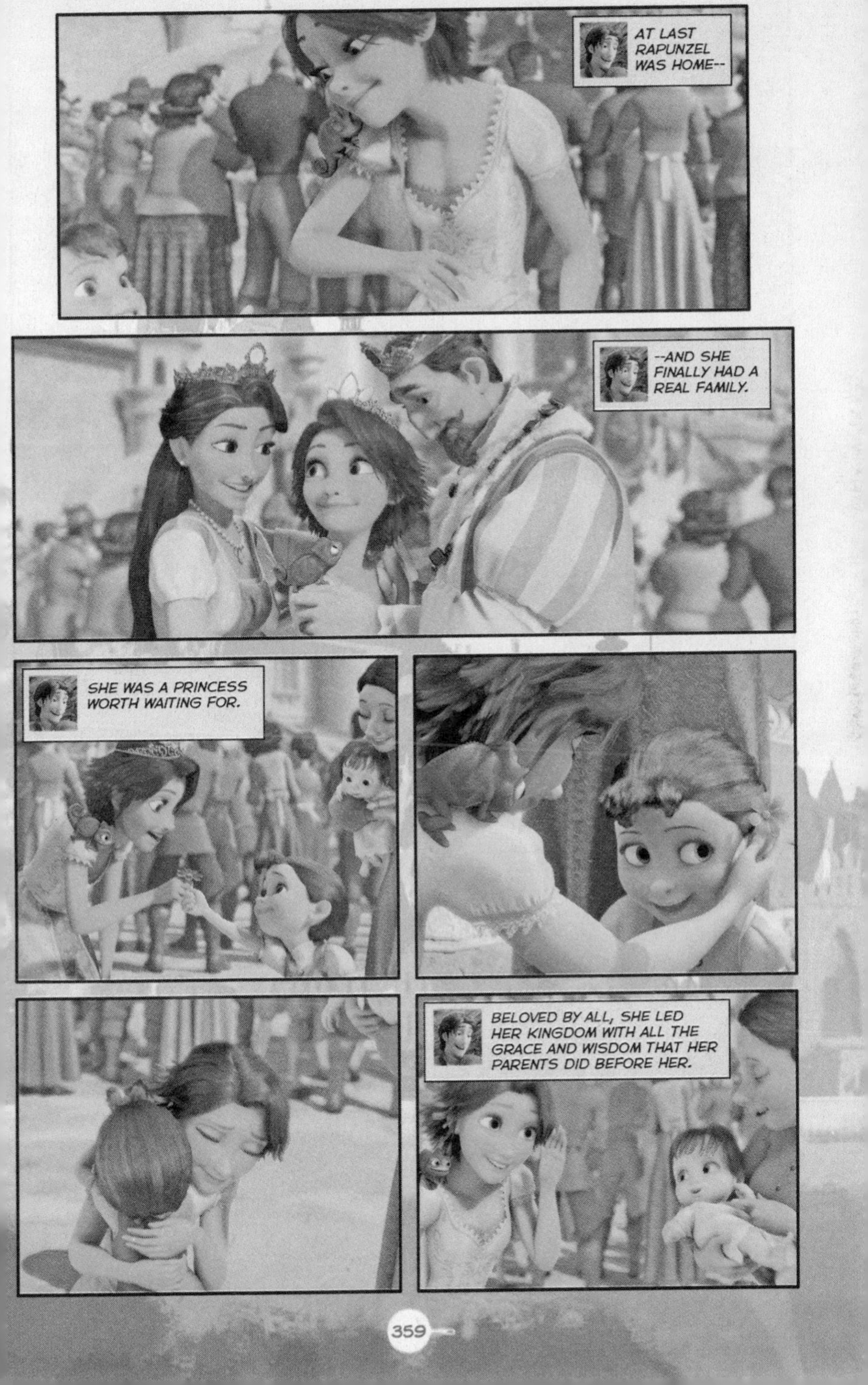
AT LAST RAPUNZEL WAS HOME--
--AND SHE FINALLY HAD A REAL FAMILY.
SHE WAS A PRINCESS WORTH WAITING FOR.
BELOVED BY ALL, SHE LED HER KINGDOM WITH ALL THE GRACE AND WISDOM THAT HER PARENTS DID BEFORE HER.

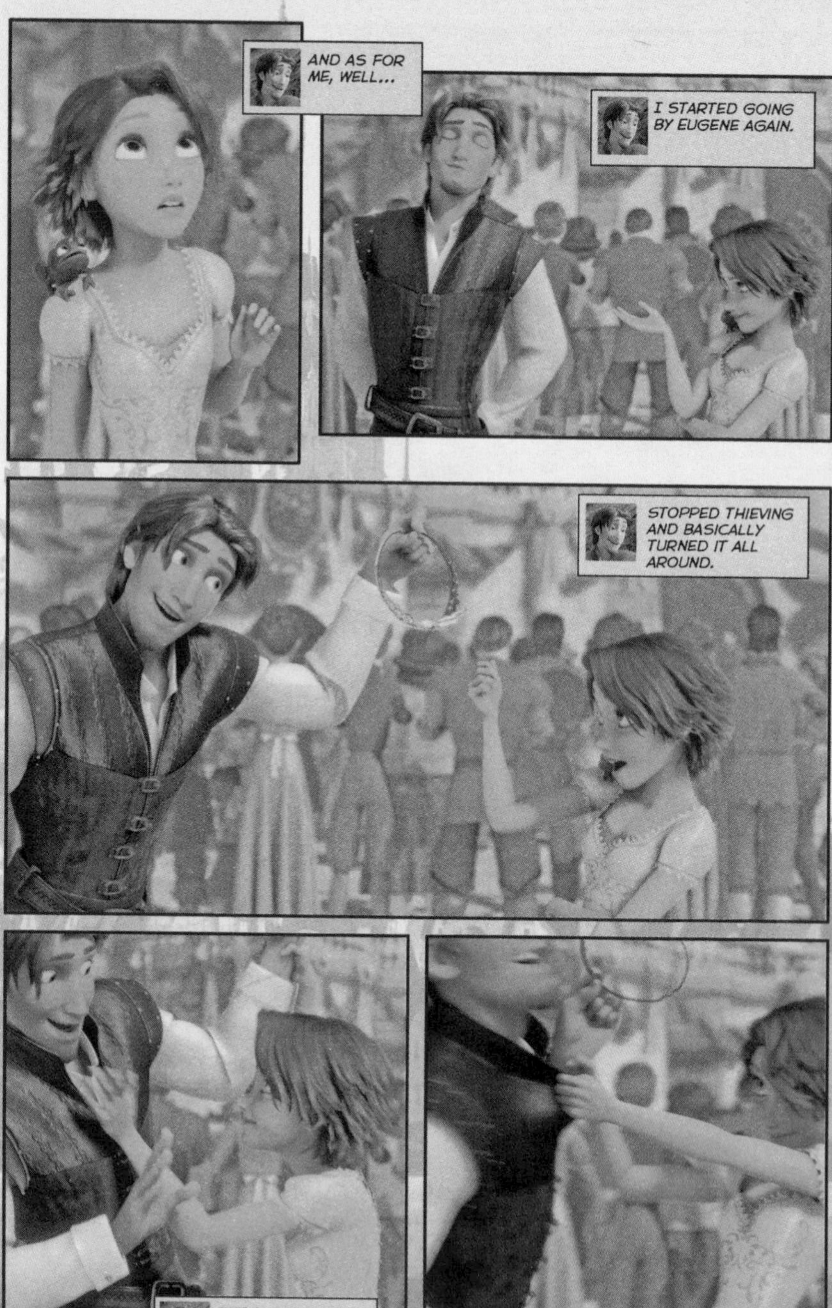
AND AS FOR ME, WELL...
I STARTED GOING BY EUGENE AGAIN.
STOPPED THIEVING AND BASICALLY TURNED IT ALL AROUND.
BUT I KNOW WHAT THE BIG QUESTION IS...

DID RAPUNZEL AND I EVER GET MARRIED?

WELL, I'M PLEASED TO TELL YOU THAT AFTER YEARS AND YEARS OF ASKING, AND ASKING, AND ASKING...

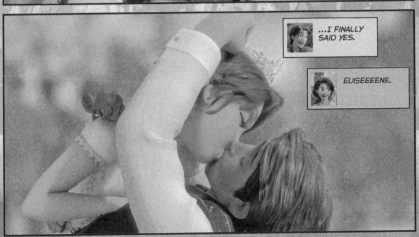

...I FINALLY SAID YES.

EUGEEEENE.

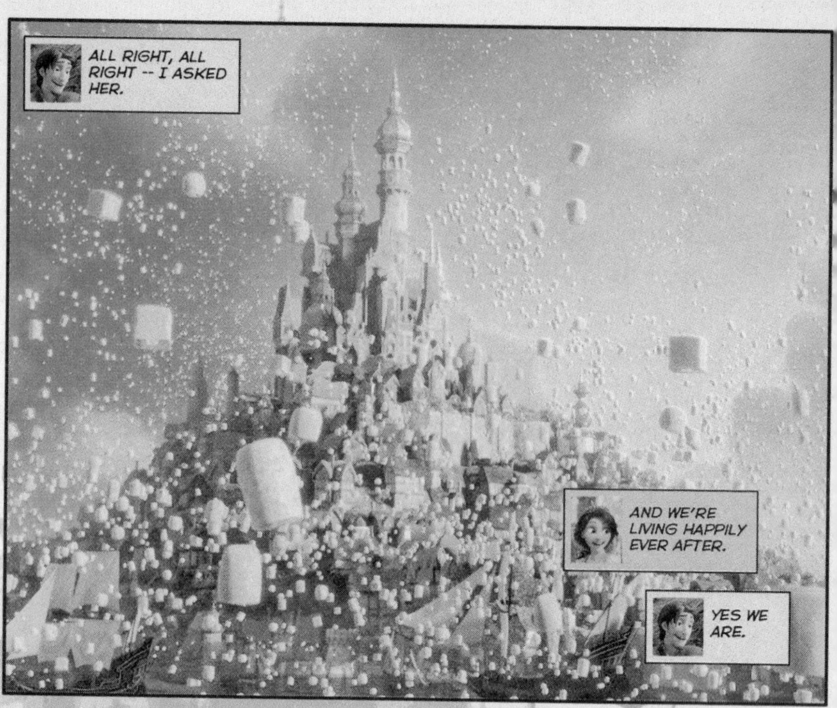
ALL RIGHT, ALL RIGHT -- I ASKED HER.
AND WE'RE LIVING HAPPILY EVER AFTER.
YES WE ARE.

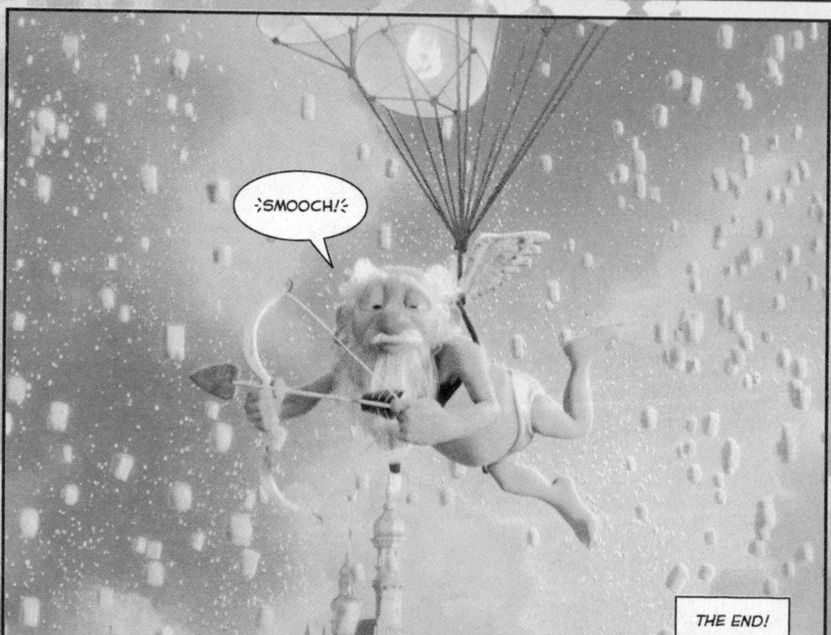
SMOOCH!
THE END!

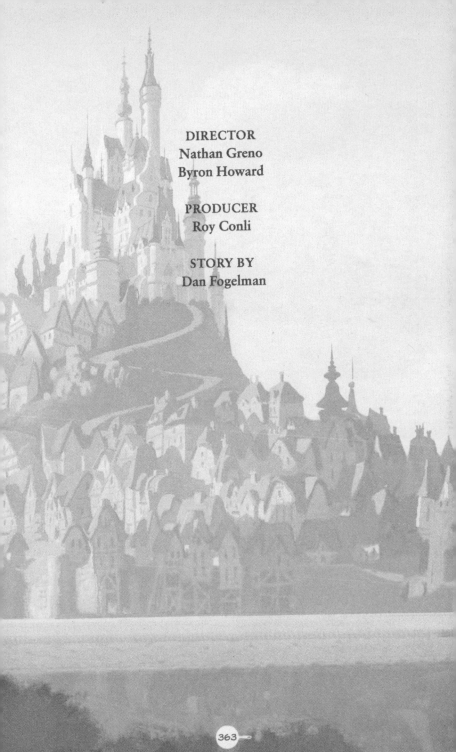

**DIRECTOR**
Nathan Greno
Byron Howard

**PRODUCER**
Roy Conli

**STORY BY**
Dan Fogelman

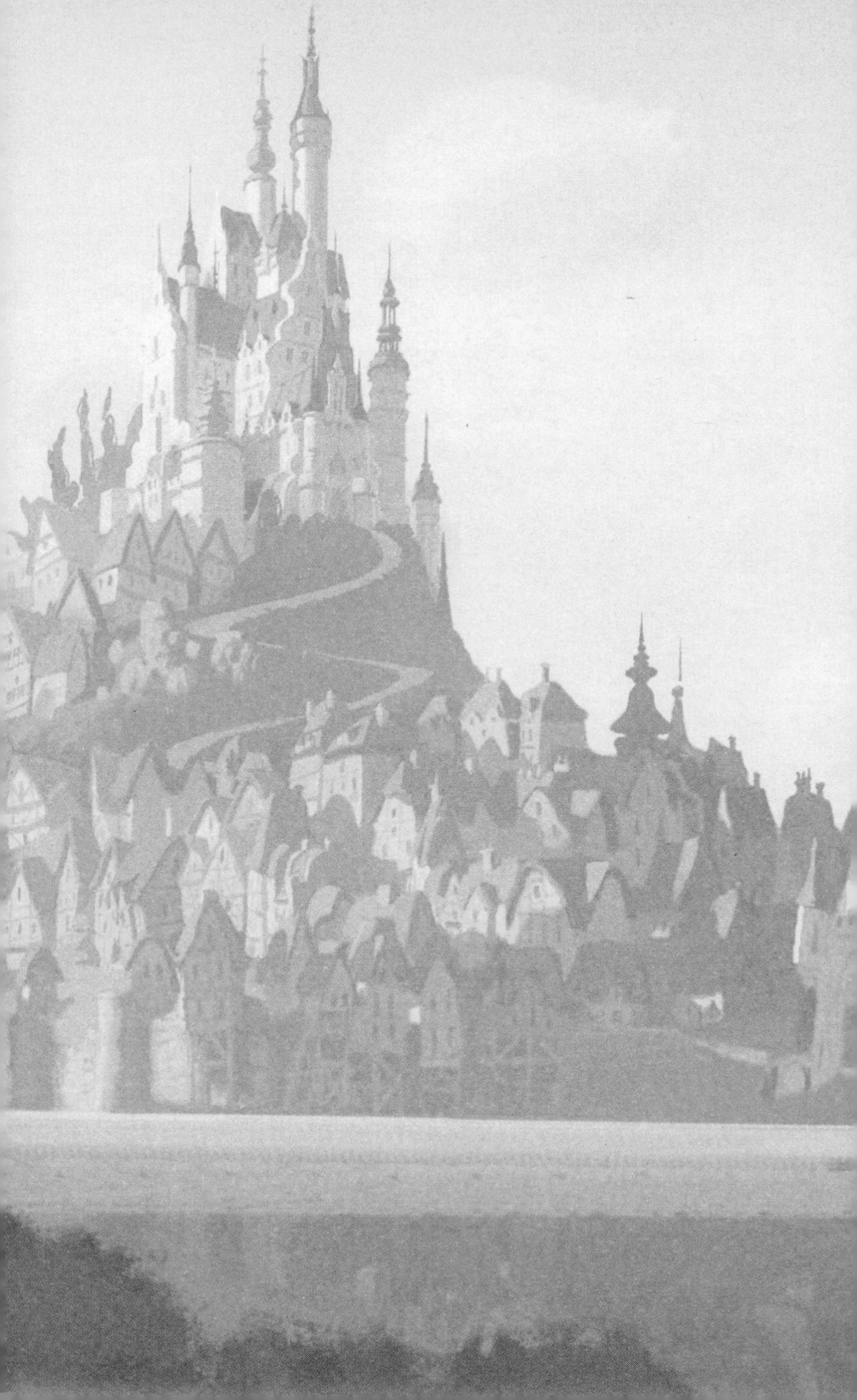

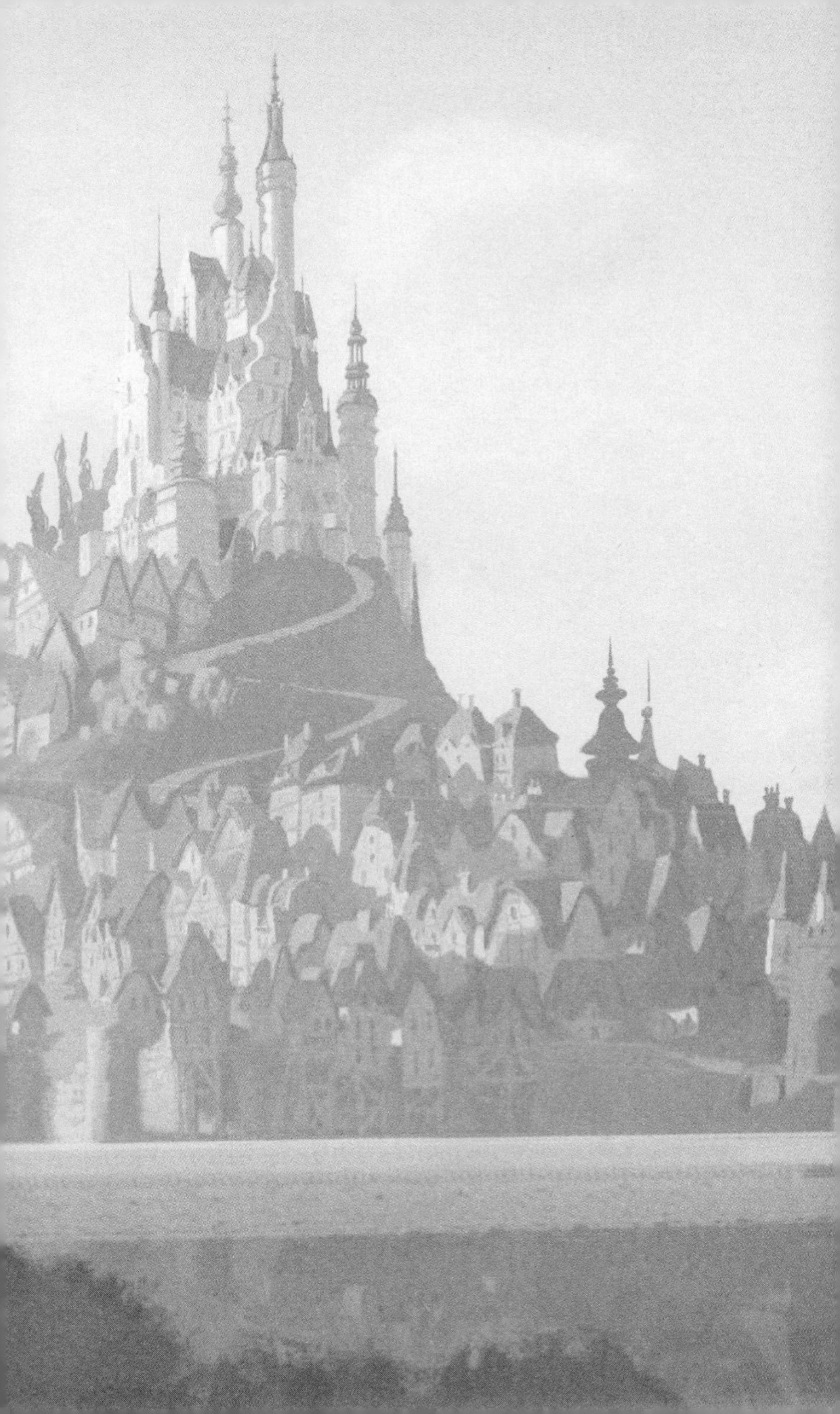

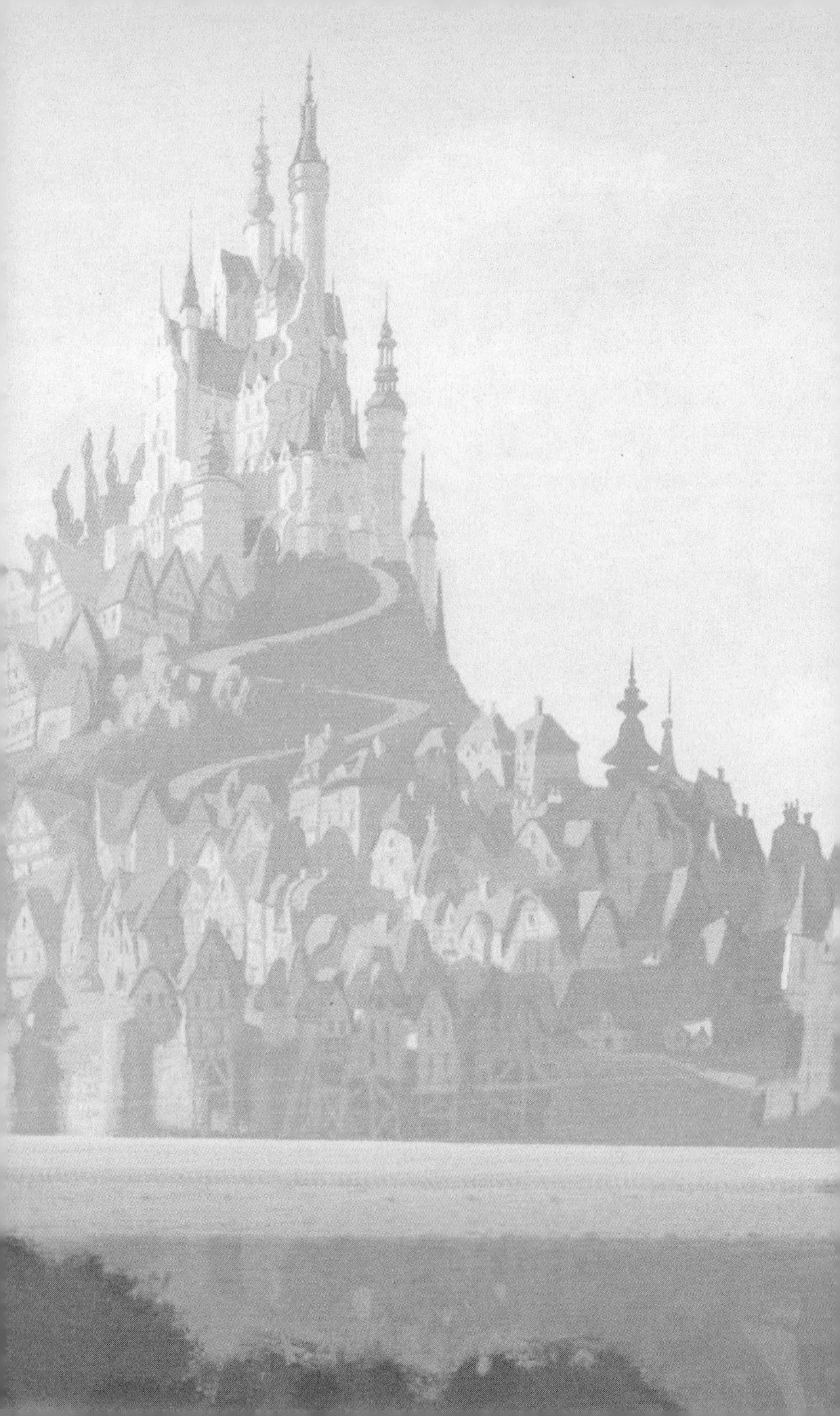

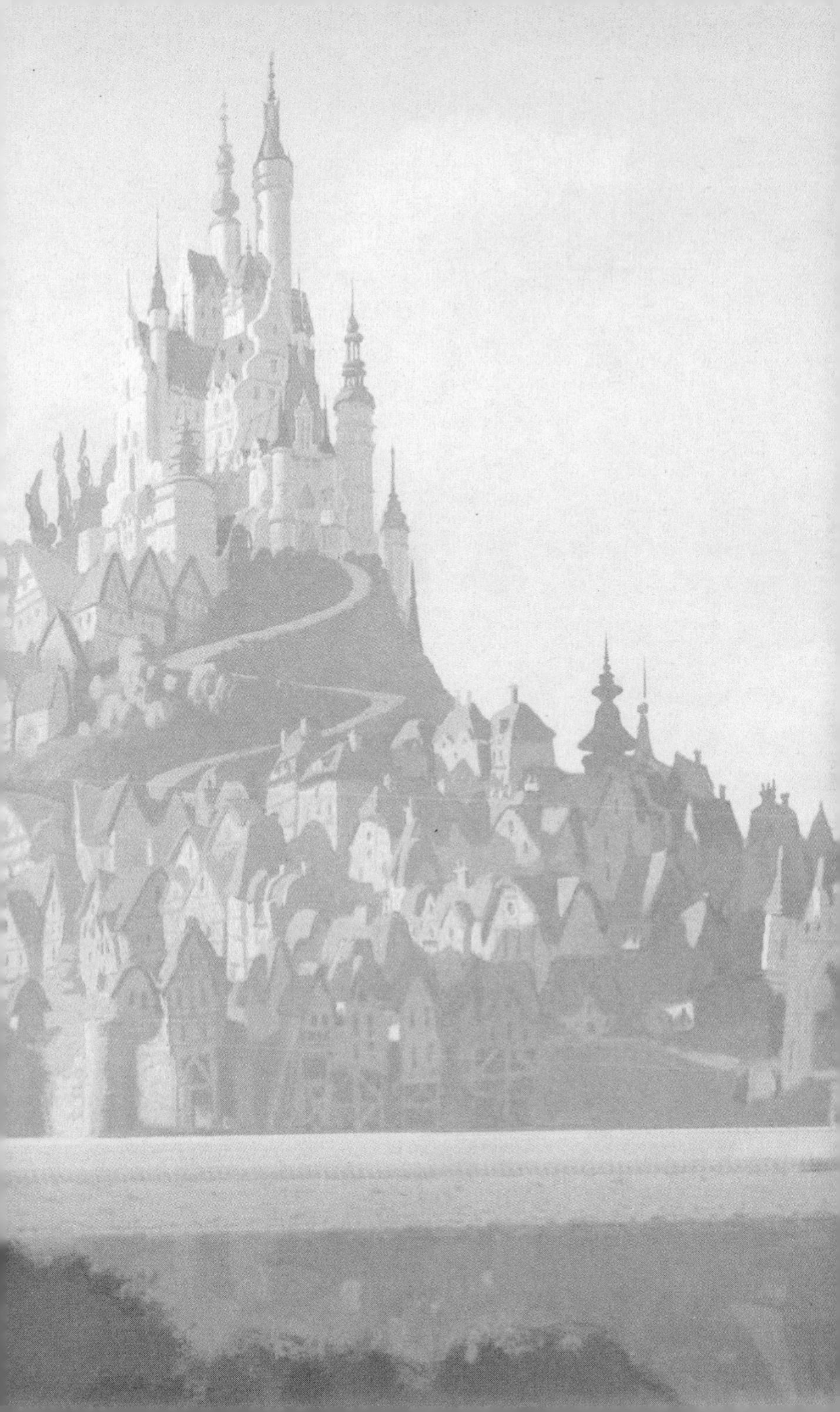

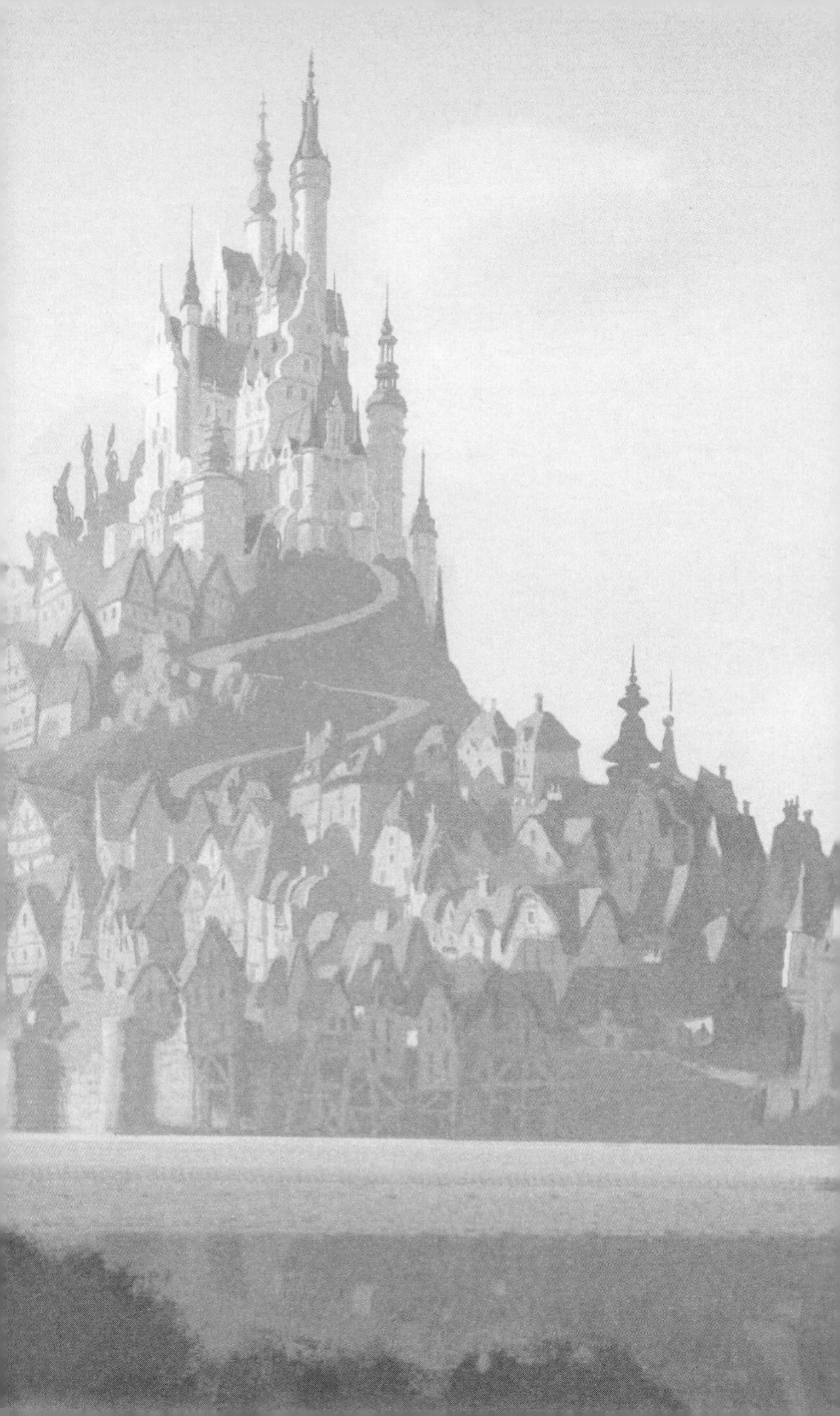

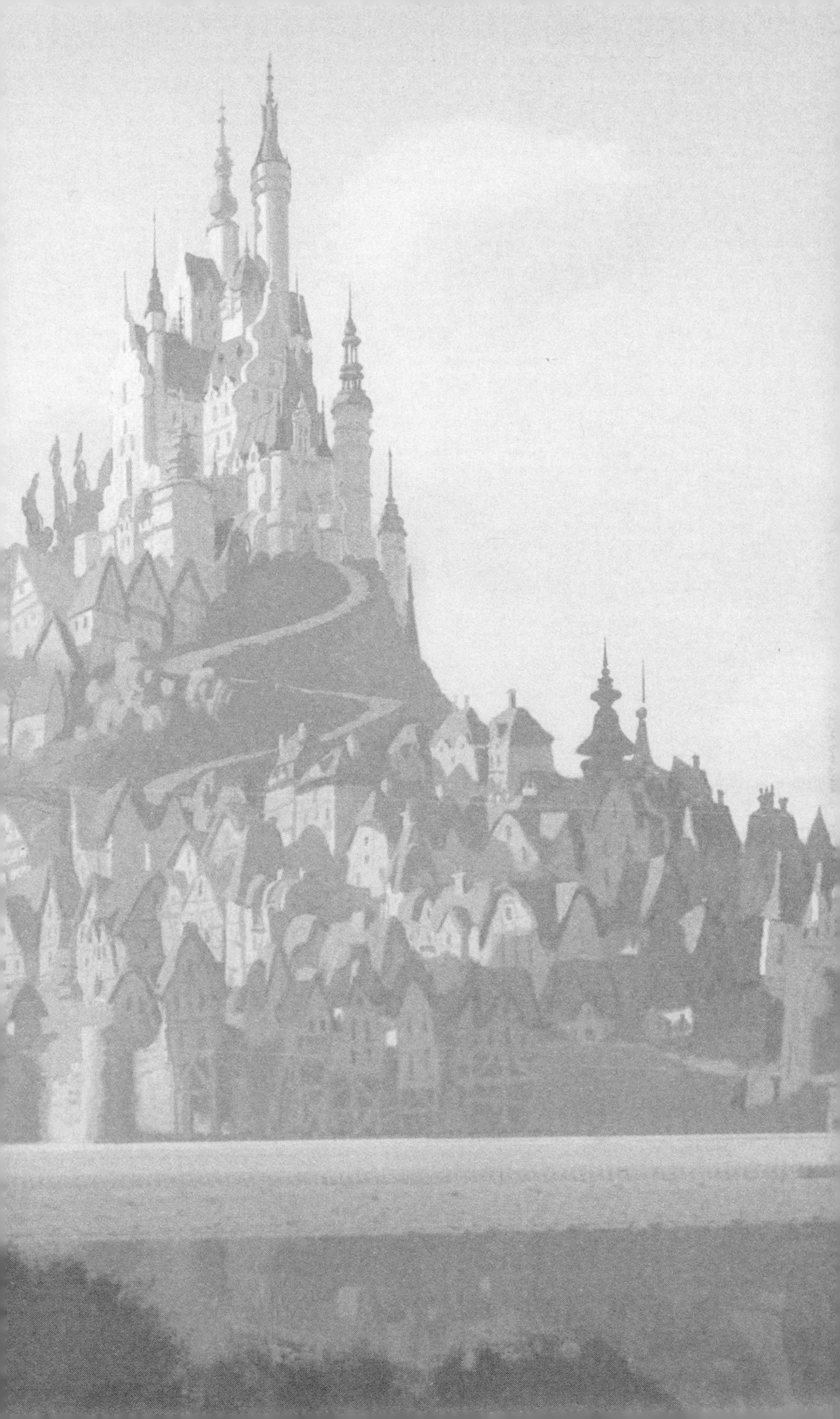

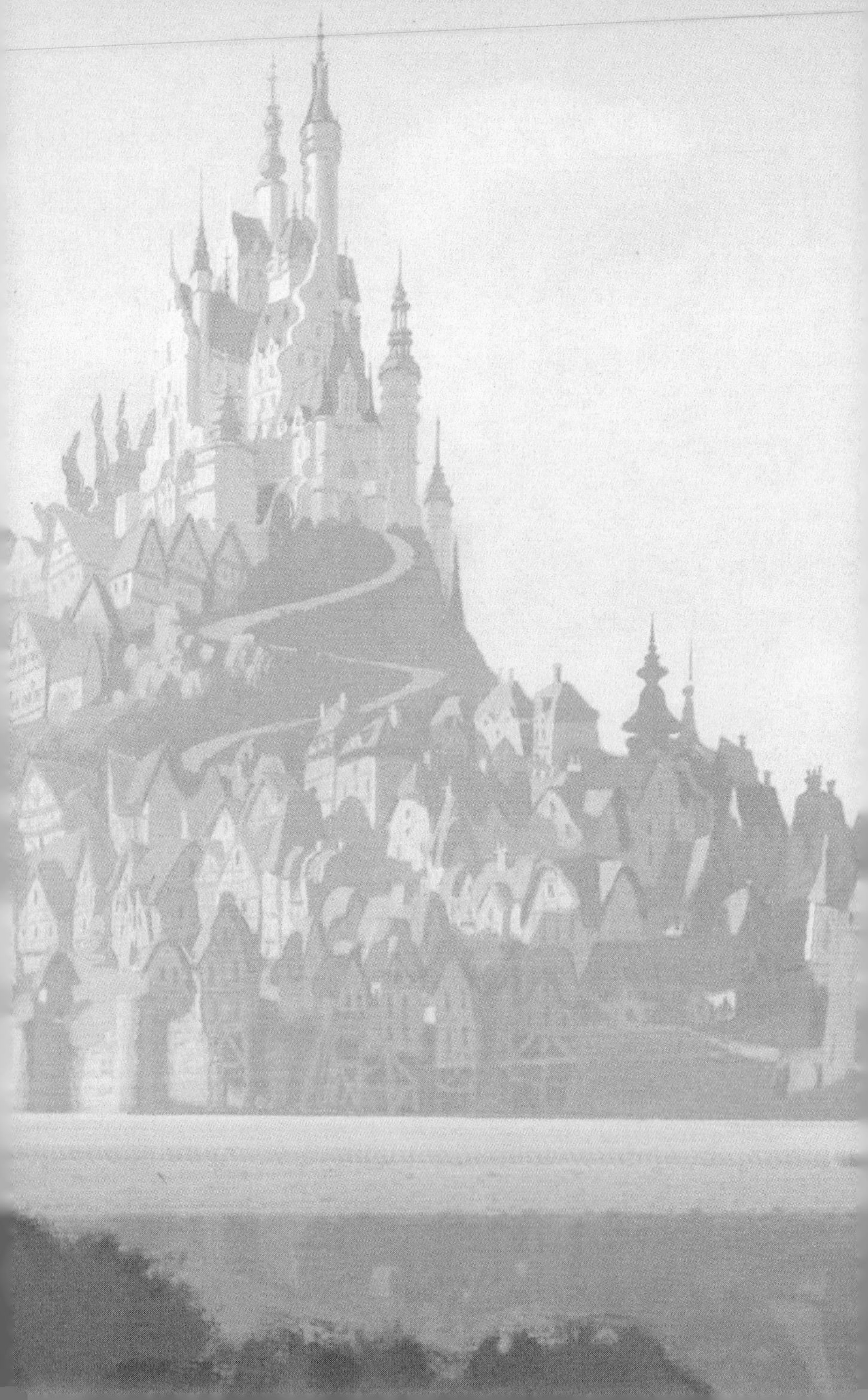

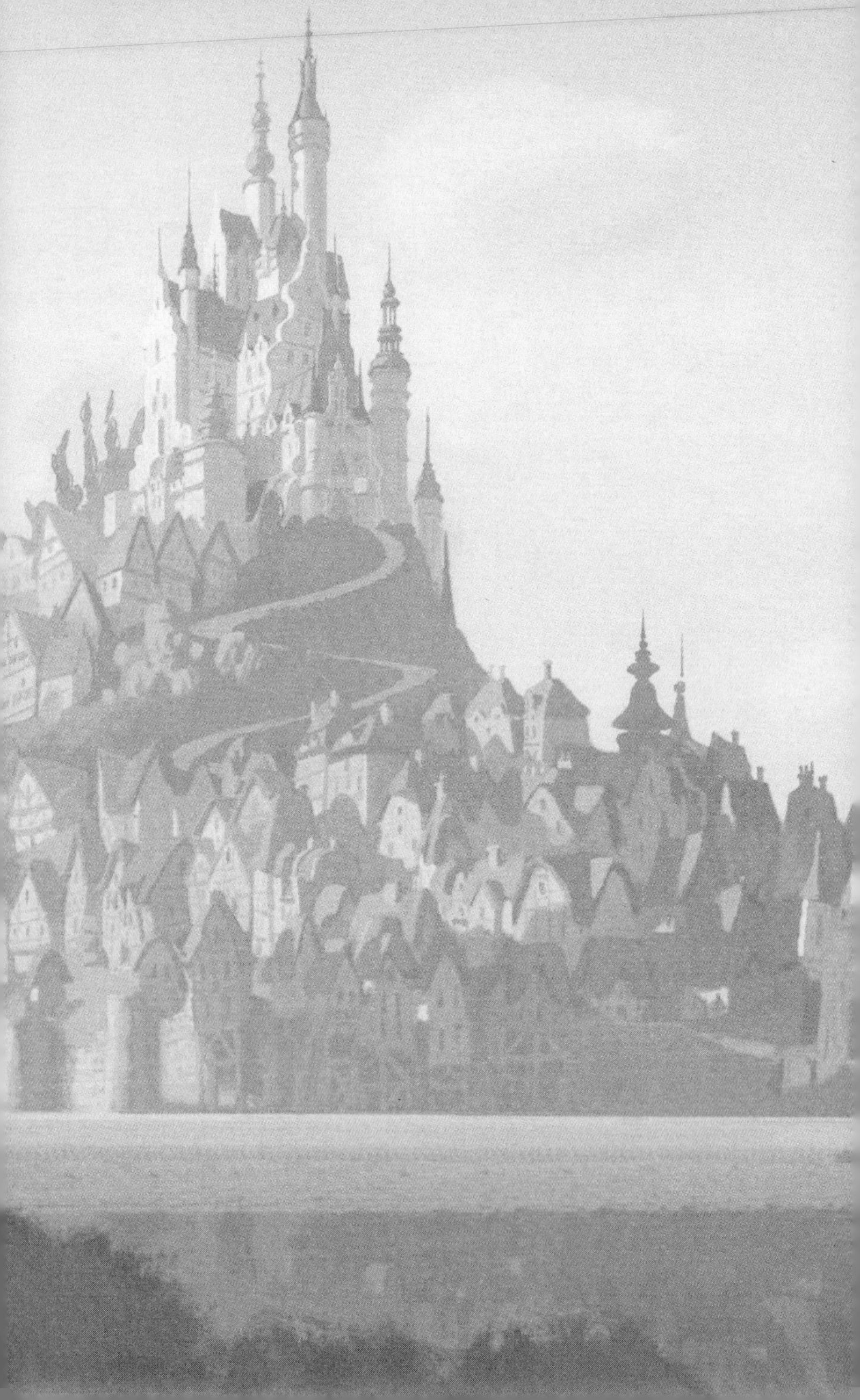

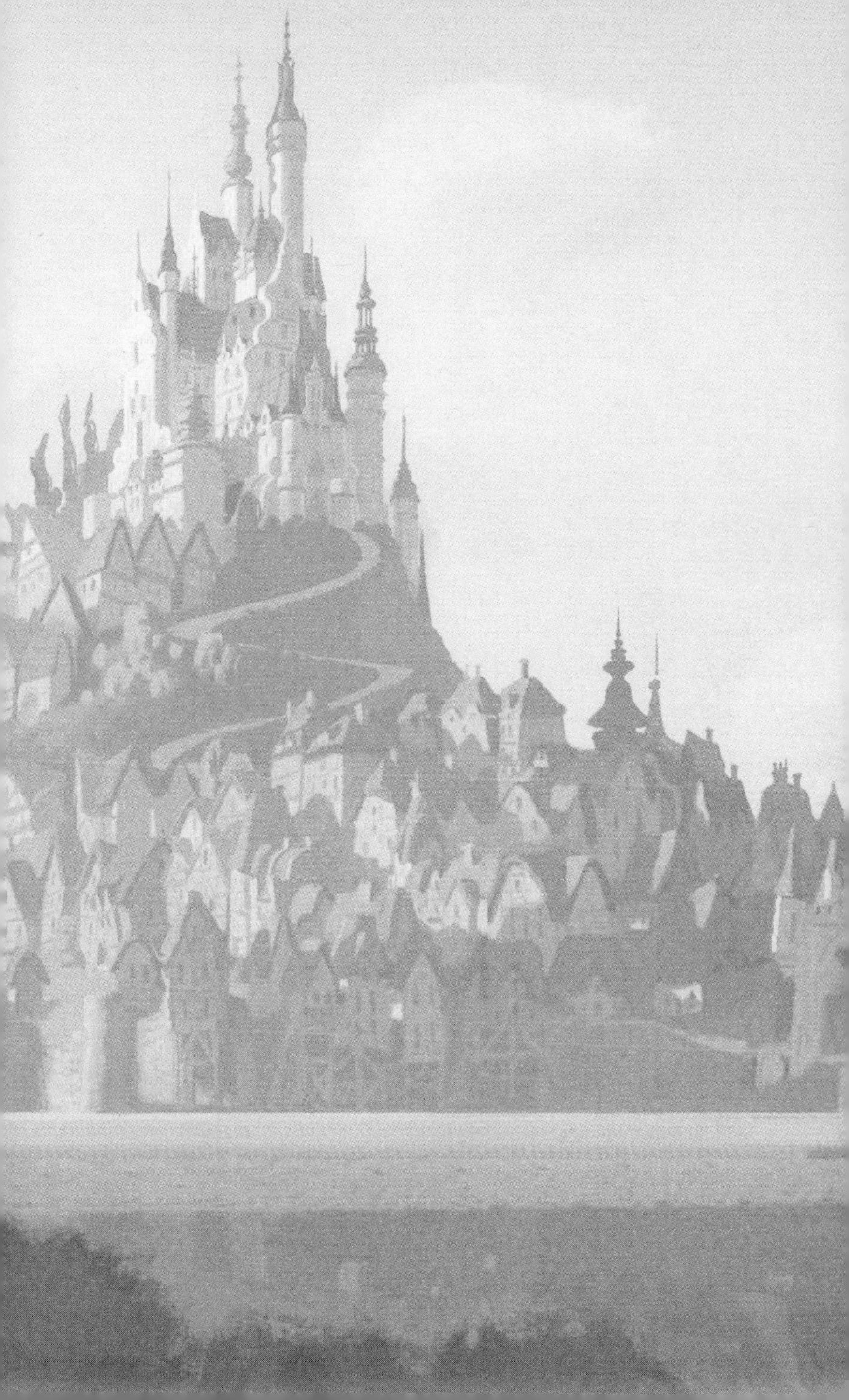

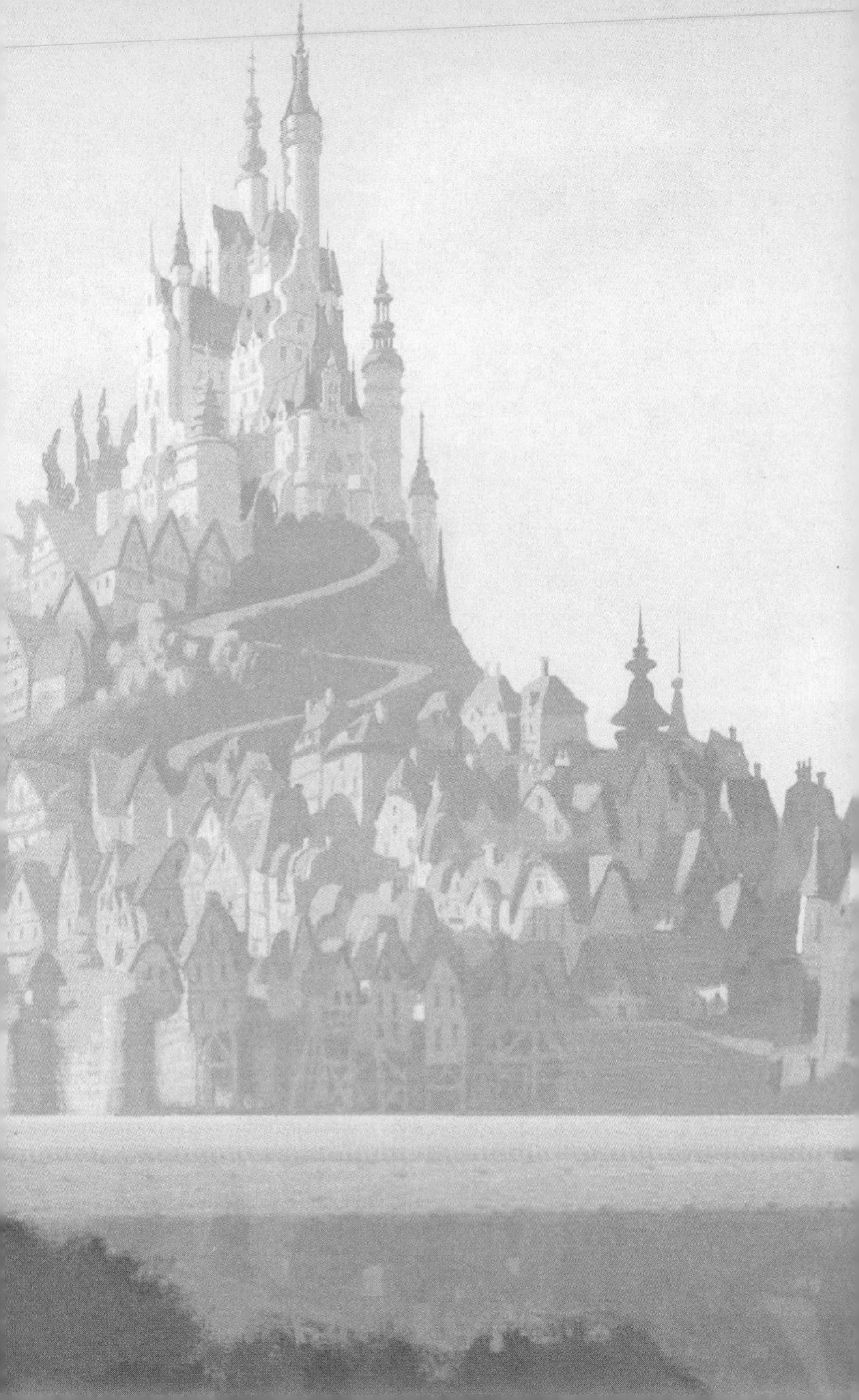

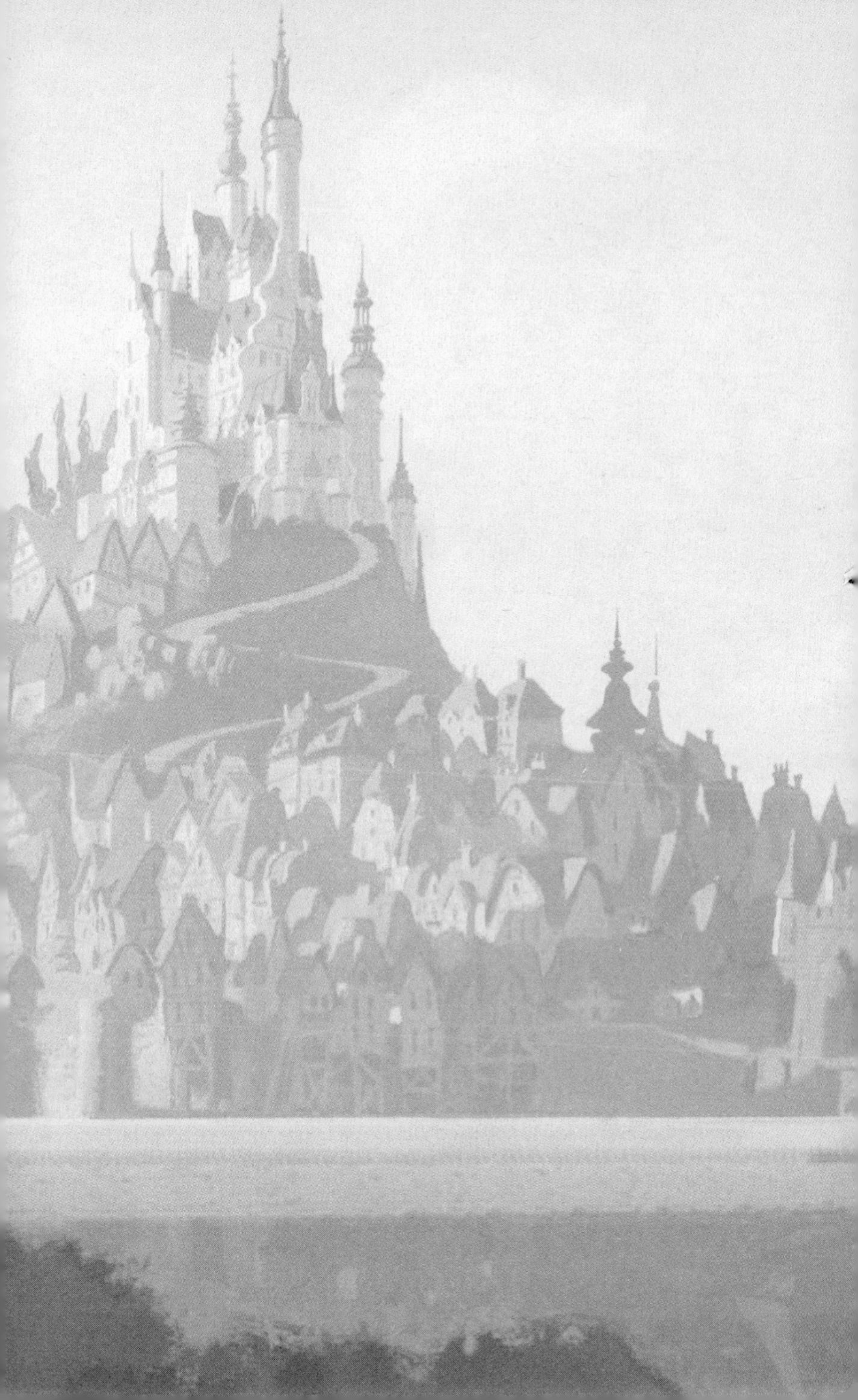

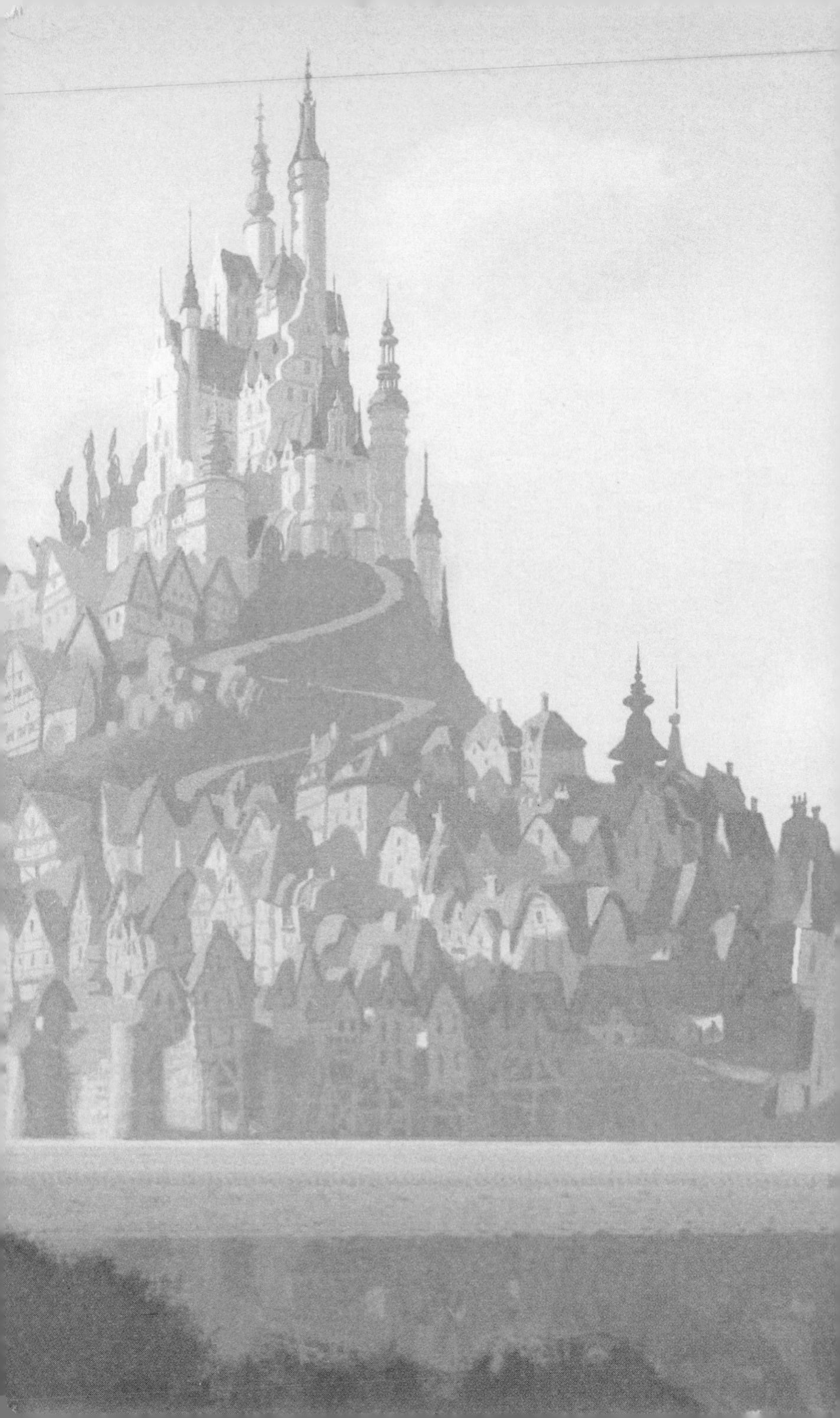

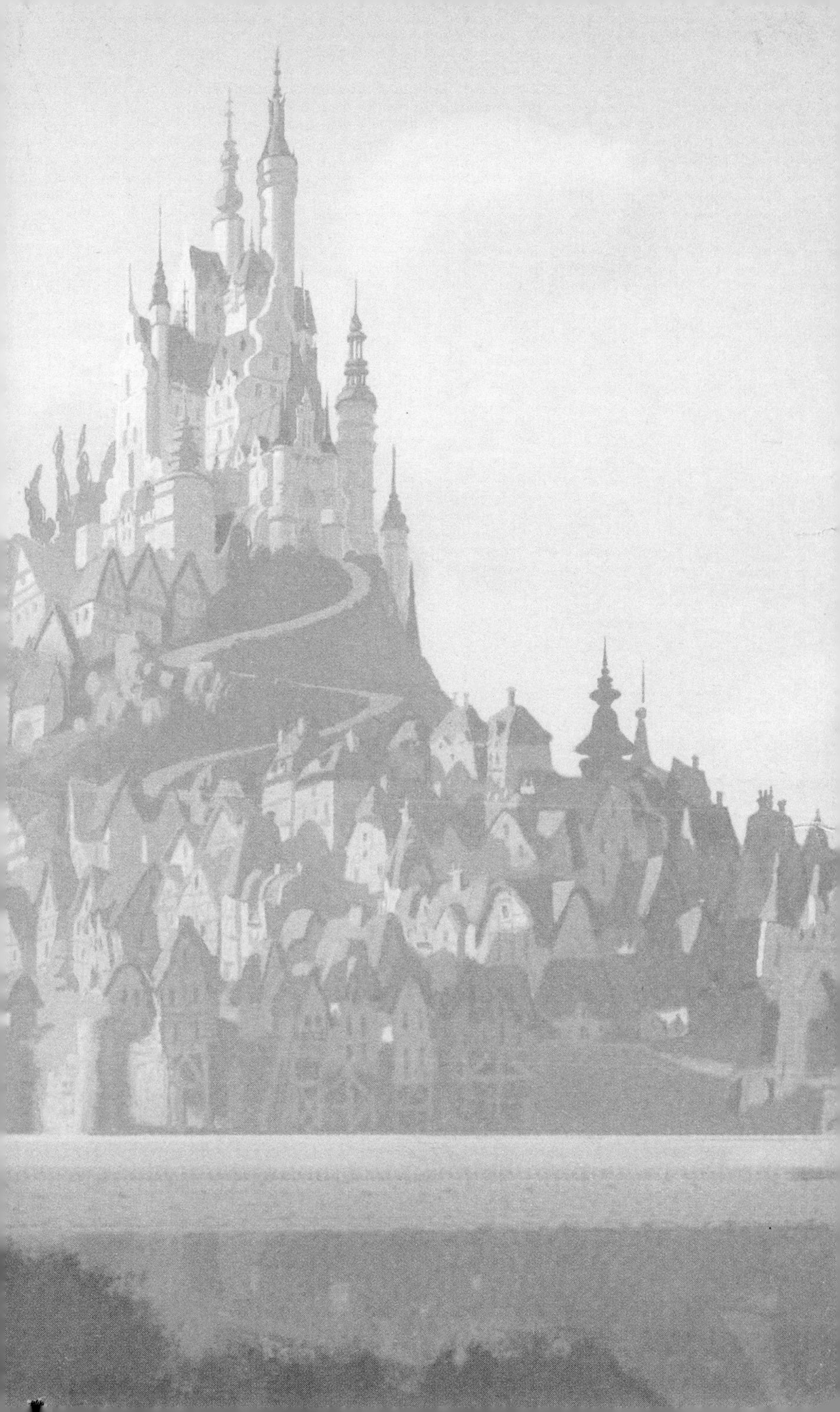

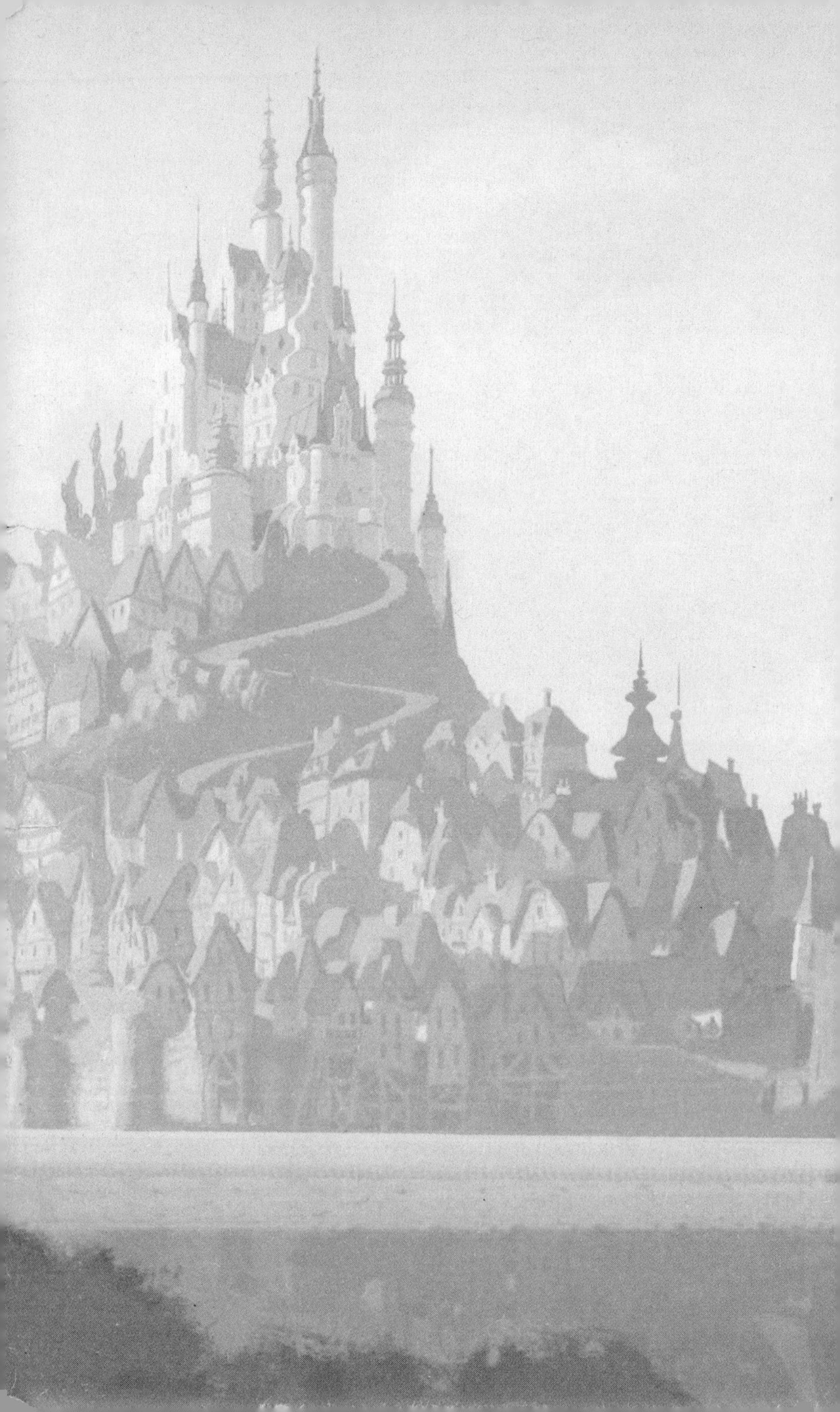